DYNASTY 25

The Question

Also in the *Dynasty* series:

DYNASTY
25

The Question

Cynthia Harrod-Eagles

LITTLE, BROWN

A *Little, Brown* Book

First published in Great Britain in 2002 by Little, Brown

Copyright © 2002 Cynthia Harrod-Eagles

The moral right of the author has been asserted.

A CIP catalogue record for this book
is available from the British Library.

ISBN 0 316 64618 0

Typeset in Plantin
by Palimpsest Book Production Limited
Polmont, Stirlingshire

Printed and bound in Great Britain by
Clays Ltd, St Ives plc

Little, Brown
An imprint of
Time Warner Books UK
Brettenham House
Lancaster Place
London WC2E 7EN

www.TimeWarnerBooks.co.uk

Select Bibliography

Margot Asquith	*The Autobiography of Margot Asquith*
Theo Barker	*Moving Millions*
Field Marshal Lord Carver	*The Boer War*
J.H. Clapham	*Economic History of Great Britain*
Sir Robert Ensor	*England 1870–1914*
Lord Ernle	*English Farming Past and Present*
Martin Marix Evans	*The Boer War, South Africa 1899–1902*
R.H. Gretton	*Modern History of the English People 1880–1922*
Stephen Halliday	*Underground to Everywhere*
Sandra Stanley Holton	*Suffrage Days*
K. Hoole	*York*
Tabitha Jackson	*The Boer War*
Donald Lindsay	*A Portrait of Britain 1851–1951*
Constance Lytton	*Prisons and Prisoners*
Victor Mallet	*Life With Queen Victoria*
Jo Manton	*Elizabeth Garrett Anderson*
Keith Middlemas	*Edward VII*
G.E. Mingay	*The Victorian Countryside*
Sylvia Pankhurst	*The Suffrage Movement*
George Plumptre	*Edward VII*
Martin Pugh	*The Pankhursts*
Antonia Raeburn	*The Militant Suffragettes*
Michaela Reid	*Ask Sir James*
Tony Rennell	*Last Days of Glory: The Death of Queen Victoria*
Giles St Aubyn	*Edward VII, Prince and King*
Giles St Aubyn	*Queen Victoria*
Marion Sambourne	*A Victorian Household*
R.A. Scott-James	*The Influence of the Press*
J.A. Spender	*Life of Sir Henry Campbell-Bannerman*
The Stationery Office	*The Boer War: Ladysmith and Mafeking, 1900*
Ray Strachey	*Millicent Garrett Fawcett*
G.M. Theal	*History of South Africa*
Stephen Trombley	*Sir Frederick Treves*
E.S. Turner	*The Court of St James's*
Ronald Willis	*The Illustrated Portrait of York*
Anthony Wood	*Nineteenth Century Britain 1815–1914*

THE MORLAND FAMILY

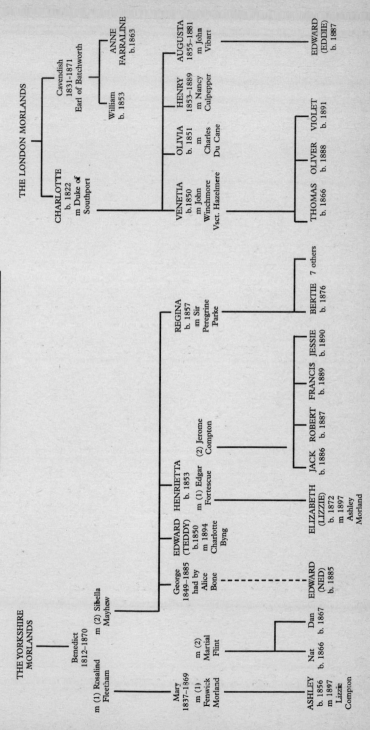

THE YORKSHIRE MORLANDS

Benedict
1812–1870

m (1) Rosalind Fleetham   m (2) Sibella Mayhew

Mary
1837–1869

m (1) Fenwick Morland   m (2) Martial Flint

George
1849–1885
had by
Alice
Bone

EDWARD (TEDDY)
b.1850
m 1894
Charlotte
Byng

HENRIETTA
b. 1853
m (1) Edgar
Fortescue
(2) Jerome
Compton

REGINA
b. 1857
m Sir
Peregrine
Parke

ASHLEY
b. 1856
m 1897
Lizzie
Compton

Nat
b. 1866   Dan
b. 1867

EDWARD
(NED)
b. 1885

ELIZABETH
(LIZZIE)
b. 1872
m 1897
Ashley
Morland

JACK
b. 1886   ROBERT
b. 1887   FRANCIS
b. 1889   JESSIE
b. 1890

BERTIE
b. 1876   7 others

THE LONDON MORLANDS

CHARLOTTE
b. 1822
m Duke of
Southport

Cavendish
1831–1871
Earl of Batchworth

William
b. 1853   ANNE
FARRALINE
b.1863

VENETIA
b.1850
m John
Winchmore
Vsct. Hazelmere

OLIVIA
b. 1851
m
Charles
Du Cane

HENRY
1853–1889
m Nancy
Culpepper

AUGUSTA
1855–1881
m John
Vibart

THOMAS
b. 1866   OLIVER
b. 1888   VIOLET
b. 1891

EDWARD
(EDDIE)
b. 1887

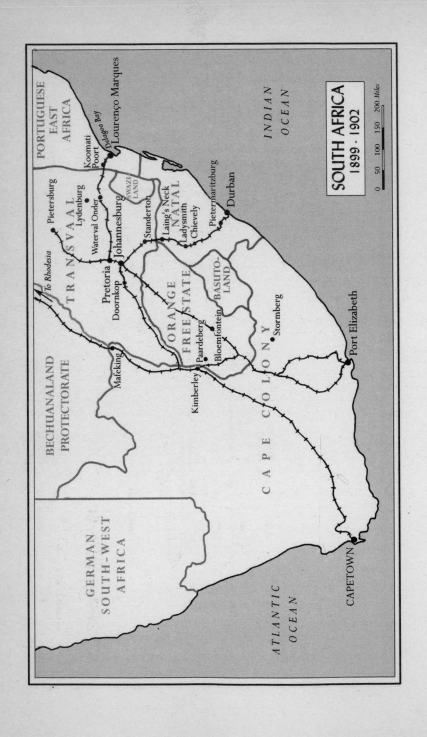

SOUTH AFRICA
1899 - 1902

0   50   100   150   200 *Miles*

INDIAN OCEAN

PORTUGUESE EAST AFRICA

Lourenço Marques
Delagoa Bay
Koomati Poort

TRANSVAAL
Pietersburg
Lydenburg
Waterval Onder
Johannesburg
Standerton
SWAZI LAND
Laing's Neck
NATAL
Ladysmith
Chievely
Pietermaritzburg
Durban

To Rhodesia
Pretoria
Doornkop

ORANGE FREE STATE
BASUTO-LAND

BECHUANALAND PROTECTORATE

Mafeking

Paardeberg
Bloemfontein
Kimberley

Stormberg

Port Elizabeth

CAPE COLONY

GERMAN SOUTH-WEST AFRICA

ATLANTIC OCEAN

CAPETOWN

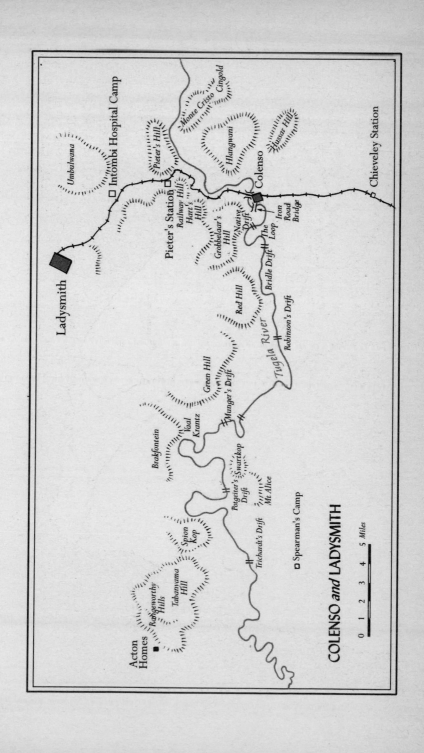

COLENSO *and* LADYSMITH

0 1 2 3 4 5 *Miles*

Ladysmith

Umbulwana

Intombi Hospital Camp

Pieter's Hill

Monte Cristo

Cingold

Hlangwani

Husar Hill

Chieveley Station

Colenso

Pieter's Station

Railway Hill

Hart's Hill

Grobbelaar's Hill

Native Drift

Iron Road Bridge

The Loop

Bridle Drift

Red Hill

Robinson's Drift

Tugela River

Green Hill

Munger's Drift

Vaal Krantz

Brakfontein

Potgeiter's Drift

Swartkop

Mt. Alice

Trichardt's Drift

Spion Kop

Tabanyama Hill

Rangeworthy Hills

Acton Homes

Spearman's Camp

BOOK ONE

Home

I know these slopes; who knows them if not I? –
But many a dingle on the loved hill-side,
With thorns once studded, old, white-blossom'd trees,
Where thick the cowslips grew, and, far descried,
High tower'd the spikes of purple orchises,
Hath since our day put by
The coronals of that forgotten time.

Matthew Arnold, *Thyrsis*

CHAPTER ONE

September 1898

The North Eastern Railway board meeting ended, and none too soon for Teddy Morland. He could never understand why certain of his colleagues seemed to take pleasure in using ten words where one would do. In fact sometimes when the one word required was 'yes' or 'no', they used a hundred and ten and never got to the one at all. Emerging into the warm hazy sunshine, and finding that his behind was as numb as his brain, he decided to stretch his legs and walk up to his club for luncheon.

He belonged to several clubs, but his current favourite was the Yorkshire, which stood beside the Lendal Bridge, just above the landing for the pleasure steamers that plied up and down the river Ouse. The Yorkshire was something of a landmark, and facing it across the river was another, Botterill's Horse Repository, a startling and ornate building in red and yellow brick. Here the gentlemen who rode or drove into York could leave their horses. The stalls were arranged on several storeys, with ramps leading up from floor to floor – the equine equivalent, Teddy supposed, of one of those new blocks of 'flats' one heard about in London – and if York grew any more crowded, they would all end up living on top of each other, like the horses, he thought.

The city within the walls was seething like a kicked bees' nest. Building was going on everywhere, leaving a film of brick and plaster dust on every surface: the very air you breathed felt gritty. The road was crammed with horse traffic and with what seemed to Teddy an inordinate number of bicycles. The whole country had gone bicycle-mad this past year, but York was particularly infested: being almost flat and in the middle of a plain it was eminently suitable to the machines. One whizzed past him now, pedalled by a ferocious-looking boy with his cap pulled down hard above his eyes. The machine had a basket fixed above the front wheel and Teddy hardly needed to look at the inscription on the cross-panel to know it belonged to Knowles the butcher.

Knowles had recently changed all his delivery boys from pony-and-trap onto bicycles. Everyone had sighed with relief at the news, believing the change could only be for the better: the butcher always had the most villainous lads and the worst-tempered ponies in Yorkshire. But Knowles's boys had amply proved that a bicycle could be put to as much nuisance as a pony.

This particular lad had pulled up as he met the tail of the traffic trying to squeeze over Lendal Bridge. But now, as Teddy caught up with him, he tired of waiting his turn, heaved his bicycle impatiently up onto the pavement, and ran straight into an old gentleman coming the other way. The crash was impressive. The old gentleman, receiving the meat-basket full in his bread-basket, went backwards a couple of feet and sat down hard, his rolled umbrella flying into the road and under the wheel of a dray.

The boy and the bicycle fell sideways, the boy banging his head on the flagstone with a sound like a walnut being cracked, and paper-wrapped parcels of meat flew out in all directions. A quick-witted dog that happened to be in the vicinity made hay and grabbed one. It laid back its ears and ran for its life across the road, dodging under the nose of a chestnut vanner and causing it to rear. The cart was full of cabbages and the tail-gate wasn't properly fastened: as the horse went up and the cart dipped backwards, the flap gaped open and cabbages rolled out like severed heads from a tumbrel and thumped into the road.

Traffic stopped. Horses whinnied, voices were raised in exclamation, and the air was blue with carters' curses. The old gentleman, purple with fury, was exercising an impressive

4

vocabulary on the boy's character and prospects. A crowd of helpful people gathered to give advice, along with various loungers and boys who were just enjoying the entertainment. Several more dogs had materialised out of nowhere, causing Knowles's boy to forget his immediate sorrows at the thought of what old Knowlesy would do to him if he lost the goods. He waved his arms at the nearest dog and shouted, 'Get out of it, you old fool!' Unfortunately the old gentleman thought the words were meant for him, provoking a fresh outburst of indignation, and earning the boy a box on the ear from a burly man in a cap who told him to 'Keep a civil tongue in your head, you young limb!'

A stout, housewifely woman, meanwhile, had understood the dog situation, and there being too many of them to hit individually, she pointed her umbrella at them and opened and shut it violently with a loud flapping noise. This didn't do much to deter the dogs, but it did startle a nearby cab horse, which shied and ran backwards, hitting the shaft of the cabbage cart and making the vanner rear again. More cabbages bounced, the carter yelled at the woman, the boy howled, dogs barked, and an ex-cavalry old gentleman with Crimean whiskers, who was descending from the cab with the intention of sorting out the mess in a proper military way, got his ankle bitten by an over-excited cur and was soon adding to the confusion, hopping about on one foot and whacking every canine in reach with his malacca.

Recognising a situation beyond help, Teddy slipped past the crowd on the parapet side and walked on. He felt inexplicably invigorated by the incident. It had proved his contention that one Knowles's boy could cause more trouble without even trying than all the Mahdi's tribesmen put together. If only the Government had thought to employ them in Egypt, he concluded, we would never have lost Khartoum.

He was almost across the bridge when a skinny pi-dog dashed past him flying a chain of sausage links naked of their wrapping. Close behind it raced three other hounds, mouths wide and tongues lolling, intent on a share of the booty. The whole circus hurtled at high speed past the legs

5

of a man who was walking slowly in the other direction, attempting to make sense of a map. When your mind is on other things, it is a shock to be brushed on either side by a dog pack and whipped around the knees by a bolas of best pork sausages. The man's arms flew up, he overbalanced, and went down awkwardly.

This time there was no-one else on hand. Teddy stepped up to him with concern. 'Good Lord, sir, that was a nasty fall! Are you hurt? Allow me to help you up.'

The man looked bewildered. 'What the devil was that?' he exclaimed. 'What sort of a place is this? Are you plagued with mad beasts?'

'There was an accident on the other side of the bridge,' Teddy said. 'A butcher's boy dropped his basket and the local curs have become – er – over-excited.'

'Thought my last hour had come,' the man said. He was still sitting on the pavement. Now he inspected the palm of his hand. He let out an oath under his breath.

'That looks like a nasty graze,' Teddy said. 'Hurt anywhere else?'

'Nothing broken, I think,' the man replied. Teddy offered him an arm and he used it to get to his feet. He was a spare, neatly built man in his forties, not tall but very upright, with thinning hair compensated by a large chestnut moustache. His clothes were the well-made tweeds of a country gentleman, and he stood brushing at them vaguely, still seeming dazed.

'I say,' Teddy said, 'you're rather upset. It must have been a shock to the system. Look here, my club's only a step over there. I was just toddling down for a spot of something. Why don't you come in and have a brandy to settle your nerves? The name's Morland, by the way.' He lifted his hat.

The man looked around for his own. It was restored to him, along with his map and pince-nez, by a passing boy, and he resumed it in order to raise it in response. 'Puddephat,' he said. 'That's very kind of you, er, Mr Morland, but—'

'Oh, not at all.' Teddy interrupted what sounded like the beginning of a refusal. 'My pleasure. Can't have visitors to

6

our fine city bein' knocked about. Give you a chance to wash the grit out of that, too.' He nodded towards the wounded hand.

'Yes, perhaps that would be wise. Thank you, sir,' the man said, and fell in beside Teddy.

'I couldn't help noticing that you were consulting a map,' Teddy said, by way of making conversation. 'Looked a bit lost. Perhaps when you've got your breath back, I can help you. I'm a native of these parts, you know. I have a house just outside the city – Morland Place, born there, ancient family seat and so on – but bein' a town bird by nature, I prefer to live inside the walls.'

'Morland Place?' said Puddephat. 'I've seen that marked on the map. Indeed, there's an entry in the guide book about it, isn't there? Quite a landmark hereabouts, I believe?'

Teddy was not immune to flattery. 'Ancient stones, you know. Any age. Been Morlands on that spot for five hundred years.'

'Five hundred years? Good heavens! You must be by way of being the – er – local squire, or lord of the manor?'

'Oh, hardly that. But everyone here knows me. Only because I'm master of Morland Place, you understand,' he added modestly. 'Never done anything else to talk of. M'father, now, he was an engineer, helped to bring the railways to York. Built the tramway for the army at Balaclava, too.'

'Indeed?' said Puddephat. His vagueness had passed, and his lean face and blue eyes were sharp with attention. 'You interest me greatly, sir. Railways and the army are two subjects close to my heart.'

Teddy beamed. 'Look here, sir, why don't you join me for lunch? The club has the best roast saddle of mutton in the Riding. Famous for it. Then we can have a good, long chinwag. I'd be interested to know what brings you to York.'

'I'd be delighted, sir,' said Puddephat.

As the train came gasping and sighing round the majestic curve of York railway station, Lizzie would have liked to hang out of the window like a schoolgirl for the first sight

7

of her mother; but given the advanced state of her pregnancy, it was not actually possible, to say nothing of propriety. As it was, she needed the help of the two gentlemen in her compartment just to get down. Ashley had wisely foreseen this, and advised her against a 'ladies only' carriage for that very reason.

Having reached the platform, she was in danger of being thrown off her feet by the crowd. The 10 a.m. from King's Cross was an excellent train, but it had no dining car, so it made a half-hour stop at platform eight in York to allow the passengers going through to Edinburgh to refuel themselves. Half an hour was not long for so many to be served, and the rush for the dining rooms resembled a stampede.

Ah, but there was her mother at last, small and neat in her brown coat and the familiar old hat Papa called her rabbit's ears, because it had a large bow on the top whose two ends stuck up one on either side. How long had she had that hat? Since before Papa went bankrupt, at any rate. There was no money for frivolities like new hats, Lizzie reminded herself, a little guiltily, as she stepped into her mother's embrace.

'Darling, darling Lizzie! Oh, it's so good to see you!' They exchanged a fierce, quick hug. 'So much to talk about – but let's get out of this crush first.'

Lizzie directed a porter towards her bags, which the helpful gentlemen had lifted down for her, and then they were walking towards the exit.

'So strange to see your name on your luggage as "Mrs A. Morland",' Henrietta said, linking arms with her daughter. Henrietta had been born a Morland. She had married first Mr Fortescue, Lizzie's father, and then Jerome Compton; and Lizzie, being first a Fortescue and then a Compton, had married a cousin from America. 'How is dear Ashley?'

'Oh, he's always well,' said Lizzie. 'He sends his love. He'll be down on Saturday, of course.'

'I'm surprised he let you travel all this way without a maid.'

'Oh, Mother! Times have changed, you know. Besides,

8

I'm a married woman, not a trembling young maiden.'

'I know, darling, but I thought Ashley was rather old-fashioned in his ideas – in the nicest way, of course.'

'Not quite so archaic as that! There wouldn't have been anyone to spare, anyway. We only have Cook and Ellen, and Ashley needs both of them to look after him. He says he could manage all alone in a log hut in the wilderness, but civilisation is more complicated! I expected Uncle Teddy to be here with you. I know how he loves meeting people from trains.'

'He'll be over later. He thought we'd like to be alone together just at first.'

'How kind he is!'

'He is,' Henrietta agreed. 'The kindest brother in the world. Wait until you see what I have waiting for us outside.'

It was a pony phaeton, low to the ground like a victoria, painted black with scarlet wheels. There was a nice bay pony between the shafts, its head being held by a boy.

'Mother! You driving? How smart!'

'Teddy thought I needed it – and I must say it has made a great difference. It did take up so much time to walk in, and it meant I couldn't carry things back but had to have them sent, which wasn't always convenient.'

'What an extravagant gift!'

'It wasn't new,' Henrietta said. 'He bought it cheaply from an old lady who'd died – well, from her son, I mean, of course, don't laugh at me – and Papa painted it for me.'

'You don't need to defend it to me,' Lizzie said, understanding the tensions involved in her mother's accepting gifts from her uncle. 'Was Papa upset?'

'Oh – well – you know how it is. He would never show it if he was. Teddy got Papa to choose the pony, because he said he didn't know anything about horses – which is not true, of course, but tactful.'

'It looks a nice little thing. What's its name?'

'I've called him Dunnock, after the pony I had when I was a little girl. He's as good as gold.' Henrietta smiled and added, 'The children were so disappointed! They were quite sure he was meant for them to ride. But I let them ride him

9

sometimes when I'm not going to use him. It has to be bare-back, of course, because there's no riding saddle for him yet, but I think that's the best way to learn anyway. I was tumbling on and off a pony's bare back almost before I could walk.'

Henrietta saw the luggage stowed, paid the boy and the porter, and climbed in beside her daughter. Lizzie watched with interest as her mother turned the pony and edged him through the press of cabs and drays, and managed the awkward right turn out of the station yard into Queen Street quite neatly. 'You're very good at it,' she said. 'I'm lost with admiration.'

'To tell you the truth, I'm quite proud of myself,' Henrietta said. 'Though I was "born on horseback", as they say, I never learned to drive until this year. But Dunnock is so good, he practically drives himself.'

They moved along slowly in the stream of traffic, with the friendly bulk of the city wall to their left, high up on its grassy bank, the grey stones warming to honey in the mellow September sunlight. As in any city, the air smelt of horse manure and coal-smoke from a thousand chimneys; but York added its own savours, sulphur and burnt soot from the railway, the tang of roasting chicory from Smith's factory in Layerthorpe, and the divine hint of warm chocolate, drifting down from the Cocoa Works.

'I always think,' Lizzie said, 'that if heaven smells of anything, it will be that.'

Driving was taking up all Henrietta's attention, and they did not speak until they had turned onto Blossom Street and passed the busy junction with Holgate Road. After that the traffic thinned considerably and the pony was able to break into a trot at last.

Then Lizzie asked, 'How is Papa?' She had always called him Papa, right from the beginning. They were very fond of each other, and while Lizzie took that for granted, Henrietta knew how lucky they had all been.

'He's well enough,' she answered, 'but he works too hard. He's out now helping the men repair fences – part of the conspiracy to let me have you to myself! But he doesn't just supervise, which is what Teddy means him to do. He *will* always take off his coat and work alongside the men, no matter what they're doing, and it isn't what he was born to. I wish he wouldn't. He gets so tired, and I'm afraid he's going to hurt himself one day. He's not a young man any more.'

Lizzie nodded. 'I suppose it's no good talking to him?'

'I've tried, but he turns it away with a joke – you know how he does – and goes on just the same. Perhaps you could speak to him? He takes more notice of you than me.'

'Oh, Mother, how can you say so?' Lizzie protested, embarrassed.

'It's true,' Henrietta said. 'You are much closer to him in some ways. You're clever and you can talk to him on his own level.' She smiled as she said it, to show it caused her no pain.

'Well, I could try, I suppose,' Lizzie said. She understood why her step-father drove himself. When he went bankrupt, they all became virtually destitute, and had Uncle Teddy not invited them to come and live at Morland Place – which was standing empty – they would have been homeless. Since then, Teddy had provided them with everything. Jerome, who had been born to money, had had to get used to being a dependant. Lizzie had read enough to know that it touched a man's pride to have someone else provide for his wife and children because he had failed to.

'It must be hard for him,' she ventured cautiously.

Her mother slowed the pony as their turning approached. 'I think the hardest thing of all for him to bear,' she said, 'was your uncle Teddy paying for your wedding.'

'Oh dear, poor Papa! But it was a lovely wedding, wasn't it? Not grand, but – elegant, I think.'

The track was off to the right opposite Tyburn – the site of the old gallows – and led across Hob Moor towards Morland Place. The pony put his shoulders into the collar and trotted along with a will, as horses do when they are heading for home, and the phaeton bounced over the uneven track, forcing Lizzie to brace herself and hold on to the side. They were on Morland land now. Once it had stretched for

miles in every direction, but now there was only the park-
land and the home farm left. All the rest had been sold to
cover the debts left by the previous master, Henrietta's and
Teddy's late elder brother George.

Lizzie looked about eagerly to see what changes there had
been. When she had left to marry Ashley and live in London,
Teddy had just begun restocking. His idea was that Jerome
should farm the place on his behalf – acting as his land
agent, in a sense – in return for which Teddy would make
Henrietta an allowance equivalent to the salary he would
have paid Jerome, if Jerome had not been a bankrupt and
therefore unable to take a job.

It was quite astonishingly tactful of Uncle Teddy, Lizzie
thought, who was a simple man and unused to mental
subtleties. He had also made a great point that it was a
shame and a sin to let good land lie wasted, and that Jerome
would be doing him and the world at large a service by
overseeing the agricultural activities for him. The trouble
was that Papa was intelligent and had a subtle mind. The
fact that what Teddy had said was quite true did not make
it any less obvious that he, Jerome, was being rescued,
propped up, bailed out – and tactfully managed into the
bargain!

Poor Papa, Lizzie thought. It was always so much easier
to be the generous benefactor than the grateful dependant.
The Bible said that it was more blessed to give than to
receive, but she had her reservations about that. Giving was
generally more fun, besides bolstering one's self-esteem. It
took a particular sort of grace to be always receiving, especially when one was a born present-giver. Jerome had always
had a genius for presents, but now he hadn't even been able
to give Lizzie her wedding. If his sense of humour didn't
support him, Lizzie thought, he'd be sunk indeed.

Here was Morland Place at last, sitting squarely inside
its moat, looking as if it had grown up out of the ground
rather than been built by man's hands. Lizzie had not been
born and raised there, had lived there for not much more
than a year, but she had heard her mother talk about it all
her life and it was a special place to her. Ashley's mother –

Henrietta's eldest sister Mary – had been born there, and he had grown up with stories of it too. It was one of the things they had in common.

They crossed the moat, passed under the barbican, and into the yard. 'You go on in,' Henrietta said, 'while I put Dunnock away. Emma will be in the kitchen getting lunch.'

Lizzie went in through the buttery door and down the corridor to the kitchen. It was just as she remembered it, the cold flagstone floor, the high ceiling with its smoke-blackened beams, the vast, ancient stove squatting under the arch of the great fireplace, the big copper pans hanging on the wall, and the smell of something delicious in the air. In the middle of the floor was the scrubbed table where the work was done and where they had so often sat to talk and eat and be comfortable. The kitchen, where past mistresses of the house would not have dreamt of setting foot, had become in these poorer days the heart of the place.

And there was Emma, dear Emma, putting down the cloth in her hands and hurrying forward, her round red face one enormous smile. 'Oh, my! Oh, my!' was all she could say.

Lizzie hugged her. 'Dear Emma! How are you?'

'Oh, I'm well, always well. But look at you – as full as you can hold! Oh, what a happy day this is.' She let Lizzie go and reached into her apron pocket for a handkerchief. Emma Holt had first come to them thirteen years ago, fresh from the country, as a housemaid. She had mutated into nanny as the children had been born, and when they had all become homeless and destitute she had stayed with them, saying only to Henrietta, 'However would you manage if I was to leave you?' As the answer to that was, 'Very badly indeed,' there had been no further argument. So here she was in Yorkshire, far away in miles and years from her native home in Norfolk.

Still, her accent had not changed – to the astonishment of the local people who had never heard words pronounced the way Emma pronounced them. 'Well, so hare you are, my dare, hoom to hev your baby,' she marvelled, when she had dried her eyes. 'That's a wonder Mr Aashley let you goo.'

13

'He didn't like it,' Lizzie confessed, 'but I told him it was traditional for girls to go back to their mothers to have their first child, and he never argues with tradition. But I don't suppose he'll let me go for the next, so you must make the most of this one.'

'Next indeed! Don't count your chickens, miss!'

'I'm not going to have a chicken, Em, just a dear little baby.'

Emma chuckled. 'Oh, you! Always funning me.'

'We will manage all right between us, won't we?' Lizzie asked, on the tail end of a qualm. Ashley had been eloquent about the convenience of London, with a doctor on practically every corner, gas lighting, domestic boilers and water that came out of a tap. Morland Place, by comparison, *was* rather primitive.

'Course we will,' Emma said. 'Didn't I see your ma through four times? And my oon mother half a dozen, 'fore I left hoom.' Henrietta came into the kitchen, and Emma went on, 'There now, hare's your ma, and we can sit down to lunch. I made you a nice steak and onion pie, seeing as you woon't have eaten since I don't know when, and that long journey besides.'

Emma's steak pie was a legend, and Lizzie didn't like to point out that since the train had left King's Cross at ten o'clock, she had not had to get up early, so had only finished breakfasting at nine – and it was barely half past two now.

The pie *was* wonderful – crisp golden pastry, tender steak, rich gravy to soak into the mashed potatoes – but perhaps Lizzie had not done enough since breakfast to work up an appetite, for half-way through she began to feel uncomfortably full. Her fork moved more and more slowly as the three of them sat around one end of the kitchen table, talking and eating. At last she was forced to admit defeat and say, 'It really is delicious, Em, but I simply can't manage any more. I'm sorry.'

Henrietta looked at her with quick concern. 'Are you all right, darling? Perhaps you ought to go and lie down.'

'I just feel rather full. I think I will lie down for a bit, though – sitting isn't very comfortable for me.'

'Your bed's all made up ready,' Henrietta said.

'Oh, I don't want to go to bed. I'd miss all the fun. Can't I just lie on the sofa while you talk to me?'

At that moment there were footsteps in the kitchen passage, and Jerome Compton came in. He was tall and dark and had been devastatingly handsome in his youth. To his women-folk he was handsome still, though his hair was greying and his eyes were netted with lines of laughter and sorrow. But they were still very blue, and his smile had all its old enmeshing charm as he raised his hands defensively and said, 'I know, I know, I'm not supposed to appear until teatime, but I couldn't wait any longer to see my favourite girl.'

'It nearly is teatime,' Henrietta observed. 'We've been sitting here well over an hour.'

'Tea?' said Lizzie, with a groan. 'We've only just had lunch.'

'What, are they stuffing you like a Christmas goose? You certainly look it,' Jerome laughed, holding out his arms to his step-daughter. 'Come and kiss me – if you can get near enough. You look like a little girl dressed up with a pillow.'

Lizzie stood up and felt a momentary dizziness, held the back of the chair for a moment, and then crossed the room to his embrace. She had reverenced rather than loved her own father, a severe and ascetic man; but Jerome was dear and close, like part of herself. She kissed his lean cheek and then rested a moment, her head against his shoulder and his face against her hair. He had always been there to comfort her; to cheer her and make her laugh.

Jerome stroked her head, and she felt the roughness of his palm snag her hair. She straightened up, took hold of his hand and turned it over. It was hard and calloused, with a long half-healed scratch across the back, an ugly black bruise on one nail, and ingrained dirt along the side of the forefinger. It was no longer a gentleman's hand. She looked up with a little shake of the head, and he smiled ruefully, but there was hurt there too. She lifted the hand to her lips and kissed it. 'I like it better like this,' she said, so that only he could hear.

15

'Little liar,' he said tenderly.

They were interrupted by another arrival: a big brindled hound appeared in the doorway. He paused cautiously, aware that something was different; and then, recognizing who it was, flung himself on Lizzie, whip-tail lashing, jaws grinning in his silent joy of reunion.

'Dear old Kithra!' Lizzie cried, catching his rough head in her hands. As she bent down he put a foreleg over her arm and washed her face enthusiastically. He had been her puppy, but she had had to leave him behind when she got married, for he was not the sort of dog who would have been happy in London. 'I've missed you, you big old fool. Ugh, don't lick my face! Oh, you bad dog, what *have* you been rolling in?'

'Cow dung,' Jerome said. 'He has a passion for it. He's been out with me all morning. He attaches himself to me as the next best thing when the children are at school. Of course, now you're here—' He saw that Lizzie was having difficulty straightening up, and caught at Kithra's collar. 'Here, let me. Come on, you unregulated cur, furl your tongue. And keep your tail to yourself. It's like being hit with an iron bar!'

Lizzie felt the dizziness again as she straightened, but almost before she had registered it, a pain like a spike stabbed her to the quick, and she gave a little cry and doubled up again.

'What is it?' Jerome asked, catching her elbow to support her.

'A pain,' she gasped.

He helped her to a chair and she sat gratefully, hunching forward as the pain spread and took hold. She felt her mother's cool hand on the back of her neck, and heard her say, presumably to Jerome, 'Give her a minute.'

The pain was ebbing now, and Lizzie drew a grateful breath and straightened up a little. She met her mother's eyes. 'Is this it?'

'It could well be,' Henrietta said. 'We shall see.'

'But it's early!' she cried.

'Only by a few days, darling. It's not an exact science.'

16

'I wanted it to come at the week-end, when Ashley's here.'

'Babies come when they want to come,' Henrietta said. 'How are you feeling now?'

'All right, I think. The pain's stopped, anyway.'

'Then we'd better get you upstairs and settled.'

'Should I carry her?' Jerome asked anxiously.

Henrietta and Lizzie favoured him with the same smile, and Henrietta said, 'I think you've got enough to handle with that dog.'

'You don't think I'm strong enough,' he said, pretending hurt.

'Not by half,' Lizzie said. She pushed herself upright with her hands on the table, and at once the dizziness struck again, accompanied this time by a swift grip of nausea. She took a few steps, searching the swaying room in dismay for escape, and then was helplessly sick on the floor. 'Oh, Emma, I'm sorry,' she gasped, and did it again. 'Oh, Mother!'

'Don't you worry. That can't be helped,' said Emma.

'It happens sometimes,' Henrietta said.

'I'd better go for the doctor, hadn't I?' Jerome asked anxiously. 'Minstrel's still saddled. I can be there in ten minutes.'

Henrietta was calm. 'Goodness, not now. Nothing's going to happen for hours yet.'

'Are you sure?'

'Of course. I have done this before, you know.'

'Don't worry, Papa,' Lizzie said, more confidently than she felt. 'We can manage.'

'That's the whole problem. You women manage everything and leave us men nothing to do *but* worry.'

'I'm sure you'll do *that* extremely well,' Lizzie said.

It was only too true. Jerome watched Henrietta help Lizzie from the room, feeling all the discomfort of responsibility without power. If anything were to happen to Lizzie, Ashley would never forgive him for having enticed her up to Yorkshire. He would never forgive himself. He was keenly aware of the lack of facilities here, compared with London. Morland Place had been built to be lived in with an army

17

of servants. Teddy had done a great deal, but he had not installed any modern conveniences; and though it was barely a mile outside York, that was a mile too far if there was an emergency requiring a doctor.

Emma was cleaning up after Lizzie and didn't want him under her feet, and Kithra was being a nuisance, so he took the dog outside and tied him up in his kennel. Then he pushed the phaeton out of the way under the open shelter they had built for it on the side of the yard opposite the stable. He checked on the pony and on his own road horse: another of Teddy's gifts, of course, though he had said – and with justice – that Jerome could not get about the estate as Teddy's agent without a mount. He loosened Minstrel's girth and took the bit out of his mouth, but otherwise left him tacked up to save time when the moment came. He filled their water buckets and gave them each an armful of hay, and went back outside, longing for something else to do.

If only the doctor were here, some responsibility would be taken off his shoulders. But Henrietta had said more than once that first babies took a long time. He thought back to the various arrivals of his own children, and remembered the same helpless waiting – though he had had Lizzie to keep him company then. And now it was Lizzie up there, undergoing that torture that women faced with such amazing calm. Surely there was something he should be doing? Wait now, didn't he remember a need for hot water? Though there was a boiler attached to the range, it was filled with rain-water, which would not be pure enough, he felt, for medical use. He went back into the kitchen and filled two kettles with drinking-water and put them on to boil. And even as he did so, he laughed at himself. Oh, well, if nothing else, he thought, at least they would come in handy when the children got home from school.

Over the past months Lizzie had had more than one sleepless night, worrying about the birth to come. Of course, once you conceived you were fairly in for it, and there was no way round it – not an entirely comforting thought. And

those women you could ask about it – Mama, and Cousin
Venetia, who was a lady doctor and thus wonderfully frank
and unembarrassed – said the same, that while it did hurt,
you forgot all about the pain the moment it was over. Lizzie
did not find this reassuring. It sounded to her like the sort
of thing grown-ups said to keep children quiet, along the
lines of the 'this-will-hurt-me-more-than-it-hurts-you'
speech. Mama had said, 'It's a different sort of pain. You
don't mind it, really,' which Lizzie thought was plainly
fiction.

But now it was actually starting, and it was a sort of relief
that the waiting was over. At first it wasn't so bad, with the
pains far apart. Once she had stopped being sick there were
things to do in between pains, getting herself and the
bedchamber ready, and she felt that, really, this thing wasn't
so bad after all, and she wondered why some women had
made such a fuss about it. But then the pains began to come
closer together and harder, and she found that when they
were going on, it was impossible to think about anything
else, and when they stopped it was impossible to think about
anything but how glad one was that they had.

After a bit she lost all sense of time. The doctor came
and was very kind, said she was going on very well. She
looked up at him with amazement as the sweat stood out
on her brow and her body seemed gripped by a force quite
alien to her. He smiled and said, 'I daresay you've never
had to work so hard for so long before. Now you know why
it's called *labour*.'

Emma was there all the time; Mama came and went.
Once she brought up a limp posy of Michaelmas daisies
and said it was from the children. 'Jessie is furious that you
began without her. She had a shocking fit of temper when
Papa said she couldn't come up and watch. I've made them
all take Kithra out for a walk.'

Another time she came in with a lamp, and Lizzie realised
that it was dark outside the bedroom window. 'What time
is it?' she asked.

'Nearly eight. I'm just going to have a little supper with
the men – Papa won't eat anything unless I sit down with

him – and then I'll come and sit with you while Emma has something to eat.'

'The men?' Lizzie queried.

'Oh, Uncle Teddy's downstairs. He's been here for a while. He sends you his best love, by the way.'

Later the doctor was there again, and she thought that she gathered she wasn't doing as well as before. But when she asked him he only said, 'Don't worry, first babies like to do things their own way.' She wanted to question him further but the pain seemed to be continuous and she hadn't the will to do anything but endure it.

Teddy had not needed a nod and a wink from his sister to know that the most useful thing he could do was to take Jerome's mind off things. Teddy was very fond of Lizzie too, but he knew it was nothing to how Jerome felt about her. Teddy, at one further remove, had no more than a reasonable amount of anxiety. Women had babies every day of the week, and the doctor had said things were going on all right, so where was the need to fret? He supposed it came from Jerome's being so dashed clever and having so much imagination. Uncomfortable thing for a man to have, imagination. All right for women and poets and such-like, but men were better off without it.

It was fortunate that he had a subject ready to hand. He waited until Jerome had furnished him with a glass of sherry and was pacing up and down the drawing-room with his own glass in his hand, and said, 'Sit down for a minute, will you, old fellow? There's something I want to talk to you about.'

Jerome raised his eyebrows. 'I hope *you*'re not going to tell me not to worry. Rather a waste of time, like telling the Thames not to flow.'

'No, no, you worry away by all means. But there's an idea that I want to put to you, about using the land. Do sit down – you're giving me a crick in the neck.'

Jerome sat and with an effort dragged his mind from the bedchamber above. 'Pigs,' he said.

'Pigs?'

'I don't know why it is, but I've always had a liking for pigs. Knowing creatures. I wouldn't be surprised if they weren't the cleverest of all the animals. Now if you were to fancy setting up in pigs—'

'Oh, no, I don't think so,' Teddy said. 'Of course, if you want to keep a house-pig, there's sense in that. Use up the kitchen waste and windfalls and so on, provide you with your breakfast bacon and sausage – fair enough . . . But it's a waste of good grazing to go in for 'em on a large scale. Everyone in York with a back yard has got his own house-pig. No market, you see. We've got to raise things people can't raise for themselves. The luxuries. Lettuces, strawberries. Lamb. That sort of tackle.'

'That's very clever thinking, Teddy.'

He looked modest. 'Oh, it's not mine! I have no brain, as you well know. I have vague ideas, but Charley puts it all into shape. She has an uncommon good head for business, Charley.'

Teddy had surprised York on two counts when he married Charley – first, because he was past forty by then and everyone assumed he was a bachelor for life, and second, because Charlotte Byng was a servant girl and only eighteen. Some elements of York society had been shocked, especially as Teddy had also recently taken into his house the bastard child of his late brother, left destitute when its mother had died. The stiffer elements had concluded that there was something lax in Mr Morland's moral standards and that there was no knowing what he mightn't do next. They told each other, bridling, that if he thought they were going to receive the new Mrs Morland into their houses and pretend there was nothing amiss with the match, he had better think again. There were even murmurings that he ought to be asked to resign from his clubs, and from the board of the North Eastern Railway besides.

But Teddy had paid no heed to any murmurings, and since Charley was circumspect in her behaviour and neither of them wanted her to cut a figure in society, the murmurings eventually died away. Teddy still attended his committees and civic functions, but he and Charley did not entertain or appear in society together. In fact, in due course the stiffer elements started to feel peeved that they were *not* asked to receive the new Mrs Morland, and to wonder whether they weren't being snubbed by the couple, who insultingly preferred their own company and fireside to anyone else's.

Teddy had found everything he wanted in his wife, who was not only lovely and loving but, freed from the drag of poverty, had proved clever and imaginative too. And, as he said, she was a good businesswoman. Teddy was inclined to be lazy and to let things go rather than face the fag of changing them. But Charley hated waste, and could not see something that needed improving without undertaking it. And being 'of the people' herself, she had a good understanding of what people wanted and were prepared to pay money for.

It was she, for instance, who had urged him to expand his drapery business and start selling ladies' ready-made dresses, for which there was a growing demand. The scheme had prospered so well he had since bought the shop next door and opened a whole new department. The dresses were cut out and made up in one of his workshops along Skeldergate, and altered to fit by two girls under the guidance of the tailoress who managed the department. A great deal of the cloth came from his own mills in Manchester, and profits were thus maximised. It was all very satisfactory.

All Teddy's businesses were thriving, and, contrary to what both Jerome and Lizzie thought, it was Charley who had urged him to invest some of his profits in Morland Place. After all, wasn't it what industrial gentlemen did, make their fortune in the factories and spend it on the land? Other wealthy factory owners had to buy a fine country estate, but Teddy had one already, his ancient family seat, and what could be better worth spending his money on?

Teddy saw the sense of that, and if it weren't for Henrietta's and Jerome's sensitivities, he would have put in an army of workmen and done up the whole house right away. But he was getting to it bit by bit, restoring the damage that had been done by a fire while the house was empty, and using the opportunity to unpick some of the changes his late brother had made that were not to his taste. Building work naturally made a mess, and he had used that as an excuse to persuade Henrietta and Jerome to let him pay the wages of an extra daily maid and a charwoman, arguing that it was impossible for Henrietta and Emma between them to keep such a large house properly at the best of times. They had enough to do with cooking and washing and taking care of the children – too much, in fact. Teddy did not want to see his favourite sister worn out with drudgery. When the moment was right, he hoped to ease a cook and laundress into the household as well, and a man to take care of Dunnock, Minstrel and the pony he intended to give little Jack and Robbie for Christmas. The expenditure was nothing to him, but Jerome was such a touchy devil – for all that he hid it with jokes – and he had to do it carefully.

He came back from his long reverie to find Jerome looking at him with wry amusement. 'So, not pigs, then. What?'

'Eh?'

'What was the idea you wanted to put to me?'

'Oh! Good Lord, miles away! Yes, well – it's horses.'

'I thought it was horses that ruined your brother,' Jerome said.

'Different sort of horses,' Teddy said. 'George was breeding racehorses. That's a rich man's hobby, not a business. No, I've a different idea. Met an interesting chap this morning, quite by accident. Name of Richard Puddephat. Nice fellow – you'd like him. Turns out he's been touring around Yorkshire looking for horses. He's an agent, buys horses, mainly for the army. Looking for new sources. Came out in conversation that we used to breed horses here and – well, one thing led to another.'

'Naturally,' Jerome said, but his eyes were thoughtful. 'Cavalry horses, eh?'

'And artillery, and baggage horses,' Teddy said. 'Good thing about it is your market's fixed – don't have to bustle about looking for customers. And there's the benefit of numbers. Like my contract with Cunard.' Teddy's mills had managed to secure the very lucrative contract for supplying bed and table linen to the new liners that carried passengers across the Atlantic.

'Breeding horses,' Jerome said. 'Now there's something I would like to get my teeth into.'

'Thought you would,' Teddy said. 'Breeding and breaking 'em. So I thought, well, we've got good grazing here, we've got the stables at Twelvetrees – need a bit of work, but they're not too bad – and, of course, there's no shortage of good men around. One thing we can pride ourselves on in Yorkshire is knowing horses. And you're a capital hand with horseflesh. So what do you think?'

'It's interesting. What sort of horses will they want?'

'Cavalry mounts are between fifteen-one and fifteen-three, Puddephat says, but they ain't particular within an inch or so. The regiments'd like to be, but they can never get enough remounts to match 'em exactly. Geldings preferred, of course, but they take mares.'

'And the colour?'

'Oh, that's easy enough. Blacks, browns and bays. The Scots Greys have greys, of course, and so do the trumpeters, so there's a market for those too, but it's mostly the dark colours they want.'

'And what about breaking?'

'Basic schooling. They take 'em at three years old, broken to ride, and finish 'em off themselves. Each regiment has a riding-master and rough riders, and they teach 'em the drills and charges and whatnot. It'd be jolly interesting,' he diverted, 'to watch that.'

'It certainly would.'

'So what do you say? Should we have a shot at it?'

'For myself, I'd like to very much. But it's going to be a long time before you have anything to sell. Are you sure it will be worth your while to invest in it?'

'Good Lord, yes! As a long-term investment, it seems to me just the thing. In fact, once it's properly under way, I think it might well take over from the market-gardening. Not so much fiddlin' about, you see, and no worries about the weather.'

'Yes, of course,' Jerome said, 'horses being waterproof.

Well, you know I am yours to command. You're the master, and if you want to try this scheme you've only to tell me what you want me to do. But I'm not sure I'd be able to supervise it and the other farming at the same time.'

'As to that,' Teddy said, 'it's only a matter of getting the right men in. You can have a farm manager under you to look after the market-gardening side while you oversee the stables. Mind, I don't want you to be picking out hoofs and mucking out stables. It's your brains I need. In fact,' he said, striking while the iron was hot, 'I always wanted you just to manage things, not go about hedging and ditching and hoeing and such-like. There's no need for you to make yourself a farm labourer. I can hire plenty of those.'

Jerome looked down at his roughened hands. 'Perhaps I needed to do those things,' he said quietly. 'You've done so much for us—'

'Oh, don't begin on that again,' Teddy interrupted hastily. 'It was all for my own good. I'm as selfish as the day is long.'

'No, you're not. I know exactly how much you do for us, out of the kindness of your heart. I'm the one who has been selfish. I wanted to toil like a labourer. I suppose I needed to punish myself for failing Henrietta and the children as I did.'

'Oh, I say,' Teddy said, alarmed at this excursion into personal revelation.

'It was always a ridiculous affectation. We all have our uses and abilities, and mine is to use the superior wits God gave me, not my very inferior muscles. I haven't been adding anything to the common weal by digging and delving. I've just been assuaging my own guilt.'

'Look here, old fellow—'

Jerome took pity on him. 'It's all right. I've done now. I'm not going to put you to the blush any more. I think this is a splendid scheme. Have you got as far as thinking about how to start?'

'I've had an idea or two,' Teddy said; and the two of them settled down into a serious and detailed discussion that was only interrupted, just after eleven, by the sudden wail of an

25

infant from somewhere upstairs. They both started, Teddy having forgotten what he was supposed to have been distracting Jerome from as completely as Jerome himself.

Ashley arrived earlier on Saturday than anyone had looked for, having been given the morning off from the office by his principal, Mr Culpepper, in honour of the occasion. Mr Culpepper sent by Ashley his congratulations and a bottle of fine port.

'How very kind,' Henrietta said. 'We must write and thank him.'

'Everyone at the office was very excited when the telegram arrived,' Ashley said. 'The fellows took me out after work for champagne at the George and Dragon, and Maltby advised me to put a notice in *The Times*. He says you get more than the money's worth in gifts from firms that advertise in it.'

'Yes, I remember that from when Jack was born,' Henrietta said. 'All sorts of things came through the post, soap and powder and patent foods. Well, come upstairs and meet your son.'

Lizzie, sitting up in bed and waiting in great excitement for the moment, almost laughed when Ashley came tiptoeing in, as though too much noise or movement would break something. But at the sight of his face laughter fled and she felt only awe that anything she could do could arouse such emotion in a great strong man. In silence she proffered the baby to him, but he did not take it, only bent over and studied the tightly sleeping face.

'He's beautiful,' he said at last. 'I thought all new babies were wrinkled and ugly, but he's quite dazzling! Like a vision. Is he really ours?'

Lizzie said, 'I know exactly what you mean. Just at first, I thought he must be an angel, and that Heaven would notice the mistake and snatch him back. But I've held him for long enough now to be sure. Here, you must hold him. Do!'

With great care, and not at all awkwardly, Ashley slid his big hands under the tiny thing and lifted him, cradled him in his arms, his eyes never leaving the beautiful face. Lizzie watched in silence, close to tears. When she was able to speak again, she said, 'I'm sorry you weren't here. I wish I could have held on until today, but he would come.'

'Never mind. I'm here now.'

'I wanted you very badly,' Lizzie pursued, 'but it was *so* comforting to have Mother and Emma here, instead of a strange nurse.'

He looked up for long enough to smile at her. 'I'm not angry about it. I know you needed to be with your mama. I'm just glad you are both all right. You look amazingly well.'

'I feel amazingly well,' Lizzie said. 'It was jolly hard work, and I was tired afterwards, but otherwise, I feel perfectly fine.'

Ashley sat down on the edge of the bed so that he could hold her hand while they both looked at the baby.

'You do think he's the most wonderful baby that ever lived, don't you?' she enquired.

'Certainly I do. Don't you?'

'Oh, yes, absolutely.'

He touched the velvet cheek with a forefinger. 'What shall we call him?'

'I really hadn't thought,' Lizzie said.

'I'd rather like to name him after my father. If you wouldn't object.'

'Martial? It's a large name for such a small fellow.'

'He'll grow,' said Ashley. 'And we can name him after your papa too, if you like.'

Lizzie smiled. 'You can suggest it, but I promise you, he'll only laugh.'

Jerome laughed. 'Lord, no, that's too much of a burden for one small child! Martial Jerome? Sounds like a French general in Napoleon's army. Thank you, Ashley, and I appreciate the honour, but spare the little chap that! Besides, I'm only Lizzie's step-father, you know.'

'But she thinks of you as her father. And it doesn't seem fair to name him only after my side of the family.'

'Well, Lizzie's real father was called Edgar, as I remember, and that doesn't sound any better. How about calling him Henry after Lizzie's favourite mother?'

Ashley's anxious frown disappeared. 'What a splendid idea, sir! Martial Henry Morland. It sounds very well, don't you think?'

'It sounds excellently,' Jerome agreed.

Morland Place had a special importance in Ashley's heart. His mother had been born there, and as she had married a distant cousin, his father's ancestors had come from Morland Place too. Through his childhood they had both talked about it as the family's long home, the well from which all Morlands sprang. Ashley had grown up with it always in the background of his mind. Far away in Carolina it had been a misty symbol, half mythical, lost and wholly desirable, like a mixture of Camelot and Eldorado. Later, when they had moved to Boston and his mother was dead, he had conceived a desire to visit it one day, as a kind of pilgrimage in his mother's memory.

It was many long years before he was able to fulfil the ambition, but at last he went there, as a tourist, in the sort of state of mind in which anything might happen. What had happened was that he had met Lizzie, and fallen in love with her instantly. She was the princess trapped in the tower whom he was fated to rescue – the tower in this case being her father's unfortunate situation.

So he did not resent her desire to go back there to have their child. Although she talked of wanting to be with her mother, in his mind it was Morland Place that was important. Their son had been born at Morland Place, and that seemed both absolutely natural and right, and like a huge portent or symbol. So it was that he asked Teddy if the child could be christened in the chapel there. Teddy saw the symmetry of it immediately: he was not of the very brightest, but he was a Morland through and through. He went off at once to see the parish priest, to ask if he could perform the ceremony the following day, before Ashley had to go back to London.

Teddy was master of Morland Place, and the priest would

have done much more than that to accommodate his wishes. The chapel had never been deconsecrated, so it was only a matter of his sparing the time. The following day at noon he came over to the house and the family gathered to receive the newest Morland into the community of the Church.

The children were scrubbed and awed into their best behaviour: Jack, Robbie, Frank, Jessie and little Ned Bone, George's bastard child, brought over by Teddy and Charley. Charley in her practical way had brought two vast baskets of provender from her own kitchen to supply a cold collation afterwards. Her cook was superb, and as Teddy had put a case of champagne into the carriage as well, the new baby was assured of a fine launching.

After the 'dipping', through which young Martial Henry slept fast, they all repaired to the dining-saloon, where Charley's offerings had been laid out in splendid array – pies, pasties, cold chicken, ham, salads and fruits – together with a jelly, a blancmange and a cake which Emma had managed to make in the short time available, determined to contribute something to the occasion. Lizzie, who had been carried down to the chapel in a chair, was installed on a *chaise-longue*, and since Jerome assured everyone that champagne was the best thing in the world for new mothers, she did not miss anything.

When sufficient toasts had been drunk, and there was a lull in the conversation, Ashley announced that he had some news. 'In honour of this great occasion, my principal, Mr Culpepper, has not only sent his congratulations, he has also given me a promotion. Old Barton is to retire and I am raised from Monday next to the position of manager of the office, with,' he added, with a significant look at Lizzie, 'a substantial increase in salary – if you'll forgive the mention of such a base subject on this auspicious occasion.'

'Nothing base about money, old fellow,' Teddy said. 'Not if it's put to good use.'

'Oh, it will be,' Ashley said cheerfully. 'I'm not just a husband now, I'm a father, with a whole new world of responsibilities. A man must take care of his family, you know. I'm sure that's why Mr Culpepper gave me the promotion.'

No-one else noticed, so engaged were they with congratulating Ashley, but Henrietta looked swiftly at Jerome, and saw the impact of the words. It was only a momentary blink, before he joined as heartily as anyone in the toasting of Ashley's success, but she knew he had felt it.

The rest of the day – and of Ashley's visit – went all too quickly. He had to catch the 8.05 train back to Town so as to be at work the next morning, and he and Lizzie parted reluctantly. She cried a little, but assured him it was her delicate condition that made her weep.

'I'll come down again next week-end,' he promised.

'I know. But that's a whole week away.'

'When will you be able to come home?'

'I'm not supposed to get up for three weeks, and then it will be another week after that before I'm allowed out of the house.'

'It seems an awfully long time.'

'I shall probably go mad,' Lizzie sighed, her tears abating. She blew her nose briskly. 'I feel well enough to get up now.'

He kissed her tenderly and removed a stray drop from her cheek with the side of his thumb. 'Take your time,' he said. 'I want you to be completely well again before you come home. And you need to learn what to do with the baby before you try it out on your own.'

Teddy and Charley took Ashley to the station in their carriage on their way home, so everyone left at once. Henrietta and Emma then had to get the children to bed, and Henrietta looked in on Lizzie and promised to bring her supper upstairs and eat with her. Only then did she have time to seek out her husband in private.

After a long search she found him in the drawing-room – not the one they used, but the original one, which was in process of being restored from the fire damage. The moon was up, a hard, bright one, and it laid squares of blue-white light across the bare floor through the uncurtained windows. The room was empty of furniture, but there were ladders and buckets and cloths, and a smell of plaster in the air.

Jerome didn't turn as she came in behind him. He was standing facing the windows and she guessed that he had been like that, unmoving, for a long time, for Kithra was lying at his feet with his nose on his paws, a posture of resignation. The dog got up and greeted her with a swing of the tail, and she put a hand down to him, but her attention was on her husband.

After a moment, she said, 'He didn't mean anything by it. It was just a little tactless, that's all.'

'Hmm?'

'Ashley likes and respects you.'

He turned his head at last and looked down at her. It was a long, searching look and, without their usual gleam of humour, his eyes seemed bleak. 'Is this what I've brought you to? To be listening out for every word anyone says in case it upsets my fine vanity?'

'Oh, no—' she began to protest, but he touched her lips with his finger to stop her.

'Vanity,' he asserted. 'Yes, you're right, it did hurt me, just for a moment. I've failed you. I threw away my fortune, and now I can't even work to support you.'

'You *do* work! Far too hard! Oh, dearest, I wish you wouldn't. You're so tired sometimes when you come in that you can't eat, and I'm afraid—'

'Yes?'

'That you'll make yourself ill. Or – or hurt yourself.'

'Yes, I know what's been in your mind, and you were not entirely wrong. Do you remember as a child when you were baulked in some way, doing something pointless and destructive which hurt only yourself? "Cutting off your nose to spite your face", as nannies say?'

'I didn't really have a nanny.'

'And I dare say, sunny-tempered little thing you no doubt were, that you never felt anything so unregulated.'

Henrietta smiled. 'You have a strange idea of me. I was a wild and wilful child, not the angel of the hearth, you know.'

'But sunny, always sunny,' he said tenderly. 'Yes, I've been working hard, doing things I'm not cut out for, and yes, there was in the back of my mind a sense of spiting Life. It had brought me low, so I was going to plumb the depths, and if it killed me then perhaps Life would be sorry. Ridiculous, isn't it?'

'I understand,' Henrietta said. She was so overwhelmingly glad he was talking to her about it at last she hardly had room for any other emotion.

'Yes, I know you do. Perhaps you should have understood me less, and given me a good shaking instead! You and Emma bore the brunt of the hardship and never used it to make martyrs of yourselves.'

'Women are different,' she said, searching for the right words. 'We don't look far ahead as men do – just the next meal and the next clean shirt.'

He put his arms round her and drew her to him, and sighed, resting his chin on the top of her head. 'You are my great comfort. And I want you to know that what you hold in your arms now is a whole new Jerome. No more nose-and-face business. No more digging ditches in the freezing rain. Vanity is cast away: I shall take pride in the future in having none.'

'What are you talking about?' She pulled her head back to look up at him, and saw with relief that the humour had returned.

'Teddy has a new scheme,' he said. 'Come, sit with me, and I'll tell you about it.'

He led her over to the window-seat, and took her onto his lap, the way they had spent many an evening when they were first married. She was a small woman, and fitted comfortably into his arms that way.

'It's a very long-term scheme,' he concluded, 'but there'll always be an army and they'll always need horses, so I think it's a sound one. And I shall throw myself into it wholeheartedly, and let him hire a man to oversee the farming.' She was silent. 'Don't you like it?'

'Oh, yes. It will be lovely to have horses on the place again. But – Jerome – don't you wonder what Teddy means to happen in the long run?'

'In the long run?'

32

'To Morland Place.'

'Darling, Morland Place isn't ours, and we have to accept that we will leave one day. The children have to be prepared to earn their own livings, and when they've flown the nest you and I will probably have to move on.'

'Yes,' said Henrietta, and the loss was in her voice along with the acceptance. She had parted with Morland Place long ago, when she first married Mr Fortescue. Coming back here was just a temporary bonus – she had always told herself so. But the heart and the mind did not always work in concert, and her heart had sung at the thought of coming home, no matter what her mind told it.

'But we'll be all right, the two of us,' Jerome said, squeezing her briefly to emphasise his words. 'We'll save a little, and we'll manage somehow. Teddy will never see us separated in the workhouse.'

'Oh, it could never come to that!'

'Well, it could, but I don't think it will,' he said. 'But I want to tell you something else. About these last two years. The work I've done here hasn't been wasted. I was always interested in Morland Place – you talked about it with so much love and such wistfulness – but since I've been here I've come to love it too. I think I know now what it means to you, and that could never have happened if I hadn't worked for it with my own hands. Every fence-post I've knocked in, every bed I've hoed, every hedge I've cut, the guttering on the stable roof I mended, the panels in the barn I repaired – all those things have tied me to it. Morland Place is *mine* now, in a way I don't think it can ever be Teddy's. The land belongs to me, and it always will, even when we have to leave it. So I don't regret my folly of the last two years. There was method in my madness after all.'

She didn't say anything, only tightened her arms round him to show she understood.

'I'm a lucky man,' he said, after a while. 'So many things to love.' And he turned her face gently to him and kissed her, long and lovingly.

And then they got up, though he kept hold of her hand.

'When the drawing-room is finished, we ought to have a celebration to launch it,' he said cheerfully.

'Like a ship,' she laughed.

'If Teddy will stump up the champagne, I promise not a drop will be wasted by breaking a bottle over anything.'

CHAPTER TWO

The noise was tremendous, and as the Thing proceeded jarringly over the track, it threw up a huge cloud of dust that followed behind and hung on the air like a bride's veil lifted by a breeze. Birds flew out of the hedges with cries of alarm, the mares in the home paddock raced away bucking, and the cows in the field by the track fled, pounding up to the far end, udders swinging, to the probable detriment of their milk. Kithra took up a brave position of defiance in the middle of the way and would have barked if he had not been of the mute breed, but leapt for safety at the sound of a warning hooter as loud as a foghorn and twice as raucous.

The Thing jerked to a halt opposite the end of the drawbridge and the children came tumbling out from under the barbican, clamouring excitedly. They stopped dead and fell silent, at the sight not only of the machine but of its riders, who appeared, horribly, to have no faces under their staring goggles. But then the hindermost put up a hand, whipped off goggles and silk dust-mask together, and revealed the familiar features of the master of Morland Place, beaming with boyish pleasure at the effect he had created.

'Uncle Teddy! Uncle Teddy!'

'It's a motor-car!'

'Gosh, what a beauty!'

'Is it yours, Uncle?'

Teddy climbed down, stripping off his dust-coat and brushing himself. 'Quite a machine, eh, boys?' He ruffled Frank's hair in greeting and swept Jessie up into his arms

35

to kiss her. 'How's my princess? How's my little fairy-cake?'

Jessie loved her uncle but felt that at eight and nearly a half she was getting a little elderly for this sort of treatment. 'Very well, thank you,' she said, with repelling politeness.

Teddy, impervious, kissed her again and put her down. 'That's right,' he said. 'Run and fetch your mother, there's a good girl. Is your papa at home?'

'He's doing accounts in the steward's room,' Jack supplied, his eyes never leaving the wonderful motor-carriage for a moment.

'Fetch him out too, then,' Teddy instructed Jessie. 'He mustn't miss this.'

They came, Henrietta wiping flour from her hands on her apron, Jerome still slipping into his jacket, and behind them, at intervals relating to their distance in the house from the summons, came Emma, Martha and Mrs Cotton, the charwoman, agog with interest.

The motor was now unoccupied, the engineer having got down from the front seat. Removing his mask and goggles, he revealed himself to be a plain and pleasant human and not at all like a hideous Morlock. The machine squatted, shuddering and growling, and occasionally letting out a cough that jarred its whole body. Henrietta, trying to assemble her scattered wits, thought vaguely that it must be the dust that troubled it.

'Won't it run off with no-one in it?' was her first spoken thought.

'Oh, no, the brake is on and the engine isn't engaged,' Teddy assured her. 'You see—'

'No, please don't tell me,' Henrietta said, with a lift of her hand. 'I haven't got a mind that can understand machines. Where did you get it, Ted?'

'Oh, it isn't mine. Belongs to Meynell – you know, chap who owns the paper mill out at Layerthorpe. I know him from the Chamber of Commerce, and he's a member of my club. Capital fellow. It's a Panhard. He took me out for a run the other day. All the way to Thirsk – and can you guess how long it took?'

'Tell us,' Jerome invited indulgently.

'One hour! And that was including stops.'

'Stops? You stopped for refreshment?' Henrietta hazarded.

'Oh! No, they were involuntary stops. Mechanical problems. Some trifling adjustment needed. But if you allow for the stops, we must have been travelling at well over twenty miles an hour.'

'Remarkable!' Jerome said.

'I tell you,' Teddy enthused, 'this is the transport of the future! It never gets tired, it can go up hills without everyone having to get out, and when you get there, you can just leave it to stand anywhere. Don't have to tie it up. Have it stand outside and wait for you for hours in the middle of winter if you want. No need to stable it or rug it up or water it.'

Henrietta nodded. 'Yes. I can see the benefits. But it is awfully noisy, isn't it? And – well, the smell is rather disagreeable.'

'Oh, you'll soon get used to that. I dare say people said the same thing about railways, but nobody thinks 'em noisy or smelly now. Or, well,' he acknowledged, 'they may be, but you wouldn't be without 'em, would you? It's a small price to pay for progress.'

'True,' said Jerome. The children were now climbing all over the machine, thrilled by the novelty, while the engineer was kindly answering Jack's eager questions. Jerome walked round it slowly. It was a large, open carriage with two long leather-covered seats, one behind the other, with the driver sitting to one side of the front one. The body was painted dark blue with black mudguards, the glossy flanks rather dimmed by dust at the moment. The engine was housed in front, under a protruding bonnet, and where it was undimmed by dust, the high gloss of the coachwork reflected the interrupted blue of the April sky. It was the first motor Jerome had been close to, though he had seen an electric brougham going along the Wetherby road about a month ago.

It was only three years since the repeal of the Road Traffic Act, which restricted mechanical vehicles on public highways to four miles an hour, and required them to be preceded by a man on foot carrying a red flag. It had been reported in the newspapers that a group of motor-owners had celebrated the repeal by gathering in London, burning a red flag and then setting off all together to drive down to Brighton. None of them got there without stops for mechanical failure, and some never got there at all, but it must have been an inspiring sight – and also, Jerome thought, a lucrative day for enterprising fellows along the route possessed of a heavy horse and some stout rope.

The speed limit had been raised at the time of the repeal to twelve miles an hour, something that did not seem to have bothered Teddy or his friend Meynell.

'So,' said Teddy, 'who's going to come for a ride with me? Henrietta, I think you should have first go.'

Henrietta drew back. 'No, I don't think so. Thank you, but I've far too much to do.'

'Nonsense! You deserve a little treat more than anyone. Housework can wait.'

This was true, and Henrietta had to own up. 'Dear Teddy, but I really don't want to. I much prefer horses.'

'How do you know, Mother, if you've never tried?' Jack said logically. His face showed naked yearning for the treat, but he was too well brought up to ask.

'I don't think I want to career along at twenty miles an hour on something that can't see where it's going. Yes,' she stemmed the protest, 'I know trains go faster than that, but they're on rails and there's nothing in their way. What will this thing do if it comes round a corner and finds the road blocked by a flock of sheep?'

There was a chorus of 'Oh, Mother!' from Jack and Robbie.

'*You*'re not scared, are you, Dad?' Jessie said confidently.

Jerome could not refuse to remain her hero. 'Certainly not,' he said. 'I'm your man, Teddy! Let it never be said that my heart failed before a challenge. Compton the Dauntless, that's how they'll remember me.'

'Remember you? Is it really dangerous, then?' Henrietta said, alarmed.

'Of course not,' Teddy said. 'He's only funning. Lord!'

38

Jack's burning desire finally overcame his self-control, and he said, 'Oh, *please*, Uncle Teddy, please couldn't I come too?'

Before Teddy could speak, Henrietta intervened. 'No, dear, of course not. It isn't a toy, you know, and Mr Meynell didn't lend it for children to play with.'

Teddy eyed his nephew with considerable sympathy, but agreed. 'Sorry, old chap. Grown-ups only. Besides, I've only got one spare set of dust-clothes. So, Jerome, you're ready for a trip?'

'Where were you planning on going?'

'How about a run out to Scarborough?' Teddy said largely.

'*Scarborough?*'

'Only take a couple of hours. That's the beauty of it.'

Jerome looked at Henrietta, who laughed. 'How could I deny you? One broken heart is enough to have on my conscience.'

'Three,' Jerome corrected, noting the passionate interest of his children in the machine.

'I don't think Frank cares much,' Henrietta said, for he had already wandered away and was examining the hedgerow for spiders.

'I wasn't counting Frank,' Jerome said.

For the rest of the day, the children talked of nothing but the motor. Jessie asked as many questions as Jack and Robbie. Few of them Henrietta could answer.

'Never mind, Mother,' Jack said kindly. 'I'll ask Dad when he comes home, and he'll explain it properly.'

They played motors in the yard all afternoon with two boxes and a hay bale to represent the carriage, a length of discarded pipe as the brake and an imaginary steering-wheel. They took it in turns to be the engineer, though Frank seemed happy to miss his turn and be the permanent passenger. The motor made appalling noises and seemed to crash and overturn with alarming frequency, tipping the passengers out into the dust, which only made Frank laugh. He was a great giggler. Robbie became a policeman summoned to deal with the accident, which meant arresting anyone he could physically overcome and throw into gaol – the end stall of the stables. Jessie, who hated a passive rôle, became a lady doctor attending to Frank's injuries. They were generally so serious they required immediate surgery, which she performed with whatever objects came to hand. She described in bloodcurdling detail what she was doing to him, but it only made Frank giggle harder.

After tea they settled down to draw at the table, Jack and Robbie devising motors of ever more fantastic elaboration, while Frank reverted to his preferred subject of soldiers and battles, and Jessie to horses. Henrietta was glad of the more peaceful occupation. The relentless crashing of the fantasy motor had played on her worst imaginings, and she did not know how she would bear the suspense until the men were safe home again – if ever they did return! Thank Heaven it was dry, fine weather; but it was only April after all, and would soon be dark, and then what would happen?

At about six the telegraph boy bicycled up to the house, giving Henrietta a bad five minutes until she read the wire from Jerome: 'Scarborough safe and sound. Dining here. Don't worry.'

Now all she had to worry about was their driving back in the dark. It was a clear night and there was a half-moon but she did not know whether the motor had lamps or not – she had not noticed – and unlike a horse the machine could not be trusted to pick its own way and avoid ditches.

To her vast relief, Jerome reappeared at last at almost ten o'clock. He came on foot, having walked from the road to save bringing the motor over the rough track. He looked bright-eyed and ruffled, and gave her a hearty hug and kiss with the words, 'Confess, now, have you been picturing yourself in widow's weeds?'

'After I got your wire? Certainly not. Why should I?'

He kissed her again. 'There was still the journey back.'

'How did you manage in the dark?'

'The thing had two lamps which fitted on the front, but we still had to go more slowly, of course. Is there any supper? I'm starved.'

'I thought you dined in Scarborough.'

'That was a very long time ago. Besides, there's something about riding a motor that stimulates the appetite.'

She provided a piece of pie and some cold potatoes, and sat with him at the table while he told the adventure.

'We had a couple of stops on the way, once for a broken tyre at Norton, which took a while to fix; and then somewhere this side of Seamer something went wrong with the engine and we just trickled to a halt. Simmons, the engineer, took a very long time to find out what it was, and Teddy and I, being complete tyros, could only sit beside the road and smoke and make sympathetic noises. The crowning humiliation came when a rustic fellow drove past in a cart with the sorriest-looking horse you ever saw between the shafts, and proposed to convey us to the railway station. He grinned in such a way as to let us know he took us for fools, and offered the information that he had seen another motor "brok' and yowsless" almost in the same spot a fortnight ago. "Tha'd be bitter off wi' owd Dobbin here," he said, and seeing the shape old Dobbin was in, we drew on our dignity and sent the fellow about his business. Besides, Teddy felt rather tender about abandoning Meynell's motor when it was only loaned to him, and I thought it would be a tame ending to our adventure, besides leaving poor Simmons in the lurch. So we sat it out, and finally Simmons managed to tinker the thing back to life, and off we went again. Only by the time we got to Scarborough it was nearly six and we were so hungry we decided to feed at the Grand before attempting the return leg.'

'It doesn't sound as though you had much fun,' Henrietta said.

'Oh, on the contrary, I enjoyed it immensely. We did the journey back without any stops, and it would have been even quicker if the roads weren't so bad. The breakdowns were rather a bore, but in between, when we were fairly bowling along, it was wonderful! Dashing down the road at anything up to twenty-five miles an hour, hedges rushing past, trees come and gone before you could see them—'

41

'Cows put off milk and horses frightened into fits,' Henrietta finished.

He laughed. 'Yes, to say nothing of the old ladies and children bowled over like ninepins by our passage! You are a Luddite, my darling.'

'I can't see the attraction of it. It looked,' she said, with dignity, 'extremely uncomfortable.'

'Well, yes, there is that. No springs to speak of, and having to be togged up like that against the dust and grit is not pleasant. But it's early days yet. I dare say they'll iron out all the problems in a few years, and motors of the future will be as comfortable as Teddy's carriage-and-pair.'

'I'll believe it when it happens,' said Henrietta.

The next day being Sunday, Henrietta forbade any discussion of motors until after dinner, which they had in the middle of the day after church. She and Jerome had early decided that Sunday mornings were to be quiet and thoughtful times, cheerful, but not noisy. The whole family walked to church, clean and tidy and in their best; the servants went in the evening. 'Wouldn't it be nice if we had a chaplain again,' Henrietta said, 'and we could all worship together at home?'

'Wouldn't it be nice if it rained gold sovereigns?' Jerome responded.

After dinner the children were allowed to take off their best Sunday clothes and be comfortable again. It was the one time in the week when Jerome was relatively at leisure, and they usually liked to do something together. Discussion of what that should be was still in progress when Teddy arrived, on horseback this time, with Ned, and motors leapt back into the conversation.

Every detail of the previous day's adventure was gone over again for the children's benefit – or such was the excuse. When paper and pencil was got out so that Teddy and Jerome between them could explain properly how the engine worked, Henrietta went to a chair by the window and got on with some mending. Her attention was drawn back to the group at the table when Teddy said, 'You seem to be

42

particularly interested in it, young Jackie. Would you like to be an engineer, do you think?'

'Oh, yes, sir,' Jack said promptly. 'Robbie and me really like engines.'

'Robbie and I,' Jerome corrected.

'I'd like to be a famous motor engineer and drive all over the world,' Robbie said.

'Me too,' said Ned. 'And I'd make lots of money and buy a big house, and it'd have a helter-skelter instead of a staircase and toy shop and a sweet shop in it.'

'I want to be a soldier,' Frank said, but no-one heeded him. He had already abstracted a stump of pencil and was drawing an artilleryman and field-gun on the corner of the sheet otherwise covered with the insides of a rapid-combustion engine.

'What about you?' Teddy asked Jack.

'I'd like to invent new engines, better ones. For motor cars or railway locomotives, I don't mind which. As long as it was something to do with engines, I wouldn't care.'

'You don't do that sort of thing at school, do you?' Teddy asked.

'They don't teach science much,' Jack admitted. 'And when they do – well, Mr Pullman doesn't seem to know very much. I mean, often when we ask questions he tells us to get on with something else, and I think it's because he doesn't know the answer.' He looked a little embarrassed as he tentatively voiced the criticism. All three boys went to St Edward's school, an ancient foundation originally endowed by the Morland family, and of which the master of Morland Place was always head of the board of governors. Being of the family, they received free schooling there, along with a number of poor boys.

But Teddy didn't seem upset. 'Hmm,' he said. 'We shall have to see about that.'

Afterwards, when the children had gone outside to play, he revived the subject. For some generations past, St Edward's had been neglected by the incumbent master. As with many of the smaller ancient grammar schools, the modern subjects were taught poorly or not at all, and the curriculum consisted largely of Latin and Greek. Teddy had only recently awoken to the state of things, and only because Ned also attended there.

'I ought to have thought about it before,' he said, 'but there's always so much else to do. And, to be frank, I've never bothered much with education. I went to Oxford, of course, but I never took my degree. In my day one went there to meet other chaps of one's own sort. Nobody thought of studying – only grinds who wanted to be dons or lawyers.'

'I remember,' Henrietta said. 'When you came home for the vacations you always talked about the dining clubs and visits to the races, never about tutorials or books.'

'And here I am, you know,' Teddy concluded. 'Lack of education never bothered me. But . . .' he paused, searching for tactful words '. . . I inherited my fortune from m'father, and all I've had to do is help it along. It's different for your lads. And the world's a different place now.'

'It certainly is,' said Jerome. 'Today motor-cars, tomorrow – what? Flying machines? Time machines?'

Teddy waved these Wellsean fantasies away. 'The country needs engineers of all sorts, and I ought to do something about having science and technology properly taught at the school. I'm going to propose to the board to build an extension for laboratories and so on. The old hospital wing could be converted. It's only used for storage now.'

Henrietta said, 'It would please Papa so much to know that you were having his subject taught properly.'

'You could call it the Benedict Morland Memorial Wing,' Jerome said. He meant it as a joke, but Teddy nodded seriously.

'Probably will. I'll have to put up the bulk of the money, of course, but that's only right. And there are government grants to be had now for teaching technology, which will help the thing along . . . Some of the other governors have been agitating about the curriculum for a while. Bayliss has been saying there's no point in keeping lads to eighteen just to do Latin and Greek. Not that many stay that long, of course.'

'But if you taught the modern subjects, perhaps they would,' Jerome suggested.

44

'Just so.'

'It seems a capital idea,' Jerome said, wondering what was coming that would affect his family. The terms of the school's trust gave members of the Morland family the right to free education at St Edward's, but only until the age of fourteen; and the Government's free elementary education stopped at twelve. Jack would be thirteen in August.

'Thing is,' Teddy went on, 'it will take time to get it set up and find the right ushers and so on. Ned's going to Eton next half, so he'll be out of it—'

'Is he?' Henrietta said with surprise. 'I didn't know.'

'Give him a little polish. He's not a great scholar, but it will do him good to mix with gentlemen's sons for a year or two. But your boys – Jack's only got one year to go. Time I've got it set up, it'll be too late for him. So I've been thinking. Bayliss says there's a very good School of Technology in Manchester. Takes boys from twelve. General education too, but the emphasis on science and so on. Little chap seems serious about this engineering business. Bright lad. What do you think?'

'Of sending Jack there?' Jerome answered. 'That we couldn't possibly afford it.'

'Oh, something can be arranged about fees. I've a large business acquaintance in Manchester, and I know a chap who knows a fellow who's on the board. Give him a bursary or some-such. As to the boy's expenses, they won't amount to much. I'll stand 'em. Least I can do.'

'No, the least you could do would be nothing at all,' Jerome said seriously.

'Well, I like Jackie. Ought to go far. Always a pleasure to help a bright lad along.'

'You are very kind,' said Jerome. 'I won't pretend we haven't been wondering what would happen to the boys when they left school. This would be a wonderful opportunity for Jack to learn something that would give him a profession.'

'He'd have to board there, I suppose?' Henrietta said.

Jerome touched her hand. 'Her next words are, "He's so young to be sent away so far from a mother's care."'

Henrietta flushed. 'I wasn't going to say that.'

'Thinking it, though,' Teddy said. 'Don't worry. Thirteen's not a baby. Do him the world of good to get away, have the corners knocked off him.'

'I like his corners,' said Henrietta, thinking how dreadful that expression sounded.

'Manchester's not the end of the earth,' Teddy went on. 'He can come home now and then on a week-end. Doesn't take long on the train. How's that?'

'Oh, Teddy, you're so good to us,' she sighed. 'What can I say but thank you?'

Much later, when Teddy had gone, Henrietta said, 'I do think it's splendid that Teddy's going to improve the school. It's taking his responsibilities seriously. The master of Morland Place ought to be more than a hunting and shooting gentleman, dedicated to pleasing himself, as Georgie was.'

'I honour him for it,' Jerome said. 'Wealth should entail obligations as well as privileges. I'm ashamed of how little I ever did for other people when I had my fortune. I was never as rich as Teddy seems to be, but still I was wholly frivolous when I was young.'

'So was Teddy. I believe it's Charley who makes him think about good works. He's always been a dear, kind person, but I don't think it would have occurred to him to do these things if he hadn't married her. It simply wouldn't have crossed his mind.'

'Were you surprised when he said he was sending Ned to Eton?'

'Yes, I was. He's a nice boy, but nothing of a scholar.'

'Do you know what I think? That he's decided definitely to make Ned his heir, and wants to polish him up for the position. Which means leaving Morland Place to him.' He looked to see if she had caught the significance. 'Which in turn means our leaving.'

'You've always said that we would have to one day,' Henrietta pointed out.

'Yes, but I don't think that it had occurred to Teddy before. I believe he's just realised the natural consequences of Ned's growing up. So he's decided to do something for Jackie, to put him in the way of a career.'

'You may be right,' Henrietta said. 'Well, we are no worse off than before. And Teddy would never turn us out onto the street.'

'I agree,' said Jerome. 'We're safe as long as Teddy lives.'

'I wish you hadn't put it like that,' Henrietta said.

Henrietta's cousin Venetia (in fact a second cousin once removed, though a dear and close friend) lived what she called a Jekyll and Hyde existence. On the one hand she was Lady Venetia Hazelmere, daughter of the late Duke of Southport and married to Viscount Hazelmere, who was equerry to and friend of the Prince of Wales and therefore moved in the highest circles of government and society. On the other hand, under the alias of Dr Venetia Fleet, she was one of the first women to qualify as a doctor. She ran a successful practice in London, operated at the Southport Hospital and the New Hospital for Women, and ran a free dispensary for the poor in Marylebone Lane.

The rapid changes of her personal landscape from the calculated butchery of the operating theatre to a gilded box at the Theatre Royal Drury Lane, from the squalid misery of the homes of her free patients to the glittering drawing-rooms of the *ton*, were enough, her husband said, to dislocate the brain. Venetia found it tiring, but stimulating, and any suggestion that she should give up any part of her professional life was met with a raised eyebrow and a 'What on earth for?'

She also had a nursery of three children of her own, plus the son of her late sister who had been left to her charge. 'Any time I feel low or distracted, half an hour in the children's company will always refresh me,' she said. But as it happened, Thomas and Eddie were away at school now, and Oliver would be going next half, so the house was too quiet for much of the time.

'We could have some more,' Hazelmere suggested blandly.

Venetia only laughed. 'At my age? I think not. No, we'll have to wait for the grandchildren to appear. And in the mean time, if I find myself growing broody, I can always borrow Lizzie's for an hour or two.'

Lizzie had run tame about Venetia's house when she was a girl, and they were very fond of each other. Venetia's connection with Ashley, apart from the Morland blood, was through Ashley's employer. Mr Culpepper, the shipping magnate, had a daughter who had married Venetia's brother, the Duke of Southport. The marriage had been an unhappy one, for the duke had already ruined his health and mind with drink and drugs, and he died before providing his wife with the heir who would have secured the dukedom to Culpepper blood for ever. Mr Culpepper was deeply disappointed, and even more angry at the way his girl had been treated; but Venetia had always been kind to the shy young duchess, and supported her through her trials. Ashley's promotion had been fully justified by his own abilities, but it was Mr Culpepper's gratitude to Venetia that had directed his eyes towards Ashley in the first place.

When in May of 1899 Lizzie wrote to Venetia to announce that she was pregnant again, Venetia sent round a note of hearty congratulations together with a bottle of Ayala for their immediate celebration. 'You must get out and about while you can. Come and dine on Tuesday. We shall be rather elderly company, I'm afraid, as it's the height of the Season and the young people are all engaged in dancing, but we may have some interesting talk.'

Venetia did not normally go in for large dinner parties in the manner that her own and her husband's rank might have suggested. She preferred an intimate gathering of eight or ten where one conversation could be held over the whole table. The Ashley Morlands knew what to expect. Though Lizzie was too diffident to talk much, she loved to listen. Ashley, being Southern born and Yankee bred, was not shy in any company, but he too preferred listening to talking, when the company comprised people who were at the heart of national affairs.

The other guests on this occasion were Venetia's cousin Lady Anne Farraline, who was very active in the Women's Cause; Peter Dorney, the Earl of Padstowe's heir, who was in love with Anne and whom Venetia hoped she would marry; the Tonbridges – Lord Tonbridge was at the War Office

48

under Venetia's old beau 'Cocky' Lansdowne – and the Campbell-Bannermans.

Venetia had known Sir Henry Campbell-Bannerman all her life. He had recently become leader of the Liberal Party; and when they were seated around the table in the candlelit dining-room in the Hazelmeres' house in Manchester Square, Anne Farraline's first question was, 'Do tell us, how was the thing arranged between you and Mr Asquith? I hear he was rather miffed to have been passed over.'

'Oh, you mustn't say that, Lady Anne,' Sir Henry said, in his comfortable way. 'Dear me, no. It was all quite amicable. Asquith is a practising barrister, you know, and he wouldn't have had time for the duties of leader. He says himself that he's a poor man and has to earn his living.' Campbell-Bannerman, son of a Lord Provost of Glasgow, had inherited a large fortune.

'So there's no hard feeling between you?' Anne pursued.

'Not the least in the world,' he said, crinkling his eyes in amusement. His slight Scottish burr became more evident with words like *world*. 'I'm sorry to spoil your fun.'

'The poor man must have need of all the briefs he can handle, with a large family to support,' said Lady Campbell-Bannerman.

'To say nothing of an expensive new wife,' Lord Tonbridge added.

'Now there *is* a story to marvel at,' Lady Tonbridge remarked. 'How he should have come to propose to Margot Tennant I shall never conceive!'

'I was never more surprised in my life,' Anne agreed.

'Don't you think widowers should ever marry a second time?' Venetia asked innocently. 'Too harsh, my love!'

'Oh, it's not that,' Anne said. 'It's just that they are so different. She's so volatile and he's so – *polite*.'

'Ah, well, they say opposites attract,' said Sir Henry.

'She is a woman I've no time for,' Lady Tonbridge said. 'So – *outré*.'

It had been quite an *on-dit* at the time of their marriage in 1894. Asquith's first wife Helen had been a gentle, shy, unambitious woman, content with the traditional rôle of

49

wife and mother to his five children. Margot Tennant was ebullient, outgoing, garrulous, flamboyant. She was passionate about hunting and outdoor sports, noisy fun, and trivial, jolly games indoors. Asquith cared nothing for the life athletic and would not break out of a walk even to catch a train. He was quiet, reserved, highly educated, a lover of books and measured conversation. His remarkably self-controlled children never cried, quarrelled or teased, while the Tennants at home spent their time alternately in floods of tears and gales of laughter. Margot was all temperament and Herbert Henry all intellect.

'I *have* heard—' Lady Tonbridge began, and Campbell-Bannerman, guessing that she was about to revive some unkind gossip, affected not to have caught her words and interrupted her with a story of his own.

'I don't know whether you heard about how the Social Democratic Federation reacted to Asquith's engagement? It was rather amusing. It seems that there was a mass meeting held on Tower Hill, and the organiser, one John Williams, told the crowd that he had seen an announcement the previous day that caused tears of joy to run down his face. He had thought the notice said, "Mr Asquith going to be murdered."' Campbell-Bannerman gave the full Scottish weight to the *r* s in the word. 'However, the fellow went on, it transpired that all the notice said was that Mr Asquith was going to be *married*. So Williams proposed that a congratulatory message should be sent, saying, "This meeting, hearing that Mr Asquith is about to enter the holy bonds of matrimony, trusts that his partner will be one of the worst Tartars in the world, and that his family troubles will compel him to retire from public life, for which he is so unfit."'

There was laughter round the table, though Lord Tonbridge shook his head a little and murmured something about damned Socialists.

Anne revived her question to Campbell-Bannerman. 'So there is no difference between you and Mr Asquith about the leadership?'

'Not the least bit in the world. Why should there be?'

'Only that one of you could be prime minister one of these days.'

'It may be a long wait,' Hazelmere said. 'The Conservatives seemed fixed for ever.'

'Oh, we shall come about,' Campbell-Bannerman said. 'We have only to wait. The people will want a change sooner or later, and then it will be our turn.'

'You're not afraid of the Socialists?' Ashley asked.

Campbell-Bannerman smiled. 'Ours is a two-party system, always was and always will be. It's the natural state of things.'

'Quite right!' Lord Tonbridge said. 'The idea of a Socialist government is enough to make the blood run cold!'

When the entrée had been brought in, the conversation turned, inevitably, to the situation in South Africa.

The British workers in the Transvaal formed the majority of the population and paid the bulk of its taxes, yet as 'Uitlanders' were denied the vote or any civil rights. The previous November a British mines engineer in Johannesburg had been shot by a policeman in circumstances that amounted to murder. The policeman, though arrested to appease the Uitlanders, had been released on a nominal bail, and in January 1899 had been tried before a jury consisting solely of Boers. They had acquitted him, and the judge, insultingly, had added a public commendation of the policeman's actions. The Uitlanders' fury had overspilled into mass agitation, which the Boers had suppressed harshly. So now in desperation the Uitlanders had got up a petition with nearly twenty-two thousand signatures, which they had sent to the Queen, begging her for protection and justice.

'But is the Government going to take up the petition?' Ashley asked the table at large.

'It must do, surely,' said Lady Campbell-Bannerman. 'How can it ignore the Uitlanders' plight?'

'It would mean war,' Hazelmere said. Campbell-Bannerman seemed to agree with this, nodding silently over his lamb cutlets.

'Oh, surely not,' Dorney said. 'A show of strength, with

real firmness behind it, ought to bring the Boers round. Don't you think?' He appealed to Tonbridge.

'That's not Milner's opinion,' Tonbridge said. Sir Alfred Milner was the High Commissioner in the Cape. 'He believes that Kruger wants to break out entirely and create an independent United States of South Africa under Transvaal domination.'

'With himself as president, no doubt?' Ashley said.

'Of course.'

Hazelmere took over. 'And with the tide of Afrikaaner feeling running his way, he's not likely to give his dream up for anything less than complete military defeat.'

'So Milner thinks, anyway,' Tonbridge finished.

'He should know how the Boers think,' said Lady Tonbridge shortly. 'He's half a German himself.'

Hazelmere chose not to see this as a criticism. 'So he understands the Boer mind. And he's the man on the spot, after all.'

'What do you think, Sir Henry?' Venetia asked. 'Is Milner right?'

'I believe so. If we take up the petition, it will mean war.'

'I gather from your tone of voice,' Dorney said, 'that you would not approve of war against the Boers.'

'I think we ought to keep a sense of proportion about it all.'

'Because it's only a few thousand British subjects in a country far away?' Anne suggested.

'My dear young lady, please don't bite my head off,' Campbell-Bannerman said, with an amused look. He laid his fork down thoughtfully. 'It's a ticklish problem. Tonbridge, I'm sure you can explain it all better than me.'

'Go ahead, old fellow,' Tonbridge said, waving his own fork delicately. 'I'm engaged with this delicious lamb. You have an excellent cook, Lady Venetia.'

'Thank you. Please go on, Sir Henry.'

'I've forgotten where I was.'

'No prevarication! The ticklish problem, if you please.'

'Very well,' said Sir Henry. 'You see, on the one hand there is the problem of British prestige. If it were seen that thousands of British subjects were living virtually as helots, to use Milner's word – ill-treated, oppressed, deprived of any voice – and that they had appealed to the Government in vain for redress, our influence abroad would be greatly damaged and respect for Great Britain would be undermined.'

'You think it a matter of reputation? I would rather say honour,' Dorney objected.

Sir Henry bowed. 'As you please.'

'Then surely we must intervene,' Anne urged.

'I have not yet given the other side of the argument,' he said. 'If we intervene, we will have to fight. And the fight, with all due respect to you, Dorney,' he inserted a bow in the younger man's direction, 'would not be a matter of merely showing our teeth. Kruger is a virtual dictator, and he has spent the last two years preparing for war. Building forts, importing huge quantities of arms; heavy guns too.'

'And he has employed German artillery officers to train and lead his men,' Tonbridge supplied.

'We can be sure,' Sir Henry concluded, 'that he has not built up so much force for nothing. He will welcome the excuse to use it, unite the Dutch behind him, and seize his prize.'

'But surely, sir, there's no doubt that we would beat them?' Peter Dorney said.

'I dare say we would,' said Campbell-Bannerman. 'But at what cost? Look here, Kruger is an old man. We have only to wait. When he dies, things will change anyway. There will be reform and the Uitlanders will have their redress without our needing to go to war. And,' he added, 'there may well be larger consequences to action against the Boers, out of all proportion to the benefit of advancing Uitlander comfort by a few years.'

'Larger consequences?' Anne said. 'What can they be?'

Venetia answered her. 'We already know that, my love. Don't you remember the Kaiser's telegram to Kruger after the Jameson Raid? That's what you mean, isn't it, Sir Henry – that war with Kruger might lead to war with Germany?'

'Germany would never fight us,' Lady Tonbridge objected. 'The Queen is the Kaiser's grandmother. Whatever his ministers might urge, he would stop short of attacking his own grandmother.'

'The truth is,' Hazelmere said, 'that we are damnably isolated at the moment. France and Russia have their entente and Germany and Austria-Hungary have their alliance, and here we are in the middle with no friends.'

'We don't need friends,' Lady Tonbridge said superbly. 'We can stand alone as we always have. Our navy rules the seas.'

'Which is precisely why the Kaiser has been building ships as fast as he can,' Hazelmere said. 'He has an army which cannot be beaten on the Continent, and now he's turned his attention to building up a navy that can challenge ours.'

'But Germany would never attack us over something like the Boers,' Lady Tonbridge protested.

'Perhaps not,' said Sir Henry mildly. 'But history shows us that it always *is* just these little quarrels that start up great wars.'

At that point Venetia changed the subject to give Campbell-Bannerman the opportunity to eat his dinner; but later, in the drawing-room over coffee, she sat beside him and revived the subject privately. 'Now, Henry, strictly *entre nous*, what do you suppose the Government will do about the Uitlanders?'

'It's Chamberlain's bailiwick. He's Colonial Secretary. I suspect he'll recommend negotiation. Certainly they must try that route first.'

'But they'll take up the petition?'

'I believe they have to. What happens after that depends on too many things for me to guess at.'

'But you think it will lead to war.'

He smiled. 'My dear Venetia, you are more in Lansdowne's confidence than I am.'

'Yes, and from what he tells me, the army is not in the best of health to prosecute a war in a place like South Africa.'

'What can you mean, my dear?'

'You know what I mean: it lacks a general staff. If only you had gone about making the reform back in 1890 when you had the chance. You managed to get rid of the Duke of Cambridge – that was so adroit of you, Henry, to do it without upsetting the Queen! I was all admiration. But you did not go far enough. Still all decisions go through the commander-in-chief, and Wolseley is almost as bad as the Duke was.'

'Oh, come!' Campbell-Bannerman protested, laughing.

'I'm quite serious, Henry. Cocky Lansdowne is no match for him. Every decision will have to go through him and there will be endless delays and muddle and shortages, just as Mama tells me there were in the Crimea. I wish you may not regret it.'

'You paint a black picture. But consider the alternative.'

'The alternative is to have a general staff, like every other country in Europe.'

'But we are not like any other country. We do not have conscript armies. We are surrounded by our sea defences and march out only at our greatest need. We are not Germany, my dear, wanting to subsume our neighbours.'

'But the general staff is the brain of an army. We have an army without a brain,' Venetia urged.

'If it had a brain, it might think too much,' Sir Henry responded. 'If we had a general staff, and there was nothing for it to do, it might *make* something to do. That is what has happened on the Continent. *You* should understand. Your father felt the same way, when he and I worked together under Cardwell. I learnt my objections from him as much as from anyone. Too much professionalism in the army is dangerous to our personal liberty. We are not a militarist power.'

'Yet we may have to fight a militarist power. I know Papa believed as you did, but he also saw the other side of the argument. He was in the intelligence division in the Crimea and he knew how important it was. How can you make a plan without intelligence? And how can you prosecute a campaign without a plan?'

'Oh, we shall come through,' he said, in his comfortable way. 'We always do.'

'At the cost of muddle and hardship.'

'It's a price worth paying for freedom. Better a little

muddle abroad than military rule at home. A dictator supported by an army? We don't have to look far to see what that is like. It must never happen here.'

Venetia had heard her father make this argument often enough in her youth, and part of her responded to it. Reports and pictures in the illustrated papers of the Kaiser in one of his many splendid uniforms, parading his vast and efficient armies with bands and banners through the public streets before a docile populace, made one glad of the stout little Queen, the peace and quiet of England, and the independent-minded British subject who hung on like a bulldog to his right to do as he pleased without interference from the Government or the Throne.

But the world had changed since her parents had witnessed at first hand the misery of the Crimean war. It had become a more dangerous place, and she was concerned that Britons might not be equipped to protect themselves in it.

There was enormous excitement at Morland Place on the day in June when Jerome brought the stallion home. He travelled down by train with it, having bought it from a breeder in Surrey, and it was a long journey, involving many shunts and long waits in sidings for the right train to come by. Then at York the horse-box was uncoupled and shunted off to another siding, where Teddy was waiting. He loved meeting trains anyway, and nothing short of imprisonment or death would have stopped him being there this time to let down the ramp and lead the animal out.

They put it into the railyard stable with water and hay to rest for a couple of hours; and then they rode home to Morland Place, leading the stallion between them. Teddy's gelding Victor and Jerome's Minstrel were both stolid, unemotional horses and were expected to have a calming effect on any temperamental outburst by the entire. But in fact they had no trouble at all until, coming along the last part of the track towards Morland Place, the stallion caught scent of the mares. Even so, there was only a trembling, a few deep whickers and some piercing neighs, which some of the mares answered. They had little difficulty in turning him off the track and over the drawbridge into the yard.

Henrietta and the servants were all waiting on the steps, having been alerted by the whinnying, along with the head man, Lelliot, whom Teddy had taken on when the first batch of breeding mares arrived.

'You didn't have any trouble with him?' Henrietta called, as they halted and dismounted.

'Not a bit. He has a wonderful temperament,' Jerome said. 'Didn't I tell you?'

Lelliot led Minstrel and Victor away and tied them up out of the way, and then came back to take the stallion's head. Jerome waved him off. 'No, no, I have him. You look him over, tell me what you think.'

'I think he's *beautiful*,' Henrietta said, as Lelliot began to walk slowly round the horse. 'The most beautiful horse I've ever seen. Does he have a name?'

'He has a stud name a yard long, but his stable name is Pasha.'

'Pasha. That's nice.' She drew her hand out of her pocket. 'I've an apple here. Do you think I could . . . ?'

'Of course,' Jerome said. 'I've been with him all the way down, and he's as gentle as a kitten. I tell you,' he enthused, 'he has the perfect temperament.'

Henrietta needed no further urging. She had been born and bred to horses, and had no fear of them. Pasha watched her approach, his nostrils fluttering to catch the scent of her. His ears went forward when he saw the apple, and he knuckered a soft greeting.

'Oh, you darling,' Henrietta said, slipping her hand under the enquiring nose, and stroking his cheek with the other. The horse felt around the apple with prehensile lips, and then bit it cleanly in half without touching Henrietta's skin. He crunched lustily, tossing his head up and down as the sweet juice teased his tongue, then nosed in for the other half.

He was a pure-bred Arabian, and in colour an unusually dark chestnut, as dark as liver-chestnut but richer in tone, with no white marks. He had all the breed's delicacy of head, the high, almost pointed quarters that made him look as though he was on tiptoe, the arching tail carriage, the slender, sloping pasterns and small, round hoofs. The eyes were large and intelligent, and, unlike some horses, he seemed to look at the people around him as if he saw them as individuals, as if he would know them again. He was, Henrietta thought, exquisite; but he was also very much a stallion, as the weight of his neck and the muscle packed over his crest and shoulders attested.

'Well, what do you think?' Jerome asked Lelliot, unable to wait any longer.

Teddy couldn't even wait for an answer. 'He's a good colour,' he put in, as if every other aspect had been mentioned already. 'Very distinguished, to have no white marks.'

'He looks healthy enough,' Lelliot said grudgingly. He was in his forties, already grizzled, and with a slight limp where a bad break had left his leg distorted. He was wonderful with horses, but sparing with his smiles and his words. 'How old?'

'Four,' said Jerome. 'All his life ahead of him.'

Lelliot sighed. 'He's too small. What is he, fourteen-two?'

'He's fifteen hands,' Jerome said. 'But—'

'Too small. You want bigger than that for army horses.'

'I was about to say, we put him to bigger mares, that's all. And the army will take anything from fifteen hands upwards. In fact, there are places bigger horses would be impractical. Look at Afghanistan!'

'Maybe,' said Lelliot, 'but the army doosn't want bits o' fancy work like this 'ere. They want working 'osses, plain and simple. Why, an 'oss like him wouldn't last five minutes on campaign.'

Jerome laughed, making Pasha jerk his head a little, his ears flicking back and forth enquiringly. 'My dear chap, you don't know Arabians! Toughest horses in the world!'

'What, wi' them skinny legs? And look at 'is little 'oofs! I reckon I could 'old two in one hand.'

'No, don't look at them – feel them! Go on! Small they might be, but they're hard as flint. Go for ever over any terrain, rock or sand, and never split. Not last on campaign?

What do you suppose the Arab people ride to war?'

Lelliot was lifting a foot with slightly increased respect, and as Pasha stood patiently to allow him, he said, 'Well, he seems kind enough, I'll give him that.'

'It'll be a good injection into army stock,' Teddy said happily, 'to have that temperament, plus that hardiness. And it will make our lives easier if we have good-tempered progeny from him.'

'Well, maister,' Lelliot said, straightening up, 'he must have cost you a pretty penny. I hope it'll pay you in the end. I never 'eard the army pays top price for its remounts.'

Teddy came forward to stroke the big neck admiringly. 'Oh, we've talked about all this before. If we're going to breed, we might as well have our own stallion as pay for someone else's to visit, and if we're going to have a stallion, it might as well be the best, not some scrawny screw that just happens not to have been gelded.'

'If you say so,' Lelliot said agnostically.

'You're the hardest man to persuade in the world,' Jerome laughed.

'Aye, well, I'm a Yorkshireman, and I reserve my judgement till I'm convinced.'

'You'll be convinced,' Teddy said. 'I don't just mean to breed army horses from him, but general riding horses as well. Everything benefits from an injection of Arabian blood. Besides, this fellow can serve any number of visiting mares as well as ours. When you see what a high stud fee he commands, and what a queue of people want to send their mares to us, you'll see his worth all right.'

Henrietta stroked the stallion's cheek again. 'Poor fellow, what a lifetime of labour lies ahead of you! I still believe,' she added, smiling at her brother, 'that it's nothing to do with business, that you just want everyone to say that the best stallion in the Ridings is at Morland Place!'

Teddy smiled and confessed, 'Why not? Not buying the best is false economy, especially with horses.'

'Are we tekkin' him up to Twelvetrees?' Lelliot asked.

'Not tonight,' Jerome said. 'I'll bed him down in the stable here. He's had enough travelling for one day.'

59

'Which means, you want the children to have a chance to see him when they get back from school,' Henrietta said.

'She sees through you, too,' Teddy nodded to Jerome.

When the children came home, they were amazed at how delicate-looking and gentle the stallion was, having never seen an Arabian before, and knowing the reputation of entire horses. Having been warned to be quiet and still, they crowded round the door of the loose-box and were thrilled when he came over to nuzzle them and accept their offerings of carrots and apples.

'He's like a fairy prince that's been turned into a horse by a magician,' Jessie said, enchanted in her turn.

'Fairy prince!' Robbie scoffed. 'He's too big to be a fairy.'

'All right, then, just a prince,' Jessie corrected. 'But a specially handsome and nice one, not the sort of person who'd steal a person's conker.'

'I didn't steal it. You lost it and I found it. Finding's keeping. Anyway, you can't prove it's yours. It could be anyone's.'

'It *is* mine. I know because—'

'Children, if you're going to quarrel, go and do it somewhere else,' Jerome commanded.

They stopped at once, and Jack asked, 'Are you going to ride him, Dad?'

'No, he's not for riding. He'll live a very different life from the other horses from now on.'

'Just think,' Jack said, 'one day our soldiers will ride his children. If we ever go to war, they might take part in the winning battle, and make all the difference because they're such good horses, and save the whole country.'

'Maybe Frank will ride one,' Jessie said.

'I'm going to be in the infantry, not the cavalry,' Frank objected.

'But if you're an officer you'll have a horse,' Jessie pointed out.

'If he's an officer, he won't have an army horse,' Jack said. 'He'll have his own private one.'

'Then it probably will be one of ours,' said Jessie, with triumphant logic.

Pasha followed the argument back and forth with his ears, then reached out and tentatively nibbled at Jessie's hair, which being fair and untidy did look rather like hay.

A fine-looking fellow lounging along Coney Street lifted his hat as Henrietta drove by, dragging her mind back from the puzzles of menus and marketing that occupied it.

'Bertie!' she said, checking the pony.

'Hello, Auntie. Shopping, or taking the air?'

'A little of both. Oh dear, we're holding up the traffic. Are you going anywhere in particular?'

'I'm as idle as the idle wind.'

'Then hop in, dear boy, so I can move off.'

He resumed his hat and hopped, disposing his limbs with exaggerated elegance in the space available, tilting his hat a little forward over his nose. He was Henrietta's nephew, eldest son of her sister Regina, who was married to Sir Peregrine Parke, the squire of Bishop Winthorpe. Bertie's name was actually Percival, but he disliked it and had insisted on using his second name ever since he went to school. He was twenty-two, tall and slim, with fine, light brown hair that would never lie down no matter what he put on it, and a healthy colour in his cheeks no matter how late he had been up the night before. Since coming down from Oxford he had grown a splendid set of moustaches, which were as fair as his hair but with just a hint of red, and they were the one thing about his physical appearance that gave him complete satisfaction.

'Actually,' he drawled, as they reached the corner of Museum Street and Dunnock automatically turned left, 'I was thinkin' of coming out to see you, only it's such a dashed long way to walk on a hot day like this.' The June sunshine was dancing on the river and reflecting painfully from every scrap of glass and metal in view. 'Frightfully hearty, this sunshine, don't you think? Drives spikes into your head.'

Henrietta glanced sideways at him. 'Were you out on the town again last night?'

'Oh, really, Aunt Hen, a lady like you shouldn't use such expressions. On the town? Whatever next?'

'Now, Bertie, don't try to bamboozle me! Tell the truth, sir. What were you up to?'

Bertie sank lower in the seat and pushed his hat further over his eyes. 'Just a bit of innocent fun. Drink or two with some fellows. Dinner at the club.'

'Ah,' said Henrietta. 'The Maccabbees, I suppose? Dinner accompanied and followed by far more wine and brandy than is good for you.'

'No, no, dash it, wine is good for the blood, and brandy settles the digestion. Most unhealthy chaps at Trinity were the teetotallers, I promise you.'

'And then,' Henrietta continued inexorably, 'a long session with the dice or cards, smoking until your head ached.'

'Baccy's meant to clear the head. All your great men like to smoke while they're thinking. Why, every don at Trinity sucked on a pipe.'

'And now you can't go home. How much did you lose?'

Bertie smiled suddenly – a smile that warmed every heart and disarmed every critic with the exception of his father – sat up properly and abandoned his affected drawl. 'You see through a fellow far too easily for a respectable matron. Makes one wonder what you can have been doing with your life.'

'One would have to be blind and deaf not to know about the sorts of foolishness young men get up to. Did you lose an awful lot?'

Bertie frowned judiciously. 'To be fair, it wasn't the dice. One has to be careful at the Maccabbees – can't get a bad name or they chuck you out. I don't play high there. But afterwards we went off to Jenkins's house to play cards, and that's where the damage was done. Trouble with June is it gets light too early, before you've fairly finished the evening, so there seems no reason to go to bed.'

'You played all night?'

'Till about eight this morning. Then Jenkins's man kicked us out. He's an awful tough, Jenkins's valet. Worse than a father to him. Said he had to get old Jenkins shaved and bathed and off to the office: he sleeps at a desk at his pater's place of business six days a week, lucky fellow. So I toddled off for a spot of breakfast, and I was just wandering along thinking about coming to visit my favourite aunt when, lo, you appeared.'

'You still haven't answered my question.'

'And I don't mean to,' Bertie said, with mock indignation. 'Think I don't know better than to mention the sordid subject of money before a lady? But to confess all, I don't want to go home for a bit. The Gov'nor don't like me gambling, as you well know, and the fact is I've spent my allowance twice over this month. Jenkins is sound enough – he knows how I'm fixed and he'll wait until I'm in funds again – but there's my bill at the club outstanding, and my tailor's out for my blood. The Gov might well think I ought to have settled accounts rather than play cards with the fellows.'

'I should think he would!'

'Yes, and what the Gov thinks, he has a vigorous way of expressing. Not a reticent man, my father.'

'Oh, Bertie!' Henrietta sighed. Dunnock was trotting along briskly now, heading for home, so she could spare attention for her nephew. 'Really, my dear, you must know it's wrong to run up bills. I don't mean to preach, but it's not manly to make tradespeople wait for their money.'

'Not manly? Oh, look here, Auntie!' Bertie protested, but his cheeks reddened.

'I mean it. They have a livelihood to make. Why should they pay for your pleasure, which is what it comes down to? Come, you know I'm right.'

'Well, yes, I suppose so. But what's a fellow to do? The Gov'nor keeps me so short, and debts of honour have to be paid first, you know. There's no help for it.'

'But why do you have to gamble, and drink, and smoke, and spend so much money on clothes and horses?'

Bertie looked at her steadily, all trace of teasing gone from his face and voice. 'What else is there to do? I must pass the time somehow.'

'You ought to have a career,' Henrietta said.

'Papa would never allow it. I'm to inherit my fortune one

63

day, and until then, I'm meant to sit about at home with my hands in my lap. Damned macabre, if you ask me,' he added, the effort of seriousness proving too much for him, 'waitin' about for the Gov'nor to hang up his tile!'

'Poor Bertie,' said Henrietta. 'I wish there were something I could do for you, but there isn't. You know I don't have any influence at the Red House.'

'There is something you can do – just take me home with you for a while,' said Bertie.

'You know you're welcome any time, and for as long as you like,' Henrietta said warmly.

'Oh, I say, thanks. You really are a trump, Aunt Hen.'

'You can repay me by telling me how your mother is,' Henrietta said.

When she had been widowed, her brother-in-law Perry had taken her and Lizzie in, and she would always be grateful to him for that. But when Jerome had begun to court her, Perry had objected. Jerome had a wife still living: in the eyes of the respectable part of society divorce was not possible and he was still married. Their crime, or sin, was compounded by the fact that Henrietta was the rector's widow, and should therefore have had higher standards than the norm. Perry had his own and his wife's reputation to consider, and the futures of his eight children. He could not afford any scandal to touch them. So Henrietta and Jerome had gone to London, and when they married – shockingly – in a register office, Perry had cast them off.

Henrietta had continued a correspondence with her sister thereafter, but Regina had never been much of a reader or a writer, and though the letters were welcomed by her, she replied only to one in three, and then sketchily and with obvious effort. When the Comptons came back to York, Teddy had thought it time the rift was healed. It was Jubilee year, and he had arranged a special celebration – a river-trip on a hired launch, with a splendid luncheon on board – and invited the families of both his sisters to join him.

Perry had grudgingly agreed that perhaps no harm could come of such a contact; but the event had not been a success. Perry had been unable to unbend towards Henrietta, and his coldness and stiffness had angered Jerome, who was always quick to his wife's defence. First obliquely and then directly he had taken up for her, and a quarrel had developed between the two men, which had resulted in the ban on any intercourse between the two families being renewed.

The squire had his worries, and no doubt they had shortened his temper. His eldest son was idle and expensive; his second, Lucas, who was at Oxford, seemed to be following in his brother's footsteps. His eldest daughter, Edith, had been in love for years with George Antrobus, the eldest son of a local landowner, and while the lad returned her affection his father was unsure about a match with a family whose two eldest scions seemed bent on dispersing the family fortune. Perry's second daughter Adelaide was nineteen and despite an expensive bringing-out had not received a single offer of marriage; and he had two sons at Eton, a third getting ready to go there, and another daughter who would need launching in a few years' time.

'Poor Perry,' had been Henrietta's comment, much though he had hurt her. But Jerome saw no poor Perry about it, and there was to be no further effort at reconciliation. Henrietta had to rely on infrequent letters and Teddy's occasional visits for news of her sister.

But Bertie, being often in York, had provided a new contact. At the Jubilee outing he had done his best to make peace, endearing himself to his aunt, and taking a fancy to her in his turn. Though he was undoubtedly adding to his father's grey hairs, he was a loveable scapegrace, charming and affectionate, and she couldn't help feeling that Perry's handling of him was unwise, keeping him idle and then objecting to the fruits of that idleness. He was a bright and high-spirited young man who needed something to occupy him.

It occurred to her now that perhaps there was something she could do, more than just giving him another lecture of the same sort he got at home. She could welcome him to Morland Place, and when he was there, try to interest him in the running of the estate. It would be good training for him for when he inherited his own land, and might keep him out of mischief at least for some of the time. And it might even help Jerome, who, it seemed to her, always had too much to do, even under the new regime.

So as she turned Dunnock onto the track she said, 'I'm glad you are coming for a visit at last. The children will be so pleased to see you. You must stay for dinner, of course. And you must have a look at our stallion. I'd be interested in your opinion of him.'

Bertie looked at her carefully. 'My opinion? Are you roasting me?'

'Not at all. You spend so much money on horses – one way and the other – that you must know a great deal about them.'

He laughed. 'Oh, you are a great gun, Auntie! I'd be delighted to see your stallion. I've heard a bit about him from Uncle Teddy. He must be something very special.'

CHAPTER THREE

In August the Hazelmeres went down to Yorkshire for what had become their annual visit to Shawes.

'It's so wonderfully peaceful here,' Venetia said. 'I feel as though I can do anything I like, without worrying about whether anyone will see me and think it worthy of gossip.'

She and her mother Charlotte were sitting alone together on the terrace overlooking the rather overgrown garden. Birds rioted about, half hidden by the unkempt foliage, and bees and butterflies moved from one spatch of colour to another, making the most of the flowers of late summer. Shawes was a beautiful little house built by Vanbrugh, its grounds bordering those of Morland Place. It belonged to Charlotte, but until the last few years she had never used it, coming to it only once before in her life.

'It's an odd thing,' Charlotte said, 'that although I've spent so little time here, this is the only place I've ever felt I could call *home*. When I was a child, we moved about a great deal, and the houses we lived in seemed like prisons rather than homes. Then, of course, as a married woman, I always lived in your father's houses, and they were not quite what one would call . . .'

'*Gemütlich*,' Venetia supplied, using one of the Queen's favourite words. She had picked it up from her sister Olivia, who was a member of the Household. 'And you think Shawes is?'

Charlotte smiled. 'Well, it's hardly a cosy cottage. But it is *mine*. I suppose that's what makes the difference. I hope you will love it too.'

'I love it now,' Venetia said. 'Haven't I just said so?'

'I mean that I hope you will love it when it is yours, when I'm gone.'

'I wish you wouldn't talk about *going* in that way,' Venetia said.

'It has to be faced, darling. Nobody lives for ever. And I've had a good, long—'

'For heaven's sake, don't say "innings"! I hate that kind of horrid, sporting talk. It's my mother you're talking about, not some silly game.'

Charlotte understood her daughter's irritability. 'You mustn't be afraid. I'm not.'

'You do feel well, don't you?' Venetia looked at her with quick concern. 'There isn't something you haven't told me?'

'I feel very well. Only the usual aches and pains. And a certain . . . weariness. When I'm sitting at ease, comfortable and happy as I am now, I sometimes feel a great disinclination to get up again. The thought of a new day bringing new challenges, which used to inspire me, now fills me with a certain reluctance.'

'Oh, Mama-duchess, everyone feels that sometimes! And you're missing Norton. It's only natural.'

Norton, Charlotte's waiting-woman, who had been with her for so many years she had been more like a personal friend, had died three months previously.

'Yes, I do miss her,' Charlotte said. 'And many others besides.' Her beloved husband, her younger brother and three of her five children had preceded her to that Far Country. And so many friends, of course. 'But,' she went on brightly, to comfort Venetia, 'I am very happy here. It is lovely to have time with you, and with the dear children, without interruption.'

'The children love it so. I wonder you never brought us here when we were little.'

'You have to remember that when I married your father railways were in their infancy and Yorkshire was a dreadfully long way away. And after that, of course, there was always so much else to do, one never had the time to go so far from London.'

68

'And now going a long way from London is the whole point of a holiday,' Venetia said.

'Yes, with this wretched South Africa business hanging over us, it's good to get away. I'm tired of people telling me why we must teach Johnny Boer a lesson.'

After the Government had taken up the Uitlanders' petition, Chamberlain had persuaded the Cabinet to enter negotiation with Kruger. A conference had been set up at Bloemfontein at the end of May; but it had broken down after five days and Milner had left the table in disgust. His was a logical, direct and disciplined mind, and he could not keep patience with the tortuous and devious obstinacy of his opponent. Hazelmere had said to Venetia at the time that it was as if Milner were playing chess and Kruger hide-and-seek: no result could ever come of such a mismatched game.

Since then there had been proposals and counter-proposals from both sides, which sometimes came close to agreement, without ever quite getting there.

'It almost seems as though both sides are just talking for talking's sake,' Charlotte said.

'I know Milner's convinced that Kruger means to go to war and that he's only delaying the start for his own purposes. And Cocky Lansdowne told me that Cecil Rhodes says the Boers are only waiting for the rains, because, being horsemen, they need the grass to be green before they can prosecute a campaign. Of course one has to give diplomacy a chance, but it would be better for us, if we are going to have to fight them, for the Cabinet to start now before the Boers are ready for us.'

'Well, public opinion is all for war, for what that's worth.'

'The Cabinet would never be swayed by public opinion.'

'Perhaps not, but with that dreadful newspaper whipping people up into a blood lust, we shall have demonstrations in the street before long if we don't go to war.'

'Dreadful newspaper? You mean the *Daily Mail*, I conclude?'

'It shouldn't even be called a newspaper!' Charlotte said wrathfully. 'It doesn't report the news at all, it – it makes it up!'

Venetia noted her mother's vehemence with amusement: this was the woman who felt too tired for life's challenges, she thought. She herself was not greatly exercised over the appearance three years ago of an entirely different kind of 'ha'penny journal'. The traditional penny broadsheets were three-quarters filled with verbatim accounts of Parliamentary proceedings, and the rest of the space was devoted to giving the full text of government reports, and telegrams, speeches, minutes of meetings and so on relating to other serious public events. This staple fare featured hardly at all in the new ha'penny paper. Instead, the *Daily Mail*'s editor picked out only the 'brightest' items of news, digested them, and rewrote them so as to turn them into 'stories'. These always had to be short, strongly prejudiced in some direction, and either sentimental or sensational. The headlines were calculated to provoke, rather than merely to suggest what the paragraph was about; scandals and crime figured largely in its pages, and for preference there must always be some figure of hatred set up like a guy to be knocked down.

It was a whole new concept of journalism, and it had met with severe disapproval from the penny broadsheets and those who read them. The idea was not to inform but to entertain, to tickle the palate and play on the prejudices of the domestic servant and the junior clerk, of that whole mass of the working classes who knew little of politics and cared less. 'Written by office boys for office boys,' had been Lord Salisbury's dismissive criticism; Hazelmere called it 'The Daily Wail' or 'The Servants' Delight'; but in its first year it had achieved a circulation double that of any other daily paper. Education reforms of the past thirty years had created a mass literacy that wanted feeding.

'I suppose they've a right to their pleasures like anyone else,' Venetia said tolerantly. 'It *is* horribly successful, and if it is what people want . . .'

'Darling, what a deplorable attitude!' Charlotte said. 'It's our duty to try to raise people, not give them what they want. If you pander to people's lowest tastes you degrade them and the whole country!'

'I wonder why the *Daily Mail* is so eager for us to go to war with the Boers?'

'Because war would give them no end of sensational stories,' Charlotte said. 'I remember the harm done by that dreadful Irishman who reported to *The Times* during the Crimean war. Imagine what use the *Daily Mail* would have made of our problems in Balaclava!'

'It may not be a question of imagining,' Venetia said. 'I'm afraid we're not much better organised now.'

'Yes, I know. The Army Medical Corps hasn't changed at all,' Charlotte said. 'There's been virtually no reform. All our efforts have gone for nothing.'

Venetia reached out and patted her mother's hand. 'Oh dear, how gloomy we've become. Let's talk about something cheerful. I'm looking forward to the races tomorrow, aren't you? What do you fancy for the St Edward Stakes?'

At the same time as the Hazelmeres' visit, Ashley and Lizzie had come to stay at Morland Place. Ashley had been allowed to take a fortnight's leave from his employment, and had timed it to coincide.

It was a wonderful time for the children. There was fishing, of which the boys never seemed to tire, boating and swimming; trees to climb, the wide countryside to ramble over, three ponies between them to take turns at riding, and all the endless variety of activity ingenious minds could devise to decorate the gloriously empty landscape of school holidays. With the four from London and the four from Morland Place plus Ned Bone, there were enough people for any game. There was a general game of cricket got up almost every day; and when the papas grew tired of playing and in their elderly way insisted on retiring to the shade of a tree for a smoke, there was still Ashley, whose energy seemed boundless, and Charley, who could romp as heartily as any child. Bertie, who was a great hero with all the little ones, was often there too, finding the company more agreeable than at home, and the pleasures much less taxing to his allowance than those of York.

Lizzie was almost sorry she was pregnant again, for it

71

curtailed her activities, and sometimes when she saw the men and the children go off on some expedition she wished she could join them. But it was pleasant to be with Henrietta and Venetia and the dowager duchess, and there was never any shortage of conversation. Little Martial Henry was taking his first staggering steps now, and his efforts were of such delight to the ladies he might have had three grand-mamas instead of one. When he had had enough of exercising his limbs, he was likely to find himself passed around from person to person as if he were something good to eat. Fortunately he was of a friendly disposition, and was happy to pull the buttons and pat the face of anyone whose lap he found himself on.

Nor did he seem to mind being lugged around by the little girls, who appeared to see him as a cross between a doll and a puppy, and would dress him up, roll about on the grass with him, haul him along in a home-made cart, pretend to feed him meals of daisies and groundsel, or install him in their bower and tell him stories. Jessie and Violet, being of an age and also the only girls in a whole pack of boys, were 'best friends', and had sworn to remain so for ever and never to love anyone else more than they loved each other. Jessie, five months the elder, was always the leader in their plays; Violet was her loyal lieutenant, and thought there was no-one cleverer or more splendid.

The Races were the ostensible reason for the family gathering – or at least it was the reason for choosing August. York always attracted a lot of visitors at that time, and Teddy was not surprised to hear that Richard Puddephat proposed to come to York with his wife and two children, and suggested he and Teddy should meet to discuss progress. Teddy went one better, and, ever hospitable, invited the whole boiling to stay at Makepeace House. They declined gracefully, saying they were already engaged to stay with friends in the area, but promised to call as soon as they arrived.

'Business or pleasure?' Teddy asked Puddephat, as they shook hands.

'Oh, a little of each. I was intending to come up this way

72

soon in any case, so I thought I might as well come during race week and make a holiday of it.'

He presented his wife, Aileen, a quietly spoken Scotswoman who had obviously been a great beauty in earlier years, and his son Raymond and daughter Maud. Raymond was seventeen, a good-looking lad between school and university; Maud, fourteen, had her mother's beauty and a tendency to blush, which colour went well with her dark hair and blue eyes.

Teddy lost no time in introducing them to the families at Morland Place and Shawes, perfectly sure that he was conveying a great favour on them by doing so. The Puddephats were easy company and made themselves agreeable all round. Aileen was soon talking to Lizzie about confinements, Raymond to Jerome and Hazelmere about the South African situation and his desire to join a regiment and teach the Boers a lesson. Maud talked to the ladies of the party in as unselfconscious a way as was possible, given that Jack seemed to have been struck dumb by the sight of her and, having fumbled his way through the ordeal of introduction, had retired to a short distance to stare at her as if she had come from another planet.

Teddy took Puddephat off to look at the mares and the stallion, and they came back full of talk and plans.

'It's a great pity we didn't meet a few years earlier,' Puddephat said. 'This South African business is bound to come to war. I can tell you, unofficially, that Brackenbury at the War Office has already completed the mobilisation plan – although to my mind the remount depots are fearfully short of horses. I'm still trying to persuade them of the folly of relying on buying them locally, in the Cape. I suspect they'll catch cold at that. And this will be a war that's hard on horses – the demand will be enormous. If only you were a few years further along, and had something to sell me!'

'I'm afraid the war won't last long enough for the first of my youngsters to be ready,' Teddy said.

'No, I imagine not. However, the demand from the regiments will always be there, even in peacetime. And,' he smiled to show it was a joke, 'we can always hope for another war to break out!'

The Puddephats joined the Morlands on several occasions during their week's stay: at the races, on one of Teddy's river-trips, and at a dinner party at Makepeace House. One day Charlotte held a picnic luncheon at Shawes, and the men and the children played cricket afterwards. On that occasion Raymond Puddephat covered himself with glory as far as the boys were concerned by scoring an unprecedented number of runs, including a six that went over the kitchen-garden wall and broke a pane in a cold frame. During the tea interval, he explained with becoming modesty that he had been in the first eleven at Winchester and, under adroit questioning from Thomas, admitted he had also been a soccer blue and was induced to recount some of his greatest triumphs in both sports. Miss Puddephat meanwhile won Jack's heart by revealing that she had once ridden in a motor-car and enjoyed it very much, and by listening with apparent interest to his rather tortuous explanation of how the rapid-combustion engine worked.

Everyone was sorry to say goodbye at the end of their stay. They were going on to Scotland to visit Aileen's relations and for the grouse shooting. Promises were made for future visits on both sides, with much more intention that they should happen than is usual in such situations.

One hot day the women were gathered under the shade of the old walnut tree. At the fringe of the shadow midges jigged up and down against the light, and beyond it the air seemed almost opaque, as though the August sunshine had thickened and coloured it. Spider threads blew shimmering by from time to time, drifting on the lightest of breezes, but nothing else moved; even the birds had fallen silent in the afternoon warmth. Kithra had come sloping back from one of his lone expeditions and crept in under the shade, his yellow eyes glowing and his pink tongue dripping. Now he was asleep, flopped over on his side on the cool grass at Lizzie's feet with the baby sleeping on a blanket beside him.

Jessie and Violet were sitting together reading a story-book in their bower, a rickety device of sticks and a long stem of green laurel bent round and tied with string, and flowers, almost dried in the heat, stuck in here and there at random. They were immensely proud of it.

The boys sat or lolled in a group on the other side of the garden, chewing grass stems and talking, their voices lowered for privacy. Oliver and Ned Bone would be going to Eton next half, and Raymond Puddephat's visit had brought the subject to the fore. Now Thomas and his cousin Eddie Vibart – Augusta's son – were telling them all they would need to know.

'You'll be Oppidans, of course, like us. Boys who win a scholarship are Collegers and live in College, but we live in houses outside, in the town, you see – *oppidus*, town. That's Latin.'

'Some houses are better than others, of course.'

'I'm in Keate, which is pretty good,' said Eddie.

'I'm in Jourdelay's, which is the best,' said Thomas.

'But you don't get to choose. They probably won't put you in Jourdelay's, Olly, because they like to keep brothers apart. But the houses are all pretty good.'

'It won't be so bad for you anyway,' Thomas said to his brother, 'having me there ahead of you. I can help you along with things even if we're not in the same house. But it'll be queer for you, Boney. I mean, you're the wrong age and everything. I dare say you'll get ragged awfully.'

'Let 'em try,' said Ned, flushed with pleasure at his recent acquisition of a nickname. He felt, rightly, that it would give him distinction at school. Already he could hear himself saying airily to a group of new acquaintances, 'The fellows call me Boney, you know.'

'I don't know how it'll be,' Eddie said, with his brow furrowed in perplexity. He was a large boy for his age, with rather protruding eyes of a startling pale blue, and fine, fair hair. 'I mean, will you be treated as a new boy or not?'

'He must be, mustn't he?' Thomas said. He was quick and dark, not tall, but with a lean, well-knit boy's body. He was good-looking, and had found himself the recipient of a great deal of inexplicable attention from some of the senior

75

boys during his first half. They had called him Thomasina and vied with each other to have him fag for them. But his straightforward, energetic frankness, combined with a soon-discovered prowess at games, particularly football, had put an end to the 'silliness', as he thought of it. He was no new boy now and he understood a little more than he had done, but he still thought that sort of thing very silly, and shrugged it off with a boy's easy acceptance. He had settled in and was well liked by his own set and by the seniors, but he could take care of himself and no-one would call him Thomasina now.

'I mean,' he continued, 'he won't know anything about College or anything, will he? You see, all new boys have to learn a terrific lot of things – a great long list of House names and colours and the proper terms for things, special Eton words, you know – and then you're given a trial to see if you've learnt it all. If you fail the trial you're given a hosing.'

'A what?' Oliver asked.

'A beating with a rubber pipe,' Thomas explained. 'But worse than the hosing is having everyone think you're a duffer. You have to fit in, you know, or the other fellows will pick on you. They do all sorts of things to you – flicking you with towels, sticking you with compasses, blotting your work to get you into trouble.'

'But you mustn't ever tell,' Eddie added earnestly. 'Peaching is the worst crime. You get non-speaks – sent to Coventry – and then, well, you might as well be dead.'

'Are the lessons hard?' Ned asked.

'Oh, no,' Thomas assured him. 'They're a frightful bore, really, but they ain't hard. Mostly Latin and Greek, and some maths and French and science. If you skew in a lesson you might get a Georgic from the beak. But that don't matter. Nobody likes you if you're a sap – you know, a grind. And there's only afternoon lessons three days a week. The other afternoons we have games. That's much more important. You've got to be decent at some game or other to get on.'

'What you mustn't do is slack at games, especially at

footer,' Eddie said. 'The prefects are down on that like a ton of bricks. Smith mi. had a terrible blister on his heel so he could hardly walk, and he didn't turn up to footer one day, but the prefects said he was slacking and dragged him out, and they fined him half a crown and gave him a beating as well.'

'Oh,' said Ned, not liking the sound of that. 'Oh, well, but I like games all right.'

'That's the dandy!' Thomas encouraged him. 'There's all sorts of things, not just footer. There's rowing, swimming, cricket and so on. And running – we have tremendous cross-country runs! There's bound to be something you can make your mark at. As long as you get into some team or other. The fellows who don't are called scugs, and they're the lowest of the low. The great men at Eton are all blues. Carlyon's the greatest hero of them all. He's in the sixth, and he's in the footer team and the first eleven and he's Captain of Boats.'

'No use telling him that,' Eddie said. 'He ain't going to be captain of anything. Starting too late. But you, young Olly – if you buckle down you could make something of yourself. Only you've got to take your lumps, you know, and not blub. And take a beating without squeaking out.'

'Is there a lot of beating?' Oliver asked nervously.

'Well, pretty much all the time,' Thomas said judiciously. 'It's just about impossible to get by without a swishing or two every week. There are so many rules, you see, and a man's bound to trip over one of 'em unless he's a complete stock. The beaks put you on the bill for breaking school rules – being out of bounds, smoking, being late and so on – but the prefects swish you for practically everything. Cheek, particularly. They call anything cheek.'

'Richardson beat me last half because he didn't like my face,' Eddie said.

'Carlyon says Richardson's a bully and a cad,' Thomas said.

'He really can whop, though,' Eddie added, as if it were a skill to admire, however reluctantly.

'Yes,' said Thomas, 'on the whole it's better to get whops

from a beak than from a pre. A beak generally has his mind on other things and don't put his heart into it. And they're all pretty ancient, too. Old Fenelon can't whop for toffee. But the sixth are pretty fit men and they like to make you know who's master. I've heard 'em talk about it. If they don't draw blood, they don't reckon they've done it properly.'

'It doesn't sound,' Ned said carefully, 'as though I shall like it much there.'

'You make me pretty glad I'm not going,' agreed Jack, who with his brothers had been listening in fascinated silence.

Thomas and Eddie looked surprised. 'Oh, but it's the best place on earth! The fellows are all tremendous! And we have the most terrific fun,' said Thomas. 'I haven't told you the half of it.'

'And if you stick it out you'll be in the sixth one day,' Eddie mentioned. 'And then – well! It's the most tremendous go in the world to be in the sixth!'

'Maybe you'll even get into Pop.' Thomas held out the golden vision temptingly. 'That's better than being King of England! The men in Pop are gods.'

Unseen by them, Jessie had crept up close to listen. She had got bored with reading and, leaving Violet in the bower alone with *The Golden Treasury*, had first of all wandered restlessly round the garden swishing at flowers with a stick, and then, seeing the boys so absorbed in their conversation, had inched closer.

Now she said, 'I wish I was going! I bet I'd get into Pop. I'd be the best at everything.'

'Don't be silly,' Robbie said at once. 'How could you be?'

'Because I'm good at things. I can run faster than you,' Jessie retorted. 'And I'm a better climber. And I'm a better rider than any of you. And I can catch fish and I know how to snare a rabbit. And when we played cricket yesterday I got more runs than Jack, even.'

'Only because Dad was going easy on you and bowling dollies,' Robbie said.

'He was not! Anyway, *you* didn't get any runs at all, so you can't talk!'

Jack intervened. 'You can't go to Eton anyway, Jess, because you're a girl, so there's no use talking about it.'

'It's not fair!' Jessie said furiously. 'Why shouldn't I go? I *hate* being a girl!'

Jack and Thomas exchanged an eye-rolling glance, the usual male dislike of a feminine 'fuss'.

Thomas tried kindly to soothe her. 'Being a girl's good too. It's just as good, really, as being a boy.'

'Of course it is,' Jack agreed quickly. 'Being a girl's very important.'

'No, it's not,' Jessie cried. 'It's stupid and hateful.'

'But – but fellows all want to have a girl of their own,' Thomas said, somewhat out of his depth. 'I know a lot of the great fellows of the sixth have girls they're sweet on.'

'Carlyon's got a photograph of a girl in his study,' Eddie put in. 'I think she's his cousin. Not his sister, anyway.'

'That's right,' Thomas nodded. 'And then, when a fellow's finished school and so on and he's set up in the world – well, fellows want to get married, you know, and there have to be girls for that.'

'Married!' Jessie almost stamped her foot in frustration. 'I don't want to be married. I want to do something exciting!'

'Girls can't do exciting things,' Robbie said scornfully.

'Why not?' Jessie demanded, with a dangerous look.

'Because they'd get hurt,' said Robbie, 'and then they'd start blubbing.'

'I wouldn't blub!'

'You're practically blubbing now.'

She was, but it was with frustration. 'I hate you!' she cried.

Jack intervened. 'Oh, lay off her, Rob. It's rotten to tease her.'

'I wasn't teasing. I just said girls blub, and they do. Girls are no use for anything except making a fuss and blubbing.'

'I'll show you,' Jessie said, with a gasp, as she forced down her tears. 'I'll show you all!' She jumped up, rubbing the tears off her cheeks with a grubby, impatient hand.

'Show us what?' Robbie sneered.

'I'll do something that none of *you* can do.'

'What thing?'

'You'll see!' And she ran off.

Thomas looked at Jack doubtfully. 'I say, is she all right?'

'She's just in a temper,' Robbie answered for him. 'She's got a terrible temper. She'll get over it.'

'If she comes back you're to be nice to her,' Jack said severely. 'It ain't manly to tease girls.'

'I didn't tease her,' Robbie said. 'She was just being silly, anyway, wanting to go to Eton.'

'Well, you're not going either,' Jack said, 'so you needn't be so uppity.'

'Dad? Can I talk to you?'

'Yes, Jack. What is it? Oh – pass me that rubber, will you?'

Jack passed the stable rubber over the top of Minstrel's withers to his father's waiting hand. Minstrel blew out heavily through his nostrils, making the dust motes leap and tremble in the slanting shaft of sunlight, and eased his weight from one side to the other. His eyes were half closed, his eyelashes long and surprisingly blond-tipped. He loved being groomed.

'What is it, then?' Jerome repeated, since his firstborn did not speak.

'It's about school,' Jack began reluctantly. 'The school I'm going to go to in October.'

'Spit it out, old lad.'

'Well – will it be anything like Eton?'

Jerome straightened and looked down at him humorously. 'Not the least little bit, I should think. And before you go on, while I appreciate that you'd like to be with your cousins, I have to tell you that it is completely out of the question. I couldn't possibly find the money to send you to Eton.'

'Oh, no,' Jack said hastily, 'I don't want to go there. I mean, I know it's supposed to be the best place in the world, and every chap who goes is bound to get on and so on, but even if you could afford it I wouldn't want to go.'

'Why on earth not?'

'It sounds to me – I mean – the things I've heard—' He

stumbled and began again. 'I don't think it can really be nice. Not really.'

Jerome gave him a long look, then bent again to rub Minstrel's legs. 'Let me guess – Thomas and Eddie have been spinning you tales.'

'I don't think they were tales. They were telling Oliver and Ned what to expect when they went up. Warning them, you know.'

'They were probably roasting them. What did they say?'

'Oh, about the bullying, and the beating, and all the rules, and how you can't help breaking them, and then you get swished. It seemed to be nothing but beatings! And seniors taking against you for no reason. And the things some of the other lads do to you just for fun – horrible things, like mediaeval torture!' He paused a moment, and went on, 'They said the worst thing of all was to peach, but I'm not peaching, am I, Dad? I mean, no-one's done anything to me. I just want to know.'

'Know what, my lad?' He tapped Minstrel's fetlock and the horse obligingly lifted his foot and placed it in Jerome's hand.

'Is it true?'

'Without having heard the precise details of what they told you, I'd say it was probably the truth, but not the whole truth and nothing but the truth.' Minstrel, his hoof comfortably cradled, began to put his weight on it and lean against Jerome. Jerome shoved back. There was always a race to pick out a hoof before one was forced to drop it. 'It's a thing lads have done since time began,' he continued, rather breathlessly, 'to try to frighten new boys with lurid tales of their suffering to come. But they're probably exaggerating, and leaving out the nice parts. I didn't go to Eton, of course, but I dare say it's pretty much the same in all the public schools.'

'Where did you go?'

Jerome dropped the hoof gratefully and straightened up again. 'Harrow,' he said. 'My father and grandfather went there so it was family tradition.'

'Did you like it?'

'It was a long time ago, of course, and I dare say things

81

are more civilised there now. We always thought ourselves pretty civilised anyway, in comparison with Westminster. Now they really *are* savage there. It's a wonder to me any boy survives the cruelties of Westminster.'

Jack looked at him, troubled. 'You're joking about it, and Thomas and Eddie were sort of laughing, but—'

'But?'

'Well, what's it *for*, Dad? It sounds to me like meanness and cruelty. And they don't seem to care much about their lessons, or learning anything. I don't understand. What's the good of it?'

'Oh dear,' said Jerome, 'you're asking me to justify a whole way of life. Customs that have built up over centuries. Tradition *is* generally thought to be a good thing, you know. And one never went for what one learnt in lessons.' Minstrel nudged him, and he scratched the bay neck absently. 'I suppose it teaches one to get on with other boys, and allows one to make friends one can keep all one's life. If you're in a sticky spot and you meet a chap from the old school, you know he'll help you. And it teaches hardiness and self-reliance, and teamwork and leadership. How to take a knock without fuss, and to get up again and fight on. How to take orders for the good of all, and to put loyalty before personal comfort. They're all good qualities to have in later life, you know.'

'I suppose so.'

'You don't sound sure.'

'Oh, well, I mean I'm sure they're good qualities, but – but is that the only way to teach them?'

Jerome patted his son's hand, which was resting on Minstrel's back. 'My lad, I don't know. I don't suppose anyone designed the schools to be the way they are – they just grew. I didn't enjoy everything that happened to me at Harrow, but you could say the same about any part of your life, no matter where you spent it. I *am* glad I went, though. And I don't know anyone who wouldn't send his son there if he could.'

Jack blushed. 'I don't mind, Dad, really I don't. I'd sooner go to the technology school, honestly.'

82

Jerome was both touched and saddened at Jack's concern for his feelings. He could imagine the boy at Eton or Harrow, imagine how he would develop through the school, his sporting triumphs, the grace with which he would hide his mental accomplishments while still passing examinations and winning prizes, his popularity as a 'great man' of the sixth, how the fags would look up to him and how kindly he would influence them for the good. He might even have risen to be head boy.

It was a great pity, a great pity. But there was no sense in repining, and he had sworn an oath to himself to throw all that baggage overboard.

'You'll do well there,' he said. 'It'll be harder work, I dare say, than Eton.'

'I don't mind hard work,' Jack said quickly.

Jerome grinned. 'Good. Then you can finish Minstrel for me.'

The afternoon was even hotter. Heat-haze dithered above the fading grass, the climbing white roses drooped and browned; even the crickets fell silent. Tea was served under the walnut tree's shade, from which the women had not moved all afternoon.

'I feel so dreadfully lazy, being waited on like this,' Henrietta said, as Venetia's maids came out with the laden trays.

'Nonsense. If anyone has a right to sit still for once in a while, it's you,' said Venetia. 'You work hard enough the rest of the year.'

'And you don't, of course,' Henrietta laughed.

'If you insist on being energetic,' Venetia said, 'you can pour out.'

The children didn't need to be called: the sight of food attracted them like wasps to jam. The men strolled up to join them too, and took the empty chairs, except for Ashley, who threw himself down on the grass at his wife's feet and scooped his baby onto his knee. Teddy lit a cigar, and the coils of fragrant smoke spiralled up slowly into the branches. Kithra woke, yawned until his jaws almost met behind, stretched front and back ends separately with slow thoroughness, then flopped back down on his other side.

'Where's Jessie?' Henrietta asked, when she had dispensed drinks of one sort or another to everyone else. No-one answered. 'Violet, dear, where's Jessie?'

'I don't know,' Violet said, sitting beside Kithra with a buttered muffin in her hand. 'I haven't seen her for ages. We were reading, but she got tired of it and went off.'

'She'll come back when she's hungry,' Charlotte said.

Henrietta said, 'She's always hungry. It's not like her to miss tea. Boys! Have you seen Jessie?' They stopped talking abruptly. 'Jack, where's your sister?'

'I don't know, Mother,' Jack answered, with shining honesty.

She looked from him to Robbie. 'You two look guilty. What did you do to her?'

'We didn't do anything,' Robbie said. 'She just ran off.'

Jack took it up like a man. It was his sister, after all. 'She got into a temper, Mother. You know how she is.'

'What was she in a temper about? Were you teasing her?'

'She was cross because she didn't want to be a girl,' Jack said.

'I'm sure she'll be all right,' Venetia said. 'Didn't you tell me you wandered these fields all alone all day when you were a girl, and came home only when you were tired?'

Henrietta smiled. 'True. But I'm a mother now. All right, I won't worry. But she always appears at mealtimes. I hope those boys haven't upset her too much.'

Jessie wandered for some time, not noticing where she was going, full of resentful thoughts. As the only girl in the household she had no standard of female enjoyment, only saw that her brothers had fun and her father did things she thought must be fun – riding about the estate and working with the horses – while her mother and Emma were always toiling in the kitchen. And in the story-books that came her way, boys had adventures while girls always had to sit about looking pretty and keeping their dresses clean. The prince got to ride off and kill the dragon while the princess stayed

84

at home waiting for him to come back and marry her.

It wasn't *fair*, she thought. She hadn't asked to be a girl. Why couldn't girls do things? She didn't *want* to get married. She wanted to do things boys did. She stamped the dusty earth and shoved through the dry, seeding grass. Above her the dense blue sky was static, opaque with heat. One or two large, half-transparent clouds were sketched against the eastern curve of the blue bowl; far above, the dark scimitars of swifts curved back and forth, too high for their cries to be heard. She had kept hold of her stick, and slashed at everything as she passed – grass, weeds, flowers, hedges. The slashing helped a lot, giving rhythm to her litany of complaint, until she overreached herself by slashing at a tree trunk, and the stick broke in two.

She threw it away in disgust and kicked the tree instead. 'You old tree! Breaking my stick! I'll show you, all right!' Everything was against her, even that old tree. 'I bet I could climb you!' She stood back and looked up at it. It was an oak, gnarled and ancient. The lowest branch was too high for her to reach even if she jumped, but it grew out over the fence. If she climbed onto the top railing maybe she could catch hold of it. It was a massive tree, tall and imposing – daunting, almost. If she could climb it, right to the top, *that* would show the boys. She'd bet none of them had ever climbed anything so high!

She tucked her skirt into her knickers, spat on her hands the way she had seen Eddie do at rounders before he picked up the bat, positioned herself, teetering on the fence rail, and jumped. Her fingers just grazed the branch without being able to catch it, and she fell to ground, landing on her feet but tipping over onto hands and knees. She got up and tried again. After several attempts, she had dirty marks down the front of her dress, a hole the size of a shilling in her stocking, and she had grazed her fingers and bruised her knee. The tree was unconquered. No use to tell herself that she could have climbed it all right if she could have got onto that first branch: she had nothing to go back to the boys with, and she had vowed that she would show them. She couldn't go back until she had *done* something

– and she became aware that it must be tea-time, because she was beginning to feel very hungry.

What could she do that would impress them? A little breeze got up and stirred her hair; she pushed back a few strands from her sticky forehead and listened, her attention caught. Somewhere nearby a lark was shrilling, hanging above the grazings on its quivering thread of song, but from beyond that in the near distance she had heard, carried on the breeze, a horse's whinny – the unmistakable call of a stallion. It came to her in that moment as clearly as if someone had whispered the words inside her head: she would ride the stallion. She would ride Pasha. *That* was something that would impress the boys! None of them had ever done it, or would dare to do it. Everyone knew the stallion was not for riding. It would prove once and for all that she was as good as them – or better.

Ten minutes later she was standing, half-hidden by the bushes, just beyond the railed paddock where Pasha was running with some mares. There seemed to be no-one about. A little further up the track was Twelvetrees, the circular stable-block along with its barns, covered school and various paddocks and yards. There was no sign or sound of activity, and she supposed the grooms must be having their tea, too. She emerged from the bushes and climbed on the lowest rail of the paddock. Pasha saw her at once. He lifted his head from grazing and looked across at her. She could see his nostrils flaring to catch her scent. For months she had been coming up to Twelvetrees after school to help with the horses, and she always stopped to stroke Pasha when he was in his box, and talk to him. She thought he must know her by now, all right. She called to him, chirruping in the way she called the ponies in their field, but he didn't come, and after a moment he put his head down to graze again.

She bent her mind to the problem. No good just going into the paddock – he wouldn't let her catch him. She had no illusions about that. Even with the ponies, if they didn't come to call it was no use going after them without something to entice them. She needed some oats in a bucket.

86

She had seen her father catch him with a bucket, so she knew it could be done that way. He was wearing a head-collar, but she'd need a rope to attach to it so that she could keep hold of him. She didn't dare try to take a saddle and bridle from the stable – and she wasn't sure she could tack him up anyway, out in the open and without a box to stand on, he being so much taller than her. But she rode the ponies bareback and with only a headstall, so she didn't see why she shouldn't do the same with Pasha. He took a step or two as he grazed, and she watched him move, and shivered a little at his power and beauty. He was so much bigger and stronger than the ponies. She would need to bring him beside the rail or she would never be able to get on.

She shook herself into action: she didn't have long, if she was to do it before anyone came. She made her way up to the stable block, not by the main entrance but through the field next to it and the side entrance, a narrow passage between the loose-boxes and the tack-room. At the end she paused, listening. The yard was quiet, shimmering in the heat, and only one horse was visible, dozing with his head over his half-door. She could hear the grooms talking in the tack-room, and guessed they were cleaning tack while they had their tea: there was an effortful rhythm to their voices, and sometimes a pause in a sentence while tea was sucked down. She imagined the big white mugs being tilted against the large moustaches all grooms seemed to cultivate; visu-alised their bare forearms, brown and muscular below the rolled-up sleeves, and the muted gleam of polished leather and the glint of bit and stirrup in the shadows. She had helped them clean tack on many an evening after school, and knew just what it was like in there, with the rich smell of linseed and saddle-soap cut by a tang of metal-polish, and the warm, rolling voices with their endless stories of horses. She loved listening to them, and she understood instinctively that they liked to perform for her; but she must not linger today.

She turned the other way, keeping close to the wall and looking into the empty boxes she passed, feeling the open tack-room door behind her that might at any moment emit a human being and end her adventure with a 'What's to do, miss?' In the third box she found what she wanted: a bucket with a handful of feed crusted round its sides, and a rope, clipped to a headcollar and lying in the straw. She slipped in, unclipped the rope, and took up the bucket, wincing as its handle dropped with a clang against its side. She crept back to the door, but she could hear the grooms still talking, unalarmed. On the opposite side of the yard the horse with its head out over the half-door woke from its doze and, probably at the sight of the bucket, pricked its ears sharply at her and whickered. Foolishly she put her finger to her lips, as if it could understand the gesture.

In a moment she was out, free and clear, hurrying back to the paddock with the rope and the bucket, her feet winged with relief. She scraped the feed down as she walked, collecting it at the bottom. It wasn't much, barely two hand-fuls. She stopped and tore up some grass, and mixed that in. She hoped it would be enough. It only had to interest him long enough for her to slip onto his back. If he would come to her in the first place!

She climbed up onto the fence and sat on the top rail, then held the bucket in full view and chirruped, and called his name. Pasha looked up at once, and this time paused only to give her one long, considering look before begin-ning to walk towards her. Elation flushed through her at this first success. The trouble was, the mares were coming too. They all knew what a bucket meant, and they had been eating the grass in this paddock for long enough to be bored with it. The whole fieldful of horseflesh was converging on her at a steady walk, the hindermost mare breaking into a trot for a few paces to catch up, afraid of missing some-thing. And then Jessie was surrounded by thrusting noses, heavy snorting breaths, bright eyes under long forelocks, pointing ears and the sweet, warm smell of horses. She was nudged and jostled; lips fumbled at her hands and teeth nibbled at her skirt as they all tried to get into the bucket; the bossier mares nipped at their neighbours and made them veer away. It was hard for Jessie to keep her balance and to keep her precious bit of feed safe, and she was afraid that at any moment a full-scale biting and kicking match would break out.

But at least there was no difficulty in getting Pasha to come close. With his stallion's authority he pushed through the middle of the jostling bunch, and they fell back for him. He came straight to Jessie as though they had arranged this beforehand, and she was thrilled at this evidence of friendliness. She slipped the bucket under his interested nose, and reached out to stroke his neck. He didn't flinch from her hand, but snorted with pleasure and thrust down into the bucket, swishing his lips around the bottom for the delicious oats. Jessie knew it would not keep him long. As he withdrew his nose to chew, she quickly clipped the rope onto the ring of the headcollar, talking to him all the while. He was not alarmed, only flicked his ears back and forth, and shoved his muzzle back in to see if there was any more.

She had to work quickly, before he moved away from the fence. So far she had done nothing he objected to, but if he pulled away from her she would not be strong enough to hold him. She moved the bucket slowly, with his nose still in it, along to the nearest upright, and hung it there by its handle. This made him take a step or two, and brought him more or less parallel with the fence, his round dark chestnut flank actually touching her leg where she sat. Then while Pasha was still nosing at the bucket with hopeful interest, she stood up on the rail, grabbed hold of a hank of his mane, and slid over onto his back.

Her heart was beating so fast that for a moment she was almost shocked that nothing happened. She had thought he might buck or rear, but he did not seem to notice that she had got onto his back, only stood still, tossing his head up and down as he pursued a fragment of something or other round his teeth. Then he blew out hard through his nostrils and put his head down to rub his muzzle against his knee – all natural, easy, familiar things that horses did. 'Good boy,' she said, pleased, and ran a hand down his neck, noticing almost subconsciously how small her hand was against the great curve of muscle. He turned his head, seemed to look back at her a moment, then turned away again to rub his itch more thoroughly on the railing. She was elated. He didn't mind her! She was sitting on his back, and he was letting her! She felt his warmth, his presence like a physical aura, more real than the heat of the sun on her bare head. She smelt his strong, sweet smell all around her, and felt a strange, thrilling surge of possessive love run through her whole body so that her cheeks seemed to burn and her toes tingle with it . . .

The mares had lost interest and were wandering off, grazing as they went. She decided she would ride Pasha once round the field if she could. She had forgotten about the boys, or that this was a 'dare' to put them in their place. There was only herself and Pasha now, there was only the two of them, and love and desire and possession. He was the stallion, the King Horse, so powerful he could kill her with one blow if he wished; but she was riding him. She held him even though she was at his mercy. Without knowing any words for it, she knew the dual rapture of simultaneously possessing and being possessed. There was no sense any more of daring or wrong-doing or even of danger. This was love, and that was all.

Holding the rope in one hand and his mane in the other, she gently pressed her legs to his flanks. Nothing happened. Pasha simply stood still, as if he were thinking. He flicked his ears back and forth against the flies, and then shook himself from ears to tail, shaking Jessie in the process, but not unseating her. She grew in confidence. She felt comfortable and secure astride his warm back. 'Walk on,' she urged him. She pressed again. Nothing happened. 'Walk on, darling Pasha,' she said, and dug in her heels.

Instantly his ears went back, flat to his skull, and he leapt forward, making her gasp. He bucked once, not very hard, and then broke into a canter. The buck jolted her but she had hold of his mane and pulled herself straight again. It was harder to stay on than she had expected, for the thrusting of his great muscles under his smooth summer hide was so powerful she could get no grip with her knees, as she did when she rode the ponies. She had to rely on balance, poising her body above his and going with him. But she was doing it! Oh, she was riding him! She was really riding him! Rapture seized her. She was carried forward with more power under her than she had ever known. She was afraid, but it was a wonderful pleasurable fear, like the delicious sinking of your stomach when you went really high on a swing – only ten times, a hundred times more so!

It was taking all her effort simply not to come off. She had no way of guiding him. But he seemed of his own accord to be cantering round the edge of the paddock; and in a moment she saw why. He cantered up to one of his mares, and as she lifted her head from the grass he snaked his head at her and nipped her neck. She squealed and jumped away, lashing out, her flying hoof only just missing Jessie's leg, and then began to canter in front of him.

Jessie knew what was happening. He was going to round them all up. And she was on his back! As his speed increased, she saw the danger. She held on grimly with both hands, her mind sharpened to the single needlepoint of concentration, trying to anticipate his direction and keep her balance, so fixed on the task that she barely had room for fear. One cool small voice from far away did say that if she came off now she would go down under more than one set of flying hoofs. There were mares to one side of her, and the paddock fence to the other – hard falling either way.

His speed increased as he gathered his wives together, and they were galloping now. The ground passed beneath in a blur, the hoofs made a soft thunder, and Jessie's mind seemed to be growing numb, dazed by the effort, the movement, the tension. She felt her muscles trembling, and wondered how long she would be able to hold on – yet with all that, her mind sang with the thrill of exhilaration. The joy of speed and movement and soft air whipping past her face was the most wonderful thing she had ever known.

And then suddenly Pasha seemed to decide that he had had enough of his passenger. A quick, double dodge shook her loose and with a hitch of his quarters he simply shrugged her off with no more effort than if she had been a fly. She had an instant to know a sharp sense of loss as she flew briefly through the air, too surprised to make any sound.

91

The earth came up and hit her, knocking the air out of her. She saw a brief confusion of legs and hoofs and heard their thunder too close, and through it someone's voice, a male voice, shouting. There was a sharp pain like a hot thread running down her face, then something hit her head sickeningly and the world went dark.

She came swimming up as from the stifling bottom of a thick stream, opened her eyes to blinding white light that hurt like jagged flints, and saw a face above her, blurred and swaying in and out of focus, a man's face, familiar, though for a frightening moment she couldn't put a name to it. Blue eyes and a full, fair moustache sparked with red. He was speaking to her and she could hear him, but she couldn't understand what he was saying. It was as though her brain had been jolted loose and all the ends had come disconnected. She felt him stroke her face, a big, dry, firm hand, and it felt so good and comforting she turned her cheek a little into it. Then she had to close her eyes. She felt dreadfully sick, and moving her head had dislodged boulders of pain, which were rolling down on top of her. She escaped into the darkness again.

It was the purest chance that Bertie, on his way to join the party at Shawes, decided to ride the longer way round by Twelvetrees. It was an idle decision that had no particular reason behind it, beyond its being a fine day and his feeling like a change. He came along the track that led past the circular stable-block towards Morland Place and knew there was trouble before his mind properly assimilated what it was. In the paddock opposite the stables the horses were running like a herd out in the wild, which was not normal. Then he took in that one of the horses was the stallion, and that there was someone on his back. He shouted out something, he didn't know what, and kicked his horse forward, pulling up sharply as he reached the fence, flinging himself from the saddle, hearing voices behind him as the grooms came running out, alarmed at last. He realised that the rider was a girl at the same moment as the stallion gave a small, almost light-hearted buck; realised that it could only be Jessie at the same moment as she disappeared, slipping into the stream of bodies like an otter going in off a rock.

Except that it was not peaceful or voluntary. The herd thundered on, leaving behind a still body on the trampled earth. He was over the fence and across to her, stumbling a little in his riding boots, before they could make another circuit. He flung himself on his knees beside her, seeing out of the corner of his eye how the herd veered away from him, slowed, and stopped with a couple of bounces on the far side.

'Jessie! Jessie!' he was saying. 'Can you hear me? Oh, Lord! What did you do it for? Oh, dear God!'

One side of her little white face was a sheet of blood. He stroked the hair away from her brow and to his almost sickening relief she opened her eyes a little, frowning up at him, pouting with pain.

'Jessie, sweetheart, are you hurt? Where does it hurt?' he said foolishly. He stroked the unbloodied side of her face helplessly, and she made a sound, as like to words as a careless ink-blot on a page, and then closed her eyes, losing consciousness again. He turned towards the grooms who were advancing across the paddock, some towards him and some, helpless with horseman's instinct, towards the horses, and shouted, 'One of you go for help. Take my horse. Everyone's at Shawes. Hurry!'

When the breathless groom on the sweating horse brought the news, there were exclamations, sharp questions, and then the rapid departure of Jerome, Ashley and Venetia to Twelvetrees to assess the situation and decide on the right action. Henrietta wanted to go, but Venetia said quickly, 'You know I am more useful in this situation than you,' and it was true.

Charlotte laid a hand over Henrietta's when they had gone and said, 'Children are very resilient. They bounce where we would break.'

Henrietta tried to smile but could not. 'I'm glad Venetia is here,' she managed to say. But in her mind was an image

93

of her little girl falling under the hoofs of a galloping herd, being tossed and rolled under them like a twig in a torrent, and when the herd had passed, lying still, her limbs at unnatural angles like a thrown-aside doll.

She and Charley went back to Morland Place to prepare as far as they were able: a bed, hot water, bandages – what else might be needed? Not a shroud; sweet Jesu, please, not that! Thank God they had a doctor to hand – the best doctor, dear, dearest Venetia. Thank God for her!

The others remained at Shawes and kept the rest of the children there to be out of the way. Violet was crying, and the boys huddled together uneasily, feeling guilty and resenting the feeling, for they hadn't done anything, had they? The baby sensed the atmosphere and began to wail. Hazelmere and Teddy debated courses of action, feeling the more helpless because they were men and there was nothing for them to do. Lizzie sat apart, her hands cupped over her belly, thinking of Jessie and trying to escape the unwelcome realisation of what grief parenthood could bring, and how fragile one's tenure might be.

At last the dismal little procession returned to Morland Place, Ashley, Jerome and two grooms carrying a door between them on which the little body lay, with Venetia and Bertie walking one to either side and steadying her. Henrietta was waiting on the steps, her face white and her eyes seeming to take up most of it.

'It's not as bad as it looks,' Venetia said at once, taking pity on her. 'A concussion and a broken wrist. And some cuts and bruises.'

'All that blood!'

'It's a cut on her cheek. Not serious.' But of course it might leave a scar. Venetia was anxious to attend to it before the edges swelled. 'The best thing is that Bertie says she did regain consciousness briefly. That's very important.'

'Is it?'

'Yes. It means I have every hope she will recover.'

Henrietta looked down at the dirty, tumbled, doll-limp body of her child and her heart swooned in her. Jessie's face was covered with blood, and there was earth and grass in her tangled hair. She wanted to touch her, but her hands were shaking too much. She wanted to say something, but her tongue clove to her dry mouth.

'I've straightened the arm,' continued Venetia, who was holding the forearm in both hands, 'and once we get her into bed I'll set it properly. It's a simple fracture, and it ought to heal all right. Children's bones knit quickly.'

Henrietta couldn't speak. She looked what she hoped was a question.

'I think the cut on her cheek and the blow to the head must have been made by the horses' hoofs. Fortunately the skull isn't fractured. It must only have been a glancing blow.'

'She's come off lightly,' Jerome said, 'all things considered.' He met Henrietta's eyes. He looked drawn, ten years older in just a couple of hours. 'It wasn't the stallion's fault,' he added. 'She was riding him and fell off. He didn't attack her. She just fell off under the mares' hoofs. They'd have tried to avoid her, you know. Horses hate to tread on any living thing.'

Henrietta placed her hand on his arm. She saw it mattered to him. 'I know,' she said. At a time like this there was no knowing what foolish thing the mind would throw up. For herself, while she waited for them to come home, she had kept thinking that it had been lemon cake for tea, Jessie's favourite, and that she hadn't saved any for her. Only let her get well, she thought now, and I'll make her a whole one to herself.

The concussion was what worried Venetia most, for the brain was an uncharted area, and the unseen damage could result in memory loss, blindness, even death. Having set the arm and stitched the cheek, she sat up with the child all night, checking her pulse and breathing at frequent intervals. In the morning she left her for a short time while she bathed and changed her clothes and took some breakfast, and when she returned she saw at once that the coma was lightening. A little while later Jessie woke and stared at her blankly.

'Well, who am I?'

Jessie licked her lips. 'Cousin Venetia.'

'Where are you?'

'At home?'

'Good.' She brought a glass of water to Jessie's lips and helped her drink.

'My head hurts,' Jessie said, when Venetia had laid her back against the pillow.

'Go back to sleep, then,' Venetia said; and she did.

When she next woke, she was clear-headed, and her head ached a little less. Venetia told Henrietta she was satisfied there was no brain damage. The wrist she was confident would heal in time; but poor little Jessie looked quite a figure, with the stitched cut down her swollen cheek.

'What the devil did you think you were doing?' Jerome asked her, frightened into anger by the sight of the hurt to her.

Jessie didn't answer, only looked up at him with large eyes. She didn't think of the boys' taunts and the dare, she only remembered Pasha, and the moment of rapturous love as she rode him. But she had no words to explain that to her father. At last she said, 'Is he all right?'

'Pasha? Yes – no thanks to you! He was running loose with a rope on his headstall. Do you know what could have happened if it had caught on something, or tripped him? He could have come down and broken his legs.'

And a broken leg for a horse meant death, she knew. Her eyes filled with tears and her chin quivered. 'Oh, Papa!' she whispered.

She hadn't called him Papa for years; it was her baby name for him. He felt a brute, was instantly all contrition. He stooped swiftly to kiss the unwounded side of her face, and his own tears wet her cheeks. 'You little fool,' he whispered. 'I might have lost you. Never do anything like that again, Jess. I couldn't bear it without you.'

Jessie thought wonderingly, *Did I almost die?* It felt important and rather frightening. 'Do the boys know?' she asked.

He straightened up and looked at her carefully, and divined her thought. 'They think you were no end plucky,' he said, and her faint, watery smile was his reward.

★ ★ ★

Teddy rode in to York to bring back a supply of ice to try to bring down the swelling of her face, and brought back grapes, too, and ice-cream, and chocolate raisins, and a picture book to beguile his niece out of any thought of dying. The boys weren't allowed in to visit her, but Jack sent his best drawing of a motor-car, Frank his favourite lead soldier, and contrite Robbie, who felt really it was mostly his fault, went out and picked her a bunch of wild flowers and sent them with the promise that she could have his pet frog when she was well again, if she wanted it.

Bertie was allowed in to see her. He came tiptoeing in towards dusk on the second day, and stood looking down at her for a while before she felt his presence and opened her eyes. 'Are you awake? I didn't mean to wake you,' he whispered.

'What time is it?' she murmured.

'It's past tea-time. Are you hungry?'

'Yes, I think I am,' she said.

'Good. That means you're getting better. Aunt Hen said I was to ask you and ring if you are. I say,' he added, 'you were a little idiot, but I must say I never saw anything so brave.' She warmed to the admiration in his voice. 'But you won't ever do anything like that again, will you? I've never had such a fright as when I saw you come off. I'm sure you must have taken years off my life.'

'Oh, Bertie,' she said, 'not really!'

'True! There you were one minute, and the next you just disappeared. Terrible shock to the system. So don't do it again, hey, Jess? Promise?'

'I promise,' she said.

He sat down on the chair beside the bed. 'Why *did* you, though?'

She was silent. She wanted to explain. Seeing Bertie close to, leaning towards her, all attention, remembering him leaning over her on that first wakening, she thought perhaps he would understand. He had been part of it, in a way. She thought of Pasha, and the hot, thrilling presence of him, and the flying, soaring, winged feeling of joy she had when she rode him, the possessed-and-possessing of love. She

97

looked into Bertie's eyes and thought that somehow he must know, that he had been there and witnessed it too. But she had no words, and trying to think of them made her head ache.

'It was a dare,' she said at last. That wasn't it, and she was cross about the words as soon as they were out.

Bertie said, 'You dared yourself.' He knew, having heard some of the explanations, that the boys emphatically denied ever having thought of the stallion, let alone put her up to it.

'Mm,' she said, but not as if that was the end of it.

His eyes crinkled into a smile. 'Was it wonderful – while it lasted?'

She smiled too. He did understand! 'Wonderful,' she said. 'Like flying.'

He nodded. The door opened and Emma came in with a tray. 'I've done you a boiled egg and soldiers, just the way you like,' she said. Her eyes were red where she had obviously been crying. 'Your own little white egg-cup. You be a good girl now and eat it all up.'

With one arm immobilised, she would have to be helped. Emma was preparing to do it, but Jessie said, in a small, rather shy voice, 'Could Bertie stay? Could he help me?'

Emma looked at him doubtfully, for he was a young man and therefore neither of the age nor sex for sick-bed nursing. Even Jessie, as witness her voice, doubted he would consent. But he said, with what sounded like pleasure, 'Yes, of course – if I'm allowed?'

Emma relinquished her place. 'I've plenty to do downstairs.' She helped Bertie to sit Jessie up a little, gave them one more curious look, reasoned that he could always ring if he got into trouble, and left them.

Bertie felt a strange, nervous shyness, something like the feeling he'd had the first time he had gone calling on a girl. This, like that occasion, was a step into an unknown situation with rules and pitfalls he had no way of anticipating. But poor little Jess had asked for him, so he took himself by the scruff of the neck and determined to do the thing properly. He spread the napkin over her chest up under her chin, carefully cut off the top of the egg, and said, 'Shall I dip a soldier first, or do you want a spoonful?'

'Soldier, please,' she said.

So with a delicate efficiency that was the more touching because he was a man, and his hands were big brown hands and his muscles strong for other uses, he fed her. He did it neatly and did not spill, and soon told himself that the trick was not to overload the spoon, and to allow enough time for chewing and swallowing.

Jessie ate obediently, hardly noticing the food, so absorbed was she with Bertie, never taking her eyes from his face, noticing, when he looked down at the tray, how long and delicate his eyelashes were, how tender-pink his lips looked half hidden by his moustache. As the dusk grew outside they were cocooned more closely in the ring of light thrown by her bedside lamp, and she imagined, vaguely, that they were sheltering in a cave together against a wild and beast-filled night outside – vaguely, because she was falling asleep.

When he was near the end of the egg, he saw her eyelids drooping, and decided she had had enough. He put the tray aside, patted her lips softly with the napkin, and stood up. Her eyes followed him, heavy but insistent. With an instinct he had not known he had, he bent over her and rearranged her pillow so that she was flatter, and then, smiling, laid his lips to her cheek. He heard her give a small, satisfied sigh, and when he straightened up, her eyes were closed.

'Sleep, then,' he said, gathered up the tray and tiptoed out.

After a day or two, when her bruises had become Turneresque but her head and arm had stopped hurting, Violet was allowed up to see her. She came in wide-eyed, and her eyes stretched even more when she saw her cousin's face.

'Oh, Jessie! You might have been killed! It was awful.'

'What does my face look like?' Jessie asked. Violet's eyes filled with tears, and her lips trembled. 'Really,' Jessie urged. 'You can tell me. Mother won't let me have a looking-glass. Does it look terrible?'

Violet nodded unwillingly. In a moment, she had control enough of her voice to say, 'But Mama says it will get better. Only—'

'Only what?'

'She says you might have a scar,' Violet said, and the tears spilled over.

Jessie put up careful fingers and touched her cheek, feeling the spiky ends of the stitches, so alien in that place which before had always just been *her*. It was frightening – more frightening than her broken arm, which could be viewed with a certain amount of detachment. Her face was where she lived. But she hated to see Violet cry, so she said boldly, 'Oh, I don't mind it. It'll be rather jolly to have a scar – like a pirate. Oh, Vi, don't cry!'

'I thought you were dead,' she sobbed.

'Don't. Don't.'

'It was so terrible! Why did you do it?'

To Violet she could only say, 'To prove I can do anything the boys can do. And more. None of them would have dared.'

'I suppose not,' Violet said. Her tears were subsiding, and she sought out her handkerchief and blew her nose. Jessie noticed that even after crying Violet did not have red eyes and a red nose. She cried like a princess in a fairy story, she thought – beautifully, like rain from a blue sky. 'But I don't understand why you want to,' Violet said at last.

'Want to what?'

'Be like a boy.'

'You don't like being a girl, do you?' Jessie said in surprise. She had assumed that all girls felt like her.

'Yes, I do,' Violet said certainly. 'I wouldn't like to be a boy. Boys are always being beaten, and they play with horrid things like insects and snakes, and they can't cry when they hurt themselves, even if it's bad. And they don't have pretty things to wear, and they can't sit on Papa's knee like me. I like the things girls do.'

'But when you grow up, don't you want to do exciting things?'

Violet thought. 'I want to get married and have six children and have a white house with green shutters like Mrs Parry's.'

'Is that all?' Violet looked a little confused at the question. 'I mean, don't you want to do something important? Be a doctor like your mama, for instance?'

'No, I don't think I'd like to be a doctor,' Violet said. 'Sick people are disagreeable, and poor people smell bad, and I'd hate to cut people up and see all the blood come out and everything. Being a doctor makes Mama so tired. And she got called out in the middle of my birthday tea and didn't come back until it was nearly all over. She has to go when she's called. I shouldn't like that. When I get married I want to stay home and look after my children and always be there when my husband comes home, not like when Papa comes and she's gone out.' She frowned in thought, and then looked at Jessie and said, 'What do you want to do, then?'

'I don't know,' Jessie said. 'But something. Not just stay at home like Mother and Emma.'

'Oh,' said Violet. They both thought in silence for a while. Then Violet said, 'But we will always be friends, won't we?'

'Of course,' Jessie said, surprised by the question. 'Why shouldn't we be?'

But she thought about the conversation for a long time after Violet had gone away. Later when Venetia came to check her over, Jessie asked as she was taking her pulse, 'Cousin Venetia, you do like being a doctor, don't you?'

'It's all I ever wanted to do.'

'Don't you think girls ought to be able to do things?'

'You mean, and not be told that they are for boys only?' Jessie nodded. 'Well, my dear, that's the great question of our time. But we live in the world as it is, and we have to get on with it. That doesn't mean we can't try to change things, of course.'

'Like you did, becoming a doctor? Was it very hard?'

'*Very* hard. You can't conceive how many people told me I couldn't do it, and tried to stop me, and called me bad names because I wouldn't be stopped.'

'But you did it, all the same.'

Venetia laid down the wrist she had been holding. 'I'll

tell you something. In my experience, there's nothing you can't do if you only want to hard enough. But you must be very sure that the thing you want is *worth* wanting. Do you understand me?'

'I'm not sure. You mean like being a doctor, but not like riding Dad's stallion?'

'Yes, exactly. Good girl! Because, you see, if you put all your efforts into doing something that isn't worth doing, you will only succeed in making yourself look foolish. And you may end up doing harm.'

'Yes, I suppose so.' She raised her eyes to Venetia's face. 'Only – didn't you ever feel you *had* to just show the boys? They were being so horrid.'

Venetia laughed. 'Boys always are. Nothing will change that. But look here, my love,' she said seriously, 'they're still free to go on being horrid to their hearts' content while you're going to be laid up for months with a broken arm. Who has showed whom, I wonder?'

Jessie sighed. 'I see what you mean.'

'I thought you would. You're a clever girl.' She looked at the poor swollen face and the glum expression with enormous sympathy. She had been just such a one, hitting her head against the invisible glass that shut her in like a poor foolish bee, until she had found her way out at last. 'I tell you what,' she said, 'when you're back on your feet, I'll invite you to come and stay in London at my house, and you and I and Violet will see if we can't have some fun together. What do you say?'

'Oh, yes, *please!*'

'It'll be something to look forward to,' she said.

She was afraid Jessie was going to need it. At that age it was hard to be laid up in plaster week after week; and she was afraid that the cut might leave a scar. In her present frame of mind Jessie would not care about that, but for a girl with no dowry her looks could be important, and in spite of the progress that had been made in the last twenty years, marriage was still the only career for most girls. Jessie might prove to be one of the exceptions, but it was too early to know if she had any particular talents other than high spirits; and even then, it was hard for a girl to get on without money behind her, either in the form of a wealthy parent, which Jessie didn't have, or a wealthy and liberal-minded husband – which brought you straight back to the scar.

CHAPTER FOUR

During the month of August 1899 various arguments were raised and quashed for sending reinforcements to South Africa. The British troops garrisoned there were heavily outnumbered by the Boers, should it come to military action. The difficulty was that Wolseley, the British army's commander-in-chief, was not on good terms with Lansdowne, the Secretary for War, while the rest of the Cabinet did not agree with Chamberlain about the importance of South Africa or the right course to take concerning it. Chamberlain agreed with Milner that a show of strength was necessary to quell Kruger's ambitions; others in Cabinet argued that it would only provoke the Boers and precipitate a war, which would be thoroughly undesirable.

But in early September a moderate and conciliatory offer to the Boers, though accepted by the Cape Dutch leaders, was rejected by Kruger, and the Cabinet lost patience. Chamberlain won his argument for reinforcements to be sent as a gesture of strength. It was estimated that Transvaal could muster 30,000 men and Orange Free State, which had thrown in its lot with Transvaal, 20,000; but Kruger had arms for 80,000 and hoped that many of the Cape Dutch would join them once war was declared. So now orders were sent to British garrisons in India, Malta, Egypt and Crete for reinforcements to be despatched direct to the Cape, which would bring local numbers up to 27,000. But though plans had been drawn up for a further field force of 47,000 under Sir Redvers Buller to be sent from Britain, Chamberlain could still not move his Cabinet colleagues to order their mobilisation.

Chamberlain had requested that Sir Redvers Buller be sent out immediately, for Buller had served in the Zulu War and knew the terrain; but Wolseley insisted Buller must remain with the field force in England. Besides, Lansdowne preferred Sir George White, an 'Indian' officer. Buller, desperately worried about the whole business, wrote direct to Lord Salisbury, complaining about the lack of preparation, the route Lansdowne was believed to have chosen in the event of a war, and urging the dispatch of his field force, arguing that threats without sufficient visible force behind them would only encourage Boer aggression. In particular he warned that White should be told not to venture north of the Tugela river until the full field force had arrived in South Africa. This bypassing of Lansdowne did nothing to endear Buller to the Secretary for War.

Meanwhile, public opinion, particularly in London, was clamouring for action, and the anti-war party was being shouted down. They were derided by the great British public as 'Boer-loving', unpatriotic, covert republicans – and probably teetotallers and vegetarians to boot! Newspaper leaders, cartoons, handbills and popular songs all wanted blood. The nation hadn't had a proper enemy to hate since the Crimea, and the young men of England were lusting for a good scrap.

The Cabinet's problem was resolved on the 9th of October, two days after General White arrived in Durban, when Kruger and President Steyn of the Orange Free State together issued an ultimatum, demanding the withdrawal of British troops from South Africa within forty-eight hours. There could be no question of compliance. The field force of 47,000 men under Sir Redvers Buller was mobilised. Canada, Australia and New Zealand rallied round and sent troops, stirred by the Motherland's determination to protect her children. The Empire was at war with the Boer republics.

Much of this passed Venetia by, for her mother died in September, at the age of seventy-seven.

Since having to give up the Dower House to her daughter-in-law, Charlotte had been living in a small way in Brook

105

Street, with just a cook, a maid and a footman, who between them, she said, could cater for her few remaining needs. The footman came round to Manchester Square very early one morning with the news. The dowager duchess had been accustomed to waking early and her maid – Vickers, who had replaced the much-missed Norton – took her up a cup of tea and some bread-and-butter at six every morning, at which point her grace was always awake and usually sitting up in bed. On this particular morning she was still lying down, and when Vickers tried to wake her she knew at the first touch that she was dead.

Venetia dressed hurriedly and went round, but there was, of course, nothing to be done. To all appearances, her mother had died quietly in her sleep.

'Not a bad way to go,' Hazelmere said, much later that day, when he tried to comfort her. 'And she—'

'If you say she had a good innings, I shall hit you!'

'I wasn't going to say that. But she had lived a full and rich life, and I expect she was ready.'

'But I wasn't,' Venetia said. Dry-eyed but bleak-faced, she stared at the fire. After being alarmed by Charlotte's words at Shawes, she had allowed herself to be reassured by her mother's apparent health, which seemed just as usual. Observing no particular symptoms, she had not been expecting her to die. 'She didn't even say goodbye.'

'Darling, she's been saying goodbye all year. Looking back I can see all sorts of signs. But we weren't listening.'

As a doctor Venetia had learnt to be pragmatic about death; as a Christian she believed in the afterlife, and that they would meet again one day. But as a human animal she grieved for the loss of one who had always been dear and had become in the past twenty years progressively dearer. It is hard at any age to lose one's mother, but she had lost also a friend and mentor and a dear companion. She felt suddenly very alone, very exposed. Her parents, both her brothers and one sister were all gone. There was only her and Olivia now.

As Anne Farraline said, when she came with her condolences, 'When you lose your last parent, it really is the end of childhood.'

106

Venetia occupied herself with planning the funeral – understanding at last exactly what funerals were for. With the permission of the new duke, Charlotte was buried in the graveyard at Ravendene, the Fleetwood family seat in Northamptonshire, beside her husband, the one love of her life.

The service was beautiful, with the moving and consoling poetry of the Prayer Book, as familiar in its way as the wedding service, the words slipping down like balm into the mind and heart into places prepared through long knowledge to receive them. Thomas read one of the lessons, and did it touchingly well, life at Eton having taught him to do that, at least. The children had all loved their grandmama, but as the eldest, he had known her best. Venetia listened, looked along the pew at the boys and Violet, and was suddenly, unexpectedly, at peace. Life begins and life ends, but always it goes on, a great unstaunchable river, that rises for each of us in a small, bright spring, that slows and broadens, and carries us down at last to the great sea where all the waters mingle and we are made One.

The duke and his family were kindness itself, and invited everyone back to the house afterwards for a cold collation. It was the first time Venetia had been in her childhood home since her brother's funeral. She looked round with interest to see what changes the new incumbents had made but apart from a lot of new 'Maples' furniture and some bright modern chintzes – which she thought looked out of place – it was much as it had always been. The duke's large family was attentive, their manners rather stiff and shy, though perhaps that was natural given the nature of the occasion.

The young dowager duchess – the former Miss Culpepper – was there, by invitation, though she had not been at the funeral service, pleading off with a slight chill, which she said her doctor advised her not to take into draughty places. Venetia suspected it had rather been diffidence that kept her away from the church, or perhaps unhappy memories. Nancy had been unhappily married to Venetia's brother for six years, and had been widowed for almost four now. Despite all she had been through she was very shy, and had seemed content to shut herself away at Ravendene for a large part of the year, despite her father's urgings that she should rejoin society. Mr Culpepper was anxious that she should marry again and give him an heir, for she was his only child.

But what Nancy's parents had been unable to achieve, the kindly new duke seemed to have managed. Venetia, taking trouble to talk to Nancy, found her not only in apparent good health but in quietly intense good spirits. It was not long before a certain name began to pop into her sentences seemingly without her volition, and always accompanied by a brightening of the cheeks and eyes. Later when Venetia excused herself and sought out the duke, she said, 'Tell me, Cousin Frederick, who is Sir William Forrester?'

The duke caught her reference at once. 'Ah, you must have been talking to Nancy!'

'From the way she manages to turn every topic round to him, I assume there is love in the case?'

'He is a well-to-do landowner, a widower of eight years, a few years older than Nancy, and altogether a thoroughly decent fellow. Hunts with the Pytcheley. I had an idea last year that they might do very well for each other, and took pains to bring them into company together, but they did the rest for themselves. I hope you don't disapprove?'

'How could I? And why should I? I would be glad for everyone to be as happy. And Nancy deserves it more than most, poor thing. Does her father know?'

'Not that they are engaged – Forrester "popped the question" only yesterday – but he has met him at my dinner table and seemed to like him. And I mistake Mr Culpepper if he does not know everything that goes on, especially concerning his daughter.' The duke looked across at Nancy, talking to the duchess with quiet animation. 'She does look happy, doesn't she? Poor young lady, she's hardly had a moment to be with her beloved since she accepted him, what with the funeral – I beg your pardon!' He caught himself up. 'How clumsy and tactless of me. Here I am talking of weddings and happiness on such an occasion. I do beg you to forgive me, Cousin Venetia.'

She laid a hand on his sleeve. 'Don't apologise. It's the

108

nicest thing that could happen, to see love blooming at my mother's funeral. Life goes on, you know. It's a blessing – and perhaps the only comfort – that it does.'

'It's very good of you to take it that way.'

'Mama was very fond of Nancy. She'd be glad to know she is happy at last. You've been a good friend to Nancy, cousin. I feel guilty that I didn't do more to try to bring her out of herself.' She smiled. 'I shall look forward to the wedding. You must see if you can't use your influence and secure me an invitation!'

His permanently anxious, rather worn face – she could never think of it as ducal, only rather clerkly and nice – smoothed out. 'How absurd you are, ma'am! As if you could ever need my help.'

The disposition of her mother's estate presented few surprises to Venetia. Rigsby, Charlotte's man of business, called on Venetia at her request to explain it all. Before she had married the duke, Charlotte had been a countess in her own right, having inherited the Chelmsford title from her father. Since this title could pass to an heir of either sex, it now passed to Venetia, together with the real estate which was entailed – Shawes in Yorkshire, and the huge Town mansion, Chelmsford House in Pall Mall, which was rented out.

'Her grace did not use the title, of course, since your late father outranked her,' Rigsby said, with a small furrow of the brow. 'In your ladyship's case, however . . .'

Venetia, as the daughter of a duke, already outranked her husband, who was only a viscount, which was why she was Lady Venetia Hazelmere and not simply Lady Hazelmere – a nice distinction her butler was very strict in maintaining, should any caller be wanton enough to forget it.

'I don't think I shall use it either,' she told the lawyer. 'It would be a little awkward to be announced as Lady Chelmsford and Lord Hazelmere – though it does sound delightfully illicit! I might almost be tempted, just to see which eyebrows it would raise.'

Rigsby coughed slightly. 'As you say, my lady. But your

husband, perhaps . . .' He was the master of the delicately unfinished sentence.

'Yes, poor Hazelmere, one must consider his feelings. He has enough to bear with a wife who insists on practising as a doctor – and him so intimate with the Prince of Wales! So, tell me, Mr Rigsby, is there much else besides the two houses?'

'Oh, yes, my lady. Her grace was in very comfortable circumstances, and since she lived in latter years in such a small way, the income has accumulated with the capital. Apart from the cash sum in the Funds, there are shares and property, mostly abroad, which bring in a very agreeable amount, and which of course are not entailed with the title. A very agreeable amount, I would say,' he repeated, with a satisfied look. 'The bulk of it comes to you, my lady. Her late grace was of the old-fashioned stamp, which believes property and title ought to go together – a very wise disposition, if I may be permitted to comment. Of course she has made a bequest to Lady Olivia, and there are pensions to various old servants and small personal gifts of chattels to friends and family.'

'I see. And what's the "demn'd total", as Mr Mantalini would say?' Venetia asked lightly.

Rigsby lifted his briefcase onto his lap and removed a sheaf of papers. 'I have the details here, my lady,' he said.

'Darling, do stop laughing. Are you hysterical, or have you been drinking?' Hazelmere said, beginning to be cross.

'Neither. Or both. I don't know. Oh, Beauty, it really is too funny!'

'I don't see why. Your mother has left you some money. You must have expected that.'

'Oh, but I haven't told you how much. We're rich, my love, horribly, horribly rich. And after all these years, first of struggle and then of getting by – it seems like a most ridiculous joke.'

'In the first place, it's *you* who are rich, not *we*. And in the second place, I don't think your mother would like you to describe her bequest to you as a joke.'

Venetia sobered, wiped her eyes, and sat down. 'No, you're quite right, of course. It was just rather a shock.'

'So, what has she left you?' Hazelmere prompted after a moment. 'I can't help admitting a normal human curiosity.'

'Oho! Is that the Devil at your shoulder? Well, my love, she had fifty thousand pounds in the Funds, of which ten goes to the Southport Hospital, thirty thousand to Olivia and ten to me, out of which I have to pay a few pensions.'

Hazelmere raised his eyebrows. 'Ten thousand pounds! Even after the pensions that should leave a very useful sum. Still, I'd hardly call it a reason for hysteria.'

'Wait, you haven't heard the rest. Apart from the cash, and her personal belongings – what Rigsby in his endearing way calls her chattels – there is a large block of railway shares in Russia—'

'Russia?'

'—also a coal mine in the Urals, a large factory near Moscow, and another, together with a block of offices, in Kiev.'

'What did—'

'Wait, I haven't finished yet. There are also shares in a steel works on the Rhine, a timber-mill in the Black Forest and a tract of farmland in Northumberland. What do you think of that?'

'Is that all?' Now Hazelmere was laughing. 'It's too absurd! What was she doing with all those Russian and German holdings?'

'"For historical reasons I won't go into, my lady,"' she said, imitating Rigsby's cadences. 'Apparently Chelmsfords of old invested adventurously in these things in their infancy, and now they have matured to produce a very healthy return. But, of course, in my father's lifetime it was all masked by his wealth, and after he died, Mama kept it secret from Harry in case he should try to borrow against it – because, of course, it would all have gone to him as her eldest son, along with the dukedom.'

'Yes, I suppose that was wise, considering how profligate your brother was.'

'The ducal fortune, being mostly in land, slumped with

111

the agricultural depression. So I am probably much wealthier now than the new duke – poor fellow.'

Hazelmere shook his head. 'I can't take it in at all.'

'That's exactly how I feel. Oh, Beauty, come and hold me, and tell me you'll still love me now I'm an heiress!'

'Didn't I swear to stick by you through thick and thin?'

'Yes, but we never anticipated so much thick!'

He held her. 'I think I can manage to see through the dazzle of your wealth to the essential Venetia underneath. And I dare say we'll learn to bear being rich. At least we shan't have to worry about finding the school fees for Oliver as well as Thomas. And we'll be able to bring Violet out in style, when her turn comes.'

Venetia, comforted by his arms, said seriously, 'I don't think we ought to tell the children about our change in circumstances. I'd hate Thomas to become expensive and idle and get into the wrong sort of company.'

'That's probably a good idea. It does a fellow no good to rely on inheriting a fortune. And who knows but what we might squander it on ourselves before he has a chance to inherit? Do you want to move to a larger house?'

'Oh, I don't think so. Not at once, at any rate. It's comfortable enough here, and convenient for us both, isn't it?'

'Your mother always wanted Violet to have her coming-out ball at Chelmsford House,' he reminded her mischievously.

'That gives us a few years in hand before we need evict the tenants.'

Henrietta was in the apple store-room picking out for an apple pie those that looked least likely to keep. A shadow fell across the doorway and she turned her head to see Charley standing there.

'Hello! I wasn't expecting you, was I? Did Teddy bring you?'

'No, I came on my own. I wanted to talk to you.'

'There's nothing wrong, is there?'

'No, no. Here, let me take those for you.' Henrietta's pick of apples was too large for her hands.

'Thank you. I forgot to bring a basket with me.' She gave

some to Charley and folded up her apron to carry the rest. Outside the sweet, dry stuffiness of the store-room the air was fresh but cool. The autumn sun did not long clear the house to brighten the inner courtyard: most of it was in shadow, the well-cold shadow of stone that is never properly warmed. Moss grew between the pavings on the dark side of the yard, and in the winter frost and ice lingered there for days; but high above it a pair of pigeons was sitting on the sunny corner of the chapel roof, preening and fluffing in the warmth.

'What are these for?' Charley asked, gesturing with her burden.

'An apple pie for dinner tonight. My pastry isn't as good as Emma's, but it's her afternoon off.'

'I know. I saw her in York, just going up the Stonebow. I recognised that hat of hers with the cherries.'

'She's going to see her friend, who's a cook for a lady in Hungate.' Henrietta looked at her curiously. 'Do I gather that's why you came, hoping to find me alone? Is it something serious, Charley? You look rather . . .' She paused. There was something different about her sister-in-law, but she couldn't put her finger on it.

'I'll tell you inside,' Charley said. They went in through the open doorway to the kitchen passage, which was always dark and smelt of damp plaster, and walked along the uneven, ancient flagstones past the various cupboards and pantries and gloomy cubby-holes and into the kitchen at last, which was light and warm, with its high windows, and the great range that never went out except when the chimney was swept. Kithra was lying on the hot stone in front of it, flat out on his side in that unnerving way of his. He got to his feet and came ambling over to greet Charley with a silent thrust of his head and a swing of his whip-hard tail.

They put the apples down on the scrubbed table and Henrietta said, 'Can I offer you anything? A glass of sherry?'

Charley laughed, dispelling Henrietta's fears that she might have some dire news to impart. 'I've never really got used to drinking wine,' she said. 'It's a great trial for Teddy, I know, and a sign of my low origins, but I can't help thinking

113

it tastes like medicine, and nasty medicine at that.'

Henrietta laughed too. 'Then I won't inflict it on you. A cup of tea, perhaps?'

'That would be nice,' Charley said. She watched Henrietta walk over to the range and push the kettle across one of the plates. 'Is it common to prefer tea to sherry?'

'Common?'

'I mean, vulgar – you know.'

'My dear girl, what a thing to ask!'

'But you were born a lady. You know about these things.'

'I should think most women prefer tea to sherry, if you could get them to admit it. There's something comforting about tea, isn't there? In any case, there's nothing common about you in that way.'

'I've learnt a lot. But still . . .'

Henrietta looked at her levelly. 'Has somebody been saying something unkind to you?'

'Oh, no. Not recently. But I think about it sometimes.'

'Well, you shouldn't. Teddy loves you and so do we all. There's nothing to be ashamed of in having been a servant. Good Heavens, are we to despise everyone who earns an honest living? The sort of people who look down on you for it aren't worth bothering about. Why should you care for the opinions of people who have opinions like that?'

'That's all very well, but didn't *you* care when they said things about you and Jerome?' Charley asked, looking down and tracing a pattern on the tabletop with her finger.

'Yes, I did,' Henrietta admitted. 'But it was stupid of me, and it's stupid of you! Besides, I had actually done something that people have reason to think is wrong. You haven't done anything except marry the man who loves you, which you and he were both perfectly entitled to do. Who has been saying things to upset you?'

Charley looked up now and smiled. 'I love it when you fluff up like that, like an angry sparrow. You really would peck them on my behalf, wouldn't you – no matter who?'

'Of course.'

'Thank you,' Charley said, with simple emphasis. 'The kettle's boiling.'

114

'So it is,' said Henrietta. She made the tea and brought the pot to the table, while Charley in her handy way, without being asked, found cups and saucers and tea-strainer, and brought the milk jug from the pantry.

'So,' said Henrietta, when they were settled, 'what did you want to talk to me about?'

Charley was silent a moment, as if trying to select the right words; but then she lifted her eyes to Henrietta's and said bluntly, 'I'm going to have a baby.'

It was the last thing Henrietta had expected; but after the shock came happiness. 'Oh, my dear! But how wonderful! Are you sure?'

'I think so. I've never done it before but – well – something that should have happened hasn't happened.' Charley's cheeks flushed as she broached this embarrassing topic.

Henrietta was touched at this reticence, and thought that Charley was a great deal more refined than many of her critics. 'How many times?' she asked gently.

'Not since August.'

'Have you any other symptoms?'

'I've been sick once or twice in the mornings. At first I thought it was something I ate, but it's not really like that. And,' she laid a hand briefly to her bosom, 'I'm quite sore *here*.'

'Well, it does sound as though you are. How absolutely wonderful!' Henrietta did a quick count in her head. 'So the baby will be here in May. I'm so pleased for you, Charley dear. What does Teddy say?'

'I haven't told him yet. I didn't want to until I was sure, in any case, but also . . .' She paused.

Henrietta looked at her closely. 'You are pleased about it, aren't you? You look worried. Is there anything I can help you with?'

'I'm scared,' Charley said bluntly.

'Oh, Charley, everyone is the first time. Lizzie was dreadfully scared, you know. So was I. But you must remember that thousands of women have babies every day. It's what we're made for.'

'Is it really –' Charley gulped '– is it really not too bad?'

115

'It isn't a bit like what you fear,' Henrietta said. 'It's one of those things no-one can tell you, and afterwards you'll understand why. But no, it's not too bad. Don't let being afraid spoil what should be a wonderful time for you.'

Charley nodded doubtfully. 'There's something else, too.'

Henrietta poured her some more tea. 'Go on.'

The confession came out in a low voice. 'I'm so afraid Teddy won't love me so much afterwards. I know that's naughty and selfish of me, but – but ever since we married he's longed so to have a child, and I think he's given up hope of it now. He's going to be so happy and excited when I tell him.'

'But that's good, isn't it?' Henrietta was puzzled.

'Oh, yes. He'll pet me and make a fuss of me and everything. But once the child comes, he'll love it so much, maybe he won't care about me any more.'

Henrietta didn't answer immediately. Charley was too clever to be comforted by an automatic rebuttal. She needed to believe whatever Henrietta told her.

'He *will* be excited,' she said at last. 'He *will* adore the child. But he'll love you even more than before for being the mother of the child. Dear Charley, if you could only hear how he talks about you!'

'But . . .' Charley said helplessly.

'Yes, I know what you mean. It will be different. But love between two people doesn't stay the same, and nor should it. It grows and changes as people do when they grow up. And if it's real love it becomes better and deeper all the time. It's another thing I can't really tell you,' she said. 'But you'll understand when it happens.'

They drank tea in silence for a while. A coal dropped inside the firebox of the range, and Kithra answered with a whimper in his sleep as his paws chased dream rabbits through the golden fields.

Charley put down her cup and said, 'I'd better go. I expect you've got a lot to do before the children get home from school.'

'Won't you stay and see them? You know how they love to see you. Of course, you won't be able to romp with them

116

any longer. You'll have to be careful of yourself for the next few months.'

'No, thank you, but I won't stay. I have to get home before Teddy knows I'm missing. And, please, you won't tell anyone?'

'Not if you don't want me to.'

'I don't want Teddy to think he isn't the first to know. So when he tells—'

'Yes, I shall be all amazement. I understand.'

They stood up, and Charley came to hug her and lay her cheek briefly against Henrietta's.

'Thank you,' Charley said. 'No-one could have a better sister than you.' And then she was gone.

Teddy, in his usual style, made an occasion of 'telling'. He invited Henrietta and Jerome to dinner at Makepeace House a few days later and, as soon as they were shown into the drawing-room, regaled them with champagne and announced the great news. Honouring her promise to Charley, Henrietta had not told Jerome, so his surprise was spontaneous, and behind it Henrietta was able to express her genuine pleasure without dissembling. Teddy's joy was so huge, so grateful and so tender that she found herself in tears when she embraced him with her congratulations. He seemed almost bewildered by the bounty suddenly bestowed on him, and when they sat down to the sumptuous meal he had ordered, he ate with an unusual air of distraction, and kept gazing down the table at Charley as if he had never seen her before.

'I meant to tease you with it,' he confessed. 'Tell you I had exciting news and then make you wait until after dinner. But I couldn't hold it back.' He beamed around the table at them. 'Some time in May, Charley tells me. I wonder if it'll be a boy or a girl? Imagine, I shall be a papa! What do you think of that? I don't know what sort of a fist I shall make of it.'

'You've been like a father to Ned,' Jerome pointed out.

'But that's different,' Teddy said, with absolute conviction. 'By the by, we must make sure poor Ned knows he's

117

not abandoned. That we shall love him just as before.'

That was like kind Teddy, Henrietta thought; but the reality was that he would not be loved exactly as before, when there had been no-one to share with. However, he would have the best that could be managed, that was sure.

In the drawing-room after dinner, Teddy sat next to Henrietta and said, 'I shall have to write to Perry and Regina, I suppose. Have you heard from Reggie lately?'

'She never was a letter-writer,' Henrietta said. 'Haven't you visited them recently?'

'Not since August. But I heard from a fellow at the club that Edith is engaged to George Antrobus at last. The wedding's to come off in March, which will be a big expense to Perry. The Antrobuses will expect something in the first style.'

'Yes, and Edith being the eldest girl—'

'I only hope Perry has long enough pockets. With those expensive boys, and all Reggie's doctor's bills to pay, a wedding's going to put a strain on the purse.' He focused on Henrietta suddenly. 'It's a damned shame that we have to hear family news at second-hand. Perry's a stiff-necked ass to keep on objectin' to your situation. But I believe the loss is his.' He placed a hand over Henrietta's. 'We're happy enough, ain't we, Hen?'

'Happier than ever,' she assured him.

'Right-ho!' Another spasm of thoughtfulness overtook him. 'You know who I keep thinking about, since Charley told me her news? Foolish, really.'

'Manfred,' Henrietta said. Manfred was their younger brother who had died at school of consumption.

Teddy seemed surprised that she guessed right. 'You too?'

'No, but I know you, Ted.'

'Oh! Well, I keep thinking about poor Manny, sent away from the family and dying all alone so far from home. I've never told you, but I always felt guilty that I didn't do more for him. In a way that's why I've taken Ned in and done what I can for him. A sort of – what's that word?'

'Atonement?'

'That's the one. And now I'm to have a child of my own,

118

I'm determined Ned shan't suffer in any way because of it. Too many outcasts in our family. Manny, and you, and Ned. Not right. Not right at all.'

Henrietta thought about it, and mentally added Regina to the list, though Regina might not view it that way. But could a busy and distracted husband with the greatest worries of fatherhood dogging his days find the same time to listen to an ailing wife's woes as a sister would? She determined to find time to write Regina a long letter, telling all the family news and asking her how she was. Even if Reggie did not answer, it must comfort her to know that Henrietta still thought about her.

On the 14th of October a huge crowd watched General Sir Redvers Buller go on board the *Dunnottar Castle* on his way to take up command in South Africa. All over the country the mobilisation was going on. Reservists had been called up, ninety-one per cent of them being passed fit for duty, along with a large number of volunteers, who were needed to supplement the regular army. In towns from Totnes to Glasgow the same scenes were repeated as troops were assembled, moved out of barracks and put on trains. People lined the streets, cheering wildly and waving flags. Some, borne away by enthusiasm, broke into the ranks and insisted on carrying the soldiers' kitbags and rifles for them. At the railway stations there were bands playing 'God Save the Queen' and 'Rule Britannia', robed mayors and aldermen, bunting and speeches; lovers taking a last, moist farewell, wives and children crying and hugging Father who was going off to war. At Waterloo, when the Guards boarded the train for the coast, all semblance of military order disappeared as the crowd broke through the police cordon and the men were swept up, some carried shoulder high by cheering strangers, some having to struggle through in single file to the train.

The troops sang 'We're Soldiers of the Queen' as the trains pulled out. They were going to 'teach those Dutch farmers a lesson', to protect the honour of the British Empire, raise the flag again over the Queen's dominions,

119

and restore equal rights between man and man, and between black man and white man. But as well as these high moral intentions, they were also setting out on an adventure to the other side of the world, no small inducement to men, many of whom had never been outside their own county. It was exciting, and it was going to be a tremendous lark. The only fear was that it would not last long enough, for how could a ragged band of Bible-wielding farmers hold out against the might of the British army? 'It will all be over by Christmas' was the phrase passed from mouth to mouth.

'I wish they wouldn't say that,' Ashley said to Lizzie. 'My father told me everyone in the South said the same thing at the beginning of the civil war, and look what happened to them.'

They had received a visit from Raymond Puddephat, on his way to join his regiment, to tell them he had volunteered. He had a few hours before his train departed, and no-one else in London to spend them with; and he had taken a great liking to Ashley at Shawes, where he had quizzed him at length about his exotic origins and the American civil war, which he had lived through as a child.

'I haven't told my father yet. Do you think he'll be wild? The thing is, so many of the chaps at Oxford are volunteering; and when it comes to it, how can grinding away at Oxford compare with going to South Africa and giving the Boers a hiding?'

'I can see it's a hard choice,' said Ashley. Playing cricket with the children at Shawes he had gained an honorary status as one of the younger set, but he was in fact a great deal older than Raymond and a father to boot. He couldn't help thinking that Puddephat *père* might have something to say about his son and heir volunteering without leave. 'Look here, old chap, you oughtn't to go without telling your pa. It's not the thing at all.'

'Oh, but he'd probably object at first, and though I know I could talk him round in the end, it would waste so much time. He'll like it all right once he gets used to the idea. You see,' Raymond went on earnestly, 'everyone says it won't last long. The Boers haven't a chance, though there might

120

be one or two stiff little shows here and there. They are awful idiots to fight, really, though we're jolly keen they should, of course. Everyone says it will be over by Christmas, and if I don't go right away, I shall miss all the fun. It'd be jolly flat to have to admit for the rest of one's life that one wasn't there, when everyone else will have been.'

Everyone, Ashley concluded, had had a great deal to say, one way and another.

Venetia learnt from Thomas, in his weekly letter home, that his great hero, Carlyon, formerly of the Sixth, had also volunteered. 'Everyone thinks he's a great gun,' Thomas wrote, rather wistfully. 'Several fellows here are talking about volunteering. I shouldn't be surprised if a lot of the Sixth don't go at any rate. I do think it's the worst thing in the world to be told you're too young for something. And with my luck, there'll never be another war, so I'll never get my chance.'

Venetia showed the letter to Hazelmere. 'I know we have to fight, but I wouldn't be a mother if I didn't think, Thank God my boys are too young!'

'I forgive you for your womanliness,' Hazelmere said.

She looked at him suspiciously. 'You aren't hankering after it yourself?'

'No, my love, I am too old and too comfortable for that now. But I was a cavalryman once, you know, and I can't help being interested, and wondering what it would be like.'

'I forgive you your manliness, or soldierliness, or whatever it is. But speaking as a doctor, I can't help thinking that if men were more realistic about wars they would never happen. My mother used to tell me what it was like nursing in the Crimea, and I saw for myself in the military hospital in Berlin during the German war with France. All these poor boys going off to South Africa look so happy, and they simply don't know what they're in for.'

Henrietta also had a visit from a young man on his way to war. Bertie arrived one day, on foot for a wonder, looking as taut as a drumskin.

'Guess what, Auntie?'

'I suppose you have lost all your money on a horse again,'

said Henrietta, but with a smile that robbed the words of any sting, for she was growing fonder all the time of her 'extra son', as she sometimes called him to Jerome.

'Very poor shot. Missed by a mile. No, I've volunteered. What do you think about that? I'm off to the Cape to fight for Queen and country!'

'Oh, Bertie!'

'Was that "Oh, Bertie, you are a hero" or "Oh, Bertie, you are a villain"?'

'I hardly know,' Henrietta said. 'What does your father say?'

'The pater's furious. Absolutely forbade me to go. Thunderous denouncement – Mater in tears, servants in hysterics, dogs barking, cocks crowing, general row all round. But then I thought, Hey, nonny, I'm over twenty-one, so he *can't* forbid me. And after all,' he said, fixing her with a pleading look, 'why all the fuss? You'd think it would be a case of "Well done, my boy, finest action a man can undertake," with rose-petals strewn and the champagne flowing about like water. But no, not in our house. Why does my gov'nor have to be so different from everyone else's? So I came to see my beloved aunt Hen, in the sure and certain knowledge that *she* would see the thing in its proper light.'

So Henrietta put her arms round the manly shoulders and kissed the manly cheek, and the hero grasped her in a rigid embrace that felt to her rather more like that of a child trying not to cry.

'You do think I'm a hero, don't you?' he asked, in a small and muffled voice.

'I'm very proud of you,' Henrietta said.

'Oh, Lord, now don't *you* start crying!' he said in alarm, releasing himself. 'I had enough of the waterworks with the mater.'

'It's a natural reaction in any mother when her boy goes off to war. I should be sorry to hear that my sister *hadn't* cried.'

'All right,' Bertie conceded. 'But why can't the pater see the thing in its proper light? Everyone's going. And everyone else treats volunteers as heroes.'

Henrietta suspected that Perry's main objection was to having his authority challenged, but she could hardly say that to Bertie. 'I don't know, my dear. Probably he's worried for your safety. You are his eldest son and he's invested a great deal in you, one way and another.'

'But he's always rating me for being idle,' Bertie said crossly, 'and when I do find something to do, he cuts up rough. It ain't fair.'

'Never mind, when you return a hero, all will be well between you. You will return a hero, won't you?' she added, and he read her eye effortlessly.

'I can take care of myself, Auntie,' he said. The anxious tension was gone from his face now, and with it the lines of cynicism, which she had been sorry to see growing over the past months. His tautness was all boyish excitement, and he looked younger than his years. He glowed like a girl on her wedding-eve. 'It's going to be such a lark! I can't wait! And we'll give those Dutch farmers such a pasting they'll be sorry they ever dreamt of thumbing their noses at the British lion.'

He talked about his arrangements. Since Perry had forbidden him to go, he could not volunteer as an officer, having no money of his own to pay for kit, horse and servant. But lots of gentlemen had volunteered as private soldiers, and he thought it was 'an even better lark'.

'Because you know the men are all such biffing chaps, and it's in the ranks you see all the real action. None of that skulking in tents sipping claret while the guns roar for *your* favourite nevvy!'

Henrietta used her wits. 'Even as a private soldier you'll need to buy some things to take with you. Are you completely penniless?'

'Flat, broke and stony,' he admitted.

'Then I had better see what I can do for you.'

'Oh, I say, Aunt Hen, you are a trump. But I didn't come here to dun you, you know. You do believe that?'

'Of course. But I can't send you off to war without a tin of cigarettes to your name. I haven't much, my dear, but I'll do what I can. And if you wait until Jerome comes home,

I dare say he'll find you something too. Stay to dinner,' she added cordially.

'I was rather hoping you'd ask me. I'm dashed hungry, and I don't have to catch a train until tomorrow.'

So he stayed to dinner, and for the night, and it was a merry and poignant evening. The children were wild with excitement at the news that Bertie was going to war, and wanted more details than he could give, so he made them up, and beguiled them with hilarious nonsense about Tommy Atkins and the Boer and camp life and what the battles would be like. Jessie listened in rapt silence – most unusual for her – and with eyes that shone with hero-worship. She crept gradually closer until she was kneeling at his feet with her elbows resting on his knees, and he dropped her a smile now and then as a man strokes his dog's head absently while he talks.

In the morning he was up very early, and in much more sober mood. Jerome saw that he had confidences to impart, shook hands with him and left him to Henrietta. She walked out with him into the still of an early, misty morning to say goodbye. Jessie, shivering in her nightgown and bare feet, watched from the window of the Blue Bedroom, but he didn't look up and see her, and in a moment they had disappeared under the barbican.

At the other side of the drawbridge Bertie stopped. 'Auntie, would you do something for me?'

'Anything I can.'

'Would you write to the mater and tell her – tell her I didn't do it to upset her, or defy Pa. Make her understand I did it for the right reasons. It *is* a good thing to do, isn't it?'

'Yes,' she said. That was what he needed now.

'So you'll write to her?'

'I'll write to her.'

'And you'll write to me?'

'If you send me your direction.'

'I'll send *you* my letters home,' he decided. 'I don't think they'll be popular at the Red House. But you'll be glad to hear from me, won't you?'

'Very glad. Write to me as often as you can. And – take care of yourself, my dear.'

He stooped and kissed her cheek, his breath misting a little on the cold air, and then, with a flash of his old grin, he left her.

She watched him stride away down the track. He didn't look back. The invisible sun was only just beginning to flush the sky with gold; to the west it was still grey and dumb with night. Bertie walked briskly, the light gilding one side of him. A little cloud of mist puffed round his head at each exhalation, and she watched until they, and he, were absorbed into the fog and disappeared.

When Sir Redvers Buller sailed from Southampton, his plan was that White should hold Natal while he with his field force of 47,000 would push up through Bloemfontein to Pretoria. Presidents Kruger and Steyn, their capitals occupied and their forces defeated, would then have to accept his terms and the war would be over.

But Cape Town was a long way away, almost ten thousand miles. The Boers moved swiftly after declaring war, and crossed at once into British territory, meaning, it was assumed, to press on to Cape Colony and raise the Dutch to join them before the main British force arrived. When Buller had urged Lansdowne to order White not to move further north than the Tugela river, it was with this very threat in mind: it was essential in his view that White should keep the available forces in a defensive position. But when he finally landed at Cape Town on the 31st of October, it was to learn that his advice had not been heeded.

The Boers had advanced from Orange Free State towards the town of Ladysmith, which was in western Natal on the vital railway from Durban to Johannesburg. The Governor of Natal, Sir Walter Hely-Hutchinson, had said that his people would not tolerate the loss of Ladysmith without some effort to save it and, thus encouraged, White had taken the Natal Field Force across the Tugela to defend the town. On the 30th of October he had met the Boers under Joubert in a series of engagements, and had been forced back into

125

Ladysmith, with the loss of 1200 men to the Boers' 200.

Thus Buller arrived to find Natal without defence and the Natal force penned up in Ladysmith under siege. Furthermore, the Boer forces had besieged two other garrisons, one at the diamond town of Kimberley, where to complicate matters there was a large civilian population, including the egregious Cecil Rhodes; and the other at Mafeking, a strategic depot on the railway from Kimberley to Bulawayo, which had been surrounded after a spirited defence of British troops under Colonel Baden-Powell.

Far from being able to advance to a swift victory, Buller now had a complex problem to solve. Distances in South Africa were so great that the railway was everything, and here were the Boers besieging three widely separated towns on the railway routes, the loss of any one of which could jeopardise the whole campaign. Moreover, Natal was almost without defence, and Joubert's forces, if they bypassed Ladysmith, might even reach Durban, which would be a disaster. Buller felt he had no choice but to abandon attack for defence; to discard his invasion plan and divide his force into three for three separate relief actions. It was not a good start to the war.

As Henrietta had anticipated, Ashley did not want Lizzie to go down to Yorkshire to have her second baby; but as Lizzie was just as keen to have her mother with her, they invited Henrietta to come to London to oversee the event. Henrietta was not sure her own home could function for a whole month without her, but Jerome encouraged her to go – 'You'll only fret yourself into a decline if you don't' – and she reasoned to herself that as long as everything went well, she would be able safely to leave Lizzie to a nurse after the first fortnight or so. Emma said largely that of course she could manage. Charley promised to keep an eye on things at Morland Place, and Jerome swore he would send a wire at once if anything happened in her absence.

Only Jessie objected strongly to the scheme. 'I wish I could go too. Why can't I go too?'

'I'm not going for a holiday, you know. I'm going there

to look after Lizzie while she has her baby, and I won't have time to take care of you as well.'

'But couldn't I stay at Cousin Venetia's, with Violet? It would be much easier for Dad and Emma to manage if I wasn't here, wouldn't it?' she added beguilingly.

Henrietta was weakening. Though her arm had healed well, Jessie was supposed to be careful with it, something that went contrary to her nature. Jerome and Emma would both be too busy to keep the same close eye on Jessie that her mother did. It would ease the burden of the household considerably to take her away, and relieve Henrietta's mind of some anxiety. She made one final objection. 'But we don't know that Cousin Venetia would want you.'

'Oh, but she does!' Jessie said eagerly. 'When I broke my arm, she said when I was well she would invite me to stay. I wouldn't be any trouble, Mother, truly I wouldn't!'

'What about school?'

'Violet doesn't go to school, she has a governess, so I could share her lessons. Oh, *please*, ask if I can go. I do so want to.'

Henrietta looked at the little urgent face, with the scar still disfiguring the smooth cheek, and relented. Jessie had had a hard time of it for one usually so active. The boredom of being so long confined to the house had been harder to bear than the pain. And now Bertie, who Henrietta knew was a favourite with her, and had come over often during the convalescence to amuse the invalid, was gone away, which must be a blow. Poor Jessie needed a change of scene if anyone did. 'I'll write to Cousin Venetia and see if she'll have you.'

Venetia had no objection – was glad, in fact, to secure the company for her daughter – and knew as well as Henrietta that an all-male household would be easier to run in the absence of the mistress. Jessie was wildly excited about the whole thing, from the packing to the train journey to the picnic lunch Emma put up for them to eat on the train – hard-boiled eggs and bread-and-butter, a slice of veal-and-ham pie, curd tarts and fruit cake: 'The best lunch I've ever had in the world!' The approach to London sent her flying from window to window, and even the unappealing backs of grimy houses did not quell her. 'It's so dirty! I don't remember this bit. Why don't I remember it? Are we nearly there?' She had been too young when they left London to remember much about it, beyond their own house and the park where she and Emma had taken their daily walks. Henrietta reflected that she was just the right age really to enjoy a 'first' visit.

The station thrilled her into silence, so much bigger than York, so much more thronged with strangers, all of them moving with such speed it was a wonder they didn't crash into each other. So many soldiers, too! She twisted her head round after every uniform, until Henrietta told her none of them could possibly be Bertie, and she must look where she was going since she had twice trodden on Henrietta's heel. Jessie was disappointed that they weren't to take a cab, for Venetia had insisted on sending her carriage for them; but the sight of Venetia and Violet waiting for them beyond the barrier made up for that. When Henrietta finally left her in Manchester Square to go on to Lizzie's house, Jessie had her head together with Violet and was talking so hard she hardly noticed her mother go.

Two days after Henrietta arrived, Lizzie had her second child, a handsome and healthy boy. There were no complications, and by the time Ashley got home from work Lizzie was sitting up in bed and taking a cup of tea. She had a fancy for the name Rupert, which was currently popular in novels and stories, and though Ashley turned up his nose at it at first, it seemed to stick, and even before he had officially agreed to it, he was referring to Baby as Rupert.

Martial Henry, brought in by his grandmama to see the new arrival, did not seem very impressed by him, and was more interested in the basket of hot-house grapes that had arrived from the Hazelmeres in response to Henrietta's immediate wire to announce the birth. Martial retired under the dressing-table with a handful, while Lizzie held court, and the maid ran up and down, answering the door and bringing in telegrams, flowers, and at one time a large cake.

'I sent off rather a lot of wires from the office,' Ashley

admitted. 'You shall have visitors as soon as you feel up to it.'

Lizzie was pleased and touched that he seemed as delighted this time as the first. Her eyes tired but bright, she watched her husband walk up and down with the new baby in his arms and little Martial toddling behind, holding onto his trouser leg; and catching her mother's eye, smiled a smile of pure accomplishment.

On Charlotte's death the Queen had sent a very kind letter of condolence to Venetia, and when the Court returned to Windsor she invited her and Hazelmere to visit her. They found Olivia in attendance, engaged in reading to the Queen. Olivia had recently been appointed an assistant lady secretary, to help Princess Beatrice. The Queen's eyesight was now very poor, and for many months past she had been badgering her staff and ministers to write more clearly, and in darker ink. But as the clouds gathered over her vision nothing helped. Still, she had not given up any part of her huge volume of work or her vast private correspondence, and reading to her and writing at her dictation were a continuous labour that had been wearing the Princess out.

'It must be a very great loss to you,' the Queen said, when Venetia had seated herself on a sofa near her chair. 'I believe you were very close to your mother, my dear. I do so feel for you. I know just how it is to lose the most precious friend a woman ever has.'

Venetia always forgot, when she had not been at Court for some time, the Queen's enormous and magnetic charm: the sheer 'presence' of this stout little old woman, the extraordinary grace of her movements, her beautiful, 'silvery' voice, her wonderful smile. Now she was moved by the real warmth in the Queen's voice, and the tears that sparkled suddenly in those round, blue eyes that were so familiar to her: bright, pale blue, like two captured patches of April sky. It was impossible to doubt at that moment that the Queen Empress of half the world really did care intensely and personally for Venetia's sadness.

'I loved her very much, ma'am, and she was a great mentor to me in every way.'

'I suppose it was because of her example that you were so determined to enter medical training,' said the Queen. 'I was never sure that it was wise, my dear, for women to meddle in men's work, but I do see that you and your colleagues do valuable work, especially in India. It's such a comfort for the poor Indian women to be able to consult a doctor of their own sex. And, of course, we quite accept female nurses now, in large part thanks to your mother. The public in general associates nursing with Miss Nightingale's name, but I don't forget that your mother did important work in that field, both here and in the Crimea. Your father served us well in the Crimea too, though in a very different sphere, naturally. I knew your father well. He advised me on many occasions concerning matters in Russia. The Prince Consort thought very highly of him.'

There was no greater accolade, Venetia knew, than the Prince Consort's approval.

The Queen questioned her about her mother's funeral, though Venetia was sure she must already have asked Olivia the same questions. When it came to obsequies, no-one had a wider knowledge or a greater interest. It was well known in the Household that she had long ago written out every detail of how her own funeral was to be conducted, and the plan was frequently re-read and minutely refined. In her presence, however, it was impossible to believe the plans would ever be needed. The Queen, surely, would live for ever.

'But your children will be a great comfort to you,' she concluded. 'Children are the life of a house, don't you think? I am never happier than when some or other of my little grandchildren are staying with me. They run into one's room in the morning and say, "Good morning, Gangan," in such an innocent, cheerful way, and it lifts one's spirit at once. You have three children, I believe?'

'Yes, ma'am. Two boys and a girl.'

'And the boys are at Eton. They will have good company there. Your sister's son – Edward, isn't it? – is also at Eton, I believe.'

130

'Yes, ma'am,' Venetia said. There was nothing to show in her voice, but her body became a little tense. Augusta and her husband had been part of the Prince of Wales's set during his wildest years. Gussie and Johnny had been at the centre of a great deal of scandal, and they had not been received at the senior Court. It was hard to believe the Queen had heard the particular gossip about Gussie's son – but, then, the Queen was always surprising one.

'What is it you call him?' the Queen asked suddenly.

'Eddie, ma'am,' Venetia said, with reluctance, for it seemed to be begging for connections to be made – that royal name, which had been the name of the Queen's favourite grandson.

'Yes,' the Queen mused. 'A good name.' She raised her head suddenly and looked directly into Venetia's eyes. 'I understand he looks very like his father,' she said.

She knows, Venetia thought. She doubted whether the Queen had ever seen Johnny Vibart, Augusta's husband, and certainly no-one would have told Her Majesty that Eddie looked like *him*. She must know that Gussie had been the Prince of Wales's mistress, and that even Johnny Vibart had never tried to pretend the child was his. Venetia had no idea what to say. The Prince of Wales had not acknowledged paternity of Eddie to Venetia or to Hazelmere, but he enquired with kindly interest after him more often than of their other children. And quite recently he had sent Francis Knollys, his private secretary, to tell Hazelmere discreetly that he intended to pay the lad's school fees.

Did the Queen know about that too? The Household always said that she knew everything, and that there was no point in trying to keep a secret from her. While Venetia was still struggling to formulate an answer, the Queen smiled at her with great sweetness and said, 'Is he a good boy? Is he good at his lessons?'

'He is a very nice boy, ma'am,' Venetia said. 'I could not say that he is of the very brightest when it comes to lessons, but he's very affectionate and good-hearted.'

'Ah,' said the Queen, still smiling, 'then he *is* like his father. I shall be interested to see how he grows up.'

And, leaving Venetia astonished, she turned her attention to Hazelmere and introduced the topic of the forthcoming visit of the Kaiser and his family.

They had tea with the Queen, and then she released Olivia from her duties for a few hours so that the sisters could spend some time alone together. Hazelmere left them in Olivia's sitting room to go and talk to Fritz Ponsonby. Olivia's husband, Charles Du Cane, looked in to say hello, and learning where Hazelmere had gone, hurried off himself to join them.

The sisters talked of personal and family matters, while consuming a second tea – it was never possible to make much of a meal in the Queen's presence. Side by side on the sofa, they did not look at all alike. Olivia was a delicately plump little matron, divinely fair, with golden hair and violet eyes, neatly dressed in an expensive but not gaudy style. Ladies of the Household were permitted to wear only black, grey, purple or mauve, so it was fortunate that Olivia looked particularly good in all those colours, since she liked to appear to advantage. Today she was in black, of course, mourning her mother, but everything about her from the lace at her neck, held with a delicate jet pin, to the soft morocco slippers on her feet was nicely calculated for its effect.

Venetia was taller, had always been slender and was now almost gaunt. Her hair was brown, inclining to red, her eyes tawny, and her thin face was full of sparks and movement and vigour, where Olivia's was sweet and placid. Her clothes were well made, but utterly plain, and gave the impression that had you put your hands over her eyes and asked her what she had on, she would not have been able to answer.

Most different of all were the hands that conveyed muffins, cheese scones, Shrewsbury cake and Battenburg into the respective mouths: Olivia's white, smooth, plump, with tapering fingers and one or two pretty rings; Venetia's strong, square, the fingertips blunt, the nails clipped back hard, and naked of ornament save the single plain wedding band – a doctor's hands.

Most of the family conversation came from Venetia. Olivia

and Charlie had never been able to have any children, and when she took up the conversation, she talked about the Court, and the Queen, which was her whole life. Venetia, not much interested in the arcane minutiae of Court protocol, gently turned her to the subject of the war.

'Oh, the Queen has known all along that it would have to come. We can't leave our own people unprotected to be treated so badly, and she says we must teach Kruger a sharp lesson. And besides, the Boers are very unkind to the Negroes, which she minds very much. She can't bear anything of that sort. So it had to be. But she hates the necessity of war. She said to me yesterday that it was the hardest of a monarch's duties, to have to send her own people to face injury and death. And the worst thing, she says, is not to be able to lead them in battle herself as kings used to do. Do you know,' Olivia added, becoming almost animated, 'she really would do it, if only she were a man. She hasn't the least particle of fear.'

'When you think of how many assassination attempts have been made on her,' Venetia began.

Olivia picked it up quickly. If the Court was her life, the Queen was her passion. 'Oh, yes. But she says she is a soldier's daughter, and it's a monarch's part to be shot at. She understands military matters so well, it is the greatest pity her ministers won't listen to her and take her advice. She says Sir Redvers won't do.'

'Why ever not?' Venetia asked, intrigued.

'She says he's a good soldier but that it's a mistake to entrust the whole campaign to someone who's never had overall command before. She thinks he understands the terrain but not strategy. She urged the Government to send out Lord Roberts and Lord Kitchener, but apparently Lord Wolseley won't hear of it.'

'Lansdowne likes Roberts,' Venetia said. 'He was commander-in-chief in India when Cocky was Viceroy.'

'Yes, and the Queen thinks he ought to have been commander-in-chief of the whole army, and not Lord Wolseley.'

'Well, of course she would think that. It's the old rivalry, between the Africans and the Indians. Wolseley and Buller are Africans, while Roberts and Kitchener are Indians, and the Queen is far more interested in India than Africa so she always favours that side. I'm afraid the whole army is divided into the two camps. It hardly gives one confidence.'

'Oh, the Queen says it will all come out right in the end.'

'I suppose things generally do,' Venetia said doubtfully. 'It's just the muddle in between one has to get through.'

They were interrupted at that moment by a summons for Olivia to go to the Queen. Olivia rose at once, but said, 'Don't go. I may not be very long. If it isn't anything important, I'll remind her gently that you are here. She is always very considerate about family, but she may have forgotten. She does tend to forget things lately.'

She went out, leaving the sitting-room door open. Venetia poured the last of the tea and wondered where Hazelmere was. Footsteps came down the passage and a male figure passed the door, and then came back to look in.

'Hullo! I heard you were here.'

It was Sir James Reid, the Queen's physician. He and Venetia were contemporaries, and old friends. He was a frank, pleasant, amusing Scotsman and a great favourite in the Household; a small man, very neat, with a balding front, large mutton-chop whiskers, and bright eyes that laughed behind gold pince-nez.

'Have you been abandoned?' Reid asked. 'I saw your husband in Fritz's room, but where's Lady Olivia?'

'Summoned to the Queen,' Venetia said. 'Come in and wile away my hours of solitude.'

'I don't suppose it will be hours,' Reid said, but he came in anyway, seating himself on the arm of the sofa and swinging one leg, like a man who might be up and off at any moment, though Venetia knew he loved to chat. 'She wants a letter written. I dare say she's forgotten you're here.'

'I understand congratulations to you are in order,' Venetia said. 'Is the Queen over the shock yet?'

'Just barely; but she's beginning to take an interest in the wedding arrangements now, which is a good sign.'

'Oh, you have a date fixed?'

134

'November the 28th is the day on which I shall be made the happiest of men,' said Reid with a smile. 'I am already the luckiest.'

In July of that year, Sir James had stunned the small world of the Court by becoming engaged to one of the Queen's maids of honour, Miss Susan Baring. He was fifty and she thirty, neither of them handsome, but alike in having intelligence, warm hearts, and a liking for chat and jokes. They had been meeting for some months – a doctor having the perfect excuse for visiting anyone without provoking gossip – and he had introduced her to his passion for bicycling, which had allowed them to get away occasionally, when she was in waiting, for private moments together. The difficulty had been that they could not marry, nor even announce the engagement, without the Queen's permission; and the Queen very much disliked any of her close attendants to marry.

The Court had been surprised that Miss Baring, who was very well connected, should accept Reid, who was a lowly born Scot. But he had recently been made a baronet, and had saved a reasonable fortune over the years of his bachelorhood, and she, without money or good looks, was unlikely at her advanced age to receive another offer. Olivia had protested indignantly that it was a love-match, and a very good and equal one, and Venetia, seeing the warmth of Reid's smile, did not doubt it.

He went on, 'I must say that we owe your sister a debt of gratitude. She was our greatest advocate. After I wrote to the Queen about the engagement, she didn't reply for *five weeks*. Not a single word! I saw her every day, sometimes many times a day, without her ever referring to the letter or the subject in any way.'

'It must have been very trying for you.'

'I was on the point of bursting out and ruining everything many times,' he said, with a smile, 'but I reflected that it was a small price to pay for a lifetime's happiness, and held my tongue. And all the time your sister was working away gently, using herself and Charlie as an example of how marriage could be to Her Majesty's advantage.'

'You're luckier than they were. They had to wait years before they could marry.'

'It *felt* like years to me, I can assure you,' said Reid. 'Even after the Queen gave her permission, she wouldn't allow it to be announced, and we were always afraid she would change her mind again.'

'And what would you have done then?'

'Defied her, I suppose,' said Reid, with a twinkle. 'She must feel she needs me about her, or she'd have dismissed me for even thinking about one of her ladies, low dog that I am, so I must have been on safe-ish ground.'

'Well, I'm delighted for you. I hope you will be very happy – and I hope you will be allowed a honeymoon!'

Reid laughed. 'She'll send for me in the middle of it, I've no doubt! In all these years I've never got through my holiday without a call; but that's in the nature of the job. One takes the rough with the smooth. And talking of jobs, I hear you had an interesting surgical case a few weeks ago – removal of a gall-bladder?'

'How on earth did you know that?'

'Oh, we hear everything at Court,' he said, amused. 'People coming and going, you know. It's the compensation for being cloistered for eleven months of the year. How is the patient doing?'

'He survived.'

'Any post-operative problems?'

'No, he looks set fair for a full recovery. I don't like opening abdomens – too much opportunity for infection – but there's no doubt that when it goes well the difference it makes is gratifyingly immediate.'

'Bellies are an interesting area,' Reid said. 'You had a run-in with the greatest belly-man of them all didn't you?'

'You mean Frederick Treves?'

'He'd be gratified that you recognised him so instantly from the description! Didn't you and he have a falling-out over hygiene?'

'I'd hardly call it that,' Venetia said. 'I'm too lowly and insignificant for the great Mr Treves to argue with me. He merely told me I was wrong, and that was that. Simple cleanliness, he says, is all that's needed, and all these modern antiseptic precautions are just a Frenchified fad.'

'Yes, I'm afraid he's rather a club man. There's the London tradition, and then there's everyone else. And everyone else doesn't count for much.'

'I have to confess I can't love him. He opposed my operating at the London Hospital, you know, many years ago.'

'What did you expect? Ye're nobbut a lassie,' said Reid, exaggerating his accent. 'But *de haut en bas*, you know. He only just nods to me, and I haven't even challenged his opinions, while you argue with him, first about hygiene and then typhlitis.'

Venetia was stung. 'He's quite wrong about typhlitis – and his ideas don't even have any logic to them. To advocate surgery during the quiescent period but only medical treatment of the acute stage is back to front and upside down.'

'Yes, you'd think a surgeon would seize any excuse to wield the knife, wouldn't you?'

'I can see you're enjoying provoking me! But the evidence from America is quite clear. In the vast majority of these acute abdomens it's the vermiform appendix that's the seat of the infection, not the caecum, and medical treatment does nothing but prolong the evil. If you remove the appendix surgically at once, you can save lives.'

Reid nodded appreciation of the point, but with a physician's disinterest. 'Certainly, waiting for a quiescent period, as Treves advocates, doesn't help the patients who die of the first acute episode.'

'Even if they don't die, their health is often impaired. Much better have it out at once and be done with it. Have you read Fitz's paper?' Venetia asked him. The American doctor Fitz had published a study in 1886 of nearly five hundred cases, had coined the term 'appendicitis', and had laid down clear guidelines for the diagnosis and treatment of the condition. The term was not much used in Britain, but typhlitis or 'acute abdomen' was responsible for thousands of deaths every year.

'I have just glanced through it,' Reid said. 'Have you had any cases yourself?'

'Yes, one or two. I operated on a little girl of nine years old earlier this year at the New. Fortunately her mother was reasonably intelligent and agreed to immediate surgery. I was able to remove the appendix before it ruptured, and she made a very quick recovery. But I suppose,' she sighed, 'if Treves is still arguing with Lister's work on antisepsis after all this time, it's not surprising that he won't accept Fitz. It takes fifty years for the medical establishment in this country to accept a new idea.'

'Unfair,' Reid laughed. 'You forget I'm part of the medical establishment.'

'Oh, no, I don't count you as establishment,' said Venetia. 'You're very nearly human.'

'Thank you,' he said, with a bow. 'Treves's trouble is that he can't accept ideas that originate outside the membership of the BMA. Doesn't like foreigners, in a nutshell. I wonder how he'll get on in South Africa? That's full of foreigners, I believe.'

'South Africa?'

'Didn't you know? He means to head a medical mission to follow our boys into war.'

'No, I didn't. I can't say I'm surprised. He must be awfully bored with life since he resigned from the London.'

'Aye, and he's hardly ever in the newspapers these days,' said Reid, with a glint in his eye. 'Don't you wish you may go with him?'

'With him? No! But to visit South Africa? It hadn't entered my mind before, but now you've put it there, I would rather like to see the country, after reading so much about it.'

'You could set up your own expedition. *You* won't need a wealthy patron to provide the funds, at all events.'

'Good God! You really do know everything, don't you?'

'Oh, it isn't common knowledge. But Olivia and Susan are friends, you know. Why don't you go?'

Venetia shrugged. 'Too old, too comfortable, too busy. Any or all of those.'

'There's always time for one more adventure,' Reid said.

'For a man, perhaps,' Venetia replied, shaking her head. 'I am but a feeble woman.'

138

'Oh, I don't count you as a feeble woman.' Reid gave her her words back. 'You're very nearly human.'

Venetia followed the progress of Frederick Treves's proposed expedition with interest and some amusement. The Duchess of Bedford was persuaded to provide the necessary finance, and Treves began to put together his surgical team, along with nurses, accoutrements, transport and servants.

'The Prince is quite struck by the idea,' Hazelmere said. 'He thinks Treves might make important discoveries, which may lead to advances in military medicine. He's going to invite him to dine at Marlborough House before he goes.' He smiled wickedly. 'I shall suggest to Francis that you should be invited at the same time. You'll have so much to say to each other, one surgeon to another.'

'You'll do no such thing,' Venetia said. 'Do you want to lose your reputation with HRH as a diplomat? But I hope Treves does learn something useful, and uses his influence to improve the army's medical corps.'

'If anyone can, he can,' Hazelmere said. 'He has the public interest, and that matters in these modern times. It's a sad fact, but solid worth is not half so effective as publicity, and since that Elephant Man business, everything Treves does is news.'

It was true that not only did the *British Medical Journal* carry an extremely detailed account of the proposed trip and the preparations being made for it, but there were long articles in all the newspapers about it. It had touched a patriotic nerve in the already over-excited public mind. On the day of Treves's departure, Venetia confessed an idle desire to Hazelmere to see what sort of fuss was made of him, and he smiled and whisked her away to Waterloo station.

It was certainly quite an occasion. By the time Treves arrived at a little after eleven, there were several hundred medical students from the various schools waiting for him. A huge cheer went up as he stepped out of his cab, and he disappeared from view, to emerge moments later chaired on the brawniest shoulders, and was carried to the train. His reserved carriage was full to overflowing with flowers sent by well-wishers and he was deposited among them by his bearers, after which the crowd surged forward, cheering and singing 'Rule Britannia' and 'For He's a Jolly Good Fellow' before his window.

There was still twenty minutes to go before the train left, and the crowd was growing all the time. The station-master was worried that someone might get hurt or that property might be damaged, and sent for the police. Hazelmere suggested to Venetia that they should leave, but she said, 'Oh, these boys are very good-natured. They don't mean any harm. I'd like to see the rest. Besides,' she added, 'I'm not sure we *could* get out now. I can see some policemen over there by the exit and they can't get any further in.'

The singing went on, broken off only for long enough, amid a chorus of 'shushing' that sounded like steam escaping from the engine, for Treves to make a short speech of thanks from his carriage window. Then the cheering redoubled, and someone started up 'Auld Lang Syne' – a tune which, once begun, is always hard to stop. It lasted until the train pulled out.

When they were finally able to leave, Hazelmere looked curiously at his wife and said, 'You *do* envy him, don't you?'

'I suppose I do,' she admitted. 'I thought, like you, that I was too old and too comfortable, but I find after all there is still a part of me that would like one more adventure, even though I know that war is terrible.'

'Now you're thinking like a man,' Hazelmere said. 'Shall we walk? I don't think we'll get a cab here.'

CHAPTER FIVE

Henrietta had no reply from Regina to her letter, long laboured-over, about Bertie. There was, however, an angry letter from Perry. He believed she was behind Bertie's decision to volunteer. He accused her of coming between father and son, of stealing Bertie's affections, encouraging him to disobedience, plotting with him to subvert Perry's natural authority, and breaking Regina's heart. Regina, he said, was so upset by the whole business that she had taken to her bed, and it would be entirely Henrietta's fault if she quit her lease altogether.

'Is she really ill?' Henrietta asked Teddy, thoroughly alarmed.

'Well, she was in her room when I visited, and the doctor had been to her, but when I went up to see her she wasn't in bed, only lying on the sofa in a sort of wrapper.' He made vague frilly gestures down his chest. 'She looked a bit seedy, poor thing, but the sawbones said it was just her usual trouble – nerves, he calls it. If you ask me, she's taken to her bed to get away from old Perry. Never saw such a fuss! There he was downstairs, marching up and down the room, pounding his palm with his fist. I half wanted to stay upstairs with Regina.'

'Oh dear,' Henrietta said. 'He's very angry, then.'

'Sheer temper, I shouldn't wonder,' Teddy said. 'Can't stand to be thwarted. I said to him, "Look here, old chap, it ain't as if Bertie's done somethin' dishonourable, like not payin' his gaming bills or gettin' a girl into trouble." I said, "The boy's done somethin' to be proud of, so why ain't you

141

proud?" But off he went again about disobedience and ingratitude and plots against him, and threatening to cut Bertie off with a shilling, so I stayed mum.'

'Oh, Teddy, how awful. I do hate to be the cause of family strife. But, really, what could I have done? Bertie wouldn't have heeded me even if I had asked him not to go.'

'Oh, quite, quite. Look here, old thing,' Teddy resumed, looking a little awkward, 'I hope you don't take a miff over it, but I didn't take your part much against Perry. Not because I don't side with you every time, but you see, if I'd made him angrier, he'd have ended by banning me from the house as well, and then poor old Reggie would have had no-one to visit her. You do understand?'

'Yes, of course. That was a good thought of yours. But, oh dear, how am I to write to Reggie now? I'm sure Perry won't let her have my letters after this.'

'Not to worry. You give your letters to me, and I'll find some way to slip them to her when Perry ain't looking.'

Henrietta would rather not have told Jerome about this new breach, but theirs was not that sort of marriage. He was very angry and wanted at first to ride over and have it out with Perry, but Henrietta persuaded him that that would solve nothing.

'I know it wouldn't, really,' he said, with a sigh, when he had calmed down, 'but it would have relieved my feelings somewhat. I hate to feel so helpless when someone is upsetting my wife.'

Henrietta managed a faint smile. 'Perhaps that's how Perry feels.'

1st December 1899
Dear Aunt,
Here I am at last! And much later than looked for, because our ship was diverted from Cape Town to Durban which is a good bit further on. The sea voyage was pretty good – almost a holiday. Felt a bit queasy once or twice in the Bay of Biscay, when the ship was either balancing on its nose or its tail like a performing dog! But after that it was like yachting at Cowes! The

grub was something of a shock to your pampered boy, however – reminded me of dear old Eton, which gave me an advantage over those volunteers who hadn't been to an English public school! But the other fellows are capital chaps, and we contrived to hole in and make ourselves comfortable with a little baccy and a few songs. One of the chaps, Fallon, has a harmonica, or mouth-organ, which he plays tolerably well. It makes a surprising amount of noise for such a small instrument. We had a good 'yarn' and learnt each other's histories. Mine turned out rather tame measured against what some of the 'lower deck' fellows had been through just to survive to volunteer age!

Durban seemed a nice enough place, quite pretty, lots of trees and white houses with red roofs, and flowering creeper – I don't know the name, but very brightly coloured – growing over the verandas. However we did not remain long enough to get to know it, but were moved out right away, heading north-east up the railway, I believe towards Ladysmith. Lord, this is a strange country! First of all, it is the space that hits you. It is so very big! One feels so exposed, even in the company of several thousand other Tommy Atkinses. The light is extraordinary, more bright than you can have any idea of, and astonishingly clear. It makes you realise how misty and foggy and smoky dear old England is. The colours are all brilliant – the sky so blue, the earth so red, and here and there patches of vivid green where the farms or riverbeds are. Because of the distances, it seems very flat, miles and miles of empty plain freckled with stones, which when you come up to them turn out to be positive boulders!, or with little green-black knobs that are actually stunted trees. And then, away on the horizon, misty mountains streaked with purple.

Lest you think all this sounds idyllic, I have to tell you that the heat is intolerable. It is summer here, strange to say! And what a baking summer! We fairly stifle in our uniforms. The flies are a great nuisance, settling on one's face and crawling into one's mouth.

But worse than either is the dust. The roads are only packed dirt, and the thumping of many army boots breaks it into fine powder which flies up and coats everything, especially one's tongue.

No more to tell you now, but I will write again soon. Please write to me, and tell me how everything is at home, and if you have heard from Mama, etc. You have no idea how much a letter would cheer – a fellow who gets one is a prince for the day. The fellows who have been on campaign before say I should ask you to send an envelope ready addressed and stamped for my reply. They say that is a great help. Also, if it is not too much of a 'cheek' to ask, some more cigarettes. One seems to smoke so much more here, and it is a comfort.

Your devoted nephew,
Bertie

A telegram came for Jerome in the middle of the morning. He was out about the estate somewhere, and Henrietta, staring at the envelope as though it might bite her, wondered what to do. There was no-one to send to look for him. She might go herself, but not knowing where exactly he was, it might take a long time to find him.

'He'll be back hoom come lunch-time,' Emma said. 'He can have it then.'

'But suppose it's really urgent?'

'That's bound to be urgent,' Emma pointed out unhelpfully, 'else they'd have written a letter.'

'Oh dear. You're right, of course.'

'What about ringing the bell, ma'am? If he's in earshot, he'll come for that, surely.'

'Emma, you're a genius. Why didn't I think of that?'

The house bell had been rung often in Henrietta's youth, not only to summon people in for meals, but to mark the birth of a child, or the passing of a soul. She couldn't remember whether she had ever discussed the significance of the bell with Jerome, but if he heard it, his wits would surely guide him to answer its summons.

It worked surprisingly quickly. She had decided to ring

it every five minutes, and she was hauling away at the rope for the third time when a quick rush of nails on the stone flags heralded Kithra, circling her with his muzzle turned up to give her the full effect of his grin. Where Kithra was, Jerome must be close behind. She let the rope run up and turned as he came in from the passage.

'I didn't think you'd get here so quickly. You must have been quite near.'

'I was in Monument paddock. There's a mare I'm not quite happy about. What was the bell for? I know it isn't Sunday and I can smell there isn't a fire.'

She gave him the telegram. 'I thought if it was urgent you ought to have it right away.'

He stared at it, the light leaving his eyes. 'I don't want to open it. I have a horrid feeling about it.'

'It can't be Bertie,' she said, betraying what had been her first fear. 'The army would send the wire to Perry – and he wouldn't wire you about it.'

He sighed. 'Only one way to find out.' He tore open the envelope and drew out the single sheet. 'Ah,' he said. He looked up at her, a slightly quizzical look, as though assessing her strength for a possible shock. 'It's from Edward Winsham.'

Henrietta said nothing, but she felt the small sinking of dread that the name Winsham always provoked in her. Edward Winsham was the older brother of Julia Winsham; and Julia Winsham was Jerome's first wife – or as many, including the Church and Sir Peregrine Parke, would say, his only wife.

Jerome spoke. 'He says, "Julia gravely ill. Asking for you. Come at once." Concise and to the point. Of course, Edward wouldn't waste words on me.'

'Will you go?' asked Henrietta, in a small voice.

'It must have almost broken his heart to send for me at all,' Jerome said. 'He wouldn't have done so unless he had to.'

'You had better go, then,' Henrietta said flatly. The fiction of their marriage was laid bare in those few words: that other woman still had the power to summon him instantly to her side.

145

'Dearest—'

'I understand,' she said. She didn't want to make it harder for him. 'Truly I do.'

'No, you don't.' Jerome took her into his arms, and Emma hurried out to give them privacy. 'I love you, you must know that. Julia doesn't mean anything to me, not in that way. But she was my wife once. And, besides, it would be heartless to ignore this plea. Whoever she was, you wouldn't want me to ignore it, would you?'

'No,' said Henrietta, but her eyes said, 'Yes.' She was half horrified by her own feelings; she had thought she had got over all that years ago. But that mad, pointless, unreasonable jealousy had not died, it seemed, only lay dormant. Now it had surged up again, freshly bitter as ever. She loved him, and it burned in her like bile that he had been someone else's before he had been hers, and that nothing could ever change that, not time nor will, not the remainder of a lifetime of being with him. That he had long ago broken his marital vows to Julia was not enough. He had made them, and that was just a fact. She wanted him now to repudiate that previous life. She wanted him to declare that he would not go, to tear up the telegram and toss the pieces away and say, 'You are all I care about in the world. Let Julia go hang!' And then, of course, she would have pushed him gently from her arms and told him that he must go, that he owed it to that poor woman, who might be on her deathbed for all they knew. But Jerome, for all his sensitivity towards her, was too honest to play such a game, and she was left struggling with her own ungraciousness.

She made a huge effort to smile and sound normal. 'You had better get the gazetteer and look up a train. And I'll pack a bag, in case you have to stay overnight.'

It was enough for him. He kissed her forehead and went straight out of the room. She clenched her fists in the effort to control herself, digging the nails into her palms. Deep breaths pushed down the tears that wanted to come. Then she called Emma back in from where she was fiddling about in one of the pantries.

'The master has to go away.' She heard her own voice

come out quite calmly, but Emma must have known it was not right, for she listened with her head a little downcast, like a berated dog, and did not ask questions. 'You'd better pack up something by way of a luncheon for him to take with him on the train. I suspect he'll leave right away.'

Jerome came back, gazetteer in hand. 'I think the quickest way will be to go to London and travel direct to Winchester from there. If I try to change and go across country it will probably take longer. I can get the noon express if we hurry.' He looked apologetic. 'No sense in wasting time. It would be awful to arrive too late.'

'I'll drive you to the station,' Henrietta said. 'If you go and harness Dunnock, I'll put a few things into a bag for you.'

'Thank you, darling. Bless you,' he said.

The house seemed empty without him. They had hardly ever been separated since they were married – only for that week after his bankruptcy when he had stayed in London to settle matters and she had brought the children down to Yorkshire. The children added to her burden when they came home from school, by being intensely interested in where Dad had gone and why. Who was the lady he'd gone to see? Had they ever met her? Was she a sort of relative? Henrietta wished fervently that Jack were home. He was always so quick to comprehend. He would have silenced them, and bustled them away to play somewhere else.

A wire came from Jerome late that evening to say he had arrived and was staying at Winsham House for the night. The dark hours seemed endless to Henrietta. She could not sleep for a long time. It was a cold night, and she could not get warm in the big bed; her feet remained like blocks of stone, quite detached from her, long after she had stopped shivering. She missed his warm body beside her; not only for his delicious heat but for the simple sense of his presence, which was her life's core; and she turned this way and that, her mind hunting back and forth like a hound in a rabbit field, following one trail then another. When she did drop off at last, she woke every quarter-hour or so, startled out of sleep by the awareness of something being different. She heard the clock strike

147

four before she fell into a heavy sleep, only to be woken again at six by the sound of Emma going downstairs to the kitchen. She felt then that she could have slept, but she couldn't leave Emma to do everything unaided, and dragged herself up.

Jerome did not come back that day. Another wire arrived in the evening saying, 'All over. Staying another night. Home tomorrow.'

He arrived late in the afternoon, looking worn out, and wearing black bands on his sleeves, which he must have bought in Winchester. He favoured her with a grim smile as he came in, and then had to fend off the embraces of Kithra and the eager questions of the children. It was a while before he could gesture to Henrietta to come away with him for a private talk. It was dark already, and sharply cold in the great hall, away from the kitchen warmth. The night candle was standing on its side table, its wavering flame throwing batwing shadows up the walls into the darkness of the upper regions. Jerome lit a candle from it and Henrietta followed him to the steward's room, which he used as a study and business-room. He lit the candles in the sconces and the dark, panelled room jumped into full being. It was cold in there too with no fire lit, only marginally less cold than the hall, and Henrietta folded her arms round herself in a defensive gesture. It was not only against the cold, but against what he might be going to tell her. She was afraid of what her own feelings might be.

He turned to face her and began at once, as though he had braced himself for the story and would have it out.

'Edward knew she was dying when he sent the wire. Some kind of wasting disease. Apparently, so Nana – her old nurse – told me, she'd been asking for me for some days, but he was reluctant to send for me. Well, who can blame him? He plainly didn't want me there. It was very awkward. Brother William was there too, and the married sister, and their respective spouses – all looking at me like the skeleton at the feast, and forcing themselves to be coldly civil if it killed them. It would have been funny if it hadn't been so painful.

'I was glad to spend most of the time in Julia's room, to

148

get away from the icy disapproval in the drawing-room. Nana was there, looking after her. She always liked me, dear old Nana. The relatives would have been glad to winkle me out, but every time one of them came in and proposed to do it, Julia would send them away and say she just wanted me and Nana. Very galling for them. But poor Julia! There was nothing left of her, just skin and bones. She looked a hundred. But she was happy to see me. I'm glad I went.' He stopped a moment, obviously reliving what he'd seen.

'Why *did* she want you?' Henrietta asked. 'You always said she was happy with the divorce.'

'Yes. She always told me that too. But perhaps living with Edward and Sophy had its drawbacks. I gathered – more from Nana than Julia – that they let her know what a disappointment she had been to them, first for marrying a reprobate, and then, even worse, for losing him. They took her in, you know, out of family loyalty, but they disapprove of divorce quite as vehemently as ever Perry could. And she had to bear it, having nowhere else to go. She had an independence, but she wasn't the sort of woman who could have lived alone, even had the family allowed her to think of it. So there she was, trapped in that stiff, proper house, being done good to. It wasn't quite so bad when she was well and active, and she enjoyed being an aunt to all the little Winshams. But then she started to feel ill, and quite soon she knew she was dying, and—'

He stopped. Henrietta shivered, and wrapped herself tighter in her arms. 'And?' she said, not in the least wanting to know.

'She thought of the times we had been happy together – just the first few weeks of our marriage. And she thought she would sooner die with me beside the bed than her relatives, who had been charitable, but had never loved her.'

'I see.'

He stared unseeingly at the cold hearth. 'It was little enough to do for her, God knows. I sat beside the bed and held her poor wasted hand and talked to her. Played the "remember when?" game. After a while she couldn't answer, but she squeezed my hand from time to time to show she was listening. I pretty soon ran out of memories, of course – we had so few – but I made them up, and I don't think it mattered. She just liked to have me there, making her feel that someone in her life had found her worthwhile.'

Henrietta's throat ached with tears. Her feelings were a turmoil of pity, jealousy and shame. She couldn't have spoken if she had wanted to.

'They had to let me stay. Sophy had a room made up for me, but I hardly used it, only lay fully dressed on top of the bed for a little. The rest of the time I sat in with Julia. She woke from time to time and liked to see me there. I was with her the next day when she died. She just sank at the end, and went quite quietly. After that, I offered to remove my loathsome self to an hotel, but the family swallowed the medicine and asked me to stay. She had told Edward before-hand that she wanted me to stay and hear her will read, you see.'

Another pause. Henrietta had questions now, but still could not speak. She did not want to hear her own voice breaking into that pitiful story.

'The lawyer came in the afternoon. I don't think he liked me much either. Old family firm. As far as possible for one in his profession, he disapproved of her testamentary dispo-sition, as he called it, but he had to follow her wishes. She left me everything.' He gave a short jerk of laughter. 'Everything! Poor Julia, perhaps she had a sense of humour after all. How Edward and Sophy wriggled! They were too well-bred to say anything there and then, but I dare say they may try to challenge the will. She left me her private fortune, which she inherited from her mother. Her jewels – the lawyer had them in his strong-box. She'd left them with him to make sure I got them, I suppose. I wouldn't put it past Sophy to have collared them otherwise. And all her goods and chattels, such as they may be, which I suppose are in her room in Edward's house. I don't think I shall apply to him to send them. Even if I were not rebuffed, I don't think I could bear to have them about me.'

He suddenly put his hands over his eyes and began rubbing them. She went to him then and touched him tentatively, and he opened his arms to her, folded her in. 'It will all go to the creditors, of course. She wanted to benefit me but it will only benefit people she never met. God,' he sighed deeply, 'what a farce, what a dreadful farce it all was. That poor woman! Little as she cared for me, little as I cared for her, the one pleasant thing she had to look back on in her whole life was me. What a poor showing for a lifetime that was.' Tears welled in Henrietta's eyes as she rested her cheek against his chest, but now they were not tears of anger or frustration, but the healing tears of a pure pity. She wept for Julia, not herself.

They didn't talk any more about it that day, and the next day Jerome seemed not to want to discuss it. He didn't raise the subject, so neither did she, but she thought about it a good deal. She watched her husband, trying to judge his mood. The first day or two he seemed quiet and rather grim – she might almost have said depressed. But then his mood began to lift. He slept more soundly, his shoulders seemed straighter, his step lighter, and some of the strain left his face. When he laughed for the first time at something Frank said, she felt he was mending. And she felt better within herself, too. Her pity for that poor woman had proved greater than her jealousy, and it washed away her shame at having had such bad feelings. Perhaps now there could be a new start for both of them.

On the Sunday, going to church seemed to affect him again, but over dinner he was his usual self, and when it was finished, as it was a fine day, though frostily cold, he proposed that they all wrapped up and took a walk together. When they were strolling, arm in arm, with the children and Kithra running back and forth around them, he said to her, 'You know what this means, don't you?'

'What?' she asked.

'That I'm a single man again. Aren't you afraid I might leave you?' He was teasing, to cover his real feelings.

'If you're single, so am I. I might leave you,' she said, equally lightly.

'True, and I'd be a fool if I didn't know which of us has more to lose. Seriously, though,' he glanced at her quickly, seeming almost shy, 'would you like to get married?'

She felt shy too, happy and unhappy, bewildered. Her feelings were a cauldron out of which anything might pop. She hardly knew what to say. 'You always insisted we *were* married,' she said.

'You know my views, as I know yours. The Church's blessing did not figure highly in my requirements, but I know it mattered to you. You were very brave, my darling – I know how brave – to take me on those terms. And you've suffered for it. We can put things right now. Would you like to? I suppose I ought to ask you properly.' He stopped and turned to face her. Above him the bare branches of an oak tree scraped the blank grey sky, and somewhere hidden among the twigs was a robin, singing: long, liquid phrases, interrupted by a listening pause. Such a wintry sound, she thought, but with the seeds of hope in it. When winter comes, can spring be far behind? 'Forgive me from kneeling in this frozen mud,' Jerome said, taking her gloved hands, 'but, my dearest, most beloved wife, will you marry me?'

She wanted to laugh at his words, and his eyes were merry as well as tender; but she felt much more like crying. Poor Julia, she thought. Poor all of them. You had to accept the consequences of your actions. They might marry now, but that would not really 'put things right'. You could never undo what you had done.

Yet could God really have been so very angry with them? They had suffered shame and hardship, but they had been blessed with each other and with four lovely children. Did that seem like the actions of a disapproving God? Perhaps after all Jerome had been right all along, that the Church was a thing of man's devising, which did not necessarily speak for the Almighty.

She said, 'Yes, I will marry you, my dearest husband.' Over his shoulder she could see the children running about, hear their high voices calling to each other as they gathered something in competition – sticks, or berries or whatever. For their sake, she told herself – so that no-one could ever point a finger at them. But it was not really true. Whatever the rational part of her might argue, there was deep down

152

an ache that would be healed by marrying him, properly, within the Church, now that he was as free to marry as she was. It might make no sense to a modern man, but perhaps women were beasts of a more primordial stamp, moving to darker rhythms that were felt rather than heard.

Jerome was smiling, pressing her hands. 'Very well. You shall name the day, whenever you like.'

'Soon, then,' she said. 'Only – not in York or in the parish church. I couldn't bear all the explanations.'

He thought a moment. 'Grantby was good about christening Lizzie's baby here, and he seems an intelligent and tactful sort of man. How if I ask him if he will marry us, here, in the chapel? Just ourselves, the children, and Teddy and Charley. How would that be?'

She looked up at him with shining eyes. 'To be married at Morland Place? Oh, that would be the most perfect thing!'

General Buller's response to the situation he met in the Cape had been to send the first division, under Lord Methuen, north to retake Kimberley and then Mafeking, while leaving the third and cavalry divisions, under Gatacre and French, to secure the Cape and contain any invasion from the Free State. He himself would take the remainder of the force, the largest part, north-east through Natal to tackle Joubert's force and relieve Ladysmith.

Between Buller and Ladysmith was the Tugela river, wide, slow-moving but treacherous. The road and railway crossed the river at Colenso, a small town or perhaps village, which was held by the Boers. The British railhead position was at Chievely, about five miles south of Colenso. Buller's first plan was to have part of his force stage a diversionary attack on Colenso while he made a night march upstream – westward – about eighteen miles, where there was a ford and a second road to Ladysmith, by which he could outflank the Boers.

This plan was meant to go into operation on the 12th of December. But news came in from the other divisions, that on the 10th Gatacre had been defeated at Stormberg with the loss of seven hundred men; and on the 11th that Methuen, who had been trying to relieve Kimberley, had been driven back after a bloody battle at Magersfontein, with the loss of nine hundred and fifty men. Each of these commanders was at the end of a long and vulnerable supply line, and Buller was forced to reconsider his own position. If he took the major part of his force on a long march away from his railhead at Chievely, the Boers might well take the opportunity of making a counter-attack and seizing it, which would cut him off and leave him as badly placed as the men he was supposed to be relieving in Ladysmith.

He dared not lose his railhead. He therefore decided that the only option was to attack the Boers frontally and take Colenso itself. It was a formidable task. The approach was over flat, open land, but the Boers on the other side of the river were protected by the meandering loops of the Tugela and the towering hills, Red Hill and Grobbelaar Hill, which acted like a natural fortification: the river was in effect their moat and the hills their castle, from which they could fire down on the attackers with impunity. The road to Ladysmith ran north-west between the two hills, while the railway swung north-east, following the winding course of the river, but as the railway bridge at Colenso had been destroyed by the Boers, it was the road the army would have to follow.

Apart from the iron road bridge in Colenso itself, the only way over the river was by fords, called drifts. The plan was for Hart's brigade to go left and cross the river further upstream by Bridle Drift, and then turn eastwards back towards Colenso and roll up the Boer defences along the riverbank, while Dundonald's mounted brigade attacked the Boer position to the west of the village. Hildyard's brigade and the artillery under Colonel Long were to attack Colenso itself, where there were two drifts as well as the iron bridge.

Orders were given at 10 p.m. on the 14th of December, and the attack was to begin at dawn. In the morning, Hart's brigade moved off at about four, but Long's artillery was even more prompt, setting out at three thirty and thus getting well ahead of Hildyard's, which did not move off until half past four. Things began to go wrong almost immediately. To the left, west of Colenso, the river ran straight for a little and then made a deep meander, creating a long, narrow

154

loop pointing northwards. It was to the west of this loop that Hart's was meant to cross, by Bridle Drift; but the native guide misunderstood, or did not know of it, and directed them towards a different drift, taking them into the loop, where they came under withering fire on both sides from the Boers on the further bank. To keep the men under control in the difficult circumstances, Hart grouped them tightly into quarter column, but this had the effect of making them a better target for the Boer guns as they advanced into the trap.

Meanwhile, in Colenso, Long had discovered a deep donga, or dry ravine, across his route of advance. There was no sound from the Boers and it was assumed they had fled across the river. But when two of the guns had been manoeuvred with great effort through the donga, the Boers suddenly opened fire from hidden positions with both rifle and shell. Long's were too far forward and too far ahead of the infantry, and out of reach of the ammunition wagons. After some spirited defence, they were running out of men and ammunition. Some fled, abandoning the guns; others could only take shelter from the crippling fire in the donga.

By eight o'clock in the morning Buller saw that the attack could not succeed, and the only thing to do was to try to save as much of his force as possible. He sent his reserve to try to extricate Hart's division from the Loop, while Hildyard's advanced into Colenso to cover the attempt to retrieve Long's guns and the ammunition carts. The latter were the most troublesome to recover, for owing to their size and weight it was very difficult to turn them. They had to be pulled round laboriously by hand before horses could be hitched to them, and all under continuous fire. Buller himself went forward to supervise the rescue of the guns, and some of his staff, including Lieutenant Frederick Roberts, son of General Lord Roberts, volunteered to go in.

15th December 1899
My dear Aunt,
Well, I have been in a battle, and it was not at all like one would expect. This morning we got up at 2.30 and

155

packed wagons and then got some breakfast at 3 a.m.
– tea and dry biscuit. Do I dream of bacon and
sausages? You may guess! We fell in at about 3.45. Our
company was told to stay in reserve and keep close to
the guns. Marched off at about four and were getting
up near the naval guns by dawn. It was already hot by
then. We heard that Hart's had been hard at it drilling
for an hour before they even marched off – and in such
heat and full equipment! They made the first infantry
attack and we heard the Boer guns begin over to our
left. The first shell came in amongst us at 6.30. We
were told to spread out into single rank to make a
smaller target. It was pretty unsettling at first to be
fired upon, but excitement soon made one forget any
fear. We were behind the naval guns. Col. Long took
his guns too far forward. The Boers were hidden in
trenches and a small covert and opened up, and our
men and horses were knocked over before they could
do any good. We saw some gun crews come flying back,
having left the guns, flogging the horses madly, shells
bursting just behind them – quite a sight! About 7 a.m.
half our brigade was sent off to support Hart's on the
left. They were in trouble, caught under incessant fire
but still trying to reach the river. I do not think they
ever got across it in any numbers. The rest of us were
then told to go forward, I suppose to draw the enemy
fire while an attempt was made to rescue the guns. We
marched out to the right and advanced up the railway
with the track on our left. Shells were falling around
us, also rifle fire, and our fellows were getting knocked
about. Our Captain was shot through the lungs and
had one finger shot away. Longton of ours was carrying
him back when he was shot in the neck, but refused
to drop the Capt. Also Cowey was hit pretty badly in
the thigh, and Cox was shot through the foot but
carried on. I don't know if he realised he had been hit.
The dust was choking, and the heat was beyond
anything, like being roasted on a spit. Also the Boer
fire made a terrible noise. Just the noise alone was like

being beaten with clubs – I could never have imagined it. Two fellows of ours, Lennox and Kinsey, were one either side of me and both hit within seconds of each other. I don't know how they missed me. During this time I learn that Lt Roberts, the general's son, and some others made a daring dash and saved two of the guns, but were pretty badly shot up. Roberts was so far forward when he fell they could not get to him until late this afternoon. He was lying out in the sun all day, badly wounded. Then we were told to retire but it was slow work and under constant fire. Got back into camp about 2.30 p.m., extremely done up, dirty, thirsty and tired. The water here is thick and cloudy like pea soup, but when you are as thirsty as we were, you don't care. Then little Fallon got some tea on the brew and I drank several cups, and we had some biscuit and bully beef and pitched tents and rested. I was very glad Fallon got back. He had a lucky escape. He was hit by a bullet which pierced his brace but did not enter his body because it struck his mouth-organ, which was in his pocket. He was afraid it was damaged, but tho' dented it still plays and he shows it to everyone, much amazed and pleased at his escape. So your boy has been in a battle and come through unharmed! Apart from a bad sunburn on the back of my neck, which stings somewhat. But it was all very strange. I never saw a Boer at all, and I hardly know what it was all for, as we are back where we started this morning. Must close this long letter now as it gets too dark to see. Feel strangely depressed after all the effort and noise, but don't worry, I am well.

Ever your loving nephew,
Bertie

The casualties that day were 143 killed, 755 wounded, and 240 missing – most of them captured – and the Boers had also taken ten of Long's guns. Lord Roberts's son was brought in late in the afternoon and taken down to Chievely where the field hospital was, but he was mortally wounded and died the next day. Frederick Treves and his team were working there, and Treves was with the young lieutenant when he died.

The news of the three reverses, at Colenso, Magersfontein and Stormberg, all within a few days of each other, hit those at home like an icy shock. The British public had grown used to victory whenever the army went to war; the newspapers quickly dubbed it 'Black Week'. The sum of the losses was not catastrophic in relation to the total force employed, but to a nation unaccustomed to defeat, they seemed so.

'Buller didn't help his case by wiring to Lansdowne in such gloomy terms,' Hazelmere said to Venetia as they perused the papers.

'If he says he can't take Colenso and relieve Ladysmith, I suppose we must believe him,' Venetia said. 'He's the man on the spot, after all.'

'Yes, but it does nothing for morale and confidence. And he ought to know the War Office will never take "can't" for an answer,' Hazelmere said, turning a page. 'Not that he doesn't have problems. How can any general plan a campaign on the basis of a school map that shows everything more than five miles from a road or railway as *terra incognita*? And the heat, and the lack of water – it can't be easy out there.'

'All the same, my love,' Venetia said, 'the fact remains that we've been victorious in hot countries before, even in unmapped countries. Look at the Afghan war, when Lord Roberts marched all the way from Kabul to Kandahar! I do start to wonder whether Roberts shouldn't have been made commander-in-chief instead of Wolseley.'

'The Afghan war was twenty years ago, and Roberts is – what? – sixty-seven or sixty-eight now. And no-one who isn't there can know the particular problems of the terrain and so on. Still, I know Balfour favours a change of command, and I daresay he'll persuade Salisbury to send Roberts. It will be popular with the people – he's a great hero, especially now he's lost his son, poor man. And the Government has to do something to save itself.'

'I hardly think that is the point.'

'It is to the Government.'

'Very cynical of you, darling.'

'All right, then – let's say that, politically, we certainly can't afford to lose South Africa.'

Venetia smiled suddenly. 'Did I tell you what Olivia said about the Queen? When Balfour referred to the setbacks of Black Week as disasters, she snapped his head off, and said, "Please understand that there is no-one depressed in *this* house. We are not interested in the possibilities of defeat. They do not exist."'

'Rather a pity she can't go and lead the troops herself,' said Hazelmere. 'She'd give the Boers what-for!'

Lord Roberts, a little, cherry-nosed man with large white moustaches, was very popular in the ranks, and was known affectionately as 'Bobs'. Lord Salisbury, the Prime Minister, agreed to the urgings of his nephew Balfour and of Lord Lansdowne and appointed Roberts to take over in South Africa, but stipulated that Kitchener, the hero of Omdurman, must go with him as his chief of staff. Buller was to remain in the Cape as Roberts's subordinate. This was a dreadful rebuff to Buller, but he accepted it gracefully in the greater national interest, proving himself a gentleman as well as an officer.

It was obvious that more troops were also needed, and the rest of the regulars from home were put under orders, stripping the country bare. They were still not enough; but one effect of Black Week had been to send a wave of wild patriotism and violent Boer-hatred through the country, and thousands rushed to volunteer. Buller had said that in particular more mounted units were needed, and many wealthy men funded and got together companies of mounted infantry and sharpshooters, which were brigaded together as the Imperial Yeomanry. Almost all the militias volunteered to go, and volunteers flocked to the infantry and artillery too. 'Bobs to the rescue!' was a phrase that passed around, and it always raised a smile. Patriotism boosted confidence. In the music halls there was a revival of G. W. Hunt's song, which proved hugely popular:

We don't want to fight, but by Jingo if we do,
We've got the ships, we've got the guns, we've got the money
   too!

Everyone wanted to do something for the brave boys, for
the war effort. Men volunteered, women knitted socks and
mufflers, schoolchildren made up parcels of chocolate, soap,
handkerchief and religious tracts to send out to Tommy
Atkins. Olivia told Venetia that the Queen herself knitted away
in every spare moment as if her life depended on it. Patriotism
had some odd effects, too: *couture* decreed that khaki was the
colour of the moment, and some ladies of the *ton* were seen
in Bond Street sporting large 'veldt' hats trimmed with ostrich
feathers, and boxy 'mess' jackets piped in red.

Lord Roberts set sail for the Cape on the 23rd of
December; but raising, equipping and moving troops takes
time, and he went without the reinforcements, few of whom
were likely to reach him for some months yet.

Henrietta had never been happier. That ache deep within
her, to which she had grown so accustomed that she had
ceased to notice it, had eased. Some small part of the movement of her soul had been pinched and cramped, but now
the pain was gone, and she felt released. She sang about
her work, and when Jerome came in he looked at her with
a certain delighted surprise every time, remarking that she
was growing more beautiful by the day.

Teddy approached her and Jerome with a benign plot to
save Charley trouble, which was for the Comptons to invite
the Morlands to Morland Place for Christmas dinner, rather
than vice versa. Henrietta was delighted. 'I can't think of
anything nicer. We'll make it the best ever, and have all the
things we used to have when we were children – shall we,
Ted? The Yule log and the green branches and everything?'

'And a tree,' Teddy said. 'The children will like a tree. I
know where I can get one. A good big one to stand in the
hall. After all, the last Christmas of the century ought to be
something special.' He looked at Jerome, just as Jerome was
about to speak, and said, 'I say, old chap, you're the brainiest

160

cove in the family. Can you tell me what all this stuff is I read in the newspaper, about it *not* being the new century next year? Every day there seems to be another letter, or another article, arguing this way and that. I can't make head or tail of it.'

'It's quite simple,' Jerome said. 'The first year of our era was AD 1, and the hundredth was AD 100, so the second hundred years began in AD 101. Do you see?'

'Well,' Teddy said doubtfully.

'Continue that sequence, and you will find that this century ends in 1900, and the new one starts in 1901.'

'But the number changes from 18 to 19 next year,' Teddy pleaded. 'That ought to count for something? I mean, we won't be in eighteen-something, we'll be in nineteen-something. Isn't that a new century?'

Jerome smiled. 'It can be whatever you like. After all, every year marks the end of some hundred years or other.' He saw he had lost Teddy and went on, 'The Government and all official sources stick by 1901 as the beginning of the next century, and that is the logical, mathematical decision. But I'm sure there will be lots of people – probably most of the population outside London – who will go on maintaining that this is the last year of the century, and celebrate accordingly.'

Teddy's face cleared. 'Jolly good. I knew I could depend on you to explain the difficulty away.'

Jerome laughed. 'If you think we're having difficulties now, just imagine what it will be like at the end of the next century, when the millennium changes too!'

'Well, we shan't be around to see it,' Teddy said comfortably. 'So we'll make the last Christmas of the century something special, eh?'

Henrietta discovered that Charley knew all about the plot, and was quite happy about it. 'Teddy doesn't want me worrying and working – as if the servants don't do everything! – but I think it would be lovely to have Christmas Day here, so you needn't be tactful. I do find it quite tiring to move about a great deal,' she admitted. 'Lying on the sofa knitting socks for soldiers is all I'm fit for. But if you

161

want any help, either from me or the servants, you must say so. I do so want it to be as nice as Teddy hopes.'

Henrietta promised to let her know if she needed help, but her new surge of energy said she wanted to do it all herself – with Emma's help, of course. There followed such planning, such gathering of ingredients, such baking and storing and hiding away of treats as promised a wonderful day. The children sniffed the atmosphere, literal and figurative, when they got home from school each day, and grew wild with excitement. Fortunately the house was large enough, and a great deal of it was empty enough, for them to race and romp off their excitement without damaging anything. With Jack away at school, Jessie had emerged as the leader in their plays, easily subduing Robbie who, though he argued with her furiously, was not quick-witted enough to think of alternative plans to hers. Frank was happy to follow anyone, absorbed as he was in his private thoughts so much of the time, but he preferred Jessie as his leader, since she did more amusing things, and stopped Robbie bullying him.

After a particularly trying episode when the children used the great staircase as a toboggan slope and a tin tray as the toboggan, Henrietta felt she must deflect their energy into quieter activities and set them the task of writing and rehearsing a play to be performed on Christmas Day after dinner. 'And don't forget to write parts for Jack and Ned, too,' she urged. The children were much struck with the idea, and disappeared thereafter for long hours into the schoolroom – which they used as their private sitting-room – to write, rehearse and contrive costumes and scenery. There was a great deal of giggling, even more argument, and frequent appearances in the kitchen with mysterious and vague requests.

'Mother, have you got a box?'

'What sort of box? What size do you want?'

'Oh, just an ordinary one. And some string.'

'How much string?'

'Oh, the usual amount, you know.'

Another time it was Frank with, 'Have you got an umbrella we could borry, Mother?' And again, 'Mother, can we borry

162

your scissor? We'll be most careful with it.' It was generally Frank who was sent to 'borry' things, on the grounds that, though actually a year older than Jessie, he was somehow regarded as 'the baby' of the family and the least resistible.

The scheme was a great success and kept the children well occupied, while Henrietta and Emma wrought the feast. When Jack came home on the last Saturday before Christmas, he disappeared into the schoolroom too. All the children emerged on the day before Christmas Eve to go out and fetch the Yule log home, and see it stowed in the fireplace in the great hall, ready to be set smouldering the next day. On Christmas Eve Teddy and Jerome brought in the Christmas tree, which was so large two men from the timber merchant's were needed to help them set it up. Then everyone helped to decorate it, and when the candles were lit, they all gathered round and sang carols, before opening their presents.

Dinner on Christmas Day was magnificent. An extra leaf was put into the dining-table, and Charley brought over a cloth big enough to cover it; then she and the children laid it and decorated it with holly, ivy, myrtle, and little candles in small silver holders, one to each person, as well as the three large candelabra down the centre, which were wreathed with ivy. What with going to church and the labour of cooking, dinner did not take place until three o'clock, and the short winter day was drawing in, so that once the candles were lit it became suddenly dark outside, and the family gathered round the table into a cave of candlelight and firelight. The Christmas goose was roasted to perfection, the skin golden and crisp, the sage and onion stuffing so sharp and tangy that the mere scent of it set the mouth watering. It was served in the traditional manner surrounded by roast gilded apples, and there was gravy sauce and bread sauce with cloves besides, and also a large roast rib of beef, with horseradish sauce. The plum pudding was brought in flaming, exciting the children so much they hardly made a sound, and they ate so much they were content just to loll in their seats and be quiet while the grown-ups addressed their dessert: a fine Stilton cheese and a dish of apples.

The port went round, and when the loyal toast had been

drunk – 'The Queen! God bless her!' – Jerome called to Teddy to remain on his feet and give a speech. 'Something suitable to the last Christmas of the old century,' he said, with an innocent look.

And so Teddy, glass in hand, his face red and beaming, said, 'Ladies and gentlemen, boys and girls, I would like to say first of all, God bless all of us here, and all our dear ones who are *not* here, too.'

Henrietta thought of Lizzie and Ashley and the boys. Ashley had only one day off from work, which meant it was not worth while their coming down to Yorkshire, so they were having their own celebration at home.

'It is a time of year when we also remember those dear ones who have gone before us to a better place.' A moment's solemn silence, in which Kithra could be heard gently snoring in front of the fire, having been given a larger plateful of scraps than he was used to on less auspicious days. 'But it is also a time to look forward. The year 1900 will be the first year of a new and better century. And it will be the year in which we beat the Boers!'

Cheers from the boys, and a thump of the table and a 'Hear, hear!' from Jerome.

'Which will bring a swift return of our brave lads in triumph to these shores. It will be a year in which we all grow a little older but a little wiser, and in some cases,' he glared in mock warning at the children, who giggled, 'a lot more diligent at our studies. And, keeping the best till last, it will be the year in which my beloved wife gives me a son and heir.' He smiled at Charley, who blushed a little. 'Isn't she beautiful?' Teddy demanded of the company. 'And did you ever see such a fine, promising shape?'

'Teddy, don't,' Charley said, embarrassed. She was showing now, and looking very well, Henrietta thought, though it was not usually considered polite to mention a pregnant lady's shape in public.

'Oh, we're all friends here,' Teddy said. 'So I've come to the end of my speech, and I'll just ask you all to raise your glasses to—' He paused. 'Dashed if I can remember what the toast was supposed to be.'

164

Jerome helped him out. 'To all Morlands, born and honorary! To us!'

It was a toast they could all drink with enthusiasm; and when he had sat down again, Jerome said, 'Now then, bairns, it's your turn. Your dinner ought to have gone down enough by now. You'd better go into the drawing-room and get ready for the play. Call us in when you're ready.'

They jumped up with an energy that made the grown-ups flinch, and soon splurges of talk, laughter, and irregular thumps from next door were punctuating the comfortable talk of the adults, finishing the port.

2nd January 1900

Dear Aunt Hen,

What a dismal way to spend Christmas! It was only dysentery, but it was bad enough for this poor soldier, I can tell you! Not to dwell on unpleasant things, I shall only say that it got so bad I was put on the sick list and sent down to the hospital at Chievely. I felt rather a fool being taken off active duty for something like that, when almost all the fellows have had it more or less badly, but the MO said in my case it was compounded by heat-stroke. The heat here is not to be believed! On Christmas Day a thermometer in the hospital tent measured 105.2 degrees! And even outside it is regularly 103 or 104 in the shade. A lot of fellows have got bad sunburns – the Scotch regiments in particular suffer when they have to lie down under fire as the backs of their knees below their kilts get burnt – very nasty. Their officers are trying to get them into trews, but army traditions are hard to budge even at necessity! At least in the hospital the water was better. They had rigged up filters which took much of the brownish stuff out, though there was so much of it, it blocked the filters so that they had to clean them after each bottle! My Christmas dinner was only beef tea, but very welcome as the first thing I had been able to eat for days. Mr Treves, the surgeon Cousin Venetia talks about, was there, and came through once

165

or twice to ask me how I felt. He seemed a very nice fellow and we had quite a chat when I mentioned her name. I dared to ask him what he thought of the place, and he said the things he liked least were the heat and the bully beef! He had two lady nurses with him, brought from England, and they were splendid and knew just what to do to make a fellow comfortable. One of them rather took a fancy to me, and brought me a spray of mimosa from one of the trees outside, which smelt wonderfully and a pleasant contrast to the usual hospital stink I can tell you! Mr T told me about one or two interesting cases – interesting to him, at any rate! Like one fellow who'd been hit in the top of the head by a bullet, which travelled right down through his brain and his mouth and out through the back of his neck, but left him with nothing worse than a slight headache! There were still quite a lot of wounded from the battle in the hospital, not the really serious ones – they were sent down to 'Maritzburg on the train – but those who would be back to duty soon. But most of the beds were filled with cases of dysentery, and the dreaded enteric fever and cholera. Mr T said they are the real enemy and will likely kill more Tommies than the Boers ever do. I am back in camp now, feeling a little pale but otherwise myself again. The word is that we are getting reinforcements, Warren's division, after which we will go on the offensive again, but I dare say you know more about that than we do in these tele-graph days! No-one tells us Tommies anything! Your letter arrived yesterday, also the tin with chocolate and cigarettes, for which my heartfelt thanks. Did you think about me at Christmas? I thought of you all, and espe-cially yesterday when a new century opened with me sweating in a little stifling tent under a blazing blue sky, waiting for my succulent breakfast of salty bully and hard biscuit! Did you have snow? I dream of snow.

Your loving nevvy,
Bertie

'Bobs' arrived in Cape Town on the 10th of January 1900, though his reinforcements would not be arriving for another month. Matters were becoming critical in Ladysmith: White had signalled by heliograph that he was no longer capable of assisting any attempt to lift the siege by making a sortie, as his forces were so reduced by sickness and hunger. Supplies were running out, and there were two thousand sick within the town.

But Warren's division had reached Chievely, which meant that Buller now had enough men to guard the vital railhead *and* mount an offensive, and he telegraphed Roberts for permission to make another attempt to break through the Boer lines and relieve Ladysmith. Gossip ran as freely through an army as around a tea-shop, and there was plenty of speculation over what Buller felt about having to ask permission; but he had received his demotion with outward grace, whatever his inner feelings, and no-one could accuse him of uttering a disloyal word.

Buller's plan was a variation on his first, to outflank the Boers. Between him and Ladysmith was the Tugela river and the broken ranges of hills that ran along its further bank. Beyond those the land flattened out into an open plain. If they could only get through the hills, nothing would be able to stop them advancing the last fifteen miles to Ladysmith.

About twenty miles upstream from Colenso was another road to Ladysmith, which crossed the river at Trichardt's Drift, then passed through a narrow defile between the Rangeworthy Hills and the Brakfontein ridge before swinging north-east across the plain to Ladysmith. There was a high peak on either side of this narrow pass, on the left Tabanyama Hill, and on the right Scout's Hill, called Spion Kop in the Boer language. Buller's plan was that Warren should take the main part of the force on this road, while Lyttleton led a smaller section over a different drift, Potgeiter's, further downstream, in the hope of diverting the Boers. Once across and clear they would join forces and march on Ladysmith.

To this end, the whole force moved from Chievely to

167

Spearman's camp, about five miles south of the river and between the two drifts.

Bertie wrote to Henrietta:

It was quite a sight, a train of 650 wagons, 25,000 men, eight field batteries and the Naval guns, all plodding along under the blazing sun, raising a dust you could have seen for miles. We saw movement in the hills on the other side of the river, and sometimes a flash of light, reflecting off a glass or rifle, so we guessed the Boers were shadowing us and moving into position to welcome us! But there was no helping it. Move we must, though we had no cover to hide our movements, and in that heat and on that road we couldn't do it faster. It took three days for the whole army to reach Spearman's.

The fatal flaw in Buller's plan was Sir Charles Warren.

Bertie's group of volunteers was led by a regular army officer named Jocelyn, promoted when their captain had been badly wounded at Colenso. Jocelyn had become very friendly with Bertie: they were both from the same class and discovered that they had acquaintances in common back home. To Bertie, Jocelyn could express the opinions he would have felt it disloyal to air to the rest of his section. Warren's actions – or rather inaction – filled him with frustration. Setting out from Spearman's on the 16th of January, it took Warren two days to cross the five miles of veldt, construct the pontoons and get the men across the river.

'Why doesn't he stir himself?' Jocelyn raved, as he and Bertie shared a cigarette. 'Doesn't he understand speed is of the essence? What in God's name does he think the Boers are doing all this time – having a nice sleep while he gets himself into position?'

Bertie ran a finger round inside his collar. His khaki felt prickly and heavy, and in the midday glare it was hard to keep one's eyes open. 'It's this heat,' he offered, as an excuse for the absent Warren – though God knew why he should defend him. 'Makes it hard to think.'

Jocelyn snorted. 'Think? That would be a novelty! The trouble is, Warren can't grasp this is a real war. He's a parade-ground soldier. I've heard his fellows say they can't get him out of his tent in the morning. Thinks he's still in Piccadilly. Likes a leisurely breakfast, three or four courses sitting in his silk dressing-gown, a smoke over his coffee, then takes an hour to get dressed.'

'Oh, Lord, don't talk about breakfast and coffee, there's a good fellow!' Bertie moaned. Since he had come to South Africa he was always hungry. 'Buller should chivvy him, surely?'

But Jocelyn wouldn't hear a word against Buller. All the men liked him. He was a soldier's soldier – calm, professional, just, and careful of his men. 'It ain't Buller's fault. You can't get blood out of a stone and Warren's a stone if ever there was one. Besides, the War Office has pretty well tied his hands.'

'How's that?' Bertie wanted to know.

'By making him subordinate to Roberts. Well, look, either he's got to ask permission before he does anything, which slows him down and pretty well knocks out quick reaction, or he takes the risk of Roberts saying he acted without authority if anything goes wrong. He's in a shocking bind. And Roberts ain't here – he can't know what needs doing any more than the Government back home. It's a bad business, this running a war from a distance.'

While they waited for Warren to get into position, the other part of the plan was going well. The smaller force under Lyttleton had secured Potgeiter's Drift and were holding it against the Boers, while the cavalry under Dundonald had gone out to the left and swung round the west of the Rangeworthy Hills. They drove off the Boers there, and Dundonald sent a galloper to Warren asking for reinforcements to hold the position, a place called Acton Homes. But Warren refused, and recalled the cavalry. Word soon filtered back that Warren had told Dundonald angrily he had no right to go so far: that his place was to stay close on the main force's flank to defend it, and that it was not his business to stretch out the line to such an extent.

But still Warren did not move.

'He just sits there like a toad on a stone,' Jocelyn growled. 'What's he doing? Taking the runes? Consulting the spirits about which way to go?'

By the time Warren did mount an attack on Tabanyama Hill on the 20th, the element of surprise was lost, the Boers were well entrenched, and the attack was easily repulsed. Warren sent to Buller, demanding more artillery before he made another move, and Buller sent four howitzers. But still nothing happened, no attack was mounted, and finally in frustration Buller rode over himself on the 23rd to talk to Warren and insist he must attack.

Jocelyn came back from chatting with his friend, who was a member of Buller's staff, and found Bertie sitting in the scrap of shade afforded by a rock, smoking his last cigarette. 'I was thinking I ought to save it,' he said, squinting up as Jocelyn cut out a piece of the hot blue sky above him, 'but it kept calling to me from my pocket like a lost soul, begging to join its brothers, and in the end I gave in.'

'You'll be sorry tomorrow,' Jocelyn said shortly, dropping down beside him.

'As it is my last, there was always going to be a moment of reckoning,' Bertie pointed out. 'What news from Camelot?'

'Apparently Warren said that he couldn't mount an attack on Tabanyama without artillery in a suitable position to support it, which means taking Scout's Hill first.'

'Oh, is *that* all he wants?'

'It's damned steep,' Jocelyn said. 'I say, let me have a puff of that.'

'Of this? My very last cigarette?'

'Be a good fellow. Mine are in my tent and it's too hot to fag over and fetch 'em. I'll give you one later.'

'Bargain.' Bertie handed it over.

'Buller's going to draw up a plan of attack. There's a small force of Boers up on the Kop – not much more than a picket, so I hear – but Buller wants us to go up under cover of darkness and take them by surprise. Trouble is,' he added restlessly, 'we don't know what's on the other side. That's the whole problem with this campaign – we can't get any

170

scouts far enough forward to tell us what we're walking into.'

'The *whole* problem?' Bertie queried.

'Part of the problem,' Jocelyn acknowledged, with a smile. 'Well, at least we know there's going to be some movement tonight, at last.'

'Oh, you are an energetic fellow. I'm quite happy sitting here in the shade watching you smoke my last fag.'

Jocelyn handed it back hastily, and said, 'The shade won't last long either. The sun's coming round.'

'Then there'll be no reason for you not to go to your tent for your baccy.'

In the letter he wrote later to Henrietta, Bertie said:

I was not in the first attack, but I can tell you what I saw and what I heard later from the other fellows. They set off at about 11 p.m. on the 23rd under Gen. Woodgate, 1700 infantry, a few engineers, and 200 of Col. Thorneycroft's mounted Uitlanders, who left their horses at the bottom. Spion Kop is so steep they had to climb on their hands and knees in some places, and in others clasp hands and help each other across. They disposed of a Boer picket and reached the top safely. Next they meant to dig a trench, but half the men had abandoned their tools on the climb up, because they needed both hands to get on. In any case, what spades they had were useless, as they found that the soil is only an inch thick up there, and underneath is solid rock! Also the sandbags had been left at the bottom, whether by mistake or because the men could not carry them on such a steep climb I do not know. At all events, all they could do was to build what shelter they could with loose stones and rocks and wait for dawn. When it came, there was a thick white mist around the summit of Spion Kop. From down below we could not see them nor they us: they were on a fog-bound island in the air. But when the fog lifted at last, they discovered that what from the bottom and from our side looked like a steep-sided, single hill was in fact joined by narrow necks on the other side to two other hills, on

171

which the Boers were already in place with pom-poms and long toms. As the mist was sucked up, they opened fire and raked the summit of Spion Kop. Without heavy guns, our men could not reply, and without trenches, they had nowhere to shelter, and could only lie down and hope.

Under cover of their fire, the Boers stormed the sides, and brisk fighting went on. At 9.45 a signal was received from the hill: 'Colonel Crofton to GOC force. Reinforce at once or all lost. General dead.'

Jocelyn came back from receiving orders to get his men together. 'Our turn has come. We're the first of the reinforcements. General Woodgate's been killed by a piece of shrapnel to the head, and apparently Colonel Thorneycroft has taken over and rallied our chaps. But he desperately needs more men, so we're off. On your feet, chaps, as quick as you like!'

It was ten in the morning when they left camp, and it was already hot, though Bertie knew from experience that this was nothing to the way it would be later. This was still a morning heat, with the last hint of freshness just burning out of the air. In an hour it would be stifling. The scratchy uniform, the heavy boots, the helmet all seemed to weigh more the longer they were worn; the rifle, so obedient on the parade-ground, became a perfect fiend while climbing, swinging round like a live thing bent on mischief, hampering movement, making you stumble, catching on snags of rock.

The climb was hard. Sometimes they were inching up vertical rock like mountaineers, sometimes scrambling across a grassy slope – as difficult in its own way, for the grass was dry and slippery and hard to keep a foothold on. Once Bertie slipped and went down twenty or thirty feet sliding on his face, taking the skin off his nose, which had barely recovered from sunburn. And just to make it fun, he thought as he scrambled and panted and sweated upwards, they had to do it under Boer crossfire. Bullets whizzed around them like hornets, sometimes ricocheting off a rock with a vicious ping and whine; the ones you didn't hear were often the ones that had found a softer target. The man just ahead of him, Brewer, was shot half-way up, hit in the shoulder. He cried out and lost his footing and started to roll down the hill. Instinctively Bertie started up from his hands and knees to try to catch him, but Jocelyn barked out, 'Get down, you fool!' and Bertie dropped to his face as a bullet sang through the air he had been occupying an instant before. 'He's all right,' Jocelyn said, looking back. 'He's stopped rolling.' Bertie looked back and saw Brewer lying face up across the hillside, having been stopped by an outstanding vein of rock, and already grasping at the earth to pull himself over. But even as he looked there was another crack of rifle fire, and Brewer jumped as if he were being tossed in a blanket, and then lay still.

Jocelyn's company howled at the sight.

'Some Boer shot him!'

'The filthy brutes!'

'The swine! He was helpless!'

'Get down!' yelled Jocelyn. 'Keep your heads down, you idiots! Follow me! You'll get your chance up there to show them what you think.'

It was hard to see anything, keeping nose to the ground, and they were beginning to scatter as each found his own way over the terrain. Jocelyn realised this and kept them together and following him with hunting calls. 'He's a zipping fellow,' Bertie muttered to himself. He had been afraid at first when the shot started to fly around him, but he was too hot and tired now to think about anything but hauling his body inch by inch up that hill. His hands were sore, his shoulders ached, the sweat under his uniform was making him itch, his collar had chafed the back of his neck raw, and his rifle regularly swung round and jammed itself into the flesh of his inner thigh, where he knew he would have a bruise the size of a teacup tonight. The firing had become a background noise. It was impossible to go on being afraid in the circumstances. When I have a moment to spare, he told himself, I'll be afraid, but not now.

They reached the top at last. They knew it was the top because the ground levelled out and because it was covered with dead men. Bodies were lying everywhere, heaped in places; the smell of blood was sickening, and already clouds of flies had found the feast. Bertie felt his gorge rise; the man next to him, Nicholls, choked and then vomited with a sort of surprised ease, like a dog. Fallon was cursing in a steady stream broken only by his sobs. It was clear why there had been such carnage: they were being fired on by Boer artillery, and shells were dropping everywhere, exploding on the rock and sending out shards as sharp and lethal as shrapnel.

'Keep low!' Jocelyn screamed. 'We've got to get under cover. Wait!' A shell dropped twenty yards away and there was a shrill cry, cut short. Some poor soul had caught it, Bertie thought. He tried to be afraid and found he couldn't: his mind was quite numb with shock and the horror of the death all around him. Come, that's a good thing, he told himself. 'This way!' Jocelyn yelled. 'To me, men!' And he yipped a hunting cry. Obedient as dogs, they turned towards him and crawled through the madness of fire and rock-shards and dead men staring up at the sky with that surprised look, their limbs flung out and relaxed in death as though they had fallen asleep in the sun. Bertie wanted to cry at the sight of them. It was as though they had been cheated, like children, come to sleep but having their lives stolen from them. They were harder to bear, curiously, than the ones who had been horribly mutilated. They only looked like bloody butchered hunks of meat – sickening, but without the power to make him weep.

Jocelyn found them a good position, an upright ridge of rock about two feet high. They scrabbled the earth away at its foot and piled any stones they found on top to gain every possible inch of shelter, and settled in.

'We're pretty snug here,' Fallon said to Bertie. His voice was high as a child's with strain, and his grin was unnatural. His face, Bertie noticed, was very dirty, and he supposed his own must be too. 'Our captain's a corker! I bet we've got the best place on the whole bloody hill.'

It seemed he was right, for once they had dug themselves in, they did not lose anyone more. The next company not fifty yards away lost seventeen men killed: they watched them go down like skittle pins falling, knowing there was nothing they could do to help. It was all they could do to keep their own heads on, and to fire back when they had the chance, though what good it was doing they couldn't tell. The sun beat down on them, passing slowly overhead. There was no shelter from it, no relief from the heat, or from the firing – the Boers did not let up all day.

The pangs of hunger began to gnaw at Bertie's vitals, at least providing a counter-irritant to the other discomforts; but hunger did not last long, before being ousted by thirst. As the day dragged on and the sun began to decline, thirst became all-consuming. There was no water on the Kop. In the heat and smoke, it became a torture. Bertie's mouth was so dry his tongue stuck to the roof of it and he almost had to pull it loose with his fingers. It was impossible to lick his lips, which dried and cracked in the sun, for his tongue was like a piece of wood. He longed for water with an intensity he had never felt for anything before. He felt he would willingly have given up his life shortly afterwards if only he could have as much clear cold water as he wanted first.

Exhaustion and thirst made him light-headed, and he passed into a dream, standing a little aside from himself and watching his own actions, remote from them and from fear. Now and then the Boers tried to storm the peak, and then there was frenzied activity as they repulsed the invaders. Sometimes when he fired his rifle he would see a man fling up his hands or fall immediately afterwards, but he had no idea whether it was his shot that had done it. He felt curiously detached from the notion. He wanted to beat the Boers, he wanted his side to win, but most of all he prayed for darkness, which might give them respite from the heat and the guns, and for water, water, water. His letter concluded:

Darkness came but the Boers did not stop firing, though it eased a bit. Col. Thorneycroft was the hero all day, rallying wherever things looked worst, but all his signals for big guns, ammunition and water seemed to go unheeded. Also no stretcher bearers, so after dark

175

he set the Imp Light Infantry to start moving the dead and injured. Around 8 p.m. the firing ceased at last and we could rest a little, but that's when we started to hear the cries of the wounded. It was ghastly. The Boer big guns in particular had done shocking work, and many were terribly mutilated. Then the order came to retire, and I cannot say I was sorry. It was a rough journey down and we did much of it sitting down and sliding on our hinder ends. I cut my hand pretty badly on a sharp rock but was so tired I did not even notice until I got back to camp. We passed many dead comrades on the way down. Sometimes we had to climb over them, and once I put my hand into the remains of a body wounded in the belly, which made me squirm, I can tell you! By 2 a.m. we were all down, and under cover of darkness we moved back across the river, when we were allowed to rest. Desperately tired and thirsty when we got into camp at last. I am minding your wise words about boiling all water but sometimes it can't be helped! This morning the Boers have the possession of the Kop again. I hear we lost about two thousand, dead, wounded and missing. The Lancashire regiments were the worst hit – at the end they had only one unwounded officer! Thanks to our Captain we did not do so badly. I am not injured at all, apart from my hand, sunburn on my face and neck, and also having taken the skin off my nose. I wish you could see me. I am quite a sketch! I do not know what is planned for us next. We look forward to Bobs and K arriving with reinforcements, when perhaps we may get some of our own back on these Dutch farmers! Gen. Buller is a fine general and he did his best, but was let down by Warren. At least you know we all gave of our best, and you may be proud of

Your devoted nephew,
Bertie

BOOK TWO

Abroad

Ever the faith endures,
England, my England: –
'Take and break us, we are yours,
England, my own!
Life is good, and joy runs high
Between English earth and sky:
Death is death; but we shall die
To the Song on your bugles blown,
England –
To the stars on your bugles blown!'

William Ernest Henley: 'England, My England!'

CHAPTER SIX

The February of 1900 was bitter. Heavy snows were followed by a freeze, made worse by icy winds. The walls of Morland Place were thick and insulating, but the rooms were large and the ceilings high, and to make the house tolerably warm it was necessary to keep big fires going in all the rooms. Big fires, in turn, needed a large staff to maintain them, and Morland Place no longer had its army of servants. Without fires, the overall temperature of the house gradually sank, and the chill crept slowly like fog rolling along a valley bottom. The family lived mostly in the kitchen, where the range was never out, and put on outdoor clothes to cross the great hall. In bed at night, even under a heap of bedclothes, it took a long time to get warm enough to fall asleep. Henrietta, who was a chilly creature, pushed so hard against Jerome in her sleep for his warmth, he sometimes woke up on the brink of falling out of bed.

But the children loved the weather. To them the marvellous frost patterns on the inside of their window in the morning were an unalloyed miracle, and the snow seemed to have been provided by a beneficent God specifically for their amusement. They tobogganed and made snowmen and stamped on frozen puddles and snapped off icicles and ate them, crunching zestfully. They had snowball battles and regularly came home with frozen wet hands and feet. In Jessie's case, this led to chilblains, which some evenings were so painful she could do nothing but cry. One day on the way home from school Robbie dropped an icicle down her neck and, her temper shortened by the pain of her feet, she hit him so hard he lost his balance – partly in surprise – and fell through the thin crust of ice into the beck. He arrived home soaked to the skin, teeth chattering and almost blue with cold. Henrietta and Emma dashed about with towels and hot drinks and mustard baths, terrified he would catch pneumonia; but Robbie was tremendously robust, and shook it off as a dog shakes off water, only promising some unspecified dark revenge on Jessie.

'You will not,' Henrietta said severely, 'touch your sister! I've enough to do trying to find dry clothes for you all every day when you will play with every heap of snow you see.'

Apart from the extra work involved, she hated snow, and would have been glad never to see another white winter. But even she enjoyed the day when the village pond finally froze hard enough for skating and the villagers held an impromptu party. An old man with a fiddle provided music to skate to, and soon he was joined by other musicians – a flute and a fife, a mouth-organ and a home-made drum. Someone fetched out a bale of straw and spread it for them to stand on, and their shrill efforts carried eerily on the still, frozen air. The village inn, well placed and anticipating good trade, did its part by dispensing hot potatoes and sausages and cocoa for the children, while some enterprising traders set up with braziers to roast chestnuts. As it grew dark a bonfire was lit, and lanterns on poles illuminated the edges of the lake for the skaters. Henrietta had learnt to skate as a child at Morland Place, and won a great deal of credit with her children as, after a few wobbles, she glided away with reasonable grace while they were still threshing their arms and tumbling over. She enjoyed the occasion thoroughly; but the next day was as tired of the snow as ever, and longed for spring.

One frozen day, a letter came for Jerome from Julia's solicitor, saying that he had important information and requesting that Jerome visit him at his office in London.

'Damn these cautious lawyers,' Jerome said. 'Why can't they just put things in a letter? I don't want to go trapesing off to London.'

'It might be important,' Henrietta said.

'I don't see how it can be. Julia wasn't tremendously rich or anything of the sort. She only had the money her mother left her and my settlement. And in any case, whatever she has left me, the trustee will take it for the creditors, so as far as I'm concerned, it can wait. I'm far too busy here.'

Henrietta raised an eyebrow. 'Are you? I thought there wasn't much you could do in this weather. If you went to London, you could visit Lizzie. You haven't even seen the new baby yet.'

'Babies are all the same,' he said, 'but Lizzie, now – you've tempted me with Lizzie.'

'I thought I might.'

'I'd sooner go with you.'

'We can't both be away at the same time. It isn't fair on Emma. You go. You can take a letter from me. Oh, and bring back the fullest possible report on everybody's health and looks. Not the usual vagueness about "everyone was very well", mind, but something with detail to it.'

'Only a woman can do that sort of thing,' he protested.

'Then pretend you are a woman. It won't hurt you just for once.'

So he went, sending a letter to the solicitor proposing that he call the next morning. 'Then I can catch an afternoon train back.'

'Oh, dearest, stay tomorrow night at least. Spend a little time with your daughter.'

'You want to be rid of me,' he complained.

'As soon as you're gone,' she assured him, 'I'm going to tidy all your drawers so you can't find anything.'

Two days without Jerome were hard enough for Henrietta, though at least this time he was not visiting his former wife. But as it happened, he stayed away the whole week, sending her a wire that only said, 'Important business. Staying longer. Love.' She stared at it, wishing he were not always so frugal with telegrams, though she appreciated that he had used one of the five-word minimum to send his love. But he might have said when he was coming back. The house – her life – felt so empty without him.

Teddy rode over one day while he was away to see if they

181

were all right, and said, 'Pity you haven't got a telephone machine, then he could talk to you from London. I'm thinking of getting one put in, you know.'

'No! Teddy, how modern!'

'Used it at the club the other day. Spoke to Bayliss. Quite remarkable. Heard him as clearly as I hear you. Well,' he added, compelled by honesty, 'almost as clearly. He sounded as if he was talking from underneath a tin bath. Most peculiar! But I could understand every word.'

'But if you had one put in, who would you have to telephone to?'

'Ah, that's the problem, of course. But, then, someone has to be first, or everyone'd say the same thing and no-one would ever get one.'

'What logical thinking! How was the track up from the road?'

'Pretty bad. If we get any more snow you'll be cut off to wheeled traffic. If that happens you'd better all try and get in to York and stay with us until it thaws.'

'Oh, we have everything we need. We'll be all right here,' Henrietta said.

'Won't if you run out of coal and the coal wagon can't get through,' he said. 'Bear it in mind. I shall worry about you. Of course,' he added beguilingly, 'if you had a telephone machine, you could speak to me every day, and then I'd know you were all right. Should think about getting one.'

'They're for rich people,' Henrietta said. 'Like motor-cars.'

Jerome came back on Saturday afternoon, trudging up through the encroaching dark just as it began to snow again. Feathery flakes were hanging on his hat and eyebrows and powdering his shoulders. He banged the snow off his boots in the passage, and called Robbie to help him off with his coat. 'My hands are frozen, I can't feel the buttons.'

Everyone rallied round, and shortly he was sitting in a chair pulled up as close to the range as he could bear, boots off, dry socks on, with his hands wrapped around a cup of hot cocoa. 'Ah, this is better! This is home!' he said, looking round his family with bright eyes. 'How nice it is in here with all of you around me. I wonder everyone doesn't live in the kitchen. When I think of all those years I wasted being rich and sitting in elegant drawing-rooms, when down below my feet there was a perfectly good kitchen going begging.'

'Oh, Daddy, you do talk nonsense,' Jessie said. 'Tell about London. Did you see Cousin Venetia and Violet?'

'Tell about Lizzie first,' Henrietta countermanded.

He had plenty to tell them about Lizzie and Ashley and the babies (Mart and Rupert had colds but nothing serious); about his brief call at Manchester Square, just to pay his respects (Venetia was out, visiting a case, but he chatted for half an hour with Hazelmere – what a nice fellow he was! – and no, he didn't see Violet because it was evening and she'd gone to bed); about London (do you remember how nasty snow is in London, turned to horrible slush mixed with manure by the traffic, the poor horses slipping all the time? Oh, and he had seen five motor-cars, two of them broken down!); and about the journey and the weather in general. Then he relinquished to the children the package he had not previously mentioned but which they had been eyeing with seething curiosity, and dismissed them to the table to undo it and enjoy the contents.

Henrietta drew another chair up beside him. 'No present for me?'

'I have something for you that's better than a present, which I'm going to give you now we have a little privacy.'

She examined his face. 'It's good news,' she said.

'It is.'

'About the will?'

He nodded, took another sip of cocoa, and began. 'I told you that the lawyer-bird, Tuckwell, said Julia had left me everything. I guessed Edward and Sophy would try to challenge it, but apparently Julia had anticipated that. They went to see Tuckwell last month and he told them that not only had Julia put a clause in the will to confirm that she was passing them by, but had given him a covering letter as well, and since he could attest that she had been of sound mind when she made it – he being the man who wrote it all down and witnessed her signature – he told them it must stand

183

and that it would be a waste of their time and money to argue about it.'

'I feel rather sorry for them. They did give her a home,' Henrietta said.

'She paid for her keep, though – and in more than money. I gathered from Nana that they used her as an unofficial, unpaid governess. But all that's beside the point. If they gave her a home only in the hope of inheriting her fortune, they wouldn't be worth your pity, would they?'

Henrietta looked puzzled. 'I suppose not, but – oh dear, I can't work it out.'

'Never mind. I haven't got to the best part yet. Tuckwell had been gathering together all the assets and had a rough total for me. I know I told you I didn't think that there'd be much of her fortune left, but it turns out she lived so frugally that she never touched the capital. Not only that, her investments have been doing rather well lately. Leaving aside her personal chattels and the jewellery, he told me it comes to about thirty thousand pounds.'

Henrietta put her hand to her face. 'Good heavens! But that's an absolute fortune! You can't mean it?'

'Yes, I was startled too, I can tell you! Poor Julia, I wish it had given her more pleasure. I'd really sooner she had spent and enjoyed it than left it to me.'

'But you won't be allowed to keep it,' she remembered.

'That's why I stayed on, so that I could see Forster, the trustee, and tell him about it. Now, attend! This is the really interesting part. You understand that I could not be discharged from my bankruptcy because my assets were less than ten shillings in the pound of my debts?'

'Yes, and I always thought that was cruel, considering it was that wretched man Harwood who was responsible for most of it, not you.'

'But he was my partner,' Jerome said. 'Partners share profits and losses both. And it could be argued that I should have shown better judgement in choosing him. However, the point is that Forster took kindly to my coming forward with my inheritance. We discussed it a little, and he took the view that the thirty thousand pounds would take me over the half-way mark, if you left aside the debts that were due purely to Harwood's fraud, and he was prepared to suggest to the creditors that they should take the money and recommend the Court to discharge me. And that's what he did. That's what I've been about all this week. They had a meeting and were astoundingly decent about it, thought I'd suffered enough for Harwood's sake, and pressed the matter with all speed. So the court order has been made, and I am discharged.' Henrietta only stared at him. 'Don't you understand, my love? I am free and clear!'

'I understand,' she said. She gazed at him, seeing the lines, the weariness, the grey hairs this trouble had brought. To be free of it, she thought. Free of his debts! Free of the shame! After all these years, he could hold his head up again, he could be part of the world of men. And they were properly married, too, which was the end of her shame and anxiety. Everything was now all right: but all this good, the removal of the thorns that had marred their life together, had come about through the death of Julia. She wanted very much not to be glad about the death of Julia. She was afraid of what it might do to her soul.

Jerome was looking at her quizzically. 'You don't look happy. I thought you would cheer to the rafters. Let me guess – you're thinking of poor Julia and feeling badly that she had to die to set me free.'

'How do you always know what I'm thinking?'

'Because I love you. Try to be glad. I never wished Julia harm, and I know you didn't. But this is a wonderful thing for us, and if Julia meant anything by leaving me her fortune, it was surely that it should make me – us – happy.'

What about coals of fire? she thought. But she smiled, if rather shakily, and said, 'I am glad, of course I am. It's the most wonderful thing that could have happened, your being discharged.'

'I feel like a man again,' he confessed. 'And there's more: Forster said he wasn't interested in the other things, only the thirty thousand pounds. So Julia's jewellery is mine, and it's good stuff – as I should know, having bought half of it. We can sell it, and have money in the bank again. I don't know exactly how much it will realise, but it might be as much as a thousand pounds.'

'A thousand!' This was real; this was no abstract fortune, but a sum that could be grasped and appreciated.

'I can invest it, start up a business of some kind, actually begin to support my own wife and children again!' he said.

'A business?' The thought suddenly struck her: did that mean they would have to leave Morland Place? It was selfish of her, but she didn't want to. For all the inconvenience of life here compared with a modern house, she loved it. It satisfied some deep need in her, to be home where she belonged. 'What sort of business? Not stockbroking again?'

'You don't trust me,' he said, pretending to be wounded.

'Of course I do!'

'I'm teasing, foolish! Not stockbroking. Perhaps Teddy will let me come in with him as a partner, and stay here. How would the children cope with a normal-sized house, after this?'

'Oh, do be serious!'

'I am being. I like it here. But whatever happens,' he said, catching her hand and pressing it, 'we won't be beggars any more. What do you think of that, my lady?'

To stay here, and not be dependants? Could they be so blessed? She lifted his hand to her lips, and saw the answering warmth in his eyes. He looked so handsome in the fire-glow from the stove, his hair ruffled where the snow-melt had dried; and with the strain gone from his face – suddenly younger to her, and gay, the Jerome she had fallen in love with.

He understood that thought of hers, too. 'I love you so much,' he said, softly, so that the children shouldn't hear. 'I'm a lucky fellow.'

General Robert's plan was to move his force up the western railway to relieve Kimberley, then swing eastwards, to Bloemfontein and then on to Pretoria. Buller meanwhile was to hold the Boers at the present line on the Tugela until Roberts had secured Pretoria and could march on Ladysmith.

Things in Ladysmith were very bad, but White had signalled that they could hold out another month by eating the cavalry horses – though that would definitely end all hope of making a sortie to help any rescue attempt. But it was also possible that when the Boers under Joubert learnt of the large force advancing on Kimberley and Bloemfontein, they would redirect their own men to meet the danger and abandon the siege at Ladysmith. 'Bobs' had an extra 37,000 men now: three more infantry divisions and, perhaps more importantly, a lot more mounted infantry and cavalry. These would swell the numbers of General French's horsemen to 5000. A determined thrust now of the full force must surely break the Boers: they were only farmers, after all.

Buller, however, was not content simply to wait. He had been in regular contact by heliograph with White in Ladysmith and knew it was not just starvation that faced them but sickness too. Water was short and the Boers did all they could to contaminate the supply. Besides, having so many people penned up in close contact within the walls was creating an enormous sanitary problem. As they weakened with hunger, the enteric, cholera and other fevers would only take greater hold. To wait a month was to risk having no-one left to relieve. Buller signalled a request to Roberts to make another attempt to break through the Boer lines and Roberts, somewhat distractedly, agreed.

The plan this time was to break through at Vaalkrantz, a place where a loop of the winding river took it close to the mountains, and also where the mountains themselves were at their narrowest, so the pass was short. If a sufficient force could get through that gap and onto the flat plain beyond, there would be nothing to stop them reaching Ladysmith. To this end, artillery would be mounted on Mount Alice and Swartkop, the heights on the British side of the river, to give covering fire, while Wynne, who had taken over from the late General Woodgate, took a force across by the pontoon bridge at Potgeiter's Drift. This was upstream of Vaalkrantz, and a place where the river looped in the other direction, southwards, leaving plenty of ground between the river and the mountains for assembling a division and field artillery. It was hoped that the Boers would conclude from this that an attack was coming on the Brakfontein ridge, and move their men that way. Meanwhile Lyttleton was to cross further downstream at Munger's Drift, and while the Boers were kept occupied by Wynne's division, the hill at Vaalkrantz would be stormed. Once it was taken, artillery could be set up on its summit to cover the road through the pass to the plain. It was hoped that when the Boers saw Lyttleton's forces assembling at the lower pontoon they would assume that they were going to swing west and reinforce Wynne's attack and would therefore concentrate all their defences on Brakfontein.

By the night of the 4th of February, the preliminary work had been done, and the guns had been hauled laboriously up into position on Mount Alice and Swartkop. Wynne's was in position across the river with seven batteries of artillery, and Lyttleton's, Hart's and Hildyard's were in bivouac at the foot of Mount Alice. On Monday the 5th of February the attack began: at six o'clock Wynne's began to advance towards Brakfontein under cover of bursting shells. Meanwhile the other three divisions filed out of bivouac to Munger's Drift. When they were across, the guns on Swartkop opened a bombardment on Vaalkrantz. Advancing under heavy fire from all sides, Lyttleton's reached Vaalkrantz in the early afternoon and stormed it with bayonet, swept up the slope and took the southern peak of the hill with the loss of about 150 men. Many of the Boer defenders were killed, wounded or captured, but one of their officers managed to get the pom-pom safely away, with which the Boers had caused such damage to the attackers.

Originally, Hart's brigade had been ordered to take Green Hill, the peak opposite Vaalkrantz on the other side of the road; but intelligence suggested that there were no Boers that far east, Vaalkrantz being the extreme end of their line, and they were called back before the attempt was made.

By four o'clock in the afternoon, the southern end of Vaalkrantz was secured; but there were problems. It was seen that the peak was divided only by a deep saddle from two others, hidden from the other side of the river, both of which were invested with Boer heavy artillery, and which commanded the narrow defile through which the road ran. It also turned out that there was after all Boer artillery on Green Hill, so they could attack the road from both sides. Moreover, the original plan had been to bring artillery up onto Vaalkrantz but it was now seen that it would not be possible to bring heavy guns up as the sides were far too steep.

The infantry made themselves shelters and dug in as best they could, answering Boer artillery with rifle fire. At five o'clock on the morning of the 6th, battle was resumed with heavy bursts of artillery fire. Lyttleton confirmed that it was impossible to mount guns on Vaalkrantz, so it was essential now to attack the two Boer positions, shelling them to knock out the big guns before the infantry could take them. All day the action continued, while Wynne's kept the Boers on Brakfontein busy, but there was no luck in silencing the Boer big guns. During the night Hart's and Hildyard's relieved Lyttleton's on the peak.

On the morning of the 7th, action was resumed again, the Boers concentrating their fire on Vaalkrantz. The infantry there could do little to reply, but they had sufficient cover and there were few injuries; the infantry down on the ground were not so lucky, coming under artillery and rifle fire.

At four o'clock General Buller called a meeting of his generals and asked to hear suggestions, but the situation seemed hopeless. With the road through the defile overlooked from every direction by Boer artillery, and a report of 16,000 Boer infantry waiting on the plain at the other end, to persist would be a useless waste of life. Buller gave the order for withdrawal, and when night fell and the bombardment ceased, the troops on Vaalkrantz quietly descended and the rest of the forces returned to the pontoons and retired across the river to safety.

7th February 1900
Dear Aunt,
Just a scrawl from the actual battlefield. This is the third day of this engagement, and I hope it will come out all right, but it has been pretty hot work. The first

day was a success and our fellows took the position we wanted on Vaalkrantz. On the second they got on a little and inflicted heavy losses, I believe, on Johnny Boer and today we hope to finish him off, but time is rather on his side as he seems to be very clever at moving his guns about at night. Last night we relieved the garrison on the peak – quite an exciting climb in the dark, creeping quietly and expecting any moment to be opened fire on. But we made it without waking the enemy. So here I am now in the shelter of a sangar with nothing much to do but hang on. The fire is very heavy from all sides but we are all right as long as we stay put. Now and then we pink away at them, just to let them know we are still awake! But we have no artillery up here so depend upon our long guns from across the river to knock them out. It is dreadfully hot up here. There is water and food but it means leaving the sangar to get it. Also ammunition. We take turns, but little Brown was caught in the leg by shrapnel on his run. They have made him as comfortable as possible, but there's dashed little shade up here. No getting him down until dark – those devils will not let up even for a moment.

8th February
Well, it is all over, and we have withdrawn again. Came down in the night with no casualties. Main force is already on the march back to Chievely. Ours has been detailed to help clear the camp at Spearman's Farm of stores and ammunition, after which we follow to Chievely. It is very disheartening to have failed again. Capt. Jocelyn says the problem is that the Boer up on the hills can see everything we do down below, anticipate us and move into position to oppose us almost before we have stood up. Also can get himself into impregnable positions to fire on us, whereas we only know what is up and behind the mountains when we get there. I think another difficulty is that our chain of command is so long. Spoke a little to a Boer prisoner,

190

and it seems that with them, they work in small independent units, so the general tells the unit commander, he tells his men, and off they go. Whereas with us Buller tells the staff, the staff pass it on to the generals, they tell the colonels, the colonels tell the majors and so on until at last someone moves – by which time the Boer has moved himself and his guns and is ready for us. Capt. Jocelyn says that Gen. Buller knows this, but he is dealing with the whole army protocol, and with senior officers who like things the way they are and won't stand for any change. I dare say those back home will blame Buller for another failure and say he ought to have pegged on yesterday, but it would have been a senseless waste of life, as we who are here on the spot know very well. He is a good officer and a good fellow, and all of us Tommies think the world of him. He has a way of talking to you that makes you feel he knows you personally. He is always careful of our welfare and feels any losses deeply so he will not send us to a 'glorious death' when we are outnumbered with no hope of success. The regular soldiers say that is not the way with some generals, who look on losses as if they were so many toy soldiers, knocked over in a sort of game they must win at all costs. I don't know what will happen next. Those poor fellows in Ladysmith are at the end of their tether. But however our 'good old' Gen. will not give up and there will be another attempt soon. Meanwhile back to camp for a rest and clean-up. I value your letters more than I can say – more even than the soap I hope you will send me by your next! Also writing-paper and any little thing like that will be most welcome.

Your loving nephew,
Bertie

Bertie was right that Buller would be blamed back home. The advances in telegraphy meant that news was written up on the spot every evening to appear in the newspapers in England the next morning, while advances in general literacy meant that more people than ever were hungry for news of the war. Next to a good victory, a good defeat is the best thing for selling newspapers, and in the latter case there has to be someone at whom to throw the brickbats. The papers derided Buller's failed efforts, called him 'Sir Reverse', and 'The Ferryman of Tugela' because he had crossed the river so many times. Everything looked clear and simple to the newspapermen, safe at home, with their small maps. It was impossible to understand how the cream of the British army could be thwarted by a handful of farmers with old-fashioned ideas, however modern their weapons might be. Thank God for Bobs and Kitchener, they said. Now things would start to move, they said. What was wanted was a man of decision, not someone who dithered and then pulled back as soon as the work grew hot.

Events seemed to prove the armchair experts right. Roberts moved north, heading for Kimberley, where the Boer general Cronje was lying in wait for him at nearby Magersfontein, scene of the earlier disastrous attempt by Methuen to relieve the diamond town. Cronje appeared to believe that the British would never stray far from the railway line, for he was completely taken by surprise when French's cavalry made a wide loop to the east and suddenly appeared on his flank followed by artillery and infantry. After a short, sharp engagement the Boers began to melt away. A spectacular cavalry charge broke them, though with an appallingly heavy loss of men and horses, and on the 15th of February Kimberley was relieved.

At almost the same time, disaster struck the wagon train of British supplies, which was bogged down on the river Modder in the rear. One of the changes Roberts had made on arrival in the Cape was to alter the system by which each battalion was responsible for its own supplies, and concentrate all provisions into one wagon train. The result was a long, slow and unwieldy column of ox-carts, which also proved vulnerable.

After the effort of crossing the river, the oxen were being rested and grazed, but insufficient arrangements had been made to guard them. A Boer commando made a surprise attack, scattered the oxen and the native drivers and made off with half the wagons. Roberts, short of cavalry and anxious to push on, ordered no attempt to recover them, saying the men could manage on half-rations. Cronje's force was retreating from Kimberley towards Bloemfontein, and he was anxious to intercept them before they got there.

The Boer column did not move quickly: they were travelling with their wagons and cattle, and some of the men had their wives and children, too, and all their household goods on ox-carts. Kitchener caught up with them on the riverbank at Paardeberg on the 18th of February. A battle was fought with heavy casualties, but the Boers were not defeated. On the following day, Roberts arrived in time to receive a request from Cronje for a truce to bury the dead. Roberts refused, suspecting a trick, and Cronje replied, 'If you are so uncharitable, you may do as you please. I shall not surrender alive, so bombard me as you please.'

Roberts took him at his word. The bombardment went on for days. Cronje had a good defensive position on the river, encompassing an island in the centre, with the wagons drawn into a laager, and trenches dug into the bank; but as the British gradually surrounded him, his position seemed to be a hopeless one. Nevertheless, the Boers would not surrender, and fired back ceaselessly, inflicting plenty of damage. Roberts's troops were on short rations, and the water situation was critical: the dead from the Boer laager, horse and cattle carcases, offal and rubbish, all went into the river, which was the only water supply for the British. Large numbers of British soldiers began to go down sick. But the fighting went on, and at daybreak on the 27th of February Cronje submitted, and surrendered unconditionally, and 4000 Boers were taken prisoner. British losses had been around 1300.

The newspapers back home greeted the news with huge rejoicing. By chance, the 27th of February was the anniversary of the battle of Majuba Hill, when the Boers had beaten the British nineteen years earlier, and the popular papers made full use of the fact. An old grievance was 'wiped off the slate' as they triumphantly proclaimed.

The *Daily Mail* had begun publishing a series of maps of the campaign, with flags to move around for the various forces, and Teddy bought a copy for the family at Morland Place, thinking the boys would enjoy it. It was Jessie, however, who took it over, and proved the most interested. Most evenings Jerome would sit with her at the table and go over events. She was eager for anything that might involve Bertie, but in the absence of any news from the Tugela, 'Bobs and K' would do.

In the middle of the month she caught a cold so bad that Henrietta decreed she must not go to school, and she spent her unexpected leisure poring over the paper maps so much that she reduced them to indecipherable fur. To keep her amused, therefore, through the miserable stage of her cold, Jerome helped her create a larger version of the whole South African field, painted on a square of wood. The boys grew interested in the construction, and it developed elaborations. They made mountains with papier-maché, cardboard houses to represent towns, and small model soldiers, pinched out of clay and painted, represented the various armies.

It proved a godsend in keeping the children occupied, and every spare minute was spent poring over the old atlas, wielding the paint-box, breathing heavily over newspaper reports, and arguing fiercely over the positions of railways, towns and rivers, numbers of horse and colours of uniforms. The boys and Jerome between them brought down a table from the schoolroom into the kitchen so that it could be set up and worked on without needing to be put away each day.

'Jessie's war', as it came to be known, became such a central part of their lives that even Emma would wonder over it and ask questions as she dried the dishes. Teddy proved his worth as an uncle by presenting some tiny lead soldiers to replace the clay ones, which tended to disintegrate when handled too much. Teddy was almost as fascinated as the children by the project; and Jack, home from school for the week-end, told Jessie it was a famous thing and that he meant to do one at school with some of the fellows. Jessie bloomed through her cold at the praise. Next to Bertie, she loved Jack best in the world.

Matters were desperate in Ladysmith, with White ordering the last of the cavalry horses which had been held back to be eaten. Sickness was rife and an epidemic of typhoid had struck. Buller was determined to break through, but after the failures at Spion Kop and Vaalkrantz, it was clear a new strategy was needed. He undertook a closer study of the area to the north-east of Colenso. Downstream of the village, because of the way the Tugela meandered, the Boer line was on the British side of the river, on a series of hills. Buller had too few cavalry, but had recently received new artillery, which at last gave him an advantage over the Boers. He determined now to move carefully and methodically, using the artillery to drive the Boers out position by position, concentrating on specific targets rather than laying down a general bombardment. Then as each position was abandoned the infantry could move up and the artillery go through to the next position. Once the Boers were all driven over the river, the successive hills on the other side, overlooking the line of the railway, could be attacked until the whole gorge was held and the way was clear to the plain and Ladysmith.

13th February 1900
Dearest Aunt Hen,
You will be glad to know that your boy has been promoted! We got back into camp at Chievely on the 11th and Gen. Buller actually sent for me, having learnt somehow I was not Of The People. I think Jocelyn must have told his friend on the staff. He's a capital fellow. Anyway, the Gen. asked could I ride. Born on a horse, I answered, so he asked if I would like to change my two legs for four and lead a scouting party to reconnoitre the ground. Warned me it could be hazardous work, but 'Anything is better than marching,' said I, and accepted with good grace! Have been out twice now. Have been 'sniped' at and once or twice came near to 'catching it', but so far have not been

wounded. I have a native guide attached to my party we call Wellington, his own name being unpronounceable to our unready tongues: he is tall and straight and very black, but as haughty as his namesake! I told him all about the Iron Duke and he seemed to take it as a compliment, though a well-deserved one. I also have an interpreter, Onderman, who goes between us. It's hard to say which of them despises the other more! Wellington knows the place like the palm of his own hand and generally guides us right – when the interpreter don't misunderstand!

We had some reinforcements arrive yesterday and guess who was amongst 'em? None other than young Puddephat, very glad to see a friendly face. We had a good yarn. He is in good shape, sends all suitable regards, and is enjoying himself greatly. He seems a nice lad and I hope very much for his mother and sisters he does not get 'bowled over' when we go into action again, which I guess will be in a few days' time. I have Jessie's letter and drawing, much pleased with them, and as you suggest will write her a letter of her own, so will close this now, paper being in short supply.

Your nephew,
Bertie

13th February at Chievely
My dear Cousin Jessie,
Your letter was very welcome. How well you write now! So this is a reply all for you, you need not show it to anyone if you don't like. You ask what it is like here. Well, you would not enjoy it. The skies are grey all the time, and when the clouds break there is such rain and hail as you can't imagine! At night it gets very cold, and hard to get clothes dry. The grub is very dull, too, dry biscuit and bully beef mostly, though sometimes we find a few vegetables, and add them to make a kind of stew with the bully, and crumble the biscuit in. But how I long for fruit! I dare not think of strawberries but rise about as far as a good English apple in my dreams! You

ask what Gen. Buller is like, well, he is a great big man, very broad in the chest, with a sort of square head and a kind face. He looks as if nothing could shake him. Just the sight of him makes one feel safe and comfortable somehow. I have a horse now, the nicest little mare called Dolly, nothing to look at but kind and clever, and knows her job so well. If she could talk we could send her out on her own! You want to know what the Boers are like. I have met quite a few now, some prisoners and some deserters. They are tough fellows, and ride tough little horses that can go all day over any country. They are brown as nuts and have long beards (the men, not the horses!). Some of the older ones have beards down to their waist, and they wear them tucked into their belts to be out of the way. They call us Rednecks because we get sunburnt on the backs of our necks and they think us very foolish fellows to be here at all. They carry everything on their horse with them, rifle, ammunition, water, blanket roll, even a Bible, for they are very religious and think God is on their side. They like to strike quickly and get away, and everyone says they will not stand and fight if it comes to it, but I can't say if that's true for when the fighting is on we never see them, only the flash of their fire from cover. I liked your picture of Morland Place enormously, and show it to everyone. My friend Naseby says it is remarkable and promises to draw Colenso for me to send to you. He is very good with the pencil. Must close now as duty calls.

With love from,
Bertie

Buller's new attack began on the 16th, taking Hussar Hill. On the 17th Cingolo and on the 18th Monte Cristo were taken, and on the 19th Hlangwani fell and the Boers were pushed back over the river. Colenso was now in British hands. A bridge was built across the river under the slopes of the Hlangwani, and on the 21st Lyttleton's brigade crossed and took the two hills on the other side, which they called Wynne's Hill and Horseshoe Hill.

Bertie wrote a long letter about the action, adding to it each evening.

21st February. I watched the action from the top of the hill. Buller himself was sitting on a rock nearby watching through a telescope and giving orders to the signaller by him. About 800 feet up, could see everything – Colenso down below like a toy, the river winding about, the ruins of the railway bridge. The hills on the other side topped with green trees and thick bushes, and every now and then a puff of white smoke and a roar as a Long Tom lobbed a shell at us, or into the troops down below on the riverbank. Could see all the way to Ladysmith, shimmery grey-white walls in the distance, and the mountain Umbulwana which lowers over it, looking very grim in the silvery light, topped with puffs of smoke where they were firing down on Ladysmith. Was sent down to the pontoon about 5 p.m. The fellows all in good humour as they crossed to get into the fighting. Firing eased at dusk and stopped about 9 p.m. In the dark could see little pinprick lights of the fires of our men holding the places they won during the day.

22nd Feb. Gunfire began at dawn. Wynne moving on to Hart's Hill, v. fierce fighting. Was up and down the riverbank with messages all day – hot work! Our guns throwing shells at the Boer positions, they dropping them on us. Once Dolly put her foot in a hole and stumbled, tipping me off, just in time to miss a piece of shrapnel fit to have taken my head off! How I blessed her and the pothole, once I found she was all right! From up on the height, watched our men, thin lines of khaki, going over the top of a hill to disappear behind it, while a line of Boers went scrambling up the hill beyond it, only to be driven on again. Smoke drifts about like clumps of wool, holding shape a surprisingly long time. At nightfall a downpour which left us all soaked to the skin. Wish my hair were like Dolly's mane

– rain just runs off it, so she looks as cosy as a thatched cottage under her forelock.

23rd Feb. Sent up to observe with the Irish brigade (Enniskillens and Dub. Fusiliers) to take the next hill, we call it Railway Hill. Set off at five, no time for breakfast, leaving Dolly behind, so back on my own two feet! Going up the road the Boers had our range, and shells were dropping on us, scattering us with dust and shrapnel, but did little harm, miraculous to say! Halted and took cover while our artillery shelled the hill. Got into a shell hole with a sergeant of the Skins, who brewed up some tea, very welcome, and when he heard I'd had no breakfast, found me some biscuit, good fellow, and some of the queer dried meat the Boers carry. Gave him cigarettes in return. Ordered to attack 12.30, advanced under terrible sniping. Parts of the track very wet from the rain. Passed six dead Skins in the mud at one place, sunk in by their own weight, white faces staring up as the bullets whistled overhead – awful! Up a small hill, found two Boer wagons loaded with provisions abandoned, the horses dead. Split into three columns to attack the hill, awful fire, had to lie down for a while. Charge and stop until reinforcements came up, then charge again, dreadful losses. Darkness brought some relief but the Boers still fired on anything that moved so no chance to get the wounded down, nor could get down myself to report. All dreadfully thirsty, water long used up.

24th. Threw up some sangars before dawn, to enable us to hold on. Boers came out of their trenches and advanced on us from several sides. Bullets flying in every direction. About nine o'clock ordered to retire. No officers left on my part of the hill so found myself in charge of a dozen men. Got down in a scramble to the railway line where the Dub Light Inf. had come up to cover the retreat. No water all night, got down to river and drank and bathed face. Rifle Brigade came up also and

199

position held, but many wounded Irish still on the hill. Could see men like khaki stripes clinging to the hillside. Raining all day, miserable. Took all day to get back down the line to report. Buller v. anxious about wounded, means to arrange truce for tomorrow (Sunday) for both sides to bring in wounded and bury dead.

25th February. 6-hour truce this morning. Went up to help bring down the Irish from the summit. Boers came out from their trenches and were very curious about us, chatted and were very grateful for cigarettes. Queer to be talking in a civilised manner to people who were trying to kill you only yesterday. Have Dolly again today, v. glad of her, worn out going up and down the railway. Back at Colenso before cease-fire ended and bombardment resumed. About 8 p.m. Boers stop firing and in the silence hear them singing hymns, which reminds us it is Sunday. They have some women with them, can distinguish their voices very clearly.

On the 26th a new place was found on the Tugela where a crossing could be made downstream from Railway Hill. Now larger numbers could be brought up to attack the hills on either side of the railway line where it curved north away from the river towards Ladysmith. By the afternoon of the 27th both had been taken, and the Boers were driven off the last peaks overlooking the route.

28th Feb. Ash Wednesday. Strangely quiet this morning without artillery fire. Sent off with cavalry to see where the Boers have gone. Crossed Pieters Plain, with several hills on the left – my native scout Wellington said there are seven. Got to a height overlooking the valley with Umbulwana on the other side. Laagers in the valley, about 100 Boers marching out, fired on them and they scattered. Were fired on from Umbulwana for a time before they abandoned it. Scouted forward towards Ladysmith and reported all clear. Then Col. of the Imp. Light Horse told me to come with him and the Natal

Carbineers and gallop into Ladysmith. Very proud to be in the first force to reach the town, as the Col. knew I would be – was doing me a favour, good fellow! Dolly went like a cavalry charger, kept up all the way! Mad gallop through Intombi neutral camp where the hospital is and into Ladysmith about 6 p.m. Very clean and white, no sign of bombardment, but troops and civilians very thin and weak – expected them bad, but worse than imagined, some like shadows. Terrible smell everywhere. Everyone cheering madly, though, delighted to see us. Dolly pranced along as if she thought all the cheering was for her!

The townspeople were able to report that all that morning there had been a great exodus of Boers from the plain, thousands of wagons trekking north-west. They had certainly gone, and the siege of 100 days was over. Buller entered with troops on the 1st of March and lunched with General White, and was reluctantly persuaded to make a second grand entrance two days later especially for the news cameras. On that day the garrison lined the streets in their best uniforms – uniforms generally in much better condition than those of their rescuers – but many were too weak to stand, and most of the civilians who turned out had to sit on the kerb to wave the troops past. They had expended their joyful energy on the 28th, and were mostly silent. In the event the reporters had to use their imaginations to create for their papers the ecstatic welcome the newly relieved were too worn out to supply.

The news of the relief of Ladysmith was greeted in England with huge joy. All over the land church bells were rung, and people came out onto the streets to tell one another the news, to cheer and even hug one another. The Queen received thousands of telegrams from loyal, rejoicing subjects, and that evening the public houses of the land were filled to overflowing, and red-faced patriots swung their beer-mugs, unusually, to 'God Save the Queen' and 'Rule Britannia' – as well as the ubiquitous 'Soldiers of the Queen' and the new music-hall favourite, 'Goodbye Dolly Grey'.

Teddy rushed over to Morland Place with the news, bringing Charley and two bottles of champagne for an immediate toast to the victory. He brought also copies of all the newspapers he could lay hands on, and 'Jessie's war' was dragged forward so they could all get round it and move the little soldiers and flags about. Jessie asked a great many questions on exactly where Bertie was at every moment, which no-one could answer, not having received his letter at that point. Rather than disappoint her, Teddy made things up, assuming that she would forget what he said as soon as he'd gone. He underestimated the grasp her interest in the matter had given her, and many a visit after the letter arrived found him having to explain to the solemn young woman the discrepancy between his account and Bertie's.

Two days later Teddy gave a grand celebration Ladysmith Dinner – one of many that took place in houses, clubs, town halls and hotels up and down the country. Jerome and Henrietta were invited, and when Henrietta learnt that this would not just be a family occasion, she felt rather daunted. She and Jerome had not dined in company since they had come back to Yorkshire.

'But both the reasons for that seclusion have been removed,' Jerome said to her. 'We are married and I have been discharged. No-one can look down their noses at us now.'

'Perhaps they *can't*, but I'm sure they *will*,' she said.

'Oh, stuff! If they do, who cares for them? But I'm sure Teddy won't have invited anyone who is likely to snub us. And after all, darling, what is the point in having our impediments removed if we go on behaving as if they haven't been? Don't think of us, think of the children. We must start going into society again if they are to have friends later. Think of Jessie. Who is she to dance and play tennis with and marry if we shut ourselves away like recluses?'

'You're right, of course,' Henrietta said. 'I'm being selfish. But I haven't got anything to wear.'

'Now we come to the real reason,' Jerome said, with a teasing smile. 'You must buy something, obviously. We can afford a new gown for you now.'

'There isn't time.'

'Buy something ready-made.'

'It won't fit, and there won't be time for the alterations.'

'Darling,' he said, stepping close, 'you look exactly like a frightened fieldmouse. We must take the plunge some time, and this is a good way to dip a toe into the water. It will be all right, I promise you. You always used to enjoy company. You will again.'

Teddy also invited Perry and Regina, scrupulously mentioning that the Comptons were coming. They refused, though giving as excuse Regina's indifferent health which she needed to nurse in advance of Edith's wedding. Teddy did not know whether they were really refusing to meet the Comptons; but Jerome had no doubt.

'Perry's the most stiff-necked devil in existence,' he said privately to Teddy, when they all gathered in the drawing-room at Makepeace House. 'And when I think I practically taught that boy how to shoot!'

The party was a great success, and if some of the other guests were a little stiff at first, Jerome whispered very firmly to Henrietta that it was merely shyness. He proceeded to be his most witty and amusing self, warming up the company and showing them that if they had ever snubbed the Comptons the loss had been all theirs. By the end of the main course Henrietta had relaxed a great deal, and when Mrs Bayliss leant across to say, 'What a very pretty gown! You must let me know where you got it,' she was able to believe it was a genuine compliment and not a sidelong sneer.

She had bought it from Makepeace's ready-made department, and Teddy had warned the tailoress that she must make any essential alterations on the spot, no matter what other work she had in hand. Fortunately it had fitted tolerably well, and it had only been a matter of taking the hem up at the front and the waist in a little. Henrietta was thrilled with it. Fashion had moved on since she had last had a new gown, and 'leg-of-mutton' sleeves had gone out. Sleeves now fitted all the way down, any decoration being on the lower arm and cuff. The high neckline ending right up under the chin was *de rigueur*, bodices carried all the decoration, and

203

the fullness of the back was created by deep gores rather than a bustle. Henrietta's gown was of a dusty blue taffeta, a colour that suited her, the bodice overlaid with coarse cream lace which, like a cape, fitted from the chin down the neck and over the shoulders and fell in a graceful point front and back almost to the waist. The skirt was straight at the front, and the demi-train was finished with several self-coloured tiers of frills.

The new hairstyle suited her too. These days, ladies drew up their hair from all round the head and fastened it into a knob on top; the style depended on fullness for effect, and as Henrietta's hair was very thick it piled up quite gratifyingly. After so long without anything new or pretty, Henrietta felt like a queen, an effect enhanced by the admiring looks Jerome gave her down the table. It was a fine party, and resulted in an invitation from the Baylisses to the Comptons to dine the following week.

'You see,' said Jerome, on the way home in Teddy's carriage, 'that's how the thing is done. One invitation leads to another. We'll soon be back in the thick of things.'

'You had better hope not,' Henrietta said, smiling, feeling very much happier about everything. 'One dress won't go very far.'

Little occupied the newspapers for the next few days but Ladysmith, and those papers which had dedicated themselves to criticising General Buller were rather put out that he had won through at last. They managed to solve the problem of being joyful without praising him, by concentrating on the dreadful hardships that had been endured by the besieged in Ladysmith, and the pitiful condition of White's troops when they were rescued; and by applauding General White's courage and determination in not surrendering, while conveniently forgetting that it was his misjudgement that had caused the situation in the first place.

On Thursday the 8th of March the Queen travelled from Windsor to London, where both Houses of Parliament gathered in the courtyard of Buckingham Palace to give her three hearty cheers. Afterwards she drove through the streets: down to the Embankment, along to Farringdon

204

Street, and through Holborn, Oxford Street and the Park and back to the palace. Crowds lined every inch of the way and the cheering was rapturous. Olivia was pleased to be asked to attend the Queen on the drive, and sent a note to Venetia, who took Violet and found a good place from which to watch and see her aunt drive past in glory. That evening Olivia and Charlie dined at Manchester Square, the first time they had been able to do so in over a year. Olivia told her sister that she and Charlie would be going with the Queen to Ireland for the month of April.

'I'm so excited. I've never been to Ireland before. I don't think I've ever even met anyone who has.'

The Queen had decided against her usual visit to the South of France that year because the French papers had been very hostile towards Britain over the South African war, and had said what she regarded as unforgivable things. She had also been deeply moved by the dreadful losses of the Irish regiments during the action before the relief of Ladysmith, and wanted to show appreciation of the Irish contribution to the war. So she had given up her holiday and was to spend the time in Ireland instead.

'I know some people are saying it was the Government pressed it on her,' Olivia said, 'but it was completely her own idea. I know because I was there when she thought of it.'

'I hope you'll have a kind reception,' Venetia said, a little doubtfully, for there seemed to be nothing but trouble to be expected from that tortured island.

But Olivia had no doubts. 'Of course we will. One only has to see the Queen to love her. And they'll be so pleased by the honour. We'll be going on the royal yacht to Kingstown, and then staying with the Cadogans at the viceregal lodge. I do hope the crossing will be smooth. I've heard St George's Channel can be very rough.'

'The Cadogans will make you comfortable,' Hazelmere said. 'They are great hosts.'

War news continued to be good. After a short, sharp engagement with the Boers at Dreifontein on the 11th of March, General Roberts marched into Bloemfontein, the Free State capital, on the 13th, unopposed. He had a surprisingly warm welcome from the civic authorities, who turned out in their best suits and white top hats ceremoniously to hand over the keys, while the populace lined the streets cheering. Everywhere Union Jacks were being flown, people wore red, white and blue favours, and as the troops marched past people sang 'God Save the Queen'. A celebratory luncheon followed at the English Club, and in the evening a grand dinner was held, complete with congratulatory speeches and music from the band of the Highland Brigade. For several days afterwards every appearance of Lord Roberts or any of his troops was greeted by loud demonstrations of enthusiasm.

'Though no doubt,' said Hazelmere to Venetia, 'they were cheering the Boers in exactly the same way two days earlier.'

Venetia heard from Lansdowne that Roberts had reported the condition of his troops as very poor, weak from poor rations and the extremes of weather, their clothes and boots in tatters. They were looking forward to rest and recreation in Bloemfontein; but they brought typhoid into the town with them, and within days the water supply was contaminated and the disease had spread through the army and into the civilian population. The typhoid should have come as no surprise, for since Paardeberg the soldiers had been drinking water from the Modder river, which was contaminated with dead men, horses, offal and faeces.

As a consequence of the earlier loss of the wagon train, medical supplies and staff had been cut to a minimum. A colleague of Venetia had correspondence with a doctor, Vance Phillips, in Bloemfontein. He told her that Phillips said every available building had been turned into a hospital, but that did not solve the problem of the shortage of staff and the entire lack of equipment and medicines. Appeals to Kitchener had been turned down: 'You want pills and I want bullets, and bullets come first.' The exhausted men had no resistance to sickness, and fourteen or fifteen were dying every day.

'And Cocky says Roberts has no opinion of his Surgeon General, Wilson,' Venetia told her husband. 'Says he's a poor creature with no idea of what's required. Also Wilson doesn't like the idea of lady nurses – one of the old school of army surgeons, I deduce. I will say for Roberts, he's not slow in that respect – he asked Cocky to send out forty or fifty.'

'You can't expect any army man to welcome civilians onto his territory,' Hazelmere said.

'Quite so,' Venetia agreed. 'They see too much of what's going on, and, not being under discipline, report it back to the outside world.'

'Lansdowne must be worried about the sort of scandals that were exposed during the Crimean War,' Hazelmere said, 'when thousands more soldiers were killed by disease than by the Russians.'

'In that case, it's a pity he didn't listen to Sir Walter Foster last year.'

'Foster?'

'I thought I'd mentioned it to you. He's an expert in the control of epidemics, as well as being a fine physician. He offered right at the beginning of the war to set up a sanitary commission to go out with the army. But all Cocky said was that sanitary care was one of an army doctor's most basic daily duties, so they must have plenty of experience and wouldn't need outside help.'

'I dare say nothing could have been done to stop the soldiers drinking contaminated water,' Hazelmere said reasonably. 'It's all very well telling them they must boil it first, but you can't watch every man every minute, and if they're desperately thirsty they don't want to wait. But in any case, you would expect Lansdowne to see things from the soldier's point of view rather than from the doctor's.'

'It's time someone saw things from the soldier's point of view,' Venetia grumbled.

'A war is not an exercise in philanthropy or socialism. A war is for winning. Military matters must come first.'

'Ah, but I have you there,' Venetia said. 'You can't win a war if half your soldiers are sick with dysentery and cholera and typhoid, can you? The soldier's welfare is essential to his being able to fight.'

Hazelmere laughed. 'All right, I won't argue with you. You should go and tell Cocky Lansdowne all this, not waste it on me.'

207

'I did. And I shall again,' said Venetia. 'But I wish I thought it would make any difference.'

For six weeks General Roberts remained in Bloemfontein, taking stock and consolidating his position. The march to Pretoria, the Transvaal capital, was 480 miles, and fresh supplies were needed before it could be attempted. First the railway to the south had to be put back in action, and then trainloads of boots, uniforms, ammunition, guns, horses and mules had to be brought up from the Cape.

One particular report from Lord Roberts was passed from the War Office to General Brackenbury, and thence a copy reached Mr Puddephat, who showed it to Jerome when he visited Morland Place later in March on one of his trips around the country. The report was dated the 9th of March and had been written at Poplar Grove, a place between Paardeberg and Bloemfontein.

I am anxious to bring to your attention the urgent necessity for a constant supply of horses being sent to South Africa. Owing to absence of forage and hard work a good many have been lost during the past month. 558 were lost during the relief of Kimberley, and on the 7th inst 165 were lost and 116 others were reported unfit for work. The artillery and Household Cavalry consider that English horses suit them best, but the rest of the cavalry would take any good stamp of small horse. Large numbers of smaller horses or even Burma ponies are required for the Mounted Infantry. The success of the campaign depends so materially on the mounted troops being efficient that I trust there will be no lack of good serviceable horses.

'You see how it is,' Puddephat said. 'Morland had the right idea with that Arabian stallion. There will be no difficulty about size at all. Smaller, hardy horses are exactly what's needed.'

'Yes, I see. It's only a pity, as we said before, that they won't be ready sooner,' Jerome said. 'But have you time to

208

come and see the yearlings? They're a promising bunch. This year's foals are the first by the Arabian, and I'd like you to see them, too, if you're not in a hurry. They're up at the Bachelor Hill paddock.'

'I'm in no hurry. I'd like to see everything.'

'Good. We'll be cutting the yearlings in a few weeks' time, and then they'll be ready to break in. They'll be ready for you in the spring of 1902 – too late for the war, I'm afraid.'

'Yes, it does look as though it's all over except for the clearing up. Still, the army will always need horses – and I have a few other ideas as well that I'd like to share with you.'

'We can talk as we ride,' said Jerome.

Lord Roberts certainly thought the war was almost over. On taking Bloemfontein he had issued a proclamation offering amnesty to every Free Stater, except the leaders, who laid down his arms and signed an oath of allegiance, and he wrote to the Queen that men were daily laying down their arms and returning to their usual occupations. 'It seems unlikely that this state will give much more trouble. The Transvaalers will probably hold out, but their numbers must be greatly reduced, and I trust it will not be very long before the war will have been brought to a satisfactory conclusion.'

On the 3rd of May Roberts left Bloemfontein for the long march to Pretoria, and on the same day ordered Mahon north from Kimberley to the relief of Mafeking. The small town was 250 miles north of Kimberley, on the railway and of strategic importance, close to the point where the borders of Cape Colony, Bechuanaland, Transvaal and Rhodesia met. Colonel Baden-Powell was in command, and for some reason this siege had captured the imagination of the newspapers back home and their readers, even more than that of Ladysmith. Stories were regularly printed of the British pluck and resourcefulness shown by the besieged, their stoicism and their humour in the face of adversity. Baden-Powell, who had shown inventiveness and skill in managing the problems of the siege, was a national hero. Much was made of the occasion when Kruger's grandson, who was with the besieging force, sent a facetious message to him inviting his garrison to take part in a cricket match.

Baden-Powell replied, 'I should like nothing better – after the match in which we are at present engaged is over. But just now we are having our innings and have so far scored 200 days not out against the bowling of Cronje, Snyman, Botha, etc., and we are having a very enjoyable game.'

When the relieving force, accompanied by a food convoy, came in sight of the town on the 19th of May, every roof was lined with people trying to see them. Mahon signalled, 'How are you getting on?' and Baden-Powell helio'ed back, with true British understatement, 'Welcome.' The Boers melted away and the siege was lifted without further resistance.

The news was greeted in Britain with a sort of frenzy. Newspapers were full of stories of how staid citizens, whose previous decorum had been beyond reproach, had come out of their houses to join the throngs parading the streets, shouting patriotic songs with the full force of their lungs, dancing, jumping, waving flags, screaming in a delirium of joy. Public houses were full not just that night, but night after night. In Windsor the Eton boys staged a welcome to the returning Queen that almost amounted to a riot. In London, crowds gathered in Trafalgar Square to shout and cheer the heroes of 'gallant little Mafeking'. The music halls, which had regularly been displaying, as a finale, cinematograph portraits of Roberts, Kitchener, Buller, Baden-Powell, Kruger and Joubert for the audience to cheer or boo, now had to show Baden-Powell last, as the cheering could go on for twenty minutes or half an hour before they could play 'God Save the Queen'.

The prolonged and unregulated nature of the excitement was so remarkable that 'Mafeking' became a verb, as the humorist Saki displayed in his couplet:

> Mother, may I go and maffick,
> Tear around and hinder traffic?

On the 27th of May Baden-Powell, who was now almost universally referred to as 'BP', was promoted to General, and the Queen sent him a telegram whose content was

210

proudly printed in the newspapers: 'I and my whole Empire greatly rejoice at the relief of Mafeking after the splendid defence made by you through all these months. I heartily congratulate you and all under you, military and civil, British and native, for the heroism and devotion you have shown.'

Lord Roberts's army of 30,000 men, including 11,000 horse, together with artillery and a wagon train of 8000 vehicles, advanced up the railway line towards Pretoria, with the Boers defending each river crossing before blowing up its bridge and retreating. At Doornkop – two hours' ride from Johannesburg, and the place where Jameson had surrendered after his disastrous raid in 1895 – the Boers made a stand to try to keep possession of the 'City of Gold' and its precious mines. A sharp encounter broke the Boer line, and Johannesburg lay open for the army to walk in. However, Lord Roberts was met by the town governor, Krause, who asked for a twenty-four-hour delay before the city was taken, to allow the Boer troops to leave. This, he said, would save unnecessary bloodshed, and he undertook that no damage would be done to the gold mines if only this was agreed on. Roberts agreed to the delay. The Boers did leave without damaging the mines – but they took a great deal of gold with them and were also able to remove all their guns. Many believed Bobs had been humbugged by the wily Krause.

Roberts then marched the last sixty or so miles to Pretoria, where the Boers employed exactly the same tactic, asking for delay to leave without fighting, and getting away with their guns and equipment.

In the afternoon of the 5th of June Roberts entered the Transvaal capital in triumph. General Buller, meanwhile, had been restricted by Roberts to a purely defensive role in northern Natal, but his patience gave way at last and he advanced up the railway line north of Ladysmith and by the 17th of May had taken both Dundee and Newcastle.

2nd June 1900
Dearest Aunt Hen,
I write to you from our present position north of

Newcastle. Our next object is Volksrust on the Transvaal border, but between us and that are the Boers, who have fallen back on the pass at Laing's Nek. Here the railway goes into a tunnel, which they have blocked. We are having a truce at the moment while our Chief talks to their General Botha (not the famous one, but his brother – all these Boers are related to one another!) about surrender. He will tell him that there is no point in fighting on, but privately I can tell you that he doesn't believe for a moment they will surrender. As witness, we are using the period of truce to get ourselves into position for the assault that will follow when Botha rejects our overtures. We have heard how Ld Roberts was humbugged at Jo'burg and allowed the Boers to get all their artillery away, and who knows what else besides? Also how he has been saying that the war will be over as soon as he takes Pretoria. Buller was mad as fire about it, and about being kept inactive instead of being allowed to follow up our advantage. He understands things a deal better than Bobs, and says that the Boers will let their capitals go and simply carry on fighting from wherever they find themselves. Also that showing them leniency makes them despise us as soft. Only defeating their armies so soundly they cannot go on fighting will make them yield, and unless they are well beaten there will be no leaving the place, for they will jump up again as soon as we are gone. Our Chief is such a splendid fellow it makes us mad that he is not more heeded by Bobs and K. Well, we shall have a sharp little 'do' of it here in a day or two, but don't worry, your boy knows how to keep his head down after all this time. It would make you stare to see how that idle boy has become a soldier. When we have Laing's Nek we will have to repair the railway and then on to Standerton, which is on the way to Jo'burg. By the by, you will be interested to know that young Ray Puddephat has been transferred over to my troop. Our good old Gen. arranged it himself, having heard we were friends from back home. With all he has to do, he still had time for little things like that! Puddephat is very glad to be with me – you will laugh, but he looks on me as a seasoned soldier and seems to think following me will protect him from harm! I hope he is never disabused!

8th June

I did not have time to close this letter, being busy every minute since, and just as well, for we have had our little 'do' and driven the Boer off. We are bivouac'd now for the night. It is bitter cold here, being their winter, and tents give little protection. I am more sorry than I can say to tell you that little Fallon, of whom I have often written, has been 'bowled out', shot through the head. It was rotten luck, as we took the pass with only 15 casualties, but he was one of them. There was a farm flying a white flag so we left it alone, but coming back to bivouac when we came in range a hail of bullets sang out. There were 17 Boers inside sniping at us. This is a trick they have used more than once – damn' dishonourable we call it. We cleared them out and they begged for mercy. Williams and Barrett killed one of them before they could be stopped – bad show, but all understood their wrath – the rest taken prisoner. You could say poor Fallon was avenged. This is a rotten war but don't think it will end soon. If the Boer would stand and fight we would soon have it over but with them it's snipe and run, snipe and run. It's a different kind of warfare altogether, which I don't think the bigwigs have grasped. We hear that the Boers pulled the same Jo'burg trick at Pretoria and Bobs let them go again. It makes us feel very tired to think of. He thinks they will just sit down quietly now that he has their capital city but they are not playing by his rules. No space to send Jessie anything but please give her my love and say I wear her muffler all the time now it is so cold.
    Your devoted
    Bertie

CHAPTER SEVEN

One day in May Henrietta drove into York to pay a morning call on Mrs Havergill. She felt rather nervous about it, having done nothing of the sort for many years, though in London when she and Jerome had first been married much of her life had seemed to be taken up with calling and being called on. As she drove, watching the harness bounce cheerfully on Dunnock's round rump and the V of road reeling in between his pricked yellow ears, she thought half ruefully that it had been rather nice in a way not to have to waste so much time on the pursuit. Visitors who were amusing, or real friends, were one thing, but the endless parade of married ladies who had nothing else in the world to do was a tedium she could do without. The actual stuff of life – doing the things that someone *had* to do – used up the day so much more satisfyingly.

But Mrs Havergill was kind, and the Havergills were old friends of Teddy's – probably his closest, for they had been the only people at his wedding to Charley. What Henrietta dreaded was meeting a crowd of other matrons there: she suspected Teddy of hinting Mrs Havergill into making the invitation as a first step in reintroducing Henrietta to the 'calling' circle. They would gossip about people she didn't know or subjects she had no opinion on, and she would feel like a child at a stranger's birthday party.

But when she was shown up to the drawing-room her hostess was alone, except for a pet pug dog, which she was feeding with scraps of biscuit dipped in her tea while it snuffled and grunted with accomplished greed. Mrs Havergill put the dog down at once, made Henrietta welcome and sent for fresh tea. She was a tall, square, sensible lady with well-disciplined hair and a brisk, no-nonsense air about her. Her only folly was the dog, which seemed to be the way she proved she was human and fallible like everyone else.

Having asked after Henrietta's family, she put Henrietta at ease by dropping into conversation a subject comfortably far removed from her personal problems.

'John was called out again to Hungate last night. A wretched man was found dead in the street and there was a lot of hysterical talk about "plague". These Irish are so emotional, and quite dreadfully ignorant, poor things! It wasn't a fever of any sort, as it turned out, but of course it could so easily have been, and then we would have been "for it", as my son Harry says. Really, you know, it's time the Corporation tackled Hungate properly – and the other slums.'

'It's difficult,' Henrietta said. 'The situation has existed so long, I don't know what the answer is.'

'Well, for one thing, we need a full-time medical Officer of Health. John has his own practice to run: he can't give the time to it that the job demands. And then all those places should be cleaned up. Despite all your father did in that respect with the Water Lanes, there are still dozens of insanitary courts and rookeries, all teeming with the most wretched people! It really is a disgrace. There are things to be done, if only the Corporation weren't so supine! Did you know, for instance, that we have *ninety-five* private slaughter-houses in the city, all mixed up with the houses and not a single one of them conforming to the regulations? Why don't they shut them down, to begin with? Or is it ninety-four?'

The bathos of the correction almost made Henrietta laugh. She said gravely, 'It's a great deal too many, whichever it is.'

'Well, of course you're right.' Mrs Havergill smiled at her own absurdity. 'You know, I haven't in the past been a great advocate for *public* action on these matters. I always felt it was a matter for individuals, and that charity could and should provide what help was needed to the weak and foolish. The worst thing one can ever do is to invite a government, any government, to interfere in people's private lives. But times are changing,' she went on, with a sigh that suggested she didn't entirely approve of the direction, 'and I suppose in the case of the slums it is something that affects us all – or it will if we have another outbreak of typhoid or cholera in the city.'

'Does Mr Havergill expect one?'

'Oh, not imminently. But when you have all those people crowded together in dirty conditions with no water and no sanitation, it's something that could happen any time. Did you hear, my dear, that Mr Rowntree is writing a book about poverty in the city?'

'No, I hadn't heard that. Which one?'

'Which Mr Rowntree? Seerbohm – such names these people have! Yes, he sends out investigators into the bad areas to make notes about what goes on.' She smiled suddenly. 'I can't imagine how they disguise themselves. Think what the Irish would say if they discovered a spy watching how much they drank and taking down their every word!'

'Could any disguise be adequate? The Irish must surely all know each other very well.'

'Yes, I imagine they do. And that makes me wonder whether the Rowntree approach is the right one,' she distracted herself. 'Those of his tendency always talk about "clearing out" the slums, but would it really be kind to scatter these people apart from each other and away from the little world they've built for themselves? When I've visited in Hungate, they've all seemed rather cheerful. The public houses were full and the little shops were doing brisk business, especially the fried-fish shops. The women were sitting on the kerbstones smoking their pipes while the children played around them; and sometimes there was lovely singing in the public houses – when they weren't fighting, of course.'

'It's human nature to create happiness out of the poorest materials,' Henrietta said. 'But on the other hand, the effects of that sort of poverty are dreadful – the sickness, the child mortality.'

216

'Yes. And the women die so shockingly young. If only one could help them, without destroying their spirit. I'm afraid that's what the Rowntree approach will do.'

'Mr Rowntree employs a great many of them, doesn't he? So it's right he should interest himself in their welfare.'

'True. Except that he will go on about their drinking and bad language. I'm sure he'd shut every public house if he could, and leave them with nothing to do but read the Bible all evening after a hard day's work. And,' she added, suddenly fierce, 'his own factory is no example. Cramped dark work-rooms, bad lighting, bad air, and endless flights of narrow stairs. I've heard some of the women who work there talking about Tanner's Moat as Hell itself.'

They were interrupted at that moment by the maid opening the door to introduce a new arrival. Teddy came in, his hat in his hand, and the pug trotted over to meet him, and snuffed and grunted about his boots, seeming to find the blacking irresistible.

'Ah, there you are. Good morning, Theresa! So she did come after all! Oh, look here, Duffy, don't lick the shine off, for goodness' sake!' He scooped the dog up and continued to his sister, 'I warned Theresa you might not pluck up the courage, but I'm glad you did.'

'I wouldn't be so impolite,' Henrietta began, embarrassed, but Teddy overrode her.

'Oh, we quite understand. But look, I haven't come to interrupt you, only to ask if you'll do me the kindness of calling on Charley while you're in town. She hardly goes out now, and it's dull for her at home all the time with nothing to do.'

'Of course I will. I was going to anyway,' Henrietta said. 'She is well?'

'Lord, yes. Hearty as a horse, only she can't get about much any more. And the other thing I was going to say is, have you heard of this travelling showman fellow, who's brought the cinematograph pictures to York?'

'Yes, he has a booth in the market-place,' Mrs Havergill said.

'I heard he has pictures of the war,' Henrietta added.

217

'General Roberts and the cavalry and soldiers marching past and so on.'

'My boy Harry said all the children at school were talking about it. It's quite the wonder of the age to them.'

'That's right. Would you like to see them?' He seemed to be addressing the question to both women equally.

'The pictures? I'd love to,' Henrietta said, 'but—'

'My dear Teddy, I can't imagine myself paying a visit to a market booth.' Mrs Havergill voiced the objection.

'No, no,' Teddy said, 'of course not. Wouldn't do at all. Didn't mean you to. No, my plan is to hire the fellow and his equipment to give a private showing at my house. I thought it would amuse Charley – don't you think?'

'I should think it would amuse anyone,' Henrietta said. 'Moving pictures! How very exciting!'

'What a good thought of yours, Teddy,' Mrs Havergill said approvingly. 'I know I can speak on John's behalf and say, "name the day".'

'Apparently,' said Teddy, revealing another motive under the noble one, 'he's been photographing in York, too – the railway especially. Trains coming and going, railway workers leaving the Leeman Road depot and so on. I'd dearly like to see that.'

Henrietta mused. 'You can see it in the life just by walking down the road. Strange how a moving picture of it should be so much more interesting. The power of novelty, I suppose.'

At Makepeace House half an hour later she found Charley lying on the sofa in the drawing-room.

'Oh, I'm glad you've come!' she cried, as soon as Henrietta appeared. 'I'm moped to death lying here with nothing to do.'

'Has Teddy forbidden you to get up?'

'Dr Havergill did, and I've forbidden myself. I wish I could get on and do my housework but standing or sitting are both so uncomfortable, and if I try to bend it makes me sick. So here I am lying on the sofa staring at the dust on the mantelpiece and seeing how dirty my china's getting, and wondering how I'm going to get through another day of this.'

'Would you like me to wash your china for you?'

'Oh, no, don't. Thank you, but I'd rather you sat and talked to me. Besides, if it's clean Teddy will think I got up and did it against orders, and be cross.'

Henrietta laughed. 'You don't think for a moment Teddy would notice it was clean?'

'Well, perhaps not, but sit and talk to me anyway. Did he come and check on you at the Havergills', to make sure you'd called?'

'Yes. How did you know?'

'Oh, he said he was going to. I said it would be tactless and you'd guess and be offended, and he said, no, it wouldn't be tactless because he'd tell you that was what he was doing.' She smiled, a rather tired but warm smile. 'There just isn't anyone like him, is there?'

'He's the dearest person in the world. He said—' Henrietta stopped, remembering the cinematograph show was supposed to be a surprise.

'He said what?'

'Oh, nothing of consequence.'

'If you mean the moving pictures, I know all about that. Cook's sister's son was hanging around the booth trying to find a way of sneaking in when Teddy was talking to the man about it, so it got back to me. But I shall pretend to be surprised, so don't tell him I know. I am looking forward to it. When I can admit to knowing about it, I shall try to persuade him to arrange another show later on for the children. Think how excited they'd be!'

Henrietta said, 'Oh, you are kind! My one worry about it was how I was going to be able to keep the children away from that booth when they know Jerome and I have seen them.'

'Do you miss Jack awfully?' Charley asked. 'I miss Ned so much. The house seems so empty now he's at school. I can't wait for the summer, when I shall have him for eight whole weeks! I wish Teddy had never thought of this Eton scheme. I can't believe it's doing Ned any good, judging by the letters he sends home. I'm sure he'd be happier here.'

'Teddy wants to do the best for him.' Henrietta said. 'It

219

must help him on in life, to have been to Eton. But you'll have your own baby soon,' she reminded her sister-in-law, 'and then you won't miss poor Ned a bit.'

Charley smiled. 'Yes, I know that's how it's supposed to be, but I can't really believe in this baby at all. I mean, I know I have the evidence before me,' she laid a hand on the great bulge, 'but the actual baby seems so – remote. I can't imagine it, really – what it will look like or how I'll feel about it or anything. Is that wrong?'

'It's natural,' Henrietta said. 'You're tired out with carrying it around. But as soon as it arrives, you'll feel different. You'll know it the moment you see it, and you'll wonder that you could ever have lived in a world without it. Do you think it will be a boy or a girl?'

'I'd like it to be a boy for Teddy's sake. He says he thinks it will be a girl, and, really, I can't imagine either.'

'It's bound to be one or the other,' Henrietta assured her.

'Yes, I imagine you're right! Henrietta, can I ask you something?'

'Of course. Anything.'

'When the baby starts coming, could you – would you lend me Emma?'

'Of course, if you want her to be here.' Henrietta was slightly puzzled.

'It's just that Teddy's so anxious about me, and wants me to have the best of everything, and he's arranged a midwife and a month-nurse and a specialist doctor as well as Dr Havergill, and with all those people standing around me I shall feel like a performing bear if I don't have someone of my own, someone plain and familiar and nice. I'd really feel better if I knew Emma would be there to take my side.'

'Of course she shall. But, Charley, take your side? If you don't want all these people, tell Teddy so.'

'Oh, I couldn't! He'd only worry twice as much, and anyway it would hurt his feelings if I said I didn't want the things he's arranged specially for me. It would be like – refusing a present from him.'

'Well, you must know best,' Henrietta said, though she thought privately that Teddy would soon get over any such

220

feeling, for he was never petty, and he only wanted to please her. 'At least you'll know you're in the best of hands.'

Henrietta arranged with Teddy that she would send over Emma at Charley's request, without mentioning Charley's feelings about the 'specialists'. She only said that Charley wanted a familiar face beside her at a moment like that.

'I can understand that,' Teddy said. 'I was hoping you would come and hold my hand when the show comes off. I've never gone through it before and I'm afraid I might fall into a blue funk.'

'Not you, my hero! But of course I'll come and be with you. If you hadn't asked me, I would probably have turned up anyway.'

Charley went into labour one Saturday night at the end of May. Teddy's carriage came to fetch Henrietta and Emma at about eleven o'clock, and they drove away, leaving Jerome watching from the lighted doorway, having promised him a message by one means or another the moment the baby was born. By the time they reached Makepeace House, the rest of the attendants were already there. As Emma disappeared determinedly upstairs, Teddy grabbed Henrietta's arm, his face pale and sweating with fear, so she relinquished the thought of going up to see Charley herself and settled down to talk her brother into a better frame of mind.

'Why is it taking so long? Something must be wrong!' was put to her about every half-hour, and she told him again and again, patiently, that first babies were always slow and reminded him of Lizzie's labour.

'You were so kind, keeping Jerome occupied all that time,' she said.

'I know what he was going through now, poor fellow. But it's worse for me, isn't it? I'm the one that did this to Charley, and if anything should happen—'

'Nothing's going to happen. Charley's young and strong – goodness, she's younger than Lizzie! And you've got the very best care for her.'

'Yes, Havergill and that fellow Milton know what they're about, and the midwife is the best in the country, so Havergill says. He recommends her to everyone. But why

221

is it taking so long? Something must have gone wrong!'

And so the night hours passed, and the lovely dawn of early summer came. There were stirrings in the kitchen regions, the smell of coffee flowered exquisitely through the house, and a ribboned maid with a sleepy unbreakfasted face came and drew back the curtains and put up the window to let the soft new air in. Henrietta was desperately thirsty after her long night's talking, and accepted coffee gratefully, but though Teddy let her pour him some, he did not drink it. Outside the birds were singing passionately. The sound of hoofs clopping on the cobbles heralded the milkman, and an early workman went by, whistling. A dog barked, sharply and enquiringly, and then was silent. Inside the room, the clock on the overmantel clicked, gave a preliminary whir like someone clearing his throat, and struck the three-quarters.

And then, far off and faint, like something in a dream, something not in this world, came the sound of a baby crying. Teddy's eyes widened, he jumped up and rushed to the drawing-room door to listen.

'It's born,' he said. There were no more distinguishable sounds to be heard, though he strained his ears, every part of him aching with anxiety and hope and the trembling anticipation of a delight beyond his imagination. A maid, evidently an emissary from the servants' hall, drifted past and ostentatiously dusted the vestibule table, to be on hand when the news came down.

At last there were footsteps from above, and the maid effaced herself as Teddy came out to the foot of the stairs to watch John Havergill descending with something in his arms. He smiled at Teddy, though to Henrietta he looked tired and drawn.

'I wonder why it is that babies will stick to night work? Well, my good fellow, here you are. You're the father of a fine baby girl.'

'A girl!' Teddy searched the doctor's face urgently. 'How is she?'

Havergill knew he didn't mean the child. 'She had a hard time of it, but she came through like a soldier, and she's doing well. There's nothing to worry about. Come, you haven't looked at your daughter yet.'

'My daughter?' Teddy repeated; and he looked, and then held out his arms in a gesture that was so natural that it turned Henrietta's heart over. He took the tiny bundle in his arms and gazed at the baby with a bewildered, wondering joy. 'My daughter?' he said again, but softly, to himself.

'Can I go up and see Charley?' Henrietta asked Havergill quietly.

'In a little while. They're just making her comfortable, and then she wants to see Teddy first.'

'Of course.'

'Your Emma was a tower of strength,' Havergill went on. 'Splendid woman.'

'She's been through it a few times before,' Henrietta smiled.

'Look at the little ears!' Teddy was rhapsodising. 'And the tiny fingers! She's so perfect. And beautiful! Isn't she beautiful?'

Henrietta was going to answer when there were more footsteps coming down from above – but this time running. Her attention was arrested. Havergill turned his head. A strange woman appeared at the turn of the stair – the midwife, presumably. 'Doctor,' she said, and the sharpness of her voice made them all look.

'What is it?' Havergill asked.

'Can you come?' was all she said, and her eyes exchanged some urgent message with him. He did not waste more words, but started up at once, not running, but hurrying.

Teddy stared only a moment, before thrusting the baby into Henrietta's arms and running after them.

It was all over very quickly. Charley suffered a haemorrhage so massive that she was gone in minutes, without seeing Teddy, without knowing he was standing at the door, his eyes stretched wide in horror as the crowd around the bed desperately tried to stop her life from flowing away. Only Emma spared him a wild, terrible glance of pity as she hurried past with towels. The expensive specialist, the recommended

223

midwife, trusted Dr Havergill – all the care Teddy had provided could do nothing to save his wife.

No-one could have done anything more, as Havergill tried to explain afterwards. Charley had been doing well, there had been no reason to expect any problems, but these things happened sometimes. It was God's will, if you liked, but it was outside the skill of anyone there to predict or prevent. Teddy heard him and nodded, tried to say something to let him know he didn't blame him, but he couldn't find any words. The world just then made no sense to him. Only hours ago there had been Charley, and now there wasn't, and he couldn't understand how the world could go on turning as if nothing had happened. He sat in the drawing-room while things went on around him, people coming and going, things being said and done, and none of it mattered. Why did they bother? There was no more Charley for him, for anyone, ever. He sat and rocked himself, just a little, and held the baby close against him. He hardly knew he was holding her, could spare no thought or feeling for her for the moment, but when Emma tried to take her away he shook his head slightly, frowning, and she left him alone. The baby seemed content to be there, as if knowing she had found a haven from life's storms, which had come upon her so soon. At all events, pressed close against his body by his strong arms, she slept away the first hours of her birth day.

Havergill sent a woman to lay out the body. Henrietta and Emma helped, dressing Charley in a white nightgown and arranging flowers around her head on the pillow. That was when Henrietta wept, her tears pouring like summer rain for this dear, loved, cheerful person lost, this young life snuffed out. It seemed so randomly cruel, and the beauty of the day and the flowers twisted the spike in her heart. Charley looked beautiful, too. She had lost so much blood that her skin was translucent and colourless, like immortal alabaster.

When she had regained her composure, Henrietta went downstairs to call Teddy up, but he wouldn't come, only shaking his head and rocking. She let him alone. He must come in his own time. She was aware that no message had been sent to Jerome yet; and there were home matters to consider, even at such a time. She sent Emma back to Morland Place, to tell Jerome and to take care of the children and the house.

'I have to stay here with him. I can't leave him yet.'

'I understand,' Emma said. 'Oh, ma'am, what a terrible sad thing!'

'Don't, I shall start crying again,' Henrietta said.

Jerome came up when Emma's arrival released him. By that time Teddy was dozing in the chair, still holding the baby, and Henrietta drew her husband out into the hall, not to disturb him.

'I can't believe it,' he said.

'I can't either. She was doing well, Havergill said so. Then this. It was so sudden. There was nothing to be done.'

Jerome held her for a moment, his lips trembling, close to tears himself. Then she freed herself to fumble out her handkerchief and blow her nose. The house seemed unnaturally quiet; the servants were all keeping to the servants' hall, their morning work left undone.

'What's to happen to her?' Jerome asked, nodding in the direction of the baby.

'We'll have to find a wet-nurse for her,' Henrietta said, with a note of hopelessness in her voice. She was very tired.

'I expect Havergill knows someone. I'd say we ought to take her back with us, but it would be too far for a wet-nurse to come several times a day, out to Morland Place. Poor Teddy. Poor little girl. God, this is a wretched business!'

Henrietta was crying again. A maid, looking lost and forlorn, appeared at the end of the passage, sent from the cook wanting orders about luncheon. The door, swinging closed behind her, propelled a savour of frying cabbage into the air. In a sorry and confusing world, the servants' dinner was a fixed point round which every household turned, and the cook had no doubt wanted something to do to keep herself occupied. Henrietta received Jerome's handkerchief

225

and wiped her eyes and nose, preparing to do what was necessary. So long seemed already to have passed, hours and hours rolling them all relentlessly away from the last moment when there was Charley, but it was not even twelve o'clock yet.

Teddy coped amazingly well. Everyone said so, with mingled amounts of admiration and surprise. It was not his nature to show great emotion; it was his nature to try to please others, which included not embarrassing them or being a burden on them. Jerome had to go home, having a great deal of work to do, but Henrietta had meant to stay to help Teddy with the various arrangements that had to be made. But he said, 'No, no, you have things to do at home. I shall be quite all right. It will be better for me to be kept busy. No, really – I've a houseful of servants, I shan't be alone.'
    'That's different. You ought to have someone with you.'
    'I want to be by myself,' he said gently. 'For a bit. Please. Betty will look after the baby, and Havergill's going to find a wet-nurse. I just need to be alone with her for a while. To say goodbye.'
    'I understand. I'll come back this evening, then.'
    He nodded and smiled, though to Henrietta he seemed indifferent to the idea, as if he were agreeing for her sake rather than his. Well, perhaps he was. She needed things to do, too, ways to be useful.

When she had gone Teddy drew a huge sigh and went upstairs. He had given Henrietta the conventional words 'to say goodbye' because they were an accepted code at times like this, and he had no words of his own to express what he felt. He went with the dutifulness of a well-brought-up child into the room where Charley had died and looked at the body, lying composed as a wax figure in the bed and waiting for the coffin. But there was no sense of connection in him, no feeling that this was Charley or had ever been. He could not say goodbye to it: it was not her. He wished they had not put flowers there, as if it was a person. Charley had gone, suddenly and utterly, like the night star when the dawn light pours across the sky. An after-image gleamed faintly and briefly on his memory, but soon that would be gone too, leaving nothing. He didn't know how to feel a loss so absolute, he didn't know how to mourn; he hardly knew how to breathe. He could only wait, and go on doing things, as it was expected he should, until some way of knowing this thing came to him.

It was a piece of good luck in the middle of ill that one of Havergill's usual midwives had had a baby that very morning, and was willing to take Teddy's as well; for, as he tried to explain to the bewildered father, the first-milk is all-important for preparing a baby's new, untried stomach for its job. It would give her a much better start. Often in these circumstances there was colic and sickness (and some-times, though he didn't say it, death) because even human breast-milk was no substitute for colostrum. Teddy nodded, dutifully. A farmer's son, he knew all about beestings, the rich orange first-milk cows made for their calves, perfectly designed for their first days. So humans made it too? That was interesting. He nodded like a good student, his eyes politely on Havergill's face, while inside him his soul stared helplessly into the sickening emptiness.

The drawback was that the baby had to be taken to the nurse, rather than the nurse coming to the baby. The most sensible proposition was for her to be left there until Mrs Bigelow was up and around, but Teddy came out of his blankness long enough to object firmly to the idea. He could not put it into words, but he was afraid that if the baby went away, she would become remote to him. He would lose the feeling of connection to her which he already had, and which was different from the way he felt towards Ned. He loved and cared for Ned, but Ned was not part of him as the baby was. He had lost so much; he did not want to lose that too. So a proper nursemaid was hired to release the housemaid Betty back to her duties, and she carried the baby, well wrapped up, to Mrs Bigelow to suck six times a day.

The funeral brought out, as though from hiding, a surprising number of people who felt a deep loss. Charley, in her quiet way, had touched many lives; Teddy was not aware of half the things she had done while he was out of the house about his pleasant pursuits. Coming from the slums she had gone back there when in good fortune to try to do something for those left behind. Word passed in a mysterious way about the date of the funeral, and on the day people drifted from their back-streets and formed a cluster about the door of Makepeace House. The hearse, all gleaming black lacquer and shining glass, arrived early outside the house, but there was already a crowd there, which parted silently to make room. The four black Fells champed their bits nervously at such a press of people, tossing their heads occasionally so the long black plumes flicked like squirrels' tails.

The coffin was brought out, and a very quiet, low sound came from the crowd, like a sleeper's moan. It was slid into its glass carriage and surrounded with massed flowers like Sleeping Beauty. Some in the crowd came forward humbly with their own flowers – just a single bloom in many cases – and asked to be allowed to add them. Teddy came out, in his blacks, tall hat wound with crape, and black mourning gloves, and climbed into the carriage behind. The crowd shuffled backwards as he passed, to let him by. His face was perfectly blank and he seemed not to notice anyone or anything. But the carriage had only moved a few feet when it stopped again, halted by Teddy's rapping; and the door opened and he stepped out again. He looked round the sea of faces, seeming to be seeking words. And then he said, 'Thank you. Thank you all.'

He nodded, and some of them nodded back, or bowed their heads; others tried to smile, and many wiped their eyes, which were suddenly overflowing. Then he got back into the carriage, and it pulled away again, following the hearse out onto Micklegate and through Micklegate Bar. They were going to Morland Place, where the invited guests would be waiting, for Charley was to be buried in the crypt under the chapel with the rest of the Morlands. When it had been discussed where the funeral should be, Teddy had said, 'I want to bring her home.' But as they passed under the gate and left the city walls behind, Teddy thought that, really, her home had been back there, and with that shabby crowd.

Everyone said afterwards how remarkably well Teddy had behaved at the funeral, how brave, how stoical he had been, an example to them all. But the truth of it was that the funeral meant nothing to him. It was a ritual society required him to arrange and take part in; but what they lowered into the crypt was not Charley, and he had no feelings about it at all.

By the 7th of July, Buller had taken Standerton, and Roberts in Pretoria now had two rail links, one to Cape Colony and one to Durban, to supply his army. Buller travelled up from Standerton and he and Roberts met for the first time in their lives – rather stiffly and awkwardly, for they came from different camps in the first place, their correspondence hitherto had marked several differences of opinion, and Buller was aware that Roberts had criticised him in dispatches to Lansdowne.

Nothing much seemed to transpire from the meeting. Bertie wrote:

It's my belief they don't quite know what to do next. We hear now that Smuts and his men got away with thousands of pounds' worth of gold from Pretoria while Bobs waited outside, and trainloads of ammunition and war supplies besides, so they are set up for months. We have their capitals but they don't surrender, and they move about the country so fast it takes all one's time just to know where they are. They won't stand and fight to let us finish it. Meanwhile our Chief came back from visiting Bobs in a temper, so I guess no job has been given us but to guard the railway, so we will be stuck here in Standerton for weeks more twiddling our thumbs. Supplies are going up to Pretoria now but we have still not received new winter uniforms and hard wear has left us in rags. We patch our clothes with whatever comes to hand – sacks, buck-wagon sheeting,

229

leather, sheepskin with the hair still on. We look more like Boers now than British soldiers. The other day we were reviewed – something to keep us busy, I think – and you never saw such a difference from when we left England. No bright buttons or prancing horses – our poor old gees can hardly hold their chins off the ground. Nearly all the men have beards, and our helmets are all battered and stained. We are such ragamuffins it would give the eye of mother-love a hard task to pick out her own son! We have been long enough here now for the women to catch us up – aside from those who follow close on behind. There is always a wagon of tough little 'wives' just behind us. But now they are flooding in daily. Even some of the officers have wives following, Major Ferrars of ours welcomed his yesterday. It puts a strain on the regiment, and when the men don't have enough to do there are sometimes fights. If I were Buller I would ban the whole boiling. But I suppose there would be mutiny! I enclose a separate letter for Jessie as you can't very well show her this last part. A fellow in the Dub. Fus. has a camera and has been taking snapshots. I got him to take me with Dolly. If we can find someone to develop it I will send you a picture next time. I hope you recognise me. I was so very sorry to hear about Aunt Charley. She was such a kind lady, and will be dreadfully missed. What a terrible blow for poor Uncle Teddy. Please give him my deepest condolences. I would write but have no paper suitable for it – you see what dirty scraps I have had to use for you and Jess.

Whenever Henrietta went to Makepeace House, she looked about her curiously to see if anything was different. But it seemed that Charley had ordered her household so well that it carried on exactly the same without her. The carpets were swept, the tables were dusted, the doorstep scrubbed and the brass polished, and there was no air of disintegration anywhere. The maid who opened the door was clean and smart and said and did all the right things. Only the muslin covering the mirrors and pictures and the black crape round the knocker said that this was a house of mourning.

What Teddy always did first when she arrived was to take her upstairs to see the baby. She was at home all the time now, the wet-nurse coming up to the house, and piece by piece a nursery had been arranged for her in the sunniest bedroom upstairs. The first nursemaid had been deemed unsatisfactory and sent away, and the replacement found, an Irish girl called Katy. But when she was not being washed, fed or changed, young Miss Morland was as likely to find herself being entertained by her father as by her nurse.

'Isn't she beautiful? Look how her hair's beginning to curl. And isn't she good? She hardly ever cries now.'

'Why should she? She has company every minute of the day. Teddy, is it true you get up in the night when she cries?'

Katy rolled her eyes to indicate it was true. The master in his extravagant silk dressing-gown, green with a pattern of white lilies, was a common sight prowling the house at night with the squalling red-faced mite across his shoulder. Though Katy slept in the room next door to the nursery, she hardly ever got to the cot before him.

'Who better to go to her than her father?' he asked.

'It's perfectly foolish,' Henrietta said. 'Jerome is a devoted father but he never got up in the night for one of his babies. It would never have occurred to him.'

'But they had you,' Teddy pointed out.

'Yes, of course. I'm sorry.'

'Anyway, as I said, she hardly ever wakes in the night now.'

Henrietta waved Katy away, and when they were alone she said, 'Are you really all right, Teddy? You seem remarkably well, but—'

'But what? What have I done that worries you?'

'Well, the baby is six weeks old now, and you haven't had her christened. You really must get on and do that, you know.'

'I know. I'll get around to it soon.'

'But first of all, wouldn't a name be a good thing? You always just call her "she" or "the baby". It does seem very strange to us that you haven't named her.'

He dragged his eyes from his daughter's face and looked up. 'Does it? I suppose it isn't right, but she is just "she" to me. Just herself. I can't explain it, quite. It seems odd to me somehow to think of having to name her, as if she could ever be confused with anyone else.'

Henrietta softened. 'I think I understand. But the poor child will have to go about the world one day, and she'll need a name. Can't you think of one? Wouldn't you like to name her after her mother?'

Teddy shook his head decisively. 'No. Charley was herself. There can never be anyone else with that name for me.'

'You could name her after our mother,' Henrietta offered tentatively.

'Sibella?' He laughed. 'No, she's not Sibella. Don't I tell you, she can't be named "after" anyone. No, if she has a name, it must be the plainest, simplest thing, the least thing that can come between me and her.'

What an odd thing, Henrietta thought, to talk of a name as a barrier; but she felt they were getting somewhere so she said, 'What about Jane, then? There's nothing much plainer than that.'

'No, I don't like Jane.' He was silent, and when Henrietta fidgeted restlessly, he sighed and said, 'Mary, then, if she must have something. That's a good old family name, and plain as milk.'

'Mary Morland is nice,' Henrietta said approvingly. 'I suppose she'll be called Polly, but that's nice too.'

Teddy seemed struck. 'Polly,' he said, and at that moment the baby stirred and opened her eyes. 'See how she looks at me! She knows me already. And now I think of it, she looks like a Polly, doesn't she?'

'Well, I'm so glad that's decided,' Henrietta said. 'Now you can have her christened, and then you must think about what's to become of you both.'

'*Now* what is it? I thought I'd done everything you wanted.'

'For the moment; but you must have a housekeeper in the long run, and you'd do better to get one while things are still running smoothly, before the servants start getting lazy. And the baby ought to have a proper nanny. Katy is all right as a nursery-maid, but she won't do to have sole charge.'

Teddy looked impatient. 'Oh dear, I don't want all this fuss. Why can't I just go on as I am?'

'Teddy—'

'Oh, all right. You can send me Emma if you like.'

'I'm serious.'

'So am I. She was nanny to your children.'

'But I can't possibly spare her,' Henrietta said in dismay, thinking that after all his generosity to her she ought to give him anything he asked for. But to lose Emma!

'Then the solution is simple,' Teddy said. 'We had better come and live at Morland Place.'

There was a silence as Henrietta contemplated this huge, and wonderfully simple, idea.

'You don't really mean it?' she said at last.

'Why not?'

'Well – could you really bear to leave Makepeace House?'

'Good Lord, it's only a house. It isn't anything special, not like Morland Place.' Henrietta was silent again, thinking that he must not really want to leave the home he had shared with Charley, the place that held his memories of her – not knowing, because he had never been able to explain to her, that such commonplace sentiments had no meaning for him. She had been in his life, and she was gone, and he missed her desperately, but nothing that was not her could have any meaning for him in her context, even as a reminder.

Teddy went on, with growing interest, 'Look here, this is a very sensible idea. But if you don't want me, you only have to say so.'

'Of course I want you. Besides, it's your house.'

Teddy waved the idea away. 'Forget that. This can only be if you and Jerome both agree. But, look, there's lots of empty space at Morland Place. Empty rooms. The drawing-room's been finished for ages but you don't use it.'

'We don't have any furniture.'

'Just so. But I've got enough tables and chairs and carpets and so on here to furnish all the rooms properly. And it's too much work for you, keeping the place up without servants. I can bring my whole household with me – cook, maids, men, the whole thing. Then you can let me have Emma to take care of Polly.' He said the name so easily that he did not even notice he had used it. 'We'll all live together and be snug as mice, I won't need a housekeeper, you won't have to work so hard, Polly will grow up with a family around her, and I shan't be lonely. Morland Place can be what it was again, what it was when we were children, before Mama died – only better! I'll pay all the household expenses, you can run things, Jerome and I will take care of the estate, and I'll put Makepeace House out to rent.'

He stopped, looking at her enquiringly. To him it seemed simple and obvious, but to Henrietta it was like an impossibly golden vision held out before her, too good to be true. She couldn't immediately find the words to answer, and he thought she needed further tempting. 'Think about it, Hen – there'll be horses in the stables again, and you'll be able to go out riding whenever you like, instead of toiling in the kitchen. Maids to answer bells and make up the fires, a cook in the kitchen, a man to clean the silver—'

'Silver to clean!' Henrietta laughed. 'Stop, stop, Teddy, I can't cope with any more!'

'Is that yes or no?'

'Yes, of course yes! I can't think of anything nicer. It's the perfect solution. The Master of Morland Place shall come home.'

'Yes, well, but look here, what about Jerome? I don't want to put his nose out of joint.'

'You won't. He'll be glad, too.'

'Ask him first before you say that.'

'When would you want to move?'

'Right away. There's nothing to wait for, and I'd like to be settled when Ned comes home from school. I'd like to be at Morland Place for the summer while they're all off school. What fun we'll have! But ask Jerome first.'

'I'll ask him, but he'll say yes,' said Henrietta.

On the 11th of July, the Queen held a garden party at Buckingham Palace for five thousand guests. It was a wonderful hot, sunny day – 'Queen's weather' as people said – but it was a clear heat beneath a brilliant sky, and with a gentle breeze to keep the flags moving and refresh the crowds. Not that there was much crowding, given the extent of the garden. The fringe of trees hid the walls that shut out the city, and with the immaculate green lawns stretching into vistas it might have been some Arcadian landscape far from the haunts of men. On the lake ornamental ducks and exotic waterfowl drifted and dabbled, many of them gifts from other nations. A succession of military bands played selections of favourite tunes, and the guests, the women in all their pretty colours and many of the men in bright uniforms, laid dabs and strokes of colour against the green, or clustered in groups like beds planted with summer flowers.

Where the nodding hats of the women and the bare heads of the men gathered most closely was always around the carriage, drawn by two greys, in which the Queen sat. Her usual black was brightened by white feathers and a white rose in her bonnet and pearls around her neck, and she tilted from time to time a white lace parasol against the sun. She smiled and chatted, and if she looked worn and weary, only those who knew her best noticed; for when the Queen smiled at a person, all else was driven from his mind. Her sweet, silvery voice was so clear it could always be heard above the music and the background murmur of the crowd. From a little distance it rose and flashed on the ear as a trout in a brown river catches the eye.

Hazelmere was there on duty with the Prince of Wales, who was pacing a few steps behind the carriage and holding his own cheerful, good-humoured court, his usual cigar absent from his fingers in deference to his mother's loathing of the habit, but his geniality undiminished. The Duke and Duchess of York were there too, and the duchess engaged Venetia in kind, commonplace conversation for some time: they had been presented at the same drawing-room, and she had always had a soft spot for her.

Olivia and Charlie were there as guests, and when Venetia could get away from the duchess, she met them outside one of the tea-tents, and took a stroll with them along one of the gravelled walks. July roses blazed on either side, crimson, scarlet and yellow; the distant trees rocked their heads gently in the breeze as if in time to some music only they heard.

'Did you enjoy Ireland?' Venetia asked. 'I had your letter, but you always write so politely, as if it were an exercise, I'm never sure if it reflects your real feelings.'

'You are absurd! Yes, we liked it very much. We had very nice, comfortable rooms at the Lodge, and the Cadogans were most hospitable.'

'The reception we got when we arrived at Kingstown was extraordinary,' Du Cane said. 'I think Irish people must be noisier than English. But there was no doubting their enthusiasm.'

'Oh, yes, crowds and crowds of people,' Olivia said, 'cheering and singing "God Save the Queen" – it was like that wherever we went. The students of Trinity College turned out and shouted themselves hoarse—'

'Even the Nationalists, standing in front of City Hall with banners, forgot their grievances,' Du Cane added, smiling, 'and cheered and threw their hats in the air.'

'I'm glad to hear it. From what we read the visit did a great deal of good.'

'Well, the Queen was in better health while she was there,' Olivia said. 'She always is when she's away from home. The novelty cheers her up, I think.'

'I meant, it did some good politically,' Venetia said gently.

'Oh. But how do you think she looks today?' Olivia pursued, more interested in this aspect than the other.

Venetia hesitated. 'I was quite shocked at how thin she's grown since I last saw her. I ought to have been prepared, after what you've said and what HRH has said to Hazelmere, but she really does look quite poorly.'

'She hardly eats anything,' Olivia said, her gentle face creased with anxiety. 'Her appetite is quite gone, and what she does eat doesn't settle. And,' she added, with a spurt of wrath, 'when she does fancy some little thing, the kitchen manages to forget it, or spoil it! The food is quite dreadful sometimes – even we can't eat it, in full health. The other

236

day she ordered a bowl of vermicelli for dinner, because it was all she could fancy, and it never came at all, so she had nothing! The cook ought to be executed.'

'What does Reid say?' Venetia asked. 'The last time I spoke to him, he said that if a person gets past eighty without a major illness, they may as well go on for ever.'

'He's worried about her, of course. He wishes she could be saved any anxiety, which makes her trouble worse, but the war worries and upsets her dreadfully.'

'Well, that at least seems to be going well now. Lansdowne seems to think it will be all over in a few weeks – so Roberts tells him.'

'Yes, and that will be a relief. But then there'll be the returning troops to review, and the medals to be handed out, and all the sick and wounded soldiers to visit in hospital, and the letters to the widows, and I don't know what else.'

Venetia smiled. 'My dear Livy, she is the Queen. She can never have the life of a private citizen – and I doubt very much if she ever wanted it, either.'

'I suppose you're right,' Olivia sighed.

Venetia changed the subject. 'On a lighter note, I have something to put to you. The Sandowns have asked us if we'd like to join them on their yacht for a vacation. They'll be cruising in the Mediterranean for the whole of September, and Hazelmere thinks I need the rest, though I don't know if I shall be able to get away for as much as a month. Still, I'm bound to say the idea appeals. *Tutamen* is a lovely craft, and the Sandowns are such easy company. And Lady Sandown has asked if you would be able to join us too. It will only be a small party, and a very pleasant one, I think.' It was a particular kindness on Lady Sandown's part, Venetia thought, for they did not see as much of the Du Canes as they would have liked.

'How very kind! I think that would be lovely,' Olivia said. 'Our holiday is fixed for the first two weeks of September so that would fit in perfectly. What do you think?' She appealed to her husband.

'Delightful! I like the Sandowns very much.'

'Consider it fixed, then,' Venetia said. 'We can travel down together by train and meet the yacht in Nice or Cannes or wherever it happens to be.'

'What will you do with Violet?' Olivia asked.

'I've only to ask Henrietta if she can stay at Morland Place, and she'll be in raptures.'

Bertie's photograph caused enormous interest when it arrived in a letter to Henrietta at Morland Place. There he was, in uniform, sitting on a horse, in a wide and dusty street with a single-storey, wooden building with a veranda in the background, which was not like anything in England, and so gave authenticity to the picture.

'What a sorry-looking nag,' Jerome said. 'And small – hardly more than a pony.'

'His whiskers are much bigger now,' Henrietta added, receiving the snapshot from him. 'But he hasn't grown a beard. I'm glad.'

'It's not a very good picture, is it, Mother?' Robbie complained, crowding in.

That was true – it was fuzzy and dim, too far off from the subject, and with his face hidden by the shadow of his hat brim. 'I'm afraid it could be almost anyone. I wouldn't have known it was Bertie if he hadn't sent it me,' said Henrietta.

But Jessie, when her turn came at last, didn't seem to find it lacking; and when the conversation moved on, and Henrietta was going to put the photograph away, she asked, 'May I have it, Mother? Please?'

'The photograph? Well, I don't know . . .' Henrietta began.

But Jessie fixed her with an impassioned gaze. 'Oh, *please*, Mother! Oh, do let me!'

'What do you want it for?' Henrietta asked absently. Jessie didn't answer, but when her upturned face flooded with a blush, Henrietta remembered that when *she* had been ten and a half, she had been dreadfully in love with a villainous gamekeeper in Acomb Wood, who wore moleskin trousers and an appalling waistcoat made out of rabbit skins he had cured himself. It had been a grand passion while it lasted.

His dark face and sultry eyes had haunted her dreams for
weeks, and she had spun fantasies about marrying him and
living in a hut in the woods and cooking him rabbit stew.
Even now, the sight or touch of moleskin could provoke a
small, absurd tenderness in the back of her mind.

He had been replaced as the brightest star in her heaven
when that summer ended, by the doctor, a bulky man in
tweeds with a dog-cart and a whiskery pony; but while it
lasted, a photograph of him, had such a thing existed, would
have been a treasure beyond count. She gave the snapshot
to Jessie without another word. Jessie gave her a look of
burning gratitude and ran away upstairs, clutching it close.

Moving Teddy's household into Morland Place was not as
easy as he had expected, but much easier than Jerome had
predicted. When Henrietta had put the proposition to him,
he had not leapt at it as she had. 'It's his house, of course,
so he must do as he likes,' he had said.

She had surveyed his face anxiously. 'He means us to go
on living here too,' she assured him.

'Yes, I understand that. But what if he gets married again?
It will be very awkward then.'

Henrietta looked shocked. 'He'll never marry again!'

Jerome did not press it, but said, 'Ah, well, we'll cross
bridges when we come to them. When does he want to move
in?'

'Right away. It will make everything so much easier for
us as well as for him, you know.'

'I shall be glad to have you let off all this housework,'
Jerome admitted.

'And you'll have male company of an evening, and I'll
be able to look after little Polly and give her a mother's
care.'

Jerome grinned. 'Ah, now I see it! You're hungry for a
baby in your arms. I've heard it happens to ladies of your
age.'

'Oh, how can you be so impossible!' she cried. But it was
true. When she held that tiny baby, and smelt the sweetness
of her skin, and felt the tiny fingers hold hers, it satisfied

something in her she had not known was hungry. Lizzie was too far away with her own grandchildren. 'I thought you'd be pleased.'

Jerome kissed her contritely. 'I am pleased, of course I am. I'm very fond of him, and it will fill this big empty place. The children will like having a new baby in the house. But the move will take months to organise.'

It was not quite as bad as that, but there was quite a lot more to do than Teddy had anticipated. The servants' quarters had to be overhauled, for one thing – nothing had been done to them since the previous mistress, George's wife Alfreda, had died, and she had not done much, not caring about servants' comfort. And when Teddy put it to his household, not everyone wanted to exchange Makepeace House in the middle of the city for Morland Place at the end of a long country track – a Morland Place, moreover, with no gas lighting, no water-closets, and where every drop of water had to be pumped. Some of the servants declined absolutely to move, and he had to replace them; others he had to woo with promises that Morland Place would be given some of the modern conveniences within as short a time as possible from the move.

So Teddy and his household were not in place when the long vacation started and the children finished school. They were always wild with excitement for the first few days, racing about like colts with the sheer joy of freedom, the prospect of eight glorious weeks of it stretching ahead, with the whole countryside to roam over and no lessons to do. But now there was the novelty of the move to add to their ferment. Workmen came and went, and wagons arrived with furniture to be shifted laboriously up the stairs, and the children were so eager to help that Henrietta wondered if Teddy would be in residence any time before Christmas.

In the middle of it all, Bertie arrived unannounced, having been given furlough.

'But why didn't you tell us you were coming?' Henrietta asked, after the first greetings and embraces. Jerome was up at Twelvetrees and the children were out playing somewhere, so she had him to herself just at first.

'I didn't want to put you in an awkward position,' he said. 'If you'd known I was coming you might have felt obliged to tell Pa.'

'Oh, Bertie! You haven't told them either? But you must go home. Think how badly they'll feel when they know you came here instead.'

'Now, Auntie, don't fuss, there's a dear little fluffy hen! I shall go and see them, of course I shall, but I must have a little pleasure and petting first. I am fagged to death, and I couldn't face a row in my present condition.'

'You do look awfully tired,' Henrietta said, her attention immediately diverted. 'And you're so thin, Bertie! Have you been ill?'

'Well, to say truth, I haven't been in top form recently. That's partly why they gave me leave. Dysentery wears you down, you know, and the grub ain't all it might be.'

'Oh, poor Bertie! We must feed you up while you're here.' She studied him a moment. He seemed taller than she remembered, though that must be illusion; and despite his thinness, his shoulders and chest were broader and he was altogether more muscular. His face was shockingly tanned, of course, and there were paler lines radiating outwards from the eye-corners where he had screwed them up against the glare, which brought it home to her as words never could how hot it must have been over there. His front hair and whiskers were bleached almost colourless by the African sun and, as she had noted from the photograph, his moustache had now become whiskers, which reached round his cheeks to his ears and made him look older. But no, that was not really what made him look older: it was his eyes. They had a level, grave look, a length of focus as if he was used to scanning far horizons; and they were eyes that had seen sights he would never tell her about, never tell anyone, perhaps. He had gone away a heedless boy, for all his majority, and come back a man. He was a man now she could have appealed to for help, relied on, trusted. It pleased her, for it was a good thing that he had come by maturity; but a part of her mourned, too.

He let her stare, and then said, 'Well? Do I pass muster?'

For answer she reached up and kissed his lean, tanned cheek, then rested her hand against it a brief moment. 'My dear,' she said.

The boys and Kithra entered at a run, having heard from a labourer in a field that a stranger had gone up to the Place, and expecting some new kind of workman to whom they could offer their own brand of help. But at the sight of Bertie they stopped, shocked, for an instant, and then rushed clamouring forward to pound him with questions and exclamations, all at once and at the top of their lungs, jumping up and down on the spot with the excess of their excitement, their clear young voices making the chandelier high above them ring. He laughed that they were worse than a Boer commando, answered them as best he could, cuffed them affectionately, let them examine his uniform and showed them his scar – a bullet-wound to the forearm he had never bothered to tell about in his letters – and promised variously to view their tree-house, come fishing with them, and tell them *everything* about the war.

And at last he said, 'But where's my little Jessie? Where's my correspondent?'

Until then, only Henrietta had noticed that, bringing up the rear of the group, Jessie had halted in the doorway like them, but unlike them had remained there, paralysed with a sort of breathless joy that was more like pain than pleasure. Now as he looked round for her and saw her, she came forward almost reluctantly, her feet dragging, though her eyes were fixed on his face with passionate eagerness. Finding Bertie was no longer listening, the boys dropped their clamour. It was into a small silence that Jessie, arriving at last in front of her god, said, 'You've been promoted. You're a captain.'

He nodded. Henrietta said, 'How did you know that, dear?' and the boys rolled their eyes and said, 'Oh, Mother! His pips, of course.'

Bertie said, 'Your letters were really welcome. You can't think how a fellow over there looks forward to a letter from home.'

Jessie's face shone. 'I kept all of yours. And I've made a

242

model, and drawn all your campaigns on big sheets of paper.'

'I'd like to see those,' Bertie said.

Suddenly she couldn't look into his face any more. Her cheeks burned and she lowered her eyes, and found herself looking at his forearm, where he had drawn up his sleeve to show the boys his scar. 'You're wounded,' she whispered.

'Oh, it was only a scratch,' he said. 'A bullet passed through the muscle and out the other side. Old Johnny Boer tried his best to bowl me out, but here I am, you know, still at the wicket and as good as new.'

Jessie put out a finger, very slowly, and touched the white knot of the scar in the brown skin. Her lips trembled at the thought of his being hurt. Suddenly it was all too much for her. Tears rushed up her throat, she made a choking noise, and ran from the room without another word or look.

'Girls!' Robbie said witheringly. 'I say, Bertie, tell us about the Boer guns! The Krupps 75mm aren't really better than ours, are they?'

The next morning Bertie was up very early. Henrietta had expected him to sleep in, but camp habits did not die so easily. She found him fully dressed and creeping down the stairs when she herself, always an early riser, was on her way to the kitchen.

He smiled ruefully. 'I couldn't stay in my bed any longer. I've been awake since five. I thought I'd go out for a walk.'

'You must be starved with hunger. Let me get you something to eat first.'

'Oh, no, really, I don't want any fuss.'

She looked at him with sympathy. He had a restless, unfed look, but she guessed it was not to do with food. 'You want to get out into the fresh air.'

His tense cheek muscles relaxed. 'You understand. Best of aunts! Everything in England seems so small and close after Africa. I feel as if I'm in a little box and can't move my arms and legs. I need a long horizon – as long as I can get in this dear little country.'

'All right, my dear, I won't keep you, but just let me cut you some bread to put in your pocket, for you really must be hungry. It won't delay you a minute.' She led him towards the kitchen, and added, 'Why don't you ride? You can go further from the house than on your own two legs.'

He brightened. 'I didn't know there was anything to ride.'

'You can have my pony, Dunnock.'

'Will he be up to my weight?'

'As long as you don't race him about. He's very strong. Where he comes from, grown farmers use them for herding sheep.'

'He's so small. My feet will touch the ground.'

'Oh, don't be so vain. Who is there to see you?'

He laughed. 'My vanity has all been worn away, I assure you. When you have dysentery in the middle of an action and spend the night crouching behind a rock in the rain with Boer artillery shredding the air above you, your conceit gives up and slinks away.'

She said seriously, 'Poor Bertie. Was it really dreadful?'

'More dreadful than I can ever tell you,' he said, still smiling, but with grave eyes. 'When poor Fallon was killed – I didn't say in my letter – but the shot took his head clean off. He was right beside me. I felt—' He stopped.

She laid a hand on his arm. 'You can tell me what you like, and when you like. I will always listen.'

'Well, not now, at any rate, or I shan't get out of the house before the children stir. I love them dearly, but I need a little while alone.'

'I understand. I shan't tell them where you've gone.'

'You won't know where I've gone,' he said logically.

When he returned, much refreshed from his communion with nature, and with an opinion of Dunnock that even Henrietta's could hardly top, he found Jessie hanging around in front of the barbican, lolling on the paddock rail opposite, stepping up with one foot, swinging, stepping down.

'Hullo,' he said.

She stepped off the rail and came to meet him. 'You do look funny on Dunnock.'

'He's not much smaller than Dolly, and I won't have you insult the horse I love.'

She stroked the pony's cheek and he nudged her, his mind on his manger. 'Breakfast is nearly ready. Aren't you starved?'

'As a famine wolf,' he said solemnly.

'I told Mother you'd want fruit. She's going to put a bowl on the table. And I went and picked raspberries for you – the strawberries are finished.'

It took him a moment to remember what he had said in his letter. Her eyes were fixed on his face, and her cheeks were growing pink. 'I shall savour every one. What a kind girl you are!'

'Oh, it's all right,' she muttered, looking down, unable to bear his praise. She took hold of Dunnock's rein and began to lead him in, and Bertie slipped from his back – *stepped* would be more the word – and walked on the other side. The hoofbeats clunked hollowly as they passed onto the wood of the drawbridge. 'The boys are mad that you went out without them,' Jessie went on. 'They wanted to go with you and show you things. But you wanted to be alone, didn't you?'

'Yes,' he said.

'I knew,' she nodded. 'You look as if you can't see far enough away without hitting something.'

He was struck by her perception, and wanted to thank her in some way. 'Haven't you got something you want to show me?'

She glanced up at him, one swift flash of blue like a kingfisher, and down again. 'Not with *them*,' she said succinctly. 'They laugh at me.'

'Not with them,' he agreed. 'Just you and me.'

He heard her sigh, a great heave of accomplished pleasure. 'We've been helping Dad halter-break this year's foals. Two each. We do it after school. But I go up before school, too, in the early, early morning, and my two have got on better than anyone's. They're the best.'

'I'd love to see them,' he said.

Now she looked at him properly, her whole face as open and shining as a daisy in full sun. 'There's sausages for breakfast,' she said.

'English sausages! Pinch me! I must be dreaming!'

She giggled and pinched him, and he pretended to jump

245

out of his skin and made a shocked face at her, and she giggled harder. 'Not just English sausages,' she added jerkily, 'our sausages, from our own pig!'

'I don't believe it!' He reached under Dunnock's head and tickled her, and she dodged away. Dunnock ignored all this frivolity, his pointed ears directed towards the stable indicating his thoughts as a compass needle shows north.

Bertie stayed a week before Henrietta could persuade him to go and see his parents.

'You want to see your mother, don't you?' she urged. 'She hasn't been at all well, you know.'

'Oh, yes, I want to see the mater all right. But otherwise I'd as soon stay here. I can come back afterwards, can't I? I don't mean to stay there long. Just long enough to do my duty.'

'I'm afraid they'll blame me for keeping you away.'

'I'll tell them in no uncertain terms that it's not your fault.'

'Please don't. It won't make any difference.'

'You're trying to be rid of me.'

'Bertie! You know I love to have you here, but it will upset them very much to have you prefer Morland Place to your own home.'

'That's the Gov'nor's fault! He don't approve of me and he don't approve of you, and nothing either of us does will change that. Once he sets his mind one way, you can't budge it, no matter what. Was he always so stiff?'

'No, that's the strange thing. He was quite a rip when he was a young man.'

'Ah, they say the reformed sinner is always the strictest.'

'I wouldn't say he was a sinner exactly, but he was . . . lively, you know, and always up to some prank or other. He gave your grandfather a few grey hairs. But when he married and your grandfather died and he became squire and head of the household, that was when he changed. Quite suddenly he seemed to become—'

'Full of his own importance. Oh, I know you wouldn't say anything so rude, kind soul that you are, but that's it,

246

isn't it? He stopped being a person and became a good old marble statue of himself.'

'Bertie, that's uncharitable. He had a great many responsibilities, and he's never shirked them.'

'Unlike me, you would say?'

'I think he also has a great many worries that you don't appreciate.'

'He can't bear to be crossed, that's all, especially by his son and heir. And he can't bear to think I'll get the title after him and there's nothing he can do about it.'

'He can refuse to leave you anything else, though,' she warned. 'The estate isn't entailed, is it?'

'Oh, he won't do that. Leave the estate away from the title? What would the neighbours say? Not done, you know. But he might as well do it, for all of me. I don't want the blessed thing!'

'There may not be very much to leave,' Henrietta said. 'Agricultural estates haven't been doing well for years.'

'Yes, I know, and Grandpa didn't diversify when he should have. And then the Gov would go and have such a damned old-fashioned size of a family – ruining the mater's health in the process.'

'Bertie, you mustn't say those things to me,' Henrietta said gently.

He reddened a little under his tan, and she saw that here was the source – or one source, at least – of the son's hostility towards the father, and his long desire to provoke him. But he only said lightly, 'Well, I shall have to marry an American heiress, shan't I? That's what all these great landlords are doing, according to the illustrated magazines.'

'Whoever you marry, it will break Jessie's heart.' Henrietta smiled. 'I suppose you've noticed she has a "crush" for you?'

'Dear little girl,' he said fondly. 'That model map of hers is awfully good, you know. I shall tell the lads all about it when I get back. It's remarkable how accurately she's put in the flags. I could hardly have done it better myself, and I was there.'

Jessie was inconsolable when Bertie left to go to Bishop

247

Winthorpe, especially as Henrietta had made him promise not to say he was coming back, in case he should not find it possible. 'Better not to raise her hopes and then dash them.' Jerome wondered at, and was inclined to be impatient with, her strange mood until Henrietta enlightened him as to its cause.

'Is that it?' he said. 'Well, dear me, poor child. First love can be painful, I know. And Bertie is so horribly dashing and handsome, it will be hard for anyone to eclipse him.'

'Oh, don't tease! She really feels it, however passing it proves.'

'I know. I was sincere in my sympathy. What she needs is something to occupy her while she gets over him. Leave it to me.'

He went out and found her moping on the bank of the moat, her legs dangling over the water, moodily throwing bits of twig at a pair of ducks, who were lingering in case there should be bread coming next. 'Hullo,' he said.

'Hullo,' she replied, not looking up.

He held out a hand to her. 'Come and walk with me. There's something I want to ask you.'

'What?' she asked, but he held out his hand insistently, and at last she took it and let him pull her to her feet. They went side by side along the grassy walk. Swallows were all around, scooping the air and flickering across their path almost close enough to touch. The flat, green smell of the moat was pleasantly cool to the senses, beside the hot smell of the grass. At the corner they turned into the shade of the house along its north-facing flank. Two swans were in the water on this side, feeding from the bottom, the white triangles of their rumps all that could be seen above the surface, gleaming ghostly pale in the shadow.

'I need some help, Jess, and you're the one who can give it,' Jerome said.

She looked up sidelong at him, suspicious that he was teasing or humouring her. 'How can *I* help *you*?' she asked dully, as if the answer was, 'Not at all.'

'With the horses, of course. Wake up, wooden-head!'

The faintest smile of acknowledgement touched her sad lips. 'Is it more foals?'

'No, something different. I want to start breaking the yearlings to saddle,' he said. 'I know some people leave it until they're two, but I believe the sooner you start the better, before they get any bad habits. Leave it too long and they start to think they can decide what to do instead of you. But they are very young, and still growing. Their bones are still pliable, and you can damage them by putting too heavy a burden on their backs.'

She was listening now, gravely, flattered that he was talking to her so seriously and using grown-up words.

'I'm too heavy to ride them at this age. So's Lelliot and the other grooms. But you, now, you're as light as a feather.'

'Me?'

'I want you to help me start backing them. It will mean regular work, mind – a couple of hours every morning. No running off to play. If you begin it, you must finish it with me.'

She looked shyly at him. 'Why me? Why not one of the boys?'

'The boys are too impatient, too noisy and rough. The colts will be frightened and confused. They'll need to be handled very gently and quietly until they get used to it. You're good with horses. You know how to gentle them and win their confidence.'

'Do you think so?' She was amazed and pinkly pleased that he had noticed.

'Yes, I do. I've watched you with the foals. Horses sense when you're uncertain, and it makes them nervous. And you rode Pasha. You were an idiot to do it, mind, and if you ever try it again you'll be eating standing up for a week.'

'Yes, Dad.'

'But the fact remains you did it, and I don't think anyone else could have, stupid as it was. So what do you say? Will you help me?'

She was shining again now, almost as radiantly as when she looked at Bertie. 'Yes,' she said.

'It means giving up some of your holiday time. And it will be hard work. You understand that?'

'Yes, Dad,' she said; and almost without knowing it she slipped her hand into his as they turned the next corner of the moat and came back out into the sun again.

Bertie did manage to come back to Morland Place for a few days before his furlough was up, and happily his return coincided with a visit of Richard Puddephat to York along with his wife and daughter. They came to spend a whole day at Morland Place during which time Bertie told them everything he could remember about their son's activities in South Africa, tried to recall every word he'd ever said in Bertie's presence and made up a good few in response to questions from the doting mother and sister that he could not well answer. Fortunately he was really fond of young Puddephat and could speak enthusiastically about him.

Bertie's complete unwoundedness so far – he did not mention his arm – gave the mother and sister hope that Ray would not be hurt either, and Bertie gave exaggerated accounts of how safe it was to be among the scouts rather than the front-liners. Afterwards he was afraid he had rather got carried away, but reasoned to himself that it would do the Puddephats no good to fear the worst before it happened, when it might well never happen anyway. When they said goodbye Aileen clasped his hand in both hers and thanked him for keeping her boy safe. 'I know with you as his captain he will be safe – I *know* it!'

The following day Bertie had to be off too. He said his goodbyes before he went to bed, meaning to be off at first light and avoid any prolonged partings; but Henrietta was up in time to see him off, and while he was still kissing her goodbye at the moat's end Jessie appeared, running hard across the yard in her bare feet, still in her white nightgown, her hair flying loose. She looked like the Lady of Shalott, he told her, trying to lighten the moment; but she flung herself at him and clasped him round the waist in a fierce embrace.

'You won't get hurt,' she said, muffled by his jacket. 'Promise you won't?'

'I promise,' he said, and laid a hand on the tangled fair head. She broke her grip, seized his brown hand briefly in her two little ones and kissed it, and then, tears streaming, ran back the way she had come, unable to bear another moment of her feelings.

Bertie looked after her, and then at Henrietta, with a raised eyebrow.

'She'll be all right,' Henrietta said. 'As long as you write to her sometimes. And me, of course.'

Bertie caught her chin a moment, and smiled down at her. 'Now don't you start to blub, or you'll set me off!'

CHAPTER EIGHT

Frederick Treves had returned to England after the relief of
Ladysmith, having come down with dysentery. He was therefore on hand when *The Times* fired its opening salvo in what
was to become a campaign against the RAMC and medical
conditions generally in South Africa. William Burdett-
Coutts, the MP, had gone to South Africa as special correspondent for *The Times*, and his reports had castigated the
medical service as incompetent, ill-prepared, and so bound
up in red tape as to be hopelessly inflexible when faced with
the unexpected. He said that the sick and wounded soldiers
were being treated with neglect and inhumanity.

Treves replied in a long letter, which *The Times* printed,
saying that he had seen nothing of neglect and inhumanity.
The arrangements made had been sound, the organisation
was liberal and businesslike, and the surgeons and nurses
worked with selfless devotion and tireless skill. The Army's
medical service not being endowed with the gift of prophecy,
it could not anticipate everything that happened; and the
exigencies of war sometimes required actions which would
not be acceptable at home or in time of peace.

The correspondence continued, growing sharper. Burdett-
Coutts made a speech in the House in June; he wrote to
Lansdowne; he wrote to Lord Roberts so often that Roberts
grew irritable and told Lansdowne quite sharply that he had
heard no complaints, and that the arrangements were the
best possible in the prevailing circumstances.

'There you have it,' Hazelmere said to Venetia, when
the subject came up again, as it frequently did. '"In the

252

circumstances". War is not peace, and a military campaign is not the same as life in a modern city. But the civilian can never understand military matters, and that's where all this comes from.'

'You don't try to tell me that the Army Medical Corps is everything it should be?'

'I don't think so for a moment, and I'm sure some things could have been done better. But that doesn't alter the fact that most of this fuss is made by people who simply have no understanding of war; of what it's like trying to move troops and materials about in a vast, unknown and hostile country, in the middle of unpredictable events.'

'Treves is a civilian,' Venetia said drily, 'so I suppose his opinion – that everything is all right – has no value either?'

Hazelmere smiled. 'Don't try to fight with me, my love. This is not our quarrel.'

'A person would have to be a monster to fight with you,' she said, yielding. 'But I still remember how Sir Walter Foster offered to create a sanitary commission and they turned him down, and half the casualties at least have been due to disease. Now that, surely, is a scandal. It was the same in the Crimea. Isn't it madness to lose so many fighting men to sickness?'

'True, I don't dispute it. But I do wonder what Foster could have done in South Africa that wasn't done. In the middle of the veldt, with the railway lines blown up, hundreds of miles from base, no roads, no equipment, only contaminated water to drink, and the enemy making surprise attacks from a different direction every day – I wonder what Foster's plan for that situation would have been. It's all very well for Burdett-Coutts to complain that the sick ought to have had beds, milk, clean linen, nurses and so on. We know they ought, but when the army has to move quickly, inessentials get left behind, and that means everything but ammunition and food. Sometimes even the food is abandoned. When you are under fire, you have to concentrate on firing back. The sick and wounded get put to one side and left until someone has time to care for them. That's just the brutal truth about war.'

'Hm,' said Venetia, with a mulish look in her eye.

'You're a soldier's wife, my love. You ought to see things from a military point of view.'

'I'm also a nurse's daughter,' she said, but she allowed the argument to drop. 'Of course, Treves and Burdett-Coutts are bound to be at loggerheads: both of them so addicted to publicity, and both of them with a book on the subject about to be published. Interesting, though,' she added, 'that they both have the same publisher.'

'I think the publisher is a great deal cannier than either of them,' Hazelmere said.

The campaign started by *The Times* led to the setting up of a Royal Commission to investigate the allegations, which opened in July.

'It's a very bad idea,' Hazelmere said restlessly. 'I don't know what Salisbury's about to allow it. Does the Government think no-one abroad reads our newspapers? It can only lend comfort to the enemy.'

That was also the Queen's opinion. She wrote a stiff letter to the Prime Minister, in which she said, 'Boer spies will telegraph back to South Africa and great harm will be done. You must show a firm front. An enquiry can be held after the War itself is over, but not now. No doubt the War Office itself is greatly at fault, but it is the whole system which must be changed, and that cannot be done just now.'

But the Commission went ahead. Treves gave his evidence on the 30th of July. His position was that 'war is war, and we had enormous difficulties to meet'. You could not make particular provisions for the sick when you did not know whether ten men would come in or a thousand. Sometimes there were plenty of beds, sometimes a great deficiency. In war there were long periods of inactivity and then periods of frantic activity when everything happened at once. Staffing and the number of orderlies was adequate except during the greatest emergencies, when ten times the number would hardly have sufficed. The impossibility of caring for the wounded out in the open made it essential for a field hospital to follow the army, but on occasion it was impossible for it to keep up. It was dreadful for the wounded to be jolted over rough tracks in ox-carts, but when you were twenty-six miles from the railway and there were no roads, what choice did you have?

After taking all the evidence, the Commission concluded that the military and medical authorities had not anticipated the magnitude of the war, so the RAMC had insufficient staff and equipment, and was not so constituted as to be able to make up its deficiencies promptly.

'Which is what I've said all along,' Venetia complained, putting down the paper in exasperation, 'and what Mama said forty years ago. Too much red tape, too many layers of command, too much secrecy and protection of rank. Nothing changes.'

'It may be true,' Hazelmere said, and, at a snort from Venetia, 'Very well, it probably is true, but Burdett-Coutts has done no-one any good by airing all this now. There can hardly be a family in the country that doesn't have a son or brother or uncle in South Africa, and it will do no good to morale for them to think Tommy Atkins is not being properly looked after.'

'In recognition of your heroism in admitting the truth, I will agree with you and close the subject,' Venetia said.

On the 30th of July 1900 a new kind of underground railway was opened in London, which caused quite a stir in the newspapers. Jack was particularly interested in it, and pored over every report he could find. One day in August Henrietta, seeing what he was reading, paused in passing and leant over his shoulder to read as well. It was called the Central London Railway, and it ran from Cornhill, near the Bank of England, in the east to Shepherd's Bush in the west.

'I never liked the underground railway when we lived in London – so smoky and hot and crowded,' she said, 'but I can see that it was very useful. And I think your father actually rather enjoyed it, in a strange way.'

'Oh, but this one's different, Mother,' Jack said. 'You see, there are so many pipes running just under the surface of London – sewers and gas pipes and so on – that there wasn't room for any more railway tunnels. So they've gone down

255

really, really deep this time, underneath everything, and the new railway runs through a tunnel bored through the solid clay and never comes up to the surface at all. The passengers go down from the street to the platforms in lifts.'

'Dear me, how horrid!'

'Oh, Mother!' Jack exclaimed, at this feminine nonsense. 'Why? No more than any other tunnel.'

'I should think it would be very dangerous. How would the smoke get out? How ever would you breathe? And suppose the tunnel collapsed?'

'It can't collapse. It's lined with curved cast-iron sections, so it's just exactly like a metal tube with the train running along inside it. And of course they couldn't have steam traction down there, so the whole thing is powered by electricity. No smoke, no steam – all clean and quiet. And cool, too.'

'Well, that would be an improvement,' she admitted. 'They were talking of making the Metropolitan Railway run by electricity years ago, but nothing came of it. I don't see how it would work, though. If you have electricity running through the rails, why aren't the passengers killed?'

'Oh, because the carriage is insulated. Look, I'll show you.' Enthusiastically he began to draw diagrams along the edge of the newspaper and Henrietta tried to follow, though her brain gave up the unequal struggle when he got to 'voltage conversion'. She was impressed by his grasp of the subject, and carried on nodding and saying, 'I see,' long after she ceased to, for the pleasure of hearing her clever son talk.

The promoter of this revolutionary new railway was a syndicate headed by the German banker, Ernest Cassel, who was a friend of the Prince of Wales, and a banker and businessman from New York, Darius Ogden Mills. Eight years previously, a Parliamentary committee had recommended that free wayleave should be granted to underground railways that ran directly beneath streets, in order to save them the endless delays of negotiating with every litigious landlord in their path. To take advantage of this concession, the Central London Railway had been built to follow the line of the streets above. This was easily done from Shepherd's Bush along the admirably straight and broad thoroughfares of the Bayswater Road and Oxford Street; but further into the City the roads grew so narrow that it was necessary to build two tunnels one above the other, to carry the eastbound and westbound lines separately.

Jack expounded eagerly on the interesting innovations of the line, such as the fact that the stations were built as very shallow hillocks on the line, to help the trains to slow as they arrived and accelerate as they left. He drew his mother a detailed sketch of the locomotive, a strange, hump-backed thing with two sloping 'noses', pointing in opposite directions, with a square cab joining them in the middle. This strange animal was coupled in the centre of the train to even out the traction which ever way it was going, and so that the driver and his assistant could see both ends more easily. Each train also carried two guards – one at either end – and four gatemen, who opened and shut the doors for the passengers at the stations. An elaborate system of hand signals had been devised, which passed between the eight crew members to say that it was safe for the train to depart the station.

There were detailed descriptions in the *Daily Mail*, and even drawings in the illustrated papers, of the luxurious carriages, well lit by glass-shaded electric lamps, the seats comfortably upholstered and the whole made splendid with brass and leather. The outside of the carriages was painted crimson with the railway's name picked out in prominent gold lettering, and all in all, the *Daily Mail* said, 'If this kind of thing goes on, London will become quite a nice place to travel in.'

There had been some concern in the early days of the underground railway because there was no division between first- and second-class travel, but this egalitarian system had been taken up by all the subsequent lines. So far no serious damage to the fabric of society had been noticed – although Henrietta had sometimes privately thought it was so disagreeable to travel by 'metro' that passengers were too locked into their private misery to care. But the new Central London Railway had pushed the idea further by instituting

257

a flat fare of twopence, with penny fares on the early-morning trains for the lower-paid workers going in to their employment. So from the beginning the line was always known as the 'Twopenny Tube', and from the day it opened it proved hugely popular, not only for taking people from their homes to work and back, but also because it served the West End, and could therefore deliver people from the suburbs to enjoy the shops, theatres and concert halls in Town. Just occasionally Henrietta thought with wistfulness about this aspect of London life, and remembered the plays and concerts she and Jerome had attended, and shopping in Liberty's or D. H. Evans. But she had only to wake in the luminous dark of before dawn, and hear the birdsong and smell the sweet, grassy air coming in through her open window, to know she had the best of the bargain this way.

Jack talked so much about the electric railway that she asked him if this might be an area he would like to be trained in when the time came. 'I like steam engines much more,' he said, 'but electricity is such an amazing thing, and there's so much that you can do with it.' His brow furrowed with the huge anxieties of fourteen. 'I shouldn't like to miss out on the future – I mean, it seems to me you could do almost anything with electricity if you could only work out how – but I do love steam locomotives so, and we haven't got anywhere near the perfect one yet, so there's lots still to do. I just don't know, Mother. It's hard to choose.'

'Well, I don't think you need to make the choice just this minute. There's time yet – and you never know, something else may come up that you like even more. Something even more modern and exciting.'

'Like motor-cars? No, I don't think so – noisy and feeble compared to trains, whatever Robbie says.'

'What about flying machines?' she smiled.

'Oh, I don't care about balloons,' he said. 'Too slow. Though if ever there were proper flying machines, like in *The War of the Worlds*, that would be different.'

The servants' bedrooms were finished; a new, efficient water-pump had been installed; a dumb-waiter had been set up from the laundry-room to the bedroom floor for the more convenient carriage of clean linen, together with a chute to take the soiled linen down – both of palpitating interest to the children, especially as the upper ends came out in the corridor by the nursery doors. And plans were under consideration not only for two water-closets, but for gas to be laid on at some point in the future.

'And you know,' Teddy said, 'we might even think about central heating one day. There's plenty of room in the cellar for a boiler.'

The furniture had been moved in, and the drawing-room was now fully furnished with the pieces from Makepeace House, and with two new carpets. The bits and pieces with which Henrietta and Jerome had been making do were put back where they came from, and Teddy's better items filled the rooms, along with quite a lot of new furniture that somehow got sneaked in. Teddy's modest objections to taking the Great Bedchamber were overcome, and the massive Butts Bed was reconstructed from its component parts, and given new hangings. All of his cook's own precious equipment was moved into the kitchen, her preserves and stores into the cupboards in the housekeeper's room, and after a breath-holding pause while she tried it out, she pronounced the great stove 'a marvel' and fears that she might leave in a temper were put aside.

Henrietta was extremely busy during the moving-in period. Every minute of the day someone would be coming to her with a question, a difficulty, a complaint, a breakage. The newly arrived servants had to be shown where everything was and instructed in their duties; some even had to be conducted about the house as they continually got lost, with the confusion of unlit passages and four staircases to distract them. One girl began having nightmares, and Henrietta had broken rest night after night; another, a devotee of cheap novels, began seeing ghosts and hearing 'strange knocking noises, madam, and ghostly feet walking about above my head at night'. Her nerves were not soothed by Robbie's assuring her cheerfully that the latter was 'only rats'. The children had to be banned from the kitchen, which they were used to regarding as their home, as the cook was rather a stately individual and not used to 'a pack of children trammelling up my kitchen while I'm trying to cook, madam – begging your pardon, but it's them or me'.

'You're not to go in there for any reason whatever, without asking me first,' she told them in her sternest voice, but hoping that when things had settled down, a little more flexibility might be introduced.

'Aren't we going to eat in there any more?' Jessie asked.

'No, and a good thing too,' her father said. 'You'll eat in the dining-room and learn proper manners. You all eat like wolves, and if I let you loose on society like that you'll disgrace me.'

Jerome was in two minds about the changes, although he kept his feelings to himself. On the one hand, it would be extremely pleasant to have all the disagreeable tasks done by servants again, and have the house comfortable and Henrietta relieved from the hard work and worry that had been her lot these latter years. Oh, to have fires in the winter that he hadn't had to light and carry the fuel for! To be saved the regular messy job of filling the lamps! But on the other hand, there had been a kind of freedom to it that he would miss. A household of highly trained servants was a boon, but it was also a restriction. You could not go where you wanted, do what you wanted, say what you pleased. You could not kiss your wife in front of them, eat bread and cheese at the kitchen table, roll on the carpet with the dog or demonstrate a rugby scrum to the boys with the aid of a pumpkin. You were the Master and you had to be dignified. You had to behave for them, as they had to behave for you.

Henrietta wasn't aware that there was a drawback for her in the new dispensation until after the worst of the settling-in was over and the household routine began to function. Then, like a débutante at the end of the Season when the whirl of gaiety suddenly stops and leaves her beached, she found herself with nothing – or, at least, not enough – to do.

'Good!' said Jerome decidedly. 'Sit with your hands in

your lap and twiddle your thumbs. It will do me good to watch you.'

'It won't do *me* good to be doing it,' she replied.

'Read a book.'

'I've read one.' She sighed. 'I suppose I'd better get on with the sewing I was always putting off because I hadn't enough time.'

He concealed a smile. 'You could go and see the baby first,' he suggested.

She needed no more urging.

For Emma, there had been no pain in giving up the cooking and housework for looking after baby Polly. She loved children, and the work was much more congenial. Also, she did like being known as Nanny Morland when she met other servants in York on her days off. The night nursery, built for mediaeval families of children, was vast, and though the boys had their beds at one end, there was still plenty of room to set up Polly's cot at the other. The difficulty was that Emma's bedroom was on the third floor, too far from the baby at night. In earlier generations, the nursery-maid had slept in the nursery along with all the children, with no more privacy than a screen around her bed, but that would not do in these modern times.

Teddy applied his own brand of logic to the problem when Henrietta put it to him. After brief but weighty thought, he said, 'You must move the boys out of the nursery. Give them a bedroom. You've got plenty. Put them in the North Bedroom. That's plenty big enough. Then Emma can sleep in the night nursery with the baby.'

'But she has her own comfortable bedroom upstairs. It won't be very nice for her to give that up for sleeping in that barn of a room, with nowhere to put her things.'

'Well, then, we'll *make* her a room of her own in the nursery. Put up a wall across it, turn one end into a nice bedroom – it's got windows all the way along, so that's not a problem. Then she'll be right next door to the baby – keep the door open in between, if she likes.'

It turned out to be remarkably easy to do, simply the building and plastering of a wall and the hanging of a door, and Emma had a bedroom a little larger than her old one, into which her things were moved, with the addition of a new and very comfortable armchair, a gift from Teddy, and a useful table, so that she could use it as a sitting-room as well if she liked. She expressed herself very satisfied. 'It's lighter than my old room and the ceiling's higher – and not so many stairs to climb. I shall be happy as a clam, with my new baby and all – just when the old ones were getting wore out!'

The boys were also delighted to be 'promoted' to a bedroom from the nursery, so it seemed all was well.

'You are so good at solving problems,' Henrietta said to her brother.

'Am I? I only say what seems obvious to me.' He smiled at her. 'I can solve your problem, too.'

'I didn't know I had one.'

'You feel strange and restless, with your labours taken away from you.'

'How do you know that? Has Jerome been talking to you?'

'Well, a bit. But I don't need Jerome to tell me what's before my eyes. And I know the solution. You need a horse.'

Henrietta opened her mouth automatically to refute it, and then closed it as the glorious vision flooded in on her. To have a horse of her own, a proper riding horse, and the leisure to go with it! To be able to ride all over the land she had grown up in and see the old places again! She hadn't ridden, not properly, since her first husband died and the horses were sold. She and Jerome had lived in London all their married life until his insolvency, and riding had not been a part of their life there.

Teddy was watching her face. 'You'd like it? Then it's done. It's a pity none of our own horses is ready yet, but I think I know where I can lay my hands on a nice sort of mare. Laycock was saying his wife never went out any more and he was thinking of selling her horse if he could find a good home for it. If he hasn't sold it already, we might give it a try. I've not seen it, but Laycock is a good judge of horseflesh, and he rides the nicest brown gelding I've seen in a long while.'

It was done in a remarkably short time. The mare, Elida, was a bay of fifteen hands, eight years old, well schooled and good-tempered. She had been something of a pet. Mrs Laycock parted with her in tears, but agreed with her husband that now rheumatism had stopped her riding, it wasn't kind to the mare to keep her.

Henrietta had kept her riding habit all these years, more out of sentiment than in the hope that she would ever be able to ride regularly again. She got it out and tried it on, expecting to have outgrown it. But hard work had kept her slender, and it fitted well. She turned back and forth in front of Teddy's cheval glass – the only full-length mirror in the house – and thought it made her look younger. Jerome evidently thought the same, and when she appeared before him in it, looked her up and down with an appreciation that made her blush.

On the day Teddy brought the mare home, Henrietta and the children were all waiting in the yard in a state of excitement. Jessie and Violet sat on the steps with their heads together, talking as usual; Robbie was swinging on the stable half-door making horrible faces at the girls, who disappointingly would not look up and catch them, and Frank was rewriting the scene in his head so that it was a troop of hussars they were expecting, and he was the general about to review them. Jerome was out about his business. 'I can see her later when I come home,' he said. It should be Teddy's occasion, he thought: Teddy ought to be the centre of attention.

The sound of hoofbeats on the track was quickly followed by the appearance of two horses, turning over the drawbridge and clattering in under the barbican. Teddy was riding Victor and leading the mare, who looked about her with interest and only a flickering of the ears to betray uncertainty. All the children jumped up and spoke at once. Robbie leapt off the stable door and managed to trip himself on a rake that was propped against the frame. It fell with a clatter and he fell with a thump and a yell, but the mare only jerked her head back and took a sideways step.

'Well, isn't she good?' Henrietta exclaimed. 'Another horse would be half across the county by now. Pick up that rake, Robbie, don't leave it lying for a horse to tread on.'

'Isn't she pretty?' Violet said, coming forward with a piece of carrot for the newcomer. All the children had treats for her, and she munched them and flirted her head while they crooned and petted her.

'Can I try her, Mother?' Jessie asked before long.

Teddy intervened: 'Of course not, your mother's to try her. And then she'll need to be stabled so that she can get settled in. Come on, Hen. I want to see how she goes for you.'

Henrietta was ready dressed in her habit. Robbie tightened the girths for her and linked his hands to throw her up. 'She's so tall after Dunnock!' Henrietta exclaimed, as she settled herself and found the stirrup. She leant forward and stroked the bay neck, and the mare turned her head a little to look at her. 'Poor girl, it must be confusing for you. But you'll like it here, I promise,' she told her.

Teddy turned Victor and they rode out again, followed by the children, and walked and then trotted up the track towards the Monument. There he opened the gate into an empty paddock so that Henrietta could try all the mare's paces, finishing with an all-out gallop round the boundary that flushed birds out of the hedge and almost unseated Henrietta when Elida threw in a light-hearted buck.

'She's fresh,' Teddy said, sitting on sensible Victor, who only pointed his ears and snorted at this evidence of female frivolity. 'What say we go out for a ride this afternoon? Give her a couple of hours to get used to her stall, and then take her for a good run?'

'I'd love it,' Henrietta said, panting a little as she pulled up and patted the mare's neck.

'Do you like her?'

'She's lovely. Her paces are beautiful, and she has a nice mouth.'

'Shall we keep her, then?'

'Oh, Teddy, yes! Thank you so much! You are very much too kind to me.'

'Oh, bosh,' he said. 'It was nothing at all.'

* * *

264

After lunch they saddled the horses again and went out, up the track the local people called Green Lane, skirting Acomb, passing through Ten Thorn Gap, across to Harewood Whin and then on to Marston Moor.

'All the old places, all the old sights,' Teddy said, looking round with satisfaction. 'I never knew how much I missed them. The mare's going well, ain't she?'

'Beautifully. I shall be stiff tomorrow, though – I haven't ridden this long in years.'

'That'll soon wear off. I must say,' he added, as if he'd just thought of it, 'that it's nice having old Victor living right here on the spot, instead of having to send for him from the livery stables. Just pop down any time I like and see the old fellow, saddle up and away. Of course, in the town I didn't have anywhere to ride *to*, not for pleasure. Are you ready for a canter?'

They rode as far as Wilstrop Wood, and then Henrietta worried about overtiring the mare when she wasn't fit, so they turned for home. Teddy glanced at his sister's happy face and a wave of tenderness washed over him. 'This is nice, isn't it?' he said. 'Just like when we were children.'

'Better,' she said. 'Now we're old enough to appreciate what we took for granted then. I'm so glad you've come to live here again, Ted.' He nodded, but his eyes were suddenly withdrawn, his mouth grave. She knew he was thinking that if he hadn't lost Charley it would not have happened. 'You miss her, don't you?' she said gently.

'All the time,' he said. 'I think about her all day, and dream about her all night, and then I wake up and she's not there, and she never will be there.'

'Oh, Teddy, I'm so sorry.'

'It's better here, though, at Morland Place. At least here I've got all of you around me.'

'You belong here. This is your home, and we are your family.'

He managed a smile. 'We ought to go out every day, Hen. Nothing like riding – best thing for your health. And you know what I've just thought – we might even hunt this winter, what do you say? Think the mare would go?'

265

'Like a bird.'

'I'd have to buy a hunter, though – couldn't hunt old Victor.' He slapped the warm neck affectionately. 'No reason why I shouldn't have a couple of hunters, though, is there? Plenty of room in the stables. Take the children out, too. All the children ought to have ponies. Think your little Jessie would like a pony of her own?'

'She'd swoon with delight!'

'And when Polly's old enough, I'll teach her to ride. She'll be a fine rider – she's got the hands for it.'

'Oh, Teddy, they're just fat little baby fists!' Henrietta laughed.

'A father can tell,' he said solemnly. 'Lord, there's nothing like the country after all! Why didn't I do this years ago? I can't believe I let Morland Place stand empty while I lived in a dusty, fusty town. To think I deprived Charley of all this.'

'Charley was happy where she was.'

They were just passing Huntsham Farm now, and Mrs Walton who was working in her kitchen garden straightened up to stare and then to wave when she recognised the riders. They waved back and Teddy lifted his hat courteously. 'I tell you what else, Hen,' he went on. 'If business goes on the way it's been going, I'm going to start buying back the land.'

'Teddy, really?'

'I know, everyone says farming doesn't pay any more, but it does if you go the right way about it. Got to think things through properly, not just go on doing what you've always done and hoping for the best. Can't compete with American wheat, and wool's a wash-out now, but the market-gardening is beginning to show a profit, and there's certainly a market for milk. I could run a big dairy herd on one of the farms. Then there's eggs, chickens and spring lamb for the table. And working horses – railways and omnibus companies need lots of horses. I shouldn't mind turning Morland Place entirely over to horses and moving the market-gardening to one of the other farms, where there's more room.'

Henrietta smiled at his enthusiasm, so good to see it

loosen the pinched, tight look that was so often in his face, despite his determined cheerfulness. 'You've been thinking about it a lot,' she observed.

'Oh, it was Charley made me. Charley was always so full of ideas. She wanted me to buy back the whole estate. "Don't let profit sit idle," she would say to me. "Expand the businesses to make more profit, and use the profit to buy back your land." That was her plan, and by God it was a good one! If only she could be here to see what comes of it. If only she hadn't had to die,' he finished sadly.

It was the nearest Teddy came to rebelling against the will of God, and it made Henrietta ashamed that she had ever felt hard-done-by. 'I expect she does see,' she said gently. 'And there's Polly.'

'Yes,' he said, 'Polly, my little treasure. Lord, what a ball we'll give for her coming-out!'

Henrietta laughed. 'Give the poor child a chance to grow up first. She isn't even coming out of her cradle yet!'

The new regime seemed to suit everyone, though Henrietta had been worried about how Ned would cope with the changes that had come so suddenly to his life. Charley had been like a mother to him. His own mother was a distant memory now, unreal, like a figure from a story book; and he had never had a father until Teddy took him in. Now in a short space of time he had been sent away to school, Charley was dead, Polly had appeared, and Makepeace House was no longer home. He had come back from school for the funeral, and Henrietta had kept close to him on that occasion. He had grown and put on weight in his time at Eton but, pale in his stiff new blacks, he was, she saw, just a little boy still. He had tried manfully not to cry, and when Henrietta had laid a hand on his shoulder he had stiffened and pulled away; but singing the hymn had done it, for him and for Teddy. First one and then the other had broken down; and when the coffin was lowered into the crypt there had been no more pretence at keeping a stiff upper lip. Henrietta was glad for both of them that they had cried, believing that there was healing in natural tears. After the funeral Jerome had ventured to say to her that it was inhumane to send Ned back to school, but she believed it was the best thing for him. 'He's said goodbye. Now he needs to see that life goes on.'

When Ned came back for the long vacation, Teddy had arranged that he should come straight to Morland Place, and being with his cousins did seem to cheer him up. She wondered sometimes if he remembered anything from his earliest childhood in Morland Place, but didn't like to raise the subject, especially not now. He had been a little subdued at first, as was to be expected, but after a few days he was laughing and romping with the rest. She would sometimes see him catch himself up, remembering his loss and wondering if it was all right to be happy again so soon. He did not see Polly until Teddy finally made the move to Morland Place, and when he did see her, he showed the same amount and kind of interest as the other boys had: amazement at her tiny size and the novelty of her, soon giving way to a benevolent indifference when she proved not to do anything more interesting than sleep and cry.

'But after all,' Jerome said, when she talked to him about it, 'what did you expect? Boys are never much interested in babies, and she's not his sister, only his cousin. What should he feel?'

'Oh, you know very well. Don't pretend ignorance. Charley was his mother to all intents and purposes, and Polly is her child and – well – the reason she died. And Polly takes his place now. He may resent it.'

Jerome took hold of her hand with a serious look. 'Darling, don't lay those things on the poor child's head. Ned knows Charley was not, in fact, his mother. And he trusts Teddy to do the right thing by him. I don't think he expected to be his heir. I doubt if he has ever even considered the matter – it's only we who have done that. And nobody blames Polly for Charley's death, so why should Ned? Frankly, my love, I don't think he has the imagination to think along such romantic lines. He's just a nice, ordinary, rather stolid little boy.'

'Not so little. He'll be fifteen soon.'

'But stolid all the same. He takes life as it comes – and lucky him, to have that kind of nature. It will mean a great deal less pain for him.'

Henrietta kept a close eye on Ned for a while, but she saw that Jerome was right. He had a phlegmatic temperament, and was not given to more exercise of thought than necessity demanded. She crossed him gratefully off her list of things to worry about, and looked forward instead to the visit of Lizzie, Ashley and the children, which was to be in September as Ashley could not get leave for August.

'I shall have a lovely houseful,' she said to Jerome, one evening, as they took a stroll alone together, 'and hardly have any work about it – just planning and giving orders. Goodness, what a pleasure it is to be rich again!'

'Speaking of which,' Jerome said, 'I had a letter this morning from Rundell and Bridges to say they had finished selling the jewellery.'

'Oh? You didn't say. Did it fetch as much as you hoped?'

'A little more,' he said. 'I have a very nice cheque to deposit in my bank account. It will think it must be a mistake, it has been starved so long!'

'Oh, darling, I'm very glad for you,' Henrietta said.

'Aren't you glad for you, too?'

'Of course – but someone has always looked after me. I'm mostly glad that this awful nightmare is over and you can be free of it and happy again. Do you mean to ask Teddy to let you in on the business?'

They had been walking up the slope towards the Monument, and he stopped now and turned her to face him. The sun was setting; long thin bars of cloud across the western horizon were edged with molten gold.

'That's something I want to discuss with you. I could ask Teddy if I can invest in the horse-business, and arrange with him some kind of *pro rata* share of the profits. Or I could use the money to set up something of my own – of our own.'

'And leave Morland Place?'

'And leave Morland Place. But I want to know which you would favour. I want you to think very carefully about it. I know Teddy will always be kind and generous, but Morland Place is his, not ours, and what that means with the rind off is that we have no hold on this place and no security here. We have now a small but useful amount of capital, which we could invest elsewhere, giving us independence. We could set up a home of our own, though it would not be a home like this, of course, and we would have to live in a much smaller way. No big house and dozens of servants.'

She searched his face, trying to guess what he wanted her to say. He returned her gaze steadily, not wanting to influence her, wanting to know what she truly thought. There could never have been a less demanding or more modest benefactor than theirs, and Jerome was truly grateful to Teddy and loved him as a brother; but this was a chance for him to be free of the last ties of dependency, to plough his own furrow and care for his own family as a man should. He would stand by her decision, whatever it was, but like a harnessed horse he had caught the smell of open fields coming faintly to him on the wind, and his heart turned over in him with the longing to be gone.

She said, 'I don't care about luxury, you know I don't. I just love being here. It's – oh, I can't explain it to you, but it's more than a house or land or anything like that. It's . . .' She paused, searching, and in the end could only say helplessly, 'It's home.'

'And you'd sooner be here than anywhere else, no matter what the circumstances?'

'Yes, of course. But – but don't you like it here? I thought you were happy. If you want to go, of course we will go. We'll do whatever you want. I only want you to be happy.'

So there was his answer. He managed to say, 'Of course I'm happy here. How could I not be? I'd hate to leave now I've got the yearlings under saddle, and the mares in foal again. I couldn't abandon the scheme in the middle.'

Her glowing smile was his reward. 'Oh, I'm so glad! You frightened me for a moment – I thought you really wanted to go away.' He kissed the end of her nose in place of a reply. He did not want to lie to her, and needed a moment to master his disappointment. She went on, 'Teddy was talking about starting to buy the farms back. If you invest in the horses, that will give him some capital to work with.'

He needed to change the subject. 'I had a parcel this morning, as well as a letter,' he said.

'Who from?'

'Also from Rundell and Bridges. They didn't sell quite all the jewellery. There was one piece I told them to hold back, to have it cleaned and sent here to me. It's something that belonged to my mother, so I hope you won't mind that Julia had it before you. I was going to keep it for your birthday, but I can't wait any longer.'

He took out from his pocket the jeweller's box, and opened the lid. It was a string of pearls, smooth, creamy and glowing in the sunset light.

'They're beautiful,' she breathed. 'I've never seen such lovely ones.'

'Yes, my mother adored them. They went everywhere with her. Ever since I first met you, long before I met Julia, I wanted you to have them,' he said. 'I knew how they would look round your throat. Now at last I shall see. Turn round.'

She turned, and he put them round her neck and did up the clasp, then placed a kiss on her bare neck, where the little curls that were too short to catch up nestled in a way he had always found deeply distracting. He put his arms round her and she folded her hands over his. 'I love you,' he murmured.

'I love you, too.'

He rested his cheek against hers, and together they faced the sunset. The sun was almost down, and the sky was flaming with gorgeous pinks, rich purples and bars of pure crimson, strips of cloud edged with light flying like ragged banners of fire. Once in a while, he thought, God put on a special show just to remind you who He was and what an insignificant worm you were, for all your human cleverness. He felt the warm body of the woman he loved pressed against him, and put firmly aside his faint longing for freedom, buried it and rolled a stone over it. He was lucky. He had always been lucky: fortune's favourite, his sister used to say.

24th August 1900
Dearest Aunt Hen,
Well, I am back with my khaki brothers and you may have thought your boy had forgotten you but we have been quite busy. To explain what has happened so far, our Chief has worked his way northwards through Transvaal, securing as he went. You may have heard what is going on in the Free State (Orange Colony we are supposed to call it now it has been annexed, but it don't trip off the tongue like the other!), I mean the clearances, where they burn the farms, destroy the crops, drive off the animals and leave the women and children on the open veldt with what they can carry, just enough to get to the nearest town. It is very harsh but Bobs and K think it necessary – to begin with, the Free State prisoners-of-war were released after taking an oath of allegiance not to fight again, but when they got home they armed again and straight away joined commandos, so they have broken their oath. My friend Jocelyn (who's on the Staff now) says it is the Boer women who are fiercest and drive the men to do it, so it is on their own heads when our fellows come and smoke them out. Secondly the commandos move so fast – quick strike and run – and use every homestead as a base, so the only way is to destroy the farms and so cut their supply line (just as they try to destroy ours by attacking the railway and telegraph). Well, war is war and a dirty business, and as I said, Bobs thinks it necessary. But I am glad to say that our Chief doesn't hold with burning farms and turning women out to starve. He says it ain't gentlemanly and that the only way to defeat the Boers is in the field. Also that we have to hold the land between the towns, because their capitals are just empty trophies and mean nothing to them. So we confiscate any arms and ammunition we find but don't fire the farms and the rest of it – which is a great relief to us Tommies, I can tell you.

So we have moved north and reached the railway which runs between Pretoria and the coast at Delagoa

Bay. Now Bobs has decided it is time to clear the eastern section and he's sent K to join forces with us. So we are driving eastward on a front straddling the railway, K to the north and us to the south. Botha is somewhere between Belfast and Machadorp and the intelligence is that he has 7000 men. Also there is a rumour that Kruger is somewhere about behind Botha's line and if we move fast enough we may catch him. It is strange to be back here after Yorkshire, everything so wide and empty and very little green, but in some ways it seems more natural to me than England now. I'm glad to say that young Ray Puddephat is very useful to me, having very sharp eyes, but more than that it is good to have a friend to talk to about home. My dear old Dolly was glad to see me, and I believe I stood and stroked her for half an hour at once, while she nudged and rubbed away at me and did her best to nibble off my buttons! After your efforts and those of the maids at home I am a little less ragamuffin than some of the other fellows, who look on me as quite a smart! I must tell you what the Boers do now. When they capture any of our fellows, they make them strip down to their shirts, take their boots, puttees, breeches and tunics, and give them their own rags in exchange. This shows that however shabby our fellows have become they are better off than the Boers, who being penned up all round can't get any new stuff. It does create a problem, though, in that it lets the Boers get quite close up to us at times before we can be sure they are the enemy and not our own. I will keep this letter open a day or two as we are sure to catch up with Botha soon and then I can tell you about it. If I am bowled over I have made Alderson of Ours promise to send it to you, with my love, as always.

31st August
We found the Boers dug in at Bergendal, a very good position with rocks to the north and marsh to the south and in the centre a kopje where Botha had his best

273

men, the Johannesburg Police (they call them ZARP) dug into sangars ready to biff away at us. However, the kopje was vulnerable to our artillery and we bombarded them all day. It was very hot work. Our men lying down on the ridge opposite had to be quick to raise their heads, get a round off, and duck down again, as to the Boer we were silhouetted on the skyline and there was no cover. One of the Devons said to me afterwards he just sat tight behind the largest blade of grass he could find! Our howitzers tried to shell ZARP out of the sangars but as they could not get close enough to see the target they had to fire on directions and did not manage to land on target, though their smoke gave our men some relief and allowed them to pop up and fire off. At twilight the firing on both sides grew tremendous, and then as darkness fell it all stopped dead – very queer, as your ears ring so hard for a time afterwards you keep thinking it has started up again! Our casualties were not much, about fifty I think. I was kept on the go all day and Dolly was tired out, quite something for her as usually she will go all day and still frisk a little at nightfall. It was very cold in the night and we all 'had the jumps' thinking of the Boer perhaps creeping up on us and potting us out of the dark. There was a tremendous burst of firing from the Manchesters once but no return fire so I think they were probably firing at nothing, which often happens. The next day (27th) the firing resumed. By sunset the ZARP were obviously weakened and the Skins and Rifles attacked with bayonet and overran them, though they fought like furies and few were taken prisoner. After that the rest of the Boer line collapsed and they went on the run, some north towards Lydenburg, some east towards the coast.

Even then they still had the nerve to hold on here and there. On the 29th they got a pom-pom up in the fog and shelled our column on the left, from the Lydenburg road, and got away smartly before we could take them, and yesterday at Waterval Onder, which is at the bottom of a deep valley, they were sniping from the other side of the valley at anyone going into the village. I was up with the cavalry and we got into the village ahead of the main force and had to lie low there until dark. Our fellows on the hillside shelled them but they hung on and got away after sunset without our ever having seen them. It is the most frustrating kind of war! The reason we dashed into Waterval was that intelligence said we should find Kruger there, but needless to say the bird had flown, and we hear now he is heading east for the border. Tomorrow we shall be marching towards Lydenburg in pursuit of Botha. It is mountainous country and the Chief anticipates we shall have a fight or two on the way but now we have them on the run the advantage is with us. I think perhaps the end is in sight at last. More when I have some more paper.

Your devoted,
Bertie

The railway from Pretoria eastwards to the Portuguese port of Lourenço Marques crossed the border at a town called Koomati Poort, which was the last railway station in Transvaal. News came in September that President Kruger had escaped that way on the 11th into Portuguese East Africa, along with 1500 Boers and 500 foreign volunteers. They set fire to 1500 railway wagons as they passed through, and Roberts telegraphed the Portuguese authorities to ask them to make sure the railway bridge at Koomati Poort was not destroyed, which the Portuguese agreed to do. Kruger and the foreign volunteers, mostly Dutch and Irish, reached the coast and set sail for Europe on a ship sent for them by the Queen of Holland. The Boers mostly returned home after taking the oath of allegiance, though some stayed on in small units in the hills to continue to harry 'Mr Khaki' through October.

Roberts wrote to Lansdowne that the war was all but over. Transvaal was formally annexed on the 28th of October, and the newspapers were full of victory and peace.

The Government took advantage of the temporary public approval by calling a general election – something that scandalised the highest-minded as being a degradation of politics, and not in the best traditions of fair play. The success of the ploy was not overwhelming: the Unionist Government was returned, but with only three more seats than before the election. Salisbury, who was seventy-one and growing very tired, gave up the Foreign Office, which he had been holding as well as the premiership, and passed it to Lansdowne. Those newspapers that thought the conduct of the war had been less than satisfactory disapproved vehemently of this promotion. The *National Review*'s editorial described it as 'A first-rate joke of Lord Salisbury's – one of the most cynical acts of our time.'

But Venetia said, 'Cocky will do better there. It's his natural constituency.'

And Hazelmere agreed. 'He did well in India. He's a diplomat much more than a soldier.'

General Buller came home, and while the newspapers were willing to give him a hero's welcome, having forgiven him for Spion Kop, the military authorities and the Cabinet were now all against him. He was awarded no honours, and instead of promotion was sent back to his former post at Aldershot, training the army corps. Wolseley, his patron, could do nothing for him, being himself on the way out. The 'Indian' faction was supreme. Lord Roberts was the hero of the hour, due also to come home, but to an earldom, a reward of £100,000, and succession to Wolseley's post of commander-in-chief. He had meant to leave at the same time as Buller, but was delayed in South Africa by the illness of his daughter and of the Queen's grandson, Prince Christian Victor, both with enteric fever. Kitchener was to take over from him as commander-in-chief in South Africa.

At the very end of September, pressing the Boers northwards through the mountains, Buller's division came to a place called Pilgrim's Rest. In this latter phase of the war, reconnoitring had become ever more important. Bertie's scouting party, with a support of fifteen mounted rifles under a Lieutenant Grey, was about a mile ahead of the infantry and artillery, testing out a winding road through the mountains and looking for the Boers. Bertie was ahead of the rifles, riding off to the side of the road with a small group of his scouts. It was a hot and cloudy day, rather oppressive, and the usual silence of the mountains seemed on this day brooding and strange. Everyone's nerves were on the jump; even the horses seemed restless.

Dolly pushed her way through the rough grass, her ears going back and forth, champing her bit, and the clink of the bit-rings seemed too loud against the background silence. There was no wind, and the further they went into the mountains the more stifling it became. Hordes of tiny black flies rose up at every step and would not be brushed away: Bertie found them sticking to the sweat on his face and again and again passed the sleeve of his jacket over his face to wipe it. Beyond the rustling of the grass and the soft thudding of hoofbeats he could hear nothing. Far above a bird of prey circled slowly on the wind – too far up to see what it was – but there was no other movement, which in itself was a warning. Usually there were all sorts of birds around. Had something frightened them off?

Alderson, riding beside him, touched his arm. Bertie put up his hand and they all halted. Dolly stretched her neck and sighed. One of the other horses shook its head with a jingle of bit-rings. Then there was silence. Bertie stared off in the direction Alderson had pointed. For a long time he could see nothing, and his vision began to jump a little with the effort of staring so long. He squeezed his eyes shut, then looked again. Yes, now he saw what could be people, near the top of a ridge off to the right. It was hard to tell, but it looked like something that was not a natural rock formation. And then something came over the skyline: the briefest glimpse of a silhouette, but it was enough to know it was a man and not a deer. It joined the other somethings and was still, but it had given the game away.

Bertie turned to his party. 'Puddephat, Holmes, get back to the Rifles and warn Lieutenant Grey. He'll probably want to send one of you back to the column. Don't ride straight along the road. Go down there into that gully – the trees

277

will hide you. We don't want to let Johnny Boer know we've seen him. Alderson, Pack and I will ride on a bit before we turn back, let them think we're still looking.'

Puddephat and Holmes turned their horses down to the left where a dry gully was marked by a line of thorn trees and disappeared. Bertie rode on, making a show of still looking for the enemy, really looking for a natural place to turn off the path. Then suddenly there was a crash of rifle fire – not from up on the skyline where they had seen the movement, but from behind, where the Rifles were coming up. Bertie exchanged one startled glance with his men – *ambush?* – and turned back. With a jerk of his arm he directed them into the gully: important they should have some cover if the Rifles had been ambushed or pinned down. The horses crashed through the long grass in bounds and, once in the gully, broke into a gallop; the gully bed was strewn with boulders but the horses were all natives and dodged or leapt over them with the skill of springbok.

When they got to the scene of the action it was clear what had happened. There must have been another party of Boers up above the road, hidden in a patch of scrub. When Puddephat and Holmes had brought the message, the Rifles had evidently dismounted – one of them, Biddle, had been left with the horses – and started up a slight ridge off to the right of the road to see if they could see the Boer, and as soon as they were half-way up and vulnerable, the Boer had opened fire. Now the Rifles were pinned down, lying flat on the slope without any cover while the Boer bullets kicked up dust spots all around them. Bertie could see Puddephat amongst them, but not Holmes – presumably Lieutenant Grey had sent him off to the column.

'How many, d'you think?' he said to Alderson.

'About twenty?'

'That's my guess,' Bertie said. 'God damn it! There's Grey hit!' He saw the impact of the bullet on the lieutenant's body, saw it jump in that particular way and then lie still. One of the others tried to get up and go to him and dropped down again hastily as a bullet sang past his head. Bertie saw uncertainty pass through the small beleaguered group as

278

clearly as wind passing over a cornfield. They had no officer now. Any moment they might scramble to their feet and run, and that would be fatal.

He was out of the saddle in a moment. 'Pack, ride back to the column as fast as you can and give them the new situation. Alderson, stay here and hold the horses.' And without waiting to see either order obeyed he was up out of the gully and running awkwardly through the long grass, unslinging his rifle as he went. He saw Biddle's startled face turn to him as he passed, and then he was going up the slope.

'All right, boys! Let 'em have it!' he shouted. Faces turned to see him and a cheer went up. 'Help's on the way. Just give them what for, boys! Keep low.'

They did not need telling any of those things, and yet somehow being told steadied them. All they needed was a lead. Bertie knew he had a reputation of being cool under fire – he was not sure how it had come about – and he saw how having him there cheered them. That was all the good he could do them. With no cover they could not do much against their attackers, or retreat: they could only stick it out and hope that help would arrive quickly.

And then there was a new sound: firing in a different direction, and the agitated whinny of a horse. The man nearest Bertie raised himself enough to look back and cursed vehemently. 'They're firing at the horses, God damn them!'

'Get down!' Bertie yelled at him, and he flopped just in time. But this was serious. If the horses were killed or panicked into running away, they would all be for it. He eased himself round far enough to take a look. Yes, the Rifles' horses were beginning to mill as bullets landed among them and Biddle was having difficulty holding them. Someone must go and help him. Even as he thought this, he felt himself hit. The shock was sickening, a sort of panicky, angry outrage, together with an almost childlike terror – *Mummy, I've been hurt*! The pain came moments later, a fireburst of it in his shoulder and chest and back. He heard himself cursing and, with a huge effort stopped, clamping his jaw on the useless stream of profanity. Mustn't unnerve the men!

But he heard someone shout, 'Cap'n Morland's hit!' and up ahead of him saw Puddephat turn his head then start up as if to come to him.

'Damn it, Ray, keep under cover!' Bertie yelled. 'I'm all right!' Puddephat lay down again, but kept turning his head back. Bertie could not use his rifle now; it had better be him, then, that went to help Biddle. His right arm and shoulder were a volcano of pain, but his left was unhurt: he could hold some horses with his left hand. He started crawling backwards down the slope, then lost his footing and rolled, agonisingly, for a few dozen feet, over and over on his wounded shoulder. He managed to stop himself, then crawled and scrambled the rest of the way down. He was not a moment too soon. The horses were milling now and Biddle was losing control. No time to think about the target he would make, or about his arm. He shoved himself over onto his knees with his good arm and then got to his feet. Speaking calmly he went amongst the horses. 'Ho, then, ho, then. Steady now. Stand, now.' The hornet whine of a bullet went past his head and he felt a burning followed by wetness on the top of his ear. A horse screamed. Biddle's sweating face turned towards him. One of the mounts was dragging backwards on its bridle and would soon be loose. Bertie caught the rein with his left hand and spoke soothingly to it, hoping the smell of blood about him would not do more harm than good. Biddle yielded several reins to him and redistributed the rest between his two hands. If only they could have signalled to Alderson to come and help! But Bertie had only one arm and Biddle had both hands full.

And then, quite suddenly, the firing stopped. The Boers gave up and disappeared in that odd way they had. Perhaps, Bertie thought, from their vantage-point they had seen the column coming. At all events, they were saved. Alderson reached them first, and took over the horses Bertie was holding, to his enormous relief. He took himself out of the way and sat down on a rock, feeling nauseous and faint. Some part of his mind told him to examine his wound but he could not bring himself to do it just at first. He was in a sick terror of what he would see. He knew how often wounds in the limbs led to amputation. Now the men were coming down off the ridge, carrying the wounded. He saw Grey with his eyes open, his face set with pain, but still alive. They carried him to where Bertie was sitting and laid him down. Their eyes met, but neither had the strength to speak. Another man – Cutts, was it? – had been hit in the leg, and was hopping on the other, his arms over the shoulders of two friends. And there was one other – who was it? – being carried. Very still. Awfully limp. He came nearer. Bertie knew that hair, knew it before he saw the dusty face, white under its tan. A moan escaped him that was nothing to do with his pain. They laid the body down beside him, and he knew it was dead without being told: death, he had discovered over these past months, does not much resemble sleep. Many of the soldiers he had seen killed died with their eyes open – a strange proportion of them – and the look on their faces was one of surprise, as if death was not at all like what they had expected. But Raymond Puddephat's eyes were closed, his face a blank. He looked very young, Bertie thought, through the haze of pain and weakness that was engulfing him.

The men were crowding round him now, talking, praising him for coming to their aid, for holding the horses, saying they'd have been for it if he had not come when he did. Someone gave him water. Alderson appeared beside him and said his wound wasn't too bad and that he'd be all right: Bertie had no idea if he were telling the truth or trying to comfort him. Someone contrived a sling to support his wounded arm out of a couple of knotted handkerchiefs. Someone else wet another handkerchief and cleaned the blood off his face from his grazed ear. Suddenly Holmes was at his side. The column was here, he said, and Major Archbold had sent for the ambulance wagon. 'Sir, Puddephat's dead, did you know? Shot clean through the heart.' Alderson bustled him away.

Bertie caught Alderson's attention. 'You'll write to my people, won't you? Tell them how it happened? Not just to my father and mother but my aunt Henrietta?'

'Of course I will. We promised each other.'

'You're a good fellow, Basil.'

'I'm going to ask the major if I can go in the wagon with you. It'll be a trial, over this rough road, and you'll need a friend with you.'

'Thanks,' said Bertie faintly. It seemed to be getting dark, and people were drifting farther and farther away into the unseasonal dusk. 'Tell Holmes to look after Dolly for me. Make sure she – gets—' He didn't manage to complete the sentence.

In November Venetia and Hazelmere were invited to spend a day at Windsor, and Venetia was again shocked to see the deterioration in the Queen's health. She looked quite emaciated and much more feeble than in July. It was a surprise to her when Olivia said, with a hopeful countenance, 'Oh, she's much better now. We were so worried last month, we really feared the worst, but she has picked up wonderfully. If only she will allow herself to be invalidish for a while longer! But the trouble is that as soon as she feels the tiniest bit better, she overtires herself and then she collapses again.'

'She was very upset by Christle's death, I imagine?' This was the family name for Prince Christian Victor, the Queen's grandson, who had not recovered from his fever and had died in Pretoria at the end of October.

'Oh, it was a dreadful blow! She bore it so patiently, it nearly broke my heart. She sent for me one day and just gave me her hand, and I knelt down and stroked it and she cried so quietly.' Olivia was plainly very moved. It was the first time she had ever touched the Queen, and that Her Majesty had actually invited any form of physical comfort was proof of how deeply she was grieved. 'It's been such a hard year,' she reflected. 'So much to worry her. First the King of Italy being murdered, and the attempt on the Shah, and then the dreadful attack on the Prince of Wales.'

In April a Belgian youth had shot at the Prince and Princess as they passed through the Gare du Nord in Brussels on their way to Denmark. Four shots had been fired, but all had missed, although narrowly. The Princess said she had felt one whizzing across her eyes. The Prince, ever cool in danger, said only that It was fortunate anarchists were always such bad shots.

'She was so anxious when he went abroad again,' Olivia went on. 'We told her she was quite safe in England, and she didn't say anything, but you know, we had to wonder. Things are changing so quickly these days, and one hears of such unrest in the towns, and with morals and manners declining, and people not believing in God any more, I wonder really whether any of us is safe anywhere.'

'These are troubled times,' Venetia agreed.

'Then there was the Duke of Coburg's death, and now we hear the Empress Frederick is worse and can hardly survive many weeks longer, poor dear lady.'

The Duke of Coburg – the Queen's son Prince Alfred – had died of cancer of the throat in July. It was hard for the Queen to bear the knowledge that she had outlived three of her children – Alice, Leopold and now Alfred; and the Empress Frederick, her daughter Victoria and perhaps the dearest of her children, was dying of what they referred to in their letters to each other as 'lumbago' but both knew was cancer of the spine.

Venetia had known the Empress in her youth, and had received much kindness from her, and was very sorry that she was suffering so much. 'It's a sad thing,' she concluded, 'that the concomitant of great longevity is witnessing more and more of your relatives' deaths. No wonder the Queen seems depressed.'

'And yet, you know,' Olivia said, 'she has such great spirit. She said to me the other day that when the Prince Consort died she wanted to die too; but now she wants to live as long as possible so she can do all she can for the country and the people.'

Venetia saw that her sister took comfort from that, so did not ask the question that was in her mind: *what will you and Charlie do when the Queen dies?* As a doctor she could see that the Queen was frail and failing; but as an ordinary person, she could not believe that the Queen could ever die, that there could ever be an England without Victoria. A person must be pretty aged to remember any time before

283

Queen Victoria came to the throne; and it would take a foreigner to imagine a time after her.

Sir Redvers and Lady Buller were guests at luncheon, and Venetia was pleased to be seated next to him so that she could talk to him about the war. She asked him how soon it would be over, and he gave her a half-stern and half-twinkling look under his eyebrows and said, 'When Roberts has left!' As he was in candid mood, she asked him what he thought of Kitchener.

'His handling of Paardeberg was deplorable. He's a man of determination, but his judgement is poor – both in action and in strategy. Look at what is happening now – this plan of his to burn all the homesteads and starve the Boers out. It won't do – won't do at all. It's not warfare as we have always known it. It will only make the Boer more determined, and it will sow great bitterness which we will have to harvest in the future.'

'And Baden-Powell? What's your opinion of him?'

'I have no opinion of him. He's a man of straw. He dresses up and plays at soldiers, that's all.'

'Dear me, Sir Redvers, you are very frank,' she said with pleasure, almost managing a dimple in her desire to keep him talking; but at that moment Lady Erroll, sitting on his other side, demanded his attention in order to deliver a tirade on temperance, her hobby-horse. Alcohol, she said, was poison to the brain and the source of every ill in the country, father to poverty and vice, and responsible for the destruction of character and ability.

Buller listened with more patience than Venetia would have expected, but at length he was driven to tell her that he had had his pint of champagne every day while on campaign. 'And very good it was, too.'

Venetia, amused, staged a rescue of him, and asked him how they had managed for provisions.

'Oh, very well indeed. We lived on the best all the time. In fact, the only thing we ever lacked that I can remember was butter. But everything else we had, and the men never went without their full ration. Of course, I never moved without my commissariat.'

'Unlike Lord Roberts, who lost his entire wagon train to the Boers on the Modder,' Venetia said mischievously. 'But, then, he was moving rather quickly, while you, I believe, were criticised for slow progress in advancing.'

Buller was not at all embarrassed by this. 'True,' he said, 'but look here, what did Roberts achieve for all his haste? Arrived in Bloemfontein with a sick army, had to leave half of them behind when he moved on to Pretoria. There was no resistance at either town, and no advantage was gained by occupying 'em. He could have taken his time about it and saved his men. It's my opinion a general should take care of his men. Can't fight a battle without 'em, you know.'

Venetia could agree with him there, and engaged him on the subject of the medical corps. She found his view soldierly, but humane. 'It's a fact, ma'am, that a civilian cannot understand what goes on out in the field, and expects a far higher standard of comfort and treatment than the soldiers ever expect for themselves. In a war fighting comes first, and the wounded know that. They lie patiently and wait until there's time to help them. But we do for them everything we can in the circumstances.'

'But the chain of command, Sir Redvers? The red tape? The impossibility of getting anything done because of the convoluted organisation of the medical corps?'

'Oh, that's bad all right, and ought to be reformed. Dare say it will be once the war's over. But even there, you know, a great deal is down to the general in the field. If he cares about the men, he can make things happen, all right. There are a great many rules and nonsenses, but in practice, whatever my surgeons wanted, they got. There was no argument about precedent and filling in the right forms!'

The Court went down to Osborne for Christmas on the 18th of December, and just before that Venetia was surprised to receive a visit from Dr Reid. He seemed a little less cheery than his usual self. 'I want to confide in you, and ask your help,' he said.

'I hope nothing is wrong? Is it Susan?' Reid's wife was

285

pregnant again, after having miscarried their first child.

'Oh, no, she's very well. Quite bonny. No, it's the Queen.'

'Ah! Yes, she did seem to have gone downhill when I saw her last month.'

'I am seriously worried about her. Although she has picked up a little in the last few days that doesn't mean all is well. She is feebler, her nervous system has been much taxed, and of course she still has great difficulty both in eating and sleeping.'

'There's no organic disease?'

'None that I am aware of. Of course,' he gave her a small, tight smile, 'I am not permitted to examine her as closely as I would like, but I would say that her condition is the effect of age – which means, naturally, that there can only be one outcome, sooner or later.'

'And you think sooner rather than later?'

'I hope not,' he said hastily, and she was reminded a little of a child crossing its fingers to ward off bad luck. 'With constant care and attention, I hope the progression may be slow – though, of course, if she were to catch some illness, in her present state she would hardly be able to resist it.'

'Quite. But what is it I can help you with? Do you wish to discuss treatment?'

'Thank you, no. There isn't much to be done for her. What she needs is food and sleep, and both are constantly denied her. I give her Dover's Powder to try to settle her when she has a bad night, but I don't like to give it too often.' Dover's Powder contained morphine. 'And on the worst occasions I have given her twelve grains of Trional, which sends her off all right, but then she complains she is sleepy all the next day, and blames me for it. As to food, it is Benger's, broth, warm milk, rice pudding and so on. I wish I could get more nourishment into her, but everything gives her indigestion now.' He frowned, thinking through his own problem, and she prompted him again.

'So how can I help you?'

'The thing is that I cannot get anyone else to realise the seriousness of the situation. I wrote to the Prince of Wales to make him aware of it, but he simply wrote back that the

Queen was a little seedy but had such pluck and vitality she would soon recover from the present indisposition. He will not understand that it is not an indisposition, and that it is precisely her "pluck and vitality" that she has lost.'

'Yes, I see. And you would like me – or Hazelmere, rather – to try to make him understand.'

'I know Hazelmere is close to him. Do you think he would?'

'I'm sure he will make the attempt, if you ask it, but I doubt whether anyone is very close to the Prince.'

Reid looked surprised. 'Do you say so?'

'He is very amiable, conversable, easy to get on with,' Venetia said, 'but as to real intimacy, or being in his confidence – he is not like you, Sir James. I don't think anyone, not even the royal mistresses, are close to him in that way.'

Reid looked as if he did not quite believe it, but he said, 'Well, I will take what I can get. If Hazelmere would undertake to try to explain it to him, I'd be grateful. I can't get anywhere with him, and Salisbury's as bad. I had a long talk with him the last time he came to Windsor, but he still talks of the Queen's going to Nice early next year. I've told him that she would never be able to stand the journey, but he shrugs it off and goes on thinking what he wants to think.'

'Lord Salisbury is the last person who will want to imagine the Queen suffering from the effects of age, given his own years and health – and having lost his wife so recently.'

'Perhaps so. But I wonder what the Prince's reason is.'

'Oh, no man ever wants to believe his mother is mortal,' said Venetia, but she met Reid's eye, and understood his thought. Later, when she told Hazelmere about Reid's visit, she said, 'I wonder whether the Prince refuses to see the truth because he doesn't want to be king.'

Hazelmere raised an eyebrow. 'That's a large supposition. Why should he not?'

'It seems to me that he has the perfect life already, according to his own lights. He has position, money, and absolute freedom to enjoy himself in exactly the way he likes, with people who think it the greatest honour in the world to be with him. He has no work, no boxes to read, no responsibilities. If he were to become king, all the disagreeable duties his mother now takes care of would fall on his shoulders.'

'Perhaps you're right,' Hazelmere said. 'I hadn't considered it, but I see the sense of what you're saying. But in that case, it will be impossible to make him know the truth about the Queen. He has a great way of ignoring what doesn't please him. How long does Reid think?'

'He wouldn't say exactly,' Venetia said. 'Too much of a courtier – and, I think, too bound up with the Queen himself to want to put it into words. But the fact that he has come to me at all means he thinks the matter is pressing. From what he said, and from what I observed myself, I would say a few months – perhaps as little as a few weeks.'

Now Hazelmere looked shocked, and Venetia saw again that curious reaction that she had had herself. It was not possible to imagine the Queen dying. More than that, it was deeply disturbing. In a way they were all children, and the Queen was the parent who stood between them and the unpredictability of life. As long as God was in His Heaven and the Queen was on the throne, all was well with the world; but remove one of those pillars, and might not everything fall into chaos?

CHAPTER NINE

The official cable about Bertie's being wounded was, of course, sent to Perry, so Henrietta learnt about it somewhat after the event, for it took Alderson a long time to write the letter, and the letter a long time to reach her.

After recounting the event, it concluded,

> Of course travelling in the wagon gave him great pain but he stuck it out with the utmost pluck and calmness. He has been hit by one ball in the right shoulder, which passed right through and missed all the bones, just nicked the cartilage and a small artery, and another, which struck under the armpit and passed through the chest cavity and out under the shoulder blade, breaking two ribs but missing all the organs, which seems a miracle. I saw him every night and helped feed him with porridge and rice and so on, and he was doing splendidly. Now he is on the last lap to hospital which he should reach today. The doctor said his arm would be stiff for a few months but that he should recover completely, so try not to worry.

It was all very well to tell Henrietta not to worry, but another matter entirely to stop her. Despite the miracle of the bullets' not touching any of the organs, she knew that a wound to the chest was extremely dangerous, for introducing a foreign body in that way was very likely to cause infection, and then mortification would act swiftly. But a week later she had a letter from Bertie himself, badly written but very welcome.

> Pls excuse scrawl but no good with left hand. Going on well, not to worry. Docs say I am very fit and will heal but it's the end for me. Will be invalided home as soon as I can travel, so should be home for Christmas. Not sorry to be leaving – things getting nasty here. Most volunteers going home now. But wish I knew what will happen to Dolly. Broke my heart to leave her.

Jessie had begun to suspect long before that something had happened, because there had been such a gap between letters. When she asked her mother why she thought Bertie hadn't written, the quick reply, 'Oh, I expect he's busy,' did nothing to reassure her. She could read in her mother's face the anxiety she did not express.

In the beginning Jessie had thought, like the boys, that it was a glorious thing to go off to war. She knew in an abstract way that wars meant fighting and fighting meant casualties, but that did not translate in her mind into any real appreciation of danger. She parted with her hero with no doubts whatever of his return. But that had changed, quite abruptly, on his last visit when he had shown them the scar on his arm. The boys had been interested in the ghoulish way boys always were about horrid things. But Jessie had seen suddenly and in that moment exactly what it could mean to be shot at, to be hit, wounded, perhaps killed. *Bertie could die. She could lose him.*

And she loved him. That realisation came as part of, as a consequence of, the other. When the letter finally came and her mother read it out to them all she listened in trembling to the end, and as her mother was saying gravely, but with a faint, brave smile, that it was good to know he was not so badly hurt after all and would make a full recovery, she could bear no more. She jumped up and ran from the room, rushed upstairs and flung herself face down on her bed, sobbing.

No use to tell herself that he would be well again. *He had been hurt.* She was in an agony of grief. Tears tore out of her in great, clotted gouts. Hurt, wounded. Pain and blood, but more than that, worst of all, that outer envelope, the visible Bertie she knew, had been breached. She had no words for it, but she knew there was an absolute wrong in tearing open that perfect capsule, which held the essence of a person captive, which stopped it streaming off into the eternal. Life was inside and death – oblivion – was outside and the body was the barrier that divided the two. The vast and wordless fears of childhood poured through her at that moment. Chaos lay beyond the few things a person knew, like the darkness beyond the circle of firelight, like the water behind a dam, pressing, pressing in. A weakness, a fracture, a small hole, and the whole structure might crumble, collapse, and one would be swept away.

When her sobs eased, she rolled onto her side and curled in on herself, and thought of Bertie, going over every memory of him, of what he had said and done. In her mind she reread his letters to her – she did not need to get them out, knowing every one by heart, knowing every line and curve of his handwriting as though the very strokes of the ink on the paper were part of the meaning, part of him. In her mind she looked again at, touched again the knotted scar on his arm, trembled in memory as she touched it, would not let herself imagine any new wound. Instead she traced the lines of his face, the way his lips curved and his eyes crinkled with laughter. She remembered the time after she rode Pasha, when he had come to her room, and kissed her cheek; and all the times afterwards when he had come up to amuse her, talk to her, play foolish games with her. It didn't matter what he did, it had been the being with him that mattered, and she wondered now in amazement how she had not *really* realised that at the time. She had been happy that he was there, but had not lived each moment of it with the intensity that she would in future, as she now examined and stroked her memories of him.

If he came back – *when* he came back – oh, then she would make sure she treasured every second he was there. She would never go through days half asleep as she thought she must have done in the past. Bertie. She touched his name with her mind, wonderingly. It was not just a word, it was a part of him, like his voice or his hands. She knew that she was too young to love him, that she was too young to have anything but a 'crush', but she loved him just the same. When he came back . . . The tears dried on her face and she slipped without knowing from day-dream into sleep.

Bertie was home by the second week in December, and his parents met him at the dock at Southampton, considerably shaken by how nearly they had lost their son and heir, and ready to make it an occasion of reconciliation. They showered every attention on him, taking him straight back to Bishop Winthorpe where they had prepared an invalid chamber and engaged a private nurse to take care of him. Bertie laughed at that, and said he didn't need any more nursing, that his wounds were healing beautifully and there was nothing more to do for him. But the sudden change in climate, together with his weakness from having been wounded, made him vulnerable, and he developed a feverish cold which gave everyone concern – and was a great trial to Bertie, as it hurt terribly to cough. The nurse was retained, and she and his mother continued to fuss over him in a way that the old Bertie would have found intolerable. But this Bertie had learnt a great deal in his year in South Africa, and held his tongue and smiled, refusing to hurt his mother's feelings when she cooed over him and stroked his head.

Bertie was out of bed by Christmas and, though lean and pale under his tan, he was evidently mending, his great natural vitality shaking off what might have killed a less fit person. Sadly, once the first shock had worn off and Bertie was on his feet again, his father tended to revert to criticising, telling Bertie that he had 'told him so', blaming him for upsetting his mother, and speculating on how they would have felt had Bertie got himself killed. Bertie bore with it patiently and refrained from quarrelling with him. But life at the Red House was hard to bear, and he could not see how it might get better. He was missing his old friends and the sense of purpose the campaign had given him. The inactivity he now endured combined with the shortness of the horizons to make him feel trapped, miserable and restless. He had no-one to talk to at the Red House, no-one who understood how he had been living or how afraid he was of the future, which seemed to offer nothing more than this soft prison, this intolerable idleness. His arm, the doctors said, would be completely healed by the summer, and then what would he do?

He did his best over Christmas, and the New Year celebration for the new century, to be cheerful, though he longed for Morland Place, for Henrietta and Jerome and the children, for the freedom of not having to guard his tongue every moment. He could not go there, of course. He was at present completely dependent, and in a chronic state of tactfulness besides, treading on eggs as far as both his father and his mother were concerned. He had no news of the Morlands or of how they had taken his wounding until Uncle Teddy rode over to see how he was doing. Bertie greeted him with almost pathetic eagerness, but now Teddy was living at Morland Place he had lost some of his neutral status as far as the Red House was concerned and he was treated by Perry with faint suspicion, which put a curb on his conversation. But he did manage to have a few minutes alone with Bertie, walking round the bare and frozen garden, and asked him if he would accept a visit from Richard Puddephat.

'The poor fellow's devastated with loss. Raymond was his only son, and deeply beloved by all of them.'

'Yes, I know. He was such a nice fellow. It shook me up dreadfully that he was killed.'

'Puddephat is anxious to know everything about what happened. The official telegram says very little.'

'I would have written to him if it hadn't been my right arm that was wounded. Of course I'd be happy to answer all his questions – provided my father allows it.'

'Oh, Perry will agree all right. He may be a crusty devil, but he knows what's right and proper. When do you think you'll be up to it?'

'Any time at all that suits him,' said Bertie.

So in the hard, grey time of mid-January Richard

Puddephat made the journey to Bishop Winthorpe; and, true to Teddy's prediction, Perry gravely made him welcome. He expressed his condolences in sincere terms, and put his own study, where there was a good fire, at his disposal for his private interview with Bertie. It was a distressing occasion for Bertie: Puddephat was plainly grief-stricken at his loss, and at one point covered his eyes with his hand to conceal his tears. Bertie's voice faltered at that; and he found that reliving it for the grieving father revived the shock he had suffered then and had only just got over. When he had told all about the incident, Puddephat turned to happier times and wanted to know anything Bertie could remember about his boy's life out there, his adventures and friendships and pleasures. He and Bertie talked for several hours, until interrupted by a maid sent to ask if Mr Puddephat would stay to luncheon.

'I'm afraid I've exhausted you,' he said, noting the lines of strain in Bertie's face.

'Not at all, sir,' Bertie said. 'If it weren't for the sadness of the occasion, there is nothing I would like better than talking about South Africa and the good fellows I've left behind.'

Puddephat eyed him keenly. 'You must miss it,' he said bluntly.

'Yes,' said Bertie. 'To be frank, I wish myself back there. I miss the fellows and I can't get used to home and – oh, I hate to be idle. It seems my soldiering days are over, but I wish I thought there was something else I could do.'

'You'd like to go back to South Africa? After the war, I mean?'

'Yes – or somewhere else. I don't much mind where. There's so much of the world out there, and I've seen so little of it. But I'm afraid it's out of the question. Travel of that sort costs too much and—' He stopped himself. It would be disloyal to mention his difficulties with his father to Mr Puddephat. But he contrasted the easy, frank and happy relationship the Puddephats seemed to have had with that within his own family, and wished that this pleasant-faced man had been his father instead.

Puddephat had guessed something of the difficulty from his brief meeting with Perry and a reading between many lines. He reached across and laid a hand over Bertie's good one. 'Bear up. You never know what the future may bring. You've had some bad luck – now perhaps it's time for some good.'

Bertie smiled faintly. 'I can only hope so.'

Puddephat straightened up. 'Now, then, is there anything I can do for you? You have been very kind in talking to me about my poor boy – and I know you were a good friend to him over there. I'd like to do something for you in return.'

'There is one thing,' Bertie said hesitantly, 'but I don't know if it's possible.'

'Speak up! If it can be done, it will be.'

'Well, sir, I'd like to know if my little mare Dolly is all right, and if she is being well treated.'

Puddephat looked surprised, and then smiled. 'That's a very modest request! A tricky one – but you've come to the right person. It may take a while, but I will see what I can do.' He took out a pocket-book. 'Give me some details, and I'll put an enquiry in train for you.' He wrote to Bertie's dictation, and a private smile playing round his lips suggested he thought Bertie a very foolish fellow indeed – but a likeable one.

It had been a sad Christmas at Osborne. The journey down from Windsor had been tiring for the Queen, for though she had her own train direct from Windsor to Gosport, where the royal yacht was waiting to take her to Trinity Dock in East Cowes, still there were railway officials and civic dignitaries to meet at every juncture, each of them eager for a word and a look from the Queen, and she was always punctilious about such duties. So she was exhausted at the end of the four-hour journey, and that night could not sleep. The routines of her life, on which she had so long relied, had been broken and scattered like shards. She could not eat, did not go down to meals, slept at odd times, and took her drives out at irregular hours, depending on when she was awake. She was restless and irritable, cross when she could not sleep, crosser still when she slept at the wrong time and her attendants did not wake her.

Yet Dr Reid could see – even Olivia could see – that the Prince of Wales still had no apprehension about her. Hazelmere's delicate and tactful efforts to enlighten the Prince had had no effect. He believed only that his mother was not eating and drinking enough to keep her strength up. The cheer of Christmas would 'take her out of herself' and a return of her appetite would have her back to normal in no time. He left for Sandringham and his own Christmas celebrations in robust mood.

On Christmas morning, just after seven, Reid was called to see Lady Churchill. She had been a lady-in-waiting and a close friend of the Queen for fifty years, going back to the time when Prince Albert had still been alive and there had been laughter and fun in the house. Jane Churchill had come as a guest to Osborne for Christmas, though the Queen had worried about her travelling at this time of year, for she had not been well lately and her heart was not strong. The maid who had taken in her early-morning tea could not wake her, and sent to Sir James. He found her dead, having died in her sleep apparently some hours earlier of syncope.

An anxious knot of people had assembled round the door of the room: several of the servants hovering in the background, Olivia, and Harriet Phipps, the Queen's Lady Secretary, to the fore. Olivia was in tears. 'She was always so kind to me. When I first became a maid-of-honour she befriended me, explained everything and made it easy for me.'

'She went quietly in her sleep, not a bad way to go,' Reid said to comfort her. 'My concern now is how we are to break the news to the Queen.'

Tears dried at once. 'It will be such a blow to her. After everything else, for this to happen on Christmas Day!'

'It will have to be broken to her very carefully,' Miss Phipps said.

'Just so,' said Reid. 'Or else we shall have two deaths on our hands instead of one.'

'Oh, don't say that!' Olivia said. 'We must work up to it

– don't you think? Tell her at first that Lady Churchill is unwell, and then, gradually, through the day—'

'Tell her she's worse, and then that she's gone,' Reid concluded for her. 'I think that's best.'

'I agree. Well, you had better go in to her as soon as she's up,' Miss Phipps said.

'Oh, no, she'll take fright at once if it's me who tells her Lady Churchill's ill,' Reid objected. 'One of the family had better broach the subject first. Princess Christian's the most tactful. She can slip it into the conversation somehow. I'll go and talk to her about it.'

The Queen had had a bad night, lying wakeful until the early hours and then falling asleep just when it was time to get up. No-one liked to wake her, so it was not until one o'clock that she went out for her 'morning' drive with Princess Christian – her daughter Helena, mother of the late Prince Christle. Princess Christian told her, as the conspirators had agreed, that Lady Churchill was ill, having suffered a heart-attack. On her return from the drive, the Queen sent at once for Dr Reid to make enquiries. Reid told her that Jane Churchill was very ill, but added nothing more.

'Take good care of her,' the Queen said. 'Give her every attention.'

'I will, Your Majesty.'

Olivia was sent for to read to the Queen for a while, but she did not get through many pages: the Queen was plainly preoccupied with the condition of her friend, and wondered constantly how 'dear Jane' was, and reminisced about things they had done together long ago. 'That was before you joined us, my dear. Oh, what fun we used to have on our expeditions at Balmoral, when the Prince Consort was alive! We used to go out in the carriage and pretend to be ordinary sightseers, and stay in a common inn, and the good people never knew who we were! So amusing! And dear Jane Churchill was always with us. How long ago it all seems now. Olivia, my dear, just ring the bell, will you, and ask for Sir James? I must know how she is going on.'

Reid appeared, and from his solemn face Olivia guessed

he had decided the time was right for the revelation. 'I was just coming to tell Your Majesty that all is over,' he said. He and Olivia both held their breath.

The Queen shook her head slowly, her eyes filling with tears. 'I knew. I was expecting it. I knew somehow that she was going. Poor Jane, poor Jane! My closest friend for fifty years. Oh, what a terrible day this is.'

She put her hand across her eyes, resting her head against it, and grieved silently; but Reid was glad to see that she took it as well as she did. Later he said to Olivia, 'I think she has had so many blows just lately, she is numb with them. Oh, Lord, whatever is going to happen next?' It was not a question, but as he met Olivia's eyes, he saw that they both feared the answer.

There was a brief service in the drawing-room, with the vicar of Windsor, who was staying as a guest, saying a few words, and Princess Beatrice playing the harmonium for the hymns. Then the Queen went back to her room to rest.

Her Majesty's Christmas Dinner was laid out in the dining-room as usual, but it was a subdued affair. The menu card was beautifully embellished with a coloured drawing of Osborne House and the royal coat-of-arms, together with a border of flowers and crossed Union Flags in the corners, and the table was decorated with flowers, myrtle and ivy. There was turtle soup, turbot, roast turkey, boar's head, game pie, plum pudding, mince pies and chocolate eclairs, as well as the traditional 200-pound baron of beef on the sideboard, sent down from the farm at Windsor, roasted and decorated with the letters *VRI* in shredded horseradish. The Queen did not appear. Upstairs in her room, she dined on Benger's Food and a few spoonfuls of broth.

The new year came in – 1901, officially the new century now – and Osborne, like the rest of the country, was lashed with gales and heavy rain. Fishermen were drowned, ships foundered and sank, rivers burst their banks, floods swept away cattle and sheep and turned farmland into lakes and houses into islands. In York the Ouse flooded, King's Staith was under water and the flood reached half-way up King

Street. And then, a week later, the wind direction changed and a bitter cold descended over the land. Even London, which was always some degrees warmer than the rest of the country, was cloaked and muffled under several inches of snow, and in Victoria Park and Battersea Park and on the Hackney Marshes ponds froze hard enough for skating.

The Times greeted the new century with a long and solemn leader about the 'great landmark on the shores of time', pondering on the glories that the twentieth century would bring, and ending with a tribute to the 'august and venerable Lady' at Osborne who would reign 'revered, beloved and supreme in all our hearts' to the last day of her life.

Lord Roberts arrived home from South Africa and went down to Osborne to attend his monarch, who greeted him in the drawing-room and conferred the Order of the Garter on him. They then had a long talk about the war, and about the death of Prince Christle and his burial in Pretoria, on which subject the Queen wanted a great deal more detail than Roberts could give.

The Queen seemed a little better after the dismal Christmas, and was still conducting government business, reading her boxes – or, rather, having them read to her – dictating her responses, following matters in South Africa and discussing with ministers what sort of honour should be given to the officers who had distinguished themselves in the Boer War. On the 14th of January Lord Roberts travelled down from London again and had a long private talk with Her Majesty. The gentlemen of the Household, together with the Queen's family and even Miss Phipps, now all agreed that the thing was to get Her Majesty out of cold, foggy England as soon as possible for a holiday in the South of France, which would set her up and make her well again.

Dr Reid went to see her virtually every hour, so he was rarely able to get home to see his wife in their small cottage. In consequence he spent most of his off-duty moments by the Du Canes' fireside in their room at Osborne House, and he complained to them bitterly how he could not get anyone to understand that the Queen would not be able to bear the journey to France.

'You don't think her better?' Du Cane said. 'She seems a little more . . .' he hesitated, searching in vain for a word '. . . a little more herself,' was all he managed in the end.

'She's eating and sleeping better,' Olivia said. 'And she has seemed less nervous lately. Things don't irritate her the way they used to.'

'That is one of the symptoms that alarms me,' Reid said. 'It seems to me that things don't irritate her because she has ceased to care. She is apathetic. Her mind wanders. The dressers say when she wakes it takes her a while to know where she is.'

'I've noticed that when she falls asleep in the chair. Just at first she seems rather dazed,' Olivia said.

'But isn't that quite usual?' Du Cane asked. 'I mean, surely old people are often like that?'

'The Queen never was,' Reid said firmly. 'Her mind was always absolutely sharp. I think it's a sign of a mental deterioration and I don't like it. The truth is that she is declining rapidly.'

Olivia didn't want to believe that. 'Perhaps when the good weather comes . . . ?' She looked at the doctor hopefully.

'I cannot hold out any hope that she will ever be her old self again.' He took a deep breath and ventured the words out loud. 'A few months is all that's left to her, in my opinion.'

Olivia stared, as the realisation belatedly came home to her. 'You don't mean – you don't think she's – *dying?*'

'That,' said Reid grimly, 'is what I've been trying to tell you.'

Du Cane pondered the information in silence a moment, shaking his head slowly. 'Have you told Fritz what you've just told us?' he asked.

'More than once. He thinks I am an alarmist.' Reid stared into the fire. 'The problem is, you see, that she makes an effort with anyone but the dressers and me, so no-one else sees her real condition.'

'But if she has the spirit still to put on a show in that way, perhaps she will rally,' Du Cane said. 'This dark time of year depresses us all. You can't rule that out as a factor, can you?'

'Any rally can only be temporary,' Reid said. 'Don't you understand?'

'Yes, yes, old fellow, but for all of us, even a temporary rally will be a godsend,' Du Cane said gently. 'How can we even think of life without her?'

On the 16th of January, the Queen's dressers, who went in to her in the morning, were alarmed to find they could not wake her properly. She kept saying in a confused way that she must get up, but then could not do so, and seemed to be drifting in and out of sleep. Mrs Tuck, the senior dresser, sent for Dr Reid, who was so alarmed by the report that he insisted he must see her for himself. The dressers were shocked. This was unprecedented. Sir James had never been in the Queen's bedchamber, had never seen Her Majesty in bed. Always before he had examined her fully dressed and sitting very upright in a chair in the sitting-room. Any actual night attendance at the bedside had been directed by him, but undertaken by the dressers, who relayed questions and answers for the doctor to make his diagnosis and issue his instructions at arm's length, as it were. The women argued fiercely for a while, but her condition so alarmed them that they relented at last, saying that the Queen was so drowsy, perhaps she would not even know he was there.

'She looked so very small in that great bed,' Reid told the Du Canes afterwards. The bed – the same that Prince Albert had had built for them – was six feet wide and seven feet long; the Queen was tiny, less than five feet tall, and had lost so much weight over the past year that without the padding of her day clothes she barely made a hump under the bedclothes. It moved the doctor inexpressibly to be seeing her in this way at last. There was little for him to do. Her pulse was strong and steady, but she could not seem to wake fully. She slept on and off all day, and finally got up at around six p.m., and was wheeled into the sitting-room, where Reid saw her again. Her colour was good, but she seemed dazed and confused, and her speech, which had always been so bell-like and clear, was indistinct. He feared she might have suffered a stroke.

301

The next morning, relying on the new precedent, he slipped into her room early. He found her drowsy, confused and wandering in her mind, and there was a new symptom: the left side of her face had dropped a little. It seemed to confirm his suspicion that she had indeed suffered a stroke. He thought she might be slipping into a coma, and went straight to the Princesses Beatrice and Christian, to ask that Sir Douglas Powell, the Physician-in-Ordinary, should be sent for.

The Queen got out of bed in the evening as before. Reid wanted Powell to see her but was afraid of upsetting her in her delicate mental condition. He went in to her and told her carefully that Sir Douglas Powell was on the island and had called to visit him, and that as he was in the house, he hoped that she would see him. It was very casually done, as though there were no great importance about it; but still he found it worrying that the Queen seemed neither alarmed nor surprised, as she would normally have been, by the news of Powell's presence, and agreed without much interest to receive him. During the brief visit, she said nothing, only answered Powell's few questions rather incoherently. Reid was more worried than ever, for it was the first time she had not made the effort to appear normal in front of a 'stranger'.

'Powell says there is no doubt about the cerebral degeneration,' Reid said, snatching a cup of tea in the Du Canes' room. 'He thinks the condition precarious, but not yet hopeless.'

'Oh, then perhaps it is not the end,' Olivia said, gazing at him beseechingly.

Reid rubbed his eyes. 'We may all hope, I suppose.'

'You're very tired,' Du Cane said. 'This is a strain for you, on duty every hour, never able to get home to rest – or to see your wife.'

'That is the worst part,' Reid admitted. 'Susan would be such a comfort to me, but I dare not leave the house as things are.'

Olivia said nothing, but a while later, when Reid had left, she went to see Princess Beatrice, with the result that the princess summoned the doctor shortly afterwards to say that Susan Reid must come up to the house as often as she wished, and stay as long as she liked during the present crisis.

On the 19th, Reid thought the Queen worse: she was weaker, and though she was taking food, it was in an automatic way, her mind wandering so that she was not aware of eating. Princess Christian, however, saw only that the Queen had slept and was eating, two essentials that had been difficult for her for months, and she wrote her daily telegram to the Prince of Wales saying that the Queen was better and that she felt happier about her. Reid happened to go into Sir Arthur Bigge's room before this telegram was sent, just as Bigge received a telephone call from Francis Knollys at Marlborough House, asking on the Prince's behalf how his mother was and whether it was safe for him to go down to Sandringham. Bigge asked for and then relayed Reid's opinion, that the Prince ought to stay in London and be ready to come at any moment, as the Queen's condition was serious and she might die within days.

'But look here,' said Bigge, when he had hung up, 'you say that the Queen is dying, and here's a telegram from Princess Christian for me to put in cypher and send off, saying she's better. Something of a contradiction, don't you think?'

'You know she doesn't want the Prince and Princess of Wales in the house.' There was a long-standing rivalry between brother and sister. 'She sees what she wants to see. I've told you my exact opinion, I can do no more.'

Bigge stroked his chin thoughtfully. Sir James was a forthright person, and had set certain backs up before now, mostly backs that did not care for egalitarian manners from the lowly born. But this was a serious matter. 'Is it Powell's opinion too?' he asked.

'Certainly,' said Reid.

'Then I had better go and see the princess,' said Bigge.

Soon afterwards Reid was summoned to the princess's room, and after a short and rather angry exchange, the princess was convinced of the truth. Shaken, she said that

303

the Prince of Wales had better come, and wrote a new telegram to be substituted for the other.

At luncheon, it was heard that the Kaiser had left Berlin on his way to London, accompanied by the Duke of Connaught – the Queen's son Prince Arthur – who had been staying with him.

'Now, however did the Kaiser hear about it?' Miss Phipps exclaimed. 'This is dreadful! The last thing we want is to have him here, throwing his weight around. I wonder if he can be stopped?'

'The thought of him and the Prince of Wales arriving on the doorstep at the same moment chills the blood,' said Fritz Ponsonby.

'Oh, surely they will make common cause at a time like this?' Du Cane said.

'But if the Queen knew he was coming, it might alarm her and make her worse,' Olivia said.

'Will she know it, Sir James?' Miss Phipps asked. 'Can she grasp what is going on?'

'As she is at the moment, I doubt it,' said Reid.

Du Cane looked at him sharply – there was something in his tone and expression that attracted his attention. After luncheon he caught up with him in the corridor and said, 'Now then, Jamie – the truth, if you please! Was it you told the Kaiser? I know you and he were very friendly at one time, and there was that occasion at Cowes—'

'For God's sake, don't let anyone hear you say that!'

'Of course I won't tell – but did you telegraph him?'

'I promised him years ago that if anything happened I'd let him know. Well, he's not liked by his cousins, and they might omit to tell him until it was too late. So I cycled down to Cowes yesterday afternoon and sent off a wire.'

'God! You were taking a risk!'

'The Kaiser adores his grandmother. There's good in him, whatever anyone says. But you won't mention to anyone . . . ?'

'Not a word. But you had better hope *he* doesn't, or the family will have your scalp.'

The Prince of Wales arrived from London at five o'clock;

the princess was still travelling from Sandringham. At six Reid went in to see the Queen and found that her mind had cleared, and though she was very weak, and spoke with difficulty, she was quite lucid.

'I have been ill, haven't I? Am I better?'

'Yes, Your Majesty has been very ill, but you are now better,' Reid said.

'You must be very tired,' she said. 'You must not break down, Sir James. You ought to have someone to help you.'

'Sir Douglas Powell is in the house, Your Majesty. He is a great help to me.'

'Good. Good. I am glad.' After a pause she said, 'I think the Prince of Wales should be told that I have been ill. He will feel it very much.'

'His Royal Highness does know, and is anxious to come to Osborne as soon as Your Majesty would like to see him. Would Your Majesty like him to come now?'

'Certainly,' the Queen said, adding, 'but he need not stay.'

Later again, when Reid went in with Powell, she sent everyone away except Sir James and then said to him earnestly, 'I should like to live a little longer, as I have still a few things to settle. I have arranged most things, but there are still some things left undone, and I want to live a little longer.'

Afterwards, he told Olivia, 'She said it with such trust, as if she thought I could make it so. It was indescribably pathetic.'

The improvement in the Queen's mental condition had been reported by the princesses to the Prince of Wales, who now believed, as they did, that their mother was not *in extremis* but that Reid was a panicking fool. The Prince felt he had been dragged down to Osborne for no reason. In that case, the best thing he could do would be to return to London to try to intercept the Kaiser and prevent his going to Osborne, where he could cause nothing but trouble.

That evening a more cheerful bulletin was issued to the nation. One of the difficulties of the situation was deciding exactly what to make public. If the news were kept cheerful and the Queen died, all those concerned would be blamed;

305

but if they alarmed the whole country and the Queen recovered, they would not be forgiven either. So the bulletins were couched in deliberately vague terms, and the newspapers were consequently full of fervent hopes and pious prayers that the Queen's health, which was 'giving cause for alarm', would soon be restored. On the whole the papers were buoyant, believing that it was only a matter of time before she recovered; and some remarked that the Queen was the hardest-working person in the world and that her holiday plans should be accelerated so that she could take a well-earned rest as soon as the present indisposition was over.

But during the night the Queen grew worse, and Reid and Powell began to give her oxygen. They were with her all night, and in the morning, the 20th, she was prostrated, unable to move herself or to speak. As she seemed only vaguely conscious of her surroundings they took the opportunity of moving her into a smaller bed, to make it easier to care for her. The Prince of Wales had left for London in the morning, and met the Kaiser from the train at Charing Cross in the afternoon, taking him back to Buckingham Palace. In the evening Reid telephoned from Sir Arthur Bigge's room to Marlborough House to recommend that the prince expedite his return to Osborne and bring the Kaiser with him. Francis Knollys, who took the call, said that the prince was exhausted and needed a good night's sleep before setting out for Osborne again. Would it be soon enough, if he took the 8 a.m. train and arrived in the forenoon? Reid and Powell consulted together and said that they thought it would be all right.

When Reid had put the telephone down, he and Powell remained in Bigge's room with Ponsonby, Charles Du Cane and Lord Edward Clinton, the Master of the Household, talking over the situation.

'She could well die in the night,' Reid said. 'There's no way to be certain. But her determination is enormous.'

'The Bishop of Winchester voiced a different worry to me earlier,' said Ponsonby. 'What if she survives, but in such a condition as not to be able to discharge her duties? If there had to be a regency—'

306

'She would never allow it,' said Du Cane. 'She would never hand over the reins like that.'

They looked at each other nervously, recalling the situation when poor George III had gone mad.

'If it went on for years, like the last time, it would be a disaster for the monarchy,' Bigge said.

'I think that of all outcomes, that is the least likely,' Reid said. 'Even if she survives the night, the end can't be far off.'

'But what happens when she does die?' Du Cane asked suddenly. 'What are the procedures? Does anyone know what to do?'

'It's over sixty years since the question last arose,' said Ponsonby rather grimly. 'Gentlemen, there are constitutional issues which *we* will have to face. I wish there were someone we could consult. Personally, I don't feel in the least up to it. I haven't slept in days.'

'If she dies while the Prince of Wales is still here, does he go back to London to speak to the Privy Council, or does he summon them here?' Bigge asked.

'Here, I think,' Ponsonby said. He looked at Reid. 'You believe she may go at any time? Then I think either Bigge or I should be on hand at all times. We can take watch and watch, Arthur. I'll sit up tonight while you get some sleep, and then you can relieve me, if nothing has happened, at, say, six o'clock.'

There was no sleep for Reid or Powell that night. They were with the Queen the whole time, giving oxygen frequently; but towards morning she rallied. Through the forenoon of the 21st the Queen came gradually to consciousness, and was able to speak and swallow more easily. She asked to have her dog Turi brought to her, and he was put on her bed for her to stroke, which seemed to comfort her. The Prince of Wales and the Kaiser arrived in the late morning, along with the Duke of Connaught and the Duke and Duchess of York, and each in turn was taken to the foot of her bed. Even had she opened her eyes, she could not have seen them, for her eyesight had deteriorated to virtual blindness; but she had her eyes closed, as if asleep,

307

and Reid advised that they did not speak or disturb her.

The Monday papers were full of nothing but the Queen's critical condition, the hopes and prayers for her recovery, and accounts of the sorrow and anxiety exhibited in city after city in countries all over the world. Other news barely featured. The bulletins issued from Osborne House and commentary on them filled all the space. The prince and the Kaiser walked in the grounds in the afternoon, a sight which encouraged the reporters gathered around the gates, for they did not think the end could be very near if those two were able to be absent from the bedside. They walked all the way down to East Cowes to visit a convalescent home for soldiers and talk to some of the wounded from South Africa, took tea with the matron, and strolled back slowly. As if to confirm what their lack of hurry suggested, the five o'clock bulletin was more cheerful, saying that the improvement of the morning had been maintained.

Charles Du Cane went along to Powell's room when he saw the bulletin, and finding Reid and Powell together there asked them if there was really room for hope. The two men looked at each other. 'That bulletin was not our idea,' Reid said. 'We issued it at the specific request of the Prince of Wales.'

'You mean it isn't true?'

'Of course it's true,' Reid said sharply.

'The form of the words,' Powell said, 'the likelihood of raising false hopes – that was not what we would have wished.'

'For God's sake, Jamie,' Du Cane appealed, 'what am I to tell Olivia? What are the prospects? Suppose she were not the Queen but a Mrs Smith of Anytown, what would you say about her prospects?'

'I don't know any Mrs Smiths,' Reid said irritably.

But Powell took pity on him. 'I suppose I would say I should expect her to live perhaps for four or five days.'

'Thank you,' said Du Cane. He passed a hand across his eyes. 'This is a hard time for all of us, but for you gentlemen most of all, I know.'

In the evening the Prince of Wales was taken in again to

see the Queen, and this time she was awake, and knew him. They spoke to each other quietly, and she kissed his hand and asked him to kiss her cheek. Reid left them alone together and went out into the dark, narrow corridor outside the Queen's room. He found Olivia hovering there, looking agitated, her hands clasped so tightly her knuckles were white. He had never seen her anything other than calm and composed, and it cut through the numbness of his own weariness. He felt her pain with his own.

'Charlie told me – you said she might live four or five days more,' she said, turning a face of urgent appeal on him.

He sighed deeply. 'Nothing is certain. At the moment she seems stable, that's all I can say. But it could change from moment to moment.'

'I want to see her,' Olivia said, and – shocking Reid – tears broke from her eyes and spilled over onto her cheeks and she sobbed. 'Oh, why can't I see her? Please let me see her.'

'You know that I can't. The prince is in there. You should not even be here,' he said, but kindly.

'She doesn't ask for me?'

'She doesn't ask for anyone.' He could not bear the agonised eyes on him. 'She is not dying this moment. If – when – the moment comes, I will try to let you come in and see her before the end. That's all I can say.'

It had to be enough for Olivia. She nodded and turned away.

Another night followed, and while the household slept, Reid and Powell kept vigil, giving oxygen and liquid, but there was nothing more they could do. The Queen was growing weaker, though she knew Reid, and spoke to him often, as if his presence reassured her. Another dawn came, and the grey light of the 22nd of January crept in under leaden, forbidding skies. Reid left the Queen to Powell's care while he went to his room to wash and change his clothes. While he was doing so Powell rushed in and asked him to hurry back as he thought the Queen was dying. The same message was taken all over the house, and princes and princesses flung on dressing-gowns and hurried to the Queen's room, while members of the Household gathered anxiously in the drawing-room. The Bishop of Winchester stood off to one side saying prayers for the dying, while Reid leant over the bed giving oxygen. The room, though large enough for a bedroom, was not designed for state occasions, and there was hardly room for all the family members who were crowded into it, along with Reid, Powell, Mrs Tuck and the trained nurse.

The Queen's daughters, Helena, Louise and Beatrice, spoke their names to her, and told her the names of the others who were there, but omitted the name of the Kaiser. They did not wish to show him any warmth or favour, and the Prince of Wales told Reid not to mention him to the Queen in case it excited her too much. Outside the gates, growing numbers of journalists from all over the world were gathering, and the pessimistic first bulletin of the day, together with the fact that the vicar of Whippingham was seen hurrying in through the gates in response to a summons, persuaded them that the end was in sight.

But the Queen rallied again. The doctors asked everyone to leave so as to let her rest, and when they had gone, she spoke to Reid coherently, and when he asked if she would take food, smiled at him and said patiently, 'Anything you like.' When she needed to be turned, she told Mrs Tuck and Nurse Soal that she would like Reid to do it – the first time he had been allowed to do so. As her mind seemed so much clearer, he went to the Prince of Wales to ask if he might take the Kaiser in to see her, and the prince gave his permission. Reid took the Kaiser up to her bedside and told her he was there, then ushered the maids out so that grandmother and grandson were alone together for five minutes. When Reid went back in, she smiled at him and said, 'The Emperor is very kind.' He wondered, though, if she had really known which emperor it was: 'kind' was not the word most people would apply to the Kaiser.

She slept for a while, and Reid, remembering his promise to Olivia, had a message sent to her, and allowed her to come in and stand by the bedside a moment. One by one the others of the Household who had been close to her – Clinton, Bigge, Ponsonby, Du Cane, McNeill, her Master of Horse – came to say their goodbyes, unseen and unknown by the Queen. Each came in, stood a moment, and then quietly left, to go back downstairs to the drawing-room and wait. The princesses were waiting in the Queen's sitting-room, the princes in the Prince Consort's writing room, where they used Albert's desk in turns to write letters and telegrams for Bigge to send off. The morning was gone; the weak sun began to slide down the far side, and the Queen's brief rally petered out. She grew obviously weaker, and the four o'clock bulletin said, 'The Queen is slowly sinking.' In the gathering darkness the reporters at the gate knew this was the admission that there was no more hope.

After sending the bulletin, Reid went back in to see the Queen alone for a few minutes, then called for the family to come back in. He knelt at one side of the bed, supporting her with his left arm, his right fingers holding her wrist to feel her pulse. The Prince of Wales drew up a chair just behind him; the Kaiser and the Princess of Wales stood at the other side of the bed with the nurse and Mrs Tuck, and the rest of the family grouped themselves round the room. Other family members were arriving all the time, and as there was not room for everyone at the same time there was a continual coming and going. The Queen was conscious, but kept her eyes turned towards her doctor, saying his name from time to time, and once, 'I am very ill.' He said, 'Your Majesty will soon be better.' Her breathing grew more laboured, though her pulse was steady. Then suddenly she opened her eyes very wide. She stared past Reid and the Prince of Wales at some-thing – or nothing – beyond them, and the last breath she had drawn in sighed slowly out, and the pulse under Reid's fingers faded away. It was half past six. Reid gently withdrew his supporting arm, letting the head down onto the pillow, and kissed the hand before laying it down. He turned to the man behind him, who as of that instant was King and Emperor, and prompted him to close his mother's eyes.

There was so much to be done. In the Equerries' Room Ponsonby, Bigge and Du Cane, together with Lord Clarendon, the Lord Chamberlain, and Arthur Balfour, who

311

had arrived during the afternoon, discussed what the procedure ought to be, and sifted through old documents and books in the hope of finding some precedent in accounts of the deaths of William IV and George IV. Essential telegrams had to be encrypted and sent before the news was issued generally, and orders had to be given for the inner shell of the coffin to be made by a local carpenter and sent up to the house within thirty-six hours. The outer coffin would be made by the royal undertaker in London as usual.

After a snatched dinner Sir James Reid hurried back to the Queen's room to help her dressers and the nurse to prepare the body. It had to be lifted off the divan and back onto the great bed, which had to be pushed into the proper position under the canopy; then it had to be dressed and arranged and surrounded with flowers. At ten fifteen the family gathered in the room with the Bishop for prayers; and just before midnight, on his way to bed at last, Reid brought Olivia in to see the Queen and say her last goodbye.

The body was so tiny in the great bed, it seemed no larger than a child's. Olivia crept up to look, and drew in a breath. It was like a marble statue, she thought, perfect, white and smooth, with no sign of illness or age: beautiful, and in its perfection almost youthful. Yet it was still very much the Queen, and she felt as much awe as if she had been approaching her mistress alive. A few flowers and palms were lying loose around the body, most vivid among them the deep blue hyacinths brought in by Princess Beatrice, which scented the air. It was all so complete, so perfect, that it brought it home to her again that there was nothing for her to do, no service she would ever again be required to perform for the mistress to whom she had given her whole life since she was seventeen. She left the room and went back to her own. When Charlie came up at last he found her sitting by the dying fire, staring blankly, unable to think what the future might hold now that her service of over thirty years was ended.

Telegraph and telephone spread the news as fast as thought across the country. Newspapers were rushed out onto the streets and people emerged from their homes, from restaurants and public houses, offices, shops and factories to buy them. Everywhere there was a feeling of bewilderment as well as a deeply personal sorrow. Even those who had never seen the Queen in the flesh felt their connection to her; even those who did not revere the monarchy felt that the cornerstone of the country had been suddenly removed.

As the news spread, darkness followed it like a shadow as lights were extinguished, blinds drawn and shutters closed. Public entertainments were interrupted by the news – *Cinderella* at the Pavilion Theatre, London, *Aladdin* at the Theatre Royal, Manchester, a concert in Aberdeen, a lecture in Salford, a mission meeting in the Mile End Road, plays in Drury Lane and Shaftesbury Avenue – and in every case the performance was abandoned and the audience filed out in silence, heads bowed. Traffic stopped to listen, and then melted away as everyone went home. Restaurants and gentlemen's clubs emptied. In Oxford the students walked aimlessly about the streets, muffled up and silent as ghosts, the only sound in the city the tolling of the great bell of Christ Church. Flags sank to half mast on public buildings, shops hung their windows with crape; in remote villages the notice was put up on the post-office door, and tearful crowds gathered round to read.

And in the streets of London silent crowds began to coalesce around three buildings. At Buckingham Palace there had been a crowd before the gates all day, waiting for each fresh bulletin to be posted. The first indication of the dire news came when the blinds in the windows on the front façade were suddenly pulled down. The Palace could not lower any flag because, as the principal royal residence, the only one it ever flew was the Royal Standard, and then only when the monarch was in residence. The Royal Standard could never be flown at half mast because there was never an empty throne: on the instant of the Queen's death, the Prince of Wales was King and the Standard became the indicator of his presence. The lowered blinds, darkening the building, were the signal that the end had come, but it was another hour before a policeman crossed the forecourt to fix

313

the new notice on the gates. Previous bulletins had been framed in red; this one was framed in black, and a sound like a moan ran backwards through the crowd. Those at the front read it out and the word passed in a low murmur from person to person: 'The Queen died peacefully at six thirty.'

In the City of London a crowd numbering in thousands had gathered before the Mansion House. Just after seven o'clock the Lord Mayor appeared at the open window of his parlour, in evening dress and black tie, and at once a hush fell over the crowd, and in a ripple and whisper of movement, like wind blowing over a cornfield, every man removed his hat and bared his head. The Lord Mayor's voice carried on the still air. 'Fellow citizens, it is with deep sorrow I have to read to you a telegram which has just reached me from the Prince of Wales. "Osborne, 6.45. My beloved Mother, the Queen, has just passed away, surrounded by her children and grandchildren – Albert Edward."'

Having spoken, he left the window, and the blind was pulled down after him. There was no sound from the crowd: no-one spoke a word; but into the silence came the deep notes of Great Tom, the ancient tenor bell of St Paul's, which tolled only for monarchs. Many of those standing outside the Mansion House turned to listen, and then, as if drawn by the sound, began to trudge up the hill in its direction, to join the third great mass of people, who had gathered on the steps of the cathedral, waiting for that brazen voice to announce the news.

Women wept, and comforted each other; men stood with heads bowed; and with the sorrow came a strange and formless apprehension. It had been impossible to imagine life without the Queen at the centre of it. The world was a dangerous and uncertain place, and growing more so all the time, and they had just moved into the *terra incognita* of a new century – and now she was gone. What would happen to them now? They had defined themselves by her, as Victorians, and it had been their pride. There was a sense in most hearts that it was more than a woman and a queen who had passed away, but an age.

*　*　*

314

On the morning of the next day, Wednesday the 23rd of January, London seemed like a different place. Traffic, both pedestrian and horse-drawn, was lighter as many shops, offices, factories and workshops remained closed. The theatres, which had closed voluntarily the night before, would now remain dark by order of the Lord Chamberlain; the Stock Exchange opened only to close again immediately. Cab and omnibus drivers had tied black crape round their hats and black bows on their whips, flower girls wore black ribbons on their bonnets. Everyone was suddenly wanting black: the only busy shops were those selling mourning clothes and accoutrements. In Harvey Nichols, Whiteley's, Peter Robinson's, women queued silently for ready-made black skirts, coats, dresses. One outfitter's in the Strand set up a row of looking-glasses along the counter so that gentlemen purchasing a black tie could put it on at once. Court mourning was usually three months, but for the first time it seemed that there would be public mourning at every level of society. Nobody had ordered it, but for weeks to come, at least until after the funeral, perhaps for longer, every soul in the country would be wearing black.

At Manchester Square, Venetia looked out her mourning clothes, including the plain wool black dress and coat she would wear for 'work' – sickness was one thing that would not stop for the period. This was a busy time of year, when influenza was added to the usual list of ailments. Last January there had been an epidemic in London that had killed fifty a day; and though cold weather was usually better for the huge population of tuberculosis sufferers, the dense fogs that were prevalent between January and April often saw them off.

'Of course we'll have to do something about blacks for Violet. She's grown out of the things she had when Mama died. I shall have to send Nanny out with her to Liberty's – I simply won't have time to go myself.'

Hazelmere was dressing to go to Marlborough House, for the Prince of Wales was due back there from Osborne this morning. 'The King, I mean,' he corrected himself.

Venetia looked up. 'That sounds so strange. No-one has

said "His Majesty" for sixty years. It will take some getting used to.'

'And singing "God Save the King".'

'Poor fellow! He'll have a hard time of it, following her. Everything he says and does will be compared and criticised – I can just hear them saying, "The Queen wouldn't have done it like that"!'

'He'll do very well,' Hazelmere said. 'You'll see. He'll have his own way of doing things, but he won't disgrace the Crown. He has a very firm idea of his kinghood, and what's owing to it and to England.'

'I'm glad you think so. What name will he take, do you know?'

'Oh, just Edward. He told Francis long ago that he'd drop the "Albert" as soon as his mother was dead. Not English enough – and our kings have never had two names. He'll be Edward VII.'

'It sounds well. Edward VII. And Queen Alexandra – she will be perfect in the rôle. What will be happening today?'

'Meeting of the Privy Council at St James's Palace. Proclamation there and at Temple Bar. Swearing in of the Council. Cabinet ministers to attend to receive their seals of office. Then this afternoon both Houses of Parliament will take the Oath of Allegiance and sign the Roll, and when that's done there'll be an eighty-one gun salute in St James's Park – one for each year of the Queen's life. Then the King goes back down to Osborne to see the body put in the coffin.'

'Ah! It sounds as though I shan't see much of you today.'

'I'm afraid not. And, of course, if he wants me to go to Osborne with him, or sends for me there, you'll see even less.'

'If he wants you, of course you must go,' Venetia said. 'At least you'll be able to see Olivia for me, and find out how she's managing. She must be quite devastated. It's been her whole life.'

'And then there'll be the funeral to arrange,' Hazelmere went on, with a gloomy look. 'I foresee not only endless work, but endless arguments over who's in charge of what.

It's fortunate that she wrote down every detail of how it's to be done, or we'd never get on at all.'

The Queen had decreed that her funeral colour was to be white, not black: she was going to be with Albert, in death a widow no more but a bride again, so her mourning black must be cast off. And as she was a soldier's daughter, she had ordered a military funeral. The coffin was to be carried from Cowes to Gosport on the royal yacht, passing through a line of warships, which would fire a solemn salute across the water. The following day the coffin would be taken by train to Victoria and there placed on a gun-carriage and covered with a white silk pall, on top of which would be laid the imperial crown, orbs, sceptre and collar of the Garter. The gun-carriage would be drawn by the Queen's own eight cream-coloured horses through the streets from Victoria to Paddington, to be put on the train for Windsor where the actual funeral and interment were to take place. The date was set for Saturday February the 2nd, which left ten days to make everything ready.

The Duke of Norfolk – Earl Marshal of England, whose responsibility for all such royal ceremonies was by hereditary right – was in charge of the funeral, and went down to Osborne with Lord Roberts to discuss plans with the King. It wasn't long before Hazelmere was summoned to help. The Duke was not a very able man, and had areas of ignorance about surprisingly basic things, such as the geography of Windsor itself. His first plan for the funeral had it going straight from the station to the castle, a route so short that, as Hazelmere gently pointed out, the front of the procession would reach St George's Chapel before the coffin had left the railway platform, so it would be unable to move at all. The King kept Hazelmere at his side during all subsequent discussions. 'I need you to exercise your tact,' he whispered to him. 'You must stay.'

Osborne was already bursting at the seams with extra visitors, and Lord Edward Clinton acknowledged himself at a loss for a place to put him. Hazelmere said he would be happy sharing Du Cane's quarters, so a temporary bed was put up for him in the sitting-room. At least he could see something of his in-laws that way. Though both Charlie and Olivia were officially without a position since the Queen died, in effect the Household was still functioning, as the King's people felt delicate about taking over basic duties so soon. There were endless letters and telegrams to be sent, instructions to be copied out, invitations to the funeral to be addressed. And every day masses upon masses of flowers arrived, which all had to be taken in and put somewhere. From simple bunches of violets from grateful widows to whom the Queen had once sent a comforting message, to the vast floral tributes of regiments, city councils and official bodies like the Royal Mint and Trinity House, the whole country seemed to want to mark its love and respect with flowers. The market at Covent Garden had never been busier; florists worked around the clock. An urgent request was sent out through the newspaper for flowers to be sent to Windsor, not to Osborne, but still they arrived in hourly deliveries from Cowes.

Friday the 1st of February was a clear, cold day, the sky over the Isle of Wight flawless and the pale sun glinting on the Solent. The sailors from the royal yacht in their blue jackets carried the coffin out from the house and placed it on the gun-carriage, and it set off towards the main gate along an avenue of soldiers, heads bent, rifles reversed. Ponsonby, Bigge, Du Cane and other senior equerries of the Queen's Household walked beside the coffin; the King walked behind, with the Duke of Connaught and the Kaiser beside him. The other princes, the princesses, and the King's equerries followed, and the rest of the Queen's Household brought up the rear. The bagpipes of the Black Watch broke into that most poignant of laments, 'The Flowers of the Forest.' The schoolchildren, villagers, estate workers and servants watched from the lawns on either side, most in tears. All down the hill towards Cowes the road was lined with the residents of the island, watching in absolute silence as their Queen, so particularly their own, passed for the last time. Few doubted that the new King would abandon this particular residence and that Wight's days of glory were over.

318

The walk to Trinity Pier was long and tiring, and by the end of it the Princess of Wales – as she still called herself – was pale and plainly exhausted. Everyone was glad to go on board the yacht and sit down, and to warm his feet and hands. It took an hour for the royal yacht to cross the Solent between the moored battleships and to receive their salutes, and as the escort of small destroyers led her into Portsmouth harbour, the sun was beginning to set. Along the horizon the sky was a blaze of flame and crimson, the sea a shield of gold; high overhead, in the clear translucence, the moon showed faintly. On the shore a vast crowd, all dressed in black, waited in uncanny silence. The garrison battery fired a salute, the sound echoing flatly across the water. As the royal yacht anchored, the sun slipped below the horizon, lights began to twinkle from the ships, and the sea shivered into ashy grey. It was an eerie moment.

Saturday dawned bitterly cold in London, grey and misty, so that trees and buildings at any distance were ghostly, looking as if they had been sketched in with soft pencil and then half erased. Troops were in place all along the route by eight o'clock, but the crowds were there before them, some having arrived at four in the morning. A million people lined the way; there were sixty thousand in Hyde Park alone; windows and even accessible roofs were let out at high prices. It had been decreed a day of national mourning, and shops, public houses and everything else was closed. But an appeal in various newspapers for respectful behaviour had not stopped the swarms of street-sellers, hawking everything from special newspaper supplements, coloured pictures, black-and-purple rosettes and commemorative mugs to memorial watches, onyx shirt-links, and plaster busts of the Queen from pocket- to near life-size.

But the crowds waited in seemly quiet, though the day remained dankly cold and the wait was long before the cortège finally came into view. The honour guard, swords and rifles reversed, preceded the gun-carriage with its eight cream horses, the scarlet vests of the postillions making a vivid splash of colour in the dull day. Ponsonby and the same Household officers walked beside it, with the addition

319

of Sir James Reid, who had begged permission of the King to be there for this one last time. Behind the coffin came the King on a bay horse, with the Kaiser on a grey just behind and to one side of him, and then a glittering cavalry of forty kings, princes and royal dukes in their various uniforms; and behind them the various detachments of soldiers and sailors.

All passed in an uncanny quiet. The road had been sanded, the gun-carriage specially fitted with rubber tyres. There was no sound in the half-light of the winter day but the jingle of swords and curb-chains, the muted clatter of horses' hoofs, and the distant booming of the guns. The horses' breath smoked up into the chill, misty air. The black wall of the crowd waited in silence; only as the coffin approached a long, sighing whisper, 'The Queen! The Queen!' ran before it, and died down as it passed. So small it looked, white and gold, with the glitter of the crown on its crimson cushion fixing the eye. How could the loss of only that, the contents of that small thing, make such a difference? But there was a sense everywhere that life would be altered from now on.

When the last of the procession had passed, the troops lining the route were marched off and the crowds could at last move and disperse. The sun, which had never broken through all day or supplied the faintest gleam of warmth, began to decline behind the grey veil of clouds, the mist thickened and the cold intensified. Most of the crowd had had neither food nor drink all day, but nothing was available until two o'clock when the tea rooms in the park opened, to the benefit of those still queuing to get away. The mood was still sombre. Even when the public houses opened again at three, there was no reaction against the restraint of the day. Men and women talked in low voices, and there was no laughter; after an hour or so most of them drifted away into the gathering dusk to go home. It was the quietest Saturday night in London's memory.

At Windsor the funeral service in St George's Chapel began at three o'clock when the coffin arrived. Hazelmere and

Charles Du Cane were still on duty, and Venetia and Olivia had both been invited and had seats on the specially built stand in the chilly chapel. Dusk came on while the service was under way, and the candles gleamed brighter as the windows darkened. Afterwards the coffin was carried into the small chapel at the rear, and the Hazelmeres and the Du Canes were able to escape at last to their quarters to seek food and rest after the long, cold, exhausting day. The Du Canes went to bed early as did many of those who had come up from Osborne that day. Hazelmere was summoned to see the King about some arrangements, and Venetia went back to London alone by an evening train so as to have Sunday with the children.

The coffin remained in the chapel through Sunday, and on the cold, misty Monday afternoon it was drawn on a gun-carriage through Windsor Great Park to the mausoleum at Frogmore, to be laid in the tomb beside that of the Prince Consort. One by one the family, and then the Household, filed by for one last look, and then it was all over. As they walked back through the park to the castle afterwards, the bitter sky broke at last and a fine dusting of snow began to fall.

Venetia looked up at the sky, and a faint smile touched her lips. 'Look,' she said, 'God's making sure she has her white funeral.'

And then as her sister began to cry again, she slipped an arm through hers and supported her as they hurried back towards light and warmth and shelter.

CHAPTER TEN

No-one who had known Sir Peregrine Parke in his youth would have thought him cut out to be an ogre. He had been idle, affable and carelessly generous. With his future pre-ordained – to follow in his father's footsteps – he had had no ambition but to be liked by everyone. His heedlessness and expensive tastes had cost his father a great deal one way and another, but he had never in the least intended to cause the old man grey hairs, having a great and pious respect for him. Perry grew up at a time when a father's authority was absolute: a summons to the pater's study filled him with fear and trembling, belated contrition and a heart-felt wish that he had never been so bone-headed as to have done whatever it was.

Sir John's sudden and early death had shocked him, and thrown him abruptly into a position of authority he had not even begun to think about, let alone prepare for. He found himself a baronet and squire of the village, looked up to and expected to lead in all things. He was master of a large estate and guardian to his younger sisters. He now had extensive responsibilities, which he was not equipped by nature to discharge. His mental attainments were few, his education almost non-existent. He read laboriously, could not add up even with the aid of fingers, knew nothing of farming, had never learnt to concentrate, and had an aver-sion to sustained mental effort that almost amounted to terror.

Had the dibs remained in tune, he might have done well enough in the long run, for he was good-hearted and wanted to do the right thing. But his coming into his inheritance coincided with the agricultural slump, and he saw his income declining year on year without in the least understanding why, or knowing what to do about it. He married a woman – Henrietta's sister Regina – as good-natured and ignorant as himself, and proceeded to father a string of children. He loved them dearly, but they had ruined his wife's health and, as they grew, began to cost him money he could not afford.

Little by little, he retreated from the casual good humour of his salad days. He seemed to be struggling in a nightmare, having to make decisions without understanding and pay bills without money, appealed to by servants, estate workers, tenants, villagers and family members for help and advice at every turn, worrying where the next sovereign was coming from, seeing all too clearly where the last had gone. As his worries increased, his temper shortened. He had a large house to keep up, but tenants came to him complaining of leaking roofs and leaning fences, while asking to be let off their rent. His position in society demanded lavish entertainments he didn't enjoy and large contributions to charitable causes he didn't believe in. His wife had no notion of economy – nor would he have wanted her to, for that would have touched his pride – and now the doctors' bills were beyond anything. His sons were as troublesome and expensive as he had been. His second son Lucas, having spent more at Oxford even than Bertie, was going into the Church, of all things, and needed to be set up. His third son, Peg – the family's abbreviation of Peregrine – was just about to go up and promised to be the wildest of them all. There were two more sons at schools whose fees were ruinous, and his daughters wanted weddings and dowries. Was it any wonder he lost his temper sometimes? It would have been enough to try a saint.

His feeling of resentment grew. No-one seemed to understand the plight he was in; no-one had any sympathy for *him*. They came to him for money as if it grew on trees, and looked offended when it was not to be had. Everyone thought it was such a fine thing to be Sir Peregrine, when the truth was it was nothing but worry: he lay awake at nights sick with anxiety about the future. And the final straw was that his sons did not treat him with the awe and respect that he had felt for his father. The times had changed, so people said: there was no longer that unthinking obedience, that instinctive piety. He had to maintain standards, both moral and material, and be Sir Perry as his father had been Sir John, but his children defied him and spoke back to him as he would never have dreamt of doing. They got into the scrapes *he* had got into, but they did not bear their carpetings with downcast eyes and trembling cheeks. They were as likely to look him straight in the eye and tell him it was his fault for not giving them a bigger allowance!

It was natural that his resentment should focus on Bertie, who would have to take his position after him, and be Sir Percival as he was Sir Perry. He wanted to help Bertie, to warn him, to prepare him; he had to be stricter with him than with the others; and all he got from Bertie was defiance and disobedience. It hurt him when Bertie looked at him without love, and hurt made him all the sterner. He did not know how else to cope with the multiple anxieties and disappointments of his life, and the sheer terror of chaos, than to try to control, and to punish when he could not.

He was sitting in his study in the Red House one morning in late March, trying to make sense of an essay on drainage that had been recommended to him. The Red House was large and square and built in a period no longer much admired. It was early Georgian, faced as the name suggested in red brick, utterly without decoration or embellishment, depending for its beauty on its perfect symmetry and the pure mathematical relationship of its proportions. Mathematics being as closed a book to him as music to the tone-deaf, he thought it ugly, and it was an additional irritation that he had to find the money for the upkeep of a place he did not even admire. It had no gas, no lavatories, no bathrooms. It cost a fortune in coal to heat, and even then the rooms were so large they were never warm: beyond a small radius of any fire, a dank cold struck deep to the bones. But it would have been unthinkable to move out, sell it, buy somewhere smaller and prettier and more modern.

The Red House was ugly, draughty and inconvenient; but the Parkes had lived there for nearly two hundred years, so that was that.

Today it was grey and blowy outside, with occasional faint beams of sunshine, interspersed with lowering darkness when the window would be spattered with cold rain. Just beyond his window the rolling green lawn was fringed with dancing daffodils, bright as flames against the dark of neatly clipped yew hedges, but he had no eye for them. Despite the large fire his study was barely warm, and the chill seemed to weight his brain, so that he read the same paragraph again and again without understanding a word. Only his feet were warm, thanks to the devotion of an elderly spaniel, which had forsworn the comforts of the hearth rug to lie across them.

His eye ranged across the words on the page without any meaning passing into his brain. He was thinking about his troubles in general, and about Bertie in particular. The boy had recovered now from his wound. Perry remembered only too well the violent shock of the news, the gnawing anxiety of waiting for developments. In those weeks of waiting for Bertie to be brought home he had swung from fury to dismay so often that he felt quite sick with it, and by the time he went to meet the boat, he had passed into a kind of exhausted numbness. But the sight of that drawn face and the dreadful bandages had thrown him into a sharp awareness that was like a physical pain. His boy, his son, had been hurt, had almost died; was still in pain, might still decline and die. All his love had crowded up into his throat so that he could not speak, only lay a trembling hand on the unwounded shoulder, and try not to weep.

As time passed and he was able to believe that Bertie would not die, that he would recover fully, Perry had hoped that there would be a new beginning between them, that they would become what father and son should be. But as Bertie's strength returned it became clear that nothing had changed, and that his experiences in South Africa had only made him more restless and independent-minded. Last night, as on so many occasions recently, there had been a

325

row at the dinner table. Perry had been talking about the war, and Bertie had disputed with him. Heat had grown on both sides, until Bertie had said – it made Perry shake even to think about it – that his father did not know what he was talking about, and that he had no right to an opinion founded, as it was, on ignorance and prejudice. Perry had exploded in wrath and sent Bertie from the table; it only added to his fury to know that it was an imploring look from his mother that had made the boy leave without further argument.

Indigestion and sleeplessness had followed for Perry. Regina had retired early, looking so sickly he had not had the heart to go to her room to talk about the incident, so it had revolved in his mind without any way to get out. This morning neither she nor Bertie had been at breakfast – she still in her room and Bertie, he was told, having gone out very early for a ride. Ridden over to Morland Place, Perry supposed bitterly, to tell them all about it. Filial piety and family loyalty meant nothing to him; nothing would prevent him telling all and sundry that he thought his father a fool.

A tap at the door broke into his repetitive circle of bitterness, and he would have been glad of the interruption had the door not opened to admit Bertie, his face set in an expression of determination that boded no good. 'Can I talk to you, Father?'

Perry pretended to be reading. 'I am busy. Another time.'

'It's rather important,' Bertie said. He came in and shut the door behind him.

This ignoring of his wishes fired Perry's resentment, but he was not feeling in top form, and wished rather for peace and quiet than a renewed row, so he said, 'Very well, then, but be brief. I have a great deal to do.'

'I will be brief, if you will listen to me,' Bertie said quietly. That made Perry look up. The boy's face was set and determined. It did not occur to him that Bertie was no longer a boy, but a grown man who had been to war: to his father he was permanently sixteen. 'About last night,' Bertie resumed.

'I have no wish to talk about it,' Perry interrupted coldly. 'Your behaviour—'

'I want to apologise,' Bertie said. 'It was wrong of me to lose my temper and I'm sorry.'

Perry stared, trying to detect a trap. 'Very well,' he said. 'If that is all—'

'No, it isn't all. I *am* sorry, but I can't promise it will never happen again, and that's what I want to talk to you about.'

'You are impertinent. I have nothing more to say to you on the subject. Please leave.'

'No, I won't. We have to have it out, Father.'

'Do you defy me, sir?' said Perry, his voice rising.

'I'm not a boy any more,' Bertie hurried on desperately. 'I'm a grown man. That's why we argue. That's why it will happen again. I can't go on like this. I hate to make you and Mama unhappy, and that's all I'm doing by staying here. So I have to go. That's what I've come to tell you.'

'*Tell* me? Who do you think is master in this house? Whether you go or stay is for me to decide.'

'You see,' Bertie said hopelessly, 'we are arguing again already.'

'No, sir – *you* are arguing. I suppose that is what they teach you at Morland Place, to defy your father. You were there again this morning – couldn't wait even for breakfast to rush over there and air your family's private business.'

'I didn't go to Morland Place this morning,' Bertie said, sounding so puzzled Perry knew it was the truth, and was momentarily ashamed. 'I just went for a ride around the fields so that I could think.'

'And what did you think? Nothing to any purpose, I am quite sure,' Perry said – coldly, but with a step back from anger that allowed Bertie to go on.

'Will you listen and let me tell you something?' he said, and when Perry neither agreed nor refused, he went on, 'There's a Mr Puddephat, a friend of Uncle Teddy's, who is an agent for providing horses for the army.'

'Yes, yes, I know who Puddephat is. What of it?'

Bertie went on that he had met Puddephat a couple of days ago, had taken luncheon with him in the Same Yet – the village inn – by arrangement.

'Why there? Why not here?' Perry asked sharply. Here were underhand goings-on, he was sure, more insults to his authority.

Bertie looked faintly guilty at the question, but he only shrugged. The truth was that Puddephat had been quite prepared to come to the Red House, but Bertie wanted to get out, and speak to him where there was no chance of being overheard. He had something in his mind he wanted to ask him.

'He wanted to talk some more about his son Raymond,' he said, as if that were an answer. 'And he has been taking an interest in my progress since I came home. There has been some correspondence between us—'

'More letters to this Puddephat person than you sent to your own parents,' Perry could not help interjecting resentfully.

'I'm sorry, Father. Please, let me go on.'

'Be brief.'

Bertie was brief. Puddephat had spoken of how Raymond would have been following in his father's business had he not died in South Africa. It now came about that Puddephat needed to go to India and Tibet to find new suppliers of small horses and ponies, but his wife was so poorly he could neither take her with him nor feel comfortable about leaving her. The business was too important to send a hireling, and it was just such a job he would have entrusted to Raymond, had he lived, and had he been home from the army. It was the sort of trip that would have served very well as an apprenticeship into the business, though Puddephat would have had to send an older man along with Ray, given his extreme youth and inexperience in the world.

Bertie paused at this moment in the narrative, remembering the occasion. In the private parlour of the Same Yet, Tudor-panelled, cosy, with the crackling of a large fire and the soft ticking of an ancient clock for background, the conversation had waxed warmer and more kindly by the moment. So it had not been a great surprise to Bertie when Puddephat suggested he might like to take on the task. He liked Puddephat so much, and then, as now, he reflected

328

briefly on what it might have been like to have a father like him. His own father was staring at him with that boiled look of suppressed fury he knew so well, as he anticipated what was coming. Bertie drew up his courage and told him what he had guessed already.

'He offered me a proper salaried position, and hinted that I might become his partner at some point in the future. I don't know about that – but I would like to accept his present offer.'

Perry did not hesitate. 'Out of the question,' he said.

Bertie persisted. 'He would want me to leave in about a month's time. The doctor says my arm will be sound enough by then. It would mean being away for about two years. I should like very much to see India, and this is an excellent chance to travel all over it, all expenses paid, and to visit parts I would not otherwise have the occasion to.'

'Did you not hear me? I said it's out of the question.'

'Why?' Bertie asked. Perry did not answer. He had drawn the paper towards him and was pretending to read, though his hands were shaking. Bertie drew a tight breath and said, with quivering politeness, 'Father, would you be so kind as to tell me why it is out of the question?'

Perry slammed his hand down on the desk, and felt the spaniel on his feet flinch. 'Why will you always argue and dispute? I do not have to explain myself to you, sir!'

'In this case I think you do!'

'Don't answer me back! Have you no respect? I would not have dared to speak to my father the way you speak to me.'

'I *do* respect you—'

'Then you should show it! A good son would try to help his father.'

'I want to help you, but you won't let me,' Bertie said. 'You have never allowed me to do anything. Even now you won't let me take over any part of running the estate.'

'You know nothing about estate management! You would bring us to ruin in five minutes.'

'How can I know anything when you won't let me learn?' Bertie cried in frustration. 'I've asked you again and again to let me help—'

'Help? You can help by obeying my orders without question. Obedience is all that is required of you, and a simple enough thing, one would have thought, but it appears to be beyond you. All I get from you is defiance and expense.' Perry sought a paper from amongst those on his desk and slapped it down in front of him. 'Look at this! Doctor's bills – for treating you! With all the troubles you must know I have on my plate, you can think of nothing better to do than present me with more bills.'

Bertie was outraged. 'I didn't ask to be wounded! Do you think I took a ball in the shoulder for fun?'

'You wouldn't have been wounded if you had not run off and volunteered without my permission! Without even asking – and why did you not ask? Because you knew I would not have agreed!'

'That's right! I knew you would refuse me, just as you refuse me everything! You call me expensive, but you won't let me earn my keep. You call me idle but you won't let me do anything. Lucas is going into the Church, Peg is for the law, but you wouldn't let me have any profession, and when I tried to become a soldier you did everything you could to oppose it.'

'You are not to have a profession! You will be Sir Percival Parke! The estate will be yours. Your place is here at home.'

'But *what for*? To sit at your feet drooling like that damned dog? You hold the inheritance over me like a threat. I'd sooner not have the damned thing than be blackmailed with it!'

'How dare you? How *dare* you speak to me like that?' Perry bellowed, suddenly losing his temper. The spaniel crept out from under the desk and oozed across to the dark corner beside the fireplace. 'I will not be abused by my own son in my own house! Good God, has it come to this? Your impiety, sir, is beyond tolerance.'

Bertie drew himself back. 'I'm sorry, Father,' he said quietly. 'That was wrong of me. I beg your pardon. But why won't you even consider this? It's something I can do well, and be useful about.'

'Is that your idea of loyalty? Taking the place of another man's son? To be to him what you refuse to be to me?'

'*No*, Father! It's got nothing to do with loyalty. I would be employed, that's all. I'd be earning a salary – and saving you the expense of my keep too.'

'I won't have you taking a job like some – some common person.'

'Why should I not have a job? Haven't I the right?'

'No, you have not. You will be Sir Percival Parke. A gentleman hasn't the right to take a job someone else might do.'

'But it isn't ungentlemanly work, and it's for the good of the country – the army needs horses more than ever now. You ought to be glad that I want to do something patriotic.'

'Don't tell me what I ought to think.'

'No, sir. Of course not. But, Father, I'm twenty-five years old. I must *do* something. I hate living a life of idleness. And I'm only too aware that I cost you money without contributing anything. Won't you let me be useful in this way?'

'Yes, that's what it comes to,' Perry said bitterly. 'It has to be "in this way". Don't you think I know where you get your ideas? Morland Place means more to you than your own home. Your aunt and uncle mean more to you than your own parents.'

'That's not true—'

'Would you give me the lie to my face? It's they who corrupt you. It was always them. They were outside society, no decent people would know them, but you fawned on them as though they were royalty. You cared nothing about reputation, the family name, your mother's credit, or your sisters' prospects. You did not care if they shamed us.'

'They're married now,' Bertie said, foundering. 'They're perfectly respectable now. But in any case, it has nothing to do with them. Puddephat—'

'He's *their* friend, isn't he? It's all part of the same thing. You learnt impiety and ingratitude at their feet, you learnt to ignore and despise your own parents, and now you want to be a son to this Puddephat instead of to me.'

'Oh, *Father*! It's not that. It's just something I can do, a chance to travel and—' He hesitated, fatally.

331

'Well?' Perry barked.

'A chance to get away. I can't go on like this, idling my life away, making you angry. I can't bear more evenings like last night. One way or another I must get out, and this is a way to do it usefully and with honour.'

'Honour? You think it honourable to defy your father and break your mother's heart?'

But this time Bertie did not flinch. He stood four-square in front of his father, his hands clasped behind his back, and his face was firm, his eye steady. Perry saw, suddenly, not his son but a stranger, a man with a soldier's ability to endure. He had faced shot and shell. Perry would not be able to shout him into submission.

'I will go, Father,' he said quietly. 'I'd like to do it with your blessing, but one way or another I will go.'

Perry stared at him in silence. He felt a wave of weariness come over him. He had cared and struggled so long, and suddenly he felt he could not care any longer. His son, his first-born, did not love him, had no natural piety or gratitude, wanted nothing but to get away from him. He had gone to Africa to escape his father and his home. Now he wanted to escape to India. The effort of trying to make Bertie love him was breaking his heart. He had too much else to worry about, and there was a seductiveness to the idea of giving up, of ceasing to care, that he was too tired to resist any longer.

'Go, then,' he said.

Bertie was not sure if he was being given permission or merely being dismissed from the room. 'Sir?'

'Go to India. Go wherever you want. Do as you please.'

'Do you mean you don't mind? I don't want to upset you, but it is something I—'

Perry roared, 'God damn it, will you argue with me even when I agree? Go, get out of here, leave me. I have work to do. Go to India if that's what you want. I don't care any more. Just go away.'

Bertie stared a moment, biting his lip, but his father had bent his head and was appearing to read again, resolutely ignoring him. It seemed ill advised to pursue the matter further. He had his permission, however unhappily phrased, so his best course seemed to be to go before the Gov'nor changed his mind. He went out and closed the door quietly behind him, and when the hollow and quaking feeling he always got when arguing with his father had subsided, he began to feel the pleasure. He would be able to get away from this glum prison of a house, travel, see new places, have adventures. Most of all, he would be able to be active again, to do something useful. He wished his father had been able to be gracious about it, but perhaps that was too much to expect. When the Gov'nor had enjoyed the peace and quiet of two years without him, and noted the relief to his expenses, perhaps he would see sense and let him find some more work to do on his return.

Perry waited only to be sure Bertie was not coming in again, and then stopped pretending to read, shoved the paper away from him and rested his head wearily in his hands. Outside the study window a blackbird sang in a sudden gleam of sunshine, a liquidly beautiful and yet somehow melancholy sound. Perry found himself, absurdly, struggling with tears. He pressed the heels of his hands against his eyes to force them back, and no sound escaped him. After a moment or two, the spaniel came back, stump tentatively wagging, and when his master made no further movement, it crept under the desk and with a sigh lay down across his feet again.

When Kitchener had taken over command from Roberts in South Africa in November 1900, everyone thought the war was as good as over. The Boer armies had been defeated, the military leaders were on the run, Kruger had fled the country, and there remained only to clear up the commando raiding units which, like small scattered beads of mercury, had been left by the breaking up of the enemy armies.

Though Milner was urging a civic settlement to remove the justification for resistance, Kitchener's plan was to concentrate on military action to eliminate the commandos. His desire was above all to bring the war to a speedy conclusion. The Government was anxious for an end, for the war

333

was proving wildly expensive, and they were afraid of what the public would say when they realised that 200,000 British soldiers were being employed in chasing at most 20,000 Boers. Kitchener wanted a quick end for his own sake, too, for he had his heart set on the commander-in-chief post in India. He begged for reinforcements: because of the size of the terrain and the distances involved, communication and logistical requirements took up most of his army, leaving him only about 22,000 men for his offensive. But the war was costing a million and a quarter pounds a week, and far from sending him reinforcements the Cabinet pressed him to send home 60,000 of the men he already had.

Attempts were made through January and February 1901 to negotiate with the Boer leaders, but Boers who had surrendered and who agreed to act as emissaries were only executed as traitors when they reached their own side. Eventually General Joubert acted as a go-between and a meeting took place between Kitchener and Botha on February the 28th. No agreement could be reached. The Boers, Botha said, were fighting for their independence; they would not accept the annexation of the republics, even with guarantees of full citizenship; neither would they accept the equal rights for blacks on which the British Government insisted. On the other side, the British Government would not agree to the total amnesty, which Kitchener had promised on their behalf. So the talks broke down, and hostilities continued.

It was a hard sort of action to counter. The Boer commandos moved fast, making lightning strikes from concealed positions, attacking supply columns, blowing up bridges and tearing up railway lines. These were known as 'guerrilla' tactics, from the Spanish word meaning 'little war': they had been used against Wellington's troops in the Peninsular War. The intention was to wear out the British with these small but irritating attacks until they tired of the whole thing and sued for peace on Boer terms.

For Kitchener, the problem was easy to express but hard to solve: how to pin down and kill or capture these roving commandos, in areas so vast the public at home simply had no concept of them. The widely scattered farms were the commando bases, where they could shelter, hide arms and ammunition, and revictual themselves and their horses. Kitchener's strategy was therefore to destroy the farms and confiscate the supplies and arms they contained. He built stone and concrete blockhouses, linked by barbed-wire fences, to section off the vast areas he had to control, and used them both to reduce the commandos' mobility and supply his own columns. In this way he intended gradually to move the Boers in his chosen direction, either to 'corral' them so that they could be surrounded and eliminated, or drive them out into the remote and unpopulated fringes of Transvaal and the Free State where they would become irrelevant.

In the course of these 'game drives', the British learnt the skills the Boers already knew, and their columns rapidly became more mobile and more effective. The officers learnt to dress like the men so that they would not be targets for snipers; and both they and the privates abandoned helmets, lances, swords and other identifying marks so that, in khaki, puttees and slouch hat, with a cross-belt of ammunition and a Lee-Enfield to hand, they looked much like anyone else on the veldt. They learnt to travel quickly, to find cover, to manage water use, to react and adapt.

Little by little they were closing down the Boer operation, but it was slow and hard work. Guarding railway lines and stations and supply depots was employing a huge number of British soldiers. Add to that the hostile foreign press, and it was not surprising that the war was not wholly popular at home. There had always been a pro-Boer, anti-war element both in politics and in the population at large, and it seemed to be growing.

One consequence of the campaign of burning farms was that a large number of non-combatants – women, children, and black servants and slaves – was left homeless. Some of these were able to make off in wagons with a few possessions to seek shelter of friends and relatives in the towns. The rest, it was felt, could not be left to starve on the open veldt: they had to be taken care of. Refugee camps were set up all over the country where at least they could be given shelter under canvas and be fed.

Little information came back to England about these camps, which was of concern to the pro-Boer parties, and particularly worried the South African Women and Children Distress Fund. This organisation sent out a mission in February 1901, led by Miss Emily Hobhouse, a clergyman's daughter from Cornwall, and the Quakers Isabella and Joshua Rowntree. They took with them a quantity of groceries and bales of clothing to be distributed to the needy, and on arrival at the Cape secured Kitchener's brusque permission to visit as many of the camps as they pleased.

In May 1901 they returned to England on the same ship as Milner, who was going home on leave. Miss Hobhouse buttonholed him and indignantly recounted what she had seen of conditions in the camps. He was so struck by what she told him – especially given that there was no love lost between him and Kitchener and that he had always opposed the farm-burning strategy – he helped her to obtain an interview with St John Broderick, the War Minister. Broderick expressed himself politely distressed but unable to do anything; and, baffled by the red tape and entrenched secrecy of the military authorities, Miss Hobhouse felt there was nothing to do but make her report public.

It was published in June. The news shocked the nation. The camps were ill organised, insanitary, poorly supplied, and the mortality rate was appalling – somewhere around thirty per cent, and most of them under sixteen. The anti-war newspapers printed large sections of the Hobhouse report verbatim, with vitriolic leaders. Foreign newspapers picked them up and thundered out anti-British propaganda. Someone called the refugee camps 'concentration camps'. This referred to the *reconcentrado* camps which the Spanish General Weyler had established in Cuba during the guerrilla uprising of 1896–7. Something like 200,000 people had died in Weyler's camps, and his methods had been internationally condemned, so the term was one of horror and abuse, and the pro-Boer factions made sure that it stuck.

Questions were asked in the House. Two Members in

particular – Campbell-Bannerman and Lloyd George – spoke out vehemently. Campbell-Bannerman condemned the 'methods of barbarism' being used, a phrase the newspapers picked up gleefully. St John Broderick was forced to defend the Government's conduct of the war. He argued that extreme measures were needed to combat the extreme guerrilla tactics of the Boers; and that the women in the camps had been left to starve by their own people, so that the camps were fulfilling a humanitarian function. Although the Government won the forced vote, the matter had been put clearly in the public view, and it would no longer be possible to bury it without any action being taken.

Venetia was shocked, but not entirely surprised. At a small dinner party – family only, as Court mourning was still in force – she said, 'You only have to look at the mortality rates among the soldiers to know that the army – and particularly the RAMC – is not good at keeping its own men healthy. Ten times the number of soldiers die of disease than of wounds. How should they do better with thousands of civilians suddenly left on their hands? And the organisation of food and supplies have been bad throughout the war.'

Her cousin, Anne Farraline, who had been mildly pro-Boer throughout, was incensed by the news. 'It is a deliberate policy to wipe out the Boers altogether. It is genocide, plain and simple. Kitchener is a foul butcher, and this government supports his policy.'

'Oh, Anne, you can't really believe that!'

'Miss Hobhouse believes it. Have you really not read her report?'

'I dare say there is much that's exaggerated in it. The tone does strike one as rather hysterical, and there are some passages – for instance—'

Anne, over-excited, interrupted: 'I know you are always in sympathy with the military, but I hardly expected to hear you condone this appalling mistreatment of non-combatants.'

'I don't condone it,' Venetia said patiently. 'I only say I understand how it has happened. It should not have, of course, and if the army reforms had been carried out when they should have been, things might have been different.

But all the same, when thousands of people are suddenly made homeless, the best organisation in the world won't prevent all suffering. War always means suffering. The idea wasn't just invented, you know.'

Ashley Morland agreed. 'I remember my father saying that the same sort of thing happened in the civil war. When the Yankees swept across the South thousands of black slaves were made homeless, and northern armies gathered them together in camps, where two-thirds of them died. But what else were they to do?'

'Not make them homeless in the first place,' said Anne.

'Well, as a Southerner born, I have to agree that the Yankees had no right to invade us,' Ashley said, in an attempt to lighten the atmosphere.

But Anne said, 'And we had no right to invade South Africa. Now you see the consequences of this unwarranted interference in the affairs of an independent nation. How many must die for this government's folly?'

'Oh, it's folly, is it? I thought you believed they were being killed deliberately,' Venetia said. Hazelmere looked at her reproachfully. She took a more conciliatory tone. 'But, clearly, something must be done. The best thing would be to take the camps out of the control of the army. They simply haven't the organisation or flexibility to cope with them. I wonder whom we might speak to?'

'No use speaking to anyone in the Government,' Anne said, slightly mollified. 'You need a radical, someone in the anti-war party.'

'What's needed, I suggest,' said Hazelmere, 'is a little more dispassion and cool-headedness. Miss Hobhouse might be a well-meaning lady, but she does seem to have approached the matter with a determination to believe all evil of one side and all good of the other. It's hard not to conclude that she has sometimes been deceived by agitators.'

'You'll be denying next that there's anything wrong at all!'

'No, I wouldn't say that,' said Hazelmere gently. 'I'm sure things could be better organised, but we ought to understand the facts of the matter before we make judgements. I think I might have a word with Chamberlain, and see what he thinks. South Africa is very much his hobby-horse, and if anyone can find out the truth, he can.'

At the beginning of July, Sir Henry Campbell-Bannerman came to see Venetia at home. She was busy making preparations to go down to Shawes for the summer, but she greeted him warmly and offered him sherry, and they chatted for a while about the Eton and Harrow match at Lord's, which she had attended with her sons, and the prospects for fine weather at Goodwood.

He asked after Olivia, who had retired with Charlie to a cottage in Northamptonshire near to Ravendene, her childhood home. With the money she had inherited from her mother and Charlie's small independence, they could have lived in greater style; but they seemed perfectly happy in their rural retreat. They spent their time creating a garden, and occasionally advising the new duke on matters of protocol and estate tradition which, as he had been a suburban clerk before his elevation, sometimes baffled him. In return he had given Olivia and Charlie the run of the park and his stables, and more invitations to dinner than they cared to accept.

'So really,' Venetia concluded, 'she has all the benefits of the ducal condition and none of the pains. She says it's quite like being a girl again. But I'm sure you didn't come here to discuss my sister, Henry,' she added, eyeing him shrewdly. 'What can it be, I wonder? That was a fine speech you made, by the way, about the camps. "Methods of barbarism", indeed! I suspect your words will be repeated in more places than you anticipated.'

'I hope they are,' he commented. 'You know I was always against this war, and look what it is costing us. We haven't a friend in Europe, and we've sown the seeds of enmity in South Africa for generations to come.'

'Well, I won't argue with you on that head. I'm not a soldier or a politician, thank God, just a woman and a doctor.'

'It was rather that which I wanted to speak to you about,' he said, settling himself comfortably. Even in the heat of argument, he was never flurried or undignified. 'I've been talking to Chamberlain about this business – unofficially, you understand.'

'Oh, quite. It would be awkward for you in party terms to be known to be fraternising with the enemy, wouldn't it?'

He smiled. 'Enemy, indeed! You will have your little joke. But where there's good to be done, sides don't matter. And in any case, on this head there's more common ground between Chamberlain and me than between me and some of my own party.'

'You interest me, Henry. Tell me more.'

'Oh, no,' he said, 'I'll not put myself further in your power! I discovered, of course, that Hazelmere had had a word with Chamberlain before me, suggesting he thought he was the man to do something about the camps – in which I concur. Obviously the Cabinet won't be swayed by someone in the Opposition: it has to come from their own side.'

Venetia's bright eyes sharpened. 'Is something in the wind?'

'Something is, and I've been asked to act as a sort of go-between, to ask a favour of you. On Chamberlain's urging, the Cabinet has agreed to send out a commission to South Africa to inspect the camps, report on conditions and make recommendations. It's to number six, all ladies—'

'An all-woman commission? Good Lord! You are not serious?' Such a thing had never happened before: for any commission to consist solely of women was unprecedented, but for one that would be under such intense public scrutiny, and carrying the burden of the country's international esteem, it was even more extraordinary.

'Oh, but I am,' Campbell-Bannerman said, wagging his large, handsome head. 'It was a little notion of my own, to further the women's Cause.'

'But however did you persuade Chamberlain?'

'Oh, there's good political reason for it, too. If we send men, the agitators and complainers will say that men are bound to side with the military, and no-one will believe anything they say.'

'You don't mean you want the commission to find no fault?'

'I want to know the truth, whatever it is. Miss Hobhouse is a very good sort of person, but she comes from a sheltered background, and she was perhaps a little biased, so she might have been mistaken in some things. But I have no doubt that there are very grave problems, and the only way to get matters put right is to find out the sober, ungarnished facts.'

'So there is not to be a whitewash?'

'Indeed not! Did you think I would lend myself to one? And, moreover, it must be understood by all that there is none, which is why we must send women – for the credibility, you understand.'

'Yes, I see.'

'They must be level-headed, intelligent women, with enough experience in the world not to be bowled over by what they see, and the ability to remain cool and detached in horrid situations. Otherwise we shall not get to the bottom of it. It's not a matter of avoiding, nor of apportioning, blame. What we want is to make things right.'

'That, if I may say so, is the right attitude. And am I to understand that you want me to go?' Venetia asked.

'If you please,' he said, as though he were asking her to post a letter for him.

'Well, Henry, I don't know. It's rather a large request. Who else have you approached?'

'Mrs Fawcett is to lead the party.'

'Excellent choice,' said Venetia.

'I know, of course, that she is an acquaintance of yours. And then there is Lady Knox, whose husband is a brigade commander out there.' Venetia nodded, with an inward smile, for General Sir William Knox, she knew, was known as 'Nasty' Knox, to distinguish him from the other General Charles 'Nice' Knox. 'And we wish two of the other four to be doctors and two nurses. That's most important. Lay people will not be able to give us the detailed reports we require. So, as you are the most eminent lady doctor in the country—'

'Next to Mrs Anderson, perhaps,' Venetia said drily.

Campbell-Bannerman gave himself away. 'Mrs Anderson is a wee thought too old for the trip.'

341

'You've already asked her?'

'She declined, but she suggested you herself, and Mrs Fawcett is eager that we should secure you. On an expedition like this, you know, for the members to get on with each other is everything.'

Venetia saw the point of that. She nodded, but said, 'Well, I am rather *bouleversée*. I hardly know what to say.'

'I don't expect you to give your answer at once. Take a day or two to think about it – but we would be glad to have things settled as soon as possible, and the commission on its way before the end of the month.'

'A day or two to decide? You are so generous,' she said, with a smile.

She talked it over with Hazelmere as soon as he came home. He was rather taken aback. 'It was your own idea,' she reminded him.

'Up to a point,' he said. 'I did urge Chamberlain to send a commission and I did suggest it would be a good idea to include some ladies, but this! And my own wife! It's too much.'

'I dare say they thought it was what you meant,' Venetia said. 'But the question is, what am I to do about it?'

'I don't think anyone will blame you for refusing. It won't be a very pleasant task.'

'Millicent Fawcett has accepted.'

'She's younger than you.'

'Only by three years. Does that make me an old woman who ought to be let off?'

'You know I didn't mean that. But you've all your summer plans made. The packing's done, you're on the point of closing up the house and going down to Yorkshire, and I shall be going to Homburg with the King.' He broke off, frowning. 'Do you mean you *want* to go?'

'I think this commission is rather more important than my holiday plans,' she said.

'Of course it is, but it will happen whether you go or not.'

'I know, and there's a part of me that shies away and thinks that someone younger could do it. But there's another, larger, part that wants to go, that rebels at the idea

342

of comfort as an end in itself. Don't you have that little demon of mischief in you, Beauty, that urges you always to try something new?'

'I suppose so.'

'And besides, this is important work. I've lived my life on the principle that what I do matters in the long run. It was worth upsetting my parents for—'

'To say nothing of the world at large. You even jilted *me* for it,' he said. 'Drove me away with harsh words.'

'True,' she said, moving closer. 'I'm so lucky that you developed a taste for abuse and came back for me.' He put his arms round her and kissed her, and she rested her head comfortably against his shoulder, marvelling that after all these years the sheer closeness of him filled her with such deep and satisfying pleasure. 'Yes, I think I do want to do this, Beauty. It's something that ought to be done, and I don't know anyone who could do it better, so it's my duty to go. And as well as that . . .' She hesitated, seeking the words.

'You want an adventure?' he suggested.

'Yes,' she said. 'One last adventure. What do you think?'

He thought of the dangers she would no doubt face, quite apart from the hardships, and hoped fervently that it would not prove to be the 'last' adventure. But he would never try to forbid her, especially when the object was good in itself. 'I think we should put every effort into finding out what you need to take with you.'

'Thank you, darling,' she said. She kissed him gratefully, and then released herself, energy surging through her at the thought of all there would be to do.

'What are we going to do with the children?' was Hazelmere's first question.

'Oh, the boys are always being invited to stay with one schoolfriend or another – I half think that's what we pay the school fees for! And Violet can go to Morland Place. She's always happy there.'

'Did Campbell-Bannerman say how long the commission would last?'

'Not precisely – it will depend on what we find out, I

suppose. But it's bound to be several months at least.'

'Will Henrietta be willing to have Violet for so long?'

'I'm sure she will. And Vi will love it. You can go off to the Continent with a clear conscience, darling.'

'It will be the first time I shall have been on a different continent from my wife.'

Venetia took time out from her preparations to take Violet down to Yorkshire herself, not only to see her settled but to have at least a brief moment in Henrietta's company. Violet was delighted, as she had expected, to be staying at Morland Place instead of Shawes, and assured her mother she would be happy to stay there 'for ever'. Jack, Robbie and Ned were disappointed that the boys were not going to visit as well, but were more interested in the forthcoming trip and asked questions Venetia had no hope of answering. Frank was in his own dream world as usual; Teddy wanted to show off baby Polly and collect some more compliments to add to his hoard.

Venetia admired the baby wholeheartedly – she was a very fetching little thing – and gravely approved the new portrait of Charley over the drawing-room fireplace. Teddy had had it done to mark the first anniversary of Charley's death in May – which was also Polly's birthday, of course. The portraitist had copied a photograph of Charley for the face, and had used a model for the body. Venetia privately thought it a poor piece of work, but she would not have dreamed of saying so, of course.

Teddy was also eager to talk about the new plans for the estate. Jerome had sunk his money into the horse-breeding part of the business, taking shares in it with Teddy, and Teddy was now negotiating to buy back Huntsham and Eastfield farms from the bank, which was eager to be rid of them, as they had proved so unprofitable. 'And that will allow us to expand into sheep and cattle,' Teddy concluded happily.

Henrietta's happiness was less material. 'It's wonderful that so much of the estate will be restored to Morland ownership. Those farms cover the core land, the oldest part. I'll be able to ride out over our own land again.' And she had a private satisfaction that she did not speak about – that Jerome's investing his inheritance meant that they would definitely be staying here. It tied them, and she was happy with the bonds.

Venetia felt it was good to be at Morland Place again, and she enjoyed her brief visit. Everything was so lively here, and so much more informal than at home, and she thought how pleasant it was to have a houseful of people, especially so many children. They had the day-nursery as their own private play-room, but they had grown used to being all together during the years of poverty, and the children were just as often in the drawing-room with the adults – when they weren't out of doors – as anywhere else. So while she sat talking to Henrietta, she was interrupted by Jessie who wanted to show, with wistful sighs, her maps of Bertie's campaign, and by Frank asking the meaning of a long word in the book he was reading; and she interrupted herself to look at Jack's drawing, which he was making at the table nearby. She was intrigued because she thought he was drawing an angel, which she thought an odd choice of subject, but it turned out to be his interpretation of Lilienthal's bi-plane glider of 1894.

'Is that what you're studying at engineering school?' she asked, a little surprised.

'Oh, no, it's just something I'm interested in,' Jack said. He turned the drawing so that she could see properly. She saw now that the man was hanging by a harness round his shoulders attached to the two pairs of flimsy wings: really, she thought now, he looked more like a dragonfly than an angel. 'He did actually fly with this one,' Jack went on. 'He ran down a steep hillside and launched himself off into the wind.'

'And stayed up?'

'Oh, yes, for – well, I don't know how long, but long enough to know he was really flying and not just falling. And he managed to guide it a bit, before it came down.'

'Good Heavens. It must have been very dangerous.'

'Well, I suppose so. He was killed in 'ninety-six trying to

345

fly a mono-plane glider,' Jack admitted reluctantly. 'But he showed it can be done, that's what matters.'

'Do you really think man can ever fly properly?' she asked.

'Oh, yes,' he said with confidence. 'We will have flying machines one day, I know it.'

'It's his ruling interest,' said Henrietta. 'He'll talk about it for ever if you encourage him.'

Jack held his ground. 'This is just a beginning. Lilienthal was getting close, and once the principle is worked out, there's no limit to what can be done. From gliders to powered flight will only be a short step.'

'Really?'

'Oh, yes. But not steam-powered. There've been lots of experiments with steam-powered aeronautics, and they're a waste of time. It stands to reason they can never be any good.'

'Why so?' Venetia asked.

'Well, because the fuel plus the water and the boiler are too heavy. You'd use up all your power just trying to get off the ground. Even if you managed to get airborne, you'd never be able to carry enough fuel to fly any useful distance. No, it's got to be something light and powerful, like a gas.' He frowned, his pencil busy. 'Just think how easy it would be for you to get to South Africa, Cousin Venetia, if you could fly instead of going by sea. You could get there in days rather than weeks.'

Venetia shuddered. 'I'll stick to a nice safe ship, thank you. I don't think I like the idea of a great heavy machine hanging in the sky. It's not natural.'

Jack looked up with a flash of humour. 'But you know, if you were a jungle native and you'd only ever seen a wooden canoe, you wouldn't believe a great heavy ship made of metal could possibly float, would you?'

Venetia turned to Henrietta. 'I can see you'd never be short of food for thought in this house. It will be an education for Violet just being here.'

'I'll try not to send her back babbling of flying-machines,' Henrietta laughed.

'Oh, I shouldn't mind that,' Venetia said. 'She doesn't

want to be a doctor, and it would be a new field for women to conquer.'

Venetia had only ten days to make all her preparations, before the commission sailed, taking passage on a troop ship and arriving in Cape Town in the second week of August. The group comprised Mrs Fawcett and Lady Knox, a Dr Jane Waterston, whom Venetia knew slightly – and who was rather in awe of her at first, being much younger than this great legend of the pioneering days – and two trained nurses, Miss Katherine Brereton and Miss Lucy Deane. Lady Knox had brought a lady's maid with her – something Venetia wondered she had not thought of herself. Miss Deane was accompanied by her sister, and Mrs Fawcett had brought her daughter Philippa, who insisted on 'earning her keep' by acting as maidservant to her mother and any of the other ladies who would let her, and energetically made beds, fetched and carried and waited at table when she was allowed.

On their arrival in Cape Town, they were surprised to find themselves not only expected but the centre of attention throughout Cape Town society. Everyone wanted to entertain them, and they were somewhat bewildered at the clamour of invitations. They soon learnt, however, that it was not to provide them with amusement that they were sought out but to enlist them into one faction or another. Cape Town was seething with rumours, gossip, and stories that were pure invention; riven by factions so mutually hostile that there was practically a second war going on. Criticism of the camps was more violent than anything they had heard in England – Miss Hobhouse herself was almost indifferent by comparison – but the criticism seemed to be arranged along factional lines. The pro-Boer ladies believed everything and the anti-Boers nothing. To belong to one faction was to hate, despise and vilify the other, and to swallow wholesale and without criticism whatever the party line was deemed to be.

This had a serious effect, which the commission discovered before they left Cape Town. They had brought with them a sum of money provided by private charities which they wanted to spend in Cape Town on whatever was most needed in the camps, so that they could take it with them for immediate relief. But nowhere could they get sensible answers as to what they ought to buy, and the most influential ladies actually concealed information from them rather than admit there was anything right about the camps. The commission ladies concluded that what these people were interested in was not helping the inmates, but keeping hold of a good stick to beat the Government with.

'It's an attitude I encountered a lot in England, and I have no patience with it,' Mrs Fawcett said. 'Especially when it's combined with that perverted form of patriotism which extols every country but its own.'

'Well, we shall be off tomorrow,' said Venetia, 'and then we can forget about them – for the time being, at least.'

They had a railway carriage to themselves – but that was all they had. Over the next weeks and months it was to become first horribly, irksomely familiar, and then curiously homelike and almost dear, as they ate, slept and worked within its confines. There was a saloon with a table where they ate their meals and held their meetings, though the space around it was so cramped that each person had to go in turn to take her place – there was no possibility of passing one another. In the sleeping-carriage each had a screened-off space just large enough for a bunk and a locker, and clung to this small private place as a sanctuary, for it was the only way to get away from the others. It was lucky that they were all sensible, even-tempered people, for in such close confines a bad-tempered or demanding companion would have added greatly to the hardship.

It was a hard time for all of them until they adjusted to it; and even after that, much of their mission was tedious, as the train puffed its way agonisingly slowly across the flat and empty country, uninteresting after the first surprise of novelty. For mile after mile the scenery would be unchanged, the stony veldt reaching into the distance to a blurred suggestion of mountains on the horizon. Beside the tracks the telegraph wires looped along monotonously, the black shadow of the train itself waxing and waning with the progress of the sun, the endless barbed-wire fencing interrupted only by the intermittent blockhouses and the occasional relics of military action – broken wagons, derelict buildings, the burnt-out corpse of a railway engine fallen beside the track, the bleached skulls of oxen, white and dramatic against the tan-coloured veldt.

They saw few signs of life, except around the blockhouses, and where the railway crossed one of the wide, mud-coloured rivers. Then sometimes there would be a reed-bed, sometimes a patch of green and a row of stunted trees; and there would be birds flitting about, soldiers watering horses, blacks watering cattle or goats, and always a mongrel dog standing in the sun panting and watching them go by. Venetia, in her state of near mesmerism, began to believe it was always the same dog: compactly built, close-coated, brown and white, with a curly tail arched over its back. Perhaps it was a sign of the laws of evolution, that such a dog, most fitted for the life, was the only one to survive and pass on its blood.

The only compensation for the tedium of the long hours of journeying were the wonderful sunsets. In that flat place they seemed to go on for ever in space, though they were curiously short in time for one who was used to living in England, up on the world's shoulder, where the twilights were long. Here the sun went down so rapidly they could watch it disappear into its slot on the horizon like a gigantic red penny into a child's money-box. It was broad day, then there was a scarlet and crimson and gold and purple splendour of a sunset, and then it was dark, all in the course of a few minutes. And what a dark! With no distant lights to interrupt it, it lay up close alongside the carriage windows like a black, living beast. Only when they extinguished their own lights at sleeping-time would the great arc of stars become visible, stars so fat and brilliant you felt you might have plucked one from the sky and squeezed juice out of it.

It was winter in that upside-down place, of course – winter going into spring. The days were warm, warmer than many an English summer; but the nights were bitterly cold, and

349

Venetia was glad of the sleeping-bags they were using under their blankets rather than sheets. And then there was the rain, which fell in solid walls of water, so that it was like being inside a river, and which started and stopped with such abruptness, as though being turned on and off with a tap.

In between the tedium of the journeys there were the horrors of the camps. Over the months of their stay they visited nearly all of them, and found that conditions varied hugely from camp to camp, depending on the character and abilities of the commandant and his staff, the location chosen and its proximity to wood and water, the distance from the base from which stores were obtained, and also the date it was set up, for the earlier camps had been able to obtain items no longer available. From a distance they looked almost pretty, with the row upon row of white bell tents gleaming in the sun, so symmetrical and fresh-looking. Then, coming closer, you would see the burial place that always existed on the edge of the encampment, with its row upon row of graves marked with stones or with tin cans – rarely with wooden crosses, for wood was scarce and needed for other purposes.

The problems were many. To begin with, most of the camps were overcrowded, having been set up for hundreds but having thousands dumped upon them. The tents, even when in good condition, were of little value as shelters – stiflingly hot and airless during the daytime and bitterly cold at night – and many were so old they were full of holes. When the rain came, most of them leaked. The positions chosen for the camps were often inappropriate, and no-one seemed to have the initiative or perhaps the will to move them. One they visited had been set up in a shallow dip, so that every time it rained the water lay in sheets, sometimes for hours, sometimes for days, and there was no way for the inmates to keep dry. All they could do was to put the babies and little children up on boxes and tables at night to sleep. Sometimes camps were built in exposed places without a stick of shade, or on rocky slopes where the tents would not stand up properly. Some were so far from clean water that it was a permanent labour for women, in any case in poor health, to fetch enough to drink, let alone to wash anything.

The food rations were minimal, mostly of salt meat or bully and biscuit, like soldiers' rations – unsuitable for women and impossible for small children. Fresh fruit and vegetables were almost unheard-of; milk and eggs and fresh meat a rarity. In some camps a more intelligent or energetic commandant had found ways to supplement the diet, but it was not satisfactory that it should be left to chance like that. Together the commission worked out a tolerable basic diet, and this was transmitted at once to Milner and Kitchener, without waiting for the final report.

In many cases they were able to effect changes on the spot that would give immediate improvement, such as the siting of latrines, the quality of sanitary arrangements, the building of ovens and boilers. It was astonishing to Venetia how often some simple remedy had been ignored through apathy and sometimes stupidity: in one camp they ordered the hospital tent turned through ninety degrees so that the cooling breeze passed through it rather than uselessly flapping its walls. They had to recommend the removal of some camp super-intendents and doctors for inefficiency that came close to the criminal. In one camp, constant and often fatal dysentery was being caused by the latrines having been dug to drain into the river, *upstream* of the place from which the women fetched their drinking-water.

But it was clear that many of the problems were caused by the Boer women themselves, though it was hard to blame them. Torn from their homes, many of them were so sunk in apathy they would do nothing to help themselves; others so deeply resented being in the camps they would refuse to obey any order or suggestion from the camp staff, even when it was plainly for their own good. In other cases, the problem was simpler: out on their farms they had commanded hosts of blacks who had done everything for them. Now that those had been taken away from them, they did not know how to do things for themselves, or simply never thought of doing so.

Their previous lives out on the wide veldt had severe

351

medical consequences, too. For a hundred years the rural Boers had been isolated from the rest of the world; now they were suddenly brought into contact with a large influx of people from outside, who brought with them disease-causing organisms to which they had no resistance. Measles, pneumonia and dysentery were the scourges of the camps, and the children in particular were vulnerable. The diseases rampaged through the tents unchecked, laying waste thousands of little lives.

Venetia found the attitude of the Boer women to illness difficult to overcome. Living in isolated communities, they were used to doctoring themselves for the most part; and where they did have doctors, those doctors had not had the benefit of modern medical training and relied on seventeenth-century traditions, which were hopelessly inadequate. Most of all, the idea of treatment in a hospital was alien to the women. When a child fell sick, and one of the authorities came to the tent to say that the child must be taken away, they did not understand the necessity, or the principles of isolation and quarantine. They only knew that their children were taken from them, that they were not allowed to visit them in hospital, and that, more often than not, in a few days the child would be dead. It was a horrible plot, a punishment, an attempt at genocide in their eyes. They mistrusted and hated the English medical staff, and would frustrate their attempts to provide 'proper' medical treatment. When a child fell sick they did everything in their power to conceal the fact, hiding it amongst the other children, forcing it to play, holding it up when it couldn't walk – and, of course, this concealment helped to spread the sickness.

While many of their recommendations could be acted on immediately, the decision over extra food allocation for the camps rested with the commander-in-chief, Lord Kitchener, and it was necessary for the ladies of the commission to seek an interview with him when they reached Pretoria. They were rather nervous about it, for Kitchener had the reputation of being abrupt, difficult, and impatient, and was also a known woman-hater, having the lowest opinion of the abilities of the female sex. Their anxieties seemed confirmed when, in reply to their letter asking for an interview, he wrote that he would be obliged if only two of them should make up the deputation.

'Women are such loathsome creatures, you see, two is all he can bear,' Venetia said, amused. 'Obviously one must be you, Millie.'

'And Lady Knox the other,' said Miss Deane.

But Lady Knox shook her head. 'I think the other one should be Venetia. It is important that a doctor should be on hand to explain things, if he becomes difficult.'

Mrs Fawcett agreed, and so it was decided. When the two of them arrived at headquarters, they were taken to an ante-room, and as the door to Lord Kitchener's room was opened by an aide, they heard him say rather testily, 'How many of them? I did say two only. Are there two only?' The women looked at each other and exchanged a wry smile.

But the interview went unexpectedly well. Though not by any means warm or charming, Kitchener was perfectly polite, and to Venetia it was a relief to be with a man who was prepared to be businesslike and leave aside flowery speeches, 'dear ladies', and mock-gallant references to femininity and weakness. Lord Kitchener seemed prepared to accept them on their own terms, and the conversation was pursued with a brisk efficiency that wasted no time and used not a single unnecessary word. Venetia liked him for his straightforwardness, and Mrs Fawcett said afterwards that he was far easier to deal with than any politician she had had to speak to in London. Perhaps his lordship was equally glad to find them such equals, for having had the discussion with the sample of two of them, he invited all six to dinner on the next day.

Their work went on for three months. In that time winter turned to spring – the brief, but enchanting South African spring. The coffee bushes burst into starry white flower, the grim thorny acacias put out little wrinkled curls of leaf, bright yellow-green against the black, the tall feathery mimosa trees blossomed, filling the air with a scent almost painfully delicious. Grass spread like a mist over the grazing

353

farms, and sometimes they would pass a sudden sea of bright, multi-coloured daisies, some with unexpectedly blue eyes, where before there had seemed to be only desert.

For just a few weeks the climate held a delightful equilibrium of warm days and cool nights; and then it was over. Summer came, bringing with it intolerable parched heat, glare, dust, and hordes of insects. By December the commission had done its work, visited almost every camp, assessed the situation and made its recommendations. The report they had written between them was factual, unemotional, conscientious. They were satisfied that they had done what was required of them, that material improvements had already been put in train and that more would follow. They were ready to go home.

Venetia was more than ready. She was very tired, and what interest the country had had for her had faded in the grimness of their task and the monotony of the weather and scenery. She was tired of sweat running into her eyes, tired of always tasting dust, tired of continuously waving flies from her eyes and mouth. She wanted different clothes and shoes, a bed with sheets, proper food. She wanted to see her home and her husband and her children. She wanted to see *green* again – lots and lots of green.

'But it has been quite an adventure,' she said to Mrs Fawcett on their last evening. 'How do you think they will receive our report at home?'

'Well, I hope,' she said, but there was a shadow of doubt in her voice. 'At least, the sensible people will see we have done our job. But there are the other ones – you know who I mean.'

Venetia nodded. 'Yes, like those women in Cape Town. I'm afraid they will not like the fact that we haven't blamed the Government for everything and called it genocide.'

'Ah, well, even if we are cut by some of the pro-Boers, they will soon forget it. These things blow over more quickly than one ever expects.'

'I only wish we had been able to inspect some of the black camps. I'm sure things are much worse in them.'

'It wasn't part of our remit,' said Mrs Fawcett. 'It's a hard

354

thing, but we could only do what we were paid to do. Otherwise, we would lose all power with the authorities and nothing would be done at all.'

It was the way her sister Elizabeth, Dr Anderson, had always worked – like a carpenter, with the grain of the wood not against. It had annoyed some of her more fiery colleagues, who wanted confrontation and no compromise; but with greater age Venetia could see the wisdom of it.

'And,' Mrs Fawcett went on, her eyes brightening, 'we have done a very great thing for women. The first all-woman commission, and entrusted with such an important piece of work! It is a step forward.'

'A small one,' said Venetia. 'I can't imagine them rushing to give us the vote on the strength of it.'

'Every long journey is made up of small steps,' said Mrs Fawcett.

As a result of the commission's work, Lord Kitchener issued an order in December that, unless they were starving, no further women and children were to be taken into the camps. This worked unexpectedly to his benefit, because leaving the women on the veldt meant that their own men had to take responsibility for them, which hampered their military mobility. Conditions inside the camps improved enormously, and the death rate fell to two per cent, less than that of most industrial cities. Nevertheless, over the year to February 1902, 20,000 camp inmates had died, a testament to incompetence and mismanagement.

The war dragged on three months more, long enough for the first batch of Morland army horses to be shipped out, for it was still a war very expensive in horseflesh. The Boers struggled on, despite increasing numbers being 'rounded up': the 'bag' averaged 2000 a month. There was growing bitterness on both sides. The Boers did not hesitate to shoot those of their own people they believed to be traitors; and blacks who helped the British – and they were many, for the Boers were not kind masters – were massacred, sometimes tortured and mutilated first.

On the British side, the hard-living, fast-moving units that the soldiers had become were increasingly unwilling to take prisoners. This worried the military authorities very much, and there were several show trials of British officers in an attempt to demonstrate to the Boers, and to the world, what the British thought of their own men who did not 'play the game'. At one such trial two lieutenants, Morant and Handcock, gave as their defence that shooting prisoners had become standard practice, and that they were only following orders. Both were found guilty and shot. Their trial was a curiosity because it was interrupted by a Boer raid. Both men were given rifles and joined the fighting. When the Boers had been beaten off, the trial resumed.

But the Boers were running out of men and out of room, and conditions for civilians on the veldt were worse even than they had been in the camps before the improvements. There was nowhere to go and no hope of winning. On the 23rd of March 1902 the Boers indicated that they wanted to talk about peace terms.

On the 11th of April Smuts, De Wet, Botha, Steyn and Burgher arrived in Pretoria by train, and talks began. They were very protracted, and eventually a deadline had to be set and somewhat of a fudge had to be accepted on one or two points, but a treaty was finally signed on Saturday the 31st of May by Burgher for the Transvaal and De Wet for the Free State, and by Kitchener and Milner for Britain. The war was over.

BOOK THREE

Away

You took my heart in your hand
With a friendly smile,
With a critical eye you scann'd,
Then set it down,
And said, 'It is still unripe,
Better wait awhile;
Wait while the skylarks pipe,
Till the corn grows brown.'

Christina Georgine Rossetti: 'Twice'

CHAPTER ELEVEN

The last year of the war had coincided with a period in which the country had felt itself to be in mourning for the old Queen. Perhaps had the war not been on, gaiety would have returned sooner. As it was, the signing of the peace was a release from both conditions. Almost immediately on succeeding, the King had decided that it would be inappropriate to hold the Coronation while the country was at war, and there had been a tacit public approval of the decision. But once the peace was concluded, there was a feeling that the war and the mourning had been one, and were both over. A date for the Coronation was set for the 26th of June. Dark clouds had rolled away, and everyone seemed to blink in the sudden sunshine and discover themselves more than ready to have some fun.

The King himself had signalled the beginning of a new era, and a departure from the stiffness of royal etiquette. He enjoyed smoking, he visited race-meetings and went to the theatre. As Prince of Wales he had broken with custom by giving dinner parties on Sundays, and from the start of his reign he dined in subjects' houses and included commoners in his circle of friends. To the fury of certain parts of Society, some of his closest friends were even Jews – Alfred Rothschild, George Lewis (the Society solicitor), and Ernest Cassel, whom the wags called Windsor Cassel. The King encouraged conversation at the dining-table and even joke-telling; he liked rich food, card games, gambling. An invitation to dine at Windsor or Balmoral was likely in future to be pleasurable rather than merely flattering.

The King was modern-minded: he was a lover of motor-cars and at ease with the telephone. The royal palaces were to be modernised and made comfortable, fitted with wash-down water-closets, bathrooms, central heating and even electric light. One of his first orders as King was the discontinuance of the frugal supply of newspaper squares to palace WCs in favour of proper toilet paper.

The Coronation was to be a very grand affair, with royalty from all over the world attending, and a fourteen-course banquet for two hundred and fifty following the protracted ceremony in the Abbey. There was, as usual, a Coronation Honours List, and the King bestowed a life peerage on his faithful private secretary, Francis Knollys. Knollys came to see Venetia and Hazelmere in Manchester Square with the news, well before it was publicly announced.

'I'm delighted for you, Francis,' Venetia said. 'No-one deserves it more.'

'I wouldn't say that,' he replied, 'but I am pleased, of course. The King is not the sort of master who doesn't let you know he is satisfied with you, but it is gratifying to have a public acknowledgement like that.'

'A monarch needs good friends around him,' Hazelmere said. 'The King knows that.'

They had known already that the Prince of Wales was loyal to those who served him well, so it was no surprise that all his old attendants had been offered posts in his new Court – including Hazelmere himself. Venetia had noted particularly that Sir Francis Laking was to remain his personal physician – a pleasant, ineffectual sheep of a man of whom neither she nor Sir James Reid had any opinion – and that Frederick Treves, whom the King had long admired, was appointed sergeant-surgeon.

This honour was apparently triggered by Treves's performance at a dinner-party, where he had told an amusing story. It was about an officer who had been shot in the head in South Africa and had been sent back to England to be seen by Treves. He performed a trepanning and discovered extensive injuries, requiring the removal of the greater part of the brain. He hardly expected the patient to survive, but the officer made a full recovery. Treves told him frankly that he feared he would have difficulty following his profession since the larger part of his brain had been removed. The officer said, 'It's very kind of you to take so much interest in my welfare, but thank God my brain is no longer wanted – I've just been transferred to the War Office.' The King had laughed until he cried at this story, and Treves was thereafter firmly in favour.

Venetia remembered that at many a dinner she had entertained the Prince of Wales and made him laugh, and that he had told Francis Knollys (who had obligingly repeated it) that he regarded her as one of the wittiest women of his acquaintance; but he had never considered giving her any medical appointment. Because she was female it would simply never have occurred to him: in Court circles she was Hazelmere's wife, that was all.

But Francis had further news for Hazelmere, which was the purpose of this particular visit. 'The King wanted me to tell you before it was announced that he intends to give you an earldom in the Coronation honours. You will need to give some thought to what title you will adopt. The College of Arms will advise, of course: the Herald in Waiting will attend you at any time to discuss it.'

Hazelmere looked surprised. 'An earldom? My dear Francis, whatever for?'

'Oh, for services rendered and to be rendered,' Knollys said mildly, 'like everyone else.'

'A life viscountcy for you, after all you've done, and an earldom for me?'

'You start from higher up the ladder,' said Knollys. 'I'm perfectly content, I assure you. And there are special circumstances – I'm sure I don't need to elaborate. There's a grant of a thousand a year that goes with it.' He smiled suddenly. 'My dear fellow, don't look so bemused. Discretion is something kings value highly; and you've performed many discreet services over the years. He wants to thank you – thank both of you.' He looked at Venetia. 'The honour may be to Hazelmere but he thinks of you both. Levelling out

361

the discrepancy in your ranks is something he regards as a benefit to you, Venetia.'

Venetia replied graciously, for Hazelmere's sake, and because she liked Francis; but inwardly she reflected wryly that everything she had achieved in her life in the medical field counted for nothing in this context, against the mere fact of taking in and bringing up her late sister's child. Hazelmere had indeed performed services of tact and discretion to the Prince of Wales, but her share of the compliment derived from her fostering of one of Edward's bastards. If social advancement had been her goal, she might as well have saved herself the pain of becoming a doctor.

When Francis had gone, Hazelmere turned to her, guessing, because of their closeness, what she must be thinking. 'Are you cross, darling?' he asked cautiously.

'Cross? Oh – no. No, of course not. That would be dog-in-the-manger, wouldn't it?'

'I know that you are the most generous of people. But it would be natural to resent it a little.'

'Oh, Beauty, of course I don't resent it. Kings reward the services they value, and there have been rewards for far less worthy services than yours to Tum.'

'And yours.'

'Well, darling, I didn't do it for him,' Venetia said reasonably. 'I did it for poor Gussie, and the boy. It didn't matter to me who the father was. I didn't like Vibart, but if he'd been Eddie's father I would still have taken him in.'

'You're a saint!'

'I'm a pragmatist.'

'Well, we must think what title we would like.'

'It has to be territorial, doesn't it? Otherwise you could be the Earl of Winchmore – Beauty Winchmore again, which is how I always think of you.'

'Do you, darling? How gratifying! I suppose Overton is the most obvious choice,' Hazelmere said. Overton was where the Hazelmere country seat had been, before it had had to be sold.

'It sounds quite well. The Earl of Overton. Lord Overton.'

'But you would still be Lady Chelmsford in your own right,' he objected. 'I wonder if we could join them together?'

'Overton and Chelmsford? There are precedents, of course.'

'I think it would have to be Chelmsford and Overton, wouldn't it? Chelmsford is the older title.'

'Sounds clumsy. But the College will advise us. I wonder who's in waiting at the moment?' She smiled suddenly. 'I suppose this means that Hazelmere becomes the cadet title, and Thomas will be able to use it. I wonder how he'll like that.'

'Very much, I should think, if it gets him a seat in the Abbey for the Coronation,' said Hazelmere.

The arrangements for the Coronation were well under way when on the 14th of June the King attended a military review at Aldershot. At dinner afterwards at Buckingham Palace Venetia – who was a guest with Hazelmere – noted that he looked ill, his face pale and moist, and with a distracted, preoccupied expression as though he was in pain. In the drawing-room she mentioned it to Knollys, who said that the King had been suffering from abdominal pain since the evening before, but had insisted on attending the review against the advice of Laking.

'What sort of abdominal pain?' she asked. Knollys hesitated. 'Oh, come on, Francis, you can tell me. I'm a doctor. Are we talking about indigestion?'

He relented. 'No, it's worse than that. It's very severe, and localised. I must say I'm worried. He's very stoical in general, which proves it must be bad, or he wouldn't have mentioned it at all.'

'What has Laking diagnosed?'

'He didn't say anything specific. Just recommended a milk diet and bed rest.'

Venetia frowned. 'Abdominal pain can be very serious. It's never something to take lightly.'

Knollys spread his hands. 'I'm worried too, but Laking's the doctor. We must go by his advice.'

Venetia said nothing. It would be bad medical etiquette

363

for her to give her opinion of Laking to Francis, and it would have served no purpose anyway. She knew that the King valued him highly. At last she said, 'As a favour to me, Francis, would you keep me informed? I promise absolute discretion, but I have a particular interest in abdominal cases, as perhaps you know. I ask you as a friend.'

'As a friend,' Knollys agreed. He searched her face. 'Do you think I should be worried?'

'Let's wait and see.'

That night the King was in severe pain. His abdomen was distended and there was marked tenderness on the lower right side. He suffered a fit of violent shivering and his temperature was raised. Laking called in Sir Thomas Barlow, another physician favoured by the King, and the two insisted on bed rest and ordered a light diet. The King's engagements were cancelled for the day, and by lunchtime the press was demanding an explanation. Laking issued a statement that the King was suffering from lumbago.

Hazelmere brought the information home to Venetia.

'I don't like the sound of this,' she said seriously. 'Distension, pain, tenderness in the lower right side, raised temperature – you know what that sounds like.'

'Some sort of colitis?'

'They are all symptoms of appendicitis.'

Hazelmere could not but be aware of Venetia's opinions on that subject. 'Do you think so? But it could be other things too, could it not?'

She shrugged with impatience. 'I can't tell without examining the patient. There is a specific spot on the abdomen – McBurney identified it, so in America they call it McBurney's point – which is indicative if there's pain present. That separates appendicitis from colitis, or inflammation of the ureter or gall bladder or kidneys.'

'Wouldn't Laking and Barlow know that?'

'I don't suppose so. The medical establishment in general – and physicians in particular – pay no attention to American research findings.'

'I'm sure they'll give him the best of care,' Hazelmere said helplessly

364

She looked at him eloquently. 'He's sixty years old. Time is of the essence in these cases.'

The following days were a time of frustration for Venetia. As a woman doctor she was more open to new ideas than the British medical establishment, of which she could never be a part and was therefore not at pains to defend. She had been impressed by the American research, which agreed with her own surgical experience. Furthermore, she was very fond of the King, who had been kind to her in many ways. If it was appendicitis, early intervention was essential, in her opinion. If the appendix ruptured, peritonitis would follow, and in an elderly man who was not in any case in the best of health, that could mean death.

But Laking and Barlow continued with their regime of bed rest and milk diet, though the King was in such pain they had to give him opiates to enable him to travel down to Windsor – he could not have endured the journey otherwise. It was not until the 18th of June that Laking felt the lack of any improvement suggested that the condition was beyond a physician's skill, and told the King that a surgeon should be consulted. Frederick Treves was sent for.

'Treves, of course,' Venetia said. 'Naturally it would be Treves.'

Hazelmere was in attendance on the King, and Venetia had cancelled her own engagements and gone down to Windsor with him. Though she could do nothing, she wanted to be on the spot.

Treves arrived incognito – under the name of Mr Turner – in order to keep it from leaking out that the King's condition might be serious. Preparations for the Coronation were extensive, elaborate and well advanced, and the press was already so concentrating on royal affairs that it would leap on any titbit of royal news. As Knollys reported later to Venetia, Treves discovered 'an ill-defined, somewhat firm swelling in the right iliac fossa'. There was tenderness on pressure, and the temperature was raised. He said he had no difficulty in diagnosing perityphlitis.

'I suppose we must be grateful that we have got so far,' Venetia said. 'But you know, Francis – or perhaps you don't

– that Treves advocates operating in the quiescent phase, and not in the acute.'

'I don't know what that means,' Knollys said apologetically, 'but Treves doesn't recommended immediate surgery. He says we should wait and see.'

'Of course he does,' Venetia said.

'You disagree?'

'I think he should operate at once. But my opinion doesn't matter.'

'It matters to me. But, you know, to operate now would mean cancelling the Coronation, and that's an awfully big step to take. And the King seems a bit better this evening. If the attack is over and he recovers enough for the Coronation to go ahead, Treves can operate afterwards and everything will be all right. Surely that's the much better option? You could be wrong, you know.'

'Of course I could, especially as I haven't been able to examine the patient. And if the appendix hasn't yet ruptured, the attack may pass. It *is* a large responsibility to take, to postpone the Coronation. But if it does rupture, the King may die, and that's an even larger one. Early intervention is always best.'

Knollys shrugged. 'Even if Treves recommended surgery, I doubt if the King would agree to it now, not when he's feeling a bit better. He's terrified of the idea in general, and he'd have to think there was no alternative before he'd consent to it.'

The King's fever had abated somewhat, and this improvement lasted three days. But on the 22nd his temperature was up again, his abdomen was distended and he was in great pain. On the 23rd, in accordance with the Coronation programme, the King was to travel up to London. The doctors recommended he go by road so as to avoid unnecessary transfers from one vehicle to another, but the King would not hear of changing the schedule. He travelled by train to Paddington and then drove in an open carriage through the streets with a cavalry escort to Buckingham Palace. Venetia could guess what determination this took on his part. Even so, the press and the crowds lining the route noted his appearance of illness, and in the Lords that afternoon Salisbury was asked about the King's health.

By the evening everyone in the Household knew what pain the King was in. Venetia saw him only briefly as he passed up the stairs to his private apartments, but she thought he looked near death. Hazelmere confirmed everything she suspected about his symptoms. She could bear it no longer. 'Beauty, you must do something!'

'What can *I* do?'

'Talk to Francis. Talk to Laking. The King has acute peritonitis, which means the appendix has ruptured. The next stage is blood poisoning and death. Make them see that he must be operated on. Make them persuade Treves to it. He can't go on procrastinating, or the Coronation won't be postponed, it will be cancelled!'

'I can't interfere between the King and his doctors. Laking wouldn't listen to me anyway. You know that.'

'Then at least talk to Francis. He's clever and subtle. He'll know some way round it. Please, Beauty. Tell him. Make him talk to Laking.'

Hazelmere said he would do what he could, and Venetia waited, in a state of frustration and anxiety. It had never been harder to be a woman. Though one doctor could not interfere with another's patient, had she been a man she could at least have talked to the other doctors, expressed an interest, and perhaps have found an opportunity to give an opinion. They might even have been glad to solicit one. As it was, she could only wait and hope for second-hand reports, dependent on Hazelmere and Knollys, neither of whom understood what they passed on to her.

She paced about her sitting-room restlessly. It was the same one that Olivia had used when at Buckingham Palace, which she had decorated so prettily, so it seemed familiar and home-like. That it was now hers was another example of the King's extreme kindness and thoughtfulness in the smallest matters. What other monarch would have taken the trouble to see that it was allocated to her, rather than any other room? Now she believed he was in danger of his life, and she could not act to save him because she was a woman.

367

But Francis must have managed to convince Laking of the gravity of the case – or else he came to the opinion himself that something must be done. That evening, Laking proved his worth. His skills as a physician might be in question, but his skills as a courtier were not. It was he who broke it to the King that an immediate operation was necessary. The King refused outright to break faith with his subjects by cancelling the Coronation, and furiously ordered Laking from the room. But Laking stood his ground, and told him that without an operation he would die in the Abbey, if not before. Gently but persistently he worked on the King, emphasising his disinterested devotion as a long-serving dependant, urging until he brought the King to agreement.

In the morning the three sergeant-surgeons – Treves, Thomas Smith and Lord Lister – were called to the King's bedroom along with Laking and Barlow to examine the patient. By now a large abscess was both visible and palpable, and though Lister was still for waiting-and-seeing, the other two surgeons agreed with the physicians that the King's life was now in danger and an immediate operation must be performed. In spite of his consent of the previous evening, the King expressed deep reluctance and argued against it, suggesting they waited a few more days until after the Coronation; but with four opinions now against him, he agreed at last.

Hazelmere hurried with the news to Venetia. 'Thank God!' she said. 'I only hope it isn't too late.'

At ten o'clock that morning a bulletin was posted at the gate of the Palace for the public to read.

The King is undergoing a surgical operation. The King is suffering from Perityphlitis. His condition on Saturday was so satisfactory that it was hoped that with care His Majesty would be able to go through the Coronation Ceremony. On Monday evening a recrudescence became manifest rendering a surgical operation necessary today.

In the House of Commons the announcement was made, questions were put, and medical MPs were able to take the floor and explain at length and with varying degrees of accuracy the disease, the operation and the likely outcome. In the Lords the Bishop of Stepney saw the hand of God in the King's illness. The country had been approaching the Coronation with undue levity, and the call had come, in this postponement, to remember the Lord God, and bear in mind that the Coronation was a Holy Sacrament, not an exhibition of imperial greatness.

In the palace, everyone was waiting on tenterhooks. Knollys called briefly on Venetia, mostly, it seemed, to comfort himself. She had never seen the calm, capable Francis so agitated.

'Treves is as nervous as an actress,' he reported. 'I believe he thinks he has left it too late. You don't think so, do you? And the poor King is convinced he has cancer of the stomach, no matter what I say. He's terrified of cancer. He doesn't believe he will survive this operation. But he will, won't he?'

Venetia put a hand out to him. 'Treves is a good surgeon,' she said.

He took the hand and pressed it painfully hard. 'But not as good as you?'

'Francis, I can't possibly say that. Treves is an excellent belly-man, no matter that he and I don't agree on certain subjects. He'll do a first-rate job. And the King has a great natural vigour.'

He gave her a faint, brief smile. 'Thanks,' he said, and was gone.

Venetia had given him what reassurance she could, but her own view was not sanguine. The King was not a good surgical risk: he was old, greatly overweight, and his heavy smoking had impaired his respiratory system. He suffered from frequent bronchitis and catarrh, which made anaesthetising him hazardous. The delay in operating had weakened his general condition, and his own nervousness might well make him panic as the anaesthetic was administered. In spite of her frustration at being forced to inaction, she

369

was glad it was Treves who was doing the operation and not her. It certainly needed a particular kind of temperament, of which perhaps the publicity-loving Treves was an outstanding example.

At twelve twenty the King in his dressing-gown walked into the bedroom which had been prepared by Treves's theatre nurse from the London Hospital, Nurse Haines. To everyone's alarm, the Queen was with him, and seemed disposed to stay. The King was helped up onto the table (a billiard table that had been pressed into service and adapted), and the anaesthetist Hewitt stepped up to administer the chloroform. Almost at the first whiff the King began to throw his arms around and struggle, and soon began to turn blue in the face. The Queen, trying to restrain him, cried out, 'Hurry, hurry! Why don't you begin?' Hewitt flung a desperate look at Treves. Treves himself was unwilling to take off his coat, roll up his sleeves and start cutting while the Queen was watching. He applied himself to persuading her to wait in the next room with the Prince of Wales. By then the King had stopped breathing and had to be revived, so a state of extreme nervousness prevailed.

Once the King was under, Treves made an incision a little above Poupart's ligament on the right side and cut down to four and a half inches, where he found the abscess. He evacuated the pus and inserted two rubber drainage tubes into the cavity, and closed up. The operation took forty minutes, and apart from another episode when the King stopped breathing, it was straightforward.

It was not to be hoped that Venetia would learn any of the medical details from Treves himself, but she received a visit soon afterwards from Tommy Smith, who had no love for Treves either. Though with Lister he was one of the other sergeant-surgeons, he had not been allowed to assist at the operation: Treves had brought in his associate Hodgson instead.

'Treves and Laking rule the roast. They want to make sure they get all the glory,' he complained, leaning against the mantelpiece with his foot on the fender. There was no fire, of course, and the grate was hidden behind a painted screen of Olivia's delicate work, decorated with roses and butterflies. Tommy Smith, with his burly shoulders and bushy hair, was the greatest possible contrast to its femininity. 'They're behaving very badly by Lister and me, keeping us out of it,' he went on. 'But Hodgson is a good fellow. He's told me everything, otherwise I should be as much in the dark as you.'

He gave her all the details of the affair that she so craved. Surgeons tended to be less grand than physicians anyway, and Smith was much less grand than some of the great surgeons like Treves and Lister. He had read some of her papers and had complimented her more than once when they met at various functions.

'So he didn't remove the appendix?' she said, when he had finished.

'No, he didn't think it necessary.'

'A mistake in my view. If it has been infected once, it could be so again.'

'Oh, but you can't disagree with the great belly-man,' Smith said ironically. 'Anyway, it proved to be a case of "just in time". The King would certainly have died if it had been left any longer. The peritonitis was well advanced. It remains to be seen, now, how he recovers. His age and his respiratory condition may pull him back.'

'He came round from the anaesthetic all right?'

'Oh, yes. Asked for the Prince of Wales straight away, and then complained about the hammering outside – they're building stands for the Coronation. Nothing wrong with his wits. They didn't tell him he'd almost snuffed out, so don't you.'

'Me? I shan't be asked. I'm just glad he's come through it.'

Smith nodded, and then looked gloomy. 'The devil of it is that if the King recovers – as we hope and pray – Treves will be confirmed in the public's eye as the world's greatest authority on typhlitis, and the finest cutter in the land to boot. There'll be no living with him. The King's already promised him a baronetcy. Lister and I will be nothing. Treves'll keep the King all to himself from now on.'

The following day the King was reported to be reasonably comfortable. The abdominal pain had been relieved, and he only had pain in the wound when it was dressed. His temperature was down to normal. Another nurse from the London, Nurse Tarr, was brought in to help look after him, and the Queen was constantly by his bedside – so constantly that Knollys told Venetia privately the King sometimes pretended to be asleep when she came into the room, because trying to talk to her through her extreme deafness exhausted him.

Venetia was wryly amused at the jealousy the business had stirred up in the medical world. Smith and Lister were both required to sign the daily bulletins on the King, but neither was permitted by Treves to see the King or examine the wound. Sir James Reid and Sir William Broadbent, the other physicians-in-ordinary, were treated even worse. When Reid came to Buckingham Palace, at Laking's invitation, to have lunch with the other doctors, he called on Venetia afterwards, and told her that he and Broadbent were not even told about the operation beforehand, let alone consulted.

'I wouldn't be here even now except that the Kaiser telegraphed Metternich at the Embassy and told him to ask me for information. I had to say I hadn't any, so the pressure was put on Laking to tell me all about it, hence this luncheon. Barlow was rather apologetic: hinted that he thought Broadbent and I should have been brought in, but was overruled by Laking. And Laking hinted it was all Treves's doing that we were left out – it seems he said five doctors by one bedside were enough!'

'I suppose it's something to know they have you on their conscience.'

'Oh, Barlow didn't like it, that was obvious, but he's too weak to assert himself, and Laking's so thick with the King he has the whip hand in everything. And you know what Treves is like.'

'Yes. Tommy Smith came to tell me Treves won't let him or Lister near the King.'

'He said the same thing to me at luncheon. Seems to feel it deeply! Apparently the King did suggest beforehand that

Treves might have Smith or Lister to help him at the operation, but Treves said, "Sir, you don't want the entire College of Surgeons," and kept it all to himself.' He shook his head. 'What a man!'

'He's one of a kind, all right,' said Venetia.

'Smith and Lister are so disgusted, they think they might get out of it now and give up the post.'

'And what about you?'

'Oh, I'm an easy-going sort of chap. I believe in getting on with everyone if possible.'

'Which makes you invaluable, I should think, in this world of medical conceit,' Venetia said.

'It must be hardest for you, though, being here and yet completely out of the circle,' Reid said sympathetically. 'At least I was asked to lunch! But never mind, the King is going on as well as possible, that's the great thing.'

The King's operation wound required constant attention, but by the middle of July he was recovered enough to go for a three-week convalescent holiday on the royal yacht *Victoria and Albert* in the Solent, and a new date was set for the Coronation, for August the 9th. The postponement had caused great loss and inconvenience to some sections of the country. The Ritz and Claridges had emptied overnight of foreign royalty, most of whom were unable to make a second trip – there had been visitors from as far away as Russia, Korea and Zanzibar, as well as from all over Europe. Makers of commemorative china and other souvenirs now had huge stocks on their hands embellished with the wrong date. One monthly magazine had to go to considerable expense to retrieve copies of the issue containing the article, 'How I Saw the Coronation, by A Peer's Daughter'. And in the royal kitchens, someone had to decide what to do with 2500 quails, 300 legs of mutton, mountains of *foie gras*, caviare, asparagus and strawberries. While the King was undergoing surgery, far below him in the basements servants were packing up hampers of food to be distributed to the poor. That night soup kitchens in the East End were serving *consommé de faisan aux quenelles*, and the ragged homeless of Whitechapel and Stepney dined on sole poached in

Chablis and garnished with oysters and prawns.

During the King's convalescence, a small stream of visitors was invited to the royal yacht to keep the invalid amused. Venetia and Hazelmere were invited for a week at the beginning of August. The invitation was formally expressed, but accompanied by a scribbled note from Francis Knollys saying, 'Do come. I must have someone I like here to talk to.'

'He can hardly think you'd refuse,' Venetia said. 'Surely an invitation from the King is a summons. You are a member of the Household, after all.'

'I fancy the plea is directed to you, my love,' Hazelmere said. 'You will come?'

'Of course. I won't let you down – though I had been looking forward to staying with Olivia and Charlie. But I dare say we can go to them after the Coronation instead.'

'What about the children? I don't suppose Olivia will want to take charge of them without you.'

'Oh, I don't see why not. Miss Miller will look after Violet, and the boys will have the whole of the Ravendene estate to roam over, and there'll be the Duke's children to keep them all company. I don't suppose they'll be in the house more than an hour a day.'

Hazelmere accepted this, but said, 'It's something we will have to think about for the future, my love. Now that Tum is King and not just Prince of Wales, these summonses are going to become more frequent. I'm going to have to spend a lot of time away, and we need to think how we are going to arrange things if we are ever to see each other.'

Venetia sighed. 'Yes, I know. I've been thinking about it too. And I suppose the only answer is that I must give up some of my work.'

Hazelmere tried not to look glad that she had suggested it first. 'Should you mind? I've thought for some time that you really are trying to do too much, with the practice, the surgery *and* the dispensary and your poor patients. To say nothing of teaching and lecturing.'

'I don't do much of that. Not as much as I'd like.'

'Well, then, why not give up the general work and

concentrate more on that side, which is more predictable? You can arrange it for when we're not needed at Court.'

She looked at him cannily. 'I know you too well. You're thinking that it isn't seemly for the wife of a courtier to go about the back slums and listen to old ladies' chests.'

'Well, there is that aspect of it,' he admitted. 'And not only the seemliness, either. There's danger in it, too.'

'You think I might be attacked by a drunken labourer or a disease-maddened prostitute? It's possible, I suppose, though it's never happened yet – at least, not to me.'

'No, I was thinking of something worse than that. Suppose you picked up a flea and I passed it on to the Queen?'

She laughed. 'A flea? I'm sure that's happened before. In fact, I seem to remember Papa telling me that the Court was infested one time after the Russian Tsar and his entourage had visited. But I could pass on much worse things than fleas if I put my mind to it. How about measles or chicken-pox? They wouldn't go down too well at Sandringham.'

'So you will think about it?'

'Yes, I'll think about it. After twenty-four years there are some aspects of practice that have lost their charm. But I don't want to give it up altogether. You know I should go mad with nothing to do but play cards and gossip all day.'

'I know that. I wouldn't suggest it.'

Despite her fears to the contrary, Venetia enjoyed the week on the royal yacht. The weather was fine, and though they did not do any serious sailing, only pottered about, it was pleasant to sit and watch the world go by. Though she would not admit it, she was tired and needed a rest. The *Victoria and Albert* was a pleasant vessel, spacious and well appointed, handsome with her wood panelling and brass, crystal and silver, scrubbed decks and shining paintwork. They found the King in astonishingly good shape. They were taken straight to him when they arrived on board, and found him sitting in the sun on the afterdeck in a large, specially constructed deck-chair on wheels, dressed in his yachting clothes and white yachting-cap, with his writing-case on his knee.

'Ah, there you are, there you are!' he cried, beaming a smile, and insisted on struggling courteously to his feet. 'Give me a hand, Hazelmere. No, no, I insist. I am quite able to stand. I walk around a little every day now. Treves says I have recovered more quickly than any patient he has ever known! I've a remarkable constitution, he says. What do you say to that? Lady Venetia, so glad you could come. We are very dull and need you to brighten our dinner-table. Now then, you will want to refresh yourselves after your journey, but when you are ready, come and join me here, and tell me what's been happening. In half an hour? Excellent! We shall have some tea, then. Let Francis know if your cabin lacks anything.'

Venetia and Hazelmere were given a comfortable cabin with every appointment they could have expected in any of the King's houses, down to the desk supplied with pen, ink, and a supply of notepaper printed at the top with the name and a small engraving of the ship. They changed their clothes and returned to the King, to find a tea-table just being laid and chairs set out for them.

'There now, will you sit here, Lady Venetia, and pour out for us? Always think it's a strange custom, to make the guest do all the work, hey? But that's the way of it. I shan't ask you to sing for your supper, at all events!'

Venetia sat, and said how glad she was to see the King looking so well.

'Think so? I feel well. Feel astonishingly well. I've lost weight, you know. Can you see it?'

'Indeed, yes. I noticed it straight away,' Venetia said.

'I'm on a very sparse diet. Hardly anything at all – positive starvation. I've lost two stones, you know. And eight inches around the waist. Eight! Would you believe it?'

'I would believe it. You're looking very well indeed, sir.'

'Francis says I look ten years younger,' the King chuckled, 'though I dare say you'd be too tactful to say that, hey? Sleep well, too. Eight hours a night without moving – not done that for years! Fact is, I've been living too hard. Yes, I see it now. If I'd gone on as I was doing, who knows what would have happened? This illness was a warning. Queer thing – in the long run it may prove to have saved my life. What do you think of that?'

They chatted for a while, telling him what had been happening in London in his absence, until the Queen joined them, along with Francis Knollys, and Charlotte Knollys, his sister, who was one of the ladies-in-waiting. Then it was necessary to try to engage the Queen in conversation, which resulted in fifteen minutes of nervous strain before she retreated, smiling, into her tower of deafness and began to arrange a game of patience on a small table before her, which released them to talk at a normal pitch among themselves again.

Over the course of the week, Venetia had several private conversations with both King and Queen. The Queen was easier to talk to when it was *tête-à-tête* and there was only one face to watch and set of lips to try to read. She talked about the improvements they were making to the royal palaces, and the plans for the Coronation. 'I have had my robes planned these six months and more. Not that there haven't been attempts to bully me, by silly antiquaries who find dusty old documents to say this or that ought to be done or can't be done. As if I did not know better than them what's right and proper! I shall wear exactly what I like, and so shall my ladies.'

The Queen was six years older than Venetia, and looked six years younger. Her remarkable beauty had never faded. Though she was not very intelligent and had very childish tastes and sense of humour, she was very dignified, gracious and self-confident in her rôle, and seemed already every inch a queen. She had determined from the beginning that she would *not* be called Queen Consort, but simply 'The Queen', and what she wanted, she would have. She was remarkably, notably stubborn, and if all else failed – against the King, for instance, who liked his own way quite as much as she did – she was not averse from using her deafness as a weapon of last resort. The King was in any case a roarer by nature, and he could be brought to near apoplexy by her refusal to hear him when they had a difference of opinion.

With the King, Venetia's conversations were wider-ranging.

He had always liked the company of women, and on several days he had her with him on the afterdeck alone for a couple of hours, the two of them sitting side by side and watching the light sparkle on the water and the gulls wheel above their slight wake, talking about whatever came into their heads. He was by no means an intellectual, but he had enormously wide-ranging experience. His ready sympathy enabled him quickly to grasp the matter of what was said to him; and, like many who read little, he had a tenacious memory. They touched on medical matters, the South African war, horse-breeding, motor-cars, housing conditions in the slums, education for girls, radio waves and whether they would prove to have any commercial use, and the deplorable decline in the wearing of silk hats by gentlemen in Town. Venetia found him very easy to talk to. Once her initial nervousness had worn off, she almost forgot he was the King and talked to him as she might to any man of her acquaintance, which was what he enjoyed most about her.

In due course they came round, quite naturally it seemed, to her plans for her future, which she and Hazelmere had been discussing on and off since the subject was first raised. The King nodded with approval when she said she was thinking of giving up some of her practice. 'I thought when you came back from South Africa that you were looking fagged.'

'It was a very tiring three months,' she said. 'Tiring and distressing.'

'You did good work there – all you ladies did important work. But it takes its toll. You must not neglect your health. You have done your share over the years: let someone else have their turn. There are plenty of young doctors coming out of the medical schools now. Slum doctoring is young people's work.'

'I believe you're right, sir. But I won't give up all my work. There are still many advances to be made in surgery and I should like to keep up with them.'

He shook his head. 'Surgery, now – I don't know how you can! How any lady could bring herself to cut up a body is beyond me.'

378

Venetia said demurely, 'Well, sir, it used to be quite traditional, when there were two joints at the table, for the lady of the house to carve one of them.'

He gave a short bark of laughter. 'I hope you never had live joints at your dinner-table! Well, I suppose one must be grateful that anyone is prepared to do it, or where would we be now? I have to confess I was in an awful funk that morning when Treves proposed to chop me up, but I'd still sooner have been me than him! Can't you just read about it, if you want to keep up with developments?'

'I'm afraid surgery is something you have to practise to retain your skill.'

He shook his head. 'Still, I don't like to think about it.'

'Well, sir, I do think there have to be female surgeons. Most women who are unfortunate enough to need surgery much prefer the thought of having a woman perform it than a man.'

'Hmm,' said the King, unconvinced. 'My mother never consulted any but a man – wouldn't have thought of it. However, you may be right, you may be right. But I tell you where you should put your efforts – research. Not enough first-rate minds concentrating on it. So many dreadful diseases in the world. Cancer, for instance. A man – or woman – might have every advantage, wealth, position, everything, but in the face of disease they are reduced to just nothing at all. If we can conquer disease, we will really be masters of the game, and not helpless pawns. Research is the key. Concentrate on research, that is my advice to you.'

'I have, in fact, been thinking a little along those lines, sir,' Venetia said. 'But a woman faces great difficulties in the field. The medical establishment would be loath to accept anything a woman discovered.'

'But you are not to be put off by a little difficulty like that,' the King retorted. 'You would not be where you are today without determination. Is there some particular field in which you are interested?'

'There are several. But perhaps the most urgent is tuberculosis. I don't know if you are aware, sir, but the scale of

379

the problem is huge: fifty thousand deaths a year in this country – fifteen thousand in London alone! We have no cure, hardly any treatment, and diagnosis is so random it is generally too late by the time it's discovered. That is an area where research is desperately needed.'

'I had not thought of it – but you are right. You are right.'

'I have been wondering lately whether there could be any future in using Roentgen rays in the process of diagnosis.'

'Roentgen rays? I thought they only showed up bones and such-like,' the King said, revealing again the remarkable extent of his general knowledge. Roentgenology was a very new science and was only just being applied by a very few practitioners in London.

'That's true, but there is a professor at Harvard Medical School in America, Walter Cannon, who made an interesting discovery just a couple of years ago. He found that if he fed a barium solution to geese, he was able to get a clear Roentgen picture of the creatures' gullets. Just think, sir, if we could find a way to see what was going on in the soft tissues without having to cut the patient open, what an advance it would be! And if the process could be adapted in some way to see into the lungs, we might be able to detect tuberculosis much earlier.'

The King smiled. 'There, then, you have your field already mapped out. So perhaps from now on you can give up running about the back slums with your little black bag!'

Venetia laughed and agreed, and wondered privately if that had been the whole object of the conversation, and that the King was more interested in the propriety of her behaviour than her possible services to medical science. Well, she thought, he was not the first man to think like that, and would certainly not be the last. Even her dearest Hazelmere, who tried so hard to be modern-minded, would be happy to let some miraculous discovery wait a generation if it would keep her from unladylike conduct. She supposed that, underneath, all men wanted their wives to be wifely, and that was the way it would always be. At least, though, it didn't make her mad any more. Perhaps it was a sign of age, or at least of growing up at last, the acceptance of the fact that while there were many things in the world one could do something about, there was nothing to be done about the basic nature of the male half of creation.

At the end of their stay on the yacht, both King and Queen took a kind farewell of them. The King accompanied them to the gangplank and said, 'We shall see you in London soon. The Coronation next – hey-ho! I have asked Francis to make sure of a good seat for you, by the by.'

'Thank you, sir. You are very kind.'

'You've decided on your title?'

'Yes, we talked it over with the Herald and decided on Overton, sir,' Hazelmere said. 'We shall both be Overton, and our son will be Overton and Chelmsford.'

The King nodded. 'Most satisfactory. He's doing well at Eton, your boy? And that other lad of yours, your foster-son – do you have good reports of him?'

'Eddie's a good boy, sir, though no great scholar.'

'Well, well, neither was I. But that's no great disadvantage if a fellow has something to do that's within his powers. I must see what I can do for young Vibart when the time comes.'

'Thank you, sir.'

The King waved thanks away with a slightly embarrassed look, which rather touched Venetia. He turned to her, then, and said, 'I've enjoyed your visit. You must come and see us more often. Yes, yes, I don't like to see poor Hazelmere always *en garçon*. Not comfortable for a man. You must come and visit us at Balmoral after the Coronation – and at Sandringham later. Come and stay, and bring your children too. We like to have children about the place. Our grandsons are a little young for 'em, but it won't hurt 'em to take an interest in the young entry.'

He was smiling throughout this speech, but his pale, bright eyes looked down into Venetia's with an insistence that reminded her he was every bit as stubborn as the Queen, though he had his different methods of getting his own way. She had been right to guess that, now Hazelmere had been ennobled, she would be expected to toe the line.

As she settled into the carriage that was to take them to

the railway station, she said to her husband, 'We ought to look into a good boarding-school for Violet for the autumn.'

'Boarding-school? Why not a day-school?' Hazelmere said, a little surprised.

'No, my love, it will be better for her to board if we are to be away a great deal. I don't want her to be moved about from pillar to post, left with this person and that like a parcel.'

He looked at her carefully to see if she was angry. 'You've taken your orders very well, I must say.'

'No sense in struggling against the inevitable,' Venetia said. 'And you are my husband, after all – I owe you *some* duty.'

'Who is this meek and conformable woman? I hardly know you!'

'Not meek, just pragmatic. Besides, I've been thinking for some time that Violet ought to go to school. She's very much alone now the boys are away all the time.'

'That,' said Hazelmere, 'is what I call making a virtue of a necessity.'

There were no further delays to the Coronation, and it took place as arranged on the 9th of August. Although the foreign royalties had gone away (all except the representative from Abyssinia, who did not dare to return home with the news that he had not attended the Coronation after all) the colonial representatives had by and large stayed, which made the occasion seem much more like a 'family' celebration, just for Britain and the Empire. This pleased the crowds very much, and there was a turn-out and atmosphere that rivalled that of the Jubilee five years before.

The weather was fine as the King and Queen set out from Buckingham Palace in a golden coach drawn by eight cream-coloured horses. It was not seven weeks since the operation, and the crowds were delighted to see the King looking so well, and cheered and shouted tirelessly. At the Abbey, where kings and queens of England had been crowned for eight hundred years, the form of service had been shortened because of the King's health, but he refused to compromise the dignity of the occasion with anything like a ramp up which he could be pushed to save him having to climb the steps. Bells pealed, the trumpeters reeled out a fanfare like a brazen ribbon, and the King and Queen entered through the great door: she in a shimmering gown of gold tissue, looking as young and slender as if a magic spell had frozen time around her; he dignified and imposing in uniform with a purple velvet mantle and a cape of ermine, pacing slowly, head up, eyes solemn and distant as the choir sang the anthem.

Lord and Lady Overton – as they were since the investiture the day before – had their good seat, as promised, where they could see everything. The occasion, though deeply sacred and moving, was not without its lighter moments. On the King's instructions a special pew had been reserved for Mrs Keppel, Sarah Bernhardt and a number of other ladies whose claim to be present was their enjoyment of the King's favour, past or present. Overton whispered into Venetia's ear that it was 'the King's Loose Box', which almost made her snort with laughter.

In the Royal Box, Venetia noted the presence of the Prince of Wales's two eldest sons, Prince Edward and Prince Albert, aged eight and six, dressed in identical Balmoral kilts and jackets with Eton collars. They whispered and fidgeted all through the ceremony, and when Princess Beatrice dropped her heavily embossed Order of Service over the edge of the box so that it fell with a clang into a large gold vessel below, they dissolved into a prolonged and helpless fit of giggles.

The Prince of Wales – formerly the Duke of York – was there too, of course, looking nervous, and Venetia remembered Francis telling her how frightened he had been when the King was taken ill, and how the Princess of Wales had told Francis that he had said he was not ready to be king. So far he had led a blameless (and, Venetia thought, paralysingly dull) private existence of shooting birds while outdoors and collecting stamps while in. He and his wife lived in York Cottage, a tiny, cramped and dark house on the Sandringham estate, which had been furnished like a middle-class villa in Purley, with Maples furniture and nice chintzes. This, Venetia privately agreed, did not constitute much of a rehearsal for kingship.

The prince seemed too preoccupied to notice his sons' misbehaviour, but the Princess of Wales – Princess May – frowned at her boys fiercely as she could not reach them to silence them. She seemed to be following the ceremony closely as if to memorise it – she was a great stickler for form and precedent, Venetia remembered. She was also noticeably pregnant with her fifth child, so the long day must have been trying for her.

The main anxiety during the ceremony was the frailty of the eighty-year-old Archbishop Temple, who looked so tottery many wondered if he would survive to the end. His eyesight was so poor he made several mistakes in the rite, despite its having been specially written out in large letters for him. He almost stumbled on his way from the altar carrying the Imperial Crown, and it was only with a great effort that he managed to raise it above the King's head, arms visibly trembling. Even then he put it on the wrong way round and the King had gently to lift and turn it for him. As the rite demanded, the Archbishop was the first to kneel and pay homage, and having spoken the ritual words he added in a burst of spontaneous warmth, 'God bless you, sir, God be with you!' He struggled to rise, but his legs had insufficient strength, and the King had to stand and give him both his hands to raise him up, while three nearby bishops rose from their knees to help him back down the steps.

But it all went through without any serious hitch, and to more trumpets and an even more glorious peal of bells, the King and Queen processed down the aisle and out to the carriage for the circuitous drive back to the palace, with ecstatic crowds lining every inch of the route. Venetia and Overton waited their turn to file out (only the Duchess of Devonshire had the bottom to shove her way through out of turn, defying the gentlemen-at-arms as only old ladies can – and almost falling down the steps which their bulk had concealed from her) after which they made their way home to change for the banquet. The following day they were to travel down to Ravendene to stay with Olivia and Charlie and be reunited with the children. They would have a blessed month to themselves, before going to Balmoral, where they were expected on the 9th of September.

And that was how it was going to be, Venetia thought, with a faint sigh. Though she had been born a duke's daughter, she had never been a natural courtier, like the affable Beauty. It was an irony to her that after all the struggles and achievements of her life she seemed to have ended up exactly where her father would have liked her to be all along.

Teddy celebrated the Coronation with a large Coronation Dinner where they sat down thirty to the table – the first time in many years, and the first time at Morland Place that Henrietta had been hostess to such a large dinner party. All their new friends were there, with the exception of the Meynells: Meynell had died unexpectedly of a heart-attack, and Mrs Meynell was still in mourning. On the Saturday following, Morland Place held a cricket match with a large *al fresco* luncheon and picnic tea. This was intended to be the children's share of the festivities. The two teams were drawn from Morland Place servants, tenants and dependants on the one side, and employees of Teddy's businesses and tenants of his properties in York on the other. Ned was chosen to bat for the Morland Place side, and Jack, Robbie and Frank were very impressed by the fact, though Jessie, out of loyalty to Jack, was rather dismissive and said that it was only because he had been to Eton and that all Eton boys played cricket all day long so they could hardly help being good at it.

'If you'd been to Eton you'd be much better than him,' she said stoutly.

'He is awfully good,' Jack demurred.

'I wish Bertie were here,' Jessie said. 'I bet he'd have played instead of Ned. Bertie's the best cricketer in the world.'

'Oh, Jess, how do you know? You've never seen him play cricket properly, only our silly games at Shawes sometimes.'

'I can tell from that,' Jessie said. 'I wish he would come back. Why should he stay away now the war's over?'

'Why shouldn't he? The army still needs horses even in peacetime. And you know Mr Puddephat thinks there's a future in breeding polo ponies too, and he wants Indian pony mares for that. Besides, if I were Bertie, I wouldn't come hurrying home, when someone's paying me to travel in India. What wouldn't I give to be with him now?' In his latest letter, Bertie had said he was going north of Darjeeling into the Tibetan mountains in the search for a certain kind of pony: the tea-planters, who were very fond of polo, recommended it highly for speed, hardihood and nimbleness. Mr Puddephat's idea was to cross a mare of this breed with Teddy's Arabian stallion to produce the perfect English polo pony.

Lizzie and Ashley came to stay in late August, bringing Martial and Rupert with them, now aged four and three. Henrietta noted that there had been no more pregnancies and that Lizzie did not talk of having any more children, so she supposed that Lizzie and Ashley were one of the very modern couples who not only thought two children quite enough but were willing to use artificial methods to keep it that way. It made her a little sad, but she had only to look at her sister's failing health to see where unlimited childbirth led.

The Ashley Morlands were on hand to witness Teddy's latest piece of extravagance, which he brought home proudly one day at the very end of August. It was a motor-car – 'But not just any motor-car,' he added. 'It's a Gardner-Serpollet!'

The British rights for this wonder had been bought by a small York engineering firm, the British Power Traction and Lighting Company Limited, with a factory in Hull Road. The children were both fascinated and surprised by it, for it was driven by steam power.

'It's a beautiful thing,' Henrietta said, walking round it as it sat in the courtyard, gleaming in the sun. 'I do like the colour – very restful!' The coachwork was a very dark green, like holly leaves, and glossy as glass.

Teddy beamed. 'I had a fancy for it. They'll paint it in any colour you ask for, of course, livery and coat-of-arms if you like. I did think of having the Morland coat-of-arms, or at least the crest, put on the doors – only a guinea or so extra. But then I thought how Charley would laugh at me for it, and I held off. But it's got all the extras, you know: bevelled plate-glass windguard and side curtains, detachable waterproof front canopy, side lamps for electric light, signalling horn with two different noises, one for town and one for country.'

'And who is going to drive it?' Jerome asked.

'Ah! I've thought of that. Mrs Meynell is going to let me have Simmons, and he's quite willing to come. She's selling their motor-car – never liked it, you know. Meynell could never get her into it. Simmons is going to take some lessons from the engineers up at the factory, because it works a little differently from the other sort of motor, but he's a clever cove, so he ought to master it in no time. And,' he concluded with an air of hoping to surprise, 'I'm going to have him teach me how to drive it.'

'Uncle Teddy! You driving a motor-car! How dashing,' Lizzie cried, jigging Rupert against her shoulder as he stared doubtfully at the gleaming machine, unsure whether to be alarmed or not.

'Well, why not? Simmons says there's nothing to it.'

'But why a steam car, Uncle Teddy?' Jack asked. 'Why not the ordinary sort?'

'Oh, this is much better! It has every advantage. It turns in the same circle as any horse-drawn carriage, and it's guaranteed to be instantly responsive to the will of the driver. It will take reasonable hills at full speed and long difficult hills at twelve miles an hour. But best of all, it's virtually silent while running. All you hear is the slightest hiss of steam from the burner.'

'What's the fuel?' Ashley asked.

'Ordinary paraffin oil,' Teddy said triumphantly. 'Lamp oil, which is readily available even in the smallest villages, so you've no worries about running out wherever you go. How many times in the last year have you seen some

387

wretched motor engineer tramping along a road carrying a tin can, looking for somewhere to buy his horrid petrol?'

'I should imagine the engine is more reliable,' Ashley said, 'given that steam traction is a tried and tested science.'

'Yes, and not only that, it's powerful, runs evenly, and gives out no disagreeable smell. I've tried both sorts of motor-car, and believe me, this is the way of the future: smooth, silent, comfortable, it's the very pinnacle of motoring. By contrast the petrol car is rough, noisy, smelly and uninteresting!'

Henrietta laughed. 'You sound like a convert to a cause.'

'Well, I am. Only last week a horse and trap in Good-ramgate was overturned and the driver pitched out when the horse shied at a motor-car – and who can blame the poor beast, the frightful noise those things makes? My beauty,' he patted the car's bonnet lovingly, 'won't frighten the horses.'

'Well, that's definitely a consideration,' Jerome said, laughing.

'As long as they don't think it's a giant snake,' Lizzie added, 'hissing like that.'

If Teddy was extravagant, and generous with his presents and entertainments, it was not causing his bank account any unhappiness. All his businesses were flourishing, and in September he spoke to Henrietta about a new scheme he had thought of.

'It's not really my idea, not entirely. Charley was talking about it before she died – perhaps she mentioned it to you? It's a plan to expand Makepeace's. We're selling more and more ready-made clothes, and I really would like to extend that department. At the same time we have more people coming in to buy curtain material, and wanting curtains and covers made up. I thought, why not have ready-made curtains for sale? They could be in various sizes, and we could do alterations in the same way as we do for clothes.'

'Teddy, that's a very good idea!' Henrietta said.

'Do you think so? I thought I could put all that sort of thing together in one place, along with sheets and other household linens, call it the household department. People come into Makepeace's for all sorts of different reasons, so why not make sure they can buy as much as possible under the one roof?'

'Like Whiteley's, in London,' Henrietta said.

'Just so,' said Teddy, who did not know the shop, but had heard his sister talk about it often enough.

'You'll need bigger premises,' Henrietta said.

'Yes, of course. I happen to know that I shall very shortly be able to buy the shop next door.'

'Willis's, you mean?'

'That's right. The frontage isn't enormous, but it does go a long way back, which will give me enough room, and I can always open up the upstairs part. But this is the thing: I'm already in three separate shops, even if they are side by side. Should I pull down the whole thing and build one really big shop in their place, or should I just knock doors through and patch them together?'

'A new shop would be very grand,' Henrietta said. 'All in the modern style, with a turret with a flag flying on the top, maybe.'

'And electric lifts to take the patrons between floors. Lots of panelling and fancy glass lightshades and mirrors everywhere.'

'Makepeace's, the Whiteley's of York!' said Henrietta.

'But if I do that, everything will have to shut down for six months at least,' Teddy said. 'And in that time all my staff would be out of work, or they'd go and work for someone else.'

'And your customers might get used to going somewhere else,' Henrietta said. 'I see the problem. Couldn't you build the new store on a different spot?'

'There aren't really any suitable sites in York for a large building. And it would add a great deal to the costs – not good business.'

'Then you had better do it the other way,' Henrietta said. 'Join the shops together. You could adapt them inside bit by bit so that you could stay open all the while.'

'Yes,' said Teddy, sounding disappointed, 'I had rather come round to thinking I would have to do it that way. But

I really was so taken with the idea of a new big building – like a great Cunarder, all windows and lights, you know, a great ship of commerce.'

Henrietta smiled. 'How poetic of you, Ted! But you could still build it somewhere else – not in York, but in a different city altogether. Why not in Leeds? There must be enough people there who would like to have all their shopping under one roof. Why shouldn't Leeds have its Makepeace's too?'

Teddy stared, his eyes widening. 'Do you know, I think you have really struck something there! Clever old Hen! I could build one in Manchester, too.'

'Why not in London itself? Challenge the original?'

'Well, why not?' Teddy laughed. 'The world's the limit, eh? Why shouldn't I build a commercial empire for little Polly to inherit?'

Little Polly – his dearest treasure. At two she was walking and talking, full of chatter and her own little concerns. She had a way of frowning in concentration over something that had taken her attention that reminded him with sharp poignancy of her mother. And, despite all the people in the house she had to learn to recognise, every one of whom liked to pick her up and pet her and give her kisses, she still knew and loved her father best, and would light up in a special smile for him, which she gave to no-one else. Teddy thought this was not only wonderful for him, but quite remarkable. She would beam, and put out her arms, and say, 'Dad-dee!' and if he was not quick enough in coming to pick her up she would make little snatching movements of her hands with the urgency of her desire to be in his arms.

His life was rich and busy, his days crowded. He had his businesses to run, his civic duties to attend to, St Edward's School to oversee, Morland Place and the estate to improve, and all his family around him with their noise and cheerfulness and constant activity and concerns to brighten his days. And it was all because of Charley. She had come into his life of indolence and empty selfishness and shown him the pleasure of doing, of being active, of using his wealth and position to help others and improve the world.

390

He missed her dreadfully, all the time, and wondered when, if ever, the pain of loss would lessen. After two years, he still was aware every night of the empty space beside him in the bed; every mealtime her bright face was missing from those about the table. He wanted to talk to her and see her and hear her laugh, and he never could again, never. She had changed his life so much, she had filled so full of good things what he had not even known was his emptiness. He had thought when she died he could never be happy again. He was, of course – not in the same way, naturally, but happy all the same.

It was Charley's achievement, all the good of his life, the happiness he still felt, his satisfaction with what he had become, and what he now meant to those around him. It seemed, then, doubly cruel that she was not here to be happy with him, that the most fundamental thing, life, had been snatched from her – so young, so young! She would not see little Polly grow, laugh at her funny little ways, marvel at her increasing beauty. When Teddy stood and watched Polly play, sometimes he longed so to have Charley beside him that he hallucinated, imagined he felt her beside him, felt his arm circling her small waist and her slight weight leaning against him. Sometimes in bed at night – he never told anyone this – he wanted her so much he would cry, turning over on his face and weeping into the pillow so that no-one would hear.

But by day he was busy and cheerful; and that was his tribute to his beloved wife. On Polly's birthday he would get up very early and go into the chapel and put white flowers on the Lady's altar and say a prayer. He would say to Charley, *If I smile and laugh and make merry, don't think you are forgotten; never forgotten, my Charley.* And thereafter, for the rest of the day, he would be the most cheerful person in the house. Not for anything would he spoil his Treasure's special day.

As well as Teddy's plans for Makepeace's, September brought changes for two of the children. Jack had turned sixteen in August, and there was a family conference about

391

his future. He wanted more than ever to be an engineer, but his interest was in development and invention rather than any established area of mechanics. He had learnt a great deal at school and was very grateful to his uncle for having sent him, but he was restless now and eager to get out into the world and try things for himself.

'There are some things you can't really learn without getting your hands dirty,' he said, and his father nodded, understanding.

'So what about an apprenticeship?' was the question put to the conference of Jerome, Henrietta and Teddy.

'But in what field?' Henrietta asked.

'Motor mechanics?' Teddy hazarded. 'I'm pretty sure I could get him taken on by the Gardner-Serpollet factory. I happen to know they are always short of engineers, and I know the owner of the British Power Traction company – he's a member of my club.'

'But isn't that rather old-fashioned – steam-power?' Henrietta said. 'And I know he thinks that steam-power will never do for flying machines.'

'He can't very well be apprenticed to a flying-machine maker, now can he?' Jerome pointed out. 'However much he yearns for the future to happen right now, it is not yet with us.'

'He's got to start somewhere,' Teddy said, 'and an engine is an engine when all's said. Let him learn the fundamentals, and when he's older he can decide for himself where to apply them. He's still just a boy.'

'True,' Henrietta said. 'And it would mean that he could live at home, which would be nice. If he were apprenticed somewhere else he might have to live away.'

Jack thoroughly approved of these plans on his behalf. He was so eager to begin he didn't mind where it was, and he saw the sense of learning about engines from the bottom up. Being at home was an added attraction for him, too. 'I could walk there and back quite easily,' he said.

But Uncle Teddy could do better for him than that. When the matter had been settled, and Jack had been accepted by the company, Teddy bought him a bicycle of his very own, on which he could 'whistle in to work in no time!'. Jack was thrilled and deeply grateful, aware of just how much he owed his kind uncle.

There was a change for Jessie on its way, too. She had been very struck with Violet's news that she was to go to boarding-school, and though Violet was in two minds about it, part excited, part apprehensive, Jessie thought it would be quite wonderful to go and stay in a place like a hotel filled with girls of her own age. She still burned with the injustice of Ned and Thomas going to Eton, and even of Jack's going to school in Manchester. She loved her home, but Bertie's travels had given her the idea that being away was at least wonderfully romantic.

She would be twelve in December, and a decision needed to be made about her schooling. St Edward's was a boys' school, of course, so no good for her. Either she could stay on at the village school for two more years and then stay home and learn what she could on her own or from her mother; or she could be removed now to a proper girls' school. Jessie was passionate for the latter option; Henrietta had had doubts for some time that the village school was doing anything but teaching her to be rough and noisy, and was for any change at all. It would mean finding school fees, but girls' schools were much cheaper than boys', and Jerome thought they could manage to pay for something not too ambitious.

They found a school with a good reputation not too far away, in Ripon, where the building and the grounds were pleasant and the curriculum seemed interesting. Matters were soon concluded, and Jessie was to start at the end of September. She was happy and excited, and ran round the house like a mad thing, driving Kithra into a frenzy of excitement.

'I hope they know we're sending them a whirling dervish,' Jerome commented.

In her bedroom, Jessie sorted through her possessions to see what she would take. On the small table beside her narrow bed was the photograph of Bertie on Dolly, which she had begged from her mother. *Her most treasured possession.*

Naturally she would take that with her. She picked it up and caressed it with her finger, lovingly as she might stroke a horse's muzzle. It had never been a very good picture, and you would have to know it was Bertie to recognise him. Otherwise it was just an anonymous soldier on a small and scrawny horse; a man with large moustaches, his face shadowed from the bright overhead sun by the brim of his hat. She thought suddenly how there must be people all over the country who had a photograph like this, that was *their* greatest treasure She felt without words the romance of the soldier-away-at-war, and it pulled her like the tug of a kite catching the wind, high above and far away at the end of a long thread.

She tried to think of Bertie himself, but it was so long since she had seen him in the flesh, his face would not come to her. When she tried to imagine him, all she got was this faint, photographic image. Probably she would never see him again. The thought gave her a sensation of almost pleasant melancholy. To be in love was a prerequisite of life; to be in unrequited love at the age of twelve gave one a sort of inner distinction. She could say to herself, *I shall never love anyone else,* and feel that it was true and beautiful and sad, without its in any way blighting the rest of her life, or her enjoyment of the present.

She had so much else to think about just now. *She was going to school*! The excitement, the anticipation was so intense it was almost like a stomach-ache. She wanted to rush about and shriek at the top of her voice. She imagined writing to Violet with her news. And Violet would write back – she saw herself being handed the letter by a prefect, vastly impressed by her correspondence. And there would be a school uniform, so Dad said, which she thought deeply glamorous. She had read *Tom Brown's School Days*, and the adventure comics that Ned brought home, which were full of school stories: her mind was filled with japes and pranks, feasts in the dorm, tuck-boxes, arcane school rules, cross-country runs and vital matches where the unlikely hero always makes the winning score. It didn't occur to her that girls' schools might be any different. She entered, day-dreaming, a wonderful world of beaks, pre's, games captains, bullies, swots, sneaks, pals and splendid chaps. The photograph of Bertie was still held in her hand like a talisman, but it was a magic from another world, past and distant, impossibly out of reach.

CHAPTER TWELVE

In the autumn of 1905 a fire broke out in Jessie's school during the night. Though all the girls were got out safely and no-one was hurt, the building was damaged by smoke and water, and the school was forced to close while repairs were undertaken. Jessie was sent home, and arrived feeling all the cheerfulness with which youth welcomes novelty.

'I thought you liked school,' Jerome said.

'Oh, I do! But it's nice to be home, too, especially when I *ought* to be at school.'

At first Henrietta insisted she did some lessons every day but, with regular schooling, Jessie had gone past the point where Henrietta could help her much. The lessons quickly degenerated into conversation, and then Henrietta decided it would be just as useful to her in later life to accompany her mother on her normal rounds of duty. So Jessie helped her sort and mark linen, check over store-cupboards, plan menus, give orders to the servants, and go carriage-visiting. Jessie enjoyed this last because, though Henrietta did not have the instinctive dislike of Teddy's steam car that she had felt towards the petrol vehicle, she still preferred horse traction, and did her carriage-visiting literally in a carriage. Jessie liked any activity that involved horses, and persuaded her mother to allow the coachman to give her a driving lesson on their way home. Henrietta insisted that she sit inside the carriage on the way there in an attempt to preserve her in a state of neat-and-tidiness.

'I don't know how you do it,' she complained to her

daughter, 'but you seem to manage to get yourself into a mess without even trying.'

'I know. Dad says if you locked me in a cupboard too small to make any movement I could change gold into dross in five minutes. What's dross, anyway?'

'Something that isn't gold. It's not funny, though, darling. A lady must always to be particular about her appearance. Not everyone can be a great beauty, but everyone can be spick and span, and have tidy hair and neat clothes – and all their buttons done up.'

'Not a great beauty? That's me all right,' Jessie said good-naturedly. 'It isn't my fault, though. Buttons just come undone on their own. And they fall off when I'm not looking. And my hair never *will* stay tidy. I don't do anything to make it this way.'

'Well, dear, you don't do anything to help, either. I know you're not quite fifteen yet, and I don't want to stop you romping while you can, but I think you ought to start learning how to behave in company, even if it's only for an hour at a time. So when we get to someone's house, try to sit still and not fidget. Don't fiddle with your buttons or stare about you. And if you're offered anything to eat, nibble it slowly, don't wolf – and don't make crumbs.'

Jessie made a face. 'What a lot to remember! But I'll try. Do you like doing this sort of thing, Mother? Wouldn't you sooner be out riding?'

'Sometimes. Often. But everyone has duties to perform.'

'I should have thought once you were grown-up you could do as you pleased. Why go and sit in someone's stuffy drawing-room and talk nonsense when you could be out in the fresh air on a horse? No-one can *make* you do it, can they?'

'We have to think of others sometimes, and visiting gives them pleasure.'

'I bet it doesn't! How can anyone prefer it to riding?'

Henrietta laughed. 'Not everyone is like you, you know. And you'll change when you grow up, and get married and have your own home. Then you'll like having people come and visit you, and sit in your drawing-room and admire your new curtains.'

'Oh, I pray not!' Jessie said, looking alarmed. But she did her best to behave as her mother wanted, and as all the people they visited were old friends, and as she was a gregarious soul, it was not too much of a martyrdom. Even if she didn't manage to sit still and not fiddle with her buttons, she chatted cheerfully to the ladies and probably brightened their day more than if she had sat with her hands folded in her lap and her mouth daintily closed.

In addition to 'going about with Mother' there was playing with Polly to keep her amused. Polly at five was a remarkably pretty little girl, tall and strong for her age, with long straight legs like a colt and a bold temperament, which often led her into mischief. She adored Jessie, and Jessie still treated her like a personal possession. When Polly had been smaller she had been Jessie's 'own baby'; now she was her *protégée* and apprentice. It was lonely sometimes for Polly when Jessie was away at school, and as soon as she came home Polly allowed herself to be sucked up by the whirlwind that Jessie made as she rushed about trying to see and do everything at once, and trotted after her everywhere, beaming with delight.

And as well as all this, there was Outdoors just begging for Jessie's attention. Like her mother before her, she asked nothing more of life than a pony to ride and somewhere to ride it; but the best thing of all was to help her father with the horses up at Twelvetrees. From that day when he had asked her help with backing the young colts, she had taken a close interest in the whole Morland horse business, and there was always something for her to do, something within her abilities to which Jerome was happy to guide her.

As well as army horses, and general riding horses for which there was always a small but steady demand in the neighbourhood, there were potential polo ponies at Twelvetrees now. Pasha, in his prime, fathered all the colts, and it was their dams who determined what they would be. The polo ponies were bred from four Tibetan mountain ponies – Bhutias – which had been found and sent home by Bertie. He was still in India, having now set up a business of his own. He still acted as an agent for Mr Puddephat, but he travelled widely through the north of Bengal and the neighbouring provinces buying horses, and had his own place near Darjeeling where he bred and trained both riding ponies and polo ponies. Polo was a very big thing among the tea-planters and army officers, and there was a steady demand for his animals.

Jessie loved the Bhutias specially, partly for Bertie's sake, but also because they were small and clever and friendly. Though in their native land they carried full-grown adults and heavy loads, they were not much more than thirteen hands high, and in the winter when they grew their thick coats they looked like overgrown woolly dogs. Having learnt to trust Jessie, they would follow her around like dogs when she visited their paddock. They provided hardiness and nimbleness; Pasha gave their offspring extra height and finer looks. Jerome had promised Jessie that she could help with the polo training once they were old enough, and in preparation had taken her to see several matches at the cavalry barracks nearby, where there was a very keen team. During the summer Jessie had done her best to teach herself the game on her own pony, Hawthorn, using a croquet mallet and ball, and by the time she went back to school she was no longer falling from the saddle every time she attempted a shot, and Hawthorn was beginning to turn more quickly.

So she felt she had plenty to do, and when her mother came down with a heavy and feverish cold, which necessitated taking to her bed, Jessie did not see that this created a problem. 'I can look after myself,' she said, and added temptingly, 'I needn't be indoors at all, you know. I can stay out all day and you'll never know I'm even home from school.'

Had Jerome been at home, Henrietta might have agreed with this, but it so happened that Jerome had arranged to go away with Richard Puddephat on a trip to Ireland and was expecting to be absent about a week; and at the same time Teddy had to go to Manchester on business that could not be put off.

'It leaves Jessie without anyone to keep an eye on her,' Henrietta croaked to her husband. 'I really don't think that's a good idea.'

'She can't come to much harm pottering about on her pony, can she?' Jerome said.

'She can always get up to mischief, even without trying. And it is supposed to be school time. I don't think she ought to be let run wild. She should be learning something.'

Jerome did not think a complete holiday for a short time would hurt her, but he saw that Henrietta was troubled by the idea. Probably, he thought, uncomfortable and feverish as she was, she did not want the worry of Jessie being her sole responsibility when she was not in a condition to fulfil it. So he put the problem to Teddy.

'I can't take her to Ireland, and I can't put the trip off – the arrangements are all made and the passages booked.'

Teddy said straight away, 'Not to worry! I can take her with me to Manchester. It'll be educational all right, visiting the mills. She can learn a bit about how cloth's made. And it won't hurt her to see the building site: I dare say that's educational enough in its own way. She's heard so much about the new store, I expect she'll like to see it going up.'

'You really don't mind taking her with you?' Jerome said, relieved.

'Not a bit! She and I are good friends. And we can call on Jack, too, and take him out to dinner at the hotel. She'll like that.'

Jessie, who was doubtful about the first part of the plan, was persuaded by the last part. She was not sure that visiting factories would be fun, but she loved Jack and longed to see him. His apprenticeship with the steam motor-car company had not lasted long, for financial troubles had caused the firm to be wound up the following year, in 1903. Teddy had found him a place with another engineering company, but it was in Manchester, which had necessitated his leaving York. He now lived in 'diggings', and was not able to come home as often as any of them would have liked; but his letters expressed him happy, and learning a great deal. The owner of the company had taken quite a fancy to him, and had even allowed him a corner of a work-shop where he could 'fiddle about' with his own ideas during his off-duty hours. The company made marine engines and

400

he was working on a very promising improvement to one of them.

In the event, Jessie found the whole trip fun. Uncle Teddy was a pleasant and undemanding companion, and thought nothing of ordering a second portion of pudding for her in the restaurant car, when her mother would have said one was enough. Eating on the train was delightful – indeed, *travelling* on the train was a joy, for she had not yet done it often enough in her life to take away the excitement. Teddy did not keep a house in Manchester, so they stayed in an hotel, which was the first time for Jessie, and so even more exciting than the train.

Against all expectations she really enjoyed visiting the factories. In order to free himself for business, Teddy put her in the charge of a foreman with instructions to take her about and show her everything. Jessie had a quick mind and a large store of natural curiosity, and when the foreman discovered she really did want to know how things worked, he took trouble to explain everything properly, and let her poke into every corner and every process.

At the building site, where the new Makepeace's was going up, she was handed over to the architect's assistant, who showed her the blueprints and then pointed out which section of the apparent chaos related to which part of the drawings. They also visited the factories that were making the fittings, and Teddy pleased her by asking her opinion about the design of the shop counters and the colour of carpet.

The best part of all was going to see Jack in his digs, seeing his little room, meeting his landlady, and then taking him in a cab back to the hotel for proper grown-up dinner. Henrietta had insisted that Jessie's best dress was packed for the trip, and Teddy said she should wear it as he and Jack were going to change. Jessie needed the chambermaid to help her put it on, as some of the buttons were inaccessible. The maid, Doris, was friendly and also offered to do her hair for her. 'For it's a right proper rat's nest, miss, begging your pardon. What in the world have you been doing with it?'

401

'Nothing at all. It just gets like this on its own.'

Doris twinkled at her. 'My littlest sister's just the same, miss. A proper walking 'aystack.'

'Have you got lots of sisters?' Jessie asked, with immediate interest.

'Six, miss. And four brothers.'

'Oh, tell me about them!'

By the time she was dressed, Jessie knew the names, ages and occupations of Doris's entire family, and Doris, deeply flattered, was her slave. The dress was dusky pink in colour, with bishop sleeves and long buttoned cuffs. The skirt was gored at the back to give fullness, and trimmed round the hem with three rows of smart black braid. Best of all, it was longer than her skirts hitherto, coming down to the top of her boots, which made her feel, rather thrillingly, nearly grown-up. Doris brushed her hair smooth and then drew the sides back and tied them behind with pink ribbon. Jessie examined herself in the looking-glass. She was rather impressed by this new vision before her.

'How old do you think I look?'

'Eighteen or nineteen, miss,' Doris said solemnly.

'No, really,' Jessie insisted.

'Definitely sixteen, anyway. Sixteen going on seventeen.'

Jessie turned and caught the twinkle behind the serious expression. 'Oh, you're just teasing.'

'You look right nice, miss, like a real lady. I hope you have a lovely evening,' said Doris warmly.

Downstairs, as the *maître d'hôtel* bowed them to their table, Jessie felt she had entered a different world, one of excitement and glamour. Jack she thought the handsomest young man in the room in his evening dress – one of Dad's cast-offs, but no-one could have guessed, it fitted so well. Uncle Teddy looked the most distinguished, she thought; and the chandeliers, mirrors, flowers, rich red carpet and obsequious waiters were like something out of a story-book. Darling Jack chatted happily, looking around him with appreciation at this variation from his landlady's food and dining-room, but still had time to smile at Jessie and say, 'You look very splendid. I like your frock – very grown-up!'

402

She smiled back. 'I almost think it wouldn't be bad being grown-up if it was all like this.'

'Ah, if only,' Jack said, with a grin.

After such an evening, the next day was rather an anti-climax. They were to catch the train home in the evening, and it seemed flat to Jessie to be doing just the same things again on their last day. But as it happened, one of the people Teddy had planned to meet was away, so they ended up with time on their hands.

'Would you like to go to a museum or an art gallery?' Teddy asked, vaguely remembering that he was supposed to be educating his niece.

Jessie concealed her alarm and managed to say politely, 'No, thank you, Uncle Teddy. What would you like to do?'

'Oh, well, it doesn't matter to me, you see.' At that moment they turned a corner of the street and passed a billboard advertising a political meeting. The country was preparing for a general election, and there was a great deal of activity and excitement in Manchester – always a polit-ical city, but more than ever so, now that there was a defi-nite likelihood of a change of government.

Teddy seemed struck by the poster. 'By Jove,' he said, 'now I wouldn't mind going to that meeting! Sir Edward Grey and Winston Churchill to speak. Today at the Free Trade Hall – what do you say, Jess? But I suppose that would be rather dull for you, wouldn't it?'

Jessie thought it was better than a museum, at any rate. A political meeting, she had gathered from grown-ups talking, could be something of a rough-and-tumble, with hecklers, and people fighting and being thrown out. 'I expect I'd enjoy it,' she said cautiously.

Teddy beamed. 'Would you? That's the girl! It is educa-tional – democratic process and all that sort of thing. I'd like to hear what Grey has to say. And Churchill, too. Rum cove, switching sides like that.'

Winston Churchill, a junior member of the great Spencer family, had made a name for himself in the South African war as a newspaper correspondent, when he had managed to get himself captured by the Boers, escaped out of a

403

window, and later wrote a formal letter to his captors thanking them for their hospitality. He had gone into Parliament, but had recently regained his notoriety by crossing the floor from the Conservatives to the Liberals. His oddities were usually blamed on his American mother, but there was no doubt he had a superfluity of energy and ideas.

So it was to the Free Trade Hall that they went, and Teddy bought tickets for two good seats near the front so that Jessie would be able to hear and see everything. Looking around, she saw that she was the youngest person there by a long count, though there were two young women sitting further back and just to one side of them. The meeting was rather dull after all, and Jessie's attention wandered during the preliminary remarks, the introduction and the beginning of Sir Edward Grey's speech. She hoped perhaps some excitement was going to start when a man nearby stood up, but when he interrupted the speaker with a question, Sir Edward stopped, listened, and answered him seriously and politely, and the man sat down, satisfied. This happened several times more, each time Sir Edward listening and answering courteously. There was obviously not going to be heckling and fighting with everyone being so polite to each other. Jessie yawned behind her hand, and wondered how Uncle Teddy could sit there listening so attentively and nodding from time to time like a mandarin while people talked about free trade and land reform – such stuff!

Sir Edward Grey finished his speech at last, and the chairman was opening his mouth to speak when one of the young women Jessie had noticed before stood up and called out in a strong Lancashire accent, 'Will Sir Edward tell us whether the Liberal Government will give the vote to women?'

There was a brief, surprised silence, during which heads all over the hall turned in her direction, and someone at the front sniggered. Then the chairman, looking in every direction but the right one, said, 'Are there any more questions?'

The woman stood up again and said, 'I have asked a question.' The chairman ignored her, and two men sitting

404

in the row behind grabbed her arms and pulled her down into her seat.

'If there are no more questions, I propose we should continue with our next speaker,' the chairman said.

There was some sort of conferring between the young woman and her friend, and then they both stood up, unrolling between them a banner made of white calico on which in large black letters were the words VOTES FOR WOMEN.

At the sight, laughter, boos and catcalls filled the room. Men waved their hands in various gestures, not all of them polite, and shouted, 'Sit down!' and 'Rubbish!' Someone near the back shouted, 'Get off home, you baggage, and darn the old man's socks!' and there was loud and harsh laughter. The second woman shouted out, 'Why doesn't he answer my question?' Her accent was quite educated.

Jessie heard the man sitting next to Uncle Teddy say, in a surprised undertone to his companion, 'Good God, that's the Pankhurst girl, isn't it? Who's the other? I say, bad show!'

Stewards were hurrying down the aisles now, and several reached the place where the women were and forced them to sit down. Up on the platform Sir Edward Grey was sitting calmly and looking straight ahead at nothing, as though he were rather bored and waiting for nothing more interesting than the arrival of a train. Mr Churchill had his chin sunk on his chest and was glaring in the direction of the women with his lips folded tightly shut. The chairman looked exasperated, and was watching the stewards' progress.

Jessie tugged Uncle Teddy's sleeve. '*Why* doesn't he answer that lady?' she whispered. 'He answered the other questions all right.'

He bent his head to her. 'Woman aren't allowed to speak at political meetings,' he said.

'But it was so rude. He didn't even look at them, just as if they weren't there.'

Uncle Teddy shrugged helplessly, as though it were beyond him. The meeting obviously could not continue as the laughter, shouts and catcalls were not subsiding, and up on the platform the chairman was conferring with a large man with a beefy red face and enormous side-whiskers. This man now came down off the platform and made his way back to the trouble spot. 'Chief Constable of Manchester,' Jessie learnt from the man next to her uncle. Through a relay of comment it became known that he was telling the two women they must submit their question in written form. Shortly afterwards he returned to the platform with a folded piece of paper in his hand. This he handed to the chairman. Each of the gentlemen on the platform took it in his turn, read it, and passed it on, some with a smile and a shake of the head, as though it were a piece of fatuous nonsense. Finally the paper went back to the chairman, who set it aside, looked round the hall, and said, 'Now, gentlemen, shall we get on?'

'He's not going to answer it,' Jessie whispered to her uncle. 'That's not *fair*!'

Evidently the women thought so too. They got to their feet again, and were grabbed by the stewards. More men were coming down from the back – plain-clothes policemen, the relayed murmur told her. The second young woman managed to free her arms with a determined wriggle, and climbed up onto her seat so that she could see over the stewards' heads. She shouted again, 'Will the Liberal Government give votes to working women?' Her voice could hardly be heard above the derisive laughter and booing. Now both women were grabbed by several men on either side and were dragged out of their places into the aisle. As they were hurried, their clothes rumpled and their hats askew, towards the exit, the booing changed to raucous cheers, and a bellow of 'That's the way!' and 'Chuck 'em out!'

To reach the exit they had to be taken down to the front and past the platform. All the men up there were now staring rigidly ahead, ignoring the events taking place just feet away from them. As she was dragged past, the first woman shouted up to Sir Edward Grey, 'You're a coward! If I leave this hall I shall hold a meeting of protest outside!'

The second woman, managing to halt her captors in front of Sir Edward, put the same question again, in a strained but otherwise normal voice: 'Will the Liberal Government give votes for women?' Sir Edward met her eyes this time, but his expression did not change. Pale, stern and immovable, he looked like the bust of a Roman emperor – and was as silent.

After that the rest of the meeting could only fall flat, especially as a large part of the audience slipped out of the hall to follow the women, evidently anticipating more fun on the outside than the inside. Uncle Teddy got into a whispered conversation with the man next to him, of which Jessie could hear snatches. The second young woman, it seemed, was a Miss Christabel Pankhurst, daughter of the late Dr Richard Pankhurst who had stood three times for Parliament and had been a well-known liberal political reformer in Manchester. Her mother was born Emmeline Goulden and was the daughter of a local mill-owner. 'I knew Goulden,' Jessie heard Teddy remark with interest. 'He and my father were well acquainted. I think I might have met his daughter. Wasn't she sent to be finished in Paris?'

'Oh, the family's quite respectable – that's what makes it so shocking,' said the man.

'The other female's nothing but a mill-hand,' said his companion. 'Don't like to see respectable girls mixed up in that sort of thing.'

'Women ought to know their place, respectable or not. I can't think what this town's coming to,' said the first, 'when we can't have a political meeting without that kind of interruption.'

When the meeting was over and they got outside, there were lots of people still hanging around and talking about the incident with the pleasure of those who welcome any alteration to their normal daily round. It was not difficult, therefore, to discover that the two young women had started to address the crowd that had followed them out into the street, whereupon they had been seized by the police and marched off to the police station, charged with obstruction.

'I think we had better get back to the hotel and pack our bags. Once we've had a little tea, it will be time to go to the station,' said Teddy.

Jessie brightened at the thought of tea. Tea in the hotel

involved a wonderful multi-tiered cake stand, freighted with the most delicious confections, and Uncle Teddy *never* forgot to keep passing it for as long as Jessie kept accepting. He really was the best sort of uncle a person could have, she thought.

She had pretty well forgotten the meeting, until they got to the station platform and she saw another of the same posters on the wall of the waiting-room. A man was brushing paste over it, preparing to stick a new poster over the top of it.

'Uncle Teddy,' she said, 'why *wouldn't* they answer those ladies' questions? They answered all right when the men asked.'

'I told you,' Teddy said, from deep in his newspaper, 'women aren't allowed to speak at political meetings. They're only allowed in at all on condition they stay completely silent.'

'But why?'

'Because they don't have the vote.'

'Why don't they?'

'They never have had it.'

'But why?' Teddy was reading and didn't hear her. 'Uncle Teddy, why can't women have the vote?'

He looked up, distracted. 'Oh dear, I don't know. It's just the way things are, that's all. Men and women aren't the same, you know.' He saw another *why* on its way past her lips, and said hastily. 'I can't explain it to you. You'll have to ask your mother when we get home. Ah, this must be our train, coming in now! Keep close by me, Jess. Can't have you getting lost.'

The following morning Henrietta was very interested in what Jessie had to say about the meeting.

'Goodness, has that started up again? We haven't heard anything about it for years. I thought it had all died out. I took Lizzie to a meeting once, years and years ago, when she was about ten. It was all about how women should have the vote. Lizzie's papa was dreadfully angry and forbade me ever to go to anything like that again.'

408

'So it isn't a new thing?' Jessie asked.

'Goodness, no! There've been various societies trying to get the vote since – oh, well, the sixties, anyway.' She seemed struck by that. 'Goodness, forty years, and they haven't got anywhere at all! It just shows, doesn't it?'

Jessie did not enquire what it showed. Instead she asked, 'But, Mother, why don't women have the vote?'

'Well, dear, they never did have it. All through history it's been men who went out into the world, while women stayed at home and looked after the children. In fact,' she added fairly, 'that wasn't quite true among the lower classes. Lower-class women always worked – but then lower-class men didn't have the vote either. I suppose that's the trouble, really – now they've given the vote to almost all the men, it isn't fair, especially as so many women have jobs, and even professions like Cousin Venetia.'

'So why won't the men give it? And why were they so rude to those ladies? They ignored them just as if they weren't there.'

'Men don't like women to intrude into what they think of as their particular world. Lizzie's papa had his own part of the house where I was never to go – his library and study, where he could be private. Imagine the fuss if a woman went into a gentlemen's club! Well, Parliament is a bit like that. To be honest, darling,' Henrietta continued, as Jessie opened her mouth with more questions, 'most women don't want the vote. They're quite happy with things the way they are.'

'Are you?' Jessie wanted to know.

'Don't I seem happy? Most women aren't interested in politics. It's a good thing, too, because if forty years of trying haven't got women the vote, they never will have it.'

'Well, I don't think it's fair,' Jessie said.

Henrietta smiled. 'Darling, you don't really understand what the vote is, do you? You just don't like the idea of anyone telling you you can't do something. Why don't you go out for a ride? I tell you what, Elida must be longing for a good gallop after nothing but led exercise for a week. Why don't you get Potter to saddle her and take her out for me?'

Jessie was easily distracted from the topic: there was, in any case, too little time before she would have to go back to school to waste it on something so obscure.

But Teddy, having had his interest aroused, followed events in Manchester in the newspapers. Winston Churchill was standing for the Liberal Party for the constituency of North West Manchester – an important marginal seat. The organisation founded by the Pankhursts, the Women's Social and Political Union, seemed to be focusing all its efforts on having Churchill defeated. This seemed an odd tactic, given that the Liberal Party was far more likely to give women the vote than the Conservative, but there it was. Someone went about Manchester pasting 'Votes for Women' stickers over the enormous red-and-white posters put up by Churchill's Liberal supporters – the largest posters anyone had seen since Barnum and Bailey's circus had visited – and a handbill came into Teddy's possession, issued by the WSPU. It read:

> Inhabitants of Manchester, if you believe that women ought to have political freedom, better wages and fairer treatment all round, vote and work against Winston Churchill as a member of the Liberal Government.

Political meetings featuring Churchill attracted great crowds anyway, because of his recent defection from the Conservatives. Often he had to address an overflow outside the doors before he could even get up to the platform. But now that the women began to turn up at every meeting and heckle and display their banners, the excitement was almost palpable. It happened that Teddy was in Manchester again when there was a meeting at Cheetham Hill School, and he went along to see the fun for himself.

Churchill began his address to the packed school hall by attacking the record of the Conservative Government. 'The will of the people has been ignored. But now you have got your chance!'

At that point a female voice interrupted, 'Yes, we have got our chance and we mean to use it!' Teddy looked round.

A young woman had stood up, and was unfurling the familiar banner. He could see her lips moving, but what she said next was drowned by the uproar, though he guessed it was the familiar question: will the Liberal Government give votes for women?

'That's one of the Pankhurst girls,' said the man next to him. 'Sylvia, I think her name is. What names old Pankhurst gave his family! He must have known they were destined for notoriety.'

The commotion was quieted at last, and Churchill began speaking again, but he had not managed more than a sentence or two when the young woman interrupted again. This time the hall was thrown into pandemonium, with men hooting, catcalling, whistling, stamping, standing up to shake their fists at her. Stewards converged on her slight figure, but seemed unwilling to manhandle her. Teddy's companion said, 'They don't like to rough her about, given she's a lady – and old Pankhurst was well liked in Manchester.'

The man beyond him added, 'She's got supporters here, too. See those fellows at the back? They're Labour men – the Independent Labour Party. If they step in there'll be a free-for-all.'

The chairman up on the platform was vainly trying to restore order, and Teddy saw him talking earnestly to Churchill, perhaps urging him to answer the question, for Churchill was giving quick impatient shakes of the head. Finally the chairman, obviously sympathetic to Miss Pankhurst if not to her cause, invited her to come up on the platform and address the meeting herself for five minutes.

The young lady, with enormous self-possession, left her seat and walked down to the front, pausing in front of Churchill to say, 'Don't you understand what it is I want?' Churchill, his face a thundercloud, turned his head away and made an impatient gesture of rejection, to say he wanted nothing to do with her.

On the platform Miss Pankhurst did her best to make a speech, but her voice was too light to carry over the continuous bellowing of Churchill's supporters in the front rows.

411

At last when she dropped her hands and turned as if to leave, Churchill jumped up in a burst of movement, and Teddy thought for one rippling moment that he was going to hit her. But he grabbed her arm, quite roughly, and forced her to sit down on a chair at the back of the platform. 'You are not to leave until you have heard what *I* have to say!' he said in a loud, angry voice that easily carried.

The noise in the hall subsided and everyone heard what he had to say: that having witnessed the methods the women were using to disrupt and destroy great public meetings, nothing would induce him to vote for women's suffrage. A great cheer rose up at the words, and the front rows stamped their feet so hard Teddy thought the floor might give way.

'I will not be henpecked on a question of such grave importance!' Churchill added above the noise.

There was another huge cheer, and a chant began, 'Don't be henpecked, Winston! Don't be henpecked, Winston!'

For all the disruption – women attended all Churchill's rallies and displayed their banners, and either shouted out the question, or held a meeting outside – Churchill won the seat. But Manchester on the whole was sympathetic to the women, and his majority was notably small, which attracted the attention of the London newspapers. It was the *Daily Mail* – deeply scathing of the women and their cause – that coined a new and derisive term for them: the Suffragettes.

The general election was held in January 1906. The result was remarkable, and a great triumph or a great tragedy, depending on point of view. After nineteen years of Conservative government, and a general feeling that the state of affairs would endure for ever, the Liberals had not only won a majority, but had an outright majority of 84 seats over all the other parties combined. This meant that, in the House of Commons at least, they could do as they liked, carry through any legislation they wanted without having to placate any factions or lobbyists.

The other remarkable thing about the result was that there were no fewer than fifty-three Labour MPs – all of whom had been brought up in working-class homes and nearly all of whom had been manual workmen. It was the most extraordinary departure from precedent. It had been hard enough for the party grandees to become accustomed to MPs from the middle classes joining their ranks, but many now were shaking their heads and wondering if the world were coming to an end.

In the circles of women interested in the Cause – both the new generation, and the older ones who could remember back to the eighties and beyond – there was much excitement. It was on a Liberal government that they had always fixed their hopes, though some pointed out that it was a Liberal government, under Gladstone, which had refused to add the women's amendment to the franchise Act of 1884 that gave the vote to the agricultural labourer. But with an enormous majority, the Liberals could certainly do it, if they would.

On the day Parliament opened, a large meeting was held in Caxton Hall, and Mrs Pankhurst and other luminaries made speeches while they waited to hear what had been in the King's Speech. When word came that there had been no mention of the women question in the speech, hundreds of them left the hall and made their way to the Houses of Parliament. The policemen at the Strangers' Entrance refused to admit anyone, but the women stood patiently in the cold January rain until at last two relays of twenty were allowed into the Lobby. The Members who had previously pledged their support did come out to meet them, but all without exception now said there was nothing they could do, and that they could not commit themselves on the question.

Anne Farraline came to see Venetia afterwards, and for once was despondent. 'The only thing we achieved today was to hold a public meeting within a mile of St Stephen's, which lawyers now tell us is illegal on the opening day of Parliament.'

Venetia was sympathetic, but said, 'I really don't think you're going to get anywhere. After nineteen years out of office, the Liberals have got their own agenda, and a long list of legislation they want to get through. They're not going to want to be bothered with the women question.'

'Well, they're going to have to be bothered. We're going to make them bother.'

'Darling, you can't *make* them do anything. You can only persuade – and they won't be listening.'

'How can you talk like that? We can't, we simply *can't*, let another generation of women waste their lives for want of the vote. If they won't listen to us, we'll have to find other ways of making our point.'

Venetia was alarmed. 'Now, Anne, please don't think of doing anything foolish. I've seen something of the hatred men pour out against women who agitate and behave in an unwomanly way.'

'Oh, hatred? We can tell them a thing or two about hatred.'

'You don't mean that,' Venetia said, shocked. Anne did not answer, but her still-beautiful face was marble. 'Darling, I don't like to see you becoming so hard. Where's that dear, merry girl I used to know, who always had such fun?'

'She's gone,' Anne said. 'Killed by oppression and injustice.'

'Oh, don't say that! Why don't you let it alone? Let the younger women take up the fight. You've done enough. Why don't you marry Peter Padstowe? He's such a dear man, and he loves you so. He's waited for you long enough.'

'*Marry?*'

'I'm serious,' Venetia said. 'You're not getting any younger, and you can have no idea how lonely you will feel when you get old and find yourself alone. You're lucky to have someone like Padstowe who's been willing to wait all this time – and with little encouragement from you, I may add. When he inherited the title, I quite thought he would give up. Please marry him, Anne. I know he'd make you happy, and you'd make a lovely countess.'

Anne shook her head. 'I can't believe I'm hearing this from you.'

'Think of all the good you could do your cause if you were a countess. Don't forget Peter has a seat in the Upper House.'

'Do you think I'd marry him for that reason alone? I'm

414

not quite the heartless thing you consider me.' She turned her face away, but not before Venetia had seen the hurt in her eyes. 'I've told Peter I won't marry him, not ever, and he believes me at last. He's stopped pursuing me.' She walked over to the window and stared out, her back to Venetia. 'In fact, I've heard he's been paying marked attention to one of Watford's daughters.'

'Oh, Anne,' Venetia said gently, 'I'm so sorry.'

'Are you? I'm not.' After a moment, she turned to face her cousin, and said fiercely, 'Do you think I'd marry him now, at my age? He needs a younger woman who can give him sons. I'd be no use to him. I care enough for him to know that – even if he said otherwise, the idiot.' Her voice wavered, and then steadied. 'I should have married him years ago, but it's too late now,' she said quietly, 'so let's not talk about it any more.'

Venetia bent her head in acceptance, too sad to find any words just then.

She was sorry that things had taken this turn, and she felt in part responsible, since from an early age Anne had looked up to her as an example. When Venetia had been struggling to become a doctor, Anne had wanted nothing better than to follow in her footsteps as a pioneer of women's advancement. Venetia had once said incautiously that as she was conquering the sphere of medicine for women, Anne ought to concentrate on getting them the vote. The trouble had always been, she reflected, that Anne had not been given anything to do, and was too bright to fill her life with the usual, vacuous social round. She had been left from an early age in the charge of her brother William, the Earl of Batchworth, who had old-fashioned ideas about women, and who was at the same time too weak to influence Anne and too stubborn to yield to her. While he had control of her purse-strings he had kept her too confined and without occupation, so that she had plenty to rebel against as soon as she had control of her own fortune.

In recent years the women's suffrage movement had lost its force, and had seemed to confine itself to holding decorous public meetings once or twice a year, well attended by

415

the usual liberal thinkers of the professional and political worlds, but completely ignored by the press and the public at large. Venetia had hoped greater maturity and the loss of the Cause might tame Anne and persuade her to marry her faithful courtier. But the interruption of the meeting at the Free Trade Hall in Manchester had seized Anne's imagination. The two females, Miss Pankhurst and one Annie Kenney, a cotton-mill worker and trade unionist, had been charged with obstruction and, refusing to pay their fines, had been sent to prison, Kenney for three days and Pankhurst for one week. The idea of going to prison for the Cause – of really suffering – struck something in Anne's make-up, something Venetia felt was unhealthy and would never have reared its head if only she had been properly married.

Venetia hoped Anne's decision that Peter Padstowe must marry a younger woman was made before the Free Trade Hall incident rather than after: it would have been the most dismal reason for rejecting her one chance of happiness that Venetia could imagine. It was true that Anne was now forty-two, rather aged to be giving Padstowe heirs – though it was by no means impossible that she should. It was true also that Padstowe had no brothers to succeed if he did not have a son. But if he was willing to accept that situation for Anne's sake, why should she worry about it? Over the years Anne, beautiful and vivacious, had had many suitors, and though she had enjoyed their attentions, she had driven them all away in the end. Padstowe had lasted the longest by a large margin. Venetia, having seen them together on many occasions, was sure that they would have suited. But if he really was now courting another woman (and, come to think of it, had she not seen him coming out of Brooks's one day last week with the Duke of Watford, looking very 'chummy'?) it was evidently too late, and the thing was over between them.

Venetia was very sorry about Anne; but she was more sorry to see Lizzie Morland being drawn in. Ashley was doing so well and was such a favourite of Mr Culpepper that he had recently been promoted to a very high position in the company with a considerable increase in salary. In consequence, the Ashley Morlands were able to live in better style, with more servants: they had moved to a more fashionable area, and had electric lighting and even a telephone. They now had a house in Endsleigh Gardens, which meant Lizzie was much closer to Venetia's London house in Manchester Square, but even closer to Anne, who was living in Bedford Square. Also, with more household servants, her two boys of an age when they could be left with paid attendants, and her husband a great deal from home because of the demands of his career, Lizzie was finding herself with more time on her hands.

That Anne had been talking to her Venetia did not doubt when she came to call one day. After only a perfunctory exchange of family news, Lizzie jumped straight into the question of women's suffrage. 'Things are changing,' she said enthusiastically. 'More women are being educated, more and more are working and paying taxes. With the Liberal Government coming in, every political idea is going to be tested. Every economic idea too, Ashley says. So now is the time when we can really make our mark and get things moving.'

'*Our* mark?' Venetia queried.

Lizzie didn't notice the question. 'You know, the whole South African war was fought because the Transvaal refused to give the vote to English Uitlanders, and everybody agreed that the franchise was essential to them as the very basis of all other rights. Well, if the vote for Englishmen in the Transvaal was worth spending two hundred million pounds and thirty thousand lives on, what about the millions of English*women* at home? Are we to be perpetual Uitlanders in our own country?'

'Lizzie, darling, don't rant at me!'

'Oh, sorry. I didn't mean to – it's just my enthusiasm,' Lizzie said. 'But don't you think it is the perfect argument? How can they stand out against it, in logic?'

'In logic they can't,' Venetia said, 'but, then, there's never been any logic employed in resisting the Cause. Darling, I've been locked in the struggle one way and another for nearly forty years, and I know what the outcome will be – the same this year as last, and the same as every year before. I'd hate to see you waste your time on it.'

'But how can you call it "wasting time"? It's the most important, the most fundamental thing we have to fight for. And if we fight on, we must win in the end.'

Venetia shook her head. 'That's what we've been saying for forty years. I can tell you've been talking to Anne, haven't you? Look here, I'm afraid Anne is getting hold of some dangerous ideas and, much as I love her, I don't want her to be sucking you into it.'

'I'm not being sucked,' Lizzie said. 'I do have a mind of my own, you know.'

'Of course you have – and so has Ashley. What do you think he will feel about your getting involved in this sort of thing?'

'But Ashley agrees with me! Of course he does. He thinks it's terrible that women don't have the vote. Goodness, they have the vote in *Australia*! They even have it in *Russia*!'

'Darling, Ashley may agree with you in theory – many men do in theory – but that's very different from having your own wife make a spectacle of herself in public. Remember, Ashley has an employer, who might dismiss him if he gets involved in any scandal.'

'Oh, but Mr Culpepper is American, and Americans are far ahead of us in things like this. Americans think we women in this country are terribly hard-done-by, and wonder that we sit down under it.'

Venetia looked at her bright, enthusiastic face, and was reminded of Anne when she was younger. She sighed. 'I don't expect you to sit down under it, I just want to warn you not to get involved in any of the more extreme actions. You may meet a lot of women who are . . . well, not quite balanced.'

'Oh, Venetia!' Lizzie exclaimed in disappointment. 'How can you say such a thing? That's what men say about us.'

'No, men say we are all unbalanced. I only say there are some such in the movement. They have good reason to be angry – we all have – but some women lose their sense of proportion, and I should hate you to become one of them. Fight the good fight, my love, by all means, but don't get too carried away.'

Lizzie was silent a moment, looking at Venetia as Venetia imagined she might look at Mart or Rupert when they had done something foolishly naughty. 'Well, I'm sorry to hear you talk like this. I'm disappointed. You could be such a help to the Cause, with your connections and position in society. And as a pioneer woman doctor, your example is *terribly* important to all women everywhere.'

Fortunately, Venetia's sense of humour was functioning well. 'Is it? Dear me, what an enormous responsibility! All women everywhere? If I let them down it will be tantamount to genocide, won't it?'

Lizzie began to smile, too. 'Oh, well,' she said. 'Perhaps I did get on my hobby-horse a little.'

'Gave him a good gallop,' Venetia agreed. 'Will you bear in mind what I've said? I only have your best interests at heart, you know.'

'I will. I promise. But will you do something for me? Will you talk to Sir Henry Campbell-Bannerman about it?'

'Oh, Lizzie!'

'I don't mean rant at him, but just slip it into conversation. I know you and he are very fast friends, so surely he won't mind your *mentioning* it?'

'He has not been at all well lately.'

'When he's better. Please, Venetia, just when the opportunity occurs.'

'All right, I'll mention it. But I won't bully the poor fellow. That would be taking advantage of a friendship.'

'Oh dear, if you can't talk to your friends about the things that matter to you, what is friendship for?' Lizzie demanded.

The idea of talking to Campbell-Bannerman – since January the Prime Minister – about the Cause did not appeal to Venetia and she might have forgotten all about it, had not the WSPU themselves had the same idea. It was in all the papers. In February Mrs Pankhurst sent a written request for an audience to the Prime Minister's office and received

419

no reply. In March she and a small group of women walked to 10 Downing Street and asked to see the Prime Minister. They were told they could not be admitted and must submit a written request to see him. Patiently they went away and did so, upon which they were told that *all* communications with the premier must be made in writing.

Frustrated, the women arranged a peaceful deputation to 10 Downing Street. About thirty of them met at Westminster Bridge station and walked there in small groups so as not to look threatening. The press had been notified and there was a large group of reporters and photographers waiting to witness the scene. Three ladies knocked at the door, which was opened by an elderly butler to whom they gave their message. He closed the door again and they waited on the doorstep – and waited. It was three-quarters of an hour later when the door opened again and two stony-faced officials told the women that there was no reply. As the door was closed in their faces, they lost patience. One began banging on the door and shouting, 'Freedom for English women!' while another climbed onto the step of Campbell-Bannerman's car, which was parked at the kerb, and began addressing the crowd. Soon the police arrested the three ringleaders and took them off to Cannon Row police station.

They were held for an hour, but then a telephone message came through from the Prime Minister that they were to be released.

Lizzie came to see Venetia, full of the story. 'You see how it is? We are of no more importance to them than house-flies. They tell us we must go through the proper channels, but when we do, they simply ignore us! Now you must help us.'

'Must I?'

Lizzie gave her a melting look. 'Oh, I don't mean it like that. But if Sir Henry telephoned to have the women released, that must surely mean he has some sympathy. If someone he knows and respects, like you, has a word with him, it must make a difference.'

'Well, I do agree with you that the situation is beyond unfair, and I believe Sir Henry is sympathetic, so I will talk

420

to him the first opportunity I get. But don't expect too much, will you, Lizzie?'

She smiled. 'I'm remembering your words and keeping a sense of proportion,' she said.

It was not as difficult as it might have seemed for Venetia to secure a word with Campbell-Bannerman. They moved in many of the same social circles, and he had been accustomed during his years in opposition to call in on the Overtons in a casual way. At a dinner-party one night in April she said to him that she would be glad of a private word with him at some time convenient to him, and he smiled and nodded, and said he would do himself the honour of calling the next morning.

When he arrived, as it was a beautiful morning, she asked if he would care to take a stroll in the garden. 'It is no very great thing as a garden, but the daffodils are very pretty, and the air is really springlike today.'

'I should like that,' he said. 'I seem to spend so much of my time frowsting indoors these days, I hardly know what fresh air smells like.'

Out in the sunshine, she thought he was looking very worn. He had been quite ill, and as a friend, she knew that he had had heart trouble. She said, 'You look tired, Henry. I hope the rough-and-tumble of the Commons isn't tiring you too much. You could have led from the Lords, you know.'

He smiled. 'Oh, I like it in the Commons. One must be where the action is. Can't keep your finger on the pulse from a distance, now, can you?'

'You have a very full programme, haven't you?'

'Of course. After nineteen years in the wilderness, there's a lot to be done.'

'Too much to bring in anything else this session.'

'Or next.' He looked sideways at her as they strolled along the gravel path under the pale April sky. 'There's something in particular that you have in mind?'

'Well, I did ask you to come here for a purpose – beyond the pleasure of your company, that is. It's the question of the franchise for women.'

'Ah, that!' he said. 'I wish it had been almost anything else.'

'But, Henry, I know you are a liberal man, in the best sense of the word. And I know you like and respect women. You must see that it is a matter of simple justice that women should have the vote on the same basis as men.'

'That great multitude of men who go out and strive in the world the better to support their wives and children would not think so. In fact, most of mankind would tell you that women are not capable of understanding politics. Their minds don't work that way.'

'The agitations of the various suffrage societies prove that is not true.'

'They are exceptions.'

'Oh? And is it only exceptional men who have the vote? Does the agricultural labourer understand politics? Does the machine-minder? Does any man need any intellectual qualification whatever to be entitled to vote?'

He looked at her with unquenchable good humour. 'I quite agree with you that among men there are poltroons, and idiots, and asses, and men from all classes who can barely get through a newspaper. But what of it? Their nature is different, and the way in which they look at the world, and the challenges they face from day to day, which the vast majority of women never have to. It is not a matter of equality, when women are *not* equal to men.'

'I didn't say equality, I said justice,' Venetia reminded him. 'More than that, it is a matter of propriety.'

He wrinkled his brow. 'Propriety?'

'Yes, Henry – it is quite *improper* that women should be outside the franchise. Women go out to work, they pay income tax, they pay property taxes, they pay, God help us, death duties! They contribute to the Exchequer, but have no say in how the money is raised or spent. Taxation without representation is mere tyranny, nothing more. Women are obliged to live under the law, are punished under the law, but have no say in the making of the law. That is tyranny.'

He sighed. 'Yes, it's true. And strictly between us, I am very much on the women's side. I do think it is a great

422

injustice, and I wish there were something I could do about it.'

'If not you, who?'

'My dear Venetia, I may be prime minister but I am not, in fact, a dictator! However much I might want something, I can't even present it to the House unless the Cabinet is with me – and there is very strong sentiment against votes for women in the Cabinet.'

'Asquith,' she said. 'And Grey.'

He shrugged. 'Almost everyone apart from me, my dear. And even if the Cabinet were behind me, and I put up the necessary Bill, it would never get past the House of Commons.'

'You have an overall majority.'

'Yes, but the vast majority of MPs is against it, and it is not a case in which we could use the Whip. Besides, even if by some extraordinary chance we could get it through the Commons, the Lords would throw it out. They would *never* agree. And it would be an appalling waste of Parliamentary time that could be better used, to take up something that has no hope of success. I wish you would tell your campaigning friends that. There is no hope of getting any movement on this matter until it has a sufficiently large popular support. But frankly, Venetia, no-one wants this. The working classes don't want it because their wives are already too independent and they're afraid of being henpecked. The middle classes don't want it because it would simply mean an extra vote for a married man over a single man – perhaps more than one extra if he had grown daughters at home. Even most of the women in this country don't want it.'

'How can you say so?'

'Come, you know it's true. Are they all out marching in the streets demanding their rights? No. It's just a small group of educated middle-class ladies.'

'It's a vicious circle, isn't it?' Venetia said. 'Women have never had the vote so they know nothing of politics. But because they know nothing of politics, you say they don't want the vote. It was the same argument that was used against educating them. Because they'd never had the chance of education, you said they weren't capable of learning. Well, we've proved *that* one false, I think.'

'*You* have, at any rate. Look, you know that I have always believed in education for women, and I should like nothing better than to be able to give them the vote. But I can't do it, so there's no use in asking me.'

He looked more tired than ever, and she was sorry to have troubled him. 'I understand your position and I won't tease you any more. But there is one thing you *could* do – quite a small thing – and I wish you will consider it.'

'What is it?' he asked cautiously, but willing, if he could, to please her.

'Receive a deputation from the suffrage societies. They have tried every way they can to get your attention, and you can't think how humiliating it is when your lords and masters care too little even to bother to answer your questions.'

'Ah, now that was a misunderstanding,' he said. 'I never saw any of the letters – they were dealt with at a lower level. And as soon as I heard the women had been arrested I intervened to have them released.'

'Yes, I know you did, and I honour you for it. So will you, then, receive them?'

'Very well, I will try to arrange it.'

'You are very good, Henry. I know how busy you are.'

'But you know that it will do no good? I tell you now I can't promise to help.'

'Just to be allowed to make their case will mean so much, not only to the women but to the Cause. When the country at large sees that you won't even receive them, it feels licensed to despise them. If you receive the deputation, it will give them standing.'

He gave a weary smile. 'I don't know that I want to give them standing. It will only make them come after me all the more. But I've said I'll do it, and I will, if it can be managed. Oh, and on one condition.'

'What's that?' she asked, a little warily, for there was an amused gleam in his eye.

'That you will be one of the delegates.'

424

Venetia was completely taken aback. 'I – well! But I—!'

'If I have to go through with it, so shall you. What's sauce for the gander, my dear . . .'

Sir Henry was as good as his word, and the date was fixed for May the 19th, and the place the Deputation Chamber of the Foreign Office – Downing Street would have been too small for a deputation of more than a handful. The excitement was great throughout the movement, and there was a desire for the membership of the delegation to be as widely representative as possible. Mrs Fawcett, however, as the leader of the long-established and orderly National Union of Women's Suffrage Societies, expressed doubts to Venetia about the wisdom of allowing the WSPU to take a large part in it. The NUWSS was committed to quiet, reasoned persuasion and purely legal actions, while the WSPU seemed already committed to a more militant course, and didn't seem to mind being arrested for breaches of the peace. 'It only makes the men more determined to resist,' Mrs Fawcett said. 'But I suppose in justice we can't exclude them since it was their action that started the train of events.'

When the day came, there were not only representatives from all the suffrage societies, but from the trade unions too, and more than a thousand women gathered on the Embankment by Cleopatra's Needle. Women from all kinds of trades – weavers, winders, shirtmakers, chairmakers, iron-workers, cigar-makers, book-binders – gathered alongside university graduates and pit-brow women from coal mines all over the country. A contingent of women from the East End had come carrying their children to represent mothers. There was a delegation from international suffrage move-ments carrying banners. There were several bands.

The main body remained at the Embankment while the chosen deputation of about forty marched off to the Foreign Office. It comprised representatives from the trade unions, from the WSPU and the NUWSS, and several MPs, like James Keir Hardie, who had pledged their support in Parliament. There were also several pioneer suffragists – amongst whom Venetia supposed she must class herself – the

425

most senior of whom was the seventy-six-year-old Emily Davies. It had been she, remarkable to remember, who had presented the very first women's suffrage petition to John Stuart Mill back in 1866. Reflecting on that, Venetia thought how hopeless the whole business was, and regretted having let poor Henry, quite as much as herself, in for it.

After the gathering and the marching, the actual meeting was an anti-climax. The Prime Minister listened, with his usual patience and courtesy, to the various speeches, and when they were done he said, 'I am personally in favour of women's suffrage. But there is opposition in the Cabinet. It would not do for me to make any statement or pledge under these circumstances. All I can do is advise a policy of patience.'

'Patience!' one woman cried out.

He gave a faint smile. 'You must keep on pestering.'

Keir Hardie stepped forward to make his vote of thanks, and the meeting filed out, crestfallen. In the courtyard, Annie Kenney, who had come dressed in shawl and clogs as a mill-girl, stamped her foot and said, 'We are not going to stop for this! We are going on with our agitation!' Cheers answered her.

Venetia sighed and made her escape. The rest of the party were going to join with the main body again and hold a public meeting in Trafalgar Square, but she hadn't the stomach for it, for more speeches, for the anger and frustration. It was an appalling injustice that women did not have the vote but, like Elizabeth Anderson, she had carved out her own career in a man's world and it took up her time and energies. She could not care enough – or, rather, could not believe enough that it would make any difference – to bang her head against a brick wall. It would take some huge national cataclysm to reverse public opinion and get women the vote. It would not be done by speeches, deputations, or anything else these women were capable of.

CHAPTER THIRTEEN

Venetia's desire to remain detached from the suffrage agitations was not wholly indulged. She was too important a figure, if not on the suffrage question, at least in the wider cause of freedom for women. She frequently received invitations to speak at rallies, put her name to petitions and resolutions, and attend meetings and demonstrations. She refused all with the excuse that she was too busy – which was true. Though she had given up her practice and had passed the free work on to others, she still operated at the two hospitals, lectured from time to time at the London School, gave addresses, wrote papers, and was conducting her own research into tuberculosis.

The Overtons had moved to a larger house in Manchester Square, which had a fine room on the first floor at the back, which protruded over the garden and had large windows and a glass roof. This she had converted into a laboratory and study. Here from time to time came consumptives in various stages of decline or recovery. Venetia examined and photographed them, took sputum samples and recorded their case histories. The servants grew used to this, though they never liked it, not only fearing for their own health but regarding it as detrimental to their dignity. To assuage their feelings, and so as not to upset the neighbours, she had the consumptives brought in by the garden entrance and the back stairs.

She enjoyed her work, and disliked the interruptions that came from Overton's Court duties. Time spent at Windsor, Sandringham and Balmoral to her was time wasted, though she learnt to put up with it with a cheerful face. Fortunately the King's circle of friends was much more varied than the old Queen's, and there were genuinely interesting people to be met, with whom one could have an intelligent conversation. Ernest Cassel became quite a friend, and advised both her and Overton on investments. Mrs Keppel, the King's mistress, was an amusing and quick-witted woman, and so genuinely kind and good-tempered that Venetia never minded being in her company. Her least disliked parts of the royal year were the trip to Biarritz in early spring, and the August meeting at Cowes. The latter she came to regard as her real holiday, because the children always joined them. Afterwards they all went to Shawes for a further week or so, and friends visited them there for the racing. All three boys were at Oxford now, Thomas and Oliver at Christ Church and Eddie at Trinity. Violet was still at school. All of them enjoyed the yacht racing, and regarded Shawes with the same affection as Venetia, so whatever else came in by way of invitations, they never missed that fortnight.

Her life, she felt, was too full for her to work for the suffrage cause as well, though with Anne and Lizzie both involved, she could not be unaware of what was happening. Throughout 1906 the WSPU had organised demonstrations, disrupted political meetings and tried in vain to confront politicians and make deputations to Parliament. Venetia deeply disapproved of the treatment the women had received. It was not uncommon for MPs to praise in the House the far more violent protests made by Russians in their campaign to wrest political freedom from the ruling classes, but for the women of their own country they had nothing but contempt. This was proved by the harshness of their reaction to the women's disturbances. Where a man would merely have been ejected, the women were arrested; where a man, arrested, would have been let go with a caution, the women were imprisoned.

Venetia had been particularly shocked by the events of October 1906. A group of women had gone to Westminster on the opening day of Parliament, and when they were halted at the Strangers' Entrance, had requested to speak to MPs, each naming a different one. It was every citizen's constitutional right to speak to any Member, and every Member's duty to make himself available. But the women were told that only twenty of them would be allowed into the Lobby, and the twenty were selected by the officials. It was not surprising that they chose only well-dressed, middle-class ladies; but even so, none of the MPs they had named appeared in the Lobby to speak to them. The women were left waiting without explanation, the clearest possible evidence of the House's contempt for them.

Eventually, frustrated, they had decided to stage a protest. One of them climbed up onto a bench and made a speech. At this the police came into the Lobby and seized them, removed them bodily from the House, and arrested ten. At court the following day, when they were brought up for trial, no women were allowed into the public gallery, and the friends and relations of the accused were refused admittance – another infringement of normal rights.

All ten were found guilty, and were sentenced to two months' imprisonment. It was a shocking sentence, out of all proportion to their offence. Theirs had not been in any sense a moral crime, but merely a technical misdemeanour concerning the rules governing the House of Commons. Furthermore, the women were committed to the second division, as common criminals, instead of to the first division, which had always before been the case with men who committed purely political offences.

The newspapers had at first condemned and ridiculed the Suffragettes for this action, but the severity of the sentence changed their minds, especially as the women were all respectable ladies – one of them was Richard Cobden's daughter. The *Daily Mail* headed its editorial 'Cruel Treatment of English Ladies'. The *Daily News* questioned the assumption that the Suffragettes were lunatics obsessed with a silly desire for self-advertisement, and went on to speak about Mrs Despard's valuable work in the slums of Battersea and Mrs Pethick Lawrence's in the East End.

Mrs Fawcett, who had known Jane Cobden from a child, went to visit her in Holloway Prison and was appalled at the way she was being treated. She went round afterwards to Manchester Square to see Venetia and tell her, in the heat of her indignation, what she had discovered.

'A small, narrow cell, with one tiny window high up – they live in a perpetual twilight! There's no furniture, not so much as a chair, nothing to sit on but a small narrow bench without back or sides. And the food! My dear, Janie is a vegetarian, so all she had for dinner was three potatoes. She was in prison dress, marked with broad arrows. I can't tell you how it affected me! She had a horrible piece of coarse, dark cloth hanging from her waist and when I asked what it was, she said it was her handkerchief. They are not allowed their own, and the dresses have no pockets. She joked about it, and said it was lucky she hadn't a cold, as they are only allowed one a week. So brave! I took her a few flowers, but the wardress wouldn't allow her to have them. *She* was present the whole time, of course – listening to every word we said. And this is how someone is treated for trying to exercise her constitutional rights!'

Mrs Fawcett was so affected by the memory she turned away her head and had to take a minute to compose herself.

'I don't agree with the militants' ideas,' she went on, 'and I have condemned their methods from the start, but this it not to be borne. It is an appalling injustice.'

'I agree,' said Venetia. 'They have committed no criminal offence. To treat them as common criminals is beyond tolerance.'

'We must do something about it,' said Mrs Fawcett firmly.

'What had you in mind?'

'It's of no use appealing to Parliament or the law, that's plain. This is a case for personal intervention.'

Venetia looked doubtful. 'The Prime Minister won't interfere with the court's decision. I know that without asking.'

'No, of course not. I was thinking of the King.'

'The King!'

'Who else has the power?'

'But I don't think he is in favour of women having the vote.'

'Perhaps not, but he is very chivalrous, and I believe he

cannot approve of ladies being treated this way. It is sheer vindictiveness, nothing more. If we appeal to him to have them removed into the first division, I'm sure he will not refuse.'

'Perhaps an appeal for that much might be allowed,' Venetia said, though still doubtfully. 'What do you propose we should do?'

'I know you and Lord Knollys are old friends. If I write the letter, will you give it to him, with your recommendation? Otherwise I'm afraid the King may never get to see it. You know how petty officials like to shield their masters from anything troublesome that comes through normal channels.'

'Yes, that's true. Campbell-Bannerman said he never saw the letters from the WSPU asking for an audience. All right, I'll do it.'

Francis accepted the letter from Venetia with his most neutral expression, the Compleat Courtier's blank. 'I will give it to His Majesty,' he said, 'but I can't promise when he will have time to read it.'

'I know you will do your best for me,' was all that Venetia said.

Six days later, the women were all removed into the first division, where they were allowed to wear their own clothes, had better food and were allowed to receive letters. Meeting Lord Knollys shortly afterwards, Venetia held out her hand with her warmest smile, preparing to thank him, but he forestalled her quickly by saying, 'I do hope you will forgive me for not coming back to you on the subject of your letter, but I understand that the ladies in question have now been made first-class misdemeanants, so perhaps you will think that a reply is no longer necessary.'

'Just so,' Venetia said smoothly. 'Please don't trouble yourself any further with the matter, my dear Francis.' She had no doubt that the King had seen the letter and intervened, but evidently it was not to be acknowledged, and not for anything would she embarrass her old friend.

In fact, the newspaper agitation over the severity of the sentence had been so great that the Government was taken

431

aback. Though no official statement was ever made, or injustice acknowledged, all of the ten ladies were quietly released after serving only a month of the sentence.

After this brief collaboration, Venetia was not much surprised to receive another visit from Mrs Fawcett early in 1907, to ask her to take part in a demonstration on February the 9th.

'This has nothing to do with the militants,' she assured Venetia. 'This is NUWSS business – a march of the "constitutionals" only. I shall be leading it myself, and we want the largest possible attendance. We would especially like the pioneers to join us, to give the march weight and respectability. The WSPU has stirred up interest in the question, and I think it is a good time for us to make use of it, before we lose the nation's attention.'

'What do you mean to do?'

'We shall meet at Hyde Park Corner and then walk in procession to the Exeter Hall where we will have speakers. I want the march to be dignified and sober, and I would like the front rank to be made up of eminent people, so that the press can't make their usual accusations – or, worse still, ignore us! Frances Balfour has agreed to walk with me in the front row. Will you join us?' She put on her most beseeching look. 'I know you are dreadfully busy, but please, you will find time to do this for the Cause, won't you?'

'Oh, Millie! I really *am* too busy, but I don't know how anyone can ever refuse you.'

'A surprising number of people manage to,' said Mrs Fawcett.

Venetia found the experience of walking at the head of five thousand women unexpectedly exhilarating. The front row was made of up women who had achieved great things in their time, and many of those who followed were in academic dress and made an impressive sight. Some of the veterans were walking with their own grown-up daughters, evidence of how long the struggle had been going on. The procession stretched for half a mile, and there were reporters and photographers at all the key points, guaranteeing coverage in the papers. One or two rough-looking men

432

shouted out ribald remarks, but the vast majority of the crowd seemed favourably interested, and even respectful. The weather was atrocious and they gathered and walked in pouring February rain, so that the occasion became known afterwards as the Mud March. At the hall, a number of distinguished men and women gave addresses, which were reported in the papers. The whole thing had a smack of seriousness and firm intent.

Whether prompted by this demonstration or not, the Liberal MP for North St Pancras, W. H. Dickinson, who won the new session's Private Member's Bill ballot, decided he would use the opportunity to put forward a Women's Enfranchisement Bill. The debate was held on March the 19th. No women were allowed into the Gallery during the debate, which perhaps was just as well. After five hours the question was still being argued over and the Speaker refused to call a division. The Bill had been 'talked out' once again.

The disappointment throughout the movement was enormous, and for the time being the WSPU mounted no more protests. There were a number of by-elections coming up, and they concentrated instead on those, using peaceful propaganda methods. They directed most of their efforts outside London. The suffragists tended to be well received in small country villages, where the agricultural workers remembered the dark days before 1884 when *they* had had no vote. In industrial towns there was great interest, though not always sympathy. In her native Lancashire, the indomitable Annie Kenney hired a lorry and used it as a platform to address the men and women pouring out of the mills at the end of their working day, sometimes enduring fierce heckling and even missiles.

Venetia was glad that things had gone quiet. After the Mud March, when the photographs in the newspapers showed her in the front row, quite recognisable despite her large hat, there had been repercussions. If the King had intervened, as she believed, in the case of the women prisoners, it was never acknowledged, still less made public, and those close to him knew very well that he did not wish women to have the vote, and thoroughly disapproved of militancy. Sir Henry Campbell-Bannerman had supported the Dickinson Bill, but when his colleagues had talked it out, the King said to Knollys how glad he was that 'those dreadful women' had not been enfranchised. 'It would have been far more dignified,' he said, 'if the PM had not spoken on the Bill, or backed it up.' And, fixing Francis with a hard, bright eye, he added, 'I do not wish anyone connected with me, or with the Court in any way, to put themselves in a position of appearing to support these Suffragettes. It reflects badly, no matter what they may have achieved in other spheres. I cannot have it being thought that *I* have any sympathy with those women's cause.'

And so Lord Knollys, deeply embarrassed, was obliged to find a tactful and indirect way of warning Lady Overton that she had already been given as long a rope as she was going to be allowed, and that there must be no more public involvement in the women question. Venetia hated to be prevented from doing what she wanted, but she sympathised deeply with Francis for having such awkward tasks to perform. And she knew that not only would the King's disfavour with her have its effect on Overton but that it would jeopardise the children's futures.

Despite her dislike of being 'told', she was not too sorry to have a good reason to abstract herself from the movement, for she did not believe that either the sedate lobbying of the NUWSS or the stridency of the WSPU would have any effect. The time was not right: the nation as a whole was still too fiercely antipathetic to the idea. To nip any further approaches in the bud, she wrote to Mrs Fawcett saying that she could not take part in any future activities of any sort, and dropped a sufficient hint of the reason for that sharpest-witted of ladies to understand. Mrs Fawcett replied graciously, and the matter was closed. Venetia could only hope that Anne and Lizzie would prove as understanding of her position.

In the May of 1907, Regina died of what her doctor called 'nervous debility'. Over the years Henrietta had relayed to

Venetia what Teddy could describe of the symptoms, and Venetia had said it sounded like heart failure. She had no idea what 'nervous debility' was supposed to be, but there were still a great many of those old-fashioned physicians in the country, who had done their training before modern medicine was invented and had never read a thing since.

Perry was devastated. He had been devoted to Regina. They had been married for thirty-two years and he had never even thought of another woman since he had first fallen in love with her – at one of Henrietta's dinner parties, as it happened, when Henrietta was still married to Mr Fortescue, and Regina was living with them as her companion. Regina's death left him very much alone. The Red House was empty now. Bertie was in India, Lucas was attached to the diocesan staff of Bath and Wells, Peg was in chambers in Lincoln's Inn, Arthur was with Coutts's Bank in London, and all the girls were married. Only Walter, the youngest, was still dependent, but even he was away at university. To everyone's surprise he had turned out to be clever. He had gone to Eton as a Colleger, and won a scholarship to Cambridge, greatly relieving his father's mind of one worry; and by proving a prudent and scholarly undergraduate went on to relieve it of another.

Perry was too mindful of what was proper not to invite Henrietta to the funeral. Jerome suggested she go with Teddy and without him, so as not to provoke any unpleasantness, but Henrietta had pleaded with him. 'I know you mean it for tact, but it will seem as though you are keeping up the feud,' she said. 'At such a time, we all ought to show him friendship.'

'Very well. I've never wished for anything but friendship,' Jerome said. 'This foolishness has not been of my making.'

'I know.'

Perry was too distraught to want to keep up any hostility. He greeted Henrietta and Jerome vaguely, seeming almost not to know them. At any other time this might have been misunderstood as coldness, but the Comptons translated it with all possible good will. Henrietta knew it for what it was. All the time she was speaking to him, Perry had an air of abstraction, as though he were listening for some sound he expected and was afraid of missing – like someone who has long cared for an elderly relative and has lived with an ear always cocked for the bell from upstairs.

All his children except Bertie came home, with their various spouses and children, as well as his sisters and their husbands, and a vast array of old friends and neighbours. The present rector of St Mary's, Mr Chase, took the service. It was very strange to Henrietta to be in that church once again, where she had sat so many, many times listening to Mr Fortescue's rich and sonorous tones, which had so little accorded with his narrow and closed mind. Thirteen years of her life she had given him; for thirteen years she had sat in the rectory pew at least twice and sometimes five or six times a week. Now she was saying goodbye to the last of her sisters. She remembered Regina the little girl, with whom she had played in the nursery; Regina the young woman, with her harmless love of dressing-up, who had eased the loneliness of Henrietta's marriage and doted on baby Lizzie. Henrietta had helped her romance with Perry along, and she had married from the Fortescues' house. Henrietta remembered the bride, so lovely, so radiant with love and hope. And then she had disappeared into the Red House, and to a large extent out of Henrietta's life. At this last goodbye, it was the little Regina she remembered best, the close and dear companion of her Morland Place childhood, and she wept for all the sadness and distance that had come to them afterwards.

As they walked away from the graveside, Teddy, his face wet with tears, came to put his arm round her shoulder and say, 'So there's just us now, Hen. Who'd have thought it?' His voice caught a little. 'The ranks are thinning, old girl.'

She pushed down her own tears to comfort him. 'No, Teddy, don't think of it that way. Think of Polly. Think of all the children. The family's growing all the time.'

Everyone went back to the Red House for the funeral baked meats, which were lavishly provided – Perry would never stint Reggie, alive or dead, and he would always know what was due to an occasion. No-one seeing the flowing

436

wine and the array of cold food on the buffet would have guessed how bad a state his finances were in; but behind the masses of flowers that had been brought in for the occasion or sent by friends and relatives, Henrietta could see the shabbiness of things, the worn furnishings, threadbare carpet, rubbed wallpaper, and, most poignant of all, the lighter oblongs on the walls where the one or two good paintings had been sold.

Perry was surrounded by his children now, and his house was full of movement and, albeit subdued, noise; but Henrietta had a sudden vision of what it would be like for him when everyone had gone home, and he was left here all alone in this big house with no-one but the servants. She could imagine him walking from room to room with his old, near-blind spaniel tottering at his heels, always listening with that distant, half-attending look he had now for a call that never came. How empty it would seem, no sound in the house but the tick of a clock, no movement but the slow, almost invisible falling of dust.

It made her shiver to think of, and when it came time to say goodbye, she pressed his hand warmly and said, 'We've had our differences, Perry, but I hope they are forgotten now. We both loved Regina. Can't we make that reason enough to be friends from now on?'

'Oh, yes, indeed. Certainly,' Perry said; but she had no confidence he had even understood what she said to him.

As they drove away in Teddy's car, she said, 'We must make a point of trying to keep contact with him. Invite him to dinner, go and call on him.'

'Yes, poor fellow, he's very alone,' Jerome said. 'But of course he may not receive us.'

'If he won't, Teddy must work on him.'

One sultry July morning at Morland Place, Bertie crept downstairs early in his stockinged feet, his riding boots in his hand so as not to disturb anyone. The great door was still shut, and he went down the kitchen passage, hearing muted, morning voices in the kitchen, desultory talk with long spaces in between. He bypassed the kitchen and went

437

out into the yard by the buttery door. It was standing open, showing he was not the first to pass this way. Perhaps the kitchen maid had just let the kitchen cat out? He hoped no-one was there on whom he would have to expend idle chit-chat: he wanted to be alone for a little while on his last morning.

His absence from his mother's funeral was not intentional – not because he hadn't been told about it or didn't want to be there – but because of his sheer distance from England. He could not have got back in time for the funeral, and so he took a week to put his affairs in a state to be left, before beginning the long journey home. He arrived in England towards the end of June. Having attended his father and visited his sisters in the area, he had treated himself to a week at Morland Place; a week that had passed all too quickly. Time had run out. Now he had to say goodbye.

The dogs were in the yard: Kithra, who was getting old now, was walking about slowly, smelling things at his leisure with the deep, thoughtful draughts of the connoisseur. The new young hound, Fern, was trying to make him play, pawing his back, pretend-biting, bowing, her whip-tail a-lash. Both came to Bertie as soon as he appeared, Kithra walking up to thrust a nose into his hand, Fern bouncing, smiling, waggling her behind ecstatically. She lifted a forepaw to his wrist, suggesting as hard as her voicelessness could manage that it was the perfect moment to go for a walk.

Bertie was not the first in the stable. He could hear somebody moving about in there; but when he walked to the door, with Fern doing her best to trip him up, he saw it was Jessie. His face softened to a smile. 'I was hoping to ride alone,' he said, 'but this is even better.'

She was brushing Elida, and turned at the sound of his voice. 'How is it?'

'Riding with you is like being alone,' he said. 'You will ride with me, won't you?'

Her face lit up in that flattering way. 'Oh, please!' she said.

One of the most surprising things for him in this home-coming had been finding this beautiful young woman at

Morland Place. It was foolish to be surprised about children growing up, but there it was: he had almost had to check the faint, silvery scar down her cheek to be sure it was Jessie. And at their first meeting she had searched his face equally thoroughly, no doubt finding great changes in him. He was, he knew, sadly brown and leathery, and since he had been living in India he had grown a beard – it went down well with the tribesmen he often had to deal with, who thought it impious to shave. The beard had been bleached almost white in places by the sun. He had half thought of shaving it off during the long passage home, suspecting it made him look older – the journey back to India would be long enough to grow it again – but had chided himself for vanity and left it alone.

That first, long look of Jessie's had been hard to interpret: the upturned, solemn face and wide eyes had given him no clue as to whether she found him unattractive or only strange. So he had said, 'You've changed too, you know!'

And at that she had smiled – not a grown-up young lady's smile but her old urchin grin, which had given his heart a savage wrench. In that instant she had rolled back years and given him back his youth. He wanted to grab her and hug her as tightly as he could to his heart. But he had resisted *that* urge. One must be circumspect with young ladies, however well one had known them in childhood.

Now he said, 'Were you planning to go out? Where were you intending to ride?'

'Well, to tell the absolute truth, I thought you might come down early today, so I was going to get Sultan ready for you.' Sultan was Jerome's riding horse, one of the first of the home-bred horses, sired by Pasha. Jerome had put him at Bertie's service for the week. He still had Minstrel for his own use. 'I sort of hoped you might let me come with you.'

'Nothing I'd like better! Are you riding Elida?'

'Yes. Mother said yesterday she wouldn't be riding her today. Shall we go up and see the Bhutias and the three-year-olds?'

'Yes, I'd like that. Can you saddle Elida yourself?'

'Of course I can,' she said indignantly, and he laughed. 'Just being polite.'

He brushed Sultan over quickly and saddled up, and in ten minutes they were riding out over the drawbridge and into the gentle morning. It was warm already, promising a hot day; but for now the last of the morning freshness brought the scents of grass and dampness lifting from the earth, a smell combined of greenness and rich crumbly blackness, a tang of nettles and the first hint of honeysuckle – a very English smell to Bertie, which was the very essence of homesickness and longing.

A dreamy quiet lay with the last of the mist over the fields; only wood pigeons, calling liquidly from the trees, broke the silence. As the two horses turned along the track, they added their own sounds, the soft thub-dub of hoofs on the earth, the rhythmical creak of leather, the out-blown breaths as they cleared their nostrils of the night's stable dust. These sounds were poetry to the horse-lover, as the warm, sweet smell of their bodies was perfume. Long hours in the saddle in the course of running his business, often in discomfort and sometimes in danger, had not blunted his ability to ride for pleasure. In some people love of horses is so deep it is like instinct; it is an natural as breathing. Bertie had had unlimited time to think about such things up in the mountains of Bhutan and Nepal, and he concluded that the love between men and horses was of a different order, and something decreed particularly by God, to the benefit of both.

The sun was lifting, and began to burn off the milky mist. They passed out of tree-shadow and into the golden rays of young sunlight. Bertie glanced sideways at Jessie and saw how it burnished her bare head. She had braided her hair and turned the braid up neatly, as was her new style, but the sun threw into relief all the little curled and kinked hairs that would not obey the brush, so that she seemed to be wearing a halo of light. Her eyes were narrowed slightly against the brightness, and he felt a warm surge of affection for her that seemed to settle in his stomach like a hot drink. Sixteen, he thought, was a lovely age: she had a strong, young woman's body, but still the frank and eager mind of a child.

440

She felt his gaze and turned her head towards him. The low sun caught in her eyelashes turning them into a miniature golden forest. She was about to ask him why he was looking at her, but desisted in case it should stop him doing it. She loved to have him look at her, loved being with him, especially alone like this. There was something so comfortable about it – yes, like being alone; she had understood what he meant back in the stable – and yet so . . . what was the word? Thrilling? Yes, thrilling, but not in a jumpy, excitable way, more like the sort of feeling you got when galloping a good horse: doing the thing you liked best in the world to do, so that you thought about it eagerly beforehand and had the warm, deep pleasure of it for hours afterwards. Being with Bertie was like that.

When he had first arrived she had felt strange and nervous, and had hardly dared to look at him. Her memory of him had diffused as it had grown more distant, and she had not expected ever to see him again. Loving him had become something attached to her childhood, remembered but no longer acutely felt. When she looked at that old photograph it aroused nothing but a memory of affection, touched with an indeterminate, pleasant sadness.

But his sudden appearance in the flesh had thrown her completely off balance. He looked like a stranger, and yet there seemed to come off him, almost visibly like mist, a powerful aura, which was both familiar and strangely unsettling. He was so very much himself, so very *Bertie*, but that self now touched something inside her that made her quiver, like a delicate bell being struck. That burnt brown face, the beard, the extra age that had come into his lean features and body were exciting in a new way, a way that made her mouth dry; but the real him was still there underneath the newness; and it was the combination that made her vibrate in that delicious but disconcerting way.

He seemed to be able to look at her for a very long time without saying anything, and after a week she had learnt to be able to be looked at so; but she wanted to hear his voice, too, so she said, 'Tell me about Jungaipur.'

'I've told you already at least ten times,' he said.

441

'Tell me again.'

'Well, it's what they call a hill-station, about thirty miles north of Darjeeling, where they grow the best tea in the world. All my neighbours grow tea.'

'Is it very beautiful?'

'I think so.'

'Tell me about your house again,' she said, like a child asking for a familiar story.

'It's a nice white bungalow with a deep veranda all round so that I can enjoy the view in all directions – when I have the leisure. It's built on a little rise, and the gardens slope down on two sides, with steps down to the stables at the back. There are hills all around me, and everything is very green, and in the morning the air is so fresh that it jumps into your lungs and you feel as if you've never breathed before in your life. You feel that ordinary breathing ought to have a different name because it's so little like it. But that's nothing to what the air is like up in the mountains.'

Jessie's face was entranced; she was seeing it all in her mind's eye. 'Tell about the mountains.'

'Oh, they are always there in the background. Sometimes they seem to fade into the sky, so that you can only see a faint outline of them. They are so blue they seem to be transparent – you think you're looking at the sky through them. Then you think that perhaps they are asleep and gone on a long dream journey to another world. At other times they are so sharp and strong they look suddenly near, and you feel you could almost reach out and touch them. Then they seem awake and busy, and you wonder what they are hatching up. They are such a presence, you see, that you feel they are alive.'

'You miss them, don't you?' she said, looking at him.

'It's so very different here. Sometimes I half think I'm back home in India and dreaming. And then, at other times, England is so near and dear that the other place seems like a dream.'

He told her again about his early-morning rides, on his favourite pony, Nanda – small and strong like all Bhutias, clever and nimble with 'eyes in his feet', as the saying was.

442

Bertie was as fond of him as he had been of dear old Dolly, left behind in Africa. Together they would climb the steep hills that rose above the station. 'No path, however steep, ever daunts him. He's like a mountain goat.' There was a place at the top of one hill that he called the Vista, because from it he had an uninterrupted view of the country for miles around, the wooded hills and deep green valleys, and beyond that the dark, untouched jungle, all bounded by the semicircle of glittering snow-clad mountains, the Himalayas.

'We start up the steep climb in the early light, and the air has that tang that makes you gulp it down like water. You feel it cool on your face, as if it comes straight from the mountains, as if it were the touch of their breath. The shadows are still cold, but in the distance you can see the snows stained with streaks of pink and yellow and orange – it's quite amazingly beautiful. And then as the sun rises the pink slips down and the snows gradually lose that rose-blush and become dazzlingly white, like a great carpet of crushed diamonds.

'We try to get to the Vista just as the sun comes up, so that we can witness that transformation. I sit down on the turf and watch it. There's a place with wonderful moss as thick and soft as a cushion where I like to sit. And as the air warms you can smell the pine woods, and the crickets begin to chirrup.'

'It sounds wonderful,' Jessie said softly, not to break the dream.

'It's the most beautiful sight on earth, I think.'

'Do you ever take anyone else up there?' she asked.

'No, it's my special, private place. Just Nanda and I. I think he likes it as much as I do – he stands looking at the view just like a person.' He smiled at her. 'I'd take you, if you were there. You wouldn't disturb the moment. You'd know not to chatter or fidget.'

'I wish I could see it!' she said fervently.

Earlier in the week he might have said lightly, 'Perhaps you will one day,' meaning nothing very much by it. But now, on the verge of leaving, he said nothing. They rode in silence for a while, and he was very conscious of her beside him. There seemed so little time left, he felt they ought to be talking. He said, 'Tell me about school.'

'Oh, there's nothing to tell,' she said. 'It's finished now, anyway.'

'You aren't going back?'

'I don't want to be a teacher, so there's no point.'

'What will you do, then?'

'I don't know. It hasn't been decided yet. I know Dad and Mother have been talking about it. Cousin Venetia's sending Violet to a finishing-school for six months, and they were wondering whether to send me with her, but I'm not sure they can afford it.'

'Would you like to go?'

'I'd like to see abroad, and I like being with Violet. I'd like to travel. But I'm not sure a finishing-school wouldn't be wasted on me. Vi's going to have a proper coming-out next year, but I shan't be a débutante, so I don't really need finishing.'

'I should think not! You're perfect as you are. I should hate to see you given artificial manners like so many girls one sees.'

She looked at him consideringly, but said only, 'I'm something of a problem, you see. The boys are all settled now, but no-one really knows what to do with me.'

Jack was working for a marine engineering company in Southampton; Robbie, who was lazy and had no particular inclination in any direction, had been found a safe berth by Teddy in a bank in York; and dreamy Frank, who was eighteen, would be going to university in the autumn. He had turned out to have the brains of the family, and he was going to read mathematics at University College London and lodge with Lizzie and Ashley. Jerome would have liked him to go to Oxford, but felt he couldn't afford it; and Frank had said simply that he didn't mind, because he was going to university to study, not for fun.

'You'll get married,' Bertie suggested, hopeless of any other answer.

'I suppose so. I suppose that's what happens to girls,' Jessie said. He searched her voice for meaning, but it seemed quite neutral, not angry, frustrated or pleased. It was just a fact of life, she seemed to imply. Then she went on, 'Dad's threatening me with riding side-saddle this winter. He says when I'm seventeen I'll have to give up being a hoyden, at least in public. Well, I did hunt side-saddle twice last winter, when we went to the big meets, but the rest of the time I rode across. I know what Dad thinks – he thinks no-one will want to marry me if I don't ride side-saddle, and he'll never get rid of me. But Mother says I can still ride as I please when it's just on our own land and there's no-one to see me. No-one who matters, that is. Do you think it's horrible for a female to ride like this?'

She was wearing a skirt over her breeches and boots, which was split front and back so that it hung down on either side, concealing her legs – a contrivance of Henrietta, who felt tenderly towards her daughter, understanding her liking of freedom and wanting her to enjoy it as long as possible. Bertie thought she looked very nice; but he understood Jerome's concerns. She was still, just, a girl, but certainly if she were any older it would look odd and – yes – wrong.

'Not horrible,' he said, 'but I think your father's right. For a grown lady to ride like that would shock some people and might give rise to – well, improper thoughts. It may seem silly to you now, but it is important what people think of you when you're just starting out in life. You need to make the right impression.'

She smiled wickedly. 'As you did?'

He smiled back. 'It's different for boys. But whatever you do, don't take me for an example!'

They reached the paddock where the Bhutia mares grazed, each with her new foal at foot. The mares lifted their muzzles and whickered when they discovered it was Jessie. She jumped down, tied Elida to the fence, and climbed nimbly over to meet their soft, enquiring muzzles with pieces of apple – the last of the stores, too wrinkled for human consumption. The foals were growing used to her already, though they regarded Bertie with suspicion and hid behind their mothers when he got near. They were woolly, mouse-coated toys with absurdly

445

long legs, and seemed near identical to Bertie, but Jessie had pointed one out and said, 'He's going to be the best, I think. He's the pick of the whole bunch so far.'

The Bhutias were out in the furthest paddock. They rode back a different way so as to pass the paddock where the three-year olds were grazing, so that Jessie could show him, again, the polo ponies who were just beginning their training and were her particular pride and concern. They, too, came hurrying towards her as soon as she dismounted, and were given their share of her pocketful of apple pieces.

'They're looking very good,' Bertie said, not for the first time. 'It's the Arabian blood that makes the difference. I'd like to get an Arabian stallion for my own mares, but at the moment that's out of the question. One day, perhaps. You can see how it gives them the additional height, and the fineness.'

Jessie, absently caressing her favourite of the four, considered his words. 'You mean to stay on there, in India, then?' she said carefully. 'Won't you ever come back?'

'I don't know,' he said. 'I suppose I'll have to come back when the gov'nor dies, at least to settle things. But then – well, I don't suppose there'll be much left but debts. I'm not going to be able to live a life of idleness, that's for sure. And if I'm going to breed horses for a living, I might as well do it in India. I can live better there than here.'

'Better?' she queried.

'In more luxury, at any rate – I couldn't afford a place like mine at Jungaipur here in England, or as big a house or as many servants. And also there's a freedom over there I couldn't have here.'

'And adventures,' she added.

He had told her about some of them, dangerous rides over the passes, suspicious and sometimes hostile tribesmen, narrow escapes from natural hazards, from falls, the weather, and from Sikkim armed with long curving knives. He had had encounters with bandits and horse-thieves, some from as far away as Kashmir or the Afghan border – the mountain men travelled astonishing distances without thinking twice about it.

He had also told her a little of other side of his life, of the planters and army officers, of parties and dances, of polo matches in Darjeeling and Calcutta, of dinners and shoots and the other very British pleasures of the expatriates. He had shown photographs of his life over there, and Jessie had listened hard and examined the pictures with great attention, to see if there were any mention or sign of a special attachment; but most of the photographs were of scenery and horses. Those taken in civilised surroundings showed his or other people's bungalows or the grander houses in the cities, always with native people in the background, servants and syces. When a white lady appeared at all, she was spoken of casually as the wife of the fellow standing next to her, Captain Williams of the Lancers or Mr Faversham the tea-planter. When Bertie spoke of friends, it was always men or married couples he mentioned. She had paid particular notice to any mention of the bungalow, but it seemed that when he was there he lived alone, apart from native servants.

The sun was fully up now, and it was growing hot. It was going to be another lovely day. The milkiness had cleared from the sky, and it was an intense chicory blue, bright as wet paint, cloudless from horizon to horizon.

'It must be breakfast time,' Bertie said, pulling out his watch. 'I'm starving.'

'Me too,' Jessie said.

'We'd better be getting back.'

They mounted and set off homewards. Their last ride together, Jessie thought. She felt a sharp pang. The time had gone so quickly. There was a desperate need to notice and savour every second, so that she would be able to remember it properly afterwards. 'What time will you have to leave?'

'I must be on the two o'clock train,' he said. He, too, was regretting the time running out. Once they'd breakfasted and he'd packed, it would be practically time to go.

'Do you really have to? Couldn't you stay a bit longer?'

'I wish I could. But there are things I have to do, and there's only a few days to do them before my boat sails. As it is, I won't have time to visit Lucas as I meant to. He'll

447

have to make do with a letter. I don't suppose he'll mind, really – and I wanted to spend as much time here as possible.'

Jessie nodded, her throat suddenly tight. She bent her head so he wouldn't see the tears that had jumped to her eyes.

He looked across at her, and a surge of tenderness swept through him. 'I shall miss you,' he said. Her head stayed down. 'I shall miss Morland Place and everyone here, but you most of all.'

At that she lifted her head swiftly, and mastered her voice enough to say passionately, 'Take me with you!' The moment she said it she regretted it, for she saw the negative in his face before he spoke.

He said, 'I can't. I wish I could, but it's impossible.'

Well, she was embarrassed now; she could hardly make it worse. '*Why* is it?'

'The life I live – it's not the life for a female. It's hard enough for the tea-planters' families, on the hill stations, but I'm away a great deal, up in the mountains, where it's really dangerous and uncomfortable. It would be impossible.'

She said nothing more. He had hesitated before he said all that, as if it were not the real reason. She didn't now want to know the real reason. She only wanted to live with every sense each moment of this last time of being alone with him.

They came in sight of the house and she reined Elida and slid down. 'I'm going to walk from here, to make sure she's cool,' she said. Bertie dismounted too. He slipped Sultan's reins over his arm and stood before her, looking down searchingly, as though to fix her in his memory. 'I *shall* miss you,' he said.

She looked up into his face, and her stomach seemed to drop away, leaving a hollowness. Everything inside her seemed to be trembling rapidly and uncontrollably. She found a voice, but it was faint. 'I'll miss *you*, also.'

Still he looked down at her without speaking, and for one desperate moment she thought he was going to say that he would take her with him after all. But he didn't. After a long moment he bent his head and kissed her, laying his lips lightly on hers. She closed her eyes and lived the moment with everything she had. His lips were firm and smooth, his breath in her nostrils was sweet. She yearned for more, to be closer, sensing that he felt it too, hoping that at any moment his control would break. Her lips trembled under his, his warmth and the scent of him enveloped her; her tears were on his skin, warm and secret.

But it lasted only an instant. The kiss ended, he straightened up, and she swayed a little and opened her eyes, coming to her balance. She looked up at him, and cried inside, 'Oh, take me with you!' but she made no sound. She thought he was going to say goodbye, but he only gave her a faint, troubled smile, and turned to face home. They walked side by side, leading the horses, down towards the house, without speaking.

After that it was all noise and movement. The grooms were in the yard and took the horses from them, and when they stepped into the great hall a maid told them breakfast was ready and there was only just time to wash their hands before going in to join the family. Jerome and Henrietta and Teddy were all there, and Polly, cross that they had gone out riding without her, and Frank, and even Robbie, who, as it was Saturday, had been given the morning off from the bank for the occasion. The breakfast sideboard was laden with a specially wide array – sausages, bacon, fried eggs, cold ham, even kidneys and mushrooms – but though Jessie was usually a good eater, especially when she had been up early and out riding since dawn, her appetite was unaccountably gone. Fortunately no-one seemed to notice. She felt raw inside with the thought of Bertie's leaving, and was afraid to speak, in case it made her sob. Even her cup of tea suddenly reminded her of Jungaipur, and made her eyes fill with tears.

The rest of the morning fled away, and there were no more moments of being alone with Bertie. In the crowd of Morlands and Comptons, she kept herself in the background where she could look at him as much as possible without having to speak. The time ran out like sand, and suddenly it was all gone, the motor-car was at the door, and Bertie's bags were being taken out. Henrietta was going with him to the station. Jessie wanted to ask to go too, but at the last minute did not, feeling she could not bear to be with him and *not* alone, have him *not* look at her as he had been doing – or, rather, not doing – since they had got back from their ride. She said a pale goodbye in chorus with everyone else as he climbed into the car behind Simmons, and he was smiling an everyone-smile and saying a goodbye that was for all of them. Only at the last moment as the motor-car began to move he looked at her and met her eyes for a moment; and then they were gone.

As the rest of the family turned away to go in and about their business, Jessie stood where she was, feeling that her heart was literally breaking, that it would never have the strength for her to move again. The bright July sunshine fell stupidly through the clear air, as if anyone cared that it was a lovely day, *now*, when he was gone. Kithra came and nudged her and swung his tail and, getting no response, wandered off to his sunny corner where he liked to lie basking like a big cat.

And then an arm came down over Jessie's shoulder and she jumped. It was her father.

'Well, love,' he said. He squeezed her gently, and she swayed to lean against him lightly, comforted a little by his body. In fact, Jerome had noted the downcast eyes, trembling lips and lack of appetite at breakfast. He thought he had detected through the week the symptoms of that old 'crush' reviving itself, though Jessie was old enough not to be so obvious about it as she had been at eleven. When he asked Henrietta what she thought about it, she had said she thought Jessie was over it: Bertie was just a big brother to her. But Jerome wondered. And he had wondered once or twice what Bertie thought about Jessie. He had caught an expression of surprise in Bertie's eyes once or twice at how Jessie had changed. Well, it was just a good thing that Bertie knew it would never do to be dragging Jessie away to a place like that, where she would have to live alone with nothing but the servants for a good part of the year. He, Jerome, would never have consented, could not have borne to have

450

her taken so far away. And there was something else. There was a native woman in the photographs of the bungalow, who always seemed to stand a little apart from the other servants. Once when Jerome had asked who she was, Bertie had hesitated an instant before saying that she was the house-keeper. That little breath of a pause had seemed significant to him. Well, one couldn't expect a red-blooded male to stay celibate for ever. These little arrangements were not unusual, and provided there was consent and generosity on both sides, no-one was hurt by them. But it was a good thing that Jessie had never seemed to draw any conclusions.

She'd get over him, as she had before, Jerome thought. All she needed was time, and perhaps a little something to help her forget. He said, 'I've been thinking. You know I've said that you really must start riding side-saddle.'

'Yes, Dad,' she said in a dull, absent tone.

'Well, if you're going to look like a lady, you really ought to have a lady's horse of your own. There are the two nice four-year-olds that we bred by Pasha out of the thorough-bred mare.'

'Hotspur and Prince?' she said, a trace of interest germi-nating in her voice.

'Yes. How would you like to take your choice of them, and start breaking him to side-saddle?'

'You mean, I could have one for my own?'

'That's what I mean. You can school him just the way you like, and if you start now you could be hunting him this winter. How would that be?'

She turned her face up to him, the sadness still there, but the beginning of pleasure lightening it just a little. 'Oh, Dad, that would be lovely,' she said.

'You can try them both out this afternoon. I'll come up with you and bring them in to Twelvetrees, and then I can watch you try them out in the home paddock and give you my opinion – if that's of any interest to you.'

'Of course it is! Oh, Dad, you are so nice!' She reached up and kissed his cheek.

He smiled and said, 'It will be a project for you to concentrate on. You need to be doing something now you've

451

left school – not just mooning around. It will take your mind off.'

She blushed a little and looked away, embarrassed that he had fathomed her secret. But it was comforting, too, to know he sympathised, and she knew he was too tactful ever to betray her, or even to refer directly to it.

'How will I try them out?' she said, in a nearly normal voice. 'I won't be able to try them side-saddle until they've been broken to it.'

'Oh, I think I can bear to see you ride across one more time,' he said. He turned her towards the house. 'Once you and the horse are both ready, we'll have to get you fitted out with a proper lady's habit. A grown-up one – black, I think. Black suits you. With a white stock. You'll look rather splendid.'

'And a top hat?' Jessie asked.

'A top hat with a veil,' he affirmed. Talking pleasantly, they went in.

Lizzie had fallen in love with Ashley at first sight, and now, approaching their tenth anniversary, she loved him still, with a deeper, richer love than that first trembling passion, built solidly upon common tastes and experiences, the satisfying woof and warp of daily life, marriage and child-rearing. She had been happy with her husband, her two dear little boys, her nice house, and ordinary domestic things had kept her pleasantly occupied. She enjoyed, too, her visits with Ashley to the theatre and concert halls, the friendships they had developed; the annual holiday at Morland Place, and the sips and glimpses of a higher life she had when invited by Venetia to visit or dine.

So when Lady Anne Farraline began to bring Lizzie news of the WSPU on a regular basis, she was not working on a discontented or restless housewife. Still, Lizzie was clever. She had been educated in a strongly intellectual tradition first by her father and later when she attended the North London Collegiate, the most academic of girls' schools.

'All that education,' Anne would say sometimes. 'Did you never want to use it?'

And Lizzie would make some vague answer. It was hard to remember at thirty-five exactly how she had felt at eighteen, but she knew as a fact that Jerome would have paid for her to go to Cambridge had she asked for it. Her best friend, Mary Paget, had gone there and urged her to go too. But she had not asked to go. Perhaps she had felt it would be a waste of time to do all that studying when it could not result in a degree; or that it was pointless to educate herself more highly when there was no prospect of applying it except as a teacher. Mary Paget had taught for a while before she married. Marriage seemed to be the true end for a woman; and Lizzie at eighteen, like many a girl before her, had been longing for love. She had looked for it in the wrong place at first – Dodie, who had betrayed her so cruelly. Then came Papa's crash, and she had supposed she would be the penniless daughter-at-home for the rest of her life. But Ashley had come like a knight on a white horse to rescue her (the horse was a brown hireling, as she recollected, but he had looked quite astonishingly noble on it all the same) and marriage and motherhood had followed.

She had no regrets, and told Anne so.

'All the same,' Anne said, 'you do have a mind, and it must want exercise sometimes. Now your boys are at school and your domestic duties are so few, don't you long for something to get your teeth into?'

And Lizzie admitted that it was so. She was not restless or discontented, but she thought it would be fun to have a little work to do, and an aim in life. Ashley had his job, so why shouldn't she have hers? He believed that men and women were equals, and ought to be treated equally, so he couldn't possibly object.

'But what is it you want to do, darling?' he asked her, at the end of her long preamble.

'The WSPU is going to start up a monthly newspaper, and it will need staff to research and collate and typewrite and edit the material. I should like to be one of them.'

She looked at him so eagerly and doubtfully that he smiled. 'Did you think I would object? It seems respectable enough work. I presume it would not take up all your time?'

'Oh, I don't expect so,' Lizzie said. 'You don't mind, then? I thought perhaps you might think taking a job was – well – not ladylike.'

'But this is work for a cause. That's different. I shouldn't care to see you go out to work for money, of course, but this is using your abilities for something you believe in.'

'*We* believe in.'

'Of course. Do it by all means, dear, as long as it doesn't interfere with your household duties or the boys' welfare.'

'Oh, it won't. I'll see to that. Thank you, Ashley! You are a pattern of a man and a splendid husband!'

'You sound like an advertisement. Will you recommend me to others?'

'If there were more than one of you I might. But that, of course, is impossible. How could there be more than one nonpareil?' He laughed and kissed the end of her nose, and was going back to his newspaper when she said, 'There is one more thing.' He looked up enquiringly. 'I shall have to learn to typewrite. They say it isn't very difficult to learn, and there is a school that teaches it in Oxford Street – a course of daily lessons. Might I have two guineas for the fee?'

'Ha! You saved the best till last, then. Yes, I don't see why not. Typewriting is a useful skill. One day when I stand for Parliament you will be able to typewrite my speeches for me.'

Lizzie's eyes brightened. 'Do you think of standing, then? Oh, Ashley, that would be wonderful!'

'I don't think they'd have me, love,' he said gently. 'I'm a foreign national.'

'Oh! I'd forgotten. You seem so English now. You don't even have an accent any more.'

'You're firmly convinced, of course, that *you* don't have an accent?'

'Of course not, I'm English,' she said. 'English people don't have accents, only foreigners.'

Apart from the Pankhurst mother and daughters, the leading lights of the WSPU were the Pethick Lawrences. *She* had been born Miss Pethick – like Mrs Pankhurst, her

Christian name was Emmeline – and was another of those Cornish Quakers like the Miss Hobhouse who had exposed the camps in South Africa. She came from a wealthy family in Weston-super-Mare. *He* was Frederick Lawrence, a brilliant man, independently wealthy and a qualified barrister, who had devoted his life to Socialism and good works. They had met in the East End where both were involved in mission work in the slums. When they married, the putting together of their two names signalled their belief in the equality of the sexes.

As well as their Surrey home the Pethick Lawrences had a large flat at 4 Clement's Inn, above the offices of the *Labour Record and Review*, a Socialist monthly that he edited. It was this flat which had become the headquarters of the WSPU – now a large and thriving organisation, with seventy branches throughout the country. Here the regular Union administration was carried out, the campaigns were planned, leaflets and handbills were composed, visitors received, organisers exhorted and instructed, journalists briefed.

And here now the new paper *Votes for Women* was to be produced. It was the busiest place Lizzie had ever been in, and sometimes there was so much going on that she could hardly hear herself think. But it was enormously stimulating. Very soon she found herself able to typewrite an article and listen to two conversations at the same time, and even on occasion answer the telephone and talk to the caller while continuing to typewrite with the other hand. She learnt so much about the movement, politics and the law that she felt her mind stretching like a dog waking from sleep. The treatment of women that she learnt about was so abominable and unfair that she couldn't understand why the whole nation was not up in arms about it.

The first issue of *Votes for Women* had a very striking cover, a picture of the Houses of Parliament with a woman brooding over it, called 'The Haunted House'. The paper was intended to keep workers and supporters informed about the movement and to attract new supporters with intelligent and persuasive articles. There were pieces on policy and the history of the movement, reports from local

455

branches, extracts from the press, and articles by eminent writers and thinkers. Much of what Lizzie was given to type-write made her reflect, and realise that the world had changed dramatically in her own short lifetime. She found she didn't know as much as she thought she did about the way other people lived.

In one early issue, for instance, she found herself typing:

The homes must be comparatively few in which three or four maiden daughters live on with their parents. The last quarter of a century has seen the gradual uprising of the latchkey girl, who is determined to make her own living and make her own way in life. There has grown up a race of bachelor girls in flats who live on caramels and sausages. We have most decidedly changed for the better. The majority of unmarried girls now have their own employment, and as long as they do not absolutely depend on it for their bread they do very well.

When she discussed this with Anne, who was at the offices almost every day, Anne said, 'Yes, things are much easier now. I remember how hard it was for me to get permission to live in London. My brother was horrified, even though I was over twenty-one and independently wealthy.'

'But who are all these latchkey girls?' Lizzie said. 'I'm sure my mother wouldn't allow my sister Jessie to live alone, much less come and do it in London. If I had a daughter, I'm not sure I'd be happy about it either.'

'Oh, but it's largely a class thing,' Anne said. 'These are middle-class girls without great marriage expectations. They don't have to be kept in wrappers for the market.'

'But I thought we were middle class.'

Anne laughed. 'No, dear, you are old country gentry. There is always a time lapse before old families catch up with new ideas.'

From a slow start Lizzie became a very fast typewriter, and from a few hours a week, the WSPU work began to take up more and more time. She was naturally drawn into discussions with the committee and organisers who, finding she had a good mind, were glad to get her more involved. The Pethick Lawrences invited her to do some of the editing on the paper, and another task she was given – a tribute to her intellectual capacities – was to read the newspapers and extract anything of interest to the movement, either for collection in the files, for précis or full quotation in the paper, or for future action.

Naturally Lizzie took many of the news ideas and information home, and Ashley was regaled with them in the evenings. His own work was very demanding and he sometimes wished he could have had something more relaxing or jolly to greet him when he got home than the women question; but he was genuinely in support of the principles of the Cause, and he was too just to believe that only his interests should be considered in the house. Only once did he complain, when Lizzie had forgotten to order the joint as requested to by the cook, so when she got home from Clement's Inn only five minutes before Ashley, a maid had to be sent out to the butcher, and he was kept waiting an hour for his dinner.

'I'm sorry,' she said. 'I was just so busy that I forgot.'

'You did say that this work would not interfere with your household duties, and I do think it's not much to ask, to be fed when I come home from a day's hard work.'

It was a very mild rebuke, but Lizzie had been steeping all day in an atmosphere of female resentment, and she said sharply, 'I have been working hard too, and on something really important. But I suppose nothing a mere woman could do could matter as much as a man's dinner!'

Ashley's eyebrows drew down to a frown. 'I never thought I'd hear you speak like that to me.'

'I never thought *you* would turn out to be a tyrant and an oppressor.'

'How am I an oppressor?' he said, genuinely astonished.

'You think that what you do is more important than what I do, just because you're a man.'

'What I do earns the money that provides all this,' he said, waving a hand to indicate the house and everything in

457

it. 'Without my salary you would not have the leisure to help out at Clement's Inn. I was happy for you to do it, but if it is teaching you to abuse your own poor hard-working husband and call him vile names, I am sorry you ever went there.'

At that Lizzie was taken aback, and thought about what she had said. She was ashamed and went to him, her eyes full of tears. 'I'm sorry. Please forgive me, dearest Ashley! There never was a husband less like a tyrant.'

He kissed her and held her against him. 'Of course I forgive you. But I do hope this business isn't going to poison your mind.'

'No, no, it won't. It's just that being in that hive of activity all day made me over-excited. The words fly off one's tongue after a while without one's volition.'

'You are intelligent enough to keep a sense of proportion about things.'

'Yes, of course, and I will, I promise.' She released herself so that she could look up at him. 'But, Ashley, don't fall into the error of thinking that the situation is not serious. Women are treated as a different class of creature – not as the female of the human species but as if they were some kind of strange domestic animal. And so much of it is engrained and unthinking that it's hard to make the mass of men – sometimes even women – see it. *I* must keep a sense of proportion – but so must you. I must calm down, but you must – what's the opposite of calm down, I wonder?'

'Fizz up,' he said solemnly. 'Like liver pills.'

So her serious address ended in laughter, and they were friends again. She took care after that to make sure that all the necessary household orders were given before she set off for Clement's Inn. Ashley, to show his complete lack of qualification as a tyrant, went one better and told her that they could afford to engage a housekeeper. Lizzie was touched, but, feeling a little guilty, said it wasn't necessary. She did, however, give her senior housemaid instructions to ring her up at Clement's Inn on the telephone if there were any household problems during the day that the staff could not solve.

★ ★ ★

In November 1907 Sir Henry Campbell-Bannerman suffered a heart-attack. It was not fatal, but he was too ill to continue with government business, and the King advised him to convalesce in Biarritz. Sir Henry loved France: he had sometimes taken a return ticket on the cross-Channel steamer just to have luncheon in Calais. He had attended the King at Biarritz during his annual holiday each year, and the sight of the two of them strolling along in comfortable conversation, with the King's little dog Caesar running along in front of them, was one of the noted sights of the resort. Despite their differences of opinion they had got on well from the beginning, and there was liking and admiration between them.

In Sir Henry's absence, Asquith, as Chancellor of the Exchequer, took over the running of the Government.

'Oh dear, does that mean that he will become Prime Minister if Henry has to retire?' Venetia asked Francis Knollys one day at Windsor. 'I really can't like him, try as I might.'

'I *like* him,' Francis said, 'and I like Mrs Asquith – though I know many people don't – but I don't think he is quite the right stamp of man for Prime Minister.'

'I'm glad to hear you say it. Who do you favour, then?'

'Grey is obviously the best man for the job,' said Francis. 'The King could send for him and overrule his personal objections. I know HM doesn't like Asquith. He said the other day he thought him deplorably common, not to say vulgar.'

'I wouldn't go so far as that,' Venetia said, 'but he certainly doesn't have the conciliatory manners that make Henry such good company.'

'Yes, I doubt whether Asquith will be able to hold together all the disparate parts of the Liberal Party. People underestimate Campbell-Bannerman because he seems so easygoing, but who else could have kept the Government in order as he has? That takes great skill. I tell you, Venetia, if anything happens to him, the party will go to smash in six months.'

The women's movements were not too pleased, either, at

459

the idea that H. H. Asquith might become Prime Minister. Assassin Asquith – as he had been nicknamed since the death of two miners during the Miners' Strike of 1893 when he was Home Secretary – was implacably opposed to the enfranchisement of women. Campbell-Bannerman favoured the Cause, was a radical at heart and was becoming more so with every year. Once the backlog of reforms the Liberals had stored up during their years in opposition were got through, there was every hope that he would turn his genial, subtle but effective influence to improving the woman's lot. But if he were to die or retire, the Cause would suffer a setback. Asquith would set his face sternly against them; and Grey or Morley, the only other possible choices, were hardly better. That winter, to the prayers of his friends were added those of the supporters of the Cause everywhere that Sir Henry Campbell-Bannerman might fully recover.

CHAPTER FOURTEEN

In January 1908, decent people everywhere were shocked to learn that Mrs Pankhurst had been badly beaten while campaigning during a by-election in Newton Abbot.

It was a Liberal stronghold, and the Liberals were so sure of winning it they had printed a mock mourning card in memory of their opponents 'who fell asleep at Mid-Devon on January 7th, 1908'. Campaigning in Mid-Devon had always been hearty, and Liberals traditionally disrupted Conservative and Unionist rallies by rowdy heckling, pelting the speakers with eggs and rotten vegetables, and once by abducting the candidate and shutting him up in a cage – all accepted ploys, by comparison with which the Suffragettes' activities paled into insignificance.

But the WSPU campaign, urging people to vote against the Government, was surprisingly successful, and when the result was announced, the Liberals stood astounded to hear that the Unionist had won by 1280 votes. The police hustled the successful candidate away and escorted him out of town for his own safety, while the Liberals gathered in angry muttering groups, looking for someone to blame.

Mrs Pankhurst and another leading Suffragette, Mrs Martel, were walking back to their lodgings when they came upon a group of young working men wearing red rosettes. At the sight of the women someone yelled, 'They did it! Those women did it! Grab 'em!' The crowd rushed forward with a roar of anger, pelting the two ladies with eggs and sods of earth. They turned and fled. They ran into a grocer's shop for shelter, and the grocer's wife, frightened, and shocked that ladies should be so treated, took them in and locked the door after them. The mob outside howled and battered at it so violently they seemed sure to break in and wreck the shop. Mrs Pankhurst asked if there was a back way out. She and Mrs Martel were let out into a yard which gave onto a side alley, but part of the mob had already gathered at the back gate, and as soon as it was unlocked they rushed in, seized the women and began beating them with their fists. Mrs Martel managed to escape back into the shop; Mrs Pankhurst fell to the ground, dazed and bleeding, and was sure she was going to be killed; but the police arrived in the nick of time and forced a way through. Mrs Pankhurst was carried unconscious into the shop, and the police guarded it for two hours until they considered it was safe for the women to leave.

'You see!' Anne said excitedly to Venetia, when she and Lizzie were taking tea one day at Manchester Square. 'That is the sort of treatment handed out to women. Two unarmed women – ladies, not even youthful – beaten by a great mob of men.'

'It's appalling,' Venetia said, shaken by the story. How had England come to this? Violence at the hustings was not unusual, but for men to attack women in that way – it was like the end of civilisation.

'And was anyone arrested for it?' Anne went on. 'Did anyone go to prison? Yet a Suffragette gets sent down for nothing more than trying to make a speech! And now the Liberals are stopping any of us going to their meetings at all by refusing to sell us tickets – by order of Asquith the Assassin, no less!'

'I think the Liberals rather overreached themselves in Aberdeen. It will have done them no good,' Venetia said.

In Aberdeen, Asquith had been addressing a rally on franchise reform. The seating in the hall had been allocated to specially selected ticket holders, so all was going peacefully until one of the local dignitaries on the platform, a clergyman, rose to propose an amendment on women's suffrage. Asquith was clearly put out, and three burly stewards at once seized the clergyman and hustled him roughly from the hall. A Liberal woman who voiced an objection to this treatment of a man of the cloth was similarly ejected.

'Have you seen what the papers are saying about it?' said Venetia. 'They're saying that many people must have left the hall with the feeling that the suffragists had the best of it, that they had entered their protest constitutionally and respectfully but were refused a hearing. That sort of thing won't do the Government or the Party any good.'

'But what harm will it do them?' Anne said. 'One half-sympathetic report, against all the rest of the ridicule and lies poured on us by the press!'

'It adds up. Gradually, over time, there is a wearing-away of resistance—'

Anne interrupted, 'We've been wearing away for forty years and we've got nowhere. And now Asquith looks like being in charge permanently.'

'I thought the Prime Minister was back in Downing Street?' Lizzie said.

'Yes, but for how long? He's a sick man, isn't he, Venetia?' Anne said. 'And when he goes, it will be Asquith, and that will set us back years. We've got to raise our stake.'

'Well, for goodness' sake be careful,' Venetia said. 'You don't want to end up in prison, do you?'

When Anne and Lizzie left some time later, the former seemed rather thoughtful. Out in the street, she said, 'Have you time to come to my house? I've something I want to talk to you about.'

Lizzie said, 'Oh dear. I'm sorry, but I must be back for the boys when they come home from school. It's the cook's half day off, and the maids will have to get dinner, so they won't have time to look after Martial and Rupert.'

'No matter, then,' Anne said. 'I'll come home with you, and we can talk on the way. Look, here comes a cab – shall we take it?'

She hailed the approaching motor-cab and they climbed in. Lizzie hardly ever took a cab of any sort, preferring to walk when she could, and otherwise taking the bus or tube; but a motor-cab was a new experience for her. It made her realise suddenly how the composition of the London traffic had changed in the last few years. Despite her words, Anne did not seem to want to talk, being sunk in thought, so Lizzie was free to look out of the window. She counted the horse-traffic as against the motor-traffic. The former was still the majority, but only just. As well as private motors there were motor-cabs and motor-vans, and even motor-buses now, though they were terribly unreliable and therefore not popular. It seemed you hardly ever saw a motor-bus moving – they were either waiting at bus-stops, stalled in traffic, or broken down waiting for an engineer.

Lizzie remembered her mother telling her, back when they all lived in London, that the working life of an omnibus horse was only four years, because of the strain put on them by the frequent stopping and starting. They could only work for three hours a day and had to have one day off in four, so a vast number was needed to operate even a single route. Horses were therefore the most expensive component of an omnibus company's operating costs, and it would not be surprising if the companies wanted to change to motors. The horses worked in couples, she remembered, and were paired for life – like swans, she thought with a smile – and were housed in vast stables at the ends of routes, often built over several storeys. She had read somewhere that there were over fifty thousand horses in service in London – what a mountain of droppings must have to be moved every day! – though who had counted them all was not made plain. But given the terribly short life of the bus horse, she thought it would be a good thing if someone could invent a reliable motor-bus, even if it meant that someone somewhere would go short of fertiliser as a result. She had heard people say that replacing horses with motors would get rid of the smell of manure that always haunted London, but for herself she thought the smell of motor-vehicles was much worse. At least dung was a natural thing, and man had been smelling it for centuries without apparent harm.

Anne at last interrupted these idle thoughts by saying, 'I wonder if you can guess what I've been thinking?'

'Oh – er – no, not at all,' Lizzie said, hoping Anne would

464

not ask to know what had just been in *her* mind. Dung was hardly an elevated subject.

Anne fixed her burning blue gaze on her. She always looked at her most beautiful when she was excited. 'That we must *do* something for the Cause – you and I. Something more than sending out letters and attending meetings. Apart from one or two like Christabel, it's always Annie Kenney and the working women who take the direct action, and we know that our beloved government won't take any notice of them. But if some of us – rich women and middle-class women, people with good names and from good homes – got involved, they would have to take notice.'

'What do you mean by "involved"?' Lizzie asked, suspecting a bomb was about to go off beside her.

'We must do something to get ourselves sent to prison,' Anne said. 'Can you imagine the fuss in the newspapers if Lady Anne Farraline and Mrs Ashley Morland were put up in the magistrate's court and sentenced to two weeks in Holloway?'

'They might take notice of Lady Anne Farraline's name, but who would know who Mrs Ashley Morland was?'

'Oh, they'd know that she was a cousin both of Lady Anne *and* the Countess of Overton. They would certainly know that, because the WSPU would make sure they were told.'

'But, Anne, we mustn't involve Venetia. You know she's in a delicate position.'

'We won't *involve* her, but we can't help the fact that she is a relation, simply because it *is* a fact.'

Now it came home to Lizzie that Anne was really serious, and she began to think about the consequences. To go to gaol would be bad enough – terrifying thought to a gently bred, respectable woman – but what about afterwards? 'There would be such a fuss, and so much trouble,' she began hesitantly.

'Of course there will be – that's the whole point! We've got to make as much fuss as possible, in as elevated a sphere as possible. People like Asquith and Grey can ignore our demands because they can slip away into their comfortable

465

world of privilege where ordinary women can't disturb them. They don't care a dam if Annie Kenney goes to prison – or even Christabel Pankhurst. But you and I can really shake them. They know us, they know our families, we're part of their world, even if an inferior part in their eyes.' Lizzie still looked doubtful, and Anne went on, 'Of course, if you are too dainty to undertake it, I shall have to do it alone, but I'd feel much braver if you were by my side. I thought you were dedicated to the Cause, but if you haven't the stomach—'

'Oh, it isn't that. And of course I care about the Cause.'

'As long as it doesn't interrupt your comfortable routine.'

For an instant Lizzie heard Ashley's voice telling her to keep a sense of proportion. But, she thought, that was what people had always said, what they had said to Mrs Pankhurst who was beaten by a gang of Liberal supporters, what they said to women who were arrested for exercising their constitutional right to peaceful protest, what they said to women who were treated differently under the law from men – the law that was made by men and inflicted on women. A wave of anger stiffened her sinews and summoned up her blood. 'What would we have to do?' she asked. 'I don't want to do anything really bad or criminal. I have to think of Ashley.'

'Of course it won't be criminal,' Anne said eagerly, sensing victory. 'I favour something like protesting at the House of Commons, where a lot of people will know who I am. I'd like to get arrested in front of some of the MPs I'm acquainted with – that would shake them! What do you say – are you game?'

'All right, I'll do it. But, look, don't say anything to Ashley about it. I don't want to worry him just now – it's a busy time for him.'

'Better you don't tell him at all,' Anne said. 'You'd only give him the chance to forbid you.'

'Oh, I couldn't *not* tell him,' Lizzie said. 'But I'd like to choose the right time.'

In fact, as it happened, she didn't tell Ashley – or, at least, not the whole plan. She told herself there was no sense in worrying him beforehand, but in the back of her mind she knew that, really, it was because she knew he wouldn't like it.

The WSPU was to hold a 'Women's Parliament' in Caxton Hall for three days to coincide with the opening of Parliament on February the 11th. From that base, several protests were to be initiated, to take the form of deputations and petitions to Westminster. They would no doubt be ejected from the precincts and when they persisted in trying to get in there would be arrests on the grounds of obstruction or disorderly conduct – the usual pretexts. Anne's plan was that they should join one of these deputations, but slip away from the main body when they reached St Stephen's, and using their smart appearance and Anne's name, gain access to the Lobby and make a protest of their own inside. 'We may even be able to get as far as the Chamber, if we're lucky,' Anne said. 'That would be something, wouldn't it? To be arrested inside the Holy of Holies itself, the most impregnable gentlemen's club of them all!'

Lizzie told Ashley that she would be taking part in the Women's Parliament and might help carry a petition to Westminister, but she did not tell him it was her intention to get herself arrested. Ashley raised no objection to her taking part, but when she spoke of going to Westminster he said, 'You won't do anything – well – rowdy, will you? You know the police can be very rough, and I should hate you to be manhandled.'

Lizzie's conscience pricked her badly then, but she said, 'Of course I won't do anything rowdy. I don't mean to provoke the police or anyone else.' This was the literal truth – but provoked they would be, and that was the whole point. Ashley would understand afterwards and approve, she told herself.

When the day came, Anne and Lizzie joined the second wave of women trying to reach Parliament, battling through the crowds and the police barriers, while the leaders drove round and round the area in hansom cabs, using megaphones to shout slogans and encourage the troops. Anne and Lizzie were well dressed, Anne in her sable jacket, and neither wore any insignia or shouted slogans, in the hope that they would not be taken for Suffragettes. There were a great many people going in and out of the Palace of Westminster, and the police were trying to filter out the Members of Parliament and what they regarded as legitimate visitors from the protesting women. It proved to be unexpectedly easy to get past them. Anne spotted two Conservative members pushing their way through to the entrance and pulled Lizzie in behind them; and when they reached the police line she ostentatiously brushed down her fur and looked contemptuously around as if distancing herself from the rabble. In a loud voice she said to Lizzie, 'These dreadful women! Appalling! Something should be done about it.' The right voice, clothes and air of authority did the work. She gave the name of a Member of her acquaintance, and the policemen barely looked at them as they passed them through into the Lobby.

Lizzie's heart was beating so fast she could feel it pounding against her corset; yet it was strangely exhilarating to fool those policemen – to fool all these men. Inside the Lobby, she tried her best to look and move as confidently as Anne, but she felt ludicrously exposed, as if every eye must be drawn to her. She might just as well have been carrying a great banner that said STRANGER in letters two feet high. She had never been inside the Palace of Westminster before, and one part of her was staring like a tourist at the soaring, fluted stonework and mock-mediaeval decoration that made it seem like a great church. She would have liked the leisure to look around, and thought how nice it would be to be here legitimately. As it was, her nervousness was making her feel sick and, despite the cold, damp day, she could feel beads of sweat forming on her face.

Suddenly Anne decided to make her move. Perhaps she was nervous too, in spite of her appearance of calm, for she made no effort to get through to the Chamber. Instead she jumped up onto the nearest leather-covered bench seat, lifted her arms, and shouted in a ringing voice, 'Gentlemen, I crave your attention for a few words of vital importance to the welfare of this country!' The babble of voices faltered for a moment and faces turned in surprise. 'I am Lady Anne Farraline, and my father served his time and did his duty in the Upper House, as did *his* father before him. Indeed, my grandfather, the Earl of Batchworth, was instrumental in passing some very important legislation on divorce-law reform. He cared deeply about the equality of women, but his granddaughter stands here addressing you, his equal in one way only: as a peer he did not have the vote, and as a woman, neither do I.'

One person laughed at that point, but the sound was drowned by the shouts of protest. Almost as soon as Anne had begun speaking, the surprise had turned to anger as the gentlemen present realised it was another of those damned women, those damned Suffragettes! The impudence, the effrontery, to be haranguing them here, in their own place! The nuisance of them! They were as bothersome as flies – and as useless!

House officials were hurrying towards them, shouldering through the crowd. Policemen were not far behind: they had all been on the alert for anything of the sort, and it needed nothing more than the sound of a woman's voice upraised to trigger their reaction. Seeing the moment of doom fast approaching, Lizzie felt a surge of excitement rush through her, which quite washed away her fear. Her lungs seemed to fill with air, making her almost light-headed. Catching up her skirts she jumped up onto the bench beside Anne and, every eloquent thought having been expunged from her brain by nervous tension, she could only shout out, 'Votes for women! Votes for women!'

It did quite as well as anything else she might have said, since the noise was so great in the Lobby no-one could have heard her anyway. It was a magnificent moment: she was above them, looking down on the crowd of men, on the bald heads and the grey and the curly, the red faces and the white, the whiskers, moustaches, pince-nez, the high collars, ties and neckcloths, waistcoats and watch-chains, on a sea of faces every one with its mouth open in protest, every one looking at her. And this mass of mankind suddenly looked to her ridiculous; a species of ridiculousness. What silly things trousers were! How absurd were whiskers! What clumsy, awkward animals men were, lurching about on their hind legs and making ugly noises! How old-fashioned, hidebound, unable to adapt – surely destined for extinction, like the dodo! Men had no magnificent cause for denying women. All they cared for was to keep their ridiculous little world to themselves, offending justice, intellect, tolerance, liberality, mercy; rejecting everything that distinguished civilisation from the world of nature. We will win, she thought at that moment, with a thrill that rushed through her like brandy and made her very feet tingle, we will win because we are *right*!

'Votes for women! Votes for women!' she shouted again and again, in a kind of ecstasy. Anne, beside her, was still talking, but she could not hear what she was saying. She could not even hear her own voice.

It was soon over. The attendants had hesitated to seize Anne because she was a lady and a peer's daughter, but when Lizzie shouted those most hated and despised of all words, they overcame their reluctance. Hands grabbed them, faces ugly with anger were thrust close, all bristling moustaches and beads of spittle. They were dragged down from their perch. Lizzie almost stumbled, but the hard hands gripping her arms held her up. The police were there now, four of them, hot in their heavy serge uniforms. Lizzie could smell their sweat, and as they grabbed her and she stumbled before the pressure of bodies from behind, she fell against one of the constables, felt the rough material of his uniform burn her cheek, and the buckle of his belt hit her mouth painfully. She cried out, but no-one heard. With a policeman to either side she was lifted almost off her feet and hurried forward, her toes only just touching the ground. Someone hit her on the back of the head – whether deliberate or not she could not know – knocking her hat askew so that her hat-pin dragged painfully at her hair. She caught a glimpse of Anne nearby, hatless and with her hair coming down; but on her own two feet she was shorter than most people in the lobby and could see little beyond the backs and chests of the men all around her.

470

The ecstatic surge had left her, and she was frightened now. She fought to keep herself from weeping, for she did not want anyone to think her a coward. They were outside now, in the prickling rain, and there was a line of police ahead with their arms linked, and beyond them another crowd, of women this time, also with their mouths open, though she could not distinguish anything they were shouting in the wall of noise. She and Anne were being hustled away to the right. A man broke through the line and rushed up to them, shaking his fist and howling with rage, and he seemed, frighteningly, quite mad, capable of anything. But he was seized and dragged away before he could harm them. And then, there in front of them, was the Black Maria. Lizzie's stomach dropped away from her in sheer fright at the sight of it. She realised now, belatedly, that she really was going to be arrested, that it was happening, not in story or dream or idle projection, but in cold, sober reality, in that place where things hurt and consequences could not be avoided. Her legs buckled under her and she let out a sound like a sob.

'Come on, you,' said one of her guardians roughly. 'Let's be having you. Don't like it, do you? Shoulda thought o' that before you went a-making of all this trouble.'

She had imagined the inside of the Black Maria would be an open space with a bench along either side to sit on, but when the doors were opened there was a narrow central gangway between two rows of closed wooden compartments. Into one of these she was thrust. It was so narrow it was like an upright coffin, barely high enough for a grown person to sit in, and with no window but a tiny grille looking onto the gangway. She heard the door locked, and a terrible panic crowded up into her throat, which it took all her effort to fight off. Soon the outer door was shut with a slam, and darkness descended. It was like being buried alive. There was a jerk as the horses took the collar, and then they were bumping and rattling over the cobbles of the courtyard. Inside the van there was silence, except for one woman further down the row sobbing. After a bit a female voice, strained but kindly, called out, 'Is that you, Minnie? Don't cry, dear.'

471

And a rough male voice bawled, 'Shut up, you women. No talking!' and the silence fell again, even the sobbing now choked off.

They were taken to Cannon Row police station, where they were decanted into a waiting room already crowded with women waiting to be charged. Most of them were dishevelled from rough handling, some had been crying, all seemed pale and upset. There was a little whispered conversation, but mostly they sat in silence waiting for the law to take its course. There was not room for everyone to sit down, and Anne eased a way through for her and Lizzie to a piece of wall to lean against. She put her arm round Lizzie and whispered, 'Well done. We've made it! Did you know you'd cut your lip?'

Lizzie touched it cautiously. It was a little sore, and she felt dried blood. 'Is it bad?'

'No,' Anne said, and pulled out a handkerchief. 'Spit, and I'll clean you up.'

'You've lost your hat,' Lizzie whispered afterwards.

'Yes, and it was a favourite one of mine, damn them.'

Lizzie glanced at her, and saw that she was not as unmoved as she sounded. She, too, was nervous and apprehensive, but she was making a great effort not to seem so. For her, perhaps, the excitement and exhilaration of war mitigated the fear. Lizzie only felt low and depressed. 'What happens now?' she whispered.

The woman next to her heard her, and said, 'We wait here until Mr P bails us out. Then we go home. We come up in court tomorrow.'

'What will happen to us?'

'Jug,' said the woman simply.

Lizzie felt tears spring to her eyes. This was it, then. This was really it. She was very afraid. Anne fumbled for her hand and squeezed it. 'It's what we wanted,' she said.

'Silence in there! No talking!'

More women were squeezed in. Time dragged dreadfully slowly. Lizzie was terribly thirsty, but crammed in as they were there was no possibility of moving, let alone asking for anything to drink. But at least her thirst distracted her a little from her other urgent need, to urinate – even more impossible! There were fifty of them in the end, and it took time to process them all, take down their names and addresses and charge them, and for Mr Pethick Lawrence to bail them out, as he always did on these occasions, using his private fortune. The alternative to bail would have been a night in the cells with the drunks, prostitutes and robbers.

By the time Lizzie was done, word had got back to Ashley and he was waiting for her. She had never been so glad to see anyone in her life, and all but collapsed against his chest, so that he had to put his arm round her and support her. He was white with shock. 'I've got a cab waiting,' he said. Outside it was cold, very dark, and mizzling with rain. The cab was an old hansom, and he had to help her in, for her legs seemed too weak to make the awkward climb. Inside she leant back against the leather and closed her eyes, grateful that Ashley did not rail against her. In silence they jolted towards home. Only once did he speak, when he said, 'Did you mean it to happen?' She shook her head, only meaning that she could not answer; but later she realised he must have taken it for a negative to his question, and she hadn't the courage, or perhaps the energy, to take it back. She was so tired, she felt she could hardly breathe in and out. At home he had used his wits and ordered a hot bath for her as soon as she got in, and supper afterwards in bed. She saw to her surprise that it was nearly eleven o'clock. She scrubbed herself thoroughly in the bath, wanting to wash away the Black Maria and the police station, the men's rough hands and the looks of hatred. She kept thinking of Ashley's white face, and his great, great kindness. When she crawled into bed, warm and clean at last but exhausted, she couldn't manage more than a few spoonfuls of soup before unconquerable sleepiness overtook her. She knew someone took the tray away – she thought it might have been Ashley – but she couldn't raise her leaden eyelids or move her leaden lips to say thank you. And then she was asleep.

She thought about that soup many times over the next few days, wishing over and over that she had eaten it.

The next morning at Westminster Police Court all fifty women were tried in one batch – if it could be called a trial. Police evidence was taken, the prosecutor for the Crown made some disparaging remarks about the continuing disturbances, the magistrate silenced Anne tersely when she attempted to speak to make a political defence, and they were all sentenced to six weeks in the second division.

The words hit Lizzie like an electric shock. No matter what Anne had said, no matter that they had planned this, the reality was quite different when you came to it. Somehow there had always been a large, safe part of her mind that had not really believed in prison. And six weeks! It was appalling! She had thought perhaps two at the most; perhaps one week, the optimist in her had said, and how hard could that be to bear, just seven days? But six weeks! She was going to be taken away from Ashley, from her comfortable home; she would not see her little boys. She was going to be locked up in Holloway Gaol for six long, agonisingly long weeks! There was no option to pay a fine instead. Suffragettes had always refused the option, and the magistrates had now been instructed not to offer it. The Home Secretary believed that only harsh treatment would stop these protests.

The women were taken down from the dock and it was only then that Lizzie realised she was going straight to prison, without the opportunity to speak to Ashley again, to say goodbye. She flung one agonised glance over her shoulder, trying to find him in the gallery, but there was no time to single out his face before the stairs were in front of her and she was going down. Going down – that was how criminals talked about going to prison. Well, she was a criminal now! She began to cry, and tried hard to stop herself; but many of the women were weeping. Even Anne's eyes were wet. It wasn't sorrow or fear, really, but sheer emotion. That was how it affected women, she decided.

Afterwards she thought that perhaps the worst part was the beginning, another journey in the hateful Black Maria, and then being herded into the reception room at the prison. They were made to strip, and were searched. The wardresses were hard-faced, hard-handed women, and seemed determined to be unpleasant, as though that were part of the punishment. It was hard for someone who was not used to it to bear the contemptuous looks and rough words; and the humiliation of the stripping in front of and being searched by women of this sort was very great. Some of the Suffragettes, those who had been in prison before, bore it stoically, but all those of them who were new to it were weeping before long.

There was supposed to be a medical examination, but that was omitted. One of the wardresses looked briefly at Lizzie's lip, which was swollen now, but evidently decided it was nothing to make a note of. All their clothes and possessions were taken away, and they were given prison dress to put on – a coarse gown of lightish brown material patterned all over with the broad arrow, shapeless, and without belt or buttons. It came in one size, which meant that on tall women like Anne the hem was well above their ankles, while the white-haired old lady of four-foot-ten had to lift up the skirts to be able to walk. Rough, heavy prison shoes were issued as well, and then the women were taken to their cells and locked in for the night.

There was a plank bed leaning against the wall, which was to be laid on the floor, on top of which went a mattress stuffed with coconut fibre. There were coarse sheets, two blankets and a rug for bedding. Lizzie made up her bed and, there being nothing else to do, got into it. No night clothes were issued, and she felt too chilly to take off her dress, so she merely took off the shoes and climbed in as she was, another humiliation to add to the many. It made her feel dirty, soiled and abused.

She wished she were still as exhausted as she had been last night (was it really only last night?) so that she could simply fall asleep and not dream. But she was not sleepy at all, only deeply tired and very depressed and miserable. She tried to tell herself that it was for the Cause, tried to feel proud of striking a blow for womankind, but she could only think of Ashley ordering a bath for her out of his great kindness and sympathy; Ashley, whom she had deceived; Ashley, who would be lying down in his solitary bed tonight, worrying about her, missing her, needing her as much as she needed him. And the boys! What would he tell the boys? Would they understand it was for a good cause? How would they all bear the shame? She turned restlessly back and forth on the hard mattress, sleepless, longing for morning, but afraid of what morning would bring.

Venetia thought she had never seen a man more distraught than Ashley. He was pale and drawn, and though his good manners kept him in the seat she had offered him, he would plainly have preferred to be pacing about. She was shocked too, when she heard what he had to say.

'Lizzie in prison! But it doesn't bear thinking about!'

Ashley said miserably, 'We've read so much and heard so much about the other women going to Holloway, and we simply praised their courage. But things which happen to other people assume an entirely different aspect when they come right home to one's family circle.'

Venetia's shock was giving way to anger. 'Courage? This is pure folly! But I tell you what – Anne was at the bottom of this! It was Anne who planned it and talked her round to it. I've been afraid for some time that she was plotting something, but I never thought she would be so wanton as to involve Lizzie in her wild schemes.'

'She does admire Lady Anne so,' Ashley admitted, 'but she has a strong mind of her own. She couldn't be persuaded to it against her conscience. She must have thought it was a good thing to do. But what am I to do? I feel so completely at a loss. I don't even know what to tell the children. We didn't say anything to them this morning before they went off to school, but they will want to know tonight where their mother is.'

Venetia hesitated. 'I can't advise you on that point. I can only say that in my own experience it is better to tell children the truth. They always find it out in the end, and then they feel you have betrayed them by lying to them.'

Ashley nodded, looking more than ever depressed. 'It will be very hard to explain to them. And they will miss her so much. Six weeks! How can we be without her for six weeks?'

'It's an outrageous sentence!'

'It is so wrong, to treat them as criminals. Men who protest at Westminster are not sent to gaol unless they commit a criminal act.' He looked at her with the most cautious appeal. 'Is there nothing you can do? I hate to ask you, but I am at my wit's end, and I know you have a great deal of influence.'

Venetia frowned. 'I don't know. This is a very difficult time, as you probably realise. But I will see what I can do. I can't promise to be able to help, but I will try.'

'I knew you would!' he said, looking much too relieved for such a faint hope. 'You are so very good.'

She went first to Campbell-Bannerman, calling on him at Downing Street; reflecting, as she was admitted by the elderly hall porter, on how easily she gained admittance, and how often Suffragettes had knocked at that door in vain. It made her more than ever uneasy about petitioning the Prime Minister in this way – it seemed abusing her friendship with him.

He received her in his usual calm, friendly way, but she was shocked to see how ill he looked. His holiday in Biarritz did not seem to have done him any good. The flesh had fallen away from his face, leaving the bony structure visible under the skin; but more even than that, there was something in his eyes, in his expression, that stilled on her lips the question as to how he was. He was marked with death. As a doctor she had seen it before too many times to mistake it, though she could not have defined it. When he shook her hand in greeting, she kept hold of his, suddenly realising, with the full force of that word, that her friend was going to die.

'Henry,' was all she managed to say.

'Well, well,' he said kindly, reading her expression. 'It's good to see you, too. Biarritz was very pleasant, but I'm glad to be home.'

'Oh, Henry!'

'Never mind it, my dear. It comes to all of us in time. I've had a good life and done my duty before God. I'm tired now, and I miss Charlotte very much. It's time to go. All

477

things have their season.' She could not speak, and he had to prompt her. 'Now what did you want to see me about? It must be official business, if you've sought me out here at number ten.' He gave a faint chuckle. 'I wonder what Margot Asquith will make of this drab and poky place. Have you seen their house in Cavendish Square? Oh, it's very fancy, as modern as can be! She'll find this a very poor exchange, I'm thinking. Oh, Venetia, don't cry! We can't get on if you cry.'

'I'm not crying,' she said, rather rigidly.

'Yes, you are,' he replied with a gentle smile. 'Brace up, and tell me what you want.'

'I'm ashamed to ask you for favours now.'

'You might as well, or we'll have wasted all this expense of emotion. Come, my dear, out with it!'

So she told him about Lizzie. He listened gravely, but shook his head. 'I'm sorry. I'd like to help you. I am in favour of women's suffrage, you know that, and I'm sorry your young cousin is in trouble. But this is not something I dare interfere with. I can't overturn the sentence of a court.'

'But you are Prime Minister, and it was your Home Secretary who gave the order for these savage sentences.'

'Do you think if I could control that, I would have allowed it in the first place? The Cabinet is like a dozen horses harnessed to four sides of a cart and all pulling away like the devil – I beg your pardon! It's only by a monstrous effort of tact that I keep it together at all. The whole party is like that – come, you know it's true. I wish Asquith well of it when it's his turn to hold the reins.'

'I understand that. But, Henry, you know those sentences are unfair. In the interests of justice—'

'Ah, there's justice, and then there's the law. They don't always go in harness. I wish I could help you, but I can't, and that's just a fact. But, Venetia, reflect on this – isn't it part of the women's campaign, to suffer injustice? Isn't that how they hope to draw attention to the more fundamental unfairness? In a word, are you sure your young cousin *wants* to be got out?'

This gave her pause. But she said, 'Her husband and children want her back.'

'Ah,' said Sir Henry. 'Well, that's another matter, isn't it?'

Lizzie began to settle into her new life. Her cell, she discovered from the wardress, was in the new wing, for which she was told roughly she should be grateful. It was a narrow slip of a room, perfectly clean, which was a relief – she had feared fleas and rats, and there were neither – but rather stuffy, with only the one small window very high up, which did not open so admitted light but no air. In this small space she was shut alone for twenty-three hours a day with nothing to do but think, and watch the changing light in the small patch of sky she could see through the window.

The day began with restoring the bed to its daytime position and cleaning the cell. The floor had to be scrubbed, but only cold water was allowed for this. The wardresses seemed to take great delight in watching 'fine ladies' scrubbing on their hands and knees, and would taunt them, and often make them do it all again, claiming they had not been thorough. Only cold water was allowed for personal washing, too, and not much of that. Then came breakfast – a loaf of bread and a pint of tea. The bread was coarse and brown, but tasty and satisfying. Lizzie thought it very like good Yorkshire country bread and was surprised at its quality; but she supposed it might be a punishment to anyone who usually ate only white bread.

At half past eight they were herded down to the chapel. There was a service every day and twice on Sunday – with the intention of improving their morals, she supposed. Here she saw her fellow Suffragettes, and before the chaplain entered there were smiles and nods exchanged and sometimes an attempt at whispered conversation, though this was strictly forbidden. Lizzie saw two women in her row apparently exchanging messages by tapping on each other's knees with their fingertips in some prearranged code – perhaps Morse code. She never found herself next to Anne, but she saw her across the chapel, and each day Anne would smile at her comfortingly and hold up her hand with one more finger folded down. This was a great comfort to her in the first few days. After five days there were no more fingers left, and Lizzie began to lose track of time.

Chapel was the one time they saw the other prisoners, those who had been convicted of real crimes. Very few of them looked like criminals: they were almost all evidently very poor and ignorant, and seemed apathetic and miserable rather than depraved. It occurred to Lizzie that none of them would have been there if they had had the money to pay the fine instead. They did not look at the Suffragettes, seeming to have no interest in anything but surviving.

After chapel they were locked up again, and later in the morning were taken to the yard for exercise. The Suffragettes were never exercised with the other women; but there was no chance of conversation during this time, as they trudged in single file round and round the courtyard with a distance of ten feet between them, and two wardresses watching like hawks to prevent any sound or gesture passing from one to another. After this they were taken back to the cells and locked in for the rest of the day. The great stretches of time were broken only by the arrival of meals. Dinner came after exercise, and consisted of brown bread and potatoes, accompanied on two days by a watery soup, and on two an unsweetened suet pudding. On Mondays there were boiled beans and a small piece of bacon, on Thursday a slice of boiled beef as tough as the sole of a shoe but rather thinner, and on Sunday a portion of tinned meat with the most peculiar and unpleasant smell. Lizzie tried it once and was almost sick, and thereafter left it alone. The one thing about dinner was that it enabled her to know what day of the week it was, which was the only way she had of telling how long she had been there.

Supper came at four o'clock, and was the same brown loaf accompanied this time by cocoa. Both the cocoa and the tea looked, smelt and tasted like dirty water, the only difference being that the cocoa was slightly thicker. At eight o'clock the lights were turned out, and the long, sleepless night on the lumpy mattress began.

The monotony and the solitude were hard to bear at first,

and she felt as if she would go mad. Her mind rattled round and round, maddeningly pursuing the same trains of thought. She felt ashamed, humiliated, afraid of the future – what consequences would follow, what would Ashley say, what would the children think of her? Her prison sentence would attach itself to her like the mark of Cain and she would never be able to live a normal life again. She wished over and over that she had never joined the Suffragettes, that she had never listened to Anne. Sometimes she wished she had never *met* Anne, and blamed her bitterly for her plight. She spent a lot of time weeping, a lot of time pacing up and down her cell clenching and unclenching her fists. She felt trapped, and the walls seemed to be closing in on her, ready to smother and crush her. She wanted to scream and batter the door with her fists and beg to be let out, but controlled herself with a great effort, afraid of punishment but more afraid that the others would hear her and feel she had let them down.

But after a few days that very monotony came to her aid. It produced a sense of unreality, which divided her so completely from her normal life of activity and company that everything outside the prison began to seem unreal, like a dream that grew more remote as each day passed. It came to feel as if there had never been anything but this, these four walls, the silence broken only by distant sounds, the stillness broken only by the opening of the cell door to admit food or call her out to chapel or exercise. The other women, when she saw them on these occasions, began to seem unreal to her, too. She looked for Anne's smile in chapel as part of the routine, not because it meant anything to her any more. Her mind slowed to the pace of her new life, and she found herself able to stare at a single brick in her cell wall for an hour at a time, nothing its texture and imperfections almost with a kind of wonder. Sometimes she would even discover that she had 'disappeared', as she termed it to herself: she would be staring at something, and suddenly realise by the difference in the light outside the window that several hours had gone by without her noticing. Where she was during these times she could never remember. Her mind, it seemed, had been completely blank; for a little while, she had not existed.

Only in the dark after 'lights out' did she think in any coherent way, in the period between lying down and passing into her dead, dreamless sleep; and as time went on her thoughts achieved a comfortable equilibrium. She no longer felt ashamed and humiliated, or soiled by the experience – though she was definitely dirty now, there being no way to keep properly clean. Instead she felt a calm pride. She had done it for the Cause, and the Cause was right. She had fought a small battle and won; had made a tiny but important contribution to the end they all strove for. One day, when the war was won, she would be able to look back on this and know that she had made a difference; and if ever the book were written, perhaps her name would be recorded somewhere, in the list of those who had gone to prison to demonstrate the intolerable inequality that had once existed. Lizzie Morland: forty-two days and forty-two nights in the wilderness. That was her achievement. That would be her fame.

On the day Lizzie was released, Venetia offered her carriage and went with Ashley to meet her at the gates of Holloway Gaol. There was a crowd of Suffragettes, friends and relatives waiting for the release, and also a number of cabs and some other carriages, proof that this batch of prisoners had included representatives of the middle classes.

The prisoners had been allowed no visitors and no letters during their six weeks, part of the harsh treatment that was intended to deter any further disturbances. After what Campbell-Bannerman had said, Venetia had known she would not be able to do anything, but in accordance with her promise to Ashley she had approached Francis Knollys to ask, hopelessly, if the King would intervene. He had warned her, in an urgent undertone, not to mention the subject again. The King was very 'anti' the Suffragettes, and he would be very angry if she spoke out for them, or if he discovered that she was involved in even so peripheral a way. Overton added his urgings too: 'We are not free to do and say exactly as we wish,' he said. 'We've had this conversation before, Venetia. You undertook to keep away from the Cause, and not to embroil us in scandal.'

She had explained this to Ashley, feeling awkward about it, but he had understood; indeed, he had never thought she would be able to help, but had rather hoped it against reason. Her offering to go with him to the release was her way of appeasing her conscience. Her carriage was unmarked, and her coachman was not in livery. If she stayed inside the carriage, the press reporters who would be bound to be there would not know she was there.

Anne and Lizzie came out side by side, blinking like owls in the sudden light, among the crowd of women. A great cheer went up from the waiting Suffragettes and the press photographers got busy. The released prisoners beamed. Some of them waved their hands, some started running with the sheer joy of being out. There were hearty greetings, hugs and kisses, many tears. Ashley got down from the carriage and threaded his way through. Anne was laughing, being congratulated by various friends; Lizzie was hanging back a little, smiling, but searching the crowd. When she saw Ashley her face lit. No word passed between them, but despite being in a public place he enfolded her in a long and fierce embrace.

Finally he released her, and turned to shake Anne's hand and say, 'Are you coming with us? Lady Overton's carriage is waiting over there.'

Anne, beaming and elated, said, 'What? Oh, no! Thank you, but we are all going to dinner at an hotel – a celebration dinner. Imagine, proper food again! All the sisters are going – aren't you coming, Lizzie?'

'No,' Lizzie said, wondering how they could all talk so much – like the chatter of starlings. Her own voice felt so unused, she hardly knew how to speak. She was happy for them, she loved them all, but she did not want to go to a celebration dinner. 'I just want to go home.'

Anne looked at her sharply, and then at Ashley, to see if there were going to be recriminations. 'We've done something good, and important,' she said, more gently. 'You do know that?'

483

Lizzie smiled. 'Yes,' she said. 'I'll see you in a day or two. All is well.'

Ashley escorted her with his arm round her shoulder to the carriage. Lizzie climbed up. Inside, the expensive gloom smelt of sweet leather and a fragrance of verbena soap, which Lizzie now remembered was the scent that always hung about Venetia. After six weeks in a cell she was sensitive to new smells. Venetia was sitting well back in the corner, plainly dressed – no furs, just a woollen coat and a modest hat. *Ashamed of me*, Lizzie thought; and then corrected herself. *No, she has to be careful.* She was aware on the same instant of how dirty she was, and how she must smell to the others.

Venetia was shocked at how emaciated Lizzie was. Lizzie gave a faint smile as she took the other corner, but said nothing. Ashley climbed in opposite them and shut the door, and the carriage jerked into motion. None of them could think of anything to say. The occasion seemed both momentous and a strange anticlimax. At last, Venetia said, 'How was it? Was it very bad?'

'No,' Lizzie said. 'It was strange at first, but once I got used to it – no, it wasn't bad.' She thought a moment, and added, 'I missed Ashley – and the children. How are they?'

'Looking forward to seeing you,' Ashley said. 'Martial's made a banner for the drawing-room. I'm not sure Rupert really understands where you've been. They're both very excited. I've told them it must be a secret from the other children at school, but I've no confidence they'll keep it.'

Lizzie's smile faded. 'A secret? Are you ashamed of what I've done?'

'No, not ashamed,' Ashley said hastily, 'but – well—'

'You *are* ashamed.' Her eyes filled with tears. 'I should have gone with the other women after all. They understand. They're proud of me. They're celebrating the fact that we've been in, just as much as the fact that we've come out.'

'*We*'re proud of you,' Ashley said. 'We are! It took tremendous courage to do what you did, and I salute you for it.'

'But?' she said sharply.

Ashley hesitated, and Venetia spoke for him. 'You've

proved yourself, Lizzie. You've done your part for the Cause. Now you can let others take over. There's plenty you can do without exposing yourself to the risk of prison again.'

Lizzie stared, her eyes seeming too big in the carriage gloom. 'How can you say that? How can you of all people say that?'

'Because I care for you,' Venetia said. 'I know what it's like to fight against the whole of society. I've done it myself and suffered the consequences.'

'Yes, you fought for your right to be a doctor; you fought on and on until you won. I shall do the same, even if it means going to prison again. Don't you understand that our suffering is part of the fight, that nothing will happen without it?' She turned her burning eyes on Ashley. 'It's right, what I'm doing. We're fighting for justice and freedom. It's a *good* cause. Don't you believe that?' She turned back to Venetia. 'Don't you believe that?' Venetia didn't answer, her thoughts in turmoil. 'How can you advocate that I sit back at my ease and simply wait to enjoy rights other people will have fought for?'

Venetia said slowly, 'I hadn't thought of it that way. I was only thinking of you, and Ashley and the children. I care for you and want to protect you. But you're not a child any more. And the Cause is right. You've done exactly as you should, Lizzie. I'm sorry, Ashley.'

'No, I'm sorry,' he said. 'I shouldn't have asked you to interfere as I did. I wasn't thinking straight. Lizzie, forgive me. I *am* proud of you, and I support you every inch of the way. Whatever you want to do, it's fine by me.' She looked at him, close to tears, but they were tears of relief now. He smiled and reached over to press her hand. 'Let's go home and celebrate – not your release but your glorious action!' Lizzie made a sound between a sob and a laugh. 'We'll have to help Mart make a new banner. His says, "Welcome Home, Mummy", but it should say, "To the Righteous the Victory".'

He lifted her hand and kissed it, and Lizzie was beyond words, smiling at him while tears ran down her face. Venetia looked out of the window to give them the moment to themselves. She was working hard on her own mind and attitudes.

485

Perhaps she had grown too comfortable in middle age, her own battle long won, and the rest of little personal consequence to her in her comfortable niche in society. She didn't want things upset, not her own family's happiness nor Lizzie's. But the world was changing rapidly; and life was constant strife: she had forgotten that. It would take extra effort and no little ingenuity to support Lizzie's right to fight for what she believed in, while simultaneously protecting Beauty's delicate position. But if that was what was required, that was what she would have to give.

In March the King went for his usual spring holiday in Biarritz, but before leaving he called on Sir Henry Campbell-Bannerman in Downing Street, going in secretly through the garden from the Horse Guards to avoid notice. He took with him a bunch of violets sent by the Queen 'to cheer the poor patient', and spent twenty minutes with his Prime Minister, urging him if he possibly could not to retire until after Easter. The King himself was ill, his bronchitis as always aggravated by the damp foggy London weather, and his doctors had urged him to stay abroad, where he had the chance of some sunshine, for six weeks instead of his usual three.

But on the 27th of March Campbell-Bannerman sent for Asquith and told him that he was dying, and that Asquith would be invited to be the next Prime Minister. Campbell-Bannerman spoke with cheerful resignation of the plans he had drawn up for his funeral, and then in his gently firm way turned the conversation onto matters of business. Asquith left in tears; but he would not have been human had they not soon given way to a steely excitement that his moment had come at last.

On the 6th of April Asquith received a letter from the King, summoning him to Biarritz. There in the King's apartments at his usual hotel Asquith handed in his letter of resignation as Chancellor of the Exchequer and was appointed Prime Minister and First Lord of the Treasury, upon which he knelt and kissed the King's hand. The King then invited him to breakfast and they spent an hour alone going over appointments and various issues of policy. Knollys afterward confided to Overton that the King thought it 'rather dreadful' that Asquith had arrived with his entire Cabinet planned and decided views on policy changes, while his predecessor yet lived. He said it reminded him of vultures circling a dying animal. He had never liked Asquith, and the relationship did not appear destined to develop any warmth.

Sir Henry died at Downing Street on the 22nd of April, and five days later made his last journey northwards from Euston Station to his Scottish home at Belmont, there to be buried beside his beloved wife Charlotte in the churchyard. After receiving his letter of resignation in early April, the King had pondered giving him a peerage, but had changed his mind in the end, feeling that, as Campbell-Bannerman had refused from the beginning to go up to the Lords, he would not have accepted it.

CHAPTER FIFTEEN

Lizzie had requested that the news of her imprisonment be kept from her mother until she was released, when she would write herself and explain it all. She didn't want to worry her, when there was nothing she could do about it. But of course, as soon as Henrietta had the letter, nothing could prevent her from hurrying to London to see with her own eyes that her daughter was safe and well.

The news that Lizzie had been in prison shocked her profoundly. Prison was something that happened to other people, to the lowest sorts, not to decent, honest people like them. No-one in the family, no-one she was acquainted with, had ever gone to gaol. That it should be Lizzie, of all people – her clever, good daughter, always so thoughtful and helpful! And Lizzie was not only a female – it seemed somehow more shocking than if one of her sons had gone to prison, though that would have been bad enough – she was a married woman, with two small children. Henrietta did not know how to bear the idea, did not know how to think about it, and though she read the letter again and again it simply made her cry.

Jerome was equally shocked and appalled at first, but he came round to it more quickly, and it was thanks to him that when Henrietta arrived at Endsleigh Gardens she was able bravely to congratulate Lizzie rather than mourn over her. He understood at once why she had done it, and was able to separate his personal feelings for his darling daughter from the intellectual evaluation of her action.

'The worst thing you can do is to make a hullabaloo, my

love,' he told his grieving wife. 'She has done something very brave, and she will have enough people despising her for it without our being ashamed of her.'

'I'm not ashamed of her. It's just that—'

'Yes, I know,' Jerome said comfortingly. 'It *is* a terrible shock. I suppose you want to dash straight up to London?'

'Well—'

'Go, with my blessing. And tell Lizzie that Papa thinks she is wonderful.'

Henrietta leaned against him. 'You really are a remarkable man,' she said. 'The best husband and the best father in the world.'

'I'll go and look up a train for you.'

Lord Overton had gone with the King to Biarritz, but he had gone *en garçon*, Venetia having engagements in London. Lizzie telephoned her to say that her mother was coming to stay, and Venetia left them alone for a few days before inviting Henrietta, alone, to Manchester Square.

When the subject of Lizzie's adventure had been gone over at sufficient length to satisfy Henrietta, Venetia said, 'I want to turn your mind to a new and more cheerful subject. Violet will be coming home very soon. She'll be seventeen in May, as you know. Have you decided yet what to do with Jessie?'

Henrietta wrinkled her nose. 'You make her sound like a parcel. No, I haven't really thought about it. There's always so much else to do, and she seems content as she is. She was rather moody last year after Bertie's visit – I think she had a revival of her crush on him. But she cheered up after Jerome gave her a horse of her own to school. She seems to be quite happy just helping with the horses and so on – and I must say her help really is valuable. Jerome quite relies on her for some things.'

'But what about social events?' Venetia asked. 'She can't spend all her life in the stables.'

'Oh, she doesn't, of course. She's been hunting her new horse all winter.' Venetia raised an eyebrow and Henrietta hurried on, 'And there have been parties and dances and so on. There's always plenty going on in York. We give dinners from time to time, and there are plays and concerts and public balls occasionally.'

'Does she meet any young men?'

'Well, yes, sometimes. She's met some nice boys out hunting – and there are the officers at the cavalry barracks. She and Jerome go there to watch the polo quite often and we were invited to a ball there in February. That was such a nice evening! The regiment is so hospitable. Jessie danced every dance. She always seems to get on well with young men when the occasion arises. Robbie brings friends home sometimes, and Frankie had two to stay at Christmas, and she got on very well with them.'

'Is she in love with anyone – and I don't mean her childhood crush on her cousin?'

'Oh, that's all forgotten now, I'm sure. But I don't think she fancies any one man in particular. To be truthful, she doesn't take much interest in them, not in that way. But she's only just turned seventeen. There's plenty of time. This winter is the first time we've taken her to public events like that.'

'All the same, it's never too early to be thinking about marriage for her. I certainly have it in mind for Violet.'

'Really? Do you think it's important?'

Venetia smiled. 'I know what you're thinking – that it sounds strange coming from my lips! And if Violet had voiced any desire for a career, or shown any particular bent or talent, no matter in what sphere, I would have done everything in my power to help her. But she hasn't. So in that case, marriage is the only alternative. A girl must do something, and in the absence of a career, a husband, home and children are the only things that will make her comfortable and keep her properly occupied.'

'Well, I think so, of course, but I hardly expected to hear you say so.'

'Am I not a good example of a happily married woman? Have I ever spoken to you against the institution of marriage?'

'No, you haven't. I'm sorry. And of course I'd like Jessie to marry, as long as it was the right man. But as for keeping her occupied – she has so much to do at Morland Place she's never bored for an instant.'

'Yes, that's all very well,' said Venetia, 'but how long will it last? To be brutal, dear Henrietta, Morland Place is not yours, and you and Jerome won't live for ever. What will become of Jessie then, if you haven't provided for her? A young, wealthy spinster may have a certain position in society and a fair amount of fun, but an old spinster, and especially an old spinster who is *not* wealthy, is not an object of envy. You wouldn't want that for Jessie, surely?'

'No, you're quite right,' Henrietta said. Venetia's words had touched a chord. Teddy had recently been paying a lot of attention to Mrs Meynell, and it seemed to her that it was more than simply kindness towards an old friend's widow. There was no reason in the world why Teddy should not marry again, and Alice Meynell was still young enough to have children. If he did begin a new family, Henrietta would be delighted for him; and there was room enough for them all at Morland Place, as long as they were wanted. But it did, she felt, make Jessie's future more precarious. It would relieve her mind of an anxiety if Jessie could be well and happily married in the next year or so.

'We must do more to make sure she meets the right people,' she concluded. 'We shouldn't leave it to chance. You were right to warn me.'

'I've more than good advice to offer you. I'm bringing Violet out this season, which as you can imagine means a great deal of organisation and expense.'

'Yes, I believe you.' Henrietta had never been brought out, but she knew well enough what was entailed.

Venetia went on, 'It has occurred to me – or to *us*, I should say, because Beauty agrees with me completely – that neither the organisation nor the expense would be significantly greater for two than for one. So I should like to offer to bring Jessie out along with Violet.'

Henrietta had not expected this, and could only stare in astonishment while her unready tongue fumbled for the right words.

Venetia went on, 'It won't mean any trouble for you. I'll

arrange everything. Jessie will stay here with me, and I'll chaperone both of them. You don't need to be here at all unless you want to, though it's usual for the parents to attend the launch ball – and, of course, it would be lovely to have you here if you did want to come for all or part of it. But I'll make sure they go to all the right places and meet the right people – and of course I shall vet everyone Jessie meets, and particularly any young man she shows an interest in, so you can feel quite secure about her.'

'Oh – I'm sure so! It's very, very kind of you—'

'Not at all. I shall enjoy it. Ever since they were babies, I've thought that it would be nice for them to come out together one day. Do you remember that day when you first brought Jessie to my house as an infant in arms, and we fed them together?'

'Yes, I remember it very clearly. We hoped then that it would make a bond between them.'

'And it has. They love each other just as I hoped they would.'

'But, Venetia, a London season for Jessie? I hardly know what to say. We never thought of anything like that for her.'

'Well, think of it now. Why not? She will meet a much wider range of young men, and what's more, young men who know what they are there for – to look for a wife. The débutante season is the best chance of marrying off a daughter ever devised. It must be, otherwise it wouldn't have survived all these years.'

'I'm sure it is – but Jessie isn't a lord's daughter.'

'She's a gentleman's daughter. Come, don't be too modest! Jerome's family is quite as good as any she's likely to meet, and Morland blood is the equal of anyone's. Don't forget I have it myself! Goodness, if it hadn't been for Jerome's unfortunate crash, you would probably still be in London and you'd certainly be planning to bring her out yourself.'

'But he did crash,' Henrietta said, 'and – well – oh, Venetia, we couldn't possibly afford it!' She blushed at her own words, but went on, 'We expected to buy her some new clothes, of course, and take her places, and Jerome has put

492

aside something. But a London season is far out of our reach.'

'Now don't be overawed,' Venetia said firmly. 'What expense is there? Nothing at all! She'll be living here with us, so you won't have to hire a house and staff it, which is generally the biggest expense of a come-out season. You won't have to give a ball because she'll share Violet's. She'll be invited to all the same things Violet goes to, which will cover any incidental expenses like cabs, and we'll pay for any tickets that are needed. All you'll need to do is buy her clothes. Of course, she'll need quite a lot, but if she has them all made here in London when I have Violet's made, I'll get a big discount on them, so they'll probably cost less in the end than if you got them at home.'

'It would be wonderful if you chose her clothes for her,' Henrietta said, beginning to warm to the idea. 'I'm sure I'm far behind the fashion down there in Yorkshire.'

'What else is there?' Venetia went on. 'I'll be presenting Violet, of course, which is a big expense, but that won't apply to Jessie. I'd be happy to sponsor her but I don't suppose you want her presented, and I don't think there's any need for it.'

'No, not at all. It would be wasted,' Henrietta said hastily. 'She's not likely ever to move in those circles.'

Venetia smiled. 'Oh, I wouldn't say that, precisely. But she can always be presented later if it becomes necessary. And if she marries someone with a title, she'll be presented as a bride anyway.' Henrietta was staring, her eyes very large. Venetia concluded, 'I can't see any other difficulties, can you?'

Henrietta found her voice. 'No. Only that it's a great, great deal too kind of you, and – well . . .' She hesitated.

'Well?'

'I know she would enjoy coming out with Violet very much, but is it likely to come to anything? Would it be better for us to aim lower for her? Violet is Lady Violet Winchmore with a large dowry. What young man will be interested in Jessie Compton with none?'

'You'd be surprised,' Venetia said. 'There are just as many

493

untitled as titled people in our circle – far more, in fact. And as to dowry, presentation counts for a lot. It was different fifty years ago, and there are still some stiff, old-fashioned families, but in general young men expect to fall in love these days before they marry. And once a young fellow falls in love with a pretty, lively girl, he won't stop because there's no money to come with her. Jessie is a very taking young woman, and there are plenty of nice young men who will be well within her range, I promise you. Why settle for less, if you can get a man of means for her?'

Henrietta was ready to be persuaded: it seemed too fine an opportunity for Jessie for her to go on raising objections. 'Provided they loved each other, it would be a fine thing for her to marry someone well set up in life.'

'Of course it would. Naturally, there's no guarantee it will happen, but it can't hurt to put her in the way of it, can it? And I know it will make Violet very happy. They are so fond of each other, and girls who come out together have a life-long bond. Neither of them has a sister, but this will make them sisters in everything but blood. So, what do you say? Is it yes?'

'Oh, yes,' Henrietta said, 'and thank you, more than I can say.'

Two weeks later Violet was home from her finishing-school in Vienna, and Jessie arrived at Manchester Square on the afternoon of the same day. The girls embraced warmly.

'Look at you!' Jessie said, hugging her again. 'You've got more beautiful than ever. And so smart and elegant!' Violet's dress was plain but perfectly cut, her dark hair was glossy and exquisitely arranged, and though she moved with a confident grace, her face had a delicate, shy expression that made Jessie think of a young fawn, or some other dainty creature.

By contrast, Jessie was taller and stronger, and Violet thought her the epitome of vigour and vitality. She seemed more than her six months older, and while her firm-featured face was not classically beautiful, it had a life about it that made it hard to drag your eyes away from her. Venetia had

494

called her 'taking' and, seeing her now, did not regret her decision. With decent clothes and her hair properly dressed, she would pass anywhere, and be a credit to them. Her background at Morland Place – even though it did not belong to her father – would do her no discredit. And finally, Violet's shining eyes proved how much the arrangement meant to her, and Venetia was glad to make her darling daughter happy.

'Come upstairs,' Violet said to Jessie, when the greetings were finished, 'and see your room! Mama's given you the white bedroom. It's on the other side of my bathroom. There's a door into the bathroom from both, so we can come and go without going out into the corridor. Isn't it fun?'

Jessie thought it all tremendously luxurious. To have a bathroom just to themselves was wonderful enough, but it was as big as a bedroom, with an enormous bath that had all sorts of taps and nozzles to give you different kinds of spray and deluge. There was a huge fireplace, which always had a good fire in it because the rooms were on the north side of the house and never got any sun, and two big old armchairs stood to either side of it, covered with vast thick towels half as big as bed sheets.

'It's wonderful when you get out of the bath to wrap yourself up in one and curl up in a chair by the fire,' Violet said. 'The bathrooms at the school in Vienna were so cold, and they made us have the windows open all the time. Sometimes I thought I'd never get warm again.'

With both bathroom doors open, they could wander in and out of each other's rooms as they pleased. That first day Jessie sat on Violet's bed watching her put away her things, and asked her about school.

'Oh, it was quite fun, on the whole,' Violet said. 'Some of the lessons were dull – there was a lot of needlework, for instance, which I thought was terribly old-fashioned, though some of the German girls said they were still expected to be able to embroider and so on. French and German lessons were all right – it was mostly conversation, and reading books which we had to discuss afterwards, but in the language.'

'Goodness! We never had to do anything like that at my school.'

'It's supposed to give you something to say at embassy parties,' Violet said, 'but I must say I can't imagine asking Count Mensdorff if he admired Goethe more than Schiller, and I shouldn't think he'd much want me to!'

'I never did German at all, only French, though Mother's taught me a bit of Italian.'

'I think German's an ugly language, and, oh, the books are dull!'

'Tell me more. What else did you do?'

'Well, there was dancing and music, and deportment—'

'What's deportment?'

'How to walk and sit down and go up and down stairs with a train, and how to curtsy properly and how deeply to do it, depending on whether it's the King or the Emperor or whoever.'

'I didn't know there were different depths,' Jessie said, impressed and slightly worried.

'Oh, well, I don't think it matters as much as they said it did. After all, some Americans and some of the Socialists don't bow or curtsy at all, and they are accepted at Court now – or at our Court, anyway. And then there was politics.'

'Oh, I like politics. Dad reads me bits out of the papers every day and we discuss it. He says I've got a good mind.'

'Ours wasn't that sort of politics. It was mostly about royal families and who was related to whom. That was *very* dull. All those Hohenzollerns and Mecklenberg-Strelitzes, and Altenburgs and every burg under the sun! I'm glad to be done with that!'

'Did you have any riding?'

'Oh, yes. Vienna's full of horses, you know. You've heard of the wonderful Lipizzaners, of course? Austrians think themselves the best riders in the world. But our riding-master soon saw I could handle my horse, so I was put in the advanced class, which meant we just went for rides. The woods around Vienna are *lovely!*'

'What else did you do?'

'Oh, lots of things. Vienna's very gay, and there are parties and dances every day of the week, and wonderful concerts and plays, and the opera, of course. We went to receptions at Schönbrunn, and drives along the Prater, and visited museums and art galleries, and went on boat trips on the river, and picnics up in the woods.'

'It does sound nice,' Jessie said wistfully.

'It was. And some of the other girls were nice, though I didn't like any of them as much as you. I wish *you* could have been there, then it would have been perfect.'

'But did you meet any men?'

'Of course! That's what all those outings were for. Most of the girls were just man-mad. I felt a bit ashamed of them sometimes, but they seemed to think they had been sent to finishing-school purely to catch a man, and I must say the teachers seemed to agree with them. Not that there was a chance of anything *happening* – you know what I mean. We all dressed demurely and looked very innocent, and the chaperones were very strict, but the young men were always hanging round us like wasps round a jam-pot.' She laughed. 'The chaperones used to invite some of the best-behaved to accompany us, but it was the others who were much more fun, the ones who hadn't been invited but came anyway. You never saw such tricks as they got up to to find some way to meet us!'

'My life seems to have been very dull compared with yours.'

'But we are going to come out together, isn't that wonderful? Oh, Jess, I'm so excited, aren't you?'

'I'm thrilled to bits,' Jessie said. 'Your mama's so kind to do it.'

'She means to get us both married – it's a challenge to her. She gets awfully bored since she's given up her doctoring, so she needs something to occupy her mind,' Violet said. She plumped down on the bed, ready for a confidence. 'Jess, do you find you're in love with someone all the time? I can't seem to remember a time when I wasn't. And it's a different man nearly every week. Am I very fickle, do you think?'

'I think you're supposed to be, until you find the right one.'

'And then you fall in love for ever and marry him and you love each other until death,' Violet said.

'And beyond the grave too, if it's true love.'

'Yes, that's what I want,' Violet said. 'True and perfect love, not the other kind.'

'Me too,' Jessie said. She thought briefly of Bertie, and felt a pang, low down in her stomach. But Bertie was gone, for ever out of reach; and she was seventeen and ready for love. 'But until then,' she said, 'there's all the rest of it, and I mean to enjoy every bit.'

'Our coming-out ball!'

'The Season! And your presentation. Are you scared?'

'A bit. But Mama's going to arrange practices for me, so I'll know exactly what to do. All the same, I know I'm going to be shaking like a jelly. It wouldn't be half so bad if you were there. I wish you were going to be presented too.'

'Gosh, I don't! But I'm looking forward to the ball and everything, and the clothes.'

'Oh, the clothes! Don't you think there's nothing more wonderful in the world than new clothes?'

'Well, I haven't had as much experience of them as you, but I must say I do. Clothes and horses. They do take one's mind off wonderfully.'

Violet's attention was caught by the words. 'Are you in love with someone now, this minute?' she asked suddenly. 'Jess, it's not still Bertie, is it? I heard Mama saying something to Papa.'

Jessie nodded. 'But I know it's hopeless.'

'It's very romantic to have a hopeless passion,' Violet said, with a sigh. 'I wish I had one.'

Jessie giggled. 'Do you remember when I stayed here that time and you were in love with the postman? That was a hopeless passion if ever there was one! He was married and had ten children, one of the maids told me.'

'Well, that was a different sort of hopeless,' Violet said. 'We were so young then. But Bertie—'

498

'I don't suppose I shall ever see him again,' Jessie said. 'And even if I did, he wouldn't want me. So if someone else comes along, I shan't refuse to fall in love.'

'Oh, someone will,' Violet said. 'For both of us. I'm sure of it.'

Jessie was very interested in Violet's presentation, the one part of the coming-out she would not share. She went to all the fittings with Violet of her Court gown, and discussed cut and trimmings with the dressmaker with the earnestness of an acolyte. The most expensive part of the dress was the train, which Venetia had ordered from Vienna through a friend at the Embassy and which had travelled back with Violet in her luggage, occupying a small trunk of its own. Jessie was present when it was unpacked for the first time, and she and Violet walked round it in a marvelling silence. Court regulations stated that the train had to be at least three yards long and made of velvet, silk or lace. There was always great rivalry to have the most splendid train of the Season. Much thought went into the decoration of them with embroidery and semi-precious or even precious stones.

Violet's was of crimson silk figured with elaborate gold embroidery, and sewn with crystal and seed pearls.

'It must have cost hundreds and hundreds of pounds,' Jessie said in awe.

'And all just for one wearing!' Violet said.

'What will you do with it afterwards?'

'It's a mystery,' Violet said, walking round the bed to look at it in another light. 'Mama says her father's mother turned hers into a cover for the grand piano, and that *her* mother made hers into curtains – but she unpicked the jewels first, because it was sewn with diamonds. Only imagine, real diamonds! I'd have been scared to death to wear it in case one came unstitched and got lost.'

Presentation these days was not just an ordeal, but an enjoyable social occasion too. Venetia told the girls that things had changed since her day, when Queen Victoria's drawing-rooms were held in the early afternoon.

'It meant you had to start dressing straight after breakfast, and there wasn't time for any lunch before you went to the palace. There were no refreshments served there, so you spent the whole time terrified your stomach would grumble in front of the Queen, or that you'd faint from hunger. And it meant you had to travel through the streets to the palace in the middle of the day, all in your Court dress and plumes and jewels and everything, which made you feel very out of place. When your carriage got stuck in traffic, as it always did, the boys and louts would come up and peer at you through the window and laugh at you, and shout, "Mothballs!" It was all most embarrassing. And then at the palace you had to wait on rows of little hard chairs in a waiting room with all the other girls and their mamas. The longer you waited the more nervous you became, and the more you thought they all looked better than you, and the more you remembered how formidable everyone said the Queen was. By the time your turn came you'd be almost paralysed with fright. But afterwards you'd come back home so relieved that it was over, you'd feel quite light-headed. And then you'd have a "train tea", which was lovely. All your friends would be invited and you'd show off your Court dress and have lovely things to eat.'

But Queen Alexandra had changed the afternoon drawing-rooms to evening Courts, where there were ample refreshments and where, having been presented, the débutantes could go on to enjoy the rest of the function. It also meant the journey to the palace was much less conspicuous – though it did mean no more train teas, which Jessie thought was a pity. She very much enjoyed the two rehearsals Venetia arranged, where she played the part of one of the royal princesses to Venetia's Queen Alexandra. Violet had to make her entrance and walk up to the throne, curtsy, and move away, and keep doing it until she could manage her long, heavy train, fan, bouquet and three plumes with something approaching grace. The first two times she caught her feet in her train and fell over, and the third time her plumes fell off when she bent her head, though Venetia said that wasn't her fault and they should be more firmly fixed thereafter. The next few times, although she didn't drop anything, trip or poke her plumes into the Queen's face, Venetia said she went down and got up like a cow in a byre, and wondered why they'd sent her all the way to Vienna to learn to curtsy. When they were just finishing for the day, Lord Overton came in and, abstracting Violet's fan and bouquet, said he would show her how to do it, and put up such a comic performance that they were almost sick with laughter by the end.

At the next day's rehearsal Violet did better and by the end Venetia pronounced herself satisfied and said, with a note of pride in her voice, that she would be the prettiest and most graceful girl there. Violet was pleased with the compliment, and seemed much less apprehensive – even seemed to be looking forward to it. Still, Jessie was quite glad she was not being presented herself, and saw Violet off on the night without envy.

Their own ball was the focus of her excitement. Venetia had long half planned to hold it in the ballroom of Chelmsford House, her own house, which was rented out, but when the time came the tenants were not the sort of people she could ask for the favour. But the Duke of Southport, gently nudged into it by Olivia, had come forward and offered Southport House, which was also in Pall Mall and was even more impressive than Chelmsford House. Its ballroom was larger – though Venetia said it was not as pretty – and, as the house was kept in readiness with a skeleton staff at all times, it required no great cleaning or preparation. All that was needed was for the chandeliers to be cleaned and tuned, the floor french-polished, the orchestra hired, the flowers arranged, the supper ordered, the sitting-out and card rooms prepared, the extra staff hired, the police informed, and the invitations sent out.

The dinner beforehand Venetia had intended to be quite small, meaning to hold it at Manchester Square for convenience, but when the duke offered the house for the occasion, he also asked to have the honour of hosting the before-ball dinner himself. Venetia suspected more of Olivia's delicate prompting, but she was very pleased to accept the offer, not only because it relieved her of a very

501

large chunk of arranging, but because it would add enormous cachet to the launch of both girls to be thus patronised by the Duke of Southport.

He asked her to invite whomever she pleased, and submitted to her, very properly, a list both of those he meant to invite to dinner, and those he would like to bring to the ball. It was an excellent list, including among others the most eligible bachelor of the last three seasons, the handsome Lord Brancaster, heir to the Earl of Holkham, which would ensure her ball was thought a success. She was pleased for Violet's sake, though she suspected that many of the young men on Southport's list would be too rich for Jessie's blood. But you never knew, she told herself, and said later to Overton. Stranger things had happened, and Jessie was such a pretty, lively girl, it would not be the most unexpected thing in the world if she caught the attention and the heart of someone well above her social station.

Jessie might have spent most of her leisure moments for the past few years with horses, but she was girl enough, or perhaps young woman enough, to be thrilled to the core about the ball. She appreciated the difference the duke had made quite as well as Venetia. It was going to have been marvellous before, but this had raised it into something approaching a fairy-tale. She relished every detail of the preparation, and could not have enough of reading over the list of acceptances with Violet, studying the supper menu, helping to plan the flowers, choosing the music. The girls would sit up late into the night on the bed of one or the other, talking about how it would be, who they would dance with, what they would say, who would take them to supper, and whether anyone would invite them out on the balcony. Jessie was wise enough to know that the anticipation was a great part of any pleasure; young enough to hope that the eventual pleasure would be even better than her imaginings.

Two days before the ball, the dresses came home, delivered in enormous, thrilling, flat white boxes. Venetia, who was in some ways an admirable grown-up, insisted that the girls should try them on at once, and told the maids to carry them up to her own bedroom, where there was room for all of them, including the maids, who would be needed to help them dress. The maids were enjoying the whole thing as much as anyone, and carried the boxes with a flourishing ceremony. Jessie, bringing up the rear of the procession, was deeply happy. She knew that this was one of the pivotal moments of the whole affair, something she would remember always. She would remember that it was a hot, sunny day outside, that the dressmaker's van was painted a smart, shiny dark green, that the two bay horses had thrown only a short shadow onto the dazzling pavement. She would remember how the maids smiled, and how one of them winked at her, tempted out of her usual well-trained neutrality by a joint female pleasure in the occasion.

She would remember that Venetia had sent one of the maids for the cheval glass from Lord Overton's dressing-room to augment her own 'so that you can see your back view, girls'. Oh, she would remember for ever the moment of taking the lids off the boxes, and seeing the folds of material nestling inside, swathed in layers and layers of tissue paper! The clean smell of the paper, and the whispery rustle of it as they pulled it away, and the heavy, slithery movement of the material as the gowns were lifted up and out, unfolding themselves like magician's flowers, on and on, into beauty!

Violet's gown was of white lace over pale pink satin, so that the white seemed to blush with rose as she moved. It reminded Jessie of Bertie's description of the sunrise on the Himalayan snows. White, she had learnt from Venetia, was not a colour everyone could wear – it would, for instance, have made Jessie look unpleasantly sallow – but Violet looked divine in it. With her dark hair, deep blue eyes, perfectly porcelain-white skin, and the delicate flush of health in her cheeks, she looked almost ethereally lovely in white.

'You will make all the other girls in their pinks and blues and mauves look insipid,' Venetia said, with satisfaction. 'Very few will wear white, and those who do will look dull beside you.'

Violet blushed at the praise, and Jessie said, 'I really think

503

you will be the most beautiful girl of the Season – don't you, Cousin Venetia?'

Venetia had too much respect for Jessie's intelligence to deny it. 'She is quite lovely. But you have your own sort of beauty. Let's see you in your gown now.'

Jessie's gown was of a delicate pale yellow, in the new long, slender, high-waisted 'empire' style that had just come in, which suited her slim, athletic body so well. It was of soft silk crêpe-de-Chine with a swathed bodice and short turk's-cap sleeves, which were edged with delicate fringe, embroidered with gilt threads and tiny crystal beads. The skirt was quite plain except for a row of self-coloured silk knots round the hem, but at the back from the high waist fell the deep inverted pleating that gave the wonderful full-ness to the skirt behind, so that it made a kind of swirl around her whenever she moved.

'It's the loveliest thing I've ever seen,' she said, with deep satisfaction, gazing and gazing at her back view. 'I never, ever imagined wearing a gown like this.'

'That colour is perfect for you,' Venetia said. 'You look lovely.'

'I *feel* lovely,' Jessie confessed.

Violet thought her friend looked suddenly grown-up, much older than her, and, in spite of her words, strangely confident, as if she had been going to balls dressed like this for years and years. Violet had a moment of feeling left behind. Gazing at Jessie's preoccupied face as she looked at her reflection in the mirror, she wondered suddenly what went on in Jessie's mind, and for the first time doubted that it was exactly the same as what went on in her own. There was something about Jessie that suggested she knew things, or had done things, or had a secret that set her apart. It was, Violet thought, very attractive and romantic.

On the day before the ball Venetia and the girls drove over to the great old mansion in Pall Mall to try out the floor and check the arrangements. They went in Lord Overton's motor-car rather than Venetia's carriage, as they didn't know how long they would be inside, and it was too hot to have the horses stand and wait. The striped awning

504

was already up, leading from the kerb to the great door, and as the motor drew up, one or two passing people stopped to look, making the girls feel very special as they descended and trod under the canopy where the carpet would be on the night.

The Duke and his family had not yet arrived from the country, but the house was full of servants, florists and caterers, all bustling about. Four housemaids were on their hands and knees brushing the carpet up the great stairs from the hall. They stepped between them, Jessie feeling guilty about treading where they had just brushed, but they glanced up and smiled at the girls as they passed, as warmly as if they were relatives. Everyone, Jessie thought, seems to love us because we're débutantes.

They glanced into the supper-room, where maids were spreading white damask table cloths so fresh and stiff they almost crackled. They inspected the cloakroom arrangements: the padded satin hangers, the looking-glasses, powder-boxes, pin-cushions and sewing-baskets. They looked into the card room where the suppliers were setting up and brushing the green baize tops of the hired tables and laying out new packs of cards, the crisp edges looking somehow delicious to Jessie, as though one were going to nibble them like chocolate.

And they arrived at last in the ballroom.

'Goodness,' Venetia said, 'this takes me back! I had my own coming-out ball here, you know, girls. And your aunt Olivia had hers here, Vi. I wish Grandmama could have been here to see you come out in this same ballroom.'

It looked very different now from when Venetia had inspected it a few weeks ago. Then it had looked cold, dark and, frankly, a little shabby, with nothing to distract the eye from scratches, scuff-marks and the age of the curtains. But now the magic of the coming ball had changed all that. Great potted plants and banks of flowers in the corners and surrounding the orchestra dais brightened it. The chandeliers and mirrors sparkled, there was an agreeable smell of wax polish and french chalk in the air, and the hundreds of little rout chairs that lined the walls on three sides of the floor looked pretty and inviting with their gilded legs and crimson velvet seats.

The fourth wall was pierced with a row of french windows leading out onto the terrace, which overlooked the garden. It was rather overgrown and neglected, but that would not be apparent on the night, and in the dark. Coloured lanterns were to be placed here and there in the trees and bushes, and a row of electric globes was to be strung along the balustrade edge for the benefit of those taking the air.

The girls were silent and shiny-eyed with excitement as they examined each delightful detail, and tried out the floor for spring and slip. Each in her imagination whirled in the arms of the perfect man, who was going to fall in love at once, and want to marry her – but not actually propose until later in the Season, they had agreed, so that they could have the fun of dancing and flirting with a lot of other men first.

Henrietta and Jerome arrived that evening; Teddy was not coming until the following afternoon. Thomas, who was now known as Viscount Hazelmere, had gone into the Blues after university, and was on duty that evening, but would be coming to the ball. Oliver and Eddie had both come up from Oxford for the occasion. The first thing Henrietta did was to present Jessie with the flat velvet-covered box in which lay the beautiful pearls that had belonged to Jerome's mother. 'Just to borrow, for the evening, darling,' she said to Jessie.

And Jerome added, 'Pearls are just the right thing for a girl on her coming-out evening.'

'They'll go beautifully with your dress,' Venetia commented. 'How perfect they are!'

Jessie could only hug her mother and then her father, too excited and pleased to speak.

There was a family dinner party that night to which Olivia and Charlie and Lizzie and Ashley came. Overton had suggested taking everyone out to the theatre and a restaurant, but Venetia had said that if the girls had too much excitement the night before their ball they wouldn't sleep and she would be bringing them out with black circles under their eyes.

'My love, with all the dancing until dawn they're going to do, they aren't going to get much sleep for the rest of the Season,' he pointed out, amused

'Never mind,' Venetia said. 'They'll be launched then, so it won't matter. At our ball everyone will be inspecting them and passing judgement, and I want them to look and behave perfectly.'

'Violet *is* perfect,' Overton said. 'And I must say, little Jessie improves on one with every meeting. It's a shame about the scar.'

'Oh, Beauty, you can hardly see it! For heaven's sake, don't let her hear you mention it. She's absurdly sensitive about it.'

'Of course I won't. But, really, she would do better to make up an interesting story about it. She could say it was a duelling scar – that would lend her distinction.'

'You are absurd.'

'Not at all. Young men are wild for novelty, and people will always latch on to anything they think you are ashamed of. Much better brazen it out.'

'Nobody will even know it exists,' Venetia said firmly.

It was a very pleasant dinner, and the boys were easy and amusing company, and did the girls a great deal of good with their teasing compliments. Oliver declared that they were the two prettiest girls of his acquaintance; and it was evident from the way Eddie kept staring at Jessie that he had been agreeably surprised by the change in her since they last met. After dinner the girls were advised to go off to bed early, and they obeyed dutifully.

'But I bet the boys go off somewhere exciting as soon as we've gone,' Violet said to Jessie, as they climbed the stairs. 'I'm glad they're coming to the ball, though – and Thomas especially. They can dance with us if we don't have partners.'

'Oh, Vi, of course we'll have partners! It's our ball. Your mother will make sure of it. We won't need relatives.'

'But Tommy's got very handsome lately,' Violet said. 'I've sometimes thought it would be nice if you married him, then we could be properly sisters.'

507

'Or you could marry Jack – except that I think he's in love with Maud Puddephat. They seemed awfully close in the summer, and I overheard him saying he was going to write to her.'

They went to bed, but it wasn't long before Violet wandered through the bathroom to Jessie's room. 'I can't sleep – can you?'

'No. I'm not a bit sleepy.'

Violet got into bed beside Jessie, folded her hands over the counterpane and stared up at the ceiling. 'I don't see how I'm ever going to sleep. There's too much to think about. Tommy Fairbanks is going to be at the ball tomorrow, and I've half decided I might fall in love with him. I met him in Vienna at the Emperor's reception. He's such fun.'

'I thought you were going to fall in love with Lord Brancaster,' Jessie said, staring dreamily out of the window at the soft darkness. She imagined herself standing on the terrace of the ballroom, with the warm night air on her skin and the brilliant summer stars pulsing in the black velvet above her. She was standing with – who? The perfect man, of course; and if in her imagination he always looked a little like Bertie, that was just habit. She was quite prepared to fall in love with someone else, and was excited at the prospect. Bertie was a remote, almost pleasurable ache. She did not mean to let it affect her enjoyment of this unexpected gift of a Season, stop her dancing and flirting with a great many agreeable young men, or spoil her chances of meeting and marrying the one she was destined for. Her broken heart, she felt, only gave her a kind of distinction over other girls. She and Violet believed in love. They also believed in destiny, that there was one person who was right for you and who would find you at last, impelled in the right direction by unavoidable fate.

'Well, yes, I have thought about Brancaster,' Violet was saying. 'He would be a feather in one's cap. All the girls in Vienna – even the foreign ones – were wild about him. But probably he'll be too much run after to notice me.'

'Oh, Vi! You are the prettiest girl in London,' Jessie said. 'All the men are going to run after you.'

And what of me? Jessie thought. Jessie Compton, who was a nobody from Yorkshire – who would run after her? In the dark she raised a hand to her face and touched her cheek. She couldn't feel the scar any more, and Violet said it didn't show, but she knew it was there. She was not beautiful like Violet, but she knew she was attractive. She had already seen it in Yorkshire: she had something that made the young men turn and look at her, and want to talk to her and dance with her. It had excited her, that sense of power over them. It was thrilling. She knew she was going to enjoy dancing and flirting, was looking forward to it as she looked forward to the hunting season starting. Thinking about it gave her a quivering feeling somewhere deeper than her stomach. But London young men – rich, sophisticated, exacting – what would they think of a girl with a scar? They would dance with her, she knew that – it was her ball, and she would dance every dance – and they would flirt. But would they fall in love? That was the Question. It was her business to be fallen in love with at some point during the Season; she felt it her duty, or all the money spent on her would have been wasted.

She indulged a fantasy for a moment of the desirable Lord Brancaster catching sight of her across the ballroom and stopping dead, struck through the heart with Cupid's little arrow – 'Who is that remarkable girl? I've never seen such eyes!' – and hurrying through the crowds to claim her hand. And then she laughed at herself, and shook the thought away. But there were plenty of others who might fall in love with her. Cousin Venetia had talked about them; had invited them specially for her. George Cooper, the banking heir; Henry Fossey, secretary to an MP and bound for a seat himself one day, and a very nice boy from a good family. There was Willie Hunter, who was a captain in the Blues and a friend of Thomas's; Peter Grey-Gardner, whose family had a large estate in Surrey. And lots more she couldn't remember just now. In spite of everything, she was growing sleepy. Violet had stopped talking, and she thought she was asleep. She wriggled lower on her pillows, and thought, *Tomorrow is our ball!*

509

'It's going to be wonderful,' she whispered into the secret darkness; and closed her eyes. She imagined herself floating round the ballroom floor to a wonderful waltz. The orchestra was playing, and she was moving so gracefully, without effort, as though her feet did not touch the ground, whirling, twirling, round and round. She would never be tired, she would dance all night. A strong arm was round her waist, her hand was in the white-gloved hand of her partner, tall and strong and handsome, so handsome, and looking down at her with eyes that shone with suddenly discovered love . . . Foolish, just romantic nonsense. But it was so nice to dream. Round and round . . . The music went on, sparkling music, reeling out like ribbon, like the dark sky crusted with stars, like a carpet of crushed diamonds. 'You are so beautiful,' Bertie murmured, his lips against her ear. She slept.

And now the moment had come. It had really come. It was happening now, this minute!

They had stood with their parents and the duke and duchess at the head of the stairs while the glittering company came up the wide crimson-carpeted staircase like a rising sea of delicate pastel-coloured silk and satin, of evening dress and uniform, of diamonds and pearls, tiaras, orders, ribbons, medals. The cream of London Society, from the worlds of politics, fashion and the aristocracy, were here. Jessie had only to look at her parents' rather stunned expressions to know how exalted the company was. It was a great and glittering occasion, and it was all for them, for Violet and for her! That made it more amazing than any dream.

Everyone looked at them, greeted them, inspected them, smiled at them. Everyone was nice to them. Violet looked like an angel in her white lace, with white roses in her dark hair. She smiled and blushed beautifully, and everyone looked at her with a sort of pleased, sentimental indulgence. She was everyone's ideal of a débutante, pretty, modest, shy and good.

But they had looked at Jessie, too – with interest. She could almost hear them thinking, Who is this girl alongside Lady Violet Winchmore? Who is this unknown who had attracted the patronage not only of the Overtons but of the Duke of Southport? The Interesting Unknown, that's who she was. The Mysterious Stranger. She remembered the story of Cinderella from the long-ago book that she and Violet had read in their bower at Shawes; how no-one had known who she was when she arrived late at the ball, which only made the prince more eager to meet her. The beautiful Princess Incognita. No, she checked herself, that was going too far. The Interesting Unknown it was.

And beautiful? Why not? She felt beautiful. The thrill of the occasion was tingling inside her from the crown of her head to the tips of her toes. She felt she could dance on air tonight, could probably fly, might well float up to the ceiling if she weren't held down! Oh, she was so excited and happy she could barely breathe! It was happening, it was really happening! They were in the ballroom, the orchestra was playing, the ball was about to begin. This was her night, perhaps the best night of her whole life, and something she could never have imagined even a few months ago. She knew it was special and not to be repeated and that she must savour every second and every nuance, because in real life she was not a princess and there were no fairy godmothers, only kind Cousin Venetia, who was giving her this one season. She must remember everything, so that she could think about it for the rest of her life.

Dad glanced at her, so proud of her he looked as though he might burst, and she smiled back at him. She had a moment of being intensely aware of everything, of being absolutely *there*. She felt herself living inside her own body, as though every inch of her was hyper-sensitive. She felt against her skin the divine silkiness of her new underwear, bought for the occasion, finer and softer than anything she had ever had before. She felt the rigid bones of her corset gripping her hard from below the bust to her hips, and that was a pleasurable feeling too, a sort of perverse deliciousness. She felt the wonderful weight of her skirt's great fullness at the back as if it were a part of her, as she imagined a cat must feel its own tail. She moved her hips a little and felt it move in response. When she danced it would swing and swirl with a great wonderful swishing movement. Oh, how she longed to dance!

It was beginning. The Duke of Southport had led his eldest son, Lord Turnhouse, up to Violet, and he was bowing and preparing to lead her out to begin the ball. Violet's cheeks were delicately flushed and she smiled as she laid her hand on his arm, looking tiny beside him. There was a spattering of applause as they took the floor. And now it was her turn. She glanced again at her father and saw he was as nervous as a horse before a race. He smiled and mouthed something at her, but she didn't know what. The tall, stooped duke came towards her with a young man, thin and plain-faced but pleasant. She knew who it was, because this had all been arranged. The duke bowed to her and said, 'May I present to you as a partner Lord Freshwater? Freshwater, Miss Jessamine Compton.'

The man bowed and offered his arm with a kindliness that told her instantly that he was doing this because he had been asked and not because he had any interest in her. Viscount Freshwater was the eldest son of Lord Tonbridge, Cousin Venetia's friend, and a suitable person to lead off the ball with her, that was all. She was perfectly content with the arrangement. The first dance was a show-piece, for her and Violet to be looked at, and she was nervous enough not to want any extra excitement yet. She wanted to be sure she *could* dance without tripping over her own feet or mismanaging her train, and was actually glad of her partner's neutrality.

He danced well, competently, and it was comfortable to be guided round by him – almost, she thought with an inward smile, like dancing with her father! She could trust him and dismiss him from her mind while she catalogued the new sensations. Yes, she could dance! She would not trip or stumble, and would be ready next time to add an exciting partner to the pleasures of the activity. Freshwater circled her carefully, making a few commonplace remarks, which she hardly had to reply to, and when the music stopped managed to have her back at exactly the right spot in the ballroom, just in front of her parents. She appreciated

the skill involved in that, and smiled up at him and thanked
him warmly.

'My pleasure entirely,' he said, and she saw that her smile
had changed something, that he was looking at her differently, as though he thought it might have been a pleasure
after all instead of just a duty. He was going to say something else when a drawling voice interrupted him. 'Hogging
the best spot as usual? Can't have that. Introduce me,
Freddy, introduce me!'

A man was standing beside Lord Freshwater, tall also,
but well-built, younger than Freshwater but still a little older
than most of the others who had been invited 'for' Jessie
and Violet. He was in the usual black and white of evening
dress, but his seemed to fit him as a horse in the peak of
condition fits into its skin. His hair was dark and his face
lean, and he carried himself like a handsome man, like a
man who is used to being looked at and admired. You saw
the same thing in beautiful horses, she thought. He had
'presence' – like Pasha.

'Miss Compton, may I present Viscount Brancaster?' Lord
Freshwater said, not with any great enthusiasm.

Brancaster, she thought. He must have only just arrived.
He had not been presented at the receiving line. Her first
partner seemed to disapprove of him somewhat, but she had
no time to pursue that line in her mind. Brancaster bowed
to her, and as he straightened, smiling faintly, she was able
to see his face properly for the first time.

His eyes were blue, as blue as Violet's but brighter, sapphire
blue; but it wasn't that which made her catch her breath,
nor even that he was so very handsome, which he was –
reputation had not lied. It was that he was *real*, not an imaginary, perfect fairy-tale prince, but a real man. She could feel
the warmth of his body radiating from beneath his shirt-
front; see the texture of his skin, the fine bone of his jaw-
line, a tiny crescent scar just above one corner of his mouth.
She could see the creases in his lips, the feathery curve of
his eyelashes, the way the hair grew springingly at his temples.
Behind him the great space of the ballroom waited under
the glittering chandeliers. Around it there was the mass of

513

murmuring, pretty-coloured people – she caught the flicker of fans and the movement of faces turned from side to side in conversation, like the swaying of weed in the tide – but now all that was indistinct, an unimportant background. What was real and important – all that was real and important – was this man before her.

'Miss Compton,' he said. She felt she had known the instant before she heard it what his voice would sound like; that she would have recognised it anywhere. 'My dance, I think?' he said, with superb confidence. He held out his arm before him and she was about to place her hand on it. And then their eyes met, and something seemed to happen between them. It was a sense of connection, almost of recognition, and she felt it deep in her stomach with a sort of thump that was both shocking and pleasurable. It was something immediate and almost palpable, and also somehow implacable, like the soft clunk a clock makes when the strike mechanism engages, that says something is going to happen and cannot be avoided.

She saw his eyes fix a moment, and knew that he felt it too. He looked just faintly surprised – or no, perhaps, rather, absently puzzled, as a person might half listening to a piece of music and trying to remember where they had heard it before. They seemed to go on looking at each other for a very long time, although really it could not have been more than a few seconds – unless it was that time had stopped just around them for a moment. Then she completed the action of laying her hand on his sleeve.

They crossed the shining spaces of the floor, and there was a little applause from the crowd around the edges, gloved applause that sounded like rain on canvas. Now she could see normally again, and the strangeness of those few seconds was gone, replaced by a deep and vibrant happiness. Violet was also walking out onto the floor with her second partner, a fair young man in cavalry uniform. She saw Violet turn her face to smile at her as she reached the middle, and make a little raised-eyebrows face which said as clearly as if she had spoken the words, *Look who you've caught*! Jessie smiled back, then turned to her partner, and felt him slip his arm round her waist. She was tingling with an excitement that was not now to do with the ball, but to do with him. She was so happy, *happy*, that she was going to dance with him. She looked up into his eyes and laughed with sheer joy.

He did not seem to find her laughter odd. She felt a sympathy with him, as though he must understand exactly what she was feeling.

He said, 'That was lucky, my arriving just as I did, or you'd have been off again and I'd have missed my chance. I hope you won't think me too forward if I say that I believe I'm dancing with the prettiest girl in the room.'

She was meant to hang her head shyly and blush when men complimented her. She and Violet had discussed it all at great length in bed during those long nights beforehand. And they had both agreed that the more extravagant compliments from the worst, known flirts – men like Lord Brancaster – must be rebuffed with a gentle, refined coolness, to show that they were not to be taken advantage of. But she was too happy for any of that. She responded exactly as was natural to her.

'But you aren't dancing yet,' she laughed.

The music struck and his arm tightened round her as he pulled her into motion. 'I am now,' he said.

Her body went with him, knowing his movements before he made them, and they turned and turned up the room, her wonderful skirt swinging heavily after her with a soft and delicious weight. She never took her eyes from his face, and he seemed not to mind it, gazed back at her, smiling, at ease, as though they had done this before.

'You dance awfully well,' he said.

'So do you,' she said.

He smiled quizzically. 'You are a funny girl! I hope you'll give me another dance later?'

'Yes, I'd like that,' she heard herself say with wonderful calm. This is really happening, she reminded herself. This is no dream, it's really, really happening.